The Mam

Pulp
Action

Also available

THE MAMMOTH BOOK OF

Pulp
Action

Edited by Maxim Jakubowski

CARROLL & GRAF PUBLISHERS
New York

Carroll & Graf Publishers
An imprint of Avalon Publishing Group, Inc.
161 William Street
16th Floor
New York
NY 10038–2607
www.carrollandgraf.com

First published in the UK by Robinson,
an imprint of Constable & Robinson Ltd 2001

First Carroll & Graf edition 2001

Collection and editorial material
copyright © Maxim Jakubowski 2001

ISBN 0–7867–0920–0

Printed and bound in the EU

Contents

Introduction

Pulp fiction never dies!

In the footsteps of our initial volume of THE MAMMOTH BOOK OF PULP FICTION, which has enjoyed great popularity and several reprints, here is another cornucopia of fascinating tales by some of the greatest storytellers of yesterday and today.

Whether one defines pulp fiction as stories originating in the erstwhile magazines printed on pulp paper, or a tradition of storytelling whose roots lie in hardboiled fiction populated by tough guys, cops, villains and *femmes fatales* of the parish, there is no denying that they are invariably stories where action and thrills are paramount and the reader is trapped in a whirlwind of adventure and suspense.

In a way, pulp fiction is then an attitude, but first and foremost it is a grand demonstration of the art of storytelling at its best. And in these packed pages, writers of the golden age blend effortlessly with newer talents and contemporary stars who are respectful of the lessons of the past. From Prohibition days to up-to-the-minute tales of the hood, from highways to motels and Arabian desert capers, here is a mighty selection of pulp action at its best.

And yes, they do still write them like they used to!

Maxim Jakubowski

Acknowledgments

THE KID CLIPS A COUPON by Erle Stanley Gardner, © 1934 by Popular Publications. First appeared in DETECTIVE FICTION WEEKLY, April 1934. Reprinted by permission of Curtis Brown Ltd.

GOODBYE, HANNAH by Steve Fisher, © 1938 by Steve Fisher. Reprinted by permission of Scott Meredith Literary Agency, Inc.

SINNERS' PARADISE by Raoul Whitfield, © 1929 by Raoul Whitfield. First published in BREEZY STORIES, 1929.

MOTEL by Evan Hunter, © 2000 by Hui Corporation. First appeared in PLAYBOY, German edition, 1978. Reprinted by permission of Curtis Brown Ltd, London, on behalf of Evan Hunter.

SMILE, CORPSE, SMILE! by Bruno Fischer, © 1960 by Bruno Fischer. First appeared in DETECTIVE TALES December 1960. Reprinted by permission of Ruth Fischer, on behalf of the Estate of Bruno Fischer.

THE PULP CONNECTION by Bill Pronzini, © 1978 by the Pronzini-Muller Family Trust. First appeared in ELLERY QUEEN'S MYSTERY MAGAZINE. Reprinted by permission of the author.

BRUSH BABE'S POISON PALLET by Bruce Cassiday, © 1949 by Popular Publications, Inc. First appeared in ALL-STORY DETECTIVE, August 1949. Reprinted by permission of the author.

THE GANGSTA WORE RED by Michael Guinzburg, © 2000 by Michael Guinzburg. First appeared as GANGSTER EN ROUGE in Librio (France). Reprinted by permission of the author.

CARAVAN TO TARIM by David Goodis, © 1946 by David Goodis. First appeared in COLLIER'S, October 1946. Reprinted by permission of Ballard Spahr Andrews & Ingersoll LLP, on behalf of the Estate of David Goodis.

THE LADY WHO LEFT HER COFFIN by Hugh B. Cave, © 1936 by Popular Publications, Inc. First appeared in DIME DETECTIVE MAGAZINE, June 1936. Reprinted by permission of the author.

DEATH AT THE MAIN by Frank Gruber, © 1936 by Standard Magazines, Inc. First appeared in THRILLING DETECTIVE, December 1936. Reprinted by permission of the Scott Meredith Literary Agency, Inc.

RED GOOSE by Norbert Davis, © 1934 by Keith Alan Deutsch from BLACK MASK issue 16, No. 12 (February 1934). Copyright 1934 by Pro-Distributors Publishing Company, Inc. Copyright renewed © 1962 by Popular Publications,

Inc. Assigned to Keith Alan Deutsch. Reprinted by special arrangement with Keith Alan Deutsch, proprietor and conservator of the respective copyrights and successor-in-interest to Popular Publications, Inc.

THE FIRST FIVE IN LINE by Charles Willeford, © 1999 by Betsy Willeford. First appeared in ORANGE PULP. Reprinted by permission of Abner Stein Limited.

WHERE THERE'S A WILL, THERE'S A SLAY by Frederick C. Davis, from BLACK MASK, British edition, October 1953. © 1953 by Popular Publications, Inc. Copyright renewed 1962, 1970 by Popular Publications, Inc. Assigned to Keith Alan Deutsch. Reprinted by special arrangement with Keith Alan Deutsch, proprietor and conservator of the respective copyrights and successor-in-interest to Popular Publications, Inc.

RIDE A WHITE HORSE by Lawrence Block, © 1958 by Lawrence Block. First appeared in MANHUNT, 1958. Reprinted by permission of the author.

BEST MAN by Thomas Walsh from BLACK MASK issue 17, No. 4 (October 1934). Copyright 1934 by Pro-Distributors Publishing Company, Inc. Copyright renewed © 1962 by Popular Publications. Assigned to Keith Alan Deutsch. Reprinted by special arrangement with Keith Alan Deutsch, proprietor and conservator of the respective copyrights and successor-in-interest to Popular Publications, Inc.

DOG LIFE by Mark Timlin, © 2001 by Mark Timlin. Original to this collection. Reprinted by permission of the author.

DON'T LOOK BEHIND YOU by Fredric Brown, © 1947 by Davis Publications, Inc. First appeared in ELLERY QUEEN'S MYSTERY MAGAZINE, 1947. Reprinted by permission of Scott Meredith Literary Agency, Inc.

COLLEGE-CUT KILL by John D. MacDonald, © 1950 by John D. Mac-Donald. First appeared in BLACK MASK DETECTIVE MAGAZINE, 1950. Reprinted by permission of Vanessa Holt Limited.

THE LOST COAST by Marcia Muller, © 1994 by the Pronzini-Muller Family Trust. First appeared in DEADLY ALLIES 2. Reprinted by permission of the author.

THE PIT by Joe R. Lansdale, © 1987 by Joe R. Lansdale. First appeared in THE BLACK LIZARD ANTHOLOGY OF CRIME FICTION. Reprinted by permission of the author.

CLEAN SWEEP by Roger Torrey from BLACK MASK issue 16, No. 12 (February 1934). © 1934 by Pro-Distributors Publishing Company, Inc. Copyright renewed © 1962 by Popular Publications, Inc. Assigned to Keith Alan Deutsch. Reprinted by special arrangement with Keith Alan Deutsch, proprietor and conservator of the respective copyrights and successor-in-interest to Popular Publications, Inc.

EYE OF THE BEHOLDER by Ed Gorman, © 1997 by Ed Gorman. First appeared in CEMETERY DANCE. Reprinted by permission of the author.

All efforts have been made to contact the respective copyright holders. In some rare cases, it has not proven possible to ascertain the whereabouts of authors, agents or estates. They are welcome to write to us c/o the publishers if we have inadvertently made use of a story they control rights in.

The Kid Clips a Coupon

Erle Stanley Gardner

I
The Clue of the Jam

Dan Seller lounged in the big chair and listened as Police Inspector Phil Brame recounted the circumstances of the crime for the edification of the small group of cronies who frequented the choice corner of the club.

"Just a plain case of murder," Inspector Brame was saying, "and a bit of strawberry jam is going to send the guy to the chair."

"I don't think Dan Higgins intended to commit murder when he broke into the place. Mrs Morelay, paralyzed from the hips down, was in the living room, seated in her wheelchair, going over a bunch of account books. Higgins broke in to get some food. Mrs Morelay heard him moving around in the kitchen. There was a telephone attached to her wheelchair. She called police headquarters and reported someone in her kitchen, stealing food.

"Higgins heard her telephoning. It sent him into a furious rage. The man was a hungry. He dashed into the room and split the woman's head open with a hatchet he had picked up in the kitchen. Then he helped himself to food. He spread some homemade strawberry jam on a slice of bread and ate it. He spilled some jam on his necktie without knowing it. He had gone less than a block from the place when the police radio car came along.

"Higgins looked like just the type who would be stealing food – a half-starved chap with clothes that were pretty much the worse for wear. Our men stopped and picked him up on suspicion and then went to the house and found that murder had been committed. Higgins denied he'd been near the house, and he'd evidently learned his lesson about fingerprints, because there were no fingerprints on any of the stuff in the kitchen. The police found a pair of dirty gloves in his pocket. Evidently he'd worn those while he was eating. But there was strawberry jam on his tie. The jam was analyzed. The amount of sugar it contained was carefully noted by the police-chemists, and then an analysis was made of the strawberry jam in the jar in the sink. The jam on the tie Higgins was wearing at the time of his arrest came from that jar of homemade jam."

"Wasn't there someone who saw him leaving the house?" Renfroe, the banker, asked.

"Yes," Brame said. "Walter Stagg, the man who acts as manager for Mrs Morelay, drove up to the house in his automobile. He arrived there almost at the same time that the police did. He was just coming up the cement walk when the police car rounded the corner. He said that he had seen Higgins coming around the back of the house, as though he had either slipped out of a window, or had been snooping around the house. Stagg said he intended to unlock the front door – which was always kept on a night latch – and see if anything was wrong. If anything was missing, he was determined to jump into his car and follow the man until he could notify a policeman. Stagg was unarmed so he didn't want to encounter an armed crook unless he had an officer handy."

Bill Pope, the explorer, stared steadily at the curling smoke of a cigarette.

"It seems strange," he said, "that a man would have gone ahead and eaten heartily after having committed a murder, particularly the murder of a helpless old woman who had done nothing to injure him."

"She telephoned for the police," Inspector Brame said. "Don't forget that."

"But," Dan Seller pointed out, "if that was the motive for the crime and the man knew she had telephoned for the police, he'd have been doubly foolish to have murdered her and then gone on eating, knowing that the police were on their way in a radio car."

Inspector Brame's face flushed.

"More of *your* amateur detective stuff," he said. "It's an easy thing for you wealthy young coupon-clippers to construct theories proving that the police are always wrong. Doubtless, an attorney for the defence will try to bamboozle a jury into believing the police got the wrong man. But he won't be able to – not with that strawberry jam on the man's necktie."

"Was there," asked Bill Pope, "robbery as well?"

"Apparently not. Higgins had nothing in his possession when he was arrested. He might have taken something from the body and buried it somewhere in the vicinity. She was supposed to have a large sum of cash money which she always kept on hand, but there wasn't any money found on her body.

"Higgins was wise. He didn't leave a single fingerprint. We fingerprinted everything about the body, and didn't find a thing. The books that were open in front of her didn't have a single fingerprint on the page other than the prints of Walter Stagg, the manager, who kept all the books and submitted them to Mrs Morelay for examination."

"Perhaps a draught of wind might have blown one of the pages," Dan Seller said. "Did your men take prints on the other pages to see if that had happened?"

"As it happens, my bright young man," the inspector said, "we did that very thing, although we didn't need to, because when the woman's skull was split open, blood spattered upon the pages of the open account book, and we had no difficulty in telling what page was in front of her at the time."

"Very clever detective work, inspector," Renfroe, the banker, said. "Undoubtedly the man will go to the chair on the strength of that strawberry jam."

"Mrs Morelay was wealthy?"

"Quite wealthy. She leaves no will. The property goes to a niece, Tess Copley. She's the only surviving relative."

"Live here in the city?" Renfroe asked.

"Yes."

"They found the weapon with which the crime was committed?" Bill Pope inquired.

"Oh, yes, of course. It was there in the room. There could be no question about it. A blood-stained hatchet that had been taken from the kitchen."

Bill Pope's clear eyes surveyed Inspector Brame.

"You should feel pretty happy, inspector," he said, "but you seem to be down in the dumps."

Inspector Brame sighed.

"It's that damned Patent Leather Kid," he said.

"What about him?" asked the explorer.

"He's been meddling again. The man is a crook, a gangster, a public enemy. And yet, he appeals to the public. He tries to pull some of this Robin Hood stuff, and the people fall for it. Slowly but surely he's becoming a public hero, and he's making the police appear ridiculous."

"Why don't you catch him," asked the banker, "and put him away?"

"Have you," asked Bill Pope, "got anything definite on him? His methods are irregular, perhaps illegal, but can you get him on any specific felony and make it stick?"

Inspector Brame's voice was ominous.

"Listen," he said, "when we get that guy, we'll make something stick. Don't worry about that. I wouldn't want to be quoted publicly on the thing, you understand, but that fellow has been a thorn in the side of the Police Department long enough. It wouldn't take very much framing to pin a good murder case on him."

"Don't you think framing him for murder is pretty steep?" the explorer asked.

"Well, perhaps not for murder," Inspector Brame said. "I was speaking impulsively. But I can promise you this, that if we ever get our fingers on The Patent Leather Kid, he'll go away for a long, long time."

Dan Seller arose, yawned, and took a cigarette from a hammered silver case.

"Referring to that murder case once more, inspector," he said, "didn't Walter Stagg agree to notify Tess Copley, and fail to do so?"

"Notify her of what?" the police inspector asked.

"Of her aunt's death."

"He promised to go and get her, but he had some trouble starting his car. His battery was weak, and in the end the police telephoned and had a messenger sent to her. Tess Copley was working in a place where the girls weren't allowed to receive telephone calls."

"Then," Dan Seller said, "her aunt didn't part with any money while she was alive."

"I'll say she didn't," Inspector Brame said. "She was as tight as the bark on a tree – one of those misers who salted money away in gold coin. She'd been collecting gold for some time."

"And hadn't turned it in?"

"No."

"What was the amount of the money?"

"I don't know exactly. No one does. She had been collecting it for years."

Dan Seller lit his cigarette, nodded casually to the small group. "Well," he said, "I'll be seeing you later."

Bill Pope, the explorer, followed Dan Seller with quizzical, speculative eyes, but said nothing.

II
Fingerprints and a Stalled Car

The process by which Dan Seller, the wealthy club man, became The Patent Leather Kid, spectacular figure of the city's underworld, was tedious and complicated. However, it left no back trail, and when The Patent Leather Kid entered the apartment hotel where he maintained a penthouse, he might as well have appeared from thin air for all the trail he had left.

The manager greeted The Kid with deference.

Gertie, the telephone operator, flashed him a glance from eyes that were starry, as she reached for the switchboard to notify Bill Brakey that The Kid was on his way up.

The Kid's private elevator whisked him directly to the roof. Bill Brakey, ensconced behind bullet-proof doors, made certain that The Kid was alone, and that there was no trap laid by police or gangster enemies before he opened the door.

Bill Brakey's face never showed the slightest nervousness. Only his hands and his eyes betrayed the everlasting watchfulness, the readiness to explode into instant action.

"You made a short trip this time, Kid," he said.

"Yes," The Kid told him. "Let's go in where we can have a drink and talk. I've got something on my mind."

The Kid dropped into a chair, stretched out his feet and sighed.

"Seems good to be back, Bill," he said.

Bill Brakey brought out a bottle of Scotch, drew the cork and poured out whiskey and ginger ale.

"What's on your mind, Kid?"

Brakey's eyes were not fastened upon The Patent Leather Kid, but were slithering about in a nervous survey of the windows and doors. It made no difference that he knew no one could get through the roof without a warning coming over the telephone, without an automatic alarm shrilling a strident warning should the only elevator which communicated with the pent-house start on its way without The Kid's key having first unlocked an electrical contact.

Bill Brakey's watchfulness was purely mechanical, purely a matter of long habit.

"I'm interested," The Patent Leather Kid said, "in the murder of Mrs Fannie Morelay."

"Inside stuff is," Brakey said, "that Higgins is going to the chair because he had some strawberry jam spilled on his necktie. He didn't leave any fingerprints, but it looks as though it was a dead open and shut case."

"Except for one thing," The Patent Leather Kid said, slowly.

"What's that?" asked the bodyguard.

"This fellow, Stagg."

"You mean the manager?"

"Yes."

"He's okay," Bill Brakey said. "The police looked him up just to make sure. He's got the highest references. He's been with Mrs Morelay for years. He handled all of her business affairs. You see, she couldn't get around at all by herself, and she had quite a bunch of business interests. She was worth over a million dollars. Nobody knows just how much more."

"Stagg was just coming up to the house when the police came. He'd just driven up in his car, and saw Dan Higgins moving about as though he'd been prowling around the house."

Bill Brakey flashed The Kid a sharp glance.

"Even if he was lying about *that*," he said, "the strawberry jam on Higgins' necktie is enough to send him to the chair. Higgins says he wasn't near the house. The chemists can absolutely identify that jam. No two batches of homemade jam are made according to the same actual recipe. There are minor variations of sugar content, and that sort of stuff, and –"

"That's all right," The Patent Leather Kid remarked, "but when Walter Stagg wanted to notify Tess Copley, the niece, of what had happened, his car didn't start, the battery was weak."

"Well," said Brakey, "what about that?"

"If he had just driven up to the house," The Kid said, "his car would have been warm. And, what's more, the battery would have been freshly generated from a run. It would have turned over a warm motor. The fact that it didn't turn over the motor indicates that the motor was cold. It's more probable that Stagg had left the house and was running towards the car, trying to make a getaway, when he heard the police car coming, and, knowing that he couldn't get away, turned and started back towards the house, pulling out his key to open the front door as he did so."

There was an interval of silence. The Kid sipped his highball thoughtfully.

"Of course," Brakey said, "that doesn't prove anything. It's a suspicious circumstance – that's all."

"That's why I didn't call it to the attention of the police," The Kid said. "It's something that we've got to run down."

Bill Brakey nodded.

"When do you want to start, Kid?" he asked.

"Sometime tonight," The Kid told him. Brakey's poker face did not change.

"There's a police guard at the place?"

"I presume so. I don't know. I can find out."

The Kid let smoke stream from his nostrils.

"Better slip out there this afternoon, Bill," he said. "Look the ground over and make a report. I'll get a little sleep and get caught up on some of my reading. As soon as you come back with the report, we'll have dinner and then proceed to look the premises over."

Bill Brakey nodded.

"I'll have all the low-down on it," he said.

"Another thing," The Patent Leather Kid muttered, hesitatingly, "that doesn't check, is the fingerprints on the book of accounts. They found the fingerprints of Walter Stagg on those books. No other print."

"Higgins was wearing gloves," Brakey said.

"I know," The Kid said, "but if this woman had been checking over the books of account, it's almost a cinch that *her* fingerprints would have been on the books somewhere."

"That's so," Brakey agreed.

"Apparently they weren't. Just Stagg's prints."

"What do you make of that, Kid?"

The Patent Leather Kid shrugged his shoulders so slightly that the action was all but imperceptible.

"That," he said, "is something which remains to be determined."

"They were the books she was working on, all right," Brakey said, "because there were bloodstains on the leaves. They were the books she was working on when she was murdered, regardless of who did the murder."

"Then why weren't her fingerprints on the pages, Bill?" The Patent Leather Kid pointed out.

"Gosh, Kid, I don't know," Brakey confessed.

"That's something we're going to find out."

III
Inside the Murder House

The Patent Leather Kid adjusted the black patent leather mask which covered the upper half of his features. He worked his hands into soft, pliable leather gloves, nodded to Bill Brakey.

"Ready, Bill," he said.

Bill Brakey jimmied the window.

The Patent Leather Kid was the first one through. He paused for a tense moment while he listened, then muttered to Bill Brakey: "Okay, Bill, let's go."

Brakey slid noiselessly after him.

The place was musty, with a peculiar suggestion of death. The Kid produced a flashlight.

"This the window he came through, Bill?" he asked.

"This is it."

"And the murder took place in this next room?"

"Yes. On the other side of that swinging door."

The men moved upon silent feet. The Kid pushed open the swinging door and gazed upon the room in which the crime had been committed.

Inasmuch as Tess Copley, the sole beneficiary of the estate, did not care to occupy the house, the police had left the room just as it had been found when the crime was discovered. All that had been removed was the corpse of the victim. For the rest the furniture remained undisturbed. The shades were drawn so as to shut out any light, and The Patent Leather Kid let his flashlight flicker around the room, taking in the various details.

"There's a guard in front, Bill?" he asked.

"Yes. A harness bull that was taken off his beat. He doesn't take it very seriously. He's probably dozing off right now. For some reason, the district attorney wants to keep the room just as it was so that he can show it to the jury. In order to do that, he'll have it appear that the place was guarded by an officer who will testify he was there to see nothing was disturbed."

The flashlight centred upon a lacquered box.

"What's the box, Bill?"

"That's a lock-box they found in the room. There was nothing in it. There was a file of papers by the side of it that probably were taken from the box."

The Kid knelt by the box. It was unlocked. He lifted back the lid and stared at the interior.

"Notice the way the enamel is chipped on the inside, Bill," he said. "That wouldn't have been done by papers."

He pulled the lid of the box back and looked at the metal handle.

"Notice the bulge in the top of the box," he said. "It looks as though it had been filled with something very heavy and lifted repeatedly."

"Gold?" asked Bill Brakey.

"Looks like it."

"Where was the manager's office, Bill?" asked The Kid. "Did he have one here in the building?"

"Yes, he had one way in the front."

"Let's take a look."

They traversed a corridor, went through a bedroom, and came to another room in the front of the house, which had evidently been designed as a bedroom, but which had been used as an office.

"Take it easy," whispered Bill Brakey. "The cops are right outside there on the walk."

"The curtains aren't down here," The Kid observed, in a whisper. "Why would they have the shades drawn in the rest of the house and not have them drawn here?"

"Looks as though the manager had been working here," Brakey said.

"You've got a plan of Stagg's house?"

"It ain't a house. It's a flat."

"Has he got the lower or upper flat?" The Kid asked.

"Upper. It's a three-story flat. He's on the top floor."

"An attic above him?"

"Probably. I haven't been in the place. I was waiting for you."

"Okay," The Kid said, "I've seen enough here. Let's go take a look at this man Stagg. I'd like to talk with him."

"You're the boss," Bill Brakey said.

The men left the place as silently as they had entered it. They slipped through the window, oozed through the darkness to the alley, followed the alley to a side street, and there picked up their car.

Bill Brakey drove to a district given over largely to small

apartment houses and flats. He parked the car by the kerb.

"That's the place over there," he said.

"Well," The Kid said, "there's a light on the upper floor. That means our friend will be up."

"Do we bust in on him?" asked Bill Brakey.

"I think," The Kid said, "we bust in on him, tie him up and make a search. Maybe we can throw a scare into him."

"Just what do you expect to find?" Brakey asked.

"I don't know," The Kid told him. "Maybe we'll let the police find it."

"How do you mean?"

"Go in and pull out a few drawers, mess things up a little bit, tie him up, and then notify the police. They'll start making a search to see what we took and to see whether we left any fingerprints."

"He's too clever for that," Brakey said. "If there's anything hidden there, it'll be hidden where the police wouldn't find it. The police may have made a search already. They're not so dumb."

"Inspector Brame is," The Kid said. "His whole idea of handling a case is to make a quick arrest and then make sure of getting a conviction. After a man is once arrested for a crime, Brame never bothers about any clues that don't point to the guilt of that man."

Bill Brakey opened the car door.

"Well," he said, "we might as well . . . That car, watch it."

A big sedan purred smoothly along the road and slid gently to the opposite kerb. It was a car that had been designed with plenty of power under the hood. From it a big, well-nourished man stepped to the sidewalk. For all of his size, he moved with the lithe grace of a panther.

" 'Pug' Morrison, the prizefighter who turned gangster," Bill Brakey said in an undertone. "What the hell is *he* doing here?"

"Perhaps," said The Kid, "he's looking around the same way we are."

"When that guy looks around," Bill Brakey said, "he's looking around on a hot scent."

"Uses his noodle, does he?" asked The Kid.

"He uses his muscle," Brakey said. "That bird is one of those cheerful guys that always wants to give the other fellow his cut provided his cut isn't more than one and a half per cent. Pug figures that around ninety-eight or ninety-nine per cent is his fair share of the take."

"Well," The Kid said, "he's going up."

"Hell," Brakey ejaculated, "going up! He's ringing the bell."

The door of the flat opened and the broad-shouldered form of Pug Morrison moved through the lighted oblong.

Bill Brakey slid out from behind the steering wheel. The Kid got to the ground on the other side. They had no need for words. They crossed the street with swift steps. Bill Brakey had his skeleton keys in his right hand while they were still six feet from the door. It took him less than ten seconds to find the right key and shoot back the spring latch. A long flight of stairs loomed before them – stairs which were broken by one landing.

Men's voices were audible when they were still a dozen steps from the top. The voices came from the left, and sounded only as an undertone of booming sound, interspersed at intervals by a voice that was higher in pitch, less in volume, and which spoke with nervous rapidity.

A dimly lighted reception hall was at the front of the stairs. A door opened from it to what was evidently a corridor. The door on the left was closed. From under it shone a ribbon of bright light. Evidently the conference was taking place in a front room on the left hand side.

Once more the men exchanged glances. The Patent Leather Kid adjusted the distinctive black mask of patent leather from which he had derived his name. His shoes were of patent leather. His gloves were also black.

Bill Brakey wore no gloves. At times such as these, he needed to have his swift hands, with their long, delicate fingers, where they could whip guns from the shoulder holsters without the faintest suggestion of a fumble. It was an unspoken law between them that The Kid touched those things upon which fingerprints might be left; that Bill Brakey's hands remained free to reach for and use weapons.

The Kid crossed the reception hall, twisted the knob on

the door, disclosing the long corridor which stretched the length of the flat. He picked the first door on the left, twisted the knob, and entered a bedroom. He brought his flashlight into play, slid quietly across the bedroom to a bathroom which opened to his left, entered the bathroom, and crossed to a small dressing room. On the other side of this dressing room was a door through which came the mumble of voices.

The Kid worked with swift efficiency. He gripped the knob tightly with his gloved right hand, pulled the door as tightly against the jamb as he could force it, and then twisted the knob, moving it so slowly as to make the motion all but imperceptible. When the latch cleared its seat in the jamb, there was no faintest suggestion of a click. Slowly, The Kid pushed the door open – an inch, two inches.

IV
A Playmate for The Kid

They listened to the mumbling noise of the conversation, conversation which became audible as the door opened. At the slightest break in the rhythmic flow of that conversation, The Kid would have flung the door open and crouched. Bill Brakey, a gun in either hand, would have stood in the doorway, commanding the situation.

But there was no break. The door was in a dark corner of the room; the illumination came from floor lamps. The men who occupied the room were far too engrossed in what they were saying to pay attention to the shadows of the room.

". . . kidnapping is a serious business," said the deep, booming voice of Pug Morrison. "I don't go in for it."

"You go in for making money, don't you?" asked the higher-pitched, nervous voice of Walter Stagg.

"Sure I do, but I don't go in for death penalties and life sentences."

"Oh, bosh and nonsense," Stagg said. "You go in for murder."

"Who says so?" asked Morrison, with sudden menace in his voice.

"Don't take offence," Stagg said, "I'm telling you what

everyone says. I'm not talking about any specific killing. I'm talking about the reputation you've got. Remember, I'm not trying to frame you with anything. I'm in this thing just as deep as you are."

Pug Morrison laughed.

"The idea," he said, "of a guy like you trying to frame me! I could tell you what's on *your* mind right now. You've been manager for Mrs Morelay. She was murdered. It looks like a dead open and shut case against this guy Higgins, but I'm not so certain that you ain't mixed up in it now. You've been handling all the gravy for the old woman and, now that she's croaked there's going to be an administrator appointed and you've got to make accounting. There's probably a will some place that you're holding out. It provides that the niece takes all the property, unless she should die first; and then it all goes to you. Something like that. Therefore, you want us to snatch the kid and bump her off. You'll come into the big coin. You'd better get your cards on the table, buddy. If you're playing around with the big coin, we want to know it. You can't hold out on us anyway. We'd keep coming back and shaking you down from time to time until we got a fair split, so you'd better give us a break."

Stagg's voice lost much of its assurance, but maintained its nervous, almost hysterical, rapidity of articulation.

"Now, look here," he said, "you know as well as I do, that if it's just a matter of getting somebody bumped off, I can find lots of people who are willing to do it for a thousand dollars."

Pug Morrison laughed, a laugh that contained no mirth, but plenty of scorn.

"Sucker," he said. "You'd pay a grand to have a bump-off and you'd get bled white for the rest of your life. You deal with me and you're going to pay and you're going to pay plenty. But if you're on the square, you're going to pay once and that's going to be all. You know that, and you know I can't afford to get mixed into this thing any more than you can, so you figure we're going to shoot square with each other. Now, go ahead and give me the lowdown."

"Well," Stagg said, "there was some cash in the estate.

Not liquid cash, you understand, but cash in the bank. It's stuff that I can't touch without a court order, see?"

"No, I don't see," Pug told him. "Cash in the bank doesn't mean anything to me. It's cash in my right fist that talks music."

"That's just the point," Stagg went on hurriedly. "I've got that kind of cash, too."

"Oh, you have, have you?"

"That is, I know where I can put my hand on it."

"Go ahead," the gangster said, "and get to the point."

"I figured that you could snatch this girl and make a demand on the estate for seventy thousand dollars' ransom."

Morrison's tone showed sudden interest.

"Why seventy grand?" he asked.

"Because," Stagg told him, "that's the amount I *could* raise, and that's about the amount on deposit in the bank."

"Go ahead," Morrison said, with a voice that had lost much of its mocking scorn, and was almost respectful.

"The snatching job," Stagg said, "wouldn't look like it was done by any professional gang, but it would look like it was done by a bunch of amateurs. You'd make it look that way in your ransom notes."

"That's old stuff," Pug Morrison said. "That doesn't fool anybody. All regular snatchers try to make their stuff look like the work of cranks and amateurs."

"But, this would be different," Stagg went on. "You'd be snatching a woman that you couldn't get any money out of. In other words, you'd make a demand for seventy thousand dollars, the amount of money that Fannie Morelay left in the bank. Then, no matter how badly any executor of the estate wanted to pay it, he couldn't pay it under the law. The girl would have the money coming to her, but only after the estate had gone through probate. So you'd really have snatched a girl who didn't have any money or any opportunity of getting any immediate cash. There wouldn't be any relative who could pay. The newspapers would play it up big. It would be the work of blundering amateurs."

"Go ahead," Morrison said. "Maybe you've got something in your bean after all."

"Then, of course, having snatched the girl and not being able to get any money, you'd murder her. That would account for a motive. If I had the girl killed without having some other motive for the murder, someone might start suspecting me. It would look as though I might be in a position to profit by the killing."

"I see," Morrison said, musingly.

"Now, you get your letters ready. You take the girl. You get seventy thousand dollars, and you kill the girl."

"Listen," Morrison said, thoughtfully, "how do we know we ain't going to double-cross one another?"

"You can't double-cross me," Stagg said, "because I've thought it all out in advance. I'm not going to double-cross you, but I'm going to show you how you can keep me from giving you anything that looks like a double-cross."

"Go ahead," Morrison said, "show me. I'm listening."

"You take the girl," Stagg said. "And when you take the girl, you take seventy thousand dollars at the same time. And at the same time you take the money, you deliver the letters demanding payment of a ransom."

"You mean we get the cash at the same time we make the snatch?" asked the gangster.

"That's right."

"Well," Morrison said, slowly, "that's jake with me, but how about you. You said you'd done some figuring on your own account. Let's have it."

"I'm figuring this way," Stagg said. "It's got to be a genuine snatch. Therefore, as soon as you make the demand, you're in the kidnapping racket. You don't dare to turn the girl loose then because she could identify your men and you'd be on the dodge. You've got to kill her once she finds out what she's up against."

"How are we going to work this?" Morrison asked.

"I'm going to tell you where you can contact with the girl. She's going to hire a detective."

"The hell she is!" Morrison exclaimed.

"Yes, she's going to go to the Victoria Hotel and register as Ethel Mason. She has an appointment for a detective to meet her there at eleven thirty tonight."

"So what?" asked Morrison.

"So," Stagg said, "you go there about an hour earlier – about ten thirty. The girl will be there. You tell her that you're the detective, that you got rid of the case you were working on earlier than you had expected. And that you're there to talk with her. She's going to tell you some stuff about the killing of her aunt. She's a little bit suspicious about it. You tell her you want to see the premises. You get her in your car and drive her out to the Morelay house. But don't stop. Tell her you're going on past. There's a drug store about two blocks down the street. Tell her you've seen as much of the house as you want from the outside. Stop in front of the drug store and tell her that you want to see specimens of her aunt's signature; that it's important that you see them; that you would like to see some cancelled cheques."

"Go on," Morrison said.

"The only way she can get those is by telephoning me," Stagg said. "She'll telephone me and ask me to send her some cheques and documents that are specimens of her aunt's signature. She'll make some sort of an excuse. I'll put seventy thousand dollars in currency in a black bag and send it by a messenger the girl knows. I'll try and use a girl friend of hers. You take the bag, open it, look in it, find that there's seventy thousand bucks there, and then give the messenger a note to open after she's gone five blocks from the place. That note will be a demand for ransom.

"You get out of the car when you accept the bag, and you have a mask on your face. Do you get the sketch? If you aren't wearing the mask, you don't get the bag with the seventy grand. If you are wearing the mask and make the demand for ransom, you get the bag.

"The newspapers make a big hullabaloo about it, and then some wise guy finds out that the money couldn't be paid, no matter how badly Tess Copley might want it paid. The snatching is branded as the work of amateurs. The newspapers give you the horse-laugh. You retaliate by bumping the kid off and dumping the body by the side of the road somewhere. That's all there is to it."

There was a moment of silence.

Pug Morrison's voice was low and thoughtful.

"Buddy," he said, "you've got a brain on your shoulders. We need you in our gang. You've got something that we need."

"You can't get it," Stagg rasped. "I'm a business man. I've got affairs of my own to consider."

The gangster's voice was once more filled with respect.

"You made out a fake set of books," he said. "You'd been waiting for an opportunity to substitute them. You heard the old woman telephoning for the cops when the guy got in the kitchen. You recognized that as your opportunity. You waited until the bird sneaked out of the window, and then you stuck the fake books in front of the woman, slammed the hatchet in her head, ducked out, and tried to make a getaway. But the cops came around the corner just as you were getting to your machine. So you pretended you were getting *out* of your automobile instead of getting in, and started up to the house as though nothing had happened."

"Suppose I did," said Stagg, "what of it?"

"Nothing," said Morrison, "except that you used your noodle to make maybe a couple of million dollars for yourself, to say nothing of covering up any little shortages that might exist in your affairs."

"What makes you think there are shortages?" asked Stagg.

Pug Morrison's laugh was ironical.

"Seventy thousand bucks," he said, slowly, "seventy thousand bucks that you can 'put your hands on'. And don't bother about all that elaborate program, because you ain't going to cross me – not with a murder rap I can pin on you.

"You just send out the jane with the bag. Have seventy grand in the bag unless you want to go to the chair. We'll make the snatch. You kick through with your end."

The Patent Leather Kid turned to Bill Brakey, and nodded his head.

Brakey turned and tiptoed across the floor of the bath-room. The Patent Leather Kid was at his heels. As noise-lessly as two shadows, they slipped to the back of the house, found a back door, opened it and flitted like silent shadows downstairs to a back yard which opened on an alley.

Pug Morrison was driving away as the pair reached the cross street.

"What a sweet little playmate *that* guy is!" Bill Brakey said.

"Playmate is right," The Patent Leather Kid told him, "because we're going to play with him."

V
According to Schedule

Pug Morrison was too smart to make the contact himself. The Patent Leather Kid, lounging in the lobby of the Victoria Hotel, had left word with the telephone operator that he was to be signalled when a call was put through to the room of "Ethel Mason". The flash of a detective's badge and a five-dollar tip had been all that was necessary to secure her cooperation.

When The Kid got the signal, he carefully studied the man who was at the telephone desk over which appeared the sign, "TELEPHONES TO GUESTS' ROOMS".

The man was very smooth-shaven. His hands were well manicured. His clothes bore the stamp of expensive workmanship. His shoes fitted like gloves. There was an assurance about the manner in which he held his head, a quick restlessness about his hands that was reminiscent of Bill Brakey's long, tapering hands.

The man hung up the telephone, moved with quick, nervous steps to the elevator, and was whisked up.

The Patent Leather Kid smoked in contemplative silence.

Twenty minutes elapsed before the man returned. This time there was a young woman at his side. She was wrapped in a heavy cloth coat with a wide fur collar. She wore a tight-fitting black hat trimmed with white. Her eyes were large and black. Her lips had been carefully applied so that they were quite crimson. The Kid could not see too much of her figure because of the heavy coat, but he gathered that she was slim-waisted, and she carried her head with a little tilt to one side which indicated something of the vibrant individuality which seemed to radiate from her.

The Kid got to his feet, stretched, yawned, tossed away the end of his cigarette and nodded to Bill Brakey, who was standing near the door.

The man and the young woman left the hotel, went directly to a shining closed car which was drawn up in front of the kerb. Bill Brakey, getting The Kid's signal, had placed himself in a position of vantage, where he could see the interior of the car. The Kid, standing in the doorway of the hotel, stretched and yawned, as though debating just how to spend the evening.

There was a moment while introductions were performed, and The Kid knew from the introductions that there was only one other man in the car. That man, of course, would be Pug Morrison himself. Morrison wouldn't make a contact in a public hotel with a young woman who was subsequently to be murdered. On the other hand, he would not delegate the receipt of seventy thousand dollars in cash money to any of his subordinates.

The young woman entered the car. The door slammed. The car purred away, Tess Copley occupying the front seat with the driver, who, The Kid surmised, would be Pug Morrison. The contact man occupied the rear of the car.

The car purred into smooth motion and rounded the corner. The Patent Leather Kid nodded to Bill Brakey. Bill Brakey moved over to the place where The Kid's high-powered machine was parked against the kerb. He slid in behind the wheel and had the motor started by the time The Kid jumped into the seat and said, "Step on it, Bill. I think they're going to the Morelay house, but there's no use taking chances. We'll keep them in sight until we make sure that's the way they're heading."

They swung around the corner. Bill Brakey snapped the car into high gear. They accelerated into swift speed, and within three blocks picked up the tail light of the big sedan.

"Okay," The Kid said. "Let's drop behind now."

They followed for four blocks, and then The Kid nodded.

"They're headed for the Morelay place. We can cut through on the side streets and get there a little before they do."

The Kid sat back against the cushions while Bill Brakey piloted the car with deft skill. They passed the location of the grim tragedy where Mrs Morelay had been done to death, swung up a side street, and parked the car.

The Patent Leather Kid got out.

"Let's look it over, Bill," he said.

They moved as silently as shadows down the side street to the corner, waited until they heard the sound of a car, then peered out at the headlights that showed first as two gleaming eyes of white fire, then purred past, giving them a glimpse of the big sedan as it slid smoothly to a halt, exactly as Walter Stagg had planned.

The big sedan waited, the motor running. After a few minutes, the motor was shut off. A woman crossed to the drug store and returned.

The Kid nodded to Bill Brakey.

"Looks," he said, "as though it's going through according to schedule."

A man emerged from the car as automobile headlights came in sight down the street. The man paused to adjust a mask about the upper part of his face. From the interior of the big sedan came the sound of a woman's scream, a scream that was promptly suppressed.

The masked man moved to the rear of the car, flung a cloth over the rear licence plate. The man in the driver's seat started the car. The purring sound of the running motor was audible to the waiting pair.

"Better start our car, Bill," The Patent Leather Kid said.

Bill Brakey started the powerful motor, settled down behind the steering wheel, opened the door opposite him so that The Kid could jump in without the loss of a moment.

The headlights of the other car showed more plainly, then a taxicab rattled past. A girl sat in the rear of the cab. The cab slid to a stop by the side of the big sedan. The cab driver picked up a small suitcase from the floorboards, started to step from the cab. The young woman was fumbling with the door catch.

The masked man stepped forward, so that the headlights of the taxicab showed not only his mask, but the blued-steel of the automatic which he held in his right hand. There was the sound of a scream from the girl. The taxicab driver slowly elevated his hands. The bag dropped to the street. The masked man shoved an envelope in through the partially opened window of the taxicab, motioned with his gun. The cab driver slid back to his place behind the wheel. The cab rattled into slow motion. The masked figure raised his gun and fired twice, deliberately shooting out both front and rear tyre on the right hand side. Then he scooped up the bag, turned and ran to the sedan. The sedan almost instantly glided into swift motion.

The Patent Leather Kid raised his arm in a beckoning gesture and gave a shrill whistle. Instantly, Bill Brakey shot the powerful car into motion. It slid to a stop beside The Kid. The Kid climbed the running board on the side near the wheel.

"It's going to be a gun fight, Bill," he said. "I'll take the wheel."

Bill Brakey slid over to the other seat and snapped the door closed. The Patent Leather Kid adjusted himself behind the wheel. His patent leather shoe pressed down on the throttle. The car shot ahead.

As The Kid sent the car into a turn at the corner, he snapped the band of the black patent leather mask about his forehead, adjusted the mask so that his eyes fitted the eye-holes. The car was continually accelerating its speed.

They passed the crippled taxicab and, as they passed, The Kid snapped the gearshift into the overdrive. His car swept ahead with the grace of a seagull swooping down to skim the surface of ocean waves. The big sedan rounded a corner. The Kid swung wide, skidded his car into a turn, stepped on the throttle.

"They know we're on their tail, Bill," he said. "They're going to run for it."

The sedan swung wide, swayed far over on two wheels as it took a corner. The Kid, grinning, swung his car at the same corner, keeping all four screaming wheels on the pavement. Bill Brakey slipped a heavy calibre gun from its shoulder holster, nestled it in his right hand.

"Don't shoot until they do," The Kid told him, shifting gears as he spoke.

The cars roared down a paved side street devoid of traffic, travelling at a mad pace. The Kid's car gained.

The driver of the sedan tried one more turn, not realizing that The Kid's low-hung car was far less top-heavy. The driver lost control of the sedan. It ran on two wheels, came back to four wheels with a terrific jolt which swayed the big body on its springs.

A hand knocked out the rear window. A gun spatted viciously. A bullet struck the side of the windshield support on The Kid's car and ricocheted off into the night.

"Try for the driver, Bill," said The Patent Leather Kid calmly, and swung his car wide so that Bill Brakey would have a clear shot around the side of the windshield.

Brakey's gun crashed twice. The dark hulk of the driver's body jerked and swayed. The big sedan screamed into a skid, whipped entirely around, crashed against a kerb, hung balanced for a moment, and then toppled to its side with a roar of breaking glass and the sound of grinding steel.

Bill Brakey flung open the door of the car, jumped to the ground. The Patent Leather Kid was out from behind the wheel and on the ground ahead of him. Together, they raced towards the big sedan.

"Look out!" yelled The Kid suddenly. "They've got a cover-car!"

Headlights came into view as a car skidded around the corner.

"Quick!" shouted The Patent Leather Kid. "I'll get the girl and the bag. You hold the car."

Bill Brakey dropped behind a fire hydrant. His gun crashed once. The headlights of the approaching car wobbled. The car screamed as the driver applied brakes and skidded in close to the kerb. Little flashes of gunfire spurted into the night. The Patent Leather Kid tugged at the jammed door of the sedan, finally wrenched it open.

A young woman stared at him from wide black eyes. As she caught sight of the black mask which covered the upper half of The Patent Leather Kid's face, she screamed.

"It's all right, Miss Copley," The Kid said. "I came to get you."

He leaned forward and pulled her through the doorway.

Pug Morrison was lying unconscious, his head badly gashed. The man who had been in the rear seat was making futile motions, clawing with his fingers at the upholstery on the back of the seat.

"Your friends will be here in a minute, buddy," The Kid said. "In the meantime, fork over that bag. Walter Stagg said we'd find seventy grand in it."

He caught sight of the bag, lurched towards it, and then grinned at the girl.

"We've got to make a run for it," he said. "There's a battle going on."

The street echoed and re-echoed to the sound of shots. Men had jumped out of the cover-car, taken refuge behind such protection as they could find and were directing a cross-fire at Bill Brakey.

The Kid sprinted to the car. Someone shot at the pair, but the bullets were wide of the mark. The Kid flung the girl into the seat.

"Bend over low," he said.

He jumped in behind the wheel and tooted the horn, signal to Bill Brakey.

Bill Brakey suddenly stood erect. His guns roared in a pealing crescendo of rapid fire, a fire of such scathing accuracy that it drove his enemies to cover, and in the moment when they were ducking to cover, Bill Brakey sprinted for the car.

The Kid had it in second gear. The car gave a terrific lurch and then snarled into speed.

Behind them came a burst of fire. The bullet-proof body in the rear of the car deflected half a dozen bullets that thudded into the steel.

"They'll try the gasoline tank and the tyres," Bill Brakey said, slipping a fresh clip of cartridges into his gun. "I'll give them something to keep their minds occupied."

He fired four or five well-directed shots, then slid in beside the girl.

"Here they come," he said.

"We'll make a run for it," The Kid told him. The car by this time was in high gear. The Kid waited until it was going fifty-five miles an hour before he flung in the overdrive. The car swept into instant response, screaming down the pavement at better than sixty miles an hour, a sixty which soon became seventy, eighty-five. The speedometer needle quivered around ninety miles an hour.

A car came out of a side street.

There was a moment of tense silence, but The Kid swung his car in a deft skidding turn, so that he swept past the obstructing car, the driver of which had lost his head and left the car in such a position that it blocked the intersection.

The pursuing car tried a similar swerving turn. The driver was not skilled enough. The car went out of control, swung completely around in a circle, and then crashed into an ornamental lamp post.

"Okay, Kid," said Bill Brakey, "slow down and let's introduce ourselves to Miss Copley."

VI
A $70,000 Coupon

Walter Stagg was nervously pacing the floor, cracking the knuckles of his right hand against the extended palm of his left hand. From time to time he glanced nervously at the clock on the wall.

The doorbell rang. Stagg did not wait to work the electric buzzer, but dashed madly down the stairs to open the door.

A white-faced young woman staggered in through the opening and handed him an envelope.

"Tess!" she screamed. "She's been kidnapped!"

Walter Stagg ripped open the envelope with trembling fingers and stared at the demand for ransom.

"What happened?" he asked. "Tell me about it."

"I took the papers out in a cab," the young woman said. "A man was waiting. He had a mask. He drew a gun on us and took the papers. Then he gave us this demand and told us we'd never see Tess alive again unless we did just as we were instructed."

Walter Stagg heaved a great sigh of relief. "Take this to the police at once," he said.

"But they were going to kill her if we went to the police."

"Don't be a fool!" he said. "We've got no money. The money is all tied up in the estate. We couldn't pay any ransom. We've *got* to go to the police. Did you get a description of the man?"

"He was masked," she said. "He was a big man with a black suit – I saw that much."

"Take this letter," Walter Stagg said, "and go to the police."

She hesitated a moment, looking at him in white-faced anguish.

"Tess was with them," she said, "in the car – and –"

"Go to the police," Walter Stagg told her, "otherwise you'll be compounding a felony. It's up to the police to handle the case. We can give publicity to it. The newspaper can feature the fact that none of the money can be paid out except on an order of the court, and a court can't order moneys paid from an estate."

The girl took the envelope, turned and ran to a taxicab which was waiting with the motor running. Walter Stagg stood in the doorway for a moment, watching her, then slammed and bolted the door. He walked back up two flights of stairs, and a smile of serene satisfaction twisted his lips.

He entered the living room on the front of the flat, turned and locked the door behind him, then suddenly gave a convulsive start.

A man was stooping over the wall safe, and, as Stagg looked, the lock clicked and the man pulled the door of the safe open.

Walter Stagg's hand shot to his hip. The gun at which he tugged caught for a moment in the lining of his hip pocket. Then, as he freed it, he became conscious of another figure which was seated comfortably in one of the overstuffed chairs, holding a blued-steel gun levelled steadily at him.

"Better drop it," said the voice of Bill Brakey.

The Patent Leather Kid did not even look up as Walter Stagg's hands shot into the air and the gun slipped from his nerveless fingers and thudded to the floor.

The Patent Leather Kid pulled out some papers, looked through them and chuckled.

"Here's the will, Bill," he said. "Stagg was suppressing it."

"Who the devil are you?" screamed Stagg.

The Patent Leather Kid looked up. His enigmatical eyes glittered through the eye-holes in the patent leather mask.

"They sometimes call me," he said, "The Patent Leather Kid."

He turned back to the safe.

"Good heavens!" he said, "here are the original books! The damn fool hadn't destroyed them as yet."

Stagg took two quick steps forward, stopped only when he heard Bill Brakey's voice, low with ominous menace.

"One more step," said Brakey, "and I'll shoot your legs out from under you."

Stagg stopped, his face working with fury.

"Damn you!" he said. "You'll pay for this – both of you! The police will have you for this. The Patent Leather Kid, huh? Well, this once they've got you where they want you."

"I neglected to tell you," said The Patent Leather Kid calmly, "that as soon as Pug Morrison had delivered the ransom note to the taxi driver, we rescued the girl and, incidentally, picked up the seventy thousand dollars. I inadvertently dropped a remark which makes him think we were working for you."

There was a moment of silence while the full force of The Kid's words struck home to Stagg.

"Think you're working for *me*?" he screamed.

"Yes," The Kid said, "he sort of thought you had double-crossed him. What makes it bad is that there was a cover-car following along behind. It had some of Morrison's men in it. He didn't trust you all the way. I'm afraid there'll be trouble."

Stagg's upstretched hands slowly dropped. There was not enough strength in his arms to hold them up.

"Good God!" he exclaimed. "You . . ."

Bill Brakey nodded towards the door.

"We got you into it," he said. "We'll give you a chance to get out. You can beat it if you want to."

"But it's a death sentence," Stagg said. "They'll gun me out. They'll . . ."

"Better get started," Bill Brakey told him.

Stagg turned, ran to the door, struggled with the lock with futile, nerveless fingers which simply wouldn't coordinate. Bill Brakey opened the door for him, saw him into the corridor, listened to the wild beat of his steps as Stagg dashed down the staircase and wrenched open the front door. A moment later he heard the *ker-flop, ker-flop, ker-flop, ker-flop* of his running steps on the cement sidewalk.

Bill Pope, the explorer, regarded Inspector Brame with twinkling eyes.

"At least, inspector," he said, "you've got to admit that The Patent Leather Kid did a good job this time."

Inspector Brame's face slowly flushed to a dark shade that was almost a purple.

"The damned outlaw!" he said. "He wounded one man and almost killed another in one car, and killed a gangster outright in another. He had bullets flying around the street like hail. It was the most lawless demonstration of gangster warfare that has ever been staged in the city."

Bill Pope chuckled.

"Nevertheless," he said, "the public has got a great kick out of it."

"It was murder, just the same," Inspector Brame said, "and when we get him, we'll –"

"Oh, no, it wasn't murder," Bill Pope said. "You forget that the girl testifies she was being kidnapped; that there's a letter to prove her claims. Also, a girl friend who is a witness. All The Patent Leather Kid did was to rescue the girl from the hands of her kidnappers."

"The police don't need to accept help at the hands of a crook," Inspector Brame said, with dignity.

"Where were the police at the time, inspector?"

"That's neither here nor there," Inspector Brame stormed.

"Neither were the police," chuckled the explorer.

Renfroe, the banker, clucked his tongue sympathetically against the roof of his mouth.

"I quite agree with you, inspector. It's a pretty pass when crooks have to come to the rescue of people who are being kidnapped. It's an insult to the police efficiency."

Dan Seller yawned, stifled the yawn with four polite forefingers and spoke suavely.

"Wasn't there another murder, inspector?" he asked. "Seems to me I heard something about it over the radio."

"Walter Stagg," said Inspector Brame grimly. "He was shot down by machine guns. Someone took him for a ride."

"Rather looks as though he'd been mixed up with the gangsters, doesn't it?" asked the explorer.

"Yes," Inspector Brame said, "we've got plenty on Walter Stagg. It's too bad they killed him. We could have sent him to the chair."

"What for?" asked Renfroe.

"For the murder of Mrs Morelay."

"But I thought you said some tramp killed her."

"That," Inspector Brame said, "was merely a stall we were making in order to trap the real criminal. When we went to Walter Stagg's flat, we found unmistakable evidence that he had doctored certain books of account and had prepared a duplicate set ready to be substituted at the proper moment. He found his opportunity when Mrs Morelay telephoned the police that a tramp was in her kitchen. He split her head open with a hatchet, substituted the duplicated book of accounts, and took the real one with him."

"You have evidence of that?" asked Dan Seller, almost moodily.

"I'll say we have. We searched his apartment and found the original books. They still had blood stains on them, and what's more, we found Mrs Morelay's fingerprints all over them, showing that those were the books she had been examining at the time she was killed."

Dan Seller once more stifled a yawn.

"All this talk of shooting and violence," he said, "bores me dreadfully."

Inspector Brame snorted.

"That's the worst of you young coupon-clippers," he said, "you live a life of idle ease and luxury, and don't know anything at all about what goes on out on the firing line. You should have the job I have for a while – only you wouldn't last forty-eight hours. You wouldn't have the faintest idea about how to go after a crook."

Dan Seller nodded placid agreement.

"Doubtless you're right, old top," he said, "every man to his trade, you know."

Inspector Brame's grunted comment was inaudible, but Bill Pope, the explorer, surveyed Dan Seller with watchful, appraising eyes, in which there was just the suggestion of a twinkle.

"You look tired, Seller," he said, "as though you had been through something of a strain."

Dan Seller nodded.

"Yes," he said, "I clipped a coupon – a seventy-thousand-dollar coupon."

Renfroe, the banker, stared with wide eyes.

"What kind of a coupon would that be?" he asked.

"Oh, kind of a grab bag affair," said Dan Seller, casually.

Bill Pope, the explorer, was suddenly seized with a fit of coughing.

Goodbye Hannah

Steve Fisher

T he captain said: "You've been drinking," and that
was all he said about it so Smith thought he
couldn't be looking so badly; yet Smith knew it wasn't
the whisky – or anyway, not just the whisky – that made
him look as if he had been hit in the face with a ton of wet
towels. His skin was a greyish-white; and there was that
glazed ebony in his eyes; and there were lines coming
around his mouth. Oh, he was different, everything about
him had changed, it was only that in the grey suit, and
the felt hat that was shoved back on his head, and the
unlit cigarette which hung in his mouth, he looked *somewhat* the same, so that people hadn't begun yet to really
notice.

"Listen, Smitty," the captain went on, "what I called
you about was 277, a new one, see? I want you to look at it.
It might be Hannah Stevens."

Smith grew rigid with pulse throbbing in his throat, and
light flaring in his eyes. He gripped the captain's arm, and
the captain looked around and down at where his hand was.

"What's this?"

Smith released the grip and gradually found his voice.
"You mean you think you've got Hannah here?"

"Well, we don't know. Suicide, nose dive. Battered head
– no face that you can recognize. No other identification,
either."

Breathing again, Smith said: "Oh." Then: "Let's have a
look at it."

They moved through the morgue along the rows of
numbered ice-vaults. The captain was saying: "Since

you've got that case you'd know if it was her if anybody would. You know all about her, don't you?"

He said: "Yes, all about her. What kind of perfume she used, and where she got her hair done, and what movie stars she liked the best. I know what time she went to bed every night, and what time she got up. I know what her breakfasts were, I –"

"What are you – her brother?"

"No, I've never seen her. I'd never heard of her until you handed me the case three days ago. She was just another missing person. How many thousands have we every year? She was just a name on a card –"

But he stopped talking suddenly for the captain had turned in front of vault 277 and was pulling it out. It slid like a drawer. Smith's heart was massaging his chest, but he knew he had to look down and he did. There wasn't much of a head left. The hair had been copper. The body had been beautiful and young.

The captain said: "And still they come to New York in droves every year to act or model or write or marry a millionaire. I wish they could see her."

Smith was looking at the body and saying: "It isn't Hannah Stevens."

"It *isn't*?"

"No."

"How can you tell?"

"Hannah had a scar on her little toe. The hair on her legs was lighter, and there was a mole just over her hip."

"Listen, screwball, are you sure about that?"

"Yes, I'm sure."

"Okay," the captain said, and he shoved back the drawer. "Another one unidentified, that's all." They started walking back towards the office. "What kind of a dame is this Hannah Stevens?"

Smith was looking straight ahead of him. "She's beautiful," he said. "She's the most beautiful thing that ever walked on the earth. Her parents are worth half a million. She made her debut in Boston three years ago and then her folks moved to Newport and she spent most of her time in New York with the young crowd. I have a dozen pictures of her and so have about six of the town's biggest detective agencies."

"Well, you seem to know as much about her as –"

He held up his hand. "I haven't begun to know anything about her yet. She was engaged to a young man by the name of Ronald Watt. I intend to interview him. After that –"

"Listen," said the captain, "I think you've gone wacky, but it's all right. Just keep your face clean and let me know anything new that develops."

"Okay," said Smith, and he turned the cigarette around so that the dry part was in his mouth now. He moved past the captain and through the door.

He sat in his room with a bottle of rye on the table beside him and a lot of peanut shells scattered across the floor. He sat there with his hands folded, staring at the wall, or past it; and then he got up and did a turn around the room and came back, pouring more rye. Now he fixed his gaze on the dresser where her pictures were lined like a display in front of a motion picture theatre. He picked up the first picture and looked at her shining eyes. Someone had told him they were grey and her hair was the colour of crystal-clear honey. He saw the strong cleft of her chin, and the thin, yet definite, nose line. He saw her beauty in a radiance that blinded him and he put the picture down and picked up the next.

He kept doing this, going over the pictures one by one, and then going back for another drink of rye. He had long ago ceased trying to reason with himself. He had quit looking at his vision in the mirror and saying: "You're going nuts, Johnny. They're going to come and get up and slap you in a straitjacket if you don't snap out of it." There was no longer comprehension, understanding, or sanity of motive. The pictures, her history, the fragments of things he had learned about her; the odour of her perfume that was on the handkerchief that was in his drawer; the torn stocking that he had picked out of the wastebasket in her apartment; the spilled face powder that he had scooped up and wrapped in tissue paper, all of these things he had of hers, all of the stories he had been told of her; everything secondhand, everything old and used; memories of someone he had never known, told him that he loved her.

At first it had been fascination and this had grown to obsession, and then beyond obsession, beyond all reason. When he tried to sleep he thought he heard what they had said was the rich lilt of her voice; he saw her in a shimmering gold gown, walking and talking and dancing; set against a background of a dazzling cut-glass Fifty-second Street cocktail bar, he saw the honey of hair on her shoulders, and he saw her lift a drink to her lips . . .

The clangour of the telephone jarred him. He went back to the bed and sat down. He picked up the instrument. "Johnny Smith," he said.

"This is Mrs Stevens," said a soft, restrained voice. "Hannah's mother."

"Yes, Mrs Stevens."

"I hope you don't mind – you said I could keep in touch with you. It helps, you know."

"Yes," he said, "I know it does." Then: "Have the private detectives –"

"No trace," Mrs Stevens said.

There was a silence . . .

"I see."

She lifted her voice for the first time. "We all loved her so – we all want her back so badly, I can't understand why –"

"I know," said Johnny, quietly.

"I'm sending Ronald Watt over to your hotel," she went on; "you wanted to see him."

"Yes, thanks. It may help."

He talked to her for a moment longer and then hung up. He sat there wondering if Hannah's voice had been something like that – if it had had the same softness?

He put the liquor away and cleaned up the peanuts, after a fashion, brushing them all into one corner; then he got up and straightened his tie. He stuck an unlighted cigarette in his mouth and let it dangle there. Then he went to the window, waiting; he looked down ten storeys on Manhattan. All of those lights she had known and loved. Where was she? Why had she gone?

He stood here for some time, and then there was the telephone again.

"Mr Watt downstairs."

"Send him up."

When Watt tapped on the door Johnny opened it, standing there, the cigarette in his mouth, his eyes flickering. "Come in," he said. He looked after the young man as he walked past him into the room; and then he closed the door, leaning back against it. He stood leaning against the door, not saying anything, watching Ronald Watt. Watt was wearing country tweed but he would have looked better in tails and white tie, Johnny decided; his face in one way seemed weak, and in another showed strong possibilities. He had a high forehead, and brown eyes – bleak now – a drooping, though handsome mouth. His hat was in his hand and a boyish cowlick of hair overhung his forehead. He sat down on the edge of the bed.

"She was engaged to you?"

"You mean Miss Stevens."

"I mean Hannah Stevens," said Johnny.

"Yes, we were engaged." Watt was nervous.

"When did you see her last?"

"On the night before she – she disappeared."

"Explain everything leading up to that. I know after she left you she was seen in two other places alone, at the bars. I know she got in a taxicab and said to the driver: 'Just drift around the park, please,' and that she got out of the cab, in the park, at around Ninety-sixth Street, and that no one, apparently, has seen her since. But tell me up to the point where she left you. *Everything!*"

"Why, there isn't much to tell, Mr Smith. For a month she'd been avoiding me. I kept calling at her apartment. I kept leaving messages; several times I sat all night in front waiting for her to come in, but she never did. And she wasn't at home. But finally she gave in and saw me twice for lunch – that is, twice in succession, and then she agreed to go to dinner with me. Well, we'd had dinner, and we were drinking cocktails, and everything seemed swell again; she seemed to be her old self, warming up to me, and I thought pretty soon I'd say, 'Honey, let's hurry up and get married.

I can't stand being without you.' Then she saw someone pass through the dining room."

"Who?"

"I don't know. I asked her and she laughed and said: 'Only the friend of a friend,' but after that she seemed nervous, and finally she took my hand and looked at me in the way that only she can, Mr Smith. She said: 'Angel, you're rich and spoiled, and a no-good scoundrel, but I love you. Always remember that, will you? That I love you.' She said that, and then she got up. I thought she would be right back. So I sat there. I sat there for an hour and a half."

"That's the last you saw of her?"

"That's the last," said Watt. He had noticed the pictures of Hannah on the dresser and was looking at them.

Smith said: "Why did she call you a scoundrel, Watt?"

"Just an affectionate term. Nothing –"

"Don't lie, Watt."

Ronald Watt leaped to his feet. "I'm not!"

Johnny grabbed the front of his coat and shoved him back down on the bed. "You are, you little punk, and I'm going to wallop the head off you if you don't tell me the whole truth. I told you I had to know everything. I don't know what's the matter with those private cops you've hired, but to me it's obvious that she disappeared on account of you."

"That's a –"

Johnny slapped him across the mouth. "The sooner you talk, Watt, the better."

"Let me out of here!"

"You're not going to get out, and you're going to talk if I have to kill you."

"Blast you, you let me out," Watt said between clenched teeth, and he rose, shoving against Johnny. Johnny clipped him under the jaw, and then he held him up against the wall and slapped him. When he finally let him drop to the bed Ronald Watt sat there with his face bloody and said:

"I don't know what you want me to tell you. Unless it's why Hannah turned cool towards me in the first place. I was doing a little gambling." He looked up, his face pale now. "Old story, isn't it? My family didn't know, no one did except Hannah and she found out by accident. Well, I got in pretty deeply. Damn deeply. I didn't dare open about it to my father and Nicki said I had my choice. He said welshers, no matter who they were, usually had a bad time of it, if I knew what he meant, and I did. They had *accidents*, maybe playing polo. At least that was the rumour, and I was scared stiff."

"I'll bet," said Johnny.

"So he said I had my choice, either that or – or I could work for him. My family was social and – well, he just wanted a little information now and then and – ah, letters and things I might be able to pick up."

"You mean you were to be the go-between for a black-mail racket that Nicki was running."

"Well –"

"That's what you were. Well, the last mug that did that got made the fall guy when the thing fell through – and landed in prison. But go on."

Watt's face was strained. "What could I do? I pleaded with them, and – as it turned out –"

"I suppose Nicki told you to go home and forget it. To forget you owed him money, that he had reconsidered and decided you were too nice a guy to do work like that."

"No," Watt said, "not exactly that. They let me play again one night. I won back every cent I had lost and more on top of it. So what could Nicki do? He had to let me go. That's why I saw, and still see, no reason for telling it. I never did the work. It was just a proposition, and then I got out of it by –"

"– By winning back the money. Fool! You didn't win it back. Nicki *gave* it back to you! Know why?"

"Why?"

"Hannah!"

Ronald Watt stared for a moment, and then his jaw gaped open, and his face turned crimson.

"Now get out," said Johnny. "Get out before I kill you."

When Johnny Smith got outside, it was raining. He ducked across the sidewalk and got into a cab. He slammed the door and mumbled an address, and then he sat staring at the shining streets, and the lights along Broadway, at the streetcars, and buses, at the nightclubs, and the big cars pulling up in front of theatres; he sat seeing the rain slap against the window, and hearing the music from the radio, and remembering the words Watt had told him Hannah had said before she left. He remembered that Hannah had taken his hand and said to Watt: "You're a no-good scoundrel, but I love you. Always remember that, will you? That I love you?" He thought of this, and of a song Noel Coward had written: "Mad About the Boy"; and he kept watching the rain on the window of the taxicab.

The cab stopped at an apartment on Ninety-seventh Street near Central Park West, and Johnny got out, looking at the entrance of the building. He walked across and went inside, and showed the elevator man his badge, and put a twenty-dollar bill in his hand, saying: "I want a pass-key, and directions to Nicki Spioni's apartment." He had no trouble at all. The elevator man unlocked the door for him and then beat it.

Johnny stepped inside, closing the door behind him. There were a man and two women in the living room, drinking cocktails, and then Nicki, squat, and hard-faced, came in from the kitchen with a drink in his hand. He saw Johnny and the drink slipped and fell, the glass breaking. He said:

"What is this, mister?"

"Get your friends out, Nicki," Johnny said.

"Listen to him," said Nicki.

"I came about Hannah," Johnny murmured.

Nicki's face changed. "Who are you?"

"I'm a cop."

Nicki looked at his friends and they got up, staring coldly at Johnny but not saying anything. They found their wraps and got out. Johnny locked the door. When he turned around Nicki had a gun in his hand.

"All right, copper, now you can tell me just what kind of a caper this is."

Johnny smiled thinly and put an unlit cigarette in his mouth. "Too bad you weren't at your club tonight. I telephoned, had a couple of federal men go down to look at your books; couple of city cops went along, think they might pick up a little evidence that will send you up for blackmail."

Nicki gulped, his Adam's apple bulging from his throat. "Is this – a pinch?"

"Not this," said Johnny, "the pinch will come later. But not from me."

"Get out of my way then," Nicki said; "I'm getting out of here."

Johnny put the sole of one foot against the door and folded his arms. "You aren't going yet. I have a few questions about Hannah."

Nicki's face muscles flinched. "I don't know anything about her."

"No?"

"No, I don't. And you'd better move, or one of these slugs will move you, and I'll roll you aside."

"You won't shoot," Johnny said. "You're too yellow to shoot anybody, Nicki. You go in for blackmail. You go it the dirty way. But you wouldn't kill anybody. You're too afraid of the chair. We both know that, so you can put the gun down and tell me about Hannah or you'll go to the chair anyway – for *her* murder."

"What do you mean?"

"You were the last one to see her. She got out of a cab at Central Park near Ninety-sixth, and came over here. What happened then?"

"She didn't, she – How do you know what she did?"

"Listen, Nicki, we won't go into that. I just want to know what happened."

The squat man was sweating. He put his gun in his pocket, and mopped his face with a handkerchief. But the sweat came faster then he could wipe if off. There was a wild look in his dark eyes; he raised heavy brows, said:

"What else do you think you know?"

"That you made a bargain with her. She was a pawn for Ronald Watt. What did you tell her you were going to do to Watt?"

Nicki was trembling, he seemed to go all to pieces. He suddenly put his arms up over his face and sat down on the divan; he sat there for a moment, and Johnny stood at the door watching him.

"Somebody told me – about her –" he whispered. His

fists were clenched. "I told her I was going to use Watt but if she could get the money he owed it'd be okay. She tried – couldn't get the money. Couldn't explain why she needed thirty thousand dollars. She got an allowance, but I wouldn't take payments on instalments from Watt so why from her? Then I – I got that idea – I told her after we'd used Watt awhile we'd kill him. I made her think Watt didn't have a chance, and the little punk didn't. I wouldn't have killed him, that was bluff, but *he* thought I would, and so did she –" He stopped here.

"Go on," Johnny said.

"I told her – if she'd come around – if she'd be regular to me – if she wouldn't see anybody but me for a month and –"

"Never mind the details."

"Well," Nicki went on, "that was all right. It was all right, see. I let her see Watt win back his money. I let her see that he was clear. He told her he'd never gamble again. So she thought – that she had saved his life – or I had, and –"

"So what happened?" said Johnny.

"That's it," Nicki whispered, "that's it. I've wanted to tell somebody." He pounded his chest. "It's been here, up inside me. It's been killing me. She was a good sport. She was the squarest kid that ever lived. Never a peep out of her, do you see? Never a squawk. There was never a finer woman ever lived –" Nicki's hands were in his hair now; it was awful to look at him. "Then do you know what happened –"

"Tell me," said Johnny quietly.

"I fell in love with her. Me, Nicki Spioni, I fell in love with her. I was crazy for her. I wanted to marry her. I told her I'd marry her and go straight – just run my club or go away, out West, to Honolulu, anywhere. I'd give her jewels, money, anything in the world she wanted. But she had all that. All of it. She was no cheap chorus girl. She was no Cinderella model, no ham actress. She had everything, I wasn't giving her a thing, I was taking – taking –"

"I don't want to hear that, I want to know what happened."

"The month ended, and she started seeing Watt again. She was crazy for that yellow rotter. I don't know why. She loved him like I loved her. She ate and slept and dreamed him. There wasn't anything in the world she wouldn't do for him. I had taken her pride, I had taken everything from her, but she thought she could go back to him because it had been his jam, and she had gone to bat. She figured that put them on the same plane, and they could go on and be happy even though she'd never tell him about it.

"I was insane with jealousy. I wanted to kill the guy. I wanted to shoot myself. I was going nuts. I couldn't sleep. I couldn't eat. Just the thought of her with him turned me inside out. But I couldn't do anything. She had kept her bargain and I was supposed to keep mine. I was supposed to but finally I couldn't. I couldn't, see? I cracked, do you get it? Went wacky!

"I found out where she was dining with Watt and sent one of my boys there. He passed the table and gave her a signal. When she went out to meet him he told her I wanted to see her, and double quick, or Watt was going to get bumped. Well, she went to pieces then. She had thought I'd be square, too. Oh, what a fool she was to trust *me* – to think that Nicki Spioni could keep his word!" He sucked in breath.

"Well, she came up here to have it out with me," Nicki went on; "she came up here, and I was blind drunk. She was going to marry Watt and she never wanted to see me again. I did everything to keep her. I cried. I got down on my hands and knees and begged. I crawled on the floor for her. But she wouldn't listen. I kept drinking. The room was spinning in a waltz. All I could hear was her saying: 'No! No! No!' I went out in the kitchen and got a knife and said if I couldn't have her nobody would. I said that, then I changed it and said if she went out I'd cut my throat right there in front of her. I said everything and anything that came to my mind. But she started to go anyway. She started to go, and I tried to stop her, and there was a scuffle. But she got out. I stood there looking at the door and then I came back here to the divan sobbing. Oh, I know men don't cry. But I did, I tell you. Like a damn kid. I fell on the divan crying, tearing out my heart, and then I passed out cold. I haven't seen her since."

"You didn't kill her?"

"No! I loved her! I loved her!" Nicki said.

"But more than that –?"

Nicki looked up, his face strangely white, his voice suddenly quiet. He seemed to be looking past Johnny. Then he slipped to his knees. He looked like nothing human. "One of – the boys – thought he saw her – on Seventy-second Street."

That was all he said, Johnny couldn't make him say another word. When the federal agents came about the tax evasion he was still there on his knees looking as if he had lost his mind. He didn't seem to see them at all. When they led him through the door he leaned on them for support as though the flame that was Hannah had burned his eyes from his sockets, and had taken his soul from his miserable body.

West Seventy-second Street: rain and sleet, night after night. You start at West End Avenue, at the drugstore on the corner and walk up. An apartment here, a hotel there. The corner of Broadway, the subway island, on across, the cigar store, the bank, a fur shop, the automat . . . Up and down . . . Faces, old, young, haggard, painted. Eventually a repetition of faces – the same faces, the same people, up and down . . .

Night after night.

He knew every store by name, he knew every merchant, he had been in every apartment and hotel. Over and over he had said: "Beautiful – the most beautiful creature that ever walked on this earth. Honey-blonde hair, about five feet four, carries her shoulders back, has a proud walk. Beautiful, the most beautiful creature . . ." The echo of his descriptions. Laughter. Parties. The Sunday papers on Saturday night. "Her name is Hannah Stevens, she's the most –"

He watched her name fade from the papers as other news crowded out the story of her disappearance. The last news he read was that anyone who discovered Hannah would receive ten thousand dollars reward. He read that and smiled grimly, and kept walking. At night he looked at her pictures, and talked to them. Other cases were piled a foot deep in his file. Missing persons. Family hysteria. Descriptions. Suicides. The click of ice-vaults, in and out. "Is this the man you were looking for?" "Is this the child you lost?" "Is this your mother who wandered off last Tuesday night?"

Everything in a swirl. His mind going – gradually. Hannah dominating every thought. The captain's lectures. "Lay off the drinks, Smith." The sobbing women at the office, the laughing husband. "My wife just disappeared." The cranks: "I'm going to commit suicide, so don't look for me!" The captain again: "Now, Smith, you've *got* to find this one, she's probably right over the bridge in Brooklyn; didn't she have a boyfriend who –"

But the nights were his own. Seventy-second Street. Up and down, heavy steps, nodding to the merchants.

He saw her on Saturday of the sixth week.

He had been in a market looking for her when she brushed by him and he caught the odour of the perfume and the powder, though it seemed heavier than he had imagined Hannah would use, and he turned to see her back, to see her moving off down the street. He stood watching, trembling, petrified. He had not seen her face and yet he knew that it was she. He knew her better than she knew herself.

He began following, watching the even swing of her legs. He ran a little to catch up, and he heard the click of her high heels on the sidewalk. She walked down to Riverside Drive and turned right. In a moment she entered an old apartment building. He hurried now to stop her, but the door clicked shut, and locked, and she went on in, through the inside door. He had seen no more than her back, the honey colour of her hair, but he knew it was she.

He waited there, hearing the traffic on Riverside Drive, seeing the lights on the Parkway beside the Hudson. He had always known, had always been certain that some day he would find her, but now that he had he could not diagnose his emotion beyond a feeling of great triumph. To see her, to talk to her in the flesh, not to her picture.

He climbed the steps of the apartment and scanned the names under the bells. Her name was not there, but she had changed it, of course. He rang the manager's bell. It buzzed and he went in and stood in a dimly lit hall. A fat woman clad in calico waddled out and looked him over.

"Can you tell me where I can find a blonde girl who lives here. She's the most beautiful creature that –"

"Upstairs, first door on your right. Only blonde we have in the house."

"Thank you," he said. "Thank you." He hurried up the stairs, making a lot of noise, and then he stood in front of her door. In front of Hannah Stevens' apartment. A door opened down the hall and a young woman clad in a kimono looked at him. She kept standing there. He looked the other way, and then another door opened. He did not glance towards it. Hannah's door opened finally. She was there, there in front of him. Her cheeks were rouged, and she was dressed in a red kimono.

She smiled woodenly. "Come in, honey," she said.

But he stood there, staring at her, and at a jagged knife scar that was slantwise across her cheek. It was puffed and red and made her look ugly. Words tumbled through his mind. "I had the knife and I told her I was going to stab myself, but she tried to go anyway, and there was a scuffle. . . One of the boys saw her on Seventy-second Street. . ." He remembered these words, looking at her, into her grey eyes, at her honey-coloured hair; then he remembered farther back than that, the last thing she had said to Ronald Watt: "You're rich, and spoiled, and a no-good scoundrel, but I love you. Always remember that, will you? That I love you."

"Well, are you coming in or not?"

"No, it – it was a mistake."

He fled down the steps like a fool, rockets exploding in his temples.

At the corner of Seventy-second and West End Avenue he went into the drugstore and telephoned.

"Listen, Captain," he said, "remember that old case – Hannah Stevens? Well, I've found out that I was all wet. Yeah – isn't that funny? I was screwy. First time in my life. I just found out tonight. She was the corpse in ice-vault 277 – that one with the battered head –"

When he hung up the telephone, he whispered: "Good-bye, Hannah," and then he put an unlighted cigarette in his mouth and got up and left the booth. He walked briskly towards Broadway.

Sinners' Paradise

Raoul Whitfield

I

H obart Sickler grinned broadly at his wife. But Helene
Sickler did not manage her usual smile in return. It
was a bit beyond her this morning.

"Scotch," Hobey stated in a placid voice, "is a bad drink
for women of your type, Pinky."

Pinky was Hobart's pet name for his wife. She possessed
such cute little toes, and there had been a time, two years
ago, when he had delighted in sitting on the edge of her bed
and playing with them. Pinky had come, somehow, out of
this habit.

"My type?" Helene's voice was a trifle weary. "Why *my*
type in particular?"

Hobey chuckled. He was rather inclined towards a
definite stoutness, and it seemed to Helene that in the
last year he had dropped back into his old ways – before
marriage ways.

"You're too temperamental," he stated lazily. "It affects
you too much."

Helene remained silent. Her head was splitting, and she
felt completely exhausted. And then, in spite of these facts,
she remembered that tonight Jimmy Weare was giving a
party at the Romany Inn. She smiled.

"Run along to your business, Hobey," she returned
sarcastically. "You are late as it is – and with the weather
bad it will take you an hour to get in."

Her husband smiled. "Shall I return tonight," he asked
casually, "so that I may write a few cheques for you, dear?"

But Helene was not up to his jocular mood, and she missed completely the heavy undertone of his words. Hobart Sickler was near the edge – and his wife did not notice it.

He rose leisurely from his chair at the table in the breakfast-room. Thirty-five, a trifle flabby, too good-natured, Hobart was not a particularly imposing human. But he was not as stupid as his wife imagined. For a year now he had been observing Pinky in the process of breaking loose, and had not interfered. But now –

"Leave me the closed car," she was saying in her morning-weary tone. "Delatante's coming over later. He's found an old farmhouse somewhere on the Island – and he wants to show me some antiques."

Hobey frowned. "Antiques?" he said slowly. "Are they so rare in these parts?"

His implication was obvious, but Helene disregarded it with a sigh. Delatante dabbled in art, painted a bit – it was even rumoured that one of his oils had been exhibited in Boston. He was tall, dark and handsome – and quite consistently broke.

But that never seemed to matter. He travelled with the exclusive, lively element of Long Island. He borrowed a limousine here or there; somehow he always managed to get everywhere. Better still, Delatante was interesting.

Hobey gestured impatiently with his hands. He moved slowly towards the threshold of the sun-parlour. But suddenly he stopped, faced his wife.

"Pinky," he said slowly and quietly, "you've got to cut it out. I'm getting pretty tired of this business. I was talking with Sam yesterday, and he feels the same way about Tiny. It's got to stop."

Pinky was staring at her husband in utter amazement. Was it possible that Hobey meant what he was saying?

Tiny Fenwick was her best friend, her best woman friend, at least. And Hobey had been talking to her husband, Sam. That was simply disgusting!

"Why, Hobey," she managed to say, her eyes upon his, "you're talking foolishly. What do you expect me to do all day while you're in the city? Sit and read the latest philosophical books, have no social life whatever?"

Her husband grunted. "Sit and read the latest scandals among your friends, you mean," he returned. "As for 'social life' – I guess you have plenty of it."

"I do," she admitted, "because I won't allow myself to grow old."

"Meaning that I am allowing myself to grow old?" Hobey asked.

Helene's eyes narrowed. "Exactly," she replied.

Her husband muttered something under his breath that she did not catch. There was a grim smile on his face.

"All right!" he said decisively. "If I'm growing old it's worry about you that's causing it. I've a business to attend to, and plenty to think about. I don't object to your playing around with women – and there are some decent men around here, too. But I'm getting pretty sick of this fast, noisy nightclub crowd that you and Tiny are running with. Sam's getting sick of it, too. You can go a bit too far, you know – and it's our money that you're spending."

"Hobart!" Pinky got to her feet, her eyes flashing. She was rather stunning in her dark, Oriental way, and anger gave her a hot, quick beauty that her husband was not accustomed to seeing.

"It's true," he went on. "Night after night. Parties here, parties there. The same old thing. Delatante and that Italian, Grutti, George Standing, Louis Penway. Rotters – all of them!"

"They are not rotters!" she protested hotly. "You know they are not!"

"I know nothing of the sort!" Her husband had raised his voice. Pinky was surprised to see such an exhibition of his temper; her husband was usually a very calm man. But he continued to talk now, his words booming out into the room:

"But I *do* know that this business must come to an end. I want you to stay away from Romany Inn, from that section of the Island. It's getting to be a joke – for those who aren't mixed up in it. Do you know what the columnists are calling that section?"

Pinky shook her head. She was terribly angry, and her eyes showed the fact.

" 'Sinners' Paradise'," her husband informed her. "That's what they call it."

Pinky threw back her dark-crowned head and commenced to laugh. Her laughter was silvery, and considered by many quite beautiful, but it was evident that her husband would have disagreed at this moment. Finally she stopped. There were tears of mirth in her eyes. She stared at her husband.

" 'Sinners' Paradise'," she repeated, still chuckling. "Oh, Hobey – that's *too* good!"

"It is," he agreed, in a hard tone, "but not the way you mean it. It's too good, too airy a title to give that bunch of night clubs. 'Fools' Paradise' would have been better. But that's aside from the point. I warn you, Pinky – you must keep clear of café society. If you do not –"

He broke off abruptly, dropping his hands at the sides of his immaculate grey business suit.

Pinky drew herself straight. Her husband was threatening her! Actually threatening!

"If I don't keep away – what then?" Her voice was sharp, pregnant with anger.

Hobart Sickler shrugged his shoulders.

"Then I'm through with you," he said, and walked out through the sun-parlour. Five minutes later, Pinky thoroughly astounded, heard a machine move away from the elaborate drive.

In the back seat was her husband, already reading the morning paper and – worst of all – he had taken the limousine!

II

"It's ridiculous, absurd! Just because some of the newspaper columnists term that little neck of land in the Sound 'Sinners' Paradise', because some 'blurb' writer has to earn his salary – Hobey tells me I must drop out of things." Pinky curled kittenishly on her divan, glared at Tiny Fenwick.

"Don't get so angry at me, Pinky," Tiny retorted. "Haven't I just been through the same thing? I tell you, sure as the dickens, your Hobey and my Sam have gotten together and decided to make us safe for democracy – or something like that. It's utterly silly!"

Tiny Fenwick was small and blonde. Her husband was a rather big fellow, and Pinky had always thought them thoroughly unsuited. But she liked Tiny, and they were almost always together. Pinky had cultivated Delatante, while Tiny had shown a strong liking for Louis Penway.

They were not in love with Delatante and Penway – but Sam and Hobey were businessmen. Business was a bore, particularly when it tired husbands so that they did not care to run about at night. What were the gay lights of Romany Inn, the Halfway House, Scarabin's, to tired husbands? They were certainly not a lure. Hobey and Sam detested them.

And they both had plenty of money. Of course, Pinky and Tiny spent considerable of their incomes, but neither believed that it was necessary for her husband to devote so much time and so much serious thought to business.

"The thing is," Tiny continued, stretching herself beside Pinky on the divan, "what are we going to do about it? I know Sam will be furious, wild – if I go to Jimmy Weare's party at Romany Inn tonight. And Lou's coming for me at nine. Sam's off for Chicago. But it's a masquerade – and how will anyone know?"

"Know what?" Pinky reached for cigarettes, and they both lighted up.

"Know that I'm there," Tiny replied. "You are supposed to be going with Delatante. Are you?"

Pinky hesitated. "I don't know," she said slowly. "Hobey was awfully angry when he left – and he's a good sport in a way. But he's lots older, of course, and he doesn't like running around. I wouldn't want to break with him."

"Bah!" Tiny blew a cloud of smoke above her yellow hair. "He'll never know you've gone, if you do as I'm going to do."

Pinky's dark eyes were upon Tiny's. She saw that her friend had made up her mind that she was going to Jimmy's party.

"What are you going to do, Tiny?" she asked.

"I'm going!" her friend replied. "In spite of the fact that Sam said he was sick of my running around, and would move his office to Chicago and leave me here – if I went tonight."

She chuckled. "But Sam's never going to know that I went," she stated, winking. "And after this party I'm going to be a good little girl for a while. Stay home and work crossword puzzles. Read whoever's in style –"

"How are you going to do it?" Pinky interrupted. She had heard Tiny tell of reforming plans before.

"Going to reverse the procedure," Tiny stated triumphantly. "I said a minute ago that Lou was coming for me. He's not, actually – I'm going for him."

"Going for him?" Pinky echoed.

"Just that," Tiny returned, chuckling again. I'm going to drive over for him in the roadster, picking him up at Charlie Carlyle's place. My maid hasn't seen my costume, and I'll dress alone. It's a simple one, thank the Lord!"

Pinky smiled. "It sounds great," she agreed. "I'm going as a pirate – or I *was* going as a pirate. Ninette hasn't seen the costume because it hasn't arrived yet from the city."

"Fine!" Tiny chuckled. "You can work it the same way, Pinky. Can't you pretend you're sick, and sneak away from that husband of yours?"

Helene Sickler frowned. Suddenly she jumped from the divan.

"Oh, Tiny!" she exclaimed. "I forgot. Hobey has a banquet at the club. I remember now – he told me yesterday that he'd be out for dinner. He's going to change at the club!"

"Exquisite!" Tiny breathed. "Perfectly marvellous, dear! We'll run away together. You get Delatante to go over to Charlie's place. I'll stop here, noiselessly, for you at about eight-thirty. Get Ninette away. Your butler won't say a word. That's the beauty of them. And in your pirate costume no one can be sure, positive, of your identity. Delatante and Lou will be the only ones who actually know."

"Yes, but –" Pinky broke off abruptly.

"But what?" Tiny demanded. She tapped the ashes from her cigarette with a graceful motion of her little hands.

"When we unmask," Pinky said slowly. "Everyone will know us then."

"Don't be silly," Tiny returned. "You don't think I want

to lose my happy home, either, do you? Sam's all right. But nothing doing on the unmasking, Pinky. The answer is simple – we don't unmask!"

Tiny laughed in her silvery voice. "Jimmy says the party will be fast and furious and he wants to make it a real party. Things have been a bit slow, he thinks. No one unmasks until two o'clock – and we shove off at a quarter of the fatal hour. How's that?"

Pinky smiled. "Sounds cheerful enough," she agreed, "and I'm all for it. I'd like to fool Hobey, he made me pretty mad this morning. But I –"

"Another 'but'!" Tiny interrupted, in an impatient tone. "What now?"

"Hobey's not in Chicago, you know," Helene responded. "And the chances are that he'd return from New York before two. I'd be caught getting in, of course. He always kisses me goodnight."

"Good Lord! Does he do *that*?" Tiny grimaced. "He's worse than Sam, then." She shook her adorable head. "These old-fashioned men!"

They both laughed. But Tiny was serious again. For several moments there was silence.

"I have it!" Sam's wife suddenly declared. "What could be sweeter? You are lonely – so you phone your Hobey at the office, and tell him that you are going over to my place. You suggest that he stay in at the club for the night – you're feeling miserable and think you'll stay with me."

"But won't he be suspicious?" Pinky questioned.

"Of course he will," Tiny replied. "But what of it? He'll call up the house, most likely, and if it's before I've left I'll say that you're lying down, resting – that you're going to stay all night with me. If he calls up after – well I have Koti to say that we're both retired children, and that he would hate to disturb us. He's really my boy, you know, although Sam doesn't know that. I'll say I've given Koti enough dough."

Pinky was smiling. "It's a chance we're taking," she said slowly, "but I do want one big party before I settle down. And I have an idea that Jimmy Weare's will be lively."

"Lively? That's not the word," Tiny contradicted. "Terrific – that's more like it. Then you'll go, Pinky?"

Helene Sickler nodded her head. "I'll go," she said quietly.

"Wonderful!" Tiny did a rumba in front of the divan. "We'll have a perfectly marvellous time. Call up your husband now – see how he takes it. Remember, my place for the night. You're sick and lonely. But don't let him rush back to you."

"Rush back?" Pinky laughed. "Do they do that these days outside of the movies? He was rushing *away* the last I saw of him. But I'll call him."

They walked into the reception hall, and Helene picked up the telephone. While she was calling the number, Tiny was executing a continuation of her dance. But she broke off suddenly.

"Don't talk too light-heartedly, Pinky," she warned Helene. "Remember, you're sick."

Pinky nodded. She heard Hobart's heavy voice over the wire.

"This is Pinky," she said, in a weary tone. "I feel terrible, dear – and I'm going over to Tiny's. I'm *so* lonely."

She heard him grunt something unintelligible, and continued. "I think I'll stay with her tonight, Hobey. You might stay in at the club. Your banquet won't be over till late – and I expect to climb into bed with Tiny very early."

"All right," he replied, with astonishing brevity. "If you'd cut out the parties, you might feel better. I'll stay in. See you tomorrow night."

"All right, dear," she replied. "Bye, bye."

"Bye," he muttered gruffly, and hung up. She guessed that her husband was still furious over the morning scene.

Tiny was still dancing her jig as Pinky hung up. Her face was framed in one gorgeous smile. She caught Pinky by the arm, and they both danced a few quiet steps.

"All set!" Tiny stated happily. "What's that name the newspapers have given our party neck-of-woods?"

"'Sinners' Paradise'," Pinky returned, laughing. Now that the way was clear, she felt vastly pleased.

"'Sinners' Paradise'," Tiny mimicked. "I do hope there's lots of little sinners at Romany Inn tonight!"

"Me too," Pinky agreed. "It may be our last chance to sin with the rest of the bunch!"

III

Delatante helped Helene back into Tiny's closed car. They had just arrived at Charlie's place, and had picked up Lou Penway and Del. Charlie was shoving off later, and they did not see him.

Everything had gone splendidly. Koti had definite instructions. Pinky had driven her machine over to Tiny's at seven, taking a small bag containing her costume. She would spend the night with Tiny, of course.

Both Pinky and Tiny were already masked. Their fur coats hid the costumes beneath. Delatante was attired as a devil. Lou as a slender and quite ferocious cannibal.

He jerked the machine into action, with Tiny sitting close beside him. Delatante produced a flask from his overcoat pocket, and at the same time a sinister object flashed to the car's floor-rug.

"Del!" Pinky saw that it was a revolver, but Delatante quickly stuck it back in his pocket and resumed the process of unscrewing the top.

"No use taking any chances," he whispered to Pinky. "There's been quite a few hold-ups around here lately, and I usually carry it with me."

Helene nodded. After all, there was no harm in Del's having a gun. Neither Tiny nor she was wearing any jewels, but there had been several motor hold-ups in the vicinity of the neck of land on which were scattered many road houses.

"What's Tiny supposed to be?" Del questioned, steadying himself as he poured the liquor into the unscrewed cup-cover. "I know you're a pirate bold; she told me."

"Bold is right," Pinky returned. "And remember, Del — you must never breathe a word of this to anybody."

"Not a word, Pinky," Delatante replied. He looked quite handsome in his diabolical make-up. "Again what is Tiny supposed to be?"

"A nymph," Pinky returned, smiling. "And a summer, warm-weather nymph, at that."

"Not so much in the way of costume, eh?" Del grinned, and handed her the cup-top of the flask. "Just a starter, Pinky. Jimmy's the one who is supposed to have the real stuff."

Pinky swallowed the contents, made a face and laughed. And then she made another face.

"As bad as that?" Del questioned. He poured out another drink for Tiny, who was pretending to howl for it.

"Worse," replied Pinky, but she shook her head. "No, I guess it's not bad," she told him. "I'm not a drinker, you know – and I can't get used to it."

"You don't want to get used to it," Delatante stated seriously, as he handed the cup to Tiny. "When you get used to it there's not so much fun. I'm used to it, and I don't get half the kick I got in the old days."

There was a general laugh. Tiny drank, made no comment, and Del poured out a brinker for the driver. Lou was in great humour.

He drank with practice and ease, and then half turned his head towards Pinky.

"Say," he demanded, "didn't I meet you in St Louis?"

There was a groan at this, but ancient as Pinky knew the thing was going to be, she went through with her part.

"Not I," she replied seriously. "I've never been in St Louis."

"That's right," Lou shot back. "Neither have I. It must have been two other –" A chorus of groans drowned his anticipated ending.

"That's as old as Jimmy says his liquor is guaranteed to be," Del remarked, getting down the last drink of the first round.

"Listen," Tiny stated slowly. "This is going to be Pinky's and my last party for a while. We don't want it to drag, but you two *must* stay sober. We've got to leave before the unmasking. Remember!"

"Can't we get under the weather a bit – and then sober up in time?" Lou pleaded in such a serious, grieved voice that Tiny relented.

"It's all right – if you sober up in time," she stated. "You're taking a chance, too. If our husbands learn about our being at the Romany, they'll probably start after both of you. So it's up to you to protect yourselves."

"We leave at quarter of two – and, we leave sober!" Delatante spoke convincingly. "I'm not anxious to be shot at by angry husbands."

Pinky laughed. The machine was streaking over the Long Island road, but it rode smoothly. Del commenced to pour the second round.

A cluster of lights flashed behind, as Pinky lifted her voice in song.

"Scarabin's," Lou shouted. "We're on the Neck now. Fifteen minutes and we'll be at the Romany."

"For I'm a pirate bo . . . ld, so bo . . . ld!" Pinky was feeling fine, her red lips parted. The mask over the upper portion of her face made her more alluring than ever. The others joined in the chorus. They sped on, bound for Romany Inn, and Jimmy Weare's party. Both Tiny and Pinky had forgotten their husbands. Why not? It was to be their farewell party.

IV

A yellow spotlight streaked down upon the long, narrow dance floor of the Romany Inn. The dance floor was crowded; costumes were striking, gorgeous in colour and line. The spotlight became purple. Music from the Southern orchestra flared out from the raised platform at one end. Dancers swayed to it, bent with it, jerked with it.

Pinky, held tightly in the arms of Delatante, was enjoying herself hugely. Del was a magnificent dancer, and the music was wonderful. She felt herself gripped by the spirit of the carnival, the spirit of jazz music – and adventure.

" 'Lo, Jimmy!" Del called out, as a short, stocky figure danced close to them. There was no possibility of Jimmy Weare disguising himself. His friends were many, and in spite of his depressing, gloom-costume of the much-caricatured curfew maker, he was hailed from all sides. His mask was no mask for Jimmy.

He waved back. "Who is she?" he howled in his deep voice, making no attempt to disguise it.

Del shook his head, and Pinky smiled. She did not travel, had not travelled, in spite of what her husband thought, so much with Jimmy Weare's set. They could not penetrate her disguise. She was slim and of medium height, and there were many other women of similar build on the dance floor.

And yet she was having all the fun she could desire. Twisting her head, she caught a glimpse of Tiny, dancing with Lou. Tiny was having a great old time, and her costume was one of the sensations of the party.

"Feel lively enough?" Del spoke a bit thickly, but he was able to dance in his excellent manner.

"I feel like what I'm made up to be – a pirate," Pinky returned.

"You've already stolen my heart – and made my conscience walk the plank," Del returned, laughing.

"Oh, Del – not that!" Pinky rolled her eyes roguishly.

Delatante groaned. "Not that," he muttered. "Don't look at me that way, Pinky. I feel as though I want to rip that mask from your face and kiss you on those laughing lips of yours."

"Don't!" she warned. "That would give the whole thing away."

"I know." He grinned at her. "I was simply telling you how I felt. By the way, you've the next dance with Haverstraw. He fell in love with your costume and persuaded me into giving you up for a whole dance."

The music crashed into a dynamic *finale*. It was the third encore of the piece, and the dancers walked slowly from the floor.

"Haverstraw?" Pinky repeated the name. "Isn't he the man who has just figured in the papers in the Denton shooting?"

"The same and only gentleman," Del replied suavely. "He's nice, though, and you are only dancing with him, you know."

Pinky laughed. "Oh, I don't mind that," she stated. "He'll be interesting. I don't often have the chance of dancing with a murderer."

Del looked startled. Even his mask failed to hide the expression in his eyes, the thin line of his lips.

"Not necessarily a murderer, Pinky," he returned.

"That's a bit harsh – pretty heavy. He had some reasons for shooting Denton – and he didn't shoot to kill, you see."

Pinky laughed again. "I'll be careful, Del," she returned. "I won't accuse the dear fellow of being such a person."

"That's it," her companion replied, as they neared the table at which Tiny and Louis Penway were already seated. "Keep away from the subject, and you'll have a good time. Haverstraw's a good enough fellow, and he's clever, too."

"Greetings, demon and pirate-maid! Join us in the gulping festivities – or don't either of you care to indulge?"

Lou smiled at them as they dropped into their chairs. A babble of voices filled the long room; it seemed hardly less silent now than when the orchestra was playing.

Clowns and athletes, porters and columbines, strikingly costumed males and females strode about the tables, crossed the dance floor. Laughter was the chief voice of the party, and some of it was becoming quite unrestrained now.

Suddenly the lights were dimmed. The long room was plunged into absolute darkness. Giggles, a few oaths of surprise and a good deal of laughter rose from those seated about the table.

A brilliantly yellow spotlight shone down upon the centre of the dance floor. A saxophone wailed. Into the spotlight rushed a feminine figure. Pinky suppressed a gasp of surprise. There were "Ohs!" and "Ahs!" from the tables.

The figure was clad only in a thin veil of scarlet material. She was very beautiful, and she commenced a dance that was thoroughly charming. The spotlight followed her; it was the only splash of colour in the room.

The music was working itself up into a whirl of passion. It raged, sent notes into the comparative silence in a perfect fury of sound. But the dancer kept pace with it. She was whirling now in the centre of the polished floor. Her hair was golden and long. It swirled out behind her, and then, as she reversed, covered her face.

But she was kept whirling – and the orchestra kept raging. Del leaned towards Pinky. Their table was almost in a corner at the far end of the room. She felt herself jerked towards him; her lips were being pressed against his before she realized what was happening.

The lights flashed on; there was a burst of applause. She twisted herself away from Delatante amid the laughter of the few who had witnessed what little the lights had shown.

She was furious, so furious that she could not speak. Del was grinning sheepishly. She raised her fingers to her mask. It had slipped down a little but had not, fortunately, exposed her face.

Finally she spoke. Tiny was slapping Lou on the back as if the whole thing was a tremendous joke.

"Don't you dare to do that again, Del!" she warned. "If you do – I'll walk right out of here, do you understand?"

Her sharp tone of voice sobered him. "I'm sorry, Pinky," he said, in a low tone. "It was the music and the lights being out. It won't happen again, dear."

"Don't call me 'dear'!" she commanded. She was very angry. If Hobey should ever hear of the thing – if it should ever become known that she was the pirate-maid whom several persons had seen being kissed by a well-garbed devil – well, there would be plenty of explaining to do.

Tiny shoved a drink towards her. "Come on, Pinky," she shrilled. "Don't go dead on the party. Remember, this is our farewell –"

"Not so loud," Pinky ordered. "And don't call me Pinky if you have to yell. There are probably enough people here now who *suspect* who we are. We don't want them to know it."

"That's right," Del agreed. "Let's tone down a bit. I'm not dancing the next one – I'll go out and have a smoke. We've got an hour yet – it's only a quarter of one."

"My next dance is with Ulysses," Tiny announced, laughing. "At least he's wearing a lot of armour."

Lou chuckled. "You'll be all bruises tomorrow," he grinned. "I have an idea that Ulysses doesn't even know he's away from Troy or Ithaca – or wherever he used to hang out."

The music flared into being again, as a tall man, attired in the patched costume of a tramp, touched Pinky on the shoulder.

"Hello, Stella," he said, rather eagerly. "Knew you the first time. My dance, eh?"

Pinky shook her head, amid the laughter of her three companions. "I'm not Stella," she said slowly, disguising her voice by speaking in a drawl. "And the next dance is taken."

The new arrival grinned down at her from beneath a red mask. "You win," he replied, in a light tone. "Stella never said that little at one time in her life. Sorry, she was supposed to be Peter Pan."

Tiny was screaming with laughter.

"She's not Peter Pan," she informed the tramp. "She's a pirate bold."

The tramp stared at Pinky and then joined in their laughter. "My mistake," he apologized, as he moved away. "I left my glasses on the library table."

Tiny vanished with a careless "Adios!" Her Ulysses was soberer than Lou had evidently given him credit for being.

Del had risen and was introducing Pinky to a finely attired gentleman of the French aristocracy. His powdered wig was slightly slanted on his rather large head, but it detracted little from the dignity of his whole appearance.

"A pirate bold – oh, Duke!" Del laughed, and Haverstraw led her out into the swirl of the dance floor.

"The evening is a merry one," she stated. She found herself anxious to hear what sort of a voice the murderer of Richard Denton possessed. He had only bowed when introduced.

"The *morning* gives promise of being gay," he corrected, in a rich, baritone drawl.

"It is morning," she agreed. "And time all good little pirates were in bed."

He swung her to the left quickly, in order to avoid collision with a college professor who was trying something too intricate in the way of dance steps with a Pandora who had evidently *not* lost many things besides hope.

"And time good little *wives* should be in bed, too," he supplemented.

Pinky felt a quick twist of fear strike within her. Did he recognize her? But how could he? She had never met him before. She decided that he was simply trying to be clever.

"And good little husbands?" she questioned archly. "Shouldn't they be in bed, too?"

He laughed pleasantly. It was difficult to think of him as a man who had shot down Denton. But probably, she thought, it was as Del had said. He was not, inherently, a murderer.

"Husbands," he said quietly, "should be allowed certain privileges their wives can't enjoy."

"That seems to be the general opinion – of the husbands," Pinky returned, smiling. "But the wives do not always agree."

"So I notice," Haverstraw returned, and the tone of his voice sent a little shiver through Helene Sickler.

There was a conversational silence for several minutes. The floor was fearfully crowded, and there was an atmosphere of freedom in the place. Haverstraw danced fairly well, but without particular fervour.

"And your husband?" he suddenly said. "Where is he tonight?"

Pinky held herself in control. "It's hard to say," she commented. "There are five clowns here – and three of them look very much like my clown."

Haverstraw laughed. "Nice," he commented, "but you should give him credit. It's likely he knew there would be many in clown costume – and simply made it more difficult for you to keep track of him."

"He's not that wise," Pinky returned.

"Don't you believe it," her partner stated. "All husbands are wise – some of them so much so that they make their wives think they are stupid."

Pinky felt another queer little stab of fear inside of her. Haverstraw was talking in riddles but they were vaguely annoying – and she wondered just why.

"You should know," she shot back, quite obviously.

She felt Haverstraw tighten his grip upon her. The music was playing softly, and with the perfect beat of the super-jazz orchestra.

"I *do* know," he replied grimly. "And it cost me something to find out."

"In money?" she persisted.

He laughed. "A wise little pirate was she," he said, in a quoting manner. "I see my table is unoccupied. Would you care to sit and drink this out – and listen to a story in which I feel you are interested?"

Pinky was about to decline, but she was interested in the Denton case, and she felt that Haverstraw would tell her something about it. And, too, she was a trifle tired. A drink would help.

"I'd love to!" she replied recklessly.

He smiled, and led her from the floor. His table was at the opposite end of the room from the one at which Pinky had been seated. And there was champagne. Jimmy Weare was a good friend of Haverstraw's, she remembered. He had testified for him at the trial.

They seated themselves, and Haverstraw pulled his chair close to Pinky's. The champagne was excellent, fairly seemed to sparkle her into a more vivid awareness of the gaiety of her surroundings. The place was a flare of colour, noise, excitement.

Haverstraw took her hand. "Pretty," he commented. "Shall I start at the beginning?"

"Do!" Pinky urged, making a slight effort to pull her hand away. But she *did* want to hear his story – so she let him hold her hand. He commenced to talk, his face close to hers. She was beginning to feel just a bit dizzy.

V

Balloons were floating down from the balcony that surrounded the room. They were blue and gold and red. Pinky blinked at them. Haverstraw was still talking in a monotonous drone. But he had not told her what she had wanted to know, had come to hear. He was, perhaps, a little beyond that.

She felt a desire to get back to their own table, to Tiny and Del and Lou. And she was also commencing to feel a swift regret. She and Tiny should never have come to this party.

The crowd was too lively, too fast – in the first place. In the second place, it was very likely that their husbands would be incapable of understanding. Hobey, she thought, would be rather doubtful, even if she told the truth – told him that it was a farewell party, and that Tiny had urged her to go.

She could not distinguish Haverstraw's words, but was suddenly aware that both of his arms were around her. Somehow, she got to her feet. Balloons were drifting everywhere; she brushed one away from her face.

"What's the matter?" she heard Haverstraw saying. "Thought you wanted –"

She turned away from him. They were dancing, and she was bumped several times as she walked, with a fair degree of steadiness, towards the opposite end of the room.

Suddenly, just as she had reached the end of the polished floor, she felt herself jerked about by Haverstraw.

"What's the rush?" he said casually. "I'm not through telling –"

"Let me go!" she ordered. "I'm going away from this place. "I'm sick of it – sick of all the noise and the people. Let me go!"

He laughed shortly. She could hear him more clearly now; they were farther away from the orchestra.

"It took you quite a while to get sick of it," he reminded. "And quite a bit of my champagne, my dear."

She tried to get away from him, but he held her tightly. "One more dance," he begged, "and then you can go. Be a bold, brave pirate."

Pinky was aware of the fact that he was mocking her, but that did not matter. She twisted violently, but he held her. They were attracting attention. She saw Delatante coming towards her.

A swift panic gripped her. Del had a gun; he had probably brought it with him. And Haverstraw was quick-tempered – and a murderer!

"Please let me go," she begged. "I don't feel like dancing."

"That's all right," Haverstraw commenced. "Let me see who you are? Kind of like you, bold pirate."

He made a motion as though to lift her mask, but she evaded him . . . She caught a glimpse of the red cloth of Del's Satanic costume.

"Make him let me go, Del," she begged. "He's had too much to drink – doesn't know what he's doing."

There was a sharp crack; she felt her wrist free of Haverstraw's grip. Turning around, she saw Haverstraw stretched on the floor. Delatante was standing over him, his fists clenched.

She started to run towards the table and Tiny, but the staccato crackle of a revolver jerked her about. She caught the gleam of a gun in Haverstraw's right hand, and saw Delatante sway above him.

Haverstraw had fired from the floor! The place was in a wild turmoil. There were screams, hoarse cries. Men rushed towards the prostrate Haverstraw and the swaying Delatante, obscuring Pinky's vision.

She started once more towards the table. Stumbling, her eyes wide, she reached Tiny's side. Lou was not present.

"They've killed Del!" she sobbed hysterically. But curiously enough she was not thinking as much about Del as she was about the publicity – and Hobey's ultimate discovery of the fact that she had lied to him, and had come to the place.

"They? Who?" Tiny was holding her by the shoulders. "I heard the shot – what happened, Pinky?"

Helene sobbed the story incoherently. "We've got to get away," she urged. "They'll take care of Del – there's nothing we can do. Lou can get a taxi outside. They always wait there – a few of them. Oh, Tiny – I wish we'd never come. I wish we –"

She broke off abruptly. Tiny was dragging her away from the table, towards the retiring room. She got a glimpse of the crowd, still gathered about Del, she supposed. The costumes seemed an incongruous blending of colour now, an irony.

She wondered if Delatante had been killed. Haverstraw was a good shot. That had been brought up at the trial. The chances were that –

"Where *is* Lou?" Tiny was demanding, interrupting her train of thought. "I haven't seen him since you left with Haverstraw and I with Ulysses."

"I don't know," Pinky returned. "But we can't wait, Tiny – we must get away from here. What if Del talks? Tells who we are?"

"He won't," Tiny returned. "He'll be too careful of himself. Brace up, Pinky. We'll be home in half hour."

Pinky stared into the mirror. The maid brought her coat, helped her into it. She felt years older than when she had come in. There was a faint buzzing in her ears. She could not distinguish Tiny's voice from the maid's but she could hear their words, as though from a distance.

"Come on," she urged, as Tiny jammed on her hat. "Hurry, Tiny – we must get away."

"But I must put this hat on," Tiny remonstrated, "and my eyes are none too clear."

Pinky jerked her away from the mirror. Her own eyes seemed staring at things through a thin blur.

"We should never have come," she muttered, as they moved out of the room, their costumes hidden beneath the long coats. "If Del or Lou talk –"

"They won't," Tiny replied. "I tell you, they're too careful of themselves."

"But Del may be dying," Pinky returned, "and he'd tell the police – or somebody."

She shivered as they went out through a side door towards the parking place. The night was chilly.

A form loomed up in front of them. Tiny cried out.

"Lou! We were looking for you. You've got to get us away. Del's been –"

He nodded his head and led the way towards Tiny's car. Through a blur, Pinky saw that he had his overcoat on, and his hat. And, evidently, he knew that Del had been shot. His mask was still on, and his blacking for the cannibalistic makeup.

"We'll both ride in the back seat," Tiny exclaimed, helping Pinky in before her. Pinky sank down in the soft cushions. She felt as though she were about to faint. And Del was lying back on the polished floor.

A vision of Haverstraw – with the gun in his hand – flared before her eyes. She shuddered, and Tiny held her tightly with both arms.

"Why don't we start?" she asked Lou.

He did not reply, but Tiny soothed her. "He jumped off the running-board as he was getting in," she said. "I suppose he forgot something."

Pinky was sobbing as though her heart would break. Again and again she reproached herself and Tiny for having come. "Del may be dead!" she repeated over and over.

"He may be," Tiny agreed, "but it isn't likely. The chances are that Haverstraw had been drinking too much to be able to aim very straight."

A figure lurched up to the car, and jerked open the door. It was garbed as a tramp, but looked somewhat the worse for wear.

"That Stella in there?" the man demanded. "She's got on a Peter Pan costume, and you dropped this."

He offered Tiny Pinky's small turban, which she had dropped on the way out.

"Been looking mos' everywhere for Stella," he went on, blinking nervously from behind his mask.

"You keep right on looking," Tiny advised. "This is part of our pirate costume. Your Stella's probably inside."

"Inside?" The tramp shook his head. "Never find her in there. Too much excitement. Fellow just got killed."

"Killed?" Pinky jerked herself upright, staring at the tramp.

"Killed dead!" the fellow repeated solemnly.

"You run along," Tiny advised. "This isn't Peter Pan, and I haven't the slightest idea where she is."

The tramp bowed, muttered something that sounded like an apology, and closed the machine door, walking towards the inn.

"Killed!" Pinky repeated. "Oh, why doesn't Lou come? Can't you drive, Tiny? I want to get away from here."

Tiny patted her hands. "I wouldn't want to try driving," she replied. "Although I feel pretty good. But we can't run off without Lou very well, and that fellow probably didn't know what he was talking about."

"He said he was killed," Pinky groaned.

"He said he was 'killed dead'," Tiny corrected, "and that means that he didn't know what he was saying."

More figures moved beside the car, the front-seat door was opened. Lou climbed in, squeezed himself behind the wheel.

Pinky straightened in her seat; her body became rigid. Delatante had climbed in after him. She saw that he was handling his left arm with care. He did not speak.

The machine moved slowly from the parking place; the lights of Romany Inn faded behind them.

Pinky leaned forward. "Del," she questioned, "are you hurt? Did he shoot you?"

He shook his head, but did not turn in the seat. Tiny soothed her, turning the collar of her coat up about her neck.

"There," she cheered. "I told you that fool couldn't shoot straight. He had been drinking too much, Pinky. And besides, you can't kill Del – he's too tough."

"But they'll talk," Pinky returned, recovering somewhat from her astonishment. "They'll find out, in some way, who I am. I know they will."

She was silent for several minutes as the machine sped along the smooth road.

"I think I'll go to Hobey, Tiny – and tell him the whole truth," she said suddenly. "He may believe me – and I'm sick and disgusted at the thought of what we've done."

"He *may* believe, is correct," Tiny returned. "And then again – he may not."

There was another silence. Both men sat motionless in the front seat. It was evident that they were too disgusted with events to speak.

"I don't care," Pinky finally said, with determination. "I'm going to tell my husband. He may not believe – but he's going to know the truth. I'm *through*!"

"Pinky!" Tiny was staring at her. "You mustn't. I'd like to tell mine, too – but we can't. Don't you see?"

"I don't see – and I'm going to tell!" Pinky was sitting straight. She felt better, having made the decision. "I lied – and I'm sorry."

The machine slowly jerked to a stop. Del moved his head around, lifted his hands to his mask. Pinky screamed. It was not Del – it was Hobey, her own husband!

Tiny was speechless. The driver faced her, his mask down. Sam Fenwick!

Hobey chuckled. "Well," he demanded. "Glad to see your husbands? We got you out of a nasty mess, didn't we?"

Both women were unable to speak. Pinky felt as though her throat were paralysed. Tiny was still staring at Sam, who was grinning.

"You don't know as much about valets as you think you do," Sam stated impassively. "He gave me the details and I called Hobey, who sort of figured Pinky was up to something. A phone from Chicago prevented my leaving – meeting postponed."

"But how –" Pinky, staring at her husband, was able only to manage the two words. But he seemed to understand.

"We mixed in – after we got hold of your escorts, who were outside, bragging about their achievements. They were easily convinced that it would be wise to lend us their masks and clothes. Mine's a rather tight fit, but you didn't notice it, Pinky." Hobey grinned. "Sam had to borrow some blacking.

"Haverstraw never hit me. The bullet landed in the ceiling. And that crowd never did find out who I was. Had some trouble getting out, but here we are. Nice party, eh?"

"Oh, Hobey," Pinky sobbed. "I never want to go on another. I'll stay –"

"You're darned right you will!" Hobey grinned. "Right by the radio and fireside. If we hadn't heard you – both you and Tiny – tell us how you stood, well, things might have been different. But this time we'll let you off easily, eh, Sam?"

"Guess we'll have to," Sam replied. "They had enough tonight to last for a while."

"Forever!" Pinky and Tiny chorused.

"Let's shift," Hobey suggested. He changed seats with Tiny. The machine started. But Sam drove slowly – and with one hand. A cluster of lights went slowly behind.

"The end of the Neck," Hobey whispered to his wife. "Will you be good now?"

Pinky sighed. "The end of 'Sinners' Paradise'," she said in a low voice. "You just *bet* I will, Hobey!"

Motel

Evan Hunter aka Ed McBain

I

The January wind was blowing fiercely as he put the key into the unfamiliar door lock and then twisted it to the right with no results. He turned it to the left, and the door opened, and he pushed it wide into the motel room, and then stepped aside for her to enter before him. She was wearing a short beige car coat, the collar of which she held closed about her throat with one gloved hand. Her skirt, showing below the hem of the coat, was a deeper tan. She was wearing dark brown leather boots, almost the colour of her shoulder-length hair. Her eyes were browner than the boots, and she lowered them as she stepped past him into the room. There was an air of shy nervousness about her.

Fumbling to extricate the key from the lock, Frank almost lost his homburg to a fresh gust of wind. He clasped it to his head with his free hand, struggled with the damn key again, and finally pulled it free of the lock. Putting the key into the pocket of his overcoat, he went into the room, closed the door behind him, and said immediately, "I hope you won't misinterpret this."

"Why should I?" she asked.

"Well, a motel has connotations. But I couldn't think of any other way."

"We're both adults, Frank," she said. "I don't see why it shouldn't be possible for two adults to take a room and . . ."

"That was precisely my reasoning," he said.

"So please don't apologize."

They stood just inside the entrance doorway, as though each

were reluctant to take the steps that would propel them deeper into the room. There were two easy chairs on their right, in front of the windows facing the courtyard outside. A table with a lamp on it rested between the two chairs. On the wall immediately to their left, there was a dresser with a mirror over it, another lamp on one end of it. An air-conditioning unit was recessed into a window on the wall opposite the door. The bed was covered with a floral-patterned spread that matched the drapes. Its headboard was against the wall opposite the dresser. A framed print of a landscape hung over it.

"Millie," he said, "I honestly *do* want you to see this film."

"Oh, I honestly *want* to see it," she said.

"We talked about it so often on the train that it just seemed ridiculous not to show it to you."

"Of course," she said.

"Which is why I mentioned it at lunch today, and suggested that maybe we could take a room someplace, for just a few minutes, a half-hour maybe, so I could show you the film. Still, I don't want you to think the only reason I asked you to lunch was to show you the film." He grinned suddenly. "Though I am very proud of it."

"I'm dying to see it," she said.

"I'll just be a minute, okay?" he said, and went to the door, and opened it, and stepped outside into the wind-blown courtyard, leaving the door open. She debated closing the door behind him, and decided against it. She also debated taking off her gloves, and decided against that as well. Outside, she heard the sound of the automobile trunk being slammed shut. A moment later, he came into the room carrying a motion picture projector.

"I was wondering how you were going to show it," Millie said.

"I had this in the trunk," he said, and put it down on the floor.

"Do you always carry a movie projector in the trunk?"

Smiling, he said, "Well, I can't pretend I didn't *plan* on showing you the film." He took a small reel of film from his coat pocket, held it up for her to see, and then put it on the dresser top. Taking off his coat, he went to the rack in one corner of the room, and hung it on a wire hanger. He took off the homburg and placed that on the shelf over the rack. He was wearing a dark, almost black, shadow-striped business suit.

"Did your wife say anything?" she asked.

"About the projector? Why would she say anything?"

"I guess she wouldn't," Millie said. "I guess lots of men take movie projectors to work in the morning."

"Actually, she didn't see it," Frank said. "I put it in the car last night." He looked around the room. "I was hoping the walls would be white," he said. "Well, maybe the towels are white."

"Did you plan to take a bath first?" she asked.

"No, no," he said, walking towards the bathroom door. "I just want to make a screen." From the bathroom, he said, "Ah, good," and was back an instant later carrying a large white towel. "Let's see now," he said, "I guess I can hang this over the mirror, uh? Move the table there, and set my projector on it. Uh-huh." As she watched, he went to the dresser, reached up over it, and tucked the towel over the top edge of the mirror, covering it. She had not moved from where she was standing just inside the door. Turning to her, he said, "Wouldn't you like to take off your coat?"

"Well . . . is it a very long film?" she asked.

"Sixty seconds, to be exact."

"Oh, well, all right then."

She took off her gloves and her coat. She was wearing a smart, simple suit and a pale green blouse. As she carried the coat to the rack, Frank took the lamp off the table, moved the table, set the projector down and plugged it into a wall socket.

"Isn't sixty seconds very short?" she asked.

"No, that's the usual length. Some are even shorter. Thirty seconds, some of them." He looked up from where he was threading the film. "You don't have to hurry back or anything, do you?"

"No, no," she said. "As long as I'm back before dinner."

"What time is that, usually?"

"Seven-thirty, usually. But I have to be back before then. My husband gets home at seven, you see. And he likes to have a drink first. So I should be home around six-thirty, seven. Not that I have to account for my time or anything, you understand."

"Well, even if you did," Frank said, "there's nothing wrong with two adults having lunch together."

"If I thought there was anything wrong with it, I wouldn't have accepted."

"In fact, it seems entirely prejudicial that a man and a woman can't enjoy each other's company simply because they happen to be married to other people – you didn't tell your husband, did you?" he asked.

"No. Did you tell your wife?"

"No," he said. "I never even told her I'd met you on the train."

"It's really silly, isn't it?"

"It certainly is," he said. "But you know, the truth of it is that most people just wouldn't understand. If I told my wife . . . or *anyone*, for that matter . . . that I'd taken you to lunch . . ."

"And to a motel later . . ."

"To show you a film . . ."

"Who'd believe it?"

"There," he said. "Let me just close these drapes." He pulled them across the rod, darkening the room, and then snapped on the projector. As the leader came on, he adjusted the throw and the focus, and framed the film on the centre of the towel. "Here goes," he said, just as a heraldic blast of trumpets sounded from the projector's speaker. The film appeared on the towel. There were two ten-year-old children in the film. The children were singing.

"*Hot buttered popcorn,*" they sang,
"*We like it, you like it.*
"*Hot buttered popcorn*
"*From Pike, it's*
"*Great!*"

The children were digging into a box of popcorn now. One of the children asked, "Do you like popcorn?"

"I love popcorn," the other child said.

"Me, too."

The children fell silent. On the screen, there were close shots of their hands digging into the box of popcorn, other

close shots of the popcorn being transferred to their mouths.
The camera pulled back to show their beaming faces.

"Good, huh?" the first child asked.

"Delicious," the second child said.

"What is it?"

"Popcorn. What do you think it is?"

"Yeah, but what *kind* of popcorn?"

"Hot buttered popcorn."

"I mean, the name."

"Oh. I dunno."

"Is this it here on the box?"

"Yeah, maybe."

The camera panned down to the front of the popcorn
box, and the words PIKE'S POPCORN printed on it.

"Pike's!" one of the children shouted. "*That's* the name!"

Together, they began singing again.

"*Hot buttered popcorn,*

"*We like it, you like it.*

"*Hot buttered popcorn*

"*From Pike, it's*

"*Great!*"

The screen went blank. Frank snapped off the projector,
and then turned on the room light. Millie was silent for
what seemed an inordinately long time. Then she said, "I
didn't realize it would be in colour."

"Yes, we shoot everything in colour nowadays," he said.
"What'd you think of it?"

"I don't know what to say," she said. "Did you write the
song, too?"

"No, just the dialogue. Between the kids."

"Oh," Millie said.

"It was very easy and natural for me," he said. "I have
three kids of my own, you know."

"Yes, you told me that. On the train. Two boys and a girl."

"No, two girls and a boy," he said.

"Yes. How old are they?"

"The boy's nineteen. The girls are fifteen and thirteen."

"That's older than my girls," Millie said. "Mine are
eight and six."

They looked at each other silently. The silence lengthened. And then, into the silence, the telephone suddenly shrilled, startling them both. He moved towards the phone, and then stopped dead in his tracks. The phone kept ringing. Finally he went to it, and warily lifted the receiver.

"Hello?" he said. "Who? No, there's no Mr . . . oh, yes! Yes, *this* is Mr McIntyre. The *what?* Yes, the Mercury is mine. In *what?* In the parking space for seventeen? Oh, yes, certainly, I'll move it. Thank you." He hung up, and looked at Millie. "I parked the car in the wrong space," he said.

"Is that the name you used? McIntyre?"

"Yes, well, I figured . . ."

"Oh, certainly, what's the sense of . . .?"

"That's what I figured. I'd better move the car. It's supposed to be in sixteen."

As he started for the door, she said, "Maybe we just ought to leave."

"What?" he said.

"Well . . . you've shown me the film already. And since you have to move the car, anyway . . ."

"Yes, but we haven't discussed it yet," he said. "The film. In depth, I mean."

"That's true. But we could discuss it in depth in the car on the way back to the city."

"Yes, I guess we could do that," he said. "Is that what you'd like to do?"

"What would you like to do?"

"Well, I thought I'd move the car to number sixteen, and then maybe we could discuss the film afterwards. In depth. If that's what you'd like to do."

"Well, whatever you want to do."

"Well, fine then."

"Fine."

"I'll move the car," he said quickly, and went out, and closed the door behind him. She debated sitting on the bed, and decided against it. She debated sitting in one of the chairs near the windows, and decided against that as well. She settled for leaning on the dresser. She was leaning on it when he came back into the room, blowing on his hands.

"Whoo, it's cold out there," he said. "I can't remember a January this cold, can you?"

"You should have put on your coat."

"Well, I figured just to move the car . . ."

"Did you move it?"

"Yep," he said, "all taken care of. Room sixteen in space sixteen."

"What kind of car was it?"

"Mine? Oh, you mean room seventeen. A big black Caddy. With a fat old man behind the wheel."

"Alone?"

"No, he had a girl with him. A frumpy blonde."

"Probably has a film he wants to show her," Millie said, and smiled.

"Probably," he said, and returned the smile. "So . . . what'd you think of it?" Without waiting for her answer, he said, "I got quite a bit of praise for it. In fact, the Head of Creation called me personally to . . ."

"God?"

"No, Hope. Hope Cromwell. She's the agency's creative head. That's her official title."

"What's *your* official title?"

"Me? I'm just a copywriter, that's all."

"Well, I wouldn't say *just* a copywriter."

"Well, Hope's a vice president, you see. I'm just . . ." He shrugged. "Just a copywriter."

"Michael's a vice president, too," she said. "My husband. He's a stockbroker, did I tell you that?" She paused, and then said, "Is Hope attractive?"

"No, no. Well, yes, I suppose so. I suppose you could call her attractive. I suppose you could call her a beautiful redhead."

"Oh," Millie said. "Is she a nice person, though?"

"Actually, she's a pain sometimes."

"So's Michael," Millie said. "Especially when he starts discussing futures. Are you, for example, interested in soy beans?"

"No, but men like to discuss their work, you know. I guess he . . ."

"Oh, I understand that. But I've never even *seen* a soy bean, have you?"

"I've seen soy bean sauce," Frank said.

"But have you ever seen a soy bean itself?"

"Never."

"So why should I be interested in something I've never seen in my entire life?"

"You shouldn't."

"*Or* its future," Millie said. "Of course, Michael's interesting in other ways. He has a mathematical turn of mind, you see. I'm a scatterbrain, but Michael . . ."

"I wouldn't say that."

"I am, believe me. If it weren't for Michael, I wouldn't know how to set the alarm clock. Well, I'm exaggerating, but you know what I mean. He has this very logical firm grasp on everything, whereas I just flit in and out and hardly know what I'm doing half the time. I'm very impulsive. I do things impulsively."

"Like coming to lunch today," Frank said.

"Yes. And like coming here to the motel."

"That was impulsive for me, too," he said.

"Well, it wasn't as impulsive for you as it was for me. Because, after all, you *did* put the projector in your car last night."

"That's right," Frank said. "Yes, in that respect, it wasn't as impulsive, you're right."

"What would you have said if your wife saw you putting the projector in the car?"

"I guess I'd have said I was bringing it in for repair or something."

"Would she have believed that? Does she trust you?"

"Oh, sure. I've never given her reason not to trust me. Why shouldn't she trust me?"

"Well, if you go around sneaking movie projectors into your car . . ."

"I didn't *sneak* it in. I just carried it out. She wasn't even home, in fact."

"Where was she?"

"At the shop. Mae owns a little antiques shop in Mamaroneck."

"Oh? What's it called?"

"*Something Old.*"

"Really?" Millie said. "That's a darling shop! Does your

wife really own it? I've been in there several times. Which one is your wife?"

"Well, there are only two of them in the shop, and one of them's sixty years old. My wife's the other one."

"The little brunette? She's very attractive. I bought an ironstone pitcher from her last month. What'd you say her name was?"

"Mae."

"That's a pretty name. Very springlike."

"Yes. Well, it's M-A-E, you understand."

"Oh, not M-A-Y?"

"No, M-A-E," he said, and they both fell silent.

"Well," she said.

"Well," he said.

"Did you register as Mr and Mrs McIntyre?" she asked.

"Yes. Well, I couldn't very well register as Mr and Mrs Di Santangelo, could I?"

"Why not?"

"I'd still be up there signing the card," he said, and laughed. "Di Santangelo's an unusually long name, you see."

"My maiden name was longer. Are you ashamed of being Italian?" she asked abruptly.

"Ashamed? No, no, why should I be ashamed?"

"It just seems strange to me that you'd choose a Wasp name like McIntyre . . ."

"It's not a Wasp name."

"Did you choose it last night? When you were putting the projector in the car?"

"No, I chose it when I was registering."

"My mother would die on the spot if she knew I was in a motel room with a Wasp named McIntyre."

"It's not Wasp, it's Roman Catholic."

"Worse yet," Millie said. "Is your wife Italian, too?"

"She's Scotch."

"Do you think we can get something to drink?" Millie asked.

"As a matter of fact, I have a bottle in the car," Frank said.

"My, you're very well appointed, aren't you?" she said, and smiled. "A projector in the trunk . . ."

"Well, I figured . . ."

"But maybe we just ought to leave," she said. "Find a bar on the way back."

"Oh, sure, we can do that, if you want to."

"Is that what you want to do?"

"Well, this is a nice comfortable room, we might just as well . . . *would* you like a drink, Millie?"

"I would love a drink," she said, and he rose instantly and started for the door. "But not if it's any trouble."

"No trouble at all," he said, and went outside again.

She debated taking off her boots, and decided against it. She sat on the edge of the bed instead. There was a Magic Fingers box on the side of the bed. She read the instructions silently, took off the boots after all, inserted a quarter into the box, and lay back on the bed. The bed was still vibrating when Frank came back into the room. He was carrying a brown paper bag.

"Are you having a massage?" he asked.

"It said 'soothing and relaxing.'"

"Is it?"

"It's soothing," she said. "I don't know how relaxing it is." The machine suddenly stopped, the bed stopped vibrating. "Ooo," she said. "Now I miss it."

"Shall I put another quarter in?"

"No, I think a drink might be more relaxing," she said, and sat up. "I don't ordinarily drink, you know. Michael's the big drinker. Do you have a drink when you get home at night?"

"Oh, yes."

"How many drinks do you have?"

"One or two. Usually two."

"Michael also has one or two, but usually three. For a fellow who's on such a strict diet, he sure knows how to put away his whiskey. Jewish men aren't supposed to be big drinkers, you know. There are statistics on that sort of thing." She smiled and said, "I probably married the only Jew in Larchmont who has three glasses of whiskey before dinner. *Big* glasses, too."

"Are you from Larchmont originally?" Frank asked.

"No, the Bronx. Michael was born in Larchmont, though. We met at a dance. He used to play alto saxophone in a band. Would you like to hear something strange? The first time he took me out, he told me he was going to marry me. Don't you think that's strange?"

"No, that's what I told Mae the first time I dated her."

"Really?"

"Mm-huh. Let me get some glasses and ice," he said, and went into the bathroom.

"Is there a little instruction booklet or something?" Millie asked.

"No, just the ice machine," he said. "Under the sink here."

"I mean, that you fellows consult before dating a girl for the first time. I think it's extraordinary that you and Michael would have used the same line on two separate girls. Don't you think that's extraordinary?"

"No," he said, coming out of the bathroom. "In fact, it wasn't a line with me. I really meant it." He walked to the dresser, and poured Scotch into both glasses. "I knew immediately that I wanted to marry her. Did you want water in this?"

"No, thanks," she said.

Frank handed her one of the glasses. "Well . . . cheers," he said, and clinked his glass against hers.

"Cheers," Millie said, and drank. "Wow!" she said.

"Too strong? I can . . ."

"No, no, it's fine," she said, gasping. "Before you got married . . .?"

"Yes?"

"Did you go to bed with your wife? I don't mean to be personal."

"No, no, that's a perfectly legitimate question. We're both adults, after all, and if we're going to be honest with each other, we should be entirely honest."

"Precisely," Millie said. "*Did* you go to bed with her?"

"Yes."

"A lot?"

"Every now and then," Frank said. "We were at school together, you see. The University of Pennsylvania. It was very convenient."

"It was very convenient for Michael and me, too."

"It's even more convenient for the kids nowadays. My son, for example . . ."

"How old did you say he was?"

"Nineteen. He's a sophomore at Yale."

"Does he have a beard?"

"A moustache."

"Michael has a moustache, too."

"I was saying that the kids don't give a second thought to it nowadays. It's all very natural and casual with them."

"Natural maybe," Millie said, "but I don't think casual."

"Well, it *should* be a very natural thing, you know. Sex, I mean."

"Yes, but not casual. I don't think it should be casual, do you? Sex, I mean."

"No. But I *do* think it should be natural. Would you like to take off your jacket or something?"

"It *is* warm in here, isn't it?" She took off the suit jacket, and tossed it to the foot of the bed. "You were saying about your wife . . ."

"My wife?"

"About sleeping with her all the time."

"Well, not *all* the time. But we were on the same campus for four years."

"That's a long time to be sleeping with somebody."

"Especially if her father is a Methodist minister," Frank said.

"*My* father runs a Buick agency in the Bronx," Millie said. "Did you deliberately set out to marry a Wasp? I mean, because you're ashamed of being Italian and all?"

"Hey, come on," Frank said, laughing, "I'm *not* ashamed of being Italian. And besides, I don't think of Mae as a Wasp."

"What do you think of her as?"

"A woman," he said, and shrugged. "My wife. Whom I happen to love very much."

"I happen to love Michael very much, too," she said, "though he is a pain sometimes. This is very good, this Scotch. No wonder Michael belts it down every night. Could I have just a teeny little bit more?"

He took the bottle of Scotch from the dresser and went to

her, and poured more of it into her glass, and then sat on the edge of the bed beside her.

"Thank you," she said.

"You're welcome," he said.

"That must have been very nice," she said, "going to an out-of-town college, I mean. I went to N.Y.U. I used to commute from the Bronx every day."

"When did you graduate?"

"Ten years ago. In fact, Michael and I went to a reunion just before Christmas. It was ghastly. Everyone looked so old."

"How old *are* you, Millie?"

"Thirty-two," she said.

"Do you realize that when I started at the University of Pennsylvania you were still being pushed around in a baby carriage?"

"You're how old? Forty-six?"

"Four."

"That's only twelve years older than I am," she said, and shrugged.

"Exactly my point. When I was twenty-two . . ."

"Why'd you start college so late?"

"I was in the Army. My point is that when I was starting college . . . did you want some more of this?"

"Just a drop, please," she said, and held out her glass again. He poured liberally into it, and she raised her eyebrows and said, "That's like one of *Michael's* drops."

"Anyway, when I was starting college, you were only ten years old."

"Yes, but that's not in a baby carriage."

"No, but it's very young."

Sipping at her drink, she said, "Is that why you want to make love to me?"

"What?" he said.

"Make love," she said. "To me," she said. "Because I'm twelve years younger than you are?"

"Well, who . . . well, who said anything about . . .?"

"Well, you *do* want to make love to me, don't you?"

"Well, yes, but . . ."

"Well, is that the reason?"

"Well, that's part of it, yes."

"What's the other part? That I'm Jewish?"

"No. What's that got to do with . . .?"

"If that's part of it, I really don't mind," she said. "A lot of Gentiles find Jewish girls terribly attractive. And vice versa. Jewish girls, I mean. Finding Italian men attractive."

She looked at him steadily over the rim of her glass. She rose then, and walked to the dresser, and put her glass down, and began unbuttoning her blouse.

II

The motel courtyard was washed with sunshine, the trees were in full leaf. It was April, and Millie was wearing a bright cotton dress that echoed the blues, greens, and yellows of the season. Frank was wearing a business suit, but the tie he wore seemed geared to spring as well – a riot of daisies rampant on a pale green field. He unlocked the door knowledgeably, and removed the key with familiar dexterity. Millie entered the room first. She went swiftly to the dresser and put down her bag. As Frank locked the door from the inside, she went quickly to the drapes and pulled them closed across the windows. Frank threw the slip bolt and was turning away from the door, when Millie rushed into his arms. She kissed him passionately, and then moved out of his arms and disappeared into the bathroom.

Frank went to one of the easy chairs. He turned on the lamp between the chairs, and then began taking off his shoes and socks. Millie came out of the bathroom, carrying a facial tissue. She went to the mirror and began wiping off her lipstick. Frank took off his jacket. Millie slipped out of her pumps. Frank carried his jacket to the clothes rack, and hung it neatly on a wire hanger. Millie padded over to him barefooted, turned her back to him, lifted her hair from the nape of her neck and waited for him to lower the zipper on her dress.

"What's the use?" he said.

"Huh?" she said, and turned to look at him, puzzled.

"What's the use, what's the use?" he said despairingly, and went to one of the chairs, and sat in it, and began wringing his hands. "How am I supposed to put my heart in this when my mind's a hundred miles away? She's driving me crazy, Millie. If she doesn't stop, I'll just have to leave, that's all."

"Leave?" Millie asked, surprised.

"Leave, leave, right," he said, and rose and began pacing in front of the dresser. "I've warned her. I've told her a hundred times. She can't treat me this way, damn it. I'm not some adolescent kid fresh out of college."

"You've *told* her?" Millie said, and her eyes opened wide.

"A hundred times. More often than that. Repeatedly. Over and over again. A *thousand* times. Then today . . ."

Alarmed, Millie said, "What happened today?"

"What's today?"

"Tuesday. You know it's Tuesday. We meet every Tuesday."

"I mean the date. What's the date?"

"April sixth."

"Right. So that means *she* was five days late to begin with. So what's she jumping all over me for?"

"Five days late?"

"Right. And she yells at me about it. When *she's* really the one to blame."

"Frank, I thought we agreed a long time ago that we wouldn't discuss anything like this."

"Like what?"

"Like Mae or Michael."

"Who's discussing Mae or Michael? I'm talking about Hope. Hope Cromwell. She came in first thing this morning and said, 'Where is it?' So I reminded her that she'd only told me about the damn thing Friday, five days *after* it was due, and she said it seemed to her it shouldn't take that long to do a thirty-second spot when I knew the client was waiting for a presentation, and maybe I'd get the material in on time if I didn't take such long lunch hours every Tuesday. So I told her to take a look at her *own* lunch hour, which starts at eleven in the morning and ends at three, so don't talk to *me* about long lunch hours, baby."

"Did you really say that?"

"I certainly did."

"You called her 'baby'?"

"No, no, I wouldn't call her 'baby'. The point is I don't like being bawled out for something that's not my fault. And anyway, if I want to take a long lunch hour every Tuesday, so what? I've got half a mind to tell her what she can do with the job."

"Why don't you?"

"Huh?"

"Why don't you call her and tell her what she can do with the job?"

"Tell *Hope*, you mean?"

"Sure."

"Well, she's probably out to lunch right now."

"Let's try her," Millie said, and went to the phone.

"Well, perhaps it's best not to act too impulsively," he said. "There are millions of copywriters in New York, all of them just as good as I am."

"I doubt that very much," Millie said. She lifted the receiver and handed it to him. "Call her."

"Just a second, Mil," he said. "Let me *think* about this a minute, okay?"

"What's there to think about? Just tell her, that's all."

"I'll tell her when I get back to the office."

"Do you promise?"

"I promise."

Millie put the receiver back onto the cradle, and turned her back to him again. Lifting the hair from the nape of her neck, she lowered her head and waited for him to unzip her dress. "You don't have to take that kind of abuse, Frank," she said. "You're a very *good* copywriter."

"Yeah," he said, and lowered the zipper.

"So tell her."

"I will," he said, "don't worry." He unknotted his tie and threw it onto the seat of the closest chair. Unbuttoning his shirt, he said, "I'll tell her I don't have to take that kind of abuse."

"Right."

"I'll tell her I don't like to be blamed for something that's not my fault. She should have told me about the presentation earlier."

"That's right, she should have."

"Damn *right*, she should have," Frank said. "I'll tell her there are millions of copywriters in this city, but not many of them are as good as I am. And if she continues to hand out the kind of abuse she did this morning, I'll just head over to one of the other agencies where they won't treat me like an adolescent."

"Good," Millie said, "tell her." In bra, half-slip and panties, she padded to the clothes rack and hung up her dress.

"As for the lunch hour," he said, gathering steam, "I'll tell her to stop behaving as if it's a *banquet!* It isn't a banquet, it's just an ordinary long lunch hour, and that's that." He nodded, took off his shirt, and draped it over the back of one of the chairs. Millie was silent for what seemed like a long time.

"Frank, have you ever done anything like this before?" she asked suddenly.

"With another woman, do you mean?"

"Yes, with another woman."

"Besides Mae, do you mean?"

"Yes, besides Mae."

"Never," he said. "Why? Have you?"

Millie walked to the air conditioner. "Do you think this thing works?" she asked, and stabbed at a button on its face. "There," she said, and went to the bed, and neatly folded back the spread, and then carried it to one of the chairs.

"Millie?" he said. "You haven't answered my question. Have *you* ever?"

"Have I ever what?"

"Done this?"

"With another man, do you mean?"

"Yes, with another man."

"Besides Michael, do you mean?"

"Yes, besides Michael."

"Do you want an honest answer?"

"Of *course* I want an honest answer."

"Yes," she said.

"Jesus!" he said.

"You wanted to know."

"Who was it?"

"Another man."

"I *know* that! Who?"

"You don't know him. His name is Paul."

"Where'd you meet him?"

"In the Chock Full O'Nuts on Sheridan Square."

"Having a nice long lunch, was he?"

"No, he was eating a cream cheese sandwich on toasted raisin bread."

"I don't want to know anything else about him," Frank said. "In fact, I think we'd better get dressed."

"Why?"

"Because I want to leave." He went to the chair and picked up his shirt. He started to put it on, but one of the sleeves was pulled inside out. Angrily, he shoved at the sleeve, and finally managed to get his arm through it.

"He's a sculptor," Millie said.

"I don't care what he is."

"I posed for him once. Just my belly button."

"Your *what?*" Frank said.

"He does belly buttons. Not always, you understand. That was his project at the time. When I met him. He was doing these enormous sculptures of belly buttons. It was really quite fascinating. I mean, things take on a completely different perspective when you see them larger than . . ."

"I don't want to hear about your goddamn sculptor and his belly buttons!" Frank shouted. Calming himself, he said, "Get dressed, please," and began buttoning his shirt.

"He filled a very important need in my life," Millie said softly.

"I'm sure he did."

"And I could hardly have known at the time that I was going to meet you on the eight forty-six from Larchmont. Besides, I stopped seeing him right after I met you. In February."

"That's *not* right after you met me," Frank said. "That's a full *month* after you met me."

"Well, it takes time to end things," she said.

"More time than it takes to begin them, I'm sure."

"Now you sound like Michael."

"Oh, did you tell *him* about your sculptor, too?"

"Of course not."

"How come I'm so privileged?"

"I thought you'd understand."

"I don't. Put on your clothes, and let's get out of here."

"I wasn't looking for anything, Frank, I hope you realize that. It just happened."

"How? What'd you do, show him your navel in the middle of Chock Full O'Nuts?"

"I didn't do anything of the sort."

"Then how'd he know he wanted to sculpt *your* navel? There are six million women in the city of New York, how'd he happen to pick *your* navel?"

"He picked a lot of navels," Millie said. "Not only mine."

"How many?"

"At least fifty of them."

"Now that's sordid, that's positively sordid," Frank said.

"It wasn't sordid at all."

"Where'd you pose for him?"

"He has a big loft in Greenwich Village. There. But not the same day."

"Oh, that makes an enormous difference. When *did* he sculpt you, if you'll pardon the expression?"

"A month later. On October sixth."

"You remember the exact date, huh?" Frank said. "That really *is* sordid, Millie, remembering the exact date."

"Only because it was his birthday," she said.

"What'd you do? Drop in on the loft, strip down and yell 'Happy Birthday, Paul!'"

"Not Paul's birthday. Michael's."

"Oh, Jesus!" Frank said.

"And I didn't just go there. Paul called and asked me to come."

"Oh, you gave him your number, did you?"

"He looked it up, the same as you."

"He seems to have done a *lot* of things the same as me," Frank said. "Will you for God's sake get *dressed*?"

"It was just like open heart surgery," Millie said.

"What was?" Frank asked.

"Doing my navel. I didn't have to expose any other part of me. He had me all covered up with a sheet, except for my navel. It was very professional."

"When did it start getting *un*professional?" Frank said, and whipped his tie from the seat of the chair, and walked angrily to the mirror.

"After he cast it in bronze."

"Did he put it on the living room table?" Frank asked, and lifted his collar and slid the tie under it, and then began knotting the tie, and had to start all over again because somehow he'd forgotten how to knot a tie. "I think that would've been touching," he said. "A bronze belly button instead of a pair of baby shoes."

"It would've been too big to put on a table, anyway," Millie said. "I told you, the whole idea of the project was . . ."

"The whole idea of the project," Frank said, "was to get fifty stupid housewives into *bed* with him!"

"We weren't all housewives," Millie said.

Calming himself again, carefully knotting his tie, Frank said, "In any case, Millie, I think we should leave. I don't know how to sculpt, you see. I wouldn't know how to sculpt a goddamn navel. Or how to pick up a goddamn lady in the Chock Full O'Nuts on Sheridan Square."

"You did fine on the eight forty-six from Larchmont," she said.

"Oh, *I* did. I see. *I'm* the one who seduced the innocent little housewife, led her down the garden . . ."

"Well, *I* certainly didn't have the movie projector in *my* trunk!"

The telephone rang, shocking them into silence. They both turned to look at it, but neither made a move for it. The phone kept ringing.

"Why don't you get it?" Frank said. "Maybe it's Paul. Maybe he's doing buttocks this week."

Millie did not answer him. With great dignity, she padded to the phone, and lifted the receiver. "Hello?" she said. "Who? Yes, just a moment, please." She held out the receiver to Frank. "It's the manager. He wants to talk to Mr McIntyre."

Frank took the receiver from her. "Hello?" he said. "Yes? The *what's* too loud?" He looked across the room at the television set. "It isn't even *on*," he said, "so how can it be on too loud? Well, you just tell the man in seventeen that perhaps the television on the *other* side of him is on. In eighteen, that's right. Tell him it is *not* on in sixteen. Good-bye," he said, and banged down the receiver. "Stupid ass," he said. "Good thing we won't be coming back *here* anymore."

In a very tiny voice, Millie said, "Won't we?"

They looked at each other silently.

"I didn't know you'd get so angry," she said. "I'm sorry."

"Then why'd you tell me, Millie?"

"I had to."

"Why?"

"Because of what you said."

"When?"

"Just a little while ago."

"What did I say?"

"You said this wasn't a banquet."

"Huh?"

"You said it was just an ordinary long lunch hour. Well, to me it's a banquet. And if it's just an ordinary long lunch hour to you, then you can go to hell. If you're in the habit of taking lots of women to a motel in New Jersey . . ."

"I have never . . ."

"Putting a projector in your trunk . . ."

"I have never . . ."

"And showing them your lousy sixty-second commercial . . ."

"I thought you *liked* my commercial," he said.

"Not if it's been seen by every stupid housewife in the city of New York!"

"It's been seen by stupid housewives all over *America*," Frank said. "It's been aired approximately two hundred and twenty times. Listen, Millie, how did *you* suddenly become the injured party? *I'm* the injured party here. *I'm* the one who's been betrayed."

"Betrayed?" she said. "Oh my God, you sound *just* like Michael."

"Leave Michael out of this, if you don't mind. Let's get back to Paul."

"Why? Paul was nothing but an ordinary long lunch hour."

"A little while ago, you said he filled a very important need in your life."

"That's right, he did."

"You can't have it both ways, Millie. Either he was mean-ingful or he was a cream cheese sandwich on wholewheat."

"Toasted raisin."

"Whatever."

"He was both."

"Perhaps you'd like to explain that."

"Perhaps I wouldn't."

"Fine. Let's get dressed."

"Fine," she said.

She walked angrily to the rack, took her dress off its wire hanger, and slipped it over her head. "I thought you'd understand, but apparently you've never been neglected in your own home." He did not answer. "Apparently Mae adores you completely," she said, walking to him. She turned her back to him, and he zipped up her dress. "Thank you," she said. "Apparently Mae never treated you in a way that might force you to consider addressing a stranger in Chock Full O'Nuts. But when someone is concerned solely with Puts and Takes and selling short, then perhaps a woman may feel the need for conversation . . ."

"Conversation!" Frank said. "Jesus!"

"Yes, with someone whose interests extend beyond commodities. With someone who doesn't think of a *woman* as just another commodity. Paul thought of me . . ."

"As just another navel," Frank said.

She stared at him icily, and then said, "Paul thought of me as a very exciting individual. *That's* how he filled a need in my life. And that's why I'll always be grateful to him."

"Fine," Frank said, and put on his jacket. "Are you ready?"

"Not quite," Millie said. "Which isn't to say that I didn't enjoy the other aspect as well."

"Millie," he said, "you have said it all, you have really said it all. Now let's just get out of here, okay?"

"I'm not dressed yet," she said, and sat and put on her pumps, and then walked to the dresser and rummaged in her bag for her lipstick. "Haven't *you* ever felt like going to bed with somebody?"

"I have," he said.

"Not Mae, I mean."

"Not Mae."

"Who?"

"Hope."

"Hope? The Head of Creation?"

"Yes."

"*Hope!*"

"That's right."

"That's disgusting," Millie said. "She's your *boss!*"

"She's also a beautiful redhead."

"And a Wasp besides," Millie said.

"She happens to be an atheist."

"Has Mae ever met her?"

"She has."

"Does she like her?"

"Not particularly."

"Good," Millie said, and capped the lipstick and dropped it into her bag. "I'm ready," she said.

"Let's go then."

"Let's go," she said, and started for the door, and then suddenly stopped, and turned back to look into the room.

"Got everything?" he asked.

She hesitated.

"What'd you leave?"

"Nothing, I guess," she said, and shook her head. At the door, she hesitated again, and then said, "Frank, there's just one thing I'd like to know. Why do you find Paul so threatening?"

"I do not find him in the least threatening," he said.

"Then why are you so angry?"

"I am not in the slightest bit angry," he said.

"I was stupid to tell you," she said, and shook her head again. "Michael's right. Stupid is stupid, that's all." She sighed, and then said, "Let's go."

"What do you mean, Michael's right?"

"He's right, that's all. He thinks I'm stupid, and I am."

"You are definitely not stupid," Frank said.

"Michael thinks so. Maybe that's because he's so smart."

"Has he ever actually *said* he thinks you're stupid?"

"Not in so many words. But what he does is I'll make a

suggestion about something, you know, and he'll say, '*Thank you, Millicent*,' with just the proper inflection and tone, you know, to make me feel like an absolute moron. As far as he's concerned, if I keep my mouth shut and dress the girls properly and help him watch his damn calories, that's enough. Do you want to know something, Frank? I've known you for only four months, and I feel closer to you than I do to my own husband. What do you think of that?"

He did not answer.

"Well, it's true," she said. "Which is why I can't understand why you feel threatened about something that happened . . ."

"I don't feel threatened."

"You *all* feel threatened," she said. "If I'd ever told Michael about even *posing* for Paul, he'd probably have hit me or something."

"What do you mean? Are you trying to tell me he beats you?"

"Don't be silly, he's Jewish."

"So was Louis Lepke," Frank said.

"Yes, but he got mixed up with a lot of Italians. Now don't get offended."

"I'm *not* offended."

"You *do* find it threatening, don't you?"

"No, I don't find it threatening," he said. "In fact, I find it lovely. In fact I find it delightful that you picked up a belly-button sculptor, and posed for him, and went to bed with him, and can still remember the exact date, October eighth . . ."

"Sixth," she corrected.

"Yes, I find that all perfectly damn *won*derful," he said, his voice rising. "I thought we were, for Christ's sake, supposed to be in *love* with each other! I thought we were supposed to be able to trust each other and . . ."

There was a sudden hammering on the wall opposite the bed. Frank stopped mid-sentence, and turned to look at the wall.

"The black Cadillac," Millie whispered.

There was more hammering now, louder this time.

"Stop that banging!" Frank shouted, and it stopped

immediately. "Fat bastard," he said, and Millie giggled. "Thinks he owns the place. Move the car, lower the television, bang, bang, bang with his goddamn fist!" He glared at the wall. Millie was still giggling. "Go ahead!" he shouted. "I dare you to hit that wall one more goddamn time!"

There was no further hammering. Frank turned from the wall. Millie had stopped giggling. She was watching him steadily.

"*Are* we supposed to be in love with each other?" she asked.

"That was my understanding," he said quietly.

"That was my understanding, too," she said. She walked to him, and turned her back to him, and lifted the hair from the nape of her neck. He reached for the zipper at the back of her dress, and gently lowered it.

III

It was October outside, but the drapes were drawn, and in the room it might have been any season. The bedclothes were rumpled, and a pillow was on the carpeted floor. Millie, in lavender tights and brassiere was applying lipstick at the mirror. In the bathroom, Frank was singing loudly. He sang badly off-key, and she could not recognize the tune.

"Frank?" she said.

"Mm?"

"Don't you think you should call her?"

Frank came out of the bathroom, a towel around his waist, his hair wet. He had been growing a moustache for the past month, and he wore it with supreme confidence.

"What, honey?" he said.

"Don't you think you should call Hope?"

"What for?"

"It's pretty late. She . . ."

"Hell with her," he said, and picked up his shorts and trousers, and went back into the bathroom again.

Millie put the cap on her lipstick, dropped it into the bag, and then picked up her hairbrush. Brushing out her hair, she said, "You still haven't told me why Mae closed the shop so suddenly?"

"I guess she just got tired of it," he said.

"Maybe she took a lover," Millie said.

"What?" Frank said, and came out of the bathroom in his shorts.

"I said maybe she . . ."

"I doubt that sincerely," Frank said.

"It's a possibility," Millie said, and shrugged.

"I doubt it."

"You forgot to say sincerely."

"I think she just got bored with selling antiques, that's all," he said, and stepped into his trousers and zipped up the fly.

"Probably the pitcher that did it," Millie said. "My returning the ironstone pitcher. Michael says that stores operating on a small volume . . ."

"Mae's shop wasn't Bloomingdale's," Frank said, "but I'm sure a refund on a pitcher that cost fifteen dollars . . ."

"Seventeen dollars."

". . . wouldn't drive her out of business. Anyway, why'd you return it?"

"I didn't like having a pitcher belonging to another woman."

"It didn't belong to her. The moment you bought it, it became yours."

"It still seemed like hers." Brushing her hair, evenly stroking it, she said, "Would you like to know why she sold the shop? I can tell you, if you'd like to know."

"Why'd she sell it?"

"Because of your trip last month."

"My trip?"

"Mmm. Your second honeymoon," Millie said.

"You mean the trip to Antigua?"

"Well, where *else* did you go last month?"

"That was not a second honeymoon," he said. "Have you seen my shirt? Where'd my shirt disappear to?"

"I meant to tell you, by the way, that September is the hurricane season down there. Why anyone would go to Antigua in September is beyond me."

Frank lifted the bedspread from one of the chairs; his shirt was not under it. "We had beautiful weather," he said.

"Then why didn't you come back with a tan? All you came back with was a moustache."

"I also came back with a tan. Now where the hell is that shirt?"

"Not a very good tan, Frank. Would you like to know why? Because it was a second honeymoon, that's why. It's a little difficult to get a tan when you're up in the room all day long."

"We were not up in the room all day long," he said, and got down on his knees and looked under the bed. "Now how did it get *there?*" he said, and reached under the bed.

"Then where were you?" Millie asked.

"In the water, most of the time."

"Suppose a shark had bitten off your leg?"

"There were no sharks," he said, and stood up, and shook out the shirt.

"A barracuda then. How could you have driven here to New Jersey with only one leg?"

"I'm back," he said, putting on the shirt, "and I still have both my legs, so obviously . . ."

"Yes, but you never once gave it a minute's thought, did you? When you were scuba-diving down there."

"I was snorkelling."

"What's the difference?"

"Snorkelling is recreational. That's the only reason I do it. For recreation."

"Why'd you have to go all the way to Antigua to do it?"

"Mae wanted to go to Antigua."

"So naturally, you went. Never mind me."

"Millie, I was only gone for a lousy three weeks!"

"Twenty-four days, if we choose to be precise. And you never called me once," she said, and threw the hairbrush into her bag, and crossed the room to the clothes rack, and took her blouse from a wire hanger.

"I couldn't phone," he said. "We were on the beach most of the day."

"Didn't you ever come off the beach?" Millie asked, and put on the blouse.

"We came off the beach, yes," Frank said. "But there wasn't a phone in the room. The only phone was in the lobby."

"Then why didn't you go up to the lobby and call from there?" she said, buttoning the blouse.

"Because it took hours to get through to the States."

"Oh, then you *did* call the States," she said, and turned to face him.

"Yes, I called the office once to see how the new campaign was shaping up."

"But you couldn't call me," she said.

"Millie, this was a very isolated little hotel, with these small cottages on the beach, and . . ."

"Honeymoon cottages," she said.

"Suppose Mae had seen me making a phone call?"

"You could have told her you were calling the office to check on your brilliant campaign."

"I'd already called the office, and they'd told me my brilliant campaign was shaping up fine."

"I still think you could have called me, Frank. If you hadn't been so busy growing a moustache . . ."

"A man isn't busy growing a moustache. It grows all by itself."

"Yes, and there's a very definite connection, too. Between a moustache and sexuality."

"Take Michael, for example."

"Don't change the subject. If you hadn't been so involved with Mae, if you hadn't been enjoying your second honeymoon so much . . ."

"Millie, it was *not* . . ."

"Which, of course, is why she sold the damn shop ten minutes after you got back. She simply didn't need it any more. She found her husband again."

"Millie, it was not a second honeymoon. And I don't think the Antigua trip was the reason Mae sold the shop. And I would have called you if it was at all possible; but it wasn't. Would you hand me my tie, please?"

"I still think you could have called," Millie said, and handed him the tie, and then said, "I went to bed with Paul while you were gone."

"What!" he said, dropping the tie. "Why the hell did you do that?"

"Oh, for recreation," she said airily.

He stared at her silently, and then picked up the tie, and turned to the mirror.

"I figured . . ."

"I'm not interested," he said.

"That's exactly what I figured. A man goes away for three weeks . . ."

"Twenty-four days."

"Yes, and doesn't even call the woman he professes to love so madly . . ."

"Yes, so the woman runs back to a two-bit sculptor she used to *screw* every Tuesday!" Frank shouted.

"Right!" she shouted back, and suddenly there was a hammering on the wall.

"Oh, *hell!*" Frank said. The hammering stopped. "You know what he does in there?" he asked Millie. "He's not at all interested in that frumpy little blonde he brings here every week. All he does is sit in there and wait for us to raise our voices so he can jump up on the bed and bang on the wall. You *hear* that, you fat bastard?" he shouted. The man next door immediately hammered on the wall again. Frank went to the wall and began banging on it himself. The hammering on the other side stopped at once. Satisfied, he went back to the mirror and began knotting his tie.

"It was awful with Paul," Millie said.

"Good."

"Do you know what he's into these days? Sculpting, I mean."

"Nipples, I would imagine," Frank said.

"Ears. His whole studio is full of these giant-sized ears."

"Let me know when he gets to the good part, will you?"

"These huge ears all over the place." She shook her head in wonder. "All the while we were making love, I had the feeling somebody was listening to us." She went to the clothes rack, took down her skirt, and stepped into it. "I don't know why I went there," she said. "Maybe I sensed what was about to happen."

The telephone rang. Frank went to it instantly, and picked up the receiver. "Hello?" he said. "Yes, this is Mr McIntyre. Really?" he said. "Banging on the wall?

No, I don't think so. Just a minute, please." He turned to Millie, and said, "Darling, were you banging on the wall?" Then, into the phone again, he said, "No, nobody here was banging on the wall. Maybe it's the plumbing. Have you had the plumbing checked lately? Well, that's what I would suggest. Goodbye." He hung up, went to the dresser again, scooped his change, keys, and wallet off the top of it, and put them into his pockets.

"Frank?" she said. "Do you think we're finished?"

"No," he said immediately.

"I think we are," she said.

"Millie," he said, "let's get a couple of things straight, okay?"

"Okay."

"Number one, the trip to Antigua was not a second honeymoon. The situation between Mae and me has not changed an iota."

"What's the situation?"

"Mae and I *love* each other, but we are not *in* love with each other."

"You're comfortable with each other, right?"

"Right."

"Just a pair of comfortable old bedroom slippers tucked under the bed, right?"

"Right."

"Then why didn't you come back with a tan?" Millie said.

"Millie, let's get a couple of things straight, okay?" he said.

"We already got the first thing straight," she said, "so what's the second thing?"

"The second thing is that I still feel the same way about you. I'll always feel the same way about you, in fact."

"That's very nice," she said. "How do you feel about me?"

"I'm in love with you."

"But you don't love me."

"It's the same thing, Millie. Being in love with someone and loving someone . . ."

"How come with me it's the *same* thing, but with Mae it's

a totally *different* thing? A minute ago you were a pair of old bedroom slippers . . ."

"I've known Mae for twenty-two years," he said. "I've only known you for ten months."

"And twelve days."

"Who's counting?" Frank said.

"*I* am, damn it!" Millie said.

"I don't think you understand what I'm trying to . . ."

"I understand fine," Millie said, and walked to where she'd left her pumps near one of the easy chairs. Sitting, she said, "Mae's your wife, and I'm your Tuesday afternoon roll-in-the-hay."

"Millie, that isn't . . ."

"Look, Frank, you're Italian and you've got all these romantic notions about being in love, but actually I think what you really enjoy most about coming here is the idea that I'm some kind of whore or something."

"I have never thought of you as . . ."

"Have you ever thought of me as a *mother*, Frank?"

"A mother!"

"I have two children, you know. I have two adorable little girls that *I* made. *Me*. Personally."

"With a little help from Michael, I assume."

"What would you do if, with a little help from Michael, I got pregnant again? I can just imagine how *that* would sit with you. Big fat belly marching in here every week, what would *that* do to the image of the bimbo on the Via Margherita?"

"The what?"

"The Via Margherita. That's where Italian men keep their little pastries."

"I'm not an Italian man, I'm an American man."

"Right, you're Mr McIntyre, right?"

"I'm Mr Di Santangelo, but I don't have a bimbo on the Via Margherita, wherever the hell that may be. As a matter of fact, I don't have a bimbo *anywhere*."

"As a matter of fact, you have one right here in New Jersey," Millie said. She reached down for one of her pumps, and without looking up at him, slipped her foot into it and said, "Michael wants to have another baby." She put on the other shoe and only then looked up at him.

"What should I do?" she asked.

"That's up to you and Michael, isn't it?"

"It's also up to you," she said.

"Why don't we arrange a meeting then? Three of us can discuss it, decide what we . . ."

"Do *you* want me to have a baby, Frank?"

"No," he said flatly.

"Why not?"

"I hate babies," he said.

"It wouldn't be your baby."

"I hate *anybody's* babies."

"How can a man who hates babies write a popcorn commercial with two little kids . . .?"

"That has nothing to do with it. I hate popcorn, too."

"You'd never even *see* this baby," Millie said. "All I'm trying to find out is whether you like the idea of me *having* one, that's all."

"No, I don't like the idea."

"Why not?"

"I don't like the idea of your having another man's baby."

"Another man? He's my husband!"

"Anyway, what is this, a conspiracy or something? Is everybody in the whole *world* having a baby all of a sudden?"

"What?"

"Nothing," he said, and went immediately to the clothes rack, and took his jacket from its hanger.

"*Who's* having a baby all of a sudden?" she asked.

"Millions of women," Frank said. "Chinese women are having them right in the fields. As they plant the rice seedlings, they . . ."

"Never mind Chinese women, how many *American* women are having babies that you know of?"

"Right this minute, do you mean?"

"No, I mean nine months from last month when you and Mae were in Antigua working so hard on your suntans."

"Mae, do you mean?"

"Is Mae pregnant?"

"Who? Mae?"

"Mae. *Is* she?"

"Yes," he said.

"Which is why she ran out instantly to sell her little shop, right?"

"I don't know why . . ."

"Probably at Bloomingdale's this very minute, picking out a bassinette."

"Millie . . ."

"Knitting little booties in her spare time," she said, her voice rising, "papering the guest room with pictures of funny little animals! How could you *do* this to me, Frank?"

"To *you*?"

"Yes, to *me!*" she shouted. "Who the hell do you think?"

"Please lower your voice," he said. "If he bangs on the wall one more time, he'll put a hole through it."

Whispering, Millie said, "Didn't you once consider the possibility that . . ."

"What? Now I can't hear you at all."

In her normal speaking voice, but enunciating each and every word clearly and distinctly, Millie said, "Didn't you once consider the possibility that the thought of Mae having a baby might prove distressing to your lady friend on the Via Margherita?"

"Oh, cut it out with that Via Margherita stuff."

"Didn't you?"

"Do you know what you sound like, Millie?"

"What do I sound like?"

"A jealous wife."

"I suppose I do," she said. "But I'm *not* your wife, am I? I'm no more your wife than she is." She gestured towards the wall and the room next door. "To *him*, I mean. The man who bangs on the wall."

"Millie, I don't think you need equate us with a frumpy blonde and a fat old man."

"To *him*, she isn't a frumpy blonde," Millie said. "To him, she's all perfume and lace, the girl on the Via Margherita. All right to open these drapes now?" she asked.

"Sure," he said.

She pulled the drapes back on their rod. Sunlight splashed into the room. The day outside was clear and bright, the courtyard lined with the brilliant reds and oranges of autumn. She turned from the window, the sunlight behind her.

Frank looked at his watch. "We'd better get going," he said. "Hope's got a meeting scheduled for . . ."

"Just a few minutes more, Frank," she said. "I gave you plenty of time on the train, when we were just beginning. I think you can give me a few minutes now . . . when we're about to end."

"End?"

"Yes, what do you think we're talking about here?"

"Not ending, Millie."

"No? Then what?"

"I don't know. But two people can't simply *end* something after ten months together." He looked at his watch again. "Millie, really, we've got to go now, really. We'll talk about it tomorrow, okay? I'll call you in the morning . . ."

The telephone rang.

He looked at the phone, and then he looked at his watch again. The phone kept ringing, but he made no move to answer it. Millie went to it, and lifted the receiver, and said, "Hello?" and then listened, and then said, "No, I'm sorry, Mr McIntyre isn't here." Gently, she replaced the receiver on the cradle. "The manager," she said.

"What did he want?"

"I don't know. The television's off, and neither of us is yelling, and no one's banging on the wall." She shrugged. "Maybe he just felt lonely, Frank, and wanted to say hello." She went to him. "The way we did, Frank."

They looked at each other. It seemed for a moment as though they would move again into each other's arms. But Millie turned away, and went to the dresser and picked up her bag.

"I think I'll tell Michael okay," she said.

"I think you already have," he said.

"Maybe so," she said.

She went to the door and threw back the slip bolt and opened the door wide. He came to her, and they paused before stepping out into the sunshine, and turned, and stared back into the room. Then, gently, he took her hand, and together they left the room, closing the door behind them.

Smile, Corpse, Smile!

Bruno Fischer

I am a neat, precise man. The holes I chopped in the ice were as round as man-holes, and about half the size. There were an even half-dozen, formed in a semi-circle. The flags attached to the tip-ups were gaily red and stiffly proud in the wind cutting across Teacup Pond.

I am also a man who likes comfort, even when ice-fishing. On the shore, a hundred feet from my lines, I had built a modest fire of small logs. A stump served as my seat. When one of the flags tipped, I rushed out on the ice and hauled in that line – with, I hoped, a pickerel at the end of it.

I was waiting for the thirteenth pickerel when I saw the hand.

The third flag from the left dipped. That hole was the farthest from the shore, and as I strode out to it, I recalled that it was the only one out of which I hadn't yet taken a fish.

I didn't take one out that time. There was nothing on the hook, except the wriggling minnow I used for bait. I let the line slip back and started to return to shore and the fire. Out of the corner of my eye I caught movement out to my left. Again that third flag was bobbing frantically, as if urging me to hurry before whatever was on the hook got away.

Hurriedly, I pulled up the line, and at once the lack of resistance told me that I'd drawn another blank. Something down there was playing with me, perhaps one of the large turtles that inhabited the pond. I bent far over, peering down into the clear blue water below the ten-inch shell of ice, and I saw the hand.

It seemed to be reaching up for me – not as if to grab for me, not in menace; but there was something in the curve of those soft fingers that appealed for help. It was a woman's hand, young and unlined, and the nails were painted with a bright red lacquer.

Good God! I thought. *Somebody has fallen through the ice.*

I leaned forward to grip the hand and pull up the woman who belonged to it.

I didn't. It would have been impossible to pull anybody up through that very small hole. But that wasn't it. Nobody could be down there.

I lifted my eyes. A few hundred feet away, children were skating. Across the fifty-acre pond other men were ice-fishing. There was no break in the ice anywhere. Indeed, the ice was so thick that one of the fishermen had driven his car right out on it.

My gaze returned to the hole. All I saw now was the line, wavering slightly, disappearing in the water. The tip-up was erect.

I rose to my feet, and under my fleece lined sport coat I was sweating. I laughed. In that sharp air the sound of my laughter was very loud. I did not know why it frightened me. I returned to the fire.

A woman's hand imploring me for help. Except that it couldn't have been a hand. A turtle or a fish or a rag, and the water had distorted my vision of it. So it was nothing.

Well, if it was nothing, why didn't I stop shivering? It was the wind. Then why was I sweating as I shivered?

I kept my eyes on that third flag. It remained upright. So did the other five. I lit a cigarette and put another log on the fire.

The sun was sinking over the west rim of the pond. The wind got nasty. The children who had been skating went home. The fishermen across the pond pulled up their lines. I had walked over there a while ago and had seen that their tip-ups were home-made – either brush or whale-bones from old-fashioned corsets. Only one of them used store-bought tip-ups like myself, and he was the one who had driven his car out on the ice and stayed later than the others.

He liked his comfort even more than I did. Probably he had the car heater on and was listening to a football game on the car radio as he watched his flags. That was overdoing comfort, even for an ice-fisherman.

The fish no longer bit. I decided to call it a day and went out to the tank I'd chopped in the ice, leaving two or three inches of ice at the bottom as a floor. I had filled the tank with water, and there my even dozen pickerels swam, or would have if their long, somewhat vicious-looking bodies weren't packed almost solidly. A good catch – they ran from thirteen to twenty-one inches.

I strung the pickerels on a cord and then went from hole to hole, pulling up the lines and tip-ups. I started at the left. I don't know why, but when I reached the third hole, I got down on my knees and peered. And I saw the face.

It floated just under the surface of the blue water, shimmering as if seen through a veil – or in a dream.

Did I say float? No, that gives an impression of being static, and that face was anything but that. Grave black eyes looked up at me. A small red mouth was slightly parted, as if about to speak. Long, fair hair flowed back from a smooth brow. She was rather young, with a small round chin and a rather childish pug-nose.

I had never seen anything so unutterably lovely, and perhaps it was her loveliness that was so terrifying.

I leaped up. I ran, forgetting that there was ice under my feet, and I sprawled full-length. I lay there, panting, and the coldness of the ice went through my coat, my pants, my gloves. Only it wasn't the ice. The coldness was deep inside of me.

I got up and walked to the fire and dropped down on the stump. After what seemed a long time, I heard a car start. The fisherman who liked his comfort drove his car off the ice. The sun was sinking and I was alone on Teacup Pond. I sat there.

"Jed," I heard a woman call.

For one mad moment I thought that it was the woman under the ice calling to me. It was as if I had been waiting for that, for a sign from her, wanting it and at the same time dreading it. Then I looked up, and sanity returned. Laura Machin was coming towards me across the frozen meadow which fringed that side of the pond.

Laura was an attractive woman who was married to my best – and perhaps only friend. She wore a fur coat and a scarf over her blonde hair.

"Of all the unsocial guests," she said amiably. "Here you come up for the weekend and spend all day Saturday on the pond. Do you intend to spend the night here too, Jed?"

"I was just about to leave."

Laura saw my catch on the ice and went to pick it up. I pulled up the remaining tip-ups. I saved the third from the left for last, and I hauled it up without looking down into the hole.

"How long has this pond been frozen over?" I asked Laura when I returned to shore.

"Three or four weeks, since the beginning of December."

"Frozen solid?"

"Solid enough for skating, and there's been no thaw since then. Why do you want to know?"

"No particular reason," I said.

Side by side we started to trudge up to the house.

"The trouble with you, Jed," she said, "is that you like being alone too much. Don't you ever want to have some fun?"

"I do have fun."

"You mean like fishing?" Laura snorted. "Going off by yourself and freezing in the cold and having only fish to commune with! Jed, it's not normal."

"Well, I like it," I said.

She hadn't any answer to that, so we walked the rest of the way in silence.

Dave Machin was a commercial artist who didn't have to be tied to a city by a job, so recently he and Laura had bought a house overlooking Teacup Pond. They had invited me often, but during my summer vacation I had gone fishing in Maine, and as I worked in a bank I hadn't my Saturday mornings off, which gave me too short a weekend for a three-hour train trip. But this morning I'd got off in return for a lot of overtime, and I'd come up and spent the whole afternoon on the pond.

No, I wasn't social, even with my best friends.

Laura returned to the subject, while we were eating in front of the fieldstone fireplace.

"Dave," she said, "we'll have to do something about Jed. Next time he comes up here, we'll invite a girl for him."

The corners of Dave's bright blue eyes crinkled. He was

one of those tall, thin, slow-moving, drawling men. "No soap, honey," he said. "I've tried it for years. Jed's a woman-hater."

"I don't hate them," I protested. "I merely resent their possessiveness."

"It's fun having a woman possess you," Laura smiled across the table to her husband. "Isn't it, darling?"

"Yes and no," Dave replied judiciously. "All the same, Jed, you're missing a lot."

"I suppose so," I said. And all of a sudden I saw a pair of black eyes and red lips parted as if about to speak to me, and lovely, vibrant youth. And that face, glimpsed in water, was somehow more real and more desirable than the face of any woman I had ever known.

In bed that night I still saw that face. Perhaps, as Laura had said, I was alone too much. And now I couldn't sleep because of a woman who didn't exist.

From where I lay in bed, I could look through a window and down a thousand feet of slope to the pond. Under a slice of moon, the ice was dull grey. Nothing was there. That was sure, definite, logical. All right, then, go to sleep.

I couldn't sleep. Presently I dressed and slipped out of my room. I put on coat, hat, gloves, arctics, and I took with me the short-handled axe and a flashlight.

At the pond, I found that the six fishing holes were rapidly freezing over. I knelt at the third hole and chopped through the floor of ice. The water was black in the night. My hand shook as I directed the flashlight beam down into the hole. The water was still black.

Why had I run away from her when she had been there? I had deserted her when she had come to me, and now she was gone.

I stood up, shaking my head angrily. I was being absurd, worse than absurd. There could not have been anything but water. And there wasn't.

I returned to the house. Downstairs, I shed my outer clothes and went up the stairs.

A door opened, and Dave Machin stood there in blue and white striped pyjamas. "I heard you come in, Jed," he said. "Where were you?"

"Out for a walk."

"What did he say, darling?" I heard Laura ask.

Past Dave's shoulder, I saw her sitting up in bed, with a blanket held to her throat.

"He said he went for a walk," Dave told her.

"At three in the morning?" Laura said. "He's crazy."

All right, I was crazy. Probably even crazier than she thought.

I turned towards my room, then stopped and turned back to Dave who remained planted in the doorway. "Listen, Dave," I said. "Do you know a black-eyed girl with a round little chin and a nose you could flick off with a finger? I doubt if she's more than twenty. Maybe only eighteen."

He stared at me and then looked around at Laura.

She sat up straighter in the bed. "Amelia Hopkins!" she said.

He nodded and brought his gaze back to me. "I didn't know you knew her."

"Well, I —" I said, and stopped. "What about her?"

"She lives about a mile down the road, with her parents. Or lived there. She disappeared."

I started to speak and my voice got stuck. I cleared my throat. "When did she disappear?"

"About a month ago, wasn't it?" Dave asked his wife.

"The day after Thanksgiving," Laura said. "Just about a month."

"It seems that a man she was in love with threw her over," Dave told me. "She took it hard. She walked out of her house and never came back. There was quite a search for her. She must have run off, perhaps with a man."

"No," I said. "She didn't run off."

"So Amelia Hopkins came back?" Suddenly he laughed. "Holy cats, Jed, you didn't go out tonight on a date with her?"

Didn't I?

From the bed, Laura said, "Mrs Hopkins passed the house today and stopped to talk. She didn't tell me that Amelia had returned home."

I didn't know what to say, so I said nothing. I crossed the hall to my room.

Through the walls I heard Dave and Laura talking. I couldn't distinguish their words, but I could guess what they were saying about me. I sat down at the chair by the window and looked out at the frozen pond.

When I came down late to breakfast next morning. Sunday, Laura said gaily, "You can't fool us, Jed. Amelia Hopkins is living in the city, and you met her there. Isn't that it?"

"No," I said.

She gave Dave a triumphant look. "What did I tell you? He doesn't want to talk about it because he's in love with her. Last night he took a walk to brood about her. Jed's the kind of man who'll fight falling in love and doesn't want to talk about it."

"At least you ought to let her parents know she's alive and safe," Dave advised me.

I pushed aside my bacon and eggs. "Can't you people let me alone?"

Laura opened her mouth, but Dave beat her to it. "Sorry, Jed. A man's entitled to his private life. How about some skiing this morning? I hear the snow's fine on Wicket Hill."

"I'd planned to go fishing," I said.

Laura got angry at that. She was too well-mannered to say anything, but her face showed that she considered me a hell of a guest, going off by myself and returning only for food and a bed.

The day had started out crisp and clear, but by the time I reached the pond the sky was blacked out by threatening clouds. I didn't care about the weather. I set to work chopping out the holes I'd made yesterday, now almost completely frozen, and planting a tip-up beside each hole.

I started on the extreme left hole, and at the third hole I pretended that it was nothing, that it was just another fishing hole I was cutting. But when I broke through to the water and peered down and there was no face, I was bitterly disappointed.

It was as if I had found something infinitely precious and then had lost it.

I cut the rest of the holes, baited my lines, adjusted the tip-ups, then stood there waiting on the ice. I didn't build a fire or even go back to the shore where I could sit.

Children were skating at the east end of the pond, and near the opposite shore men were fishing like me, for pickerel.

A mean wind whipped across the pond. Random snow-flakes drifted down. The children disappeared, and some of the fishermen started to pull up their lines.

Through the arctics my feet got numb. Through the woollen gloves my fingers tingled with cold. And the flags did not tip. In an hour or more I hadn't got a single bite. But I wasn't after fish. I was waiting for the third flag to signal to me.

The snow came down more heavily. The last fisherman was leaving when the third flag dipped.

I rushed to the hole, and she was there.

Her face was turned up to me just below the clear, blue surface of the water. Snow fell into the hole, and, kneeling, I bent over, protecting her face with my body. And it was as if the water were gone and everything else were gone and we were alone together. Her black eyes glowed and her red mouth parted. She smiled.

She smiled the way no woman had ever smiled to me. I smiled back. We understood each other.

Snow fell about me and the harsh wind tore at my clothes, but deep inside me I was warm. I felt a sense of well-being, of fulfilment, such as I had never known before.

I have no idea how long I knelt there on the ice before Dave and Laura Machin came down to the pond for me. I heard their voices and looked at them over my shoulder. For the first time, then, I was aware that I was covered with snow and so stiff that I could scarcely move.

I didn't want to move. I wanted them to go away.

"My God, Jed!" Dave said. He put his hands under my armpits and tried to haul me up to my feet.

I fought him. And when Laura went to his aid, I fought her, too.

"Jed, what's come over you?" Laura cried.

Her words woke me as if from a dream. All of a sudden I was ashamed and afraid. I sagged against Dave.

"I – I must have dozed off," I muttered.

"Sure," Dave said gently. "Can you walk? Here, lean on me."

I twisted my head to look down into the ice hole. She was gone, of course. They had frightened her away.

They led me back to the house. They made me comfortable in front of the fire and fed me hot coffee. There was nothing much wrong with me. Not physically. In a little while I thawed out.

Lunch was very late that day. And after we had eaten, Dave took me aside for a man-to-man talk.

"What's eating you, Jed? The way you acted last night and then today at the pond."

"I don't want to talk about it." I stood up. "I'm taking an earlier train back to the city."

Dave nodded. "I'll drive you to the station."

Laura didn't come with us; she had work to do around the house. As we drove down the road, I kept my eyes averted from the pond.

Suddenly Dave stopped the car. "I just remembered. You left your fishing tackle on the pond."

"I'll miss my train if I go for it," I said.

At the station, there was a five minute wait for the train. We stood on the platform without saying anything to each other.

The train was pulling in when I made up my mind.

"Dave," I said, "Amelia Hopkins is in the pond, under the ice."

"What?" he said.

"She's under the third fishing hole from the left, facing the lake. You'll be able to locate it in the snow because the tip-ups are still planted and showing."

The train had come to a halt before the little station.

"How do you know?" He asked, watching me intently.

I didn't want to talk about it. I wanted to get away from that town quickly and forever. I said, "I saw her," and ran for the train.

When I mounted the steps, I glanced back. Dave stood gawking at me.

On Monday evening, Dave Machin came to the small furnished apartment where I lived alone. He settled himself in my one comfortable chair, stretched his long legs, lit his pipe.

"They found Amelia Hopkins in the pond," he said solemnly.

"Yes." There was nothing else I could think of to say.

"After you left yesterday, I went to the sheriff," he told me. "The sheriff was sceptical, and, anyway, he preferred to wait till the pond thawed. I went to Amelia's parents and they insisted that something be done at once. So this morning the sheriff brought a gang of men to cut a big hole in the area of that third fishing hole of yours. They used grappling hooks and almost at once brought up the body." He paused and then added, "The pond is thirty feet deep there. You couldn't have seen that far down through the water – not even three feet down in winter through a hole."

"She floated up to the surface," I murmured.

Dave shook his head. "The body was caught in roots or some other kind of growth. The grappling iron hadn't an easy time tugging it loose."

I looked down into the bustling, noisy street.

"Obviously she committed suicide when the man she loved turned her down," Dave continued. "She drowned herself in the pond and a few days later it froze over. She'd been down there nearly a month. It required the local dentist to identify her positively, through work he'd done on her teeth. The water and the fish didn't leave much of a face – much of anything."

I wished he hadn't put it into words. I just sat there, unmoving, not looking at anything now.

Dave rubbed the bowl of his pipe against his cheek. "You've never seen her, Jed. You were never in that neighbourhood before Saturday. Yet Saturday night you described her to me perfectly."

I said slowly, "She came up to the fishing hole looking the way she had in life. She wanted me to see her the way she had been – so very beautiful."

"Cut it out, Jed!"

I said as if speaking to myself, "Don't you see that she was as lonely down there as I was at the top?"

He got out of his chair and stood staring down at me. "Jed, surely you don't believe that?"

"I don't know," I said.

The Pulp Connection

Bill Pronzini

The address Eberhardt had given me on the phone was a corner lot in St Francis Wood, halfway up the western slope of Mt Davidson. The house there looked like a baronial Spanish villa – a massive two-storey stucco affair with black iron trimming, flanked on two sides by evergreens and eucalyptus. It sat on a notch in the slope forty feet above street level, and it commanded an impressive view of Lake Merced and the Pacific Ocean beyond. Even by St Francis Wood standards – the area is one of San Francisco's moneyed residential sections – it was some place, probably worth half a million dollars or more.

At four o'clock on an overcast weekday afternoon this kind of neighbourhood is usually quiet and semideserted; today it was teeming with people and traffic. Cars were parked bumper to bumper on both fronting streets, among them half a dozen police cruisers and unmarked sedans and a television camera truck. Thirty or forty citizens were grouped along the sidewalks, gawking, and I saw four uniformed cops standing watch in front of the gate and on the stairs that led up to the house.

I didn't know what to make of all this as I drove past and tried to find a place to park. Eberhardt had not said much on the phone, just that he wanted to see me immediately on a police matter at this address. The way it looked, a crime of no small consequence had taken place here today – but why summon me to the scene? I had no idea who lived in the house; I had no rich clients or any clients at all except for an appliance outfit that had hired me to do a skip-trace on one of its deadbeat customers.

Frowning, I wedged my car between two others a block away and walked back down to the corner. The uniformed cop on the gate gave me a sharp look as I came up to him, but when I told him my name his manner changed and he said, "Oh, right, Lieutenant Eberhardt's expecting you. Go on up."

So I climbed the stairs under a stone arch and past a terraced rock garden to the porch. Another patrolman stationed there took my name and then led me through an archway and inside.

The interior of the house was dark, and quiet except for the muted sound of voices coming from somewhere in the rear. The foyer and the living room and the hallway we went down were each ordinary enough, furnished in a baroque Spanish style, but the large room the cop ushered me into was anything but ordinary for a place like this. It contained an overstuffed leather chair, a reading lamp, an antique trestle desk and chair and no other furniture except for floor-to-ceiling bookshelves that covered every available inch of wall space; there were even library-type stacks along one side. And all the shelves were jammed with paperbacks, some new and some which seemed to date back to the 1940s. As far as I could tell, every one of them was genre – mysteries, Westerns and science fiction.

Standing in the middle of the room were two men – Eberhardt and an inspector I recognized named Jordan. Eberhardt was puffing away on one of his battered black briars; the air in the room was blue with smoke. Eighteen months ago, when I owned a two-pack-a-day cigarette habit, the smoke would have started me coughing but also made me hungry for a weed. But I'd gone to a doctor about the cough around that time, and he had found what he was afraid might be a malignant lesion on one lung. I'd had a bad scare for a while; if the lesion *had* turned out to be malignant, which it hadn't, I would probably be dead or dying by now. There's nothing like a cancer scare and facing your own imminent mortality to make you give up cigarettes for good. I hadn't had one in all those eighteen months, and I would never have one again.

Both Eberhardt and Jordan turned when I came in. Eb

said something to the inspector, who nodded and started out. He gave me a nod on his way past that conveyed uncertainty about whether or not I ought to be there. Which made two of us.

Eberhardt was wearing a rumpled blue suit and his usual sour look; but the look seemed tempered a little today with something that might have been embarrassment. And that was odd, too, because I had never known him to be embarrassed by anything while he was on the job.

"You took your time getting here, hotshot," he said.

"Come on, Eb, it's only been half an hour since you called. You can't drive out here from downtown in much less than that." I glanced around at the bookshelves again. "What's all this?"

"The Paperback Room," he said.

"How's that?"

"You heard me. The Paperback Room. There's also a Hardcover Room, a Radio and Television Room, a Movie Room, a Pulp Room, a Comic Art Room and two or three others I can't remember."

I just looked at him.

"This place belongs to Thomas Murray," he said. "Name mean anything to you?"

"Not offhand."

"Media's done features on him in the past – the King of the Popular Culture Collectors."

The name clicked then in my memory; I had read an article on Murray in one of the Sunday supplements about a year ago. He was a retired manufacturer of electronic components, worth a couple of million dollars, who spent all his time accumulating popular culture – genre books and magazines, prints of television and theatrical films, old radio shows on tape, comic books and strips, original artwork, Sherlockiana and other such items. He was reputed to be one of the foremost experts in the country on these subjects, and regularly provided material and copies of material to other collectors, students and historians for nominal fees.

I said, "Okay, I know who he is. But I–"

"Was," Eberhardt said.

"What?"

"Who he *was*. He's dead – murdered."

"So that's it."

"Yeah, that's it." His mouth turned down at the corners in a sardonic scowl. "He was found here by his niece shortly before one o'clock. In a locked room."

"Locked room?"

"Something the matter with your hearing today?" Eberhardt said irritably. "Yes, a damned locked room. We had to break down the door because it was locked from the inside, and we found Murray lying in his own blood on the carpet. Stabbed under the breastbone with a razorsharp piece of thin steel, like a splinter." He paused, watching me. I kept my expression stoic and attentive. "We also found what looks like a kind of dying message, if you want to call it that."

"What sort of message?"

"You'll see for yourself pretty soon."

"Me? Look, Eb, just why did you get me out here?"

"Because I want your help, damn it. And if you say anything cute about this being a big switch, the cops calling in a private eye for help on a murder case, I won't like it much."

So that was the reason he seemed a little embarrassed. I said, "I wasn't going to make any wisecracks; you know me better than that. If I can help you I'll do it gladly – but I don't know how."

"You collect pulp magazines yourself, don't you?"

"Sure. But what does that have to do with–"

"The homicide took place in the Pulp Room," he said. "And the dying message involves pulp magazines. Okay?"

I was surprised, and twice as curious now, but I said only, "Okay." Eberhardt is not a man you can prod.

He said, "Before we go in there, you'd better know a little of the background. Murray lived here alone except for the niece, Paula Thurman, and a housekeeper named Edith Keeler. His wife died a few years ago, and they didn't have any children. Two other people have keys to the house – a cousin, Walter Cox, and Murray's brother David. We managed to round up all four of those people, and we've got them in a room at the rear of the house.

"None of them claims to know anything about the murder. The housekeeper was out all day; this is the day she does her shopping. The niece is a would-be artist, and she was taking a class at San Francisco State. The cousin was having a long lunch with a girl friend downtown, and the brother was at Tanforan with another horseplayer. In other words, three of them have got alibis for the probable time of Murray's death, but none of the alibis is what you could call unshakeable.

"And all of them, with the possible exception of the housekeeper, have strong motives. Murray was worth around three million, and he wasn't exactly generous with his money where his relatives are concerned; he doled out allowances to each of them, but he spent most of his ready cash on his popular-culture collection. They're all in his will – they freely admit that – and each of them stands to inherit a potful now that he's dead.

"They also freely admit, all of them, that they could use the inheritance. Paula Thurman is a nice-looking blonde, around twenty-five, and she wants to go to Europe and pursue an art career. David Murray is about the same age as his brother, late fifties; if the broken veins in his nose are any indication he's a boozer as well as a horseplayer – a literal loser and going downhill fast. Walter Cox is a mousy little guy who wears glasses about six inches thick; he fancies himself an investments expert but doesn't have the cash to make himself rich – he says – in the stock market. Edith Keeler is around sixty, not too bright, and stands to inherit a token five thousand dollars in Murray's will; that's why she's what your pulp detectives call 'the least likely suspect'."

He paused again. "Lot of details there, but I figured you'd better know as much as possible. You with me so far?"

I nodded.

"Okay. Now, Murray was one of these regimented types – did everything the same way day after day. Or at least he did when he wasn't off on buying trips or attending popular-culture conventions. He spent two hours every day in each of his Rooms, starting with the Paperback Room at eight a.m. His time in the Pulp Room was from noon until two p.m. While he was in each of these Rooms he would read or watch films or listen to tapes, and he would also answer correspondence pertaining to whatever that Room contained – pulps, paperbacks, TV and radio shows, and so on. Did all his own secretarial work – and kept all his correspondence segregated by Rooms.''

I remembered these eccentricities of Murray's being mentioned in the article I had read about him. It had seemed to me then, judging from his quoted comments, that they were calculated in order to enhance his image as King of the Popular Culture Collectors. But if so, it no longer mattered; all that mattered now was that he was dead.

Eberhardt went on, ''Three days ago Murray started acting a little strange. He seemed worried about something, but he wouldn't discuss it with anybody; he did tell the housekeeper that he was trying to work out 'a problem'. According to both the niece and the housekeeper, he refused to see either his cousin or his brother during that time; and he also took to locking himself into each of his Rooms during the day and in his bedroom at night, something he had never done before.

''You can figure that as well as I can: he suspected that somebody wanted him dead, and he didn't know how to cope with it. He was probably trying to buy time until he could figure out a way to deal with the situation.''

''Only time ran out on him,'' I said.

''Yeah. What happened as far as we know it is this: the niece came home at twelve forty-five, went to talk to Murray about getting an advance on her allowance and didn't get any answer when she knocked on the door to the Pulp Room. She got worried, she says, went outside and around back, looked in through the window and saw him lying on the floor. She called us right away.

''When we got here and broke down the door, we found Murray lying right where she told us. Like I said before, he'd been stabbed with a splinterlike piece of steel several inches long; the outer two inches had been wrapped with adhesive tape – a kind of handle grip, possibly. The weapon was still in the wound, buried around three inches deep."

I said, "That's not much penetration for a fatal wound."

"No, but it was enough in Murray's case. He was a scrawny man with a concave chest; there wasn't any fat to help protect his vital organs. The weapon penetrated at an upward angle, and the point of it pierced his heart."

I nodded and waited for him to go on.

"We didn't find anything useful when we searched the room," Eberhardt said. "There are two windows, but both of them are nailed shut because Murray was afraid somebody would open one of them and the damp air off the ocean would damage the magazines; the windows hadn't been tampered with. The door hadn't been tampered with either. And there aren't any secret panels or fireplaces with big chimneys or crap like that. Just a dead man alone in a locked room."

"I'm beginning to see what you're up against."

"You've got a lot more to see yet," he said. "Come on."

He led me out into the hallway and down to the rear. I could still hear the sound of muted voices; otherwise the house was unnaturally still – or maybe my imagination made it seem that way.

"The coroner's people have already taken the body," Eberhardt said. "And the lab crew finished up half an hour ago. We'll have the room to ourselves."

We turned a corner into another corridor, and I saw a uniformed patrolman standing in front of a door that was a foot or so ajar; he moved aside silently as we approached. The door was a heavy oak job with a large, old-fashioned keyhole lock; the wood on the jamb where the bolt slides into a locking plate was splintered as a result of the forced entry. I let Eberhardt push the door inwards and then followed him inside.

The room was large, rectangular – and virtually over-flowing with plastic-bagged pulp and digest-sized magazines. Brightly coloured spines filled four walls of floor-to-ceiling bookshelves and two rows of library stacks. I had over 6,000 issues of detective and mystery pulps in my

Pacific Heights flat, but the collection in this room made mine seem meagre in comparison. There must have been at least 15,000 issues here, of every conceivable type of pulp and digest, arranged by category but in no other particular order: detective, mystery, horror, weird menace, adventure, Western, science fiction, air-war, hero, love. Then and later I saw what appeared to be complete runs of *Black Mask, Dime Detective, Weird Tales, The Shadow* and *Western Story*; of *Ellery Queen's Mystery Magazine* and *Alfred Hitchcock's Mystery Magazine* and *Manhunt*; and of titles I had never even heard of.

It was an awesome collection, and for a moment it captured all my attention. A collector like me doesn't often see anything this overwhelming; in spite of the circumstances it presented a certain immediate distraction. Or it did until I focused on the wide stain of dried blood on the carpet near the back-wall shelves, and the chalk outline of a body which enclosed it.

An odd, queasy feeling came into my stomach; rooms where people have died violently have that effect on me. I looked away from the blood and tried to concentrate on the rest of the room. Like the Paperback Room we had been in previously, it contained nothing more in the way of furniture than an overstuffed chair, a reading lamp, a brass-trimmed rolltop desk set beneath one of the two windows and a desk chair that had been overturned. Between the chalk outline and the back-wall shelves there was a scattering of magazines which had evidently been pulled or knocked loose from three of the shelves; others were askew in place, tilted forwards or backwards, as if someone had stumbled or fallen against them.

And on the opposite side of the chalk outline, in a loosely arranged row, were two pulps and a digest, the digest sandwiched between the larger issues.

Eberhardt said, "Take a look at that row of three magazines over there."

I crossed the room, noticing as I did so that all the scattered and shelved periodicals at the back wall were detective and mystery; the pulps were on the upper shelves and the digests on the lower ones. I stopped to one side of the three laid-out magazines and bent over to peer at them.

The first pulp was a 1930s and 1940s crime monthly called *Clues*. The digest was a short-lived title from the 1960s, *Keyhole Mystery Magazine*. And the second pulp was an issue of one of my particular favourites, *Private Detective*.

"Is this what you meant by a dying message?"

"That's it," he said. "And that's why you're here."

I looked around again at the scattered magazines, the disarrayed shelves, the overturned chair. "How do you figure this part of it, Eb?"

"The same way you're figuring it. Murray was stabbed somewhere on this side of the room. He reeled into that desk chair, knocked it over, then staggered away to those shelves. He must have known he was dying, that he didn't have enough time or strength to get to the phone or to find paper and pencil to write out a message. But he had enough presence of mind to want to point *some* kind of finger at his killer. So while he was falling or after he fell he was able to drag those three magazines off their shelves; and before he died he managed to lay them out the way you see them. The question is, why those three particular magazines?"

"It seems obvious why the copy of *Clues*," I said.

"Sure. But what clues was he trying to leave us with *Keyhole Mystery Magazine* and *Private Detective*? Was he trying to tell us how he was killed or who killed him? Or both? Or something else altogether?"

I sat on my heels, putting my back to the chalk outline and the dried blood, and peered more closely at the magazines. The issue of *Clues* was dated November 1937, featured a Violet McDade story by Cleve F. Adams and had three other, unfamiliar authors' names on the cover. The illustration depicted four people shooting each other.

I looked at *Keyhole Mystery Magazine*. It carried a June 1960 date and headlined stories by Norman Daniels and John Collier; there were several other writers' names in a bottom strip, a couple of which I recognized. Its cover drawing showed a frightened girl in the foreground, fleeing a dark, menacing figure in the background.

The issue of *Private Detective* was dated March, no year,

and below the title were the words, "Intimate Revelations of Private Investigators". Yeah, sure. The illustration showed a private eye dragging a half-naked girl into a building. Yeah, sure. Down in the lower right-hand corner in big red letters was the issue's feature story: "Dead Man's Knock", by Roger Torrey.

I thought about it, searching for connections between what I had seen in here and what Eberhardt had told me. Was there anything in any of the illustrations, some sort of parallel situation? No. Did any of the primary suspects have names which matched those of writers listed on any of the three magazine covers? No. Was there any well-known fictional private eye named Murray or Cox or Thurman or Keeler? No.

I decided I was trying too hard, looking for too specific a connection where none existed. The plain fact was, Murray had been dying when he thought to leave these magazine clues; he would not have had time to hunt through dozens of magazines to find particular issues with particular authors or illustrations on the cover. All he had been able to do was to reach for specific copies close at hand; it was the titles of the magazines that carried whatever message he meant to leave.

So assuming *Clues* meant just that, clues, *Keyhole* and *Private Detective* were the sum total of those clues. I tried putting them together. Well, there was the obvious association: the stereotype of a private investigator is that of a snooper, a keyhole peeper. But I could not see how that would have anything to do with Murray's death. If there had been a private detective involved, Eberhardt would have figured the connection immediately and I wouldn't be here.

Take them separately then. *Keyhole Mystery Magazine*. Keyhole. That big old-fashioned keyhole in the door?

Eberhardt said, "Well? You got any ideas?" He had been standing near me, watching me think, but patience had never been his long suit.

I straightened up, explained to him what I had been ruminating about and watched him nod: he had come to the same conclusions long before I got here. Then I said, "Eb,

what about the door keyhole? Could there be some connection there, something to explain the locked-room
angle?"

"I already thought of that," he said. "But go ahead, have
a look for yourself."

I walked over to the door, and when I got there I saw for
the first time that there was a key in the latch on the inside.
Eberhardt had said the lab crew had come and gone; I
caught hold of the key and tugged at it, but it had been
turned in the lock and it was firmly in place.

"Was this key in the latch when you broke the door
down?" I asked him.

"It was. What were you thinking? That the killer stood
out in the hallway and stabbed Murray through the keyhole?"

"Well, it was an idea."

"Not a very good one. It's too fancy, even if it was
possible."

"I guess you're right."

"I don't think we're dealing with a mastermind here," he
said. "I've talked to the suspects and there's not one of
them with an IQ over a hundred and twenty."

I turned away from the door. "Is it all right if I prowl
around in here, look things over for myself?"

"I don't care what you do," he said, "if you end up giving
me something useful."

I wandered over and looked at one of the two windows. It
had been nailed shut, all right, and the nails had been
painted over some time ago. The window looked out on
an overgrown rear yard – eucalyptus trees, undergrowth
and scrub brush. Wisps of fog had begun to blow in off the
ocean; the day had turned dark and misty. And my mood
was beginning to match it. I had no particular stake in this
case, and yet because Eberhardt had called me into it I felt a
certain commitment. For that reason, and because puzzles
of any kind prey on my mind until I know the solution, I
was feeling a little frustrated.

I went to the desk beneath the second of the windows,
glanced through the cubbyholes: correspondence, writing
paper, envelopes, a packet of blank cheques. The centre

drawer contained pens and pencils, various-sized paper clips and rubber bands, a tube of glue, a booklet of stamps. The three side drawers were full of letter carbons and folders jammed with facts and figures about pulp magazines and pulp writers.

From there I crossed to the overstuffed chair and the reading lamp and peered at each of them in turn. Then I looked at some of the bookshelves and went down the aisles between the library stacks. And finally I came back to the chalk outline and stood staring down again at the issues of *Clues*, *Keyhole Mystery Magazine* and *Private Detective*.

Eberhardt said impatiently, "Are you getting anywhere or just stalling?"

"I'm trying to think," I said. "Look, Eb, you told me Murray was stabbed with a splinterlike piece of steel. How thick was it?"

"About the thickness of a pipe cleaner. Most of the 'blade' part had been honed to a fine edge and the point was needle-sharp."

"And the other end was wrapped with adhesive tape?"

"That's right. A grip, maybe."

"Seems an odd sort of weapon, don't you think? I mean, why not just use a knife?"

"People have stabbed other people with weapons a hell of a lot stranger," he said. "You know that."

"Sure. But I'm wondering if the choice of weapon here has anything to do with the locked-room angle."

"If it does I don't see how."

"Could it have been *thrown* into Murray's stomach from a distance, instead of driven there at close range?"

"I suppose it could have been. But from where? Not outside this room, not with that door locked on the inside and the windows nailed down."

Musingly I said, "What if the killer wasn't in this room when Murray died?"

Eberhardt's expression turned even more sour. "I know what you're leading up to with that," he said. "The murderer rigged some kind of fancy crossbow arrangement, operated by a tripwire or by remote control. Well, you can forget it. The lab boys searched every inch of this room.

Desk, chairs, bookshelves, reading lamp, ceiling fixtures –
everything. There's nothing like that here; you've been
over the room, you can tell that for yourself. There's
nothing at all out of the ordinary or out of place except
those magazines."

Sharpening frustration made me get down on on knee
and stare once more at the copies of *Keyhole* and *Private
Detective*. They had to mean something, separately or in
conjunction. But what? What?

"Lieutenant?"

The voice belonged to Inspector Jordan; when I looked
up he was standing in the doorway, gesturing to Eberhardt.
I watched Eb go over to him and the two of them hold a
brief, soft-voiced conference. At length Eberhardt turned
to look at me again.

"I'll be back in a minute," he said. "I've got to go talk to
the family. Keep working on it."

"Sure. What else?"

He and Jordan went away and left me alone. I kept
staring at the magazines, and I kept coming up empty.

Keyhole Mystery Magazine.

Private Detective.

Nothing.

I stood up and prowled around some more, looking here
and there. That went on for a couple of minutes – until all of
a sudden I became aware of something Eberhardt and I
should have noticed before, should have considered before.
Something that was at once obvious and completely un-
obtrusive, like the purloined letter in the Poe story.

I came to a standstill, frowning, and my mind began to
crank out an idea. I did some careful checking then, and the
idea took on more weight, and at the end of another couple
of minutes I had convinced myself I was right.

I knew how Thomas Murray had been murdered in a
locked room.

Once I had that, the rest of it came together pretty quick.
My mind works that way; when I have something solid to
build on, a kind of chain reaction takes place. I put together
things Eberhardt had told me and things I knew about
Murray, and there it was in a nice ironic package: the

significance of *Private Detective* and the name of Murray's killer.

When Eberhardt came back into the room I was going over it all for the third time, making sure of my logic. He still had the black briar clamped between his teeth and there were more scowl wrinkles in his forehead. He said, "My suspects are getting restless; if we don't come up with an answer pretty soon, I've got to let them go on their way. And you, too."

"I may have the answer for you right now," I said.

That brought him up short. He gave me a penetrating look, then said, "Give."

"All right. What Murray was trying to tell us, as best he could with the magazines close at hand, was how he was stabbed and who his murderer is. I think *Keyhole Mystery Magazine* indicates how and *Private Detective* indicates who. It's hardly conclusive proof in either case, but it might be enough for you to pry loose an admission of guilt."

"You just leave that part of it to me. Get on with your explanation."

"Well, let's take the 'how' first," I said. "The locked-room angle. I doubt if the murderer set out to create that kind of situation; his method was clever enough, but as you pointed out we're not dealing with a mastermind here. He probably didn't even know that Murray had taken to locking himself inside this room every day. I think he must have been as surprised as everyone else when the murder turned into a locked-room thing.

"So it was supposed to be a simple stabbing done by person or persons unknown while Murray was alone in the house. But it wasn't a stabbing at all, in the strict sense of the word; the killer wasn't anywhere near here when Murray died."

"He wasn't, huh?"

"No. That's why the adhesive tape on the murder weapon – misdirection, to make it look like Murray was stabbed with a homemade knife in a close confrontation. I'd say he worked it the way he did for two reasons: one, he didn't have enough courage to kill Murray face to face; and two, he wanted to establish an alibi for himself."

Eberhardt puffed up another great cloud of acrid smoke from his pipe. "So tell me how the hell you put a steel splinter into a man's stomach when you're miles away from the scene."

"You rig up a death trap," I said, "using a keyhole."

"Now, look, we went over all that before. The key was inside the keyhole when we broke in, I told you that, and I won't believe the killer used some kind of tricky gimmick that the lab crew overlooked."

"That's not what happened at all. What hung both of us up is a natural inclination to associate the word 'keyhole' with a keyhole in a door. But the fact is, there are *five other keyholes* in this room."

"What?"

"The desk, Eb. The rolltop desk over there."

He swung his head around and looked at the desk beneath the window. It contained five keyholes, all right – one in the rolltop, one in the centre drawer and one each in the three side drawers. Like those on most antique rolltop desks, they were meant to take large, old-fashioned keys and therefore had good-sized openings. But they were also half-hidden in scrolled brass frames with decorative handle pulls; and no one really notices them anyway, any more than you notice individual cubbyholes or the design of the brass trimming. When you look at a desk you see it as an entity: you see a *desk*.

Eberhardt put his eyes on me again. "Okay," he said, "I see what you mean. But I searched that desk myself, and so did the lab boys. There's nothing on it or in it that could be used to stab a man through a keyhole."

"Yes, there is." I led him over to the desk. "Only one of these keyholes could have been used, Eb. It isn't the one in the rolltop because the top is pushed all the way up; it isn't any of the ones in the side drawers because of where Murray was stabbed – he would have had to lean over at an awkward angle, on his own initiative, in order to catch that steel splinter in the stomach. It has to be the centre drawer then, because when a man sits down at a desk like this, that drawer – and that keyhole – are about on a level with the area under his breastbone."

He didn't argue with the logic of that. Instead, he reached out, jerked open the centre drawer by its handle pull and stared inside at the pens and pencils, paper clips, rubber bands and other writing paraphernalia. Then, after a moment, I saw his eyes change and understanding come into them.

"Rubber band," he said.

"Right." I picked up the largest one; it was about a quarter-inch wide, thick and strong – not unlike the kind kids use to make slingshots. "This one, no doubt."

"Keep talking."

"Take a look at the keyhole frame on the inside of the centre drawer. The top doesn't quite fit snug with the wood; there's enough room to slip the edge of this band into the crack. All you'd have to do then is stretch the band out around the steel splinter, ease the point of the weapon through the keyhole and anchor it against the metal on the inside rim of the hole. It would take time to get the balance right and close the drawer without releasing the band, but it could be done by someone with patience and a steady hand. And what you'd have then is a death trap – a cocked and powerful slingshot."

Eberhardt nodded slowly.

"When Murray sat down at the desk," I said, "all it took was for him to pull open the drawer with the jerking motion people always use. The point of the weapon slipped free, the rubber band released like a spring, and the splinter shot through and sliced into Murray's stomach. The shock and impact drove him and the chair backward, and he must have stood up convulsively at the same time, knocking over the chair. That's when he staggered into those bookshelves. And meanwhile the rubber band flopped loose from around the keyhole frame, so that everything looked completely ordinary inside the drawer."

"I'll buy it," Eberhardt said. "It's just simple enough and logical enough to be the answer." He gave me a side-wise look. "You're pretty good at this kind of thing, once you get going."

"It's just that the pulp connection got my juices flowing."

"Yeah, the pulp connection. Now, what about *Private Detective* and the name of the killer?"

"The clue Murray left us there is a little more round-about," I said. "But you've got to remember that he was dying and that he only had time to grab those magazines that were handy. He couldn't tell us more directly who he believed was responsible."

"Go on," he said, "I'm listening."

"Murray collected pulp magazines, and he obviously also read them. So he knew that private detectives as a group are known by all sorts of names – shamus, op, eye, snooper." I allowed myself a small, wry smile. "And one more, just as common."

"Which is?"

"Peeper," I said.

He considered that. "So?"

"Eb, Murray also collected every other kind of popular culture. One of those kinds is prints of old television shows. And one of your suspects is a small, mousy guy who wears thick glasses; you told me that yourself. I'd be willing to bet that some time ago Murray made a certain obvious comparison between this relative of his and an old TV show character from back in the fifties, and that he referred to the relative by that character's name."

"*What* character?"

"Mr Peepers," I said. "And you remember who played Mr Peepers, don't you?"

"Well, I'll be damned," he said. "Wally Cox."

"Sure. Mr Peepers – the cousin, Walter Cox."

At eight o'clock that night, while I was working on a beer and reading a 1935 issue of *Dime Detective*, Eberhardt rang up my apartment. "Just thought you'd like to know," he said. "We got a full confession out of Walter Cox about an hour ago. I hate to admit it – I don't want you to get a swelled head – but you were right all the way down to the Mr Peepers angle. I checked with the housekeeper and the niece before I talked to Cox, and they both told me Murray called him by that name all the time."

"What was Cox's motive?" I asked.

"Greed, what else? He had a chance to get in on a big investment deal in South America, and Murray wouldn't give him the cash. They argued about it in private for some time, and three days ago Cox threatened to kill him. Murray took the threat seriously, which is why he started locking himself in his Rooms while he tried to figure out what to do about it."

"Where did Cox get the piece of steel?"

"Friend of his has a basement workshop, builds things out of wood and metal. Cox borrowed the workshop on a pretext and used a grinder to hone the weapon. He rigged up the slingshot this morning – let himself into the house with his key while the others were out and Murray was locked in one of the Rooms."

"Well, I'm glad you got it wrapped up and glad I could help."

"You're going to be even gladder when the niece talks to you tomorrow. She says she wants to give you some kind of reward."

"Hell, that's not necessary."

"Don't look a gift horse in the mouth – to coin a phrase. Listen, I owe you something myself. You want to come over tomorrow night for a home-cooked dinner and some beer?"

"As long as it's Dana who does the home cooking," I said.

After we rang off I thought about the reward from Murray's niece. Well, if she wanted to give me money I was hardly in a financial position to turn it down. But if she left it up to me to name my own reward, I decided I would not ask for money at all; I would ask for something a little more fitting instead.

What I really wanted was Thomas Murray's run of *Private Detective*.

Brush Babe's Poison Pallet

Bruce Cassiday

I

Last-Mile Lane

It was a street of crooked turnings and twisted doorways and sagging roofs. It was a crooked street walked by crooked people and watched over by crooked devils in the sky. A brooding and evil darkness stood guard above it, shutting off the light of the heavens.

Many men had come down this twisting, narrow, tortuous lane and had never come back. It was a street of lost souls, a street of barter where the costliest memories were traded for the cheapest coin. The roadway to hell, this street.

Last-Mile Lane, Greenwich Village, Manhattan.

Five minutes from Times Square. Five minutes from the crystalline splendour of Rockefeller Center. Five minutes from eternity.

A man stood on a corner of the winding lane, staring up at the street sign. It was pitch black and heavy clouds hung under the moon, squatting over the upended, sagging eaves of the ageing structures.

The man was tall and lean and he stood there with an air of anxiety. He was a man who had read the end of a grim, grisly story on the grey etchings of a tombstone, and who must now trace through that unhappy history from its sordid beginning to its tragic end.

He snapped his thumb across a match and the flame

leaped out into the darkness. The yellow-red glow painted his face bright and fine against the dancing, grotesque shadows about him. The letters of the sign burned black in the night – *Last-Mile Lane*.

His eyes were wide and deep set, and his forehead was high and pale. His hair, even in the flickering, shimmering matchlight, was carroty red, stiff, wiry. His eyes glittered in the glowing illumination, green as the shattered glass of a beer bottle. His face was pale cream, dumped with teenage freckles that would never fade away.

Robert Sands. Red Sands.

Red Sands had a clown's face with quirks in the corners of the mouth and deep lines etched in the forehead. He also had the capacity, like any clown, of carrying an angry, determined man's spirit in a laughing, devil-may-care man's body.

Lighting the cigarette there in the dancing, inky blackness, Red Sands had the look of a lobo on the stalk, a hunter on the trail, a searcher for the lost in a barren, destroyed universe. The cold, crisp wind from down the crooked alleyway crawled along the ground, licking like a hungry puppy at the cuffs and sleeves of his suit.

And then suddenly Sands waved the match out with a desperate, almost terrified flick of the wrist. The cigarette glowed crimson in the black air. Sands sucked in air tightly to his backbone, and his hand crept into his jacket pocket. The smooth, reassuring barrel of his .38 Police Positive leaped into his shaking fingers.

Sands melted into the ebon shadows of an unpainted store front. With the sweat oozing out clammily onto his body, he pulled himself flat to the wall, listening. His heart beats slowed, his nerves tingled.

Yes. Faintly, imperceptibly, he could hear the sound down the crooked, twisting lane – the slow, measured movement of cat feet.

They had picked up his trail again. They or he. He or it. Whatever had tracked Red Sands unseen through the brilliant light of day, through the black shadows of night, through the swirling fog of morning. It had followed him here, too. Whatever it was that meant to keep Red Sands from finding the hide-out of the fugitive girl called Jennie Gomez whose sanctuary was here in the twisting wilderness of Greenwich Village. It had picked up his trail again; it was out to finish him off.

Two misses were enough. Once in the subway station in the dead of morning – a hurtling dark form coming out of a corner, stumbling into Sands, shoving him forward towards the tracks in front of the onrushing express. Again in a darkened, mist-shrouded alleyway – a violently swung wooden crate slammed into Sands's hip, sprawling him helplessly in the path of an onrushing taxi.

Two tries within the three nights of his search for Jennie Gomez.

The breath of fear crawled along the sweaty backbone of Red Sands, and he listened again. Slithering like a snake through the tar-like opaque night, the thing came towards him along the bent, broken street. Sands slid out the .38 Colt and flicked the safety. The click of the metal rattled like the devil's bones in the silence about him.

No air stirred. Blackness closed down over him like ink-soaked cotton. His eyes burnt, his chest throbbed, his soles itched. Involuntarily, Sands's mouth dropped open and a gasp grated out of his constricted throat.

The motion stopped. The monster paused. The thing considered, puckered up its brows – if it had any – and uncoiled from its unseen, imagined shape.

Suddenly, whimpering like a sickened puppy, Sands blasted away desperately in the darkness with the Colt, once, twice, three times. The blinding, infra-red mushroom of gun flame smeared the darkness with a glowing smoky paint. A towering and twisted form loomed over him. Shadow? Mass? Human?

A tremendous force like the crash of a falling building tore at his hand. The gun sailed out into the darkness, and he heard it clatter angrily down the sign: *Last-Mile Lane*. It lay still, the gun – a useless pawn in this strange, eerie game of death.

An exploding, destructive horror tore at Sands's body – a smashing, paralysing force – and he was enmeshed in its trance-like, helpless terror. His arms flailed at the thing, his hands beat at the shapeless mass of strength, his knees gouged into the monster.

The shape was not human. They were not hands coming at him. They were strange taloned tentacles – hard, brittle, horned at the ends. A viscid, almost puffy mass breathed into his face, and the breath was stale. Grunts of exhaustion and fatigue came from the strange shape, but still Sands could see nothing.

They struggled there in the dark, two half-maddened beasts – neither one able to see the other distinctly. The monster and the hunter. The hunter raged blindly, fanning his arms like windmills, smashing his tough, wiry knuckles into the monster's face, chest, stomach. Panting, terrified, hysterical with dread, Sands fought insanely, like a madman, like a wounded bobcat that would not die.

He fought desperately, crazily, fearlessly, until the blackness came, and even after he was past the realm of knowledge he was pummelling the beast entwining him with its sinewy tentacles.

Crying out suddenly with a weird coyote-like call in the night, the monster backed up, panting, breathing heavily, whimpering, and without a further attempt at assault, it slithered down the black alleyway, limping, hitching itself along like a broken-backed vertebrate.

Sands lay there in a pool of his own blood.

The bar was a pleasant little underground cellar, built in the style of an Old English country pub. Dark-oak beams, carved and ornate, gave a Victorian London tone to the bar. It was called the Thackeray Room.

A row of windows high above the back of the bar gave out onto the dark Greenwich Village street. The occasional flash of a passerby's foot moved swiftly from left to right, from right to left.

A student slumbered in the corner of the bar, over a glass of ale and a calculus manual. A pair of girls stared at each other over two enormous mugs of black brew. The sleepy barkeep drowsily moved his amber coloured eyes from one side of the bar to the other to keep awake. He wandered up and down, rubbing glasses dry with a wet towel. His barrel chest and his powerful shoulders were covered with a soiled white apron.

On the opposite wall of the tavern hung a series of twelve oil paintings.

One portrait in particular stood out from the rest. It was the portrait of a woman. She had dark eyes, brooding, liquid, expressive. On her mouth curved a mocking, magnetic smile, and her lip held a contemptuous, scornful amusement. On her face was imprinted a cursed, unnatural beauty. There was too much of it for one woman to have.

Suddenly the barkeep turned from his glasses and glanced up into the street outside, viewing the darkness through the windows above the back bar. Instantly he gasped and almost dropped the glass in his hands.

Through the window stared the bloody, torn, bruised face of a man lying stretched out there full length on the sidewalk. The man's face was pale and freckled, and his mouth was twisted and beaten in. His eyes were torn with pain, and he lifted a hand feebly to scratch on the window. Then his eyes closed and he passed out, sprawled there on the cement walk, and the blood grew in a pool around him.

The barkeep knew his onions. He filled the unconscious man with strong brandy and slapped his face. He bandaged the cut and bleeding wounds, and finally Red Sands opened his glazed eyes and groaned.

The world was swirling about him painfully, and when he could focus his eyes he made out the walnut woodwork of the bar and the amber eyes of the barkeep and the brown brandy taste in his mouth. He sat up groggily, rubbing his face with his hand. He touched bruises and bandages and dried blood.

"Thanks, pal," he whispered to the barkeep. "Thanks a lot."

Shaking his head to clear out the cobwebs, Sands looked about at the interior of the bar. The two girls were staring glassily at him, and the calculus student in the corner was dozing over his ale. Sands turned back to the barkeep and grinned.

"Sorry, pal. Guess I kind of passed out."

"Forget it," said the barkeep. "Run into an uptown express?"

Suddenly remembering something, Sands reached into his jacket pocket. Oddly his .38 Colt was there.

"Last-Mile Lane," Sands mumbled. "Last-Mile is right."

The barkeep whistled. "Rough as a cob. Stay the hell out of that hole after this."

Sands grinned, and his clown's face crinkled at all its corners. "Don't worry about that."

His voice trailed off. Inside he turned to ice and glass. There was no place for air to go in his chest. He could see it plainly, and even when he closed his eyes and shook his head and opened them again he could see it. There was no doubt about it.

He turned his dazed, staring eyes to the barkeep. "Who's that girl? Where does she live?"

His eyes followed the direction of Sands's. They both stared at the portrait of the dark, brooding girl.

It was Jennie Gomez. And seeing her there in that picture again after all these years brought the roaring back in his ears, the swimming mists in front of his eyes, and the twisting, stabbing hell in his guts. It was as if all the love and hate and joy and grief in the world had come to Red Sands from that one girl.

He remembered it all clearly from the first sight of her lovely, sad face, to the sight of the last broken, crushed cigarette butt smeared with her lipstick. The story of Red Sands, the story of the sell-out that backfired.

As an FBI agent five years ago Red Sands had been sent to find Jennie Gomez and bring her in for questioning by the Department of Justice concerning the whereabouts of her brother, Danny Gomez. Gomez was an artist – some said the best primitive oil painter of the twentieth century – but since the beginning of the Spanish Revolution he had fought in Europe and had joined the spyring of a European power.

From successful oil painter Gomez had turned into one of the most fabulous of international agents, and his score had been all ten of the US State Department operatives sent to tail him.

Sands had found Jennie Gomez, and had been suckered into the perfect sell-out double-cross. He'd run out with Jennie Gomez, but she had two-timed him and vanished. Sands had been drummed out of the FBI, escaping imprisonment only because of his record.

Danny Gomez had been killed in World War II, captured by the Germans while fighting for another European power. And then two years later ten portraits of Gomez's – owned by Hamlin Bell, a rich collector of bizarre objects of art and a nut on the subject of primitive modern oils – had disappeared from Bell's apartment in Manhattan.

Bell's private operatives had traced the theft through fences to Jennie Gomez, but she was not in the United States and could not be located. Three weeks ago, however, word crept through the grapevine that Jennie Gomez was back in the States.

Hamlin Bell, tracing through the history of Red Sands – ex-FBI agent – had hit upon him as the man to find Jennie Gomez. Sands had refused at first, but the healthy fee Bell offered had finally convinced him that stalking brunettes might be better than stalking gold in 1949, and he had taken the job.

And now here hung the portrait of Jennie Gomez. And what made Sands's jaw unhinge like a steam-shovel scoop was the fact that he recognized the artist. Jennie Gomez had painted her own portrait. And she was trying to gather in a few extra bucks by hanging it in the bar here – in case anybody wanted to buy it.

Amber Eyes was studying Sands intently. "Forget about her," snapped the barkeep. "I can't remember where she went. She ain't for sale. She's labelled poison, and she comes in doses of trouble."

Sands rubbed his bruised jaw. "How's your art appreciation?" mused Sands, watching the eyes of the bartender closely. The barkeep stared back intently.

"I don't get you."

"Let me put it this way. Go in for vegetables? Cabbage? Lettuce? Moola?"

"Moola," repeated the barkeep, rubbing his chin with his finger. "That's quite a salad. Green, ain't it? Green with alphabet noodles. V's. I's. X's. Art pictures of Washington DC celebrities."

"You've got the taste of a gourmet," nodded Sands. "Like to gum down a couple or twenty leaves of the stuff, friend?"

Amber Eyes stared into the ceiling. "You twisted my arm, buddy. Funny how my mouth keeps droolin' for that wonderful moola stuff."

Sands handed over the twenty, and the custodian of the Thackeray Room suddenly recovered his impaired memory.

II

The Big Sell-Out

Jennie Gomez was a dark, handsome girl with black eyes and black hair and a black past. She was built from head to toe with the loving care of a master craftsman. If he earned the last dollar in the world for his work he came away underpaid. She was long and graceful, and her arms were smooth and cream-coloured. Her eyes smouldered with savage fire, and her mouth was full and strong and dusky.

Inside her gnawed a futile, knowing sadness – she had too much life to live and too little time to live it in. Happiness was a fragile thing and it broke to pieces in her hands, no matter how carefully she handled it.

She was standing behind the door when she opened it for Red Sands, and he could feel the terrible jolting shock deep in his guts as he faced her and moved into the room towards her. Instinctively he knew that she felt the same thing for him.

He stepped inside and closed the door.

"Jen," he said. "You double-crossing little rat. Hello, baby."

She untied her smock and smoothed her dress as she moved away from him. She turned in the middle of the room and smiled at him.

"Sucker," she said. "So you found me after all. The big red-headed chump. Think you can bring home the bacon this time? I'll deadbeat you again, Red, I swear I will. The deck is stacked against you."

She came over to him. The smile on her face seemed pasted there. She held out one hand to him, but she did not touch him.

Sands talked and his mouth had dry flour in it. "You string along with me, Jen, and there'll be no trouble at all. I won't even stick a .38 Colt in your back if you hand over those Hamlin Bell pictures." He moved over and slowly sat on the couch, gripping the .38 tightly.

She sat down beside him, watching him. Then she turned away and leaned back luxuriously into the depths of the couch.

He went on talking. "Just between you and me and that Jennie Gomez painting there on the floor, one wrong peep, and it'll be the last. Baby, I and this .38 Special of mine ain't playing."

"Danny took all the pictures with him the last time he went to Italy. Didn't you know he was killed over there?"

He stared at her steadily. "That's a lie," he said from the troubled, hard pit of his stomach. His eyes were glassy and his jaw was built out of cement. He saw her through the tight glaze of his eyes. It was impossible that this lovely lady had sold him down the river once before. It was impossible that Red Sands was in practically the same unenviable position as before, tracking down the only girl he had ever loved, for a rich man with a penchant for the primitive oils of Gomez.

"You've got those pictures," he said huskily. "Let's stop beating around the mulberry bush. "Let's get down to brass monkeys."

She smiled and shook her head. Her face was close to his and her eyes were turned up into his pleadingly. They were warm and steady and her lips were vibrant and smooth.

Cursing raspingly, he ground out the words. "I've got to get them, Jen. I'll kill you if you try to stop me! You hear? I'll kill you this time."

She leaped back and her hand touched his. She was shaking her head slowly, sadly. "No, Red," she said. "I don't have them."

He turned to her, the flames of rage boiling up inside him. He took her shoulder in his hand.

"Oh, Red," she said. Her hand came up to his cheek.

Anger surged up in him and he wanted to cry out: "This is it, you black-haired Judas! You double-dealing Delilah! Get me those pictures or I'll blast you to hell and gone!"

He reached out his other hand and took her in his arms and kissed her, cursing to himself that it should be so, burning with a helpless anger. But he could do nothing but hold her tightly and kiss her again.

He lifted one feeble hand to his jacket pocket for the .38 Colt, but the moment his fingers touched the cold steel he knew it was no use.

He knew again that she had beaten him, that this time was the last time anyone could defeat him, that he was finished, that he was no longer a man but a beaten, trampled-on hulk, that he would never again walk with his head high.

Her soft, gentle voice came to him like silk in his ears.

"Jen," he whispered, and all the love in the world was in that one word. Inside his heart cold hate chewed and gnawed at him for the memory of the man that had been, once. . . .

He came out of it with a violent start. For a long moment he could remember nothing, and the room rocked and pitched dizzily about him. It was a tall room with an infinite blue space stretching along one entire wall. His eyes focused hazily.

A long endless sheet of glass stretched from the floor to the ceiling along one end of the room. The panes of glass were embedded in the frame of the wall with strips of lead. Through the glass he could see blue-black sky, stars by the millions, high buildings in the distance, and dark trees below.

Washington Square. Manhattan. Midnight.

He remembered the girl and he remembered the wine they had finished off – wine out of a French bottle. Rhenish wine. And that was all he could remember. That old Rhenish wine had been *vin à la Finn Mickey* – and that was the fiery, deadly liquid that had drawn the curtain of lethe over him.

Damn her. A Mickey Finn! She'd knocked him out and made off with those pictures!

He tensed to tear himself up out of the chair where he was slumped. But as he did so the sound came to him again. Startled, he realized that the rustling movement in the next room must have been the thing that had roused him in the first place.

Cold dread rinsed through him. A twisted, cockeyed picture of a darkened, crooked lane, and the hideous phantom shape that had loomed above him in the pitch black of night came back to him. The sound in the other room was the cat-like movement of that same misshapen monster.

Sands slid onto the floor and moved along the rug soundlessly. He reached for his gun, but his hand came out of his jacket empty. Cursing, he slid his hands through his other pockets. No rod.

The sound slithered closer to the door and Sands pressed himself against the wall. Jennie Gomez? Where was Jennie? Besides the clear-cut vision of her sitting across from him, sipping the lovely, killable Rhenish wine, he could bring back no other memory of her.

Creaking, the door opened a slit. Sands slid along the wall, grasping desperately for a chair that stood in his path.

It was too dark to see well, but Sands could make out the moving mass of flesh slipping into the studio room from the bedroom. With a flying lunge, Sands threw the chair down over the head, and the whole thing splintered with a tearing, ripping sound that smashed about between the tight walls of the studio. A sudden grunt, and then a low-pitched laugh from the creature filled the room.

Sands hurtled himself for the beast, but it moved swiftly across the room to the door. Sands grasped one foot, and the bare flesh trembled under his palm. The thing hitched, stumbled and smashed head first into the wall.

Guttering forth cries of pain and anguish, the creature pulled itself into a knotted, hunched ball and withdrew from Sands's groping hands. Sands jumped to his feet and dived at the crouched shape. The shape hissed and spluttered and suddenly lashed out at Sands.

A force like a speeding subway crashed into him. Sands

sprawled back across the hard oak floor, skidding along on his shoulder and spine. The hot sting of scraped flesh shot tremors through his body. Through the flashing, shattered red and black shimmering before his eyes, he could see the shape draw itself up.

Tearing open the hall doorway, the thing threw itself out into the blackened walk-up and disappeared. Sands ran into the companionway, stumbling and gasping. Dazedly he leaned far out over the ballustrade. There was no movement at all in the stair well. The darkness of endless night had swallowed the creature up.

Trembling there, Sands stood, clinging to the stair rail, listening desperately for any sound. He heard nothing.

After a long, fruitless moment, Sands moved back into the studio room, and tiny prickles of fear wormed along his spine. Jennie. Where was Jennie Gomez? Maybe she was not the one who had doped that wine. Maybe the beast had lain in wait for both of them. Maybe the thing was trying not only to kill Sands, but Jennie Gomez as well. Maybe . . .

Hastily he stepped across the room and tore open her door. Her light was on, projecting its yellow rays in a cone-like shape over her bed. He saw her all right. She was sprawled out across the bed, the covers dragged halfway with her towards the floor. The sheets were twisted about her sliding body, as if she had tried vainly to struggle out of the bed of death half unconscious, half fainting. Blood was smeared in clotting streaks.

Sands gasped and turned away, gripping the door in his hands, digging his nails into the soft wood. He steadied himself and then moved into the room. Yes, of course, he thought drearily. His .38 Colt was there, plain to see, lying in the centre of the rug.

He stooped over to pick it up.

What was the use now? The bullet would match the barrel of the gun. Even a blind ballistics expert could tell that. If he got rid of the gun they still have it on record in the New York files. He had a perfect motive. Jennie Gomez had suckered him out of the FBI. He'd found her again, they'd fought, he'd killed her.

Bell would never back him to help him out of this mess.

Bell had hired him to get pictures, not to knock off a human being.

Somebody had built a beautiful frame around him. In the shake of a dead lamb's tail they'd have that frame hanging from a scaffolding somewhere. Sands too.

I killed her all right. I killed her without pulling the trigger on a gun. I killed her by following her and getting mixed up in this damned mess.

But, he thought, *I'll be damned if I'll burn for her!* . . .

The sleeping city is made for a man hiding out from the law. A thousand alley cats walk the same streets on padded feet, and rats scuttle along the gutters. They are good companions to a man on the lam. Fear walks with a fugtive in the black of the night. Fear and helplessness and inevitable death. But with him also walks loneliness, and loneliness is the friend of a man who is haunted. A howling, eerie wind moaned along Fifth Avenue down into the park at Washington Square, and only a light here and there glistened in the city about him. A pall of sleep cloaked the city like a heavy down quilt. It was 4 a.m. In an hour the sun would be up. In two hours the city would be awake. In ten hours the whole town would be on his trail, howling and screaming for blood and vengeance. Murderer. Killer. Madman.

Sands pulled the collar of his coat up around his neck. He had one place to go to settle accounts with the one man who knew why he was tailing Jennie Gomez. The one man who knew, and who could have put a killer on his backtrail.

The clean, vigorous breeze whistled about him as he came into Central Park West. Hugging the buildings, he crossed several streets and finally stood across the street from the Tower Apartments. For a moment he stopped, surveying the giant edifice. It stretched high into the night sky, a pinnacle of steel and cement and humanity. Swank. High-toned. Big.

And on the twentieth floor – stretching from one end to the other – nestled the private suite of Hamlin Bell.

Behind the Tower Apartments stood an old theatre condemned, rusted, shut up forever, waiting to be torn down and converted into another metal mountain beside the Tower. Between the two buildings ran a small alleyway for pickups and deliveries.

Sands ducked into the narrow cut-in and the cold fingers of wind followed him, whipping his coat about his ankles. Easy. Too easy. The fire escape ladder touched the ground.

He was winded and panting when he crouched resting on the nineteenth floor cage. He looked above him, checking the exact location of the room he wanted on the twentieth floor. Bell's study.

Involuntarily he sucked in his breath. Barred! The windows of the twentieth floor were barred with wrought iron bars! Sands cursed to himself, grating his teeth together, wiping the sweat off his face. Barred! That stinking dog of a tycoon!

Sands touched the gun in his pocket. Its reassuring metallic smoothness chilled his hand. He slid it out and tested the window on the fire-escape cage beside him. The room inside it was pitch black.

Slowly, easily, the window gave. Six inches. A foot. Two feet. Pausing, Sands listened carefully. There was no noise inside but the ticking of a clock. No breathing. No sound at all but the metallic beat of time.

Peering inside, Sands made out the vague outline of a fireplace at one corner of the room, a long chaise longue by the window, and a baby grand piano across from him. It was a living room. No one would be sleeping here.

Noiselessly he slid inside the room and lowered the window behind him. Slowly, so his eyes could accommodate themselves to the darkness, he made his way across the room, step by step, prayer by prayer. When he came to the end of the room he saw two doors, one leading to the right, one to the left.

Figuring that the left door led to a room facing the street outside, and the right door led to a hallway, Sands turned the right knob and opened the door. The bolt slid noisily, and he peered out into the quiet hallway. Bull's-eye.

An instant later he had climbed the stairs to the twentieth floor and was standing in front of Hamlin Bell's private room – the room in which Bell had interviewed him several days before. Sands had the .38 out in his hands now, and he slid forward on the carpeted floor and pressed the buzzer.

Several long minutes later slippered feet padded towards him. The door opened cautiously, and a grey man with grey eyes and grey hair and a black and grey bathrobe stood there, staring out of the darkness at Sands. Instantly the grey man's eyes slitted and his mouth opened. His teeth were grey inside his mouth.

Sands shoved inside, the heavy .38 pressing into the man's bathrobe. Sands closed the door quietly. "Move, boy," whispered Sands. "Take me to Old Man Bell – and no funny business, Junior, or I'll jet-propel you to hell and gone on a fat lead slug!"

The grey man didn't shake at all. He wasn't the kind to shake without being told to. He took orders. Because a gun backed up a gentleman's orders, that had nothing to do with the fact that he was now trotting down the hallway faster than he had ever trotted before – gun to his backbone – to interrupt the irascible old man who fed him and clothed him and who had cautioned him never to break in on him in the middle of a game.

Sands grinned wryly to himself. Funny Old Man Bell didn't have himself surrounded by gunnies. He'd had enough of them out all over the city. Bell liked good appearances. Mean a lot to a big shot.

The grey man was bending over a doorway, thrusting a clattering key in a lock. The key turned, the lock snapped, the door opened. At that moment a familiar metallic, wooden crash sounded from the room, and someone inside yelled: "Strike!" Bowling pins of course; Sands recognized the sound now.

Sands thrust his way into the room, brushing the grey man aside. Bell had just turned around and was watching Sands grimly, his big hawk nose twitching in his face. His eyes were large and his eyebrows prominent so that the grey eyes inside seemed set far back into his skull. He could hide them, flash them, or bug them out. His teeth were long and they stuck out in front. His hair was steel grey and it bristled up off his head. He was sixty-five years old but he still had a crew haircut.

"Oh, you, Sands," snarled the leathery old condor. "Beat

it, Haines," he called to the grey man. The grey man dissolved and the door closed behind Sands. Sands moved his eyes from Bell's face to the gun, significantly, and stepped back an inch or two.

"Bell, you damned double-crosser, you and I are going to have a heart-to-heart talk."

Bell's face was immobile. Then the flame of a smile burned at the corner of his face. His mouth crawled up at the ends, and his grey eyes receded ten or fifteen feet into his head. Little pinpoints of light glowed inside them. The yellow fangs of teeth popped out over the top of his greyish lip. He rubbed his nose suddenly with a long horny forefinger.

Sands glanced around at the long, low-ceilinged room. It wasn't a room at all – it was a bowling alley, complete with an automatic racker at the end, and a pile of bowling balls in the corner. The bright light cast a burnished glow on the white pine and ash of the alleyway, and the automatic racker finished its work. There were no windows in the room at all, but an air conditioner blew in clean air in a steady, healthy flow.

Bell was grinning now, his teeth gleaming in the light like a mole's. "Insomnia, Sands. I can't lie in bed all night tossing and turning. I've got to get some kind of exercise – even at this hour of the morning. Mind if I go on?"

"Damned right I mind, Bell. You stand right there. I want to get some things straight, and then you can go back to your game."

Bell's eyes flashed fire briefly and then cooled down. His jaw thrust out and the smile smashed to bits. When he spoke his words came out like a whiplash. "Go on, Sands."

"She's dead, Bell. Jennie Gomez. You told me to get those pictures from her, but she never even had them. Bell, you hired me to get killed. You deliberately tailed me and –"

Bell's voice cracked out like a rifle shot. "Let's get this straight. What the devil are you talking about? You found the girl? And she is dead?"

Sands took a deep breath and held the .38 closer to his

stomach to steady it. "Yeah. Dead. And my rod killed her."

The cracked old mouth twitched into a knowing smile. "Your gun? Had a dog-fight and plugged her, didn't you, Sands?" The voice was insinuating and slimy as a snake's belly. "So now you want me to pull you out of hot water – just because I hired you."

"I didn't kill her. She was dead when I came to. I went on a Mickey Finn junket and when I came to – cold potatoes."

Bell put his big, horned hand to his face and rubbed his jowly face around. "Maybe so. What's this about me using you as a patsy?"

Sands backed up a moment, thinking hard. This old duck was a tough guy, used to fighting all ways. He was wise to the tricks. He was ruthless and hard and he had money to back every wish he made. Somehow he didn't quite add up to murder. Murder would be too complicated for him to bother with.

Sands went on. "You patsied me when you sent me out on that job. A set-up. I got down there, and you sent one of your gorillas to track me – grab my rod for a plant. Lovely little monster, too, believe me. That didn't work, and then he followed me to her place and framed me."

Bell's lip moved a bit and his tongue lolled about in his mouth. He scratched his neck with his fingernails and then ran his hand through his brittle grey hair. He chewed on his lip, hitched up his baggy Harris tweeds, and rubbed his upper lip with his knuckle.

"Okay, Sands, I ought to have told you sooner." Bell slouched onto the billiard ball rack. He took out a cigar, bit off the end, shoved it in his mouth. He lit a match to it, gasped and wheezed over it until he got it blazing away, and then his piercing grey eyes looked clean through Sands.

"Jennie Gomez was blackmailing me, Sands."

Sands moved back to the wall, his eyes hooded and his breath coming short. "Blackmailing you!"

"It all goes back to the time when Danny Gomez was still painting pictures. He joined the Spanish Revolutionists and turned spy. You knew all about that, didn't you?"

Sands lit a cigarette, slouching down on the billiard rack opposite Bell. "Yeah. Gomez was just making a name for himself as a painter when he got tangled up in politics. Then he joined the Revolutionists, became a spy-baby, and continued working during World War II. He got killed in Italy. Now his paintings are worth a couple thousand apiece. You had ten of them, and they were stolen in 1947. That right?"

"You ever see those pictures?" Bell asked after a short pause, his eyes narrowed and his lips wrapped heavily over the cigar.

"No. Landscapes. Portraits. That right?"

"That's right. Portraits."

"I don't get it. So what?"

Bell took out the stogie and surveyed it distastefully. "Believe me, I don't care what my children do to amuse themselves. But for a girl of mine to be painted by a rabid political spy along with a well-known European political figure – that's too much for me, Sands." Bell paused, stared at Sands a moment. "Red. That's your name, isn't it, Sands?"

Sands nodded, his clown face bending up into a grin. "Yeah."

"Okay, Red. My daughter married a man you've probably heard of. He's a senator in Washington, DC. Now he's heading an important political mission in direct opposition to the country Gomez worked for. I believe you have a good picture of the situation. I need that one picture in particular. My daughter means a lot to me, and I assure you this political mission means a lot to us all. I will stop at nothing to get it back."

Sands had seen pictures of Bell's daughter Lois. A madcap kid, so the story went. But now she was happily married to Senator Davison. She was the mother of two children. Bell had a decent point there.

"Why didn't you tear up those damned pictures when you had them?"

Bell shrugged his shoulders, unwrapped the cigar with his lips, and spread his hands apart. "The seeds for our own destruction lie in all of us, Sands. If I could help myself, I would have. It is not in my blood to destroy a work of art that has genius in it. Those Gomez paintings were his best. That make sense to you?"

Sands grinned. The struggle of the flesh and the will. A man always lost the battle. "Yeah. It makes sense to me. We're all half-nuts anyway, aren't we?"

Bell leaned forward. "Would you mind taking that gun off my stomach, Sands? I don't doubt it's a very neat way to rid a man of his ulcers. Me, I'll just suffer on happily."

Sands lifted the .38 and scratched his cheek with the muzzle. "Listen, Mr Bell. I'm in a rat's hole. You know what happened to me the first time I tried to turn in Gomez's sister. She got me drummed out of the FBI.

"And now this set-up. I'm the perfect patsy. Even if you come forward with your story, that won't help me a bit. They'd say that I killed her on orders from you – to stop her from milking you any more. Bell, just keep your mouth shut and let me handle this my own way."

Bell stood up, clamping the cigar between his teeth. He smiled and his eyes glittered back in his skull. "That may sound dandy to you, Red. But what about me? What about those paintings? What happens to my kid when those pictures are discovered by the cops? No, Sands. You're going to be the fall guy this time. You're going to be the cat's paw – for killing that girl. That'll stop any dragged-out investigation. I'd rather pay the price to you than let that stuff pop up in the hands of the police."

Sands stood up, and tiny prickles of fear moved up and down his neck. Chills travelled along his spine. He licked his lips with his tongue. His body was tense as a coiled spring. He suddenly realized that this had been a bad, deadly error – coming to see Old Man Bell.

"What do you mean, Bell?"

"A hundred thousand dollars, Sands," Bell murmured, his face close to Sands, the eyes blazing like coals back in his head. "I'll get you off easy. Ten years. That's not anything – for a hundred thousand dollars! I've got influence. You can count on me. How's that sound to you, Sands?"

In the silence Sands fought with his voice, fought fear and hate and a desperate urge to run. His voice was rasping. "I've seen men who've spent time in the bag, Bell. Not me! Not one damned day! Not for a million bucks!"

Bell moved towards Sands, slowly, menacingly, holding

the cigar in his hand, gesturing with it. "Too bad you don't agree with me, Sands," he smiled gently, sucking on the cigar. "I've already decided that you will. You're the man for the job. Tough, Sands. You can't fight me. I've got everything in my favour – money and power and protection. Especially protection."

Bell paused to let that word sink in.

Sands raised the .38. His breath steadied and his nerves were suddenly toned up and fit. He aimed the gun.

Then instinctively he whirled. There was someone behind him. Someone wearing a funny, spicy perfume. Coming up in back of him. He had heard no one, he had felt no one in the place, but suddenly he smelled that funny, spicy perfume.

But just as he turned, aghast, and his .38 spun around with him, he felt the blazing whir of steel wings in the air above his head, smelled the salty tart odour of fear through him, tasted the gritty slime of blood, and he spun downwards to the floor, dropping thousands of miles in a glorious flood of exploding planets and stars and galaxies.

III

Model for Murder

She was slim and neat as TNT, this one was. Her eyes were brown pools of arsenic and old French wine. She wore her blonde hair feathery and fluffy, and a thin line of dark brown tufts showed in the part. Perched on the back of her head at a jaunty angle was a go-to-hell French beret.

But she was no phoney, Sands could see at a glance. She had a pallet on her lap, a brush in her right hand, and a loaded .22 Colt Woodsman in her left. She had the paint-smeared brush aimed at the canvas on the easel, the Colt aimed at Sands's guts. The safety was off, and the lady's dainty little hands were itchy with artistic inspiration.

"Hold damned still," she said to Sands. "I want this to look just like you. I'd hate for them to get the wrong man."

Sands opened his mouth to growl at her, but the pain stabbed through him like quick lime. He groaned and leaned wearily back. His hands were shackled to the chair back and his feet were tied to the legs.

Slowly his vision cleared and he turned his aching eyes to the canvas. The sweat that had been waiting inside him beaded out on his forehead. She was the one, this lovely, rose-lipped gal. The canvas portrait she was using to paint his own face over was the smiling, dark-eyed likeness of Jennie Gomez.

Dead Jennie Gomez.

Painfully Sands moved in the chair, but the shackles bit into his wrists. He groaned suddenly and eased himself back into the chair again. The wide expense of light from the side of the room came through a big window slanted up to the sun. It was similar to the window in the studio of Jennie Gomez.

But this studio was not the one Jennie Gomez had lived in. This one was bigger, and none of Jennie Gomez's pictures were piled in the corner. No. There was only one Gomez picture in the room. That was the painting on the easel. The painting that was being done over with his own face.

The girl turned again, and her taffy-tinted hair glinted in the sudden sunlight. Her brown eyes sparkled viciously at him, and he could see her little fist tighten around the .22 in her left hand.

"Steady, boy," she purred, and her voice would have matched that of any cougar with active ulcers. "Hold real still."

"How can I look my prettiest when I'm chained in, kid?" Sands asked, grinning.

"I'm no damned kid, boy. Call me Taffy. That's my name. Get it, Red? Taffy."

"Taffy with strychnine," shrugged Sands. "What the hell. They'll do anything these days to trap an honest gee."

"To trap rats!" snapped the girl, her bright eyes flashing and her crimson lips thrust out belligerently. "Now hold still! Damn it, I'll club your face in!"

"Temper, temper," grinned Red Sands, biting down the pain in him at the quick movement of the bracelets about his hands. "What's your racket, kid? You work for Old Hawk Nose himself? Old Money Bags?"

The girl bristled and golden sparks shot from her eyes. "I don't know what you're talking about. Now hold still."

"You're a lousy little painter, or you'd have that thing finished already. I've been chained here for a couple hours."

"You shut up and don't bother me."

She clamped her lips together and grimly went on slashing strokes of oil down the canvas. The picture was coming along neatly, slickly, evenly. It was a professional job, well done, realistic, but not powerful. A good commercial job.

It looked just like Red Sands. It showed a clown's face, with the querulous quirks at the corners of the mouth, the amused sea-green eyes, the ocean of freckles smeared over the pale thin face.

"Where'd you get the portrait of the girl?" Sands asked after a moment of painful silence. The damned bracelets were tight and they wouldn't budge. No amount of slipping or sliding would shuck them off.

The girl turned her fiery little face to him, and her brown eyes were hot with excitement, and her taffy hair shot out electric voltage. Her little chin came up and her tongue lashed out at him. "It's none of your damned business, mister. I got it. I'm using it. It wasn't yours. And who the hell cares?"

Sands grinned. "Me. Listen, kid, give me a break. What happened to me? How did I get here? I wake up and I'm shackled to a chair. Last thing I knew I was talking to a friend of mine." His own eyes narrowed, and his tongue stuck to the roof of his mouth. No use telling too much. No telling how much this chick knew. Maybe nothing. Maybe everything.

She smiled brightly. "I got you. You were sent here, COD. I paid the man the two-bits and he gave me you. I was told to paint you. I was given the canvas to use. And that's all there is to know. Now shut up and hold still."

"Look, kid. What's the score? Why are you using that portrait to paint over? Can't you buy canvas any more? What's the gimmick? I don't get it at all."

She dashed some more lines onto the canvas and turned to him brightly. "You'll find out pretty soon."

Sands chewed on his teeth a few minutes and then he lapsed into moody silence. What the hell else could he do?

Taffy held up the portrait in front of her and smiled at it happily. She thrust it off from her and moved around to get it into the best light. She moved it to her and looked it over carefully from one end to the other.

"It's finished," she said.

Sands groaned. "So am I. Get me out of this chair, kid."

Taffy frowned and walked over to him. She leaned over. "Taffy," she said solemnly, "not kid."

"Taffy," snapped Sands. "Okay, Taffy. Undo me."

Taffy laughed. She said, "I've got the gun, Sands. Yours and mine too. Now don't try to get away when I do untie you. Don't try to play any funny tricks, either, or I'll smash in your freckled face. Got that?"

Sands stared at the tough little chick in front of him from the flaming top of her taffy head to the bottom of her miniature clod-hoppers of bright red leather, and he found himself grinning. "Okay, kitten."

She pulled out a long exaggerated chain from her pocket and a bunch of keys dangled from the end. She looked like a jailer in an Old Western jail house. She selected one small key and inserted it in the manacles. She snapped it to the right, then the left, and the iron hoops loosened on Sands's wrists.

Sands stood up, rubbing his wrists gingerly. They were red and sore and bruised. She slit the ropes about his ankles with a knife.

"Oh," she said with a start, staring at his wrists. "They look terrible!" And she whipped out of the room and returned with some burn ointment. Sands let her rub it into the skin, and as she worked over him like a little beaver he found himself watching her with interest.

"Now don't bang them against anything," she told him when she had finished. "Keep your wrists in your pockets, and don't get them all mussed up."

"Okay," he said. "What else, boss? What about the picture?"

"You leave that to me," said the little doll with the taffy

hair and the red leather shoes. "I'm hanging you in a minute."

Sands said, "Well, that's about the only thing that hasn't happened to me today. What time is it? I'm hungry."

"It's about eleven," she said. "Time for breakfast. I'll bring some food back with me."

"Back with you! You going somewhere?"

Taffy grinned, and her mouth, when it smiled, lit up her whole face. "Sure. I'm going out into Washington Square and hang you."

"In effigy?"

"No. In exhibition."

"What about me? The real me. The flesh and blood and hungry me?"

"You'll stay here," she said calmly.

"Oh? Will I? You don't know me, Taffy. I'm hell on wheels. Just naturally contrary. I don't think I will stay."

She smiled a smug little smile, and the dimples danced around in her cheeks. "No?"

She pulled a newspaper out from under a cushion on the chair. "Look," she said happily, handing it to him.

Licking his upper lip thoughtfully, he unfolded the newspaper. Yeah. He knew what it said. He knew what the trick was. Old Man Bell had baited the trap. With him. How long before the cops began to pour out with their blue uniforms on and their guns in their holsters?

ROBERT SANDS SOUGHT

That was the headline, three banks.

EX-FBI AGENT HUNTED IN MURDER OF WOMAN HE TURNED JUDAS FOR

That was great. There was no picture, though.

"Don't worry about the picture," the girl said. "There are a hundred cops around here who know you on sight."

"Yeah," said Sands slowly. "All right. Agreed. But what about that painting of me, kid? What're you going to do with that?"

She picked up the picture and steadied her beret on her head. A wisp of hair fell over her eye and she brushed it back and tucked it under the cap. Her face was as bright as the noon sun when she turned to him. "I'm going to exhibit it on the Square."

"But why? I don't get it. All this mess just to paint a picture!" Sands shook his head.

"No, Red. Listen. Whoever did kill Jennie Gomez knows you were with her. Right? He'll be anxious to put the cops on your tail as soon as possible, right? So you can't do him any harm by tracking him down while you're at large. Right?"

"Right." The blonde kid had him there.

"This is bait. The first strange man who asks about this painting will probably be the man we're after – especially if he asks where you are and what you're doing. Everything is centred in this neighbourhood."

"You a cop, kitten?"

She turned towards the door with the canvas under her arm. "You know these Washington Square art exhibits, don't you?"

Sands grinned. "Sure. A bunch of paintings go out every day for sale on the streets. Good publicity gag for the Village. Some suckers actually buy the damned things."

"That's right, Sands. You're going on exhibit today in public. We'll smoke him out, you and I."

"You a cop, or a federal agent, kitten? I don't quite trust the feds these day. Being as I have a kind of personal difference with them."

She smiled at him as she opened the door. "Oh, I do a lot of things. Call me a trouble shooter. Whenever there's a shooting I come around and cause trouble."

She slammed the door and Sands had to grin.

From the window he watched her walk along Washington Square South – that street of many names – until she came to the first of the picture groups leaning against the wall. Others were already hanging from grillwork fences and from window ledges.

He saw the flash of her red beret as she set the big canvas down and leaned it casually against the cement wall as if it were just another hunk of art on exhibit. She joined a small group and he could see her red beret bobbing as she talked.

He sighted along the street to the left and to the right, sizing up the buildings. There were three or four studio buildings, and their high windows glinted with the morning sunlight. A brownstone building, a grey building, a white building. Two white buildings.

The second white building – he recognized that one clearly. It was the studio building where Jennie Gomez had lived. It was only two blocks away. Right now the cops were turning that place upside down, searching for anything and everything.

They wouldn't find the pictures. Sands had searched the studio high and low before he'd left it. Between the instant Jennie Gomez had seen him and the moment she had died, she'd taken the pictures out of there and hidden them. Hidden them or shipped them on to another party – someone else who could keep the blackmail ball rolling.

This blonde chick with the taffy hair – was she the blackmail heiress?

Sands opened the closet door to the studio room and searched through the piles of canvases there. There were stacks of oils with the taffy touch, but there wasn't a Gomez in a carload. He closed the closet and stood in the middle of the the room.

He moved into the bedroom after a moment of thought, but there were no canvases there either. Prowling through the dresser drawer he came across nothing but a pencilled notation on a slip of paper. It was a series of items jotted down like a grocery list.

1. *Man in a cornfield.*
2. *Woman in front of church.*
3. *Peasants in fields.*
4. *Golden landscape – wheat.*
5. *Funeral procession through small village.*
6. *Woman in vineyards.*
7. *A wedding, interior church.*
8. *Woman asleep over wine bottle.*

9. *Children fishing in river*.
10. *Girl and politician*.

Sands's breath came faster. Ten items. Ten notations. That made plenty of sense. The little taffy twist had a curiosity the size of nine black cats.

Scrambling through the girl's papers he found a blue-lined note book. Page one was ripped out. Page two had a pencil sketch. Page three, a flower arrangement. Page four, a list of nine items.

1. *Girl. Jane with black hat*.
2. *Man with red bow tie. Mr Stanley*.
3. *Man with grey felt hat*.
4. *Mary Roberts with boyish bob*.
5. *Basket of fruit*.
6. *Three little girls in pink*.
7. *Washington Square*.
8. *Night over Manhattan*.
9. *Sally Hanson*.
10.

Number ten was blank. The figure ten was there, but nothing came after it.

Of course! Only a fool would have failed to spot the trick. The original Gomez paintings were *underneath* all those portraits Jennie Gomez had done. Underneath on the same canvases – held there with a fixative and a coating of varnish – and then painted over with the bold, less skilful portraits of Jennie Gomez. The paintings were still piled up in the studio.

List number one was a list of the original Gomez scenes. List number two contained the corresponding camouflage Jennie Gomez portraits covering the originals.

Sands cursed softly. Who was the taffy queen? How did she fit into this? Why was she looking for the picture? Had she killed Jennie Gomez for her famous brother's paintings?

Walking over to the hall door, Sands opened it. He stared at the panelling on the door. There was an engraved card pinned there – the name of the occupant. It read LUCILLE BELL.

Bell! Lucille Bell – Lois Bell's little sister! Hamlin Bell's second daughter! Taffy!

Sands slammed the door shut and slipped over to the window and looked down again into the sunlit street at the green, lovely park. The crowd had broken up a bit around the first group of paintings and there were only four people left there.

Taffy, two girls and a man. Sands could see Taffy's red beret bobbing in the sunlight, and he could picture the animation and wild, animal excitement in her face as she talked. A live kid, that one. A neat little trick indeed. And Hamlin Bell's daughter. Taffy.

No wonder she wanted to smoke out the murderer. The murderer had the tenth picture. Her sister was in it.

There was an earsplitting jangle, and Sands spun around. The phone by the easel was ringing. Sands bit his lip. Thoughtfully he walked over to it and lifted the receiver. With an instinct handed down through years and years of inherited caution, he muted his voice and said hoarsely:

"Yeah?"

A tight, electrically charged voice on the other end of the wire said, "Callahan? You there already?"

Sands chewed his lip. He nodded suddenly. "Yeah." Something prompted him to add: "Chief."

"I'm damned glad. She's all right, isn't she? You get her home here quick. And take care of Sands."

Sands held the reciver off from him. The chill icy water churned inside him. He remembered that voice. That confident, authoritative voice. That nervous, high-tensioned, demanding voice.

The voice of Hamlin Bell. A twenty million dollar voice. With tax refund.

"I never should have let her talk me into that fool trick," Bell was grating on. "Good work, Callahan. Bring them both in to me, personally. My way will be best. Sands can pay the piper."

"Sure, chief," Sands croaked.

"Why should I care who murdered that girl? I want the

police off those pictures!" Bell grumbled on, a man convincing himself that it was purely an accident he was a twelve-carat rat.

"Sure, chief," Sands muttered and hung up the receiver.

He ran to the window and looked down into the Square. The group about Taffy Bell was breaking up. Taffy waited for a moment, undecided, and then walked over to the painting, standing there looking at it.

At that instant a car drove up to the kerb beside her, and she turned around as if someone from the car had called her. Sands could not make out the expression on her face, but he saw her tense there, frozen for a long moment.

She looked quickly from left to right, saw no one, and then Sands made out the sudden sag of her shoulders. She hesitated, took a deep breath, and backed towards the picture, looking quickly up and down the street in one last desperate try.

Quickly a man got out of the car. He jumped onto the sidewalk, grabbed her wrist, and pulled her towards the car. He was holding something next to her ribs, in close. She did not protest at all. She got into the car ahead of him. The car dug out and sped down the street.

Sands could not make out the licence plate number. As he stood there, fingering his chin, whistling softly to himself, trying desperately to get his mind functioning, his eye caught another swift movement in the street. Two men stood together on the corner, not far from where his painting was leaning against the wall of the building.

One of the men nodded upwards, and the sun caught his eye at the instant he glanced up square at the window in which Sands was standing. The man with him nodded, stretched his legs for the street, crossing it and moving over towards Lucille Bell's apartment. The second man followed, after a sharp glance up and down the street. He had to get the hell out of there fast.

He ran for the door, snapped it open. And even as he did so he could hear the slow, methodical tramp of feet clumping up the five-storey walk-up.

IV

The Hunt

The noon sun shone bright and gay on the world of Washington Square. It was spring and the earth basked in the clean air like a happy bride. Bright colours and flamboyant dresses glowed in the sunshine. Groups of passersby stood in front of the oil paintings on exhibit and an air of peace and contentment and good cheer hung over the world.

In the same brilliant sunlight Red Sands toiled with a sliding window high on the top floor of the studio building. His face was covered with perspiration and it was twisted in rage and fury at the sticking, balking window.

Then suddenly the window gave and slid upwards. Furtively Sands climbed out onto the fire escape and crouched there a moment, panting. He felt inside his coat pocket and nodded briefly. With an air of intent listening, he craned towards the inside of the room. Apparently hearing just what he wanted to, he leaped carefully along the fire escape ladder. Only instead of climbing down it towards the street he climbed up.

He climbed hand over hand and made the roof in a few moments. From the roof he paused a moment, leaning down, looking at the window he had just left. Then he disappeared and darted across the roof of the building. He felt inside his coat again as he moved swiftly across the roof.

A moment later two heads peered out the open window next to the fire escape. The two heads – one fat and bullish and red as a slab of raw beef, the other narrow and pinched and wearing thick glasses – turned to each other and bobbed up and down in conversation. The man with the big face and the big body to match clambered laboriously out onto the fire escape platform and began climbing too.

The big man climbed downwards. He climbed painfully from one step to the next, every step he took a torture. His feet were tired and his face was puffed and red with exertion. He climbed down from floor to floor in his fruitless quest.

The thin face with the thick glasses watched a moment and then disappeared inside the room. And then there was no more motion for the interested sun to watch. Greenwich Village settled back into the same gay, listless, lazy existence as before. Nothing ever happened there. It was an island set off from the rest of the world – an island devoted to art and beauty and culture.

Sands had found his .38 lying on the kitchen table. Quite possibly Taffy Bell had meant for him to find it there after she had gone. Now he patted it gently where it rested inside his jacket pocket. He crouched for an instant by the door opening on the roof, and then he soundlessly opened the door. The brilliant light cut down into the stair well, painting his shadow big and black along the casement.

Sands descended cautiously. One man climbing down the fire escape. The other searching an apartment, suspicious of the obviously open window and the fluttering drapes. And Sands, the fugitive, laughing to himself, creeping down the stairs inside, floor by floor, quietly making the street without any interruption.

As Sands disappeared swiftly down the glaring bright street where anything could be seen and nothing was, he saw out of the tail of his eye the big man with the florid face moving sheepishly around front from in back of the apartment . . .

It was cool and dark and restful in the Thackeray Room and he felt safe again. It was like old home week. He sat up on the big stool and hooked his heel over the brass rail familiarly. The amber-eyed, barrel-chested man sauntered over, his eyes watching Sands closely.

"You're starting in early today," commented the barkeep, his eyes veiled and impersonal.

"Yeah," said Sands. "How about a cheese sandwich to glue down my rye and water, pal?"

"Why not?" said the barkeep, picking up a glass and wiping it. "Cheese on white," he said over his shoulder into the dark, secret innards of the bar. "You want that rye straight, don't you, pal? Seems I remember it that way."

"Seems your memory is functioning one hundred proof," Sands said. "Water on the side."

"Sure," said the barkeep, and he got the rye and water. Sands had the uneasy impression that the amber-eyed man was watching him narrowly as he worked.

"I see the oil painting of the girl is gone," Sands said offhandedly. "Sell it?"

"Yeah. Blonde kid came and bought it. She paints herself. Liked the style – said something about savages and primitive urges, or something. Me, I don't mess around none with that art and beauty stuff, but I kind of went for the style of the particular dame in the painting. Dark. Fresh. You know. Nice snazzy gal."

"Yeah," said Sands, lifting the rye to the heavens. "Well, here's to dames – snazzy and otherwise." He tossed it down.

"Too bad that kind has to die so hard, ain't it, pal?"

The amber-eyed man's face was too close to Sands. It was insolent and the grin was twisted, and the cow-catcher chin was jutting into Sands's face. Sands moved back.

"I don't get you, pal." He touched the gun in his jacket pocket absently as he spoke.

"Dame in the picture was bumped off last night. Funny, ain't it, that you was popping questions about her just before she got bumped?"

Sands set the rye shot glass down with a hard slam. "Bud, if you're trying to say something, come on out right now and say it. Otherwise, brood to yourself. It keeps the air quieter and the atmosphere cleaner."

But the amber-eyed man leaned forward further, and his bulging muscular body poised on the mahogany bar as if he were ready to fling himself over it at Sands's throat.

"I ain't suggesting and I ain't insinuating. I'm saying it right out loud, pal. You shouldn't of come back here. I'm no friend and I ain't no enemy. They're on your tail, pal. They've been coming in here. The cops."

Sands leaned back, his face white. "Who?"

"Dame came in here this morning and flashed a badge on me."

"What kind of badge?"

The barkeep frowned, his big thick eyebrows moving down over his face like a screen. "What do you mean? There's different kinds?"

Sands rubbed his upper lip. "Forget it. Then what?"

"It's the dame bought the picture. Said she seen the picture from outside in the street, and would I sell it. I said, that's my racket, and I wrapped it up and gave it to her."

Sands stared at the big man. "Why you telling me this, pal?"

The barkeep rubbed his nose enthusiastically. "There's a bit more pal, and for a bit more interest on your part – that special kind of a green-type salad interest – I might be willing to unburden my festering soul."

Sands pulled out a ten-dollar bill. "Yeah," Sands said. "Try this on your subsconscious. I never did think you guys made a living selling that rotten liquor. I figured you had angles."

"Angles all over the place," the unpleasant man smiled. "The babe with the blonde hair says don't say a word to anybody. Naturally I figure that's okay for her to say, but I figure it ain't okay for me to pay attention to that kind of talk. Especially when it ain't bought and paid for."

Sands leaned against the bar. "Anything else?"

"I took her address. For a slight financial inducement I might –"

"She gave you her address?"

The barkeep's eyes slitted over. "Sure."

Sands bit his lip. An easy trap. A come-on. A come-on and get killed. Look out, Sands. "Why?"

The barkeep suddenly grinned. "Oh, sure. I forgot to tell you. I ain't suckering you into a gun-trap, pal. Why back there when she gave me the picture in the first place, the dead babe told me to be sure and take down the address of whoever bought that painting. I asked the blonde dame and got her address."

Sands stepped back an inch or two. He tried to cover over the surprise and immediate excitement surging up in him. "Yeah? Why. Did she say why?"

The barkeep stared at the ceiling, scratching his ear. "Something about – oh, yeah. She said, 'It's the one that counts.' Or something like that. That make any sense to you, pal?" The barkeep leaned forward again, the smell of spilled beer and stale liquor and dead gin wafting up into Sands's nose.

Sands tried to keep the elated grin off his mask of a face. His eyes sparkled sea-green and bright and his lips twisted up suddenly.

"It could be," he grinned. "It could be, surer'n hell! Thanks a lot, pal!"

Sands whipped out a ten dollar bill and tossed it at the barkeep. The barkeep's amber eyes glinted gold and he leaned over to pick up the bill. He nodded to himself as he pocketed it.

"I can pick the gold ones," he muttered. "I can pick the suckers."

Sands had disappeared out the front door. Three minutes later he stood in front of the exhibit, staring at the spot where the picture of him had been leaning against the wall. There was nothing now there at all.

It was the important picture Hamlin Bell had mentioned, all right. The blackmail canvas. The other nine paintings stolen from Bell's collection had been taken to cover up the importance of the one big main one. Trust Jennie Gomez to play it smart and hide the big one in plain sight where it would never be discovered.

From all Sands could figure, Taffy Bell had discovered about the painting somehow – possibly from a talk with the barkeep – and she had immediately taken it with her. Realizing she would have to cover it up and change it or let it fall into the hands of someone in the know with Jennie Gomez, she had altered it into the portrait of Sands.

Killing two birds with one stone, so to speak. Also, Taffy Bell knew that the canvas would attract little attention sitting in the middle of an art exhibit. No one but the real murderer of Jennie Gomez would notice it. And as soon as he saw it he would ask questions, and those questions would trap him.

But no one had asked any questions. And while Taffy Bell was gone with her father's private dicks, someone who liked portraits had picked up the picture and carted it home.

Who?

Trying to keep himself as inconspicuous as possible,

Sands questioned the tall blonde girl whose paintings hung next to Taffy's. The girl's eyes widened.

"You're the man in Taffy's picture!" she gasped, startled.

"Where did the picture go? Somebody buy it?"

"Yes. An old man with a scar on his face."

"An old man?" Sands bit his lip. An old duck who liked paintings. Millions of them around the Village.

"Did he give you any address?"

"Oh, no. I didn't ask him for any. But everybody around here knows him. He lives right down this street. His name's Henry. Mr Henry."

Sands nodded and smiled. "Thanks, kid."

The blonde girl watched Sands curiously as he walked down the street. Then she shrugged and went back to work, readjusting her neatly lined-up pictures.

Mr Henry lived at Number 7, about two blocks down the street. He lived in the cellar, and there was only one entrance to the place, Sands learned from a woman in a shop. It sounded like the entrance to a dog house from the description. Sands hid the grin and thanked the old, withered-up delicatessen woman. She wagged her hooked nose at him and smiled a toothless grin.

Sands moved on down the street, and the garbage piled higher in the gutters and the cats grew tougher and scrawnier, and the kids grew greasier and dirtier. The only thing that didn't change was the stink of garlic, and that had been with him all the way.

Turning into a twisting, corkscrew lane, Sands paused a second to light a cigarette. It was Last-Mile Lane. The sign was twisted and battered in the sun light. Number 7 was at the end of the lane, and Sands studied the place carefully through half-lidded eyes. Sweat stood under his lids. There were cans of garbage strewn about the twisting lane, and boxes of trash, and a soulful dog sat in a window above a pot of geraniums, eyeing him dismally. The ramshackle place had the look of a hunted, bullet-torn, dying man.

The door was green and it was painted crudely and badly. There was no knocker and there was no bell. No breath of air stirred in the stinking, filthy lane, and Sands rapped on the wood with his bare knuckles. No sign of a face in any of the windows towering above him showed at all. It was as if he was knocking at the last door this side of hell.

Then the door opened. There was no one inside that he could see. Only blackness and a musty, dismal smell of blackness and despair. A voice inside the room said:

"Come in."

It was a pleasant voice. Somehow Sands felt the voice was assumed, painted over like a new outer coat. That the original voice was a snarl, a growl, a leer, a twisted, hating voice.

He came into the blackened room gripping his gun by the butt. There was a quick movement and the door slammed behind him. A brilliant, glaring bulb flashed on in a corner behind him with a sudden blinding explosion. The bare walls and the crude stone masonry and the sweating, hideous sewer pipes glistened in the illumination.

From behind him came the deadly purr of a voice.

"We were expecting you, Sands."

Sands turned around. And what he saw made him lose the gun from his icy grasp, made his jaw drop open, made his eyes glaze over in sudden, complete terror. The sweat tore at his skin and the hair on his head writhed.

"You!" he gasped.

The man sitting in the chair with the rifle cradled in his lap was a grotesque, grimly drawn caricature of a human being. He was an old, twisted, torn-up man and his face was a long seared scar from temple to neck. The dark, smouldering eyes were fine and deep and tempered, and the mouth was a vicious twist of brute strength and violence.

The man was smiling grimly now at Sands, and the only smile he could manage was a grim, horrible imitation of a normal one. His face was a pathetic misrepresentation of a human visage.

Red Sands took in a deep, shuddering breath and tried to steady himself against the back of the door. Once again his hot, torn eyes darted about from corner to corner, seeking a window, a door, a crevice.

There was nothing. The rifle was a sniper's gun, and the

man in the chair held it like an expert rifleman. It would be hard to tell where that man's expertness stopped. Expert in rifles. Expert in killing. Expert in such a strangely opposite talent as creative art.

The man in the chair was Danny Gomez. Danny Gomez, free of the grey powder he wore in his hair when he walked the Village streets as an old man. Free of the crumpled tramp's clothes he wore when he poked about in ash cans along West Broadway. Free of all those disguises that kept people informed he was a vagabond, a stumble-bum, a creep from way down under.

"Sit down, Sands," said Gomez with a wolfish snarl.

Gomez chuckled, and the laughter sent chills racing up and down Sands's spine. "Yeah, I'm Gomez all right. You knew that, didn't you? We know each other – from that fight in the street last night."

But now Sands's eyes were riveted with a strange and horrible fascination at Gomez's hands, the hands that lay carelessly on top the sniper's rifle in his lap. And the final link in the bizarre, unbelievable picture fell into place.

Sands gasped, and his eyes were glittering with horror.

Ruefully Gomez stared down at his hands. "Yeah," he said finally. "You've got it now, Sands. Now you see. Now you know the whole rotten story – the whole filthy joke that Fate played on me – the whole ghastly comedy of my life. Now you see it all in front of you."

Sands sat down heavily in a wooden chair, and he could not move. The two hands of Danny Gomez – the two talented, inspired hands that had painted some of the greatest paintings of the twentieth century – now lay there caressing the rifle barrel. They lay there still and lifeless – charred and twisted remains of what had once been a pair of obedient human hands, but which were now burned, scorched, scarred beyond recognition by the same fire and smoke that had twisted Gomez's face into that terrible, revolting mask.

"Don't worry, Sands," grinned Gomez, "these mitts can still shoot. Yeah that's the story. No doctor would dare do anything for them. Couldn't afford to – not work on the hands of Gomez? They were scared over there in those dead and dying countries. They were afraid the wrath of heaven would descend upon them if they failed to make me whole again, if they managed to ruin the hands of the Great Gomez. And so these twisted, scarred talons are no good to me at all now, for painting. No good to me at all, and they can never be saved! It's too late!"

The sweat was oozing out onto Sands's face and body at the violent savagery of Gomez's words. "But Gomez," he whispered, "in the United States there are surgeons —"

Gomez leaned back in the chair and his sardonic, burning eyes flared brilliantly. "You think these doctors here would risk an operation on Gomez — Gomez the revolutionist? Gomez the spy? The agent? No, my friend. You see, it is all a mockery. A jest! Life itself, indeed — as, my friend, you of all people, well know."

From ear to ear the mottled face split into a wry, rare grin.

Sands drew himself up tightly. "You've got the pictures, Gomez? It was you who took the pictures from your sister's apartment?"

Gomez nodded his head. "Yes," he said simply. "I took them away. They were painted underneath her miserable imitations! That sister of mine could never paint!" He spat violently on the floor, rubbing his face with the back of his wrist.

Sands straightened in the chair. "You've got them here, Gomez. I want the pictures. You and I both know the value of silence between us. If we could make a deal for those pictures —"

Gomez's face writhed in a crimson fury. "A deal! A deal to deliver up those paintings to you? For Hamlin Bell? No, my dear Sands, no!" Gomez was shaking with fury now, and his eyes burned and his eyebrows bristled. He leaned forward and the penetrating intensity of his words drove them out into the air like miniature explosions.

He leaned back suddenly. The silence fell about them. "Besides," he said quietly, with a leer, "they are finished now. They are gone." He smiled slowly and bitterly.

The strange bizarre terror crept along Sands's backbone again. "Gone," he repeated dully. "I don't see what you mean. You – you destroyed the canvases? You burned them up? The best of the paintings you made?" Sands was half out of his chair, the excitement in his voice carrying him forward.

Gomez hurled himself out of the chair towards the crude fireplace at the end of the room. The rifle glinted as he twirled it about with his blackened, twisted claws. "Look for yourself!" Gomez cried, springing by the fireplace, thrusting one charred hand towards the ashes in the hearth. "There lie your nine lovely paintings! The nine greatest paintings of the twentieth century!"

Gomez's voice wavered up into a half-mad laugh, and he strode back to the chair again, gripping the rifle, his eyes lidded and dark. His long slender body relaxed in the chair, slumping into a defeated, weary helplessness.

He laughed softly then, and the sounds that came from his throat were sudden music. Gentle, flowing sounds. Thoughtful, lovely laughter.

"You may be able to understand," he said. "I cannot let these things live when I cannot do better. An artist must always outdo himself with each performance. Without that dominating desire, that driving urge deep inside him, he is a sad and worthless artisan indeed. Sands, you must try to understand me! That is a fundamental truth in all great art. To surpass! To exceed! To grasp the stars, the sun, the galaxies in the very ends of the heavens!"

Sands stared at Gomez with no breath stirring in his body. The man's voice was swelling and expanding and filling the room, overflowing it, and the dynamic tension inside him was poised at the highest possible pitch.

"No, Sands," Gomez said softly. "I cannot let those pieces of art exist any longer. They must all go. I can never paint again. I was not my best when I stopped. Therefore, the world must never be allowed to laugh at my feeble, pitiful practice attempts."

His eyes stared moodily at the floor. His body loosened in the chair, and he slumped from his head to his feet. His head shook sadly. Age crept over him as he sat there. He was suddenly a hundred years old, the electric vitality gone.

He was a hulk of a man, the juice sapped from him. He was helpless, shaking, palsied. His eyes glowed dully, and his lips trembled as he smiled at Sands.

"Get out of here."

Sands rose, crossed the room and stood before Gomez. The burns had unsprung some precariously balanced artistic tension in him. The kind of man he now was could certainly be capable of killing.

Then it all came clear.

"You killed her, didn't you, Gomez?" Sands spoke the words softly and quietly, but their force was double for all the gentleness. Gomez lowered his head into his palm and shook it slowly. "You wanted those pictures from her and you tried to get them, but she wouldn't give them to you. And you killed her to get them. Right?"

Gomez clawed lightly at the rifle. "Yes," he said simply. "She was always trying to run my business! That sister of mine! That talentless, crazy, slave-driving sister of mine! I killed her! Yes! She was using my picture to blackmail a dirty old man with a spiritless, sad excuse for a daughter! Not with my pictures, Sands! Not with my paintings! Not with the priceless relics of the Great Gomez!"

Sands moved to the centre of the room again.

"Your number's up, Gomez. You've got to come with me. You killed her with my gun and planted it on her, and it's you or me. Come on. I'm loaded, Gomez. I wouldn't try any funny business. It's broad daylight outside."

Gomez smiled and the puffy face twisted sideways in mirth. "Maybe it is time to throw in the towel, eh? Maybe I've had my day. Maybe the last corner is turned."

Gomez's eyes glinted cunningly. Sands stared at him closely, and lifted the .38 out of his jacket pocket. "Move, Gomez," he said softly. "Drop that rifle and move on out that door."

Out of the corner of his eyes Sands could see the portrait of himself staring out from the wall. He would come back later and get it. Now that the murderer of Jennie Gomez was under lock and key, the picture would be safe from the cops. Sands would come down later and pick it up.

Gomez was fast. He was faster than a bobcat with a hot

foot. He spun and the rifle smashed out against Sands's chest and exploded a split second later. If it had exploded at the moment it touched his chest Sands would have been splattered over the inside of that dirty cellar like orange marmalade. But instead the flame burnt along him and the lead tore through his shoulder. Immediately hot blood surged out into his shirt.

Gomez lifted the rifle again to fire, a wild, raw hate in his black eyes. He fired and the slug missed. Sands pulled himself down into a crouch in the corner and thumbed two slugs at Gomez. One hit him in the ribs and another smashed into his leg.

The room was full of cordite and gunsmoke clouds. Gomez swept the rifle above him in a wide, murderous arc and the electric light smashed to smithereens with a splintering crash. Somebody scuttled along the darkened floor and grabbed up the painting. Then a wide slit of daylight streamed in and immediately the door slammed shut.

Weakly Sands got to his feet, swaying dizzily. Blood sopped his shoulders and chest. He pulled himself across the room, breathing in deeply, cursing to himself. That damned fool Gomez. He could never get away in broad daylight.

Sands forced the door open and blinked into the bright daylight. Lead powdered the green door by his face. The damned fool was still shooting in the alleyway. Sands sent a slug after him, but the lead pellet glanced along the side of a building and the ricochet sang into the clean bright air.

Madly Gomez staggered down the street, heading for Washington Square. The painting was under his arm, and there was no telling where he was going.

Sands stumbled along after him, every step a separate wrench on a torture rack. He levelled the Colt again and fired. The lead smashed dead on into an iron railing.

Gomez whirled about, poised the sniper's rifle and fired. Lead whistled by Sands's stomach. Gomez was aiming low. Sands ducked beside a building and fired again.

Women and kids were racing for cover in the street. At the end of the street by Washington Square, Sands made out the sudden blue of a policeman's uniform. Gomez was a dozen yards from the cop and he saw him too. Gomez, panicky, raised the rifle and fired at the policeman. The cop went down with a slug in his leg.

Gomez turned, looking about wildly. An iron-spiked fence ran along the sidewalk beside him. Past the fence lay a garden, and past the garden tenement houses. If he could get through those tenement houses he could find shelter. Already a crowd was gathering at the corner, like a huge and angry wolf pack.

Gomez scaled the iron fence expertly. One leg over, he was poised to jump down, when the cop raised himself painfully and fired. Gomez hung there, leaning into the thrust of the slug. At the same instant Sands fired and the other slug caught Gomez in the thigh. Gomez grimaced, gave a howling, maddened shout into the air, slammed the painting down onto the heavy, tough iron spike, and then, summoning up the last of his strength, he dashed himself down headfirst onto the spikes, catching his neck expertly.

Sands turned away, sick, and the crowd gave a strangled gasp . . .

"Rye and water," sighed Sands, and the amber-eyed barkeep grinned.

"You're getting to be a steady customer here, pal. Know it?"

Sands grinned at the barkeep and turned to the lady at his side. "What's for you, Taffy?"

Taffy smiled, looking at the barkeep. "Rye and water," she said. "What's good enough for this character with me is good enough for me."

Amber Eyes winked at Sands. "What you've got there mister, I'd keep if I had it myself."

Sands chucked Taffy under the chin. "I'll sure think about it."

"How's the shoulder?" Taffy asked after the first round.

"Good. Your dad get that picture all right? That was the one he wanted. I haven't had the guts to go to see him yet."

"You're coming with me. He wants to give you some kind of a bonus, he says. Thinks you're terrific. Silly man."

Sands leaned back, puzzled. "Who the hell were those monkeys that grabbed you in the car?"

She growled into her rye glass. "Oh, they're some private cops dad has working for him. See, I had to do some fast talking to make dad let me use you to spook out that killer. He got to thinking it over, and decided he was going to get me out of the trouble fast. He didn't know I'd already let you go."

"He didn't know you were using me to smoke out Gomez, huh?"

"Didn't even know Gomez was alive. I had to use the picture he wanted to lead me to Gomez. Sorry I couldn't tell you all about it either. The FBI wouldn't let me."

Sands scowled. "You permanent party in the Bureau?"

She smiled up at him. "As permanent as you were."

Sands banged for another rye. "We won't talk about that."

"I like rye and water," said Taffy Bell, and a smart little smile began in her eyes and travelled far and finally ended up on the faces of both of them.

"Then I guess that settles it," said Sands, tipping his glass to hers.

The Gangsta Wore Red

Michael Guinzburg

I

It was just one of those things. A fact of life. I was naked.
Naked and alone. I didn't hold it against Mama for
locking me up naked and leaving me alone. Wasn't her fault
there wasn't no money for no babysitter . . . That's just the
way it was . . . Like being black, being poor, being six years
old and not knowing your daddy, being locked up naked
and alone was just one of those things . . .

I understood why she locked me up. Understood she had
to go to work. Understood she didn't want me hanging out
on the block while she was off at work. Understood she had
to lock my clothes in the closet so I wouldn't get dressed
and run out into the halls and get in trouble again. So I
wouldn't kiss pretty little Shamika and feel her baby pea
breasts under the stairwell. So I wouldn't bounce dumb
onion-head Horace's onion head off the wall a hundred
times for calling Mama a crackhead ho, for calling me
"crack baby". It was just one of those things . . .

Just like Mama had to put on the starched white maid's
uniform and the spotless ugly cracked white shoes I carefully polished for her . . . Just like Mama had to take three
crowded smelly old buses – sometimes standing all the way
– cross town to where the rich white folk lived in a rich
white palace . . . Just like Mama had to smile for those rich
white folk, smile until her face hurt and speak only when
spoken to, carry heavy silver trays of fancy food out to the
big table, hold those heavy silver trays still and stand there
frozen like a statue while each individual white folk studied

the shape and size of each individual slice of meat before choosing, each individual soggy boiled vegetable, each individual cherry drowning in brandy, each individual part of Mama's pretty slim brown body in the starched white uniform and white stockings and spotless ugly cracked white shoes I polished for her . . . Just like gunshots and drugs and dead bodies on the street below, just like sirens and screams and dogs howling in the night, just like televisions blasting and cats screeching and doors slamming and toilets flushing . . . Just like big folk arguing and babies crying and radiators hissing . . . Just like crackheads piping up in the halls and rats scrambling in the walls and cockroaches crawling on your face and eating the spit off your lips when you was sleeping . . . Just like my daddy being sent to penitentiary for killing a man before I was born, born small as a baked potato with the crack addiction running hot like fever in my blood . . . Just like me rubbing Mama's aching swollen feet at the end of the night, being naked and alone was just one of those things . . .

Like the time she brought me to the big white palace when she couldn't find no babysitter – before the white folk cut her nights down and she stopped being able to afford a babysitter. How I played with little golden-headed Mary. How I ran all over the big white palace with little golden Mary. Little Mary who changed dresses every fifteen minutes . . . The long halls, the big rooms, the carpeted stairs, the closets . . . How we hid in a closet, me and Mary, a closet near as big as me and Mama's whole apartment, a closet with lights and carpets even, a closet full of bright soft clothes and pair after pair of bright shiny uncracked shoes . . . How little golden Mary found some candy hidden there and told me to eat the candy. How she giggled when I put the candy in my mouth. The big white ball of candy that tasted so bad, the candy I didn't want to eat, was about to spit out when Mary touched my arm and promised with big blue serious eyes cold and clear as the sky that if I chewed it and swallowed it she'd kiss me. How I chewed the horrible candy and fought the sickness and waited for my golden kiss. How little Mary laughed at me then, laughed at me instead of kissing me. Laughed and ran away, ran down the

hall, down the stairs, me following, holding my stomach
. . . How Mary skipped into the dinner party, me following
feeling so sick . . . How Mary announced with a big smile to
the big people at the big table that Frankie Lawrence had
eaten a mothball. How the big white folk laughed and
laughed. How Mary laughed and laughed and then ran
off to change her dress. How Mama marched me into the
kitchen and made me throw up, sticking a long thin brown
finger with a cracked fake fingernail down my throat until
the mothball and the cheese sandwich on white bread I'd
eaten at home came up, until the tears came down, flowing
free and easy and hot . . . Just one of those things.

Like the next time I went with Mama to the big white
palace and just like Mama told me I ignored Mary. Didn't
pay her no mind. Lay there on the green grass in the big
green garden off the big shiny kitchen, lay there in the cool
tickly green grass as the big orange ball of late afternoon sun
rolled sleepy behind the big green trees, lay there in the cool
tickly green grass playing with a caterpillar I called Vincent.
I wouldn't look at Mary, no way, wouldn't answer her, no
way. Even when she begged me to say something, no way.
How she begged and begged and said she was sorry about
the mothball and promised with those clear blue eyes that if
I spoke to her she would kiss me and show me her pee-pee.
How finally I spoke to her, told her to leave me and my
friend Vincent alone, that I didn't want to see her dumb old
pee-pee. How she bent down and kissed me then with her
cold cherry lips and then raised her skirt to show me her
pee-pee. How the big white lady walked out the back door
right that moment and saw Mary showing me her pee-pee.
How the big white lady turned bright pink like a giant
pencil eraser and pulled me away from little golden Mary
by the ear and almost yanked my little cookie ear off and
dragged me by the ear, me going "ow ow ow ow ow" all the
way across the lawn into the kitchen and told Mama not to
bring me any more. How Mama looked mad enough to
snatch the big white lady baldheaded but instead just said,
"Yes, Ma'am" and slapped me upside the head two or three
times, then sighed and muttered and drank a big glass of
cooking wine fast, then poured me some milk and broke out

some cookies and made me sit in the corner of the kitchen all night long . . . How I kept looking out the window, wondering where Vincent was . . . How tired Mama was at the end of that day. That day, every day. How poor we were. How tired Mama was. That day, every day. How lonely Mama was. How lonely I was. How hard life was. That day, every day . . . How Mama kept writing to Daddy in prison and how the letters were never answered . . . How one time Mama and me took that long smelly bus ride upstate to surprise-visit Daddy and bring him oranges. How when we got to the big penitentiary with the high walls and the men with guns Daddy wouldn't come out to see us. How Mama busted out crying then, cried as we walked down the street, cried as we was waiting there in the cold for the bus home, cried all the long smelly bus ride home, me hugging her, the small towns and moonlit forests outside the windows, the bag of oranges untouched on her lap, telling her it was okay, Mama, it was okay, it was just one of those things . . . How we never did eat those oranges, those bad-luck oranges shrivelling brown and dry and lifeless in the back of the fridge . . . How Mama sat there on the ratty old chair the nights she didn't work – sat there on the ratty old chair in her ratty old robe, drinking a whole jug of wine, looking over all those old newspaper clippings she kept about Daddy's trial, sat there talking to herself, laughing crazy and singing along to sad sad songs on the radio . . . She knew all the words . . . How one time I woke up in the night to go pee-pee and there was a naked man in bed with Mama and Mama was naked too, and she was smoking crack like the crackheads in the halls and the man winked at me and laughed nasty and said, "So that's the pup . . ." And Mama giggled and said, "Frankie, baby, you're dreaming, go back to sleep . . ." How sleep never did come back that night as I listened to them laugh and cough and grunt, the bedsprings singing, the sharp smell of the burning crack making me feel so sick . . .

I understood. I understood. I understood – didn't I? Mama was just trying to keep me out of trouble by keeping me in the apartment – dumb onion-head Horace with his dumb eyes like a dead sheep in the Muslim butcher's, little

Shamika and her nice warm lips and Chinese eyes and baby pea breasts under the stairwell, Malik and Jamal and all those other boys running wild and free, getting in trouble. Trouble . . . So Mama had to lock me up, lock me up naked, lock that front door from the outside. It was the only way she could be sure I wouldn't hang out in the streets and work for the bigger boys out on the corner who worked for the older men with the fine cars and fine clothes – was that what my daddy looked like? Mama laughed. There were no cars in prison, Mama said, no fine clothes. Only hard men who'd made hard choices, hard men learning hard lessons, hard men with hard eyes, hard men who'd once been little boys. Little boys like me who'd become bigger boys like the ones on the street, the ones with the hungry eyes, the ones who paid me to look out for the Man . . . I knew it was all about drugs – I wasn't no dummy – drugs and money . . . Ten-dollar bags of heroin that turned folk into snaggle-toothed grey scarecrows with wobbly heads and dead eyes, their bodies split open with crusty scabs and running sores, scratching all over like flea-bit dogs, dreaming in their vomit, waking long enough to beg change and stumble into traffic . . . And the crack, the little white five-dollar chunks of instant heaven in the little clear plastic bottles that turned folk into bright-eyed skeletons, that made them jabber like monkeys, made them rob and shoot and scream and stab you bloody, stare at you with such bright hate . . . Mama hated the crackheads, hated the crack dealers, said it was the devil's drug, that it had almost gotten her, gotten me, taken us both down for the long count . . . But there was money out there, out on the street. Money that Mama needed to pay for light, to pay for food, to pay for heat, to pay for clothes . . . But when I came back that time with twenty dollars after working lookout for a big boy, Mama didn't want the money, dirty money she called it, and she beat me then, beat me till the snot bubbled out my nose, said she was beating the devil out of me, and then she marched me back downstairs and made me point out the boy who'd paid me and made me give the money back. And the boy just laughed at Mama, laughed at Mama and winked at me and walked off to talk with one of the hard men in one of the fine cars . . . But we were so poor. It was so tough on Mama. Mama alone . . . So I understood why I was naked. Locked up naked. My clothes behind lock and key. I understood being locked up naked and alone was for my own good, like Mama said. I understood. That's just the way it was. A fact of life. Like not knowing your daddy. Like having no brothers and sisters because Mama had been hurt something awful when I was born, born the size of a baked potato and screaming for lack of crack from the git-go, spending my first four months in the hospital baking under a hot light in a glass incubator box . . . Like having no cousins or uncles or aunts or grannies or grampas because Mama had come up an orphan in foster care with bad people who beat on her like a drum, she said. Like death and drugs and the bills that kept coming and the letters from my daddy that never came, being locked up naked and alone was just one of those things, a fact of life, the way it was. And the way it was was the way it was. And the way it was? That's just the way it was.

And then it was winter. And winter was cold. The winter wind whined and wailed, whined and wailed and rattled at the window like an evil deformed baby in the night, whined and wailed and got into your bones. And Mama couldn't leave me there naked and alone, the wind in my bones. Shivering and naked when I went to make pee-pee. No. Mama loved me too much for that. Mama had to do something to keep the wind from my bones . . .

I was with her when she bought it. From the battered cardboard box outside the church thrift store. The two-dollar red dress. The bright shiny two-dollar red dress. I wondered, when she bought it, wondered that she would buy herself such a small dress. Such a shiny dress. It wouldn't fit her, I thought. It was too small. Mama was small, yes, Mama was very delicate, bones so light you'd think a strong gust of winter wind would pick her up like a candy wrapper and swirl her around in a tornado of dust and losing lottery tickets and carry her far far away, maybe back to Africa or some other nice place, someplace nice and warm where she wouldn't have to worry so much, and I would come too, I'd catch the next tornado of dust and losing lottery tickets, 'cause I wanted to be with Mama always, and I was small too . . . but the dress was too small for her . . .

The red dress . . . it fit me like a glove.

"Mama," I cried at home, the red dress fitting me like a glove, my face streaked with tears. "I don't want to wear it!"

"Frankie, we been through this," Mama said, firm. "It's cold here and I don't want the wind in your bones. And I know you're such a little tough guy you won't go out looking like this . . ."

"I'll stay in bed, Mama, please. Let me wear my Spiderman pyjamas."

Mama shook her head.

"You're a sly little man," she said, smiling, her eyes bright with fresh memory . . .

A few days before when it got so cold and she let me wear my pyjamas and I went out the window and down the drainpipe. How the police picked me up wandering around a grocery store ten blocks away, eating a bag of chips I couldn't pay for, barefoot in my Spiderman pyjamas. How they drove me to the station in the caged back seat of the police car. How that nice friendly young white Officer Charles made shadow puppets of lions and other animals on the wall before going back on patrol . . . How the police sergeant asked me the name of the white folks Mama worked for, me thinking hard and finally remembering and him whistling all impressed when he heard that fancy name and how he called Mama there. How I ate stale donuts and drank hot chocolate with the sergeant . . . How warm it was in the police station, the radiators hissing away like a bunch of happy snakes from a picture book, me falling asleep in the scratchy blood-stained police blanket that smelled of some old bum's piss and puke, a pair of huge socks from one of the police on my feet. How Mama came from work early to pick me up. How the sergeant warned her to keep me inside.

Inside. Naked. Spiderman pyjamas locked up with the other clothes. The next day, out the window again. Running to the park naked. Playing football naked in the park.

The other kids laughing at my naked ding-dong at first, then treating me normal, letting me play. And then the police car cruising by. Officer Charles and his partner watching me run the length of the field, watching me make fools of the tacklers, watching me score. The cops clapping from the sidelines.

"Good run, Frankie," Officer Charles said, before wrapping me up in another scratchy blanket and driving me to the station again. The sergeant smiling at me like an old friend and then calling Mama. Mama who had to leave work this time soon as she arrived. Leave to come pick me and my second pair of big socks up from the police.

And the next day the social worker came to see us, to "assess" the home life, she said. I wore the Spiderman pyjamas.

"He'll stay home," Mama told the hard-faced black lady, Prudence De Vore, showing her the shiny new lock she'd put on the window that day. "I promise."

"He better," said Prudence De Vore. "Otherwise this little man will end up in foster care – or, worse, Juvenile Hall. The Zoo. You don't want to go there, Frankie. It's a bad place full of bad boys."

And when the hard-faced lady was gone, Mama beat me. She beat me. With tears in her eyes, she beat me. Beating the devil out of me, she said. And afterwards, as I cried and cried, Mama cried too. She held me, and we both cried. And the winter wind whined and wailed, whined and wailed and rattled at the window like an evil deformed baby, whispering:

"Frankie, Frankie Lawrence, you're my very special little nigga, come on out and play."

And so Mama bought me the red dress. And I did stay home. Home. The front door was locked. The window was locked. I stayed home. Out of the wind. But it was cold there . . . And because it was cold, I wore the red dress.

At first the red dress made me so embarrassed. I would go in the bathroom, look at myself in the spotty mirror, see a little boy in a bright red dress and I'd feel the hot shame and I'd tear the red dress off and run into bed. But bed was boring – it was too early to sleep – boring at first and then scary there under the covers, nothing but the winter wind whispering cold at the window, so I'd get up, walk the apartment naked like an animal in a cage, dreaming of football, fine cars, pretty girls . . . But it was cold. So so cold.

So I wore the red dress. Stayed away from the window. Stared at the locked closet, the locked door, the locked window. The kids playing out there in the cold would call up to my locked window.

"Frankie! Frankie Lawrence! Where are you?"

And I'd ignore them. Go to the mirror and look at myself and see a boy in a red dress. A pretty boy who looked like a girl but a boy I knew. A boy in a red dress.

And I would go to the window on my knees, stick my chin on the windowsill, look down at the kids playing.

"What happened, Frankie, you shrink?" the kids called. "You done lost your legs? Crack baby become a shrimp?"

I just watched them.

"Shrimpie!" they called. "Crack baby! Shrimp boy!"

But it was cold. So cold. So I wore the red dress. I looked at the little girls down there, bundled fat in their winter coats, in their tassled winter hats, and I wondered what it would be like to kiss them. And I touched my little woodie through the red dress and thought of the girls.

And then one day Malik and Shamika were playing quiet in the hallway, just outside the door, when Mama came home. And when Mama came in I was standing there in the red dress waiting to give her a big hello hug and Malik and Shamika saw me in the red dress and my life was changed forever.

At the bus stop the next morning the word was out.

"Faggot! Faggot!" they sang. "Red dress! Red dress!"

I took a deep breath and ignored them. Turned the other cheek, like Mama was always telling me to. Turned the other cheek and thought about football and fine cars and Africa.

At school the word was out.

"Faggot! Faggot! Red dress! Red dress!"

By afternoon play-time I was boiling.

"Faggot! Faggot! Frankie is a faggot! Crack-baby faggot!"

I couldn't take it no more. I chased Malik. Caught him easy. Hit him hard. And the next one. Jermaine. WHAP –

upside his ear. And the girls, I smacked them too, pulled them by their pigtails. There were five crying kids when the teacher dragged me to the principal's office.

"What's wrong, Frankie?" the old lady principal asked.

I just kept my grill shut.

The principal sighed and called Mama on the phone . . .

Mama came. Asked me what was wrong.

I just kept my grill shut.

Mama sighed and took me home. Sat me down. Kneeled in front of me and looked at me with big tired dark eyes.

"Frankie, baby, why you always fightin'?"

How could I explain? Didn't Mama remember what it was like to be a kid? The way other kids smelled your soft spots and grabbed onto those soft spots and ripped into those soft spots like a pack of hungry wolves . . .?

"Mama," I said, imitating her sigh. "Like you always sayin', it's just one of those things . . ."

And Mama handed me the red dress.

"I wish my daddy was here," I said. "He wouldn't make me wear no girly dress."

"That man ain't in the picture no more," Mama said, hard and firm. "Now put it on, boy."

"Please don't make me."

"You know, baby," she said, soft. "When I was a little girl I dreamed of a red dress. I wanted a red dress so bad, so so bad, and I asked my foster mother and she just laughed. I figured, if only I could have a red dress, everything would be okay."

"But I'm a boy, Mama. It ain't the same."

"Child, this dress is magic. You wear it, you'll be safe. Now be a good little man and put in on."

"No, Mama." I was crying, holding that red dress and crying.

"Frankie, please . . . Do it for Mama. I can't go to work until you put it on . . . Please, to make Mama happy."

Finally I put it on . . .

Then she kissed me. She held me close.

'I love you, Frankie Lawrence. You got all my heart,

baby . . . Maybe you think some of the things I do are wrong. But I'm doin' the best I can."

"I know, Mama. I love you too."

And then Mama was out the door, the lock clicking. And I was there alone . . . Alone in the magic red dress. And the clock was ticking and the wind was whining and a dog started barking and the cars were roaring and a toilet flushed somewhere and an ambulance screamed and I was alone alone alone.

It started snowing. The flakes swirled fast and thick. I went to the window finally, looked out finally. No need to be on my knees any more – they all knew – so I stood . . .

Down there, Jamal, Erik, Dwayne, Abdul – throwing snowballs at the window.

"Come on down, crack-baby faggot!" called Jamal, grabbing his crotch. "Get your after-school special!"

"Go away," I said to them, though I knew they couldn't hear me through the dirty glass.

And then I sat down in the ratty old chair. I turned on the fuzzy old television. The TV screen was as snowy as the weather outside. I turned it off. Turned on the radio. Some sad sad stupid stupid song. I turned it off . . . No Nintendo, no videos. A few picture books I'd looked at a thousand times. Nothing but the wind . . .

Yellow papers sticking out of a picture book . . . The pile of crinkled old clippings that Mama read when she got all drunk and misty . . . First grade was learning me how to read . . .

"Gangland slaying," I read aloud. "Larry Lawrence charged in the brutal execution-style murder of Lucius Weathers. Lawrence is in stable condition in Mercy Hospital after undergoing three hours of surgery for multiple gunshot wounds."

Damn, I thought.

"Larry Lawrence found guilty and sentenced to twenty-five years to life . . ."

"Faggot! Faggot!" came the voices. "Red dress! Red dress!"

"Stop it," I said to the window, the clippings falling off my lap and sailing to the floor like losing lottery tickets . . .

And then the snowballs started hitting the window. One after another like dull distant gunshots. And the anger rose sour in my throat like moth-ball vomit.

"Leave me be," I said to the window, to the kids out there, to the laughing wind. "Why can't y'all just leave me be?"

But they couldn't leave me be. I'd beaten their heads at school and now brave, in a pack, they wanted payback.

At the window, eyes full of hot tears, the melted ice of cold fury. The kids down there laughing, laughing along with the wind.

"You want me? You want some of this?" I pulled the red dress up, waved my little boy penis at them through the snow-filmed dirty window.

"Suck my dick!" I screamed.

Then BOOM, an ice ball smacked the window, cracked the window, and a cold bony finger of wind snaked through the spider web of glass into the room, the evil deformed baby stroking my face, reaching under my red dress, reaching into my head, inviting me out to play . . .

"Faggot, faggot, red dress, red dress, faggot, faggot . . . Poor Frankie! Poor Frankie!"

I punched the window. The glass broke. My hand was cut, bloody. Cold wind peppered with snowflakes rushed in like water into the doomed *Titanic*. And I punched again and again until the glass was gone. And then I was out the window, hanging on the drain pipe, holding on for cheap life and the kids were gone, out of sight . . . Inside. They were inside the building, inside my head, and I was outside, on the drain pipe, above the street, the snow in my eyes, the wind in my ears. Like Spiderman, but cold. Hand bloody. Dick cold. Spiderman in a red dress. Spiderman in a red dress with a cold dick. And then I heard them again, from above.

"Faggot, faggot, red dress, red dress!" They were on the roof and I was climbing.

"Poor Frankie! Poor Frankie!"

Like Spiderman, I was shinnying up that drain pipe in the cold, the wind in my ears, cheering me on, saying:

"Go, Frankie, go!"

The snow blowing in my eyes, a trail of blood on the pipe, climbing, climbing.

On the ledge, over the ledge, on the cold roof, feet in the snow, not feeling it.

"Gotcha nasty little niggaz now," I said, huffing and puffing, grinning cold, my breath white and evil as crack smoke.

"Whatcha gonna do, faggot?" Malik was brave. Had his posse with him so Malik was brave.

"Gonna jack you up, Malik. Jack you up and shut you up."

"You and what crew?"

"Me and my shadow gonna teach you respect."

My toes were frozen numb. The wind whipped my legs, stroked my ding-dong frozen, made the red dress flap. The blood dripped warm down my arm, dripped into the snow, melted the snow into red slushy sauce.

And the boys just laughed.

"Motherfucking faggot in a red dress. The blood matches your dress, nigga."

I caught Dwayne first. Beat his head against the cold snowy roof. Erik pulled me off, rolled me in the snow, mashed my face into the roof as the others punched me. Jamal, Erik, Dwayne, Malik. Punch punch punch punch. I felt nothing. I absorbed the punches and smiled. My grill was bloody. I could taste the salty blood. I went limp and still as the little boy boots pounded my ribs, as they kicked and punched the red dress over and over . . . I felt nothing. The pain was like my daddy, locked up far far away, a total stranger . . .

"Ya mama's a crack ho," said Jamal, kicking my stomach.

"And ya daddy's a convict," said Erik, spitting on me.

"And you a faggot," said Dwayne, laughing.

And then the boys were walking away . . .

"Stay down, little red-dress faggot," said Malik, sneering over his shoulder. "It's over."

But it wasn't over. I was up and I grabbed the first boy, didn't matter which one – Malik! – and I punched and pushed, butted Malik with my head, punched and pushed and avoided his wild windmill swings, and then we were at the ledge, him and me, me and Malik, we were wrestling, dancing and . . .

"Cool it, Frankie!" called Erik.

"Chill out, nigga!" cried Jamal.

"Faggot!" screamed Malik.

"Faggot this!" I screamed back, punching . . .

And Malik . . .? His eyes were wide and full of wonder, his lips were wide and screaming as he stumbled backwards and grabbed air, and . . . he was over the ledge, out of sight, falling falling falling into empty space . . . a dull sick slamming THUMP . . .

I looked over the ledge. Malik lying there on the sidewalk, crumpled flat as a pizza, arms and legs at broken puppet angles, blood running from his grill, staining the fresh white snow.

"Malik," I whispered. "I didn't mean it. I'm sorry."

"You be in trouble now, crack baby," said Dwayne at my side. "A whole mess o'trouble." And all the other boys looked down too. "You and your muhfukkin red dress are in some serious shit."

I felt a tear run down my cheek. I was in serious shit. Me and my red dress were in some serious shit. Malik was dead and I was in trouble . . . And that's the way it was. A fact of life. Just one of those things.

And the winter wind just laughed.

II

As advertised, Juvenile Hall was a bad place. Bad food, bad beds, bad smells, bad sounds, bad vibes – a bad life for bad boys who'd done bad things . . . And as a consequence of all that badness – shit – I grew up bad.

But not at first. No. Those first few weeks I was as good as Mama told me to be. Good as a little angel . . . Break out the harps and the hallelujahs, I was all sweetness and fear . . . I'd been sentenced to the maximum – Malik's uncle was a cop and he fixed it so the juvenile court judge sentenced me to the max.

"This was no accident," said the old bald white judge, hair snaking out of his nose, his ears. "This is a case of vicious, malicious, premeditated murder. And given Mrs Lawrence's history of drugs and the lack of supervision in the home . . ."

He didn't throw the book at me, nuh-uh, that old clown threw the whole twenty-volume encyclopedia. The Zoo was gonna be my home sweet home till I turned eighteen, what they called a "full-term baby".

But I wasn't bad, nuh-uh. Not yet. With me, badness didn't come slow, no, it didn't come limping slow and loud like some fat old asthmatic club-foot thief in the night, it didn't germinate inside of me like some nasty little seed of evil, no, with me badness flowered forth instantly – like a bullet in the brain, like a thunderbolt, like death driving a Lamborghini – like true motherfucking love . . .

But I wasn't bad, nuh-uh. Not yet. Those first few weeks in the Zoo I wasn't no animal. I was still Mama's little boy, little Mr Innocent . . . I'd walk around those gloomy green-painted halls with big dark eyes full of fear – listening to the barbells clanking, the radios blasting, the basketballs bouncing, the sneakers squeaking, the laughter echoing – shivering at all the badness coming at me from every which way, all the hatred, all the despair, all the confusion, all those young twisted hearts and ancient evil souls stuck in young fresh bodies, and I'd lower my eyes and say, "Yes, sir," to anyone older than me – and that was everyone, since I was the youngest dude there. And every night as I lay there in the dark on the battered old mattress, listening to the snores and sex noises and laughs and farts, breathing the nasty night cloud of farts and sex and cigarettes, waiting for the healing grace of sleep, as I lay there on the ancient lumpy mattress mapped with the misery of a parade of pissing and weeping and drooling boys, every night I'd add a few thousand of my own hot salt tears to that mattress, every single night I'd cry myself to sleep . . .

During the daylight hours I'd go to the school rooms and I'd stare at the walls, looking for exit signs in the peeling green paint, and I'd listen to the sad desperate laughter echoing out in the gloomy green halls that smelled of chemical cherry disinfectant, the sad desperate laughter of all the sad lost boys, and the laughter would sound like the winter wind – like a bunch of evil deformed babies, like a pack of fallen angels . . . I was so scared. So so scared and so so alone.

But I wasn't bad. Nuh-uh. Not yet.

"Happy birthday to me," I said to Mama's good little brown-skinned boy brushing his teeth in the mirror one morning.

It was my birthday, my seventh birthday. Just a week into my incarceration incarnation and I was turning seven. Eleven years to go till I hit eighteen. Eleven years – count them – eleven years of three-hundred-sixty-five days of twenty-four hours of sixty minutes of sixty seconds till I was out. I'd never make it, I thought. The Zoo would eat me alive and wouldn't even burp. I didn't have what it took to ride the storm. I wasn't hard, I wasn't cold, I couldn't laugh crazy in the face of fear. I wasn't bad . . . Not yet I wasn't.

January twenty-ninth was the day. There was a cake at dinner in the cafeteria. A special visit from Mama earlier. A new, bigger pair of Spiderman pyjamas. I'd cried and hugged her. She'd cried and shushed me, told me to be brave, to be good, that she loved me and I had to stay brave and good. She read me from the Bible and told me to be brave and good, that if some boy messed with me to just give him my other cheek, like you-know-who. I cried and cried and Mama cried and cried and when our time was up I had to be dragged off.

And now the cake. I listened to the old school standard sung by those evil-eyed bad boys. Those dudes could sing, sweet as a chorus of fallen angels.

"Happy birthday to you, happy birthday to you, you look like a monkey and you smell like one too . . ."

I blew the candles out. I sliced the cake with a plastic knife. I ate my slice of cake, washed it down with a few gulps of fear and milk. I was alone. Alone and scared. But I wasn't bad. Not yet I wasn't.

And then it was night. Surrounded by sleeping boys in the dorm but alone. Alone in the dark . . . And then I wasn't alone. They came fast and furious as a bunch of hyenas. I tried to fight them but there were too many. Six big boys held me down, yanked my Spiderman pyjamas off, stuffed a dirty sock in my grill, flipped me over and tore into me like a piece of cake, busting into my tender ass from behind, passing me back and forth like a football, spitting on me, mauling me, biting my shoulders with sharp dog teeth, sneering, laughing, hitting me, slapping at my tear-stained face, singing "happy birthday" as they poked and prodded and ripped me inside, taking turns, taking second helpings, drooling all over my chewed-up shoulders, wiping their bloody greasy flesh-weapons with my pyjamas . . . And then finally, when they were worn out, when wave after wave of cruel dog orgasm had soaked into my guts, as I lay there squashed and bloody and twisted like a dead cat in the street, my ass torn wide open, my belly swollen with their hatred, the winter wind laughing at me from the window, one motherfucker delivered a parting message by pissing like a garden hose up my ruined bloody hole . . . I couldn't even scream I was so flat . . . All I could do was laugh . . . Lie there on the wet bloody mattress and laugh. And that's the way the counsellors found me the next morning. Laughing. They sent me to the hospital ward stinking of piss and jism. And I laughed. The hospital ward where the nurse sedated me, cleaned me out, shot me full of antibiotics, where the doctor sewed my ass up like a torn pair of underwear, whistling all the while, where he bandaged my shoulders, where I spent two weeks in a hospital gown, on an IV, staring at the cracked ceiling, thinking bad thoughts, not looking for exit signs, not answering questions, not naming names, listening to the wind, laughing with the wind and healing into hardness, vowing never never by God never to cry again. Never. Bad boys don't cry. They laugh. And, motherfucker, I was bad . . . The wind had dried all the tears out of me.

The last night in the hospital ward I stole the syringe. Sharp. It was sharp. Sharp and long. The needle gleamed. By the light of the diseased moon I filled the glass tube. Laughing, I filled it with yellow liquid. Carried it the next morning in my sock back to the dorm. Back to my lumpy mattress. Same old lumpy mattress – they'd just turned it over so the cockroaches had easy access to my dried crusted blood . . . Ready. Frankie Lawrence was ready. Frankie Lawrence was bad. Come on, you dog-mafockas, I thought, come on back for seconds.

And like I knew they would, they came again. That night. The same crew. The same six. They'd liked their cake and this time they expected no fight, they expected Frankie's ass as a gift. The gift that keeps on giving.

But Frankie had other plans. Oh, yeah, I had other plans. The first motherfucker got a different kind of gift – the syringe! – the syringe full of piss, he got the syringe right smack in his eye!

"Motherfucker!" I yelled, standing on the bed, and as the boy screamed I plunged the plunger and the piss streamed into the motherfucker's head and I raked that needle back and forth hard, ripping his eyemeat, laughing as I bent the motherfucking needle hard against the eye-socket bone, him screaming like death driving a Lamborghini, and I yanked with all my strength and "plop" there it was, like a motherfucking shrimp on a fork, the fucking eye.

"Piss off, nigga," I said, laughing like crazy, standing tall on the bed, showing those big bad motherfuckers the two-tone egg all goopy and shiny in the moonlight streaming through the caged window, my hand dripping piss. Showing them who was crazy, who was bad. And, laughing, I raised the eye to my grill, and, just like Mama always told me, I chewed before I swallowed.

"Better than a mothball," I said, licking my lips, laughing my ass off, feeling the hot half-chewed chunks of eye-meat gurgling nasty down into my stomach. "Sweet as motherfuckin' candy."

And as the one-eyed motherfucker rolled on the floor in agony, the piss and blood like a trail of tears on his face, his eye-socket dark and empty, the eyelid puckered like your grandpa's scrotum, the other boys looked at me with respect.

And me? I felt nothing.

I burped loud and long . . . I was bad.

*   *   *

The incident was noted on my records. Like Malik, laying there flat as a pizza on the street, just another cold hard fact in black and white.

The Zookeeper called me in, lectured me about anger, about self-control. I bowed my head, looked all sad and guilty. I kept my grill shut.

I got sent to the shrink. The motherfucker asked question after question. I bowed my head, looked all sad and guilty. I kept my grill shut.

And the counsellors, the guards, the teachers – no questions, no lectures – they kept their distance, like I was a dog with nasty foam on his lips. I could see it in their eyes, I was bad.

"Yo, little man," said Eight Ball Johnson, head of the Zoo Crew gang, swaggering up to my bed after lights-out, him and Louie Tran, his Vietnamese number-one homie. Both fifteen years old. Eight Ball in for a triple homicide. Louie the Dragon in for narcotics and extortion. Both seriously bad. "That was some wild shit you pull."

"Just one of those things," I said.

"You a little cannibal," said the Dragon.

"No, I be a Lawrence. Frankie Lawrence. My daddy Larry Lawrence."

"Larry Lawrence?" Eight Ball was impressed. "Double L? Shit, that was one legendary nigga!"

"What'd the muhfukkah do?" asked Louie.

"Check it out, Dragon. Crazy nigga try to take down Ronny Dewitt singlehanded!"

"Ronny Dewitt? Nigger Mortis? The dude run all the heroin?"

"Yeah, man. This back in the day Ronny was clockin' rock in the hood . . . Nigger Mortis and Double L was partners . . . But they had them a altercation and Larry smoked Ronny's number one nigga and was gunnin' for Ronny hisself till Ronny put five caps in the nigga's chest. Ronny skated on self-defence and the cannibal's pappy upstate doin' life."

"Ronny Dewitt," said Louie. "That's a cold nigga to cross."

"Cold and bold," said Eight Ball. "It take balls the size of Kansas City to even consider takin' down Nigger Mortis . . ."

"That's my daddy," I said, loud and proud.

"Ya daddy's a bad nigga."

Eight Ball checked me up and down.

"Yeah," he said. "That boy you fucked up was my captain of the ten-and-unders, my best little nigga . . . How you like to take his spot? You got what it takes?"

"Balls the size of Kansas City," I said.

They laughed

"Okay," said Eight Ball. "But you need a new handle. Frankie sound like some Spaghettio lounge singer."

He handed me a sharpened butter knife.

"Welcome to the monkey house, Cannibal. You in the Zoo Crew now."

So I was Frankie the Cannibal and I was in the Zoo Crew, captain of the ten-and-unders. I was bad like my daddy. My daddy who took five caps and lived to tell the tale from jail . . . And the one-eyed motherfucker whose job I copped? He came out of the hospital ward a week later wearing a black eye patch. Immediately got tagged the Piss-Eyed Pirate, shortened to just Piss.

We was in gym class that afternoon. The day Piss made his pirate-patch debut. All the ten-and-unders, shootin' hoop, taking foul shots. Piss glared at me hard from his one eye. Piss big for nine. Big and holding a grudge. Ready to explode.

The gym teacher handed him the rock just as the phone rang in the office.

"Shoot the ball, big pirate," the gym teacher ordered Piss, as he went for the phone.

Piss threw up a shot . . . Air ball. Missed the basket by five feet. Mafockas be laughin' they asses off.

"Piss sucks! Piss sucks!" the boys chanted.

Piss touched his eye-patch, then wheeled and came at me. Bull-rushed me. I sidestepped him, tripped him up, and then they was on him – all the ten-and-unders. Twenty boys had him ass-down on the basketball court. The brothers all laughing at him, taunting him as he struggled.

"Piss sucks!"

"Piss," someone said. "You blind nigga! You gonna end up sellin' pencils on the corner!"

Gym teacher in the office, on the phone. Piss on his back. Two boys on each leg, each arm. A big ten-year-old named Shaquille kneeling on his chest, pulling that dead eyelid skin back and spitting nasty clams into that empty eye socket.

"Motherfuckuh!" screamed Piss struggling, the socket spilling bubbly white snot.

Shaq snorted like a hog, hawked up some more mucus, splashed a long stringy loogie into the hole and laughed.

That's when I put the cold steel of my sharpened butter knife against Shaquille's throat.

"That'll do," I said.

"Say what?" Shaquille looked back at me.

"You heard me, fat boy," I said, pressing the edge of the shiv into his throat. "Party's over. This my nigga."

"How you feelin', homeboy?" I asked, when I went to visit my nigga that night. Came with a box of cookies I got from Mama.

Piss sat looking at a comic book on his bed.

"You took my eye, man. You took my job. Then the niggaz spit inside my head. How's I s'posed to feel?"

"Grateful, boy. I saved your ass today." I threw the cookies on his bed. I'd figured the angles. I needed this nigga.

"You took my eye, nigga," he said. "I ain't never gonna forget that."

"Yo, you took my ass . . . Anyway, nigga, it wasn't nothin' personal. You was just the closest one."

Piss laughed bitter as sour lemon candy. He was holding the box of cookies, reading the label with his one eye.

"So now I s'posed to just let it go?" he asked, looking at me cold and mad. "You ate my muhfukkin' eye, nigga, then you shit it out like some bacon and eggs . . . My eye! I s'posed to pretend like it didn't happen? Sell out for some Keebler chocolate chip cookie shit?"

"They made by elves," I said. "Listen. Lemme ask you

this, nigga – you a full-term baby – what you in for?"

"Nigga, I cracked my grandma skull with a baseball bat cause she try to wake me up early. Old bitch dead."

"See, that's the kind of cold-ass pirate motherfukkah I need to partner up with . . . You and me, Piss, we got years ahead of us behind these mafockin walls . . . We gots a choice, bro – enemies or homies. Me, I say we go for bros. All you gots to do is chill on the blame game an' we both make money."

He looked at me. I looked at him. And then he reached a decision. A sweet cold smile broke on his lips.

"Shee-it," he said. "One eye's all I need."

Piss had a beautiful, evil smile. He was rotten to the core. I loved him.

"You a bad muhfukkuh, Frankie Lawrence," he said.

"Tell me somethin' I don't know, Piss," I said. "Now break out those muhfukkin cookies."

The first few years Mama came to visit once a week. She took the bus and cried every time. I felt bad for Mama. Yeah, she was my sweetheart. Yeah, she was getting her shit together. Yeah, she was going back to school and getting her high school diploma. She'd stopped drinking the wine, she said, was getting career counselling, she said, planning for the future – her future, our future – yeah yeah yeah . . . But sure as shit ain't sugar, sure as pigs don't fly, sure as black ain't white and sure as eating pussy and drinking cognac is the breakfast of champions, I wouldn't cry. Couldn't cry. I was past crying. The wind had dried all my tears. I'd become hard. I didn't dream, I didn't hope, all I did was scheme and hustle and practise being hard and cold. All I did was stay alive and get my piece of the action . . . I was growing into the full glory of my badness like a puppy grows into his paws.

Sure, I went to school. Shit, I was a straight A student . . . Sure, I learned to smile at the teachers and counsellors and guards, at that big old Zookeeper. Shit, that was the game . . . But it was after school hours, after the books were shut and the basketballs were asleep, when the real lessons of Juvenile Hall were being laid out: how to lie, how to steal, how to get high and not show it. How to fabricate a weapon out of near anything. How to deal drugs and not get caught. How to hide a stash of drugs or a shiv in the walls or floor or your mattress. How to hide a safety razor in your grill or up your poop-chute so even in the shower you had a weapon. How to work the phone and talk in code so you could get motherfuckers on the outside to deliver you shit. How to bribe a guard to look the other way. How to make money hand over fist. How to take a cut of other dudes' cash crops. How to think clear with a head full of pills or coke or reefer or home-made liquor. How to hurt a motherfucker, physically or mentally, how to strip him of self-esteem. How to hold a secret over a motherfucker's head or sweet-talk that motherfucker into doing something he didn't want to do. Crush that nigga's spirit to the floor then raise him up an inch or two so that he'd lick your sneakers and be grateful for the taste of rubber. Intimidation and manipulation. That's how you got by, that's how you got ahead, that's how you got yours . . . The gym teacher liked to say, "The best offence is a good defence." Nuh-uh for that old school shit, Jack. Flip the mafocka for modern times: "The best defence is a good offence." Translation, dumbfuck: score enough and the mafockas'll never catch up with you. They be eating your dust till the end of time. So I went on the offensive, never gave an inch to anyone. I studied hardness and coldness – I sucked hardness and coldness from the walls, I made friends with the winter wind – and I learned my lessons well. I was the cream of the cream of the crop, as hard and cold as they came. I was Bad Frankie Lawrence, the Cannibal. A goddamn gourmet of respect.

I learned kung-fu from Louie Tran, how to kick high, punch low, take no prisoners. My fists and feet were fast as black lightning. The Dragon schooled me to the points on an enemy's body, the places you pressed that would make the nigga beg for mercy, promise obedience, vomit instantly . . .

"Boy," I said to some goggle-eyed chucklehead, some new bone-scared white mafocka my age fresh from the streets trying to be bad. "What's your name?"

"Rocco. What's it to you, black?"

"You want to see my invisible punch, Rocco?"

"Say what?"

And I threw down so fast the mafockin Wop-a-doodle-dandy never even saw it. Lights out, nobody home.

When he came back to the land of the living, groggy, pockets empty, me counting his stash of cash, I asked him: "Did you see it, Spaghettio?"

Rocco just groaned.

"That's right, nigga. No one ever saw the Cannibal's invisible punch and no one ever will. You could video the mafocka and slow the tape down and you still wouldn't see it. Not if you lived till you were sixteen or sixteen million. And, homeboy, the way you stylin' it, you won't see next week."

And I leaned down and gently touched Rocco under the collarbone . . .

"Welcome to the monkey house," I said.

And the look in that mafocka's eyes – gratitude at the softness, the reprieve, the ticket out of Pain City, but then, as I pressed the magic spot just an itty-bit harder, he turned pale green and his body heaved, he was right back in Shit Central, swimming in a sea of dark pain, the vomit bubbling ugly on his lips, and I laughed . . . Submission, motherfucker. I had another nigga for my collection.

I collected hard boys like that goofy fat Polish retard Maurice Kowalski collected rat turds. Every week another boy would join me. My junior crew was growing. As my hardness set, my crew grew.

And I listened to Eight Ball and Louie and the parade of older boys. I listened and learned. I acquired skills . . . From Julio the Blade I learned the best way to shank a guy. Right through the ribcage on the heart side, blade horizontal, wiggle the shiv back and forth, up and down, make sure those essential veins were properly sliced and diced, chopped into Big Mac meat, beyond the surgical skills of modern medicine, and then snap the blade off inside. Adios, motherfucker . . .

I learned stuff for later, for the streets. Gems of practical wisdom . . . Like when you wanted to remove a motherfucker no doubt . . . You walked up to his house wearing rubber gloves, you rang the bell, you pulled your silenced steel, and when the chump came to the door in his shorts, scratching his itchy balls, smelling like unwashed socks and ugly love, you popped a cap in the nigga's head and walked away cool and calm, put some distance between you and the cooling body . . . Then you took a file and filed the barrel so ballistics could never match the hardware and software, you burned the gloves, you dumped the file, took the gun to the river and chucked the mafocka into the cold dark deep where it would sleep innocent for about sixteen million goddamn years or eternity, whichever came first. Adios, motherfucker.

Oh yeah, Frankie Lawrence was on the offensive. I was heading for freedom and age eighteen at Lamborghini speeds. I had no brakes, but shit, the Cannibal was a helluva driver, a child of the wind, slick and crafty behind the wheel. There was no mafockin way this nigga was gonna crash . . . I was in control, on top of my game. And as my body grew into young manhood, lean-muscled, hard, slim and cool and handsome as any hip-hop nigga sucking magic money from the musical mammary, as I grew bigger and wiser and stronger with each passing day and year, my heart cold and smoking like dry ice, as the factory pumped out hard young muhfukkahs, cold and perfect as snowflakes – some graduating to the streets where they lived like kings or died like flies, some shipped off to adult institutions – and as the younger boys took their place in the food chain, I gained power, I took control. And so it came to pass, that at the age of fifteen, I, Frankie Lawrence, took over the Zoo Crew, I became the king of Juvenile Hall, the hardest, coldest, baddest motherfucker in the joint. Long live the king! If you weren't with me, you were against me. And if you were against me? Adios, motherfucker.

III

And Mama kept coming. She'd finished her studies and become a nurse. Traded one white uniform for another . . .

And then one week she came with somebody, some lean muscular nobody, an older black dude. Like a carpet that's been stepped on for years, like a dog with the mange, the old dude was all used-up.

"Frankie," the man said. He was old.

"Do I know you?" I asked. But I knew him.

The man looked into my eyes, never giving an inch. Dude had some coldness in him. But old. An old man. Must have been thirty-four.

"Do you know me?" The man raising his eyebrows.

"You hard of hearing on top of bald and ugly, old dude?"

"Frankie," Mama said. "Talk nice. This is your father."

And I just laughed and laughed. I could see the other visitors cringing at the laughter. Crazy laughter cold and bad as the winter wind.

"Mama, that ain't my father," I said, looking with contempt at the old dude's cheap new clothes, straight out of some K-Mart clearance sale. "My father don't dress like a goddamn out-of-work garbageman! My father in prison! Double L doin' twenty to life for murder one!"

"I'm out," said the old dude. "Did fifteen years hard time. I got parole."

"Shit, nigga, my daddy's parole officer ain't even been born yet."

"I'm out," the old dude said with a sigh. "That's a fact. And I'm here to make amends. I never called or wrote 'cause I wanted your mama to divorce me and find someone else. But she's stubborn."

"Like you, Frankie." Mama took the old fuck's hand. "I'm stubborn like you."

She looked at the veiny-armed jailhouse nigga with smiling love.

"Mama, you ain't fallin' for this old nigga's game?"

"I want to be in your life now, Frankie," old dude said. "Make up for lost time. Be a father to you."

"You trippin'? My father cold, he bad, he tried to take Ronny Dewitt down, he took five caps . . . You ain't him."

"Frankie," said Mama, sharp. "Don't talk to your father like that. You don't know what he done for us."

"Praise God, son, I've turned my life around."

"Old nigga, you better turn your ass around and walk it out of here while you still can."

I waved him off.

"Mama, you get that money order I sent you?"

I'd sent her another five hundred dollars that week.

Mama looked at the old dude and then pulled the money order out of her purse. She handed it to me.

"Yes, baby," Mama said with a sigh. "But Mama can't accept the money any more."

"Say what?"

The old dude put his hard hand on mine.

"Boy, no money comin' out of here is clean. Your mama don't want no dirty money."

"Man," I said, pulling my hand away. "Who the fuck are you showin' up outta the clear-blue motherfuckin' nowhere and tellin' folks how to live? Who the fuck you think you are?"

"Just a man," said the man with a sigh. "A man like the next man. Strong in some places, weak in others. But here's the deal: your mother and I are makin' a go of it. You don't have to like it, hard case, but that's the way it is."

"I don't hear nothin', old nigga, 'cept maybe a rat goin' 'cheap-cheap-cheap'. Mama, send this cheap old fool back to the boneyard."

And Mama just sighed. She got up to go.

And the next time she came, she came alone. Old Larry Lawrence never visited again.

IV

The Zoo never changed. Just a parade of miserable boys walking the one-way road to hell. In the old-school days they were mostly white, now they were mostly black. But always, till the end of time, regardless of colour, the Zoo would be hard and cold. A stewpot of old misery, a breeding ground for fresh misery. A warehouse of badness, sadness, gloom and doom. A hard cold factory that produced hard eyes and hard bodies, cold eyes and cold hearts – unsoftened by the feminine touch – hard with maleness, with macho, with attitude and anger and fear. A rumble could break out anywhere – spontaneous explosions of turbulence, testosterone, terror – even the cafeteria. Shit, especially the cafeteria. Never bother a dog when it's eating . . . The cafeteria . . . That's where the only females in the whole of Juvenile Hall worked, the cafeteria.

Hundreds of dog-mafockas and three females? Not a good idea, nuh-uh, but the females who worked the cafeteria, cooking and serving and locking away the knives between meals, a guard present at all times, the kitchen locked overnight, they musta had to show their menopause papers to get hired. Those females were way too used-up to cop even a second banana role in any teenage horndog fantasy – overweight and overworked – just your typical sad sweet old black ladies that life had been shitting on for about four hundred years, about as sexy as a bag of turkey necks rotting in the noonday sun or a hippopotamus's asshole with a wad of toilet paper hanging off it . . . One even had a full flowing Pancho Villa moustache and chin whiskers. The motherly types? More like the grand-motherly types. Hell, more like the great-great grand-motherly types . . .

And then one day – I was sixteen now, only two years till bust-out time, sixteen and riding high – I show for dinner and there was a hum in the line. Like a live electric wire there was a hum.

I went to the head of the line as always, as befits the king, and when I got to the front I saw what was makin' the niggaz jump.

She.

She was beautiful.

Ayesha was her name, said so on her nameplate. And she wasn't the grandmother type, no, not even the mother type, except for those fine big wholesome breasts that'd make any little baby nursing at its mama's titty bite his old lady's nipple off so she'd drop him and he could land like a cat and crawl over to Ayesha and hop into her arms and nuzzle at hers. She was soft and curvy and beautiful, a bubblicious twenty-five-year-old caramel princess in a white uniform that showed more than was fair for all that swingin' dick energy . . . The hormones in the place were hoppin' wild and electric like a bunch of hungry fleas on a rabid dog.

"Shut up, you knuckleheads," I said, showing Ayesha

my lovely pearly whites, noting her cheap gold wedding band. "Any of these sorry mafockas bother you, Ma'am, tell 'em you know Frankie Lawrence."

"If you say so, Mister Slim, but reality says I don't know any Frankie Lawrence."

"You do now. My name is Frankie Lawrence, honey, and I'd like some mashed potatoes." I smiled at her and she smiled back. And that wasn't any grandmotherly smile, I knew. No way no how. And as I walked off hard and cool, something soft and warm and distantly familiar was working in my guts. Like a foreign language you knew in another lifetime . . . Frankie Lawrence was in love.

She was there only until her grandma Hortense got out of the hospital. We all knew it was for a short time. We all knew she was married – shit, she wore that big gold ring like a goddamn advertisement for marital bliss. We all knew she was a dream princess come to grace us with her beauty . . . We all knew she was generous with the starch. One day it was potatoes, the next it was rice, the next it was spaghetti. She piled it on . . . But every day, between me and Princess Ayesha, on top of the starch, it was smiles and respect – an exchange – it was attraction.

I had eyes and ears everywhere in the joint. I heard the mafockas dreaming, heard them scheming . . .

Piss sat on the end of my bed, broadcasting the CNN as Black Jimmy braided my hair. My boy Piss was huge now. Six foot seven, tippin' the scales at two-hundred-forty pounds of pure muscle. No weights or steroids, just a big damn motherfucker. He'd refused a glass eye, said it looked dumb, and now, with that black eye patch and his shoulder-length dreadlocks and his size and natural coldness, he commanded instant respect. Shit, motherfucking Arnold *Swatchanigga* would pinch a musclebound log in his *diapers* he run into Piss. Huge and bad, his black eye patch embroidered with a red skull and cross bones, the fine stitch-work done by his ex-bitch Jewel – Rafael to his Mexican mama and daddy – Piss was almost eighteen, about to graduate and hit the streets. Pity the poor mafockin streets. And unlike me the motherfucker had a heart. He'd cried the day he caught that little taco-loco bitch Jewel in the shower takin' some fat nigga up the Hershey highway. Yup, he'd cried, cried with his one good eye then thrown Jewel headfirst into the shower wall. Cried some more as he kicked the shit out of the soapy nigga who'd been bangin' Jewel. Cried and then stomped that broken-neck paraplegic Jewel in the family jewels and said, "Adios, bitch."

"Word up, Cannibal. Shaq and his crew are fixin' to jump your honey freaky tomorrow night."

"She ain't my honey, brother."

"Yo, whoever she is or isn't, they plannin' a pony party. They talkin' they gonna rock that fine puddy into the next life."

I sent for Shaquille. Him and me hated each other, had never made it up since the day I saved Piss from his spit bath.

"Whussup, nigga?" I asked that cold motherfucker. Piss stood by, tall. Black Jimmy was done with my hair and was finishing up my manicure, buffing my nails mirror-bright.

"Me, always." He grabbed his business.

"Whoop-de-damn-do for you . . . Lookee here, bitch, whuss this shit I hear 'bout you and Money Johnson and Claude DeVeaux bein' all geeked up about a certain female?"

"Don't believe the lyin'-ass niggaz."

"Listen up, lame-ass – you get within spittin' distance of Miss Lovely and I'll personally chop your sorry mafockin' steroid-shrunk johnson off and put it in a bun and sell it as a midget goddamn hot dog – hold the motherfuckin' mustard. Know what I'm sayin'?"

"Why you always frontin' on me, man?" Shaq wasn't bending over easy. "Why don'tcha back off and take care of you own business?"

"This is my business, nigga."

"You think you bad?"

"No, sucker," I said. "I know it."

"I ain't one of your dumb little Zoo Crew niggaz, Frankie. I don't scare like a pussy-ass mafocka. You can't just order me around."

"I just did. You just too dumb to know it. You liftin' weights and shit but your brain still the size of a mothball.

Consider your gorilla ass warned. Now remove your stank out of my presence and lemme watch the paint peel."

I waved him away with a flash of polished nails. Piss smiled and growled.

Later on Piss and Popeye and Gangstahlove sat on my bed. We smoked a blunt full of sweet coke and sensemilla.

"I want Shaq and his niggaz shadowed."

"Toyota," said Piss, echoing an ancient ad. "*You asked for it you got it*, Toyota."

"Burger King," said Popeye, echoing another ancient ad. "*Have it your way*."

"And if they try some shit . . ." I smiled, drawing deep on the blunt.

"Nike, my brother," said G-love, echoing another ancient ad. "*Just do it*."

"Truth," I said. "Just do it."

They made their play for her the next night. It was her last night, everyone knew it. Grandma Hortense was out of the hospital and coming back.

I'd said bye-bye to Ayesha, told her to stay beautiful. Told her to be well, be happy, be happy with that lucky mafocka of a husband she had. Told her that Frankie Lawrence was her friend, her friend for life.

She'd looked at me with affection in her eyes.

"You're a gentleman, Frankie. One of the boys told me you been watching my back, and I appreciate it."

"Someone squealin'?" I faked anger. And then we both smiled.

"You stay strong, Ayesha."

"You be good, Frankie."

"Too late for that, baby," I said. "But I'll stay alive."

The word came in an hour after dinner. Just as I figured, Shaq and his boys were bustin' a move. It was Friday night and there was a Harrison Ford movie rolling in the auditorium. Most of the boys and staff were there watching old Indiana Jones do his hangdog hero thing, including the kitchen guard. I had a skeleton crew walking the halls, and two good niggaz, Spanish Jimmy and Rocco the Wop, stashed in a storage room behind the kitchen. And when

Shaq and his boys made their play, the hall boys passed the word.

This is how it went down.

Ayesha and the two grannies about to bust out. The kitchen spotless. The fridges humming. The cutlery all locked up. Ayesha looking for her purse. Not finding it. Telling the old ladies to get going, she'd be fine, just had to find her purse. Old ladies gone. Ayesha alone there looking for her purse. Looking in the changing room. Looking again in her granny's locker. Looking under the benches. Not finding it.

And then the three mafockas standing there, grinning evil. Shaquille with a sharpened spoon in one hand, his other hand stashed behind his back.

"Hello, sugartit," said that cold nigga. "You lookin' for somethin'?"

"Nothing you'd know about," she said.

Shaquille took his hidden hand from behind his broad back. The purse.

He laughed, cold and evil, and then they was on her, ripped her coat and dress off. Her titties pressing against a sheer red slip. Up against some boxes, Money and Claude pinning her still as Shaq worked his zipper and pressed the polished sharp spoon shiv to her long lovely throat.

"Oh, yummy mama, Shaqdaddy gonna eat you with a spoon! It gonna be an Olympic bonathon!"

Ayesha spat in his laughing face. Shaq slapped her hard, wiped his face, ripped that slip up and off her flailing arms. Lacy black panties and bra over ripe caramel curves. His lovestick jumpin' ready, all primed and shit.

And that's when Jimmy and Rocco busted out of the storage room, that's when me and Piss and Popeye and Gangstahlove rolled into the kitchen. Jimmy and Rocco grabbed Shaq by the arms, pulled him off. Piss wrapped a lock-arm around his throat, shut down his air. I pressed his wrist and took his shiv. Shaq's flagpole drooping to half-mast as he struggled.

"Mafocka," I said. "You been warned."

Gangstahlove and Popeye had their shivs out. They closed in on Money and Claude. Shaq's niggaz let Ayesha go and turned, stepped off, hands up. The supplication gyration.

"We just followin' orders, Cannibal."

"New orders," I said. "I want a review of the movie. You my Cisco and Egbert now, niggaz. Harrison Ford likely in some deep doo-doo by now, but it ain't within nine millimetres of the pool of shit Shaquille in."

I motioned Cisco and Egbert away. They walked. Shaq's dick was soft now. Shrivelling into grey nothingness with fear. He could hardly breathe the way Piss was clamping down on his throat.

Ayesha dressing fast, leaving the slip off, stuffing it in her coat pocket, checking her purse, that the money and ID and shit were all there.

"Frankie, thank you, but I don't want him hurt. Promise me he won't be hurt."

"You're good," I said, pocketing the shiv. "A good lady. He won't be hurt," I said. "I promise."

And then I walked her out of there. Into the back room of the kitchen. Through that back room with the dim bulb and all the boxes full of rice and shit, to the door to the hall, the hall that led to another door, a door with a guard, the door to the street, the door to goodbye . . .

"Baby," I said.

She sighed and gave me a sad smile.

"Ayesha," I said. "You know I got feelings for you."

"I know," she said, coming close, those big brown eyes burning into mine. "I think you're a very special young man . . ."

She kissed me then, pressed my lips with her soft sweet lips, a hint of tongue, the pressure of her breasts, the heat of her body . . .

"Goodbye, Frankie."

"Ayesha . . ."

"I'm a married lady," she said.

"That's the way it is," I said with a sigh. "Thanks for not sayin' anything about me bein' a kid."

"You're not a kid, Frankie Lawrence. You're a man. A man of respect. I hope from here on out life treats you with a little kindness."

"Goodbye," I said.

"Good luck," she said.

She pressed the red slip into my hands.

"Take this to remember me by. You're my knight in shining armour."

She kissed me again, quickly this time. And then she was through the door, her hot brown eyes grazing my face as the door closed and the lock clicked.

"Goodbye, Ayesha," I said, going to me knees.

I smelled the slip . . . So sweet . . . The perfume of her sweat, her thoughts, her essence . . . Ayesha, my sweet flower . . . I put my head against the door . . . I'll never make it two years, I thought, kissing the door handle, the locked handle, banging my head against the door softly. I'll never make it, not feeling like this I won't, not with this soft thing working in my guts, eating away at the hardness, not two years, not two minutes . . . Ayesha, baby, I love you I love you . . . And the walls pressed in on me, the walls just seemed to close in tight and suck all the air out of me, all the light, all the hope . . . I was in a closed coffin, no light, no air, no hope . . . And then like some ugly old demon with bad breath, the coffin walls just seemed to press in and vomit up all the stinking horror they'd been storing, all sadness and despair of the institutional life, all the violence and crazy laughter that sounded like the wind, all that crazy laughter stored in those cold hard walls, all that crazy laughter that sounded like a crew of fallen angels, like the wind, it all just came tumbling down, a tidal wave of misery pouring onto my head, into my brain, pounding at my heart and lungs, and the walls closed in and I was in the coffin and the vomit rose, the vomit and laughter and sadness and horror were around me and inside me, squeezing my heart and lungs, filling up my brain, and I couldn't breathe . . . I clawed at my shirt as the echoes sounded in my memory, echoes of boys begging, boys crying, boys screaming, all the tears I'd seen, all the screams I'd heard, all the pain I'd caused, the blood – all of it, a whole universe of hurt – and the dead bodies, they were in there with me too, crowding me, the dead with their cold dead lips and cold dead flesh, blaming me with their cold dead eyes, and I laughed, I laughed, just like the winter wind I laughed. My clothes were strangling me, I couldn't breathe, I was suffocating. I was drowning in a coffin of blood and death and vomit and mad mad laughter. I covered my ears but it did no good, the hyenas were inside of me, laughing insanely and tearing huge putrid chunks out of my rotten soul, and their laughter echo-echo-echoed in all the empty places . . . I had to get out of my clothes. I had to breathe. I tore my buttons, I yanked my shirt and pants and shorts, ripped those clothes off and sucked in huge gulping lungfuls of air. And I lay there naked, naked, smelling that slip, breathing pure sweet hope instead of sour ugly vomit, hope instead of death, hope instead of hell, touching my hardness, breathing hope and life instead of death and vomit . . . Life . . . Ayesha, baby . . . Life . . .

When Shaquille saw me standing there in the kitchen doorway in that red slip, the shiv gleaming in my hand, he laughed.

"Faggot," he said before Piss cut his air supply off, and it was like an echo, an old old song.

I smiled. Oh, man, how I smiled. That smile was feeding off his disrespect and I could feel the sweet evil percolating in my brain, bubbling mad and electric in my veins. I was charged with it.

Piss and the boys, they didn't laugh. They knew that smile. They didn't know my red dress but they knew that smile.

"I promised her I wouldn't hurt you," I said, and my face hurt from smiling. "And I won't. You see, motherfucker, pain is a privilege . . . Pain is for live niggaz . . ."

IV

The Zookeeper stood at the podium in the auditorium next morning. He was gripping the old wood hard.

"Gentlemen," he was a big old black man. Old-school dude. Old and tired, but strong. He'd seen boys come and go and come and die – he was the parade marshal checking off names as motherfuckers marched the one-way road to hell. Nothing seemed to rattle his cage. But today he was off his game.

"Gentlemen," he said. "And I use that form of address reluctantly. Last night while most of you were in this room watching Harrison Ford make the world safe for democracy, we lost a boy. This morning Mrs Wills opened up the steam table to put in the oatmeal and eggs and what did she find? Shaquille Clark in the water. His penis and testicles stuffed in his mouth. Dead? You can't get much deader . . . Now, I assure you, the hoodlums who perpetrated this monstrosity will not get off . . ."

Shit, I thought. There was no way we were gonna get busted. Not with Cisco and Egbert already in the Zoo Crew, each happy and high on some killer smoke, each with a stash of pills to sell, each of them having given thumbs-up to Harrison Ford . . . They were my niggaz now. They knew what happened to Shaquille. How he begged. How he exited soft. How he paid for fucking with Frankie Lawrence. Ain't no one was gonna drop a dime on us. Hell, no, we weren't gonna get popped . . . Not in this life, anyway.

And then it was night again, and I was alone. Naked and alone there in the dark, there in my bed, making love to my own right hand, my faithful friend and lover, my own right hand. I was stroking and squeezing and thinking of Ayesha. It was dark. My bed was off from the others, as befits the king. I had my privacy. All the solitary boys and all the loving couples were asleep and I was smelling that red slip of Ayesha's and making love to myself, listening to the wind blowing mad outside the walls. And then like magic, like going home, I slid into the silk, slid into that cool red silk, and I felt safe, I felt strong. The wind couldn't touch me and there were no walls. I was free.

Did they laugh when I started wearing that red dress full-time? Maybe behind my back they laughed. I didn't give a retarded rat's ass about behind my back. The motherfucking king wants to wear a motherfucking dress, the rest of you mafockas better get with the programme and break out your cell phones and dial Victoria's Secret and order you a dress too. Just make sure it ain't red, motherfucker . . .

The Zookeeper called me in.

"What's with the dress, Frankie?"

I kept my grill shut.

"Frankie, you're smart. Talk to me, man."

Smarter than that. I kept my grill shut.

"The young boys look up to you."

"They better not look up my dress, boss."

"You think you're funny?"

"No, sir."

"Frankie, don't screw up here, man. You've got a chance in life. I've seen smart guys like you turn it around. You could go to college."

Now that was funny. I laughed. I laughed and laughed. Me in college.

"What? And waste a perfectly good million-dollar education the taxpayers already provided me?"

The Zookeeper sighed.

"Take the dress off, man."

I shook my head.

"I like it, boss. I feel comfortable in it."

"I can make you take it off. You want that?"

"You can try," I said. "It'll be more trouble than it's worth. You don't want a war."

"War?" He laughed. "You want war? Nigger, I got the army, I got the National Guard."

"You don't need the publicity, chief."

He played his hole card.

"They'll laugh at you, Frankie. Ruin your rep as a swinging dick. You want that?"

"Let 'em. One laugh per customer."

"Shit," he said, smiling. "You're a ballsy little punk. This is going to be some entertainment. It'll be a pleasure to watch you go down."

The guards laughed. Well, one guard laughed. One guard laughed one time . . . You see, there was a catch to the system, a built in protection factor for us niggaz . . . If you were a full-term baby, any infraction – short of icing a motherfucker inside the joint – was just noted on your jacket. Maybe it caught you a beating from the guards, maybe it bought you a few days locked down in the hole, maybe you were sent to the shrink who'd look at you like some interesting frog shit under a microscope and ask a few dumb-ass questions, maybe, but they couldn't hurt you where you lived, they couldn't add time. You hit age eighteen, you passed go, you were back on the streets . . . So when the guard laughed at me and I kicked him in the jaw and then stomped him some teeth out of his head, I did a week in the hole and then was sent for a little shrink rap.

"Do you like girls, Frankie?" the new white shrink asked, his eyes behind thick glasses like giant undercooked fried eggs with wet green yolks. He was staring at me like I deformed. A freak in a soiled red dress. I could see the nasty smile bubbling ugly under the surface of his ugly rubber lips. Could smell the laugh hiding down there like a mole in a dirty hole.

"I been here since I was six, Doc. What's a girl?"

"Do you love your mother?"

"I ain't even gonna dignify that one."

"Do you have fantasies about making love with girls?"

"Do you, motherfucker?"

"How do you feel about your father?"

"He be dead."

The shrink looked at the file on his desk.

"But it says here –"

"Nigga dead," I said.

The shrink switched tactics.

"Do you like boys, Frankie?"

"Where you goin' with this, Doc? You want to know am I a faggot? Did I ever fuck a boy? That what you askin'?"

"That's what I'm asking, Frankie."

"Listen up, Doc, you a new visitor to the Zoo here, you just on a day-pass – so maybe you don't know the whole score . . ."

"I hear things. I see the results. This isn't my first institution."

"Could be your last, you don't vacate your nose from my business."

"You're a very angry young man. Do you dream at night? Dream about boys?"

"Life's a dream, Doc. Life's a stinkin' nasty bitch of a dream and then you die . . . But you, Doc, you ain't in here with us livin' the dream. You get to go home at night – you know what I'm sayin'? What you do there, I don't know. I don't want to know. Maybe you got some fat old mutant bitch of a wife with a giant hairy snappin' clam between her legs, maybe you got some slim young dude who licks you like an ice-cream cone – maybe you got both of them with lit candles up they ass plus a Pit Bull wearin' a party hat. You got needs, motherfucker – that is if you human. Urges and shit, right? Juice in your balls, right? Loneliness in your flesh, right? And flesh is flesh, right? A warm hole is just that, right? Doesn't matter it's pointed southeast or southwest . . . So what do you think goes on here? Answer your own question."

"Do you wish you were a girl, Frankie?"

"You askin' did any boy ever fuck me, Doc? You askin' me if I'm a bitch? Shit, man, we in Buttfuck City here. We in Cock-In-The-Assadelphia. You read my psych profile. It's all there in black and white. Once, motherfucker. I got fucked once, by the Wannabe-Jackson motherfuckin' Five plus one. They pulled a train on me . . . But that was a long long-ass time ago. I'm a different person now. I wasn't the Cannibal then . . . But the bottom line is this, motherfucker: No one fucks with Frankie Lawrence and no one fucks Frankie Lawrence. Period."

"Don't be angry, Frankie. I'm just paid to ask the questions. Ask questions and make recommendations. Talk to me here. I'm your friend. I'm just trying to understand your . . . fashion statement . . ."

"Listen up, 'friend'. Forget my 'fashion statement'. I got pussy on the brain 24/7. I'm normal that way."

He looked at me. That smile struggling to come out. I could see he wanted to smile. Smile at the red dress. Smile at the bad little nigger in the dirty red dress. Maybe he thought I was a joke. Me and my red dress. Maybe he thought that a boy in a dirty red dress was a joke . . . Maybe he thought I was joking. Maybe he thought all his degrees and shit made him safe. Maybe he was just textbook-smart and life-stupid, 'cause the shit-eating grin broke free on his face.

"Something here funny?" I asked.

"Frankie, the whole thing. The tough-guy act and you sitting there looking like a lingerie model!"

"Doc," I said, shaking my head. "I'd say that comment is downright unprofessional."

"Why did you kick the guard, Frankie?" he asked, still smiling. "The man's jaw is shattered. He lost two teeth."

I raised my kick and put in on the desk, leaned back in my chair. The blood was dried to black and fading, but I'd left the two big front broken fangs embedded in the rubber of the toe.

"I found them."

The doctor looked at the fronts and his smile died fast as an executed nigga.

"Doc, the guard laughed at my red dress. Someone laughs, you lash out. It's the normal reaction. I don't like people laughin' at me. You know what I'm sayin'?"

"Well . . ." He looked in my eyes. "Yeah, I guess I do."

"That's good, Doc," I said, smiling cold. "I wouldn't want to think you were laughin' at me. I mean, I'm a normal guy . . . Except for one thing. Listen up careful, mother-fucker, and take this to the bank: I ain't scared of dyin'."

The doctor turned ashy white and made notes.

"I'll recommend you be allowed to wear your red dress."

"You a good nigga, Doc. For an old white boy . . . In fact . . ." I stood up, leaned across the desk, smiling, my face inches from his. "You my nigga. You my very own private doctor nigga . . . And nigga, right about now I think I could use a prescription for Valium."

Lemme just fast-forward through those last two years of Zoo time. What's there to tell? I sent away for some red dresses by mail and I wore them. I wore red and I ruled the joint . . . And I set up an operational structure for the street. After all, what good were all the lessons of Juvenile Hall if I didn't put them to use? I had that million dollar education you taxpaying mafockas forked your hard-earned cash for and shit if I was gonna disrespect your investment . . .

Piss was out a full twenty months before me. Piss and Gangstahlove ran the show for me out there. They rented apartments. Bought the coke from the Colombians. I took a map and carved the city up into territories. Piss and G-love assigned corners and spots to the boys. They were good niggaz, those boys, true motherfucking blue. Many of them'd grown up under my protection and care, some of them was my elders too. Zoo Crew boys. My niggaz . . .

It was New Jack City out there. The rock business was booming. Niggaz just loved that shit. Poor black niggaz suckin' the welfare tit, rich white niggaz livin' champagne wishes and caviar dreams in fine cribs – they were all stone-cold dog mafockas for the smoking cocaine zap . . . The old dudes out there in the fine clothes and fine cars? Shit, they ran the heroin for Ronny Dewitt . . . Nigga Mortis still the King Kong of Dope in the hood . . . But as far as the rest of the city went, it was every ethnic posse for itself . . . The Shaghettios? Shit, those ravioli-eatin' garlic-breath cappuccino-drinkin' Woptalian motherfuckers didn't have what it took to compete anymore. Them and the Won Tons – Chinese niggaz – had been squeezed out of most of their traditional rackets by fresher, hungrier types . . . I mean, shit, now you had Jamaicans, Ricans, Dominicans, Vietnamese, Cambodians, Laotians, Koreans, Russians, Albanians, Serbs, Greeks – you name it – every motherfucking ethnic posse under the sun was working the dark side of the street, sucking cash from they own people's sorry immigrant asses. And all those hard motherfuckers from those hard motherfucking countries make us home-grown niggaz look soft with our *Big Macs* and government handouts. Hard motherfuckers from hard motherfucking countries who come up eating rats and breadcrumbs and wiping their asses with their fingers, they all come to this country and see that money tree blooming with cash and they eyes light up like Christmas morning . . . Grow up with nothing, nothing scares you . . .

But the rockpile was wide open. Gangs of hungry young-bloods springing up right and left. And the Zoo Crew was

right in there with the best of them . . . My boys were cold
and hard, ruthless, never gave an inch. Pluck that easy
money off the tree. Money tree ripe with fruit. Shake it and
take it. Pure easy money just waiting for anyone with the
balls to step up and take it. And motherfucker, under my
red dress I had balls the size of Kansas City.

So I did my time. Saw Mama less and less now, now that
she was living with whatever-that-motherfucker's-name-
was. I knew she was worried about me, me and my red
dress. I saw it in her eyes the times she came. I told her it
was cool. Gave her a history lesson. Told her all about Mel
Gibson and *Braveheart* and all those bad Scottish motherfuckers in their plaid skirts. But, really, I didn't give a fuck.
Not about what she thought, not about what anyone
thought. Thoughts untranslated into action can't hurt
you. All I wanted was respect. Man without respect not
a man. As long as I was respected, I was cool. And respect is
born of fear and fear breeds respect and mafockas fear crazy
. . . Was I crazy? Hell, no. No more than you if you was in
my shoes. If you was in my dress, haha – hey there, don't
you laugh now, nigga. I see that smile breaking ugly on your
face . . . Listen up, you, I wasn't crazy, I was bad. Crazy is a
momentary thing – like when you take a life out of emotion.
I've had my crazy moments. Maybe doing Shaq was crazy.
But it also solidified my hold on the Zoo . . . It was smart
and it was bad. And bad is just bad. I'm taking you to school
here, teaching you the facts of life – a nigga be bad enough
he get away with any damn thing. You take that basketball
nigga *Dennis Rodman. He wear dresses* too. And that bad
championship nigga got the last laugh, he laughing all the
way to the bank. All the way to fame and motherfucking
fortune. And motherfucker, that's where I was headed too.
Destination Fame and motherfucking Fortune. Shit, after
I'm dead and gone you still be talking about me. Me and my
red dress. You can take that to the bank. And when you get
to the bank, look for a bad nigga in a red dress . . . Or look
for the ghost of a bad nigga in a red dress. That'll be me,
motherfucker. Counting my money and laughing at your
ugly ass.

VI

"Adios, motherfucker," I said to Juvenile Hall from the back seat of the armoured black Benz as we rounded the corner, putting the old cold walls behind us.

G-love was driving. Piss was with me in back. Between us on the fresh baby-butt-soft black leather that smelled of new money, a bright butterscotch-skinned honey named Kali. My dress was hiked up around my waist and Kali's silky semi-pro grill was working overtime. Wet and wild. Liquid lickability factor through the roof. Maybe sixteen years old.

"Happy birthday to you, Frankie," she said, coming up for air, planting a kiss on my lovestick.

"Yeah," I said. "Blow that candle for me, baby."

It was January the twenty-ninth. I was eighteen. Eighteen and free. Eighteen and free on the back seat of a silent black Benz with smoked windows. A butterscotch honey named Kali blowing my candle . . . And here's the CNN: freedom air didn't taste no damn different than Zoo air. No different. I felt exactly the same as an hour earlier back when the Zookeeper was spilling me the canned adios lecture about accepting responsibility . . . You see, geography, walls, those bitches just an illusion. There's no real inside and no real outside. That's a fact. The road to hell is in your head. And if you walkin' that road, you walkin' that road. Just follow your feet. No detour from the facts. And when destiny calls, that nasty third-class ho calls collect . . . And it ain't like you got a choice, *nigga* just gots to accept the charges . . . Now that's responsibility.

I'd told Mama not to pick me up and not to expect me living back home. I'd visit the old lady – pretend I was kickin' it there if any authorities checked up on me – but I wasn't gonna actually put my head on no pillow there. Not while whatever-that-motherfucker's-name-was was with her . . .

We drove the city. That fly gangstah bitch Kali now high in the saddle, getting busy, working me with that slippery slidy velvet crotch glove, thumping and bumping and grinding, riding the pony to Paradise as I looked out the window and smoked a cigarette . . .

The hood hadn't modified a fraction since I'd been inside. Nothing but poor folk and wild dogs. Desperation and the wind. Winos and junkies and homeless mother-fuckers waiting for gold or death to fall out of the sky. Candy wrappers and losing lottery tickets and empty heroin bags blowing dead in the cold wind. Paper sailboats in a sea of dust and grey decay . . . Grey sky, grey buildings, grey faces. Colour and life sucked out of faces by the wind. Empty crack vials and dead syringes glittering like false promises in the gutters . . . The geography of poverty. Hopelessness reigned supreme.

There were things I wanted. A whole shopping list of things I wanted. I wanted power, I wanted money. I wanted folk to know my name. I wanted people to beg me for favours, for drugs. For rock, for heroin . . . I wanted females, females of every colour and shape. I wanted to eat them, to fuck them, to make them laugh and shiver and whine with pleasure. I wanted to blow my nose in their hair and make them cry and sigh and whisper my name with love and fear. I wanted to pop my nut a million times in a million different pussies. I wanted your wife, your girlfriend, your sister – I wanted your mother if she was fine . . . I wanted cars, cars of every make and model. I wanted to drive fast, fast as the motherfucking wind. I wanted cars, I wanted girls. I wanted fine champagne and uncut cocaine, Hawaiian herb and big screen TVs. I wanted toasted bread and clean mattresses. I wanted silk sheets and silk bitches. I wanted . . .

"You find her?" I asked as Kali pogoed up and down, sweat on her brow, making freaky yipping noises.

"Easy," said Piss. "Ayesha got a baby now. Her husband work in a damn supermarket. Stockboy."

"She happy?" I asked, squeezing a ripe Kali chest mango.

"She poor," Piss said. "Poor can't be truly happy."

"Tell me somethin' I don't know."

"Word," said Gangstahlove as we passed two scabby winos playin' tug-of-war over the dregs in a bottle. The loser crashed to the ground and watched the winner upend the bottle, two final drops hittin' the nigga's dry grey tongue.

I looked out the back window as that gymnastic Kali drew the major gush out of me. The loser was swinging a piece of wood at the winner's head. And as I popped, the winner's head popped red . . . Winner now the loser . . .

I'll tell you what it was I really wanted. All that other shit was just shits and grins, magazines in a wating room . . .

You know what I wanted. I wanted Ayesha.

Mama's toenails needed cutting. Mama's hair needed fixing. Mama's face was looking saggy and ragged, tired and cracked as an old shoe.

The apartment was same. On the surface it was changed. Different furniture, different paint on the walls, a different smell. No more little-boy-with-his-mama smell, now it had a man and woman smell. Different on the surface, but at the core it was the same. Same sadness, same desperation. Same poverty. It was the same, yeah, but I wasn't.

It was just before lunchtime and Mama was still chillin' in her robe, fresh from the sack. Me, I was in my ankle-length black chinchilla coat.

"Frankie, baby!" She hugged me hard. "Happy birthday! Welcome home!"

"Yeah yeah, Mama. Don't break my ribs . . ."

"Baby, it's good to see you."

"Mama, what's goin' on here? Why you not gettin' ready for work?" I knew she was on the swing shift.

Her face fell. "I lost my job, Frankie."

"I'll give you money, Mama. I got stupid mad money."

She licked her lips as I flashed the roll of hundreds Piss had pressed in my hand soon as I exited the Zoo.

"I can't take it," she said. But I could see she wanted to.

"Where's what's-his-name?" I asked.

"His name is Larry, Frankie. Your father's name is Larry."

"Where's what's-his-name?"

"He's working."

"When he get home? I wanna talk to the motherfucker. Give him some cash. Straighten his ass out."

"He got him a church service after work. He's workin' construction, but he got a little storefront he preaches out of."

"What's-his-name's a motherfuckin' preacher?"

She nodded.

"He a preacher, he oughta be bankin' the clink. Get him a television show. That's a good hustle."

"Your father's not a hustler. Whatever he gets he gives away. He's a righteous preacher."

"You shittin' me."

"Frankie, it's God's truth."

"Damn," I said. "Motherfucker accepted the collect call."

"Frankie, show some respect for the Lord."

"The Lord," I snorted. "What'd that skinny-ass bottom-of-the-deck-dealin' shoot-from-the-hip white nigga ever do for black folk? Pass us his motherfuckin' crown of thorns, that's what."

"Frankie, watch your language."

"Mama, I'm beyond language." I peeled her some bills. "Go fix yourself up. Get yourself a new dress. Buy you a magic red dress, okay? I want a smile on that pretty face."

As we made the rounds, touring the city, Piss never introduced me, me in my floor-length fur over a thigh-high red silk, but you could tell the motherfuckers knew who I was. The legend had arrived before I had. And motherfuckers'd been warned. The Cannibal wore red. Don't laugh. If breathing was a function you cared about, don't laugh.

We stopped at corners, at crackhouses, in a club we owned where we drank champagne and cognac. In the back room I put the wood to a *nasty little Janet Jackson-lookin' freak* whose name I never got.

"Fuck me good, bad daddy," she said. "Fuck me good with that nice big dick you got under that nice red dress."

"Toyota," I said. "You asked for it, you got it. Toyota."

*   *   *

The factory. That's where they cooked the coke. Behind steel doors, that's where they packaged it. Armed guards on the street, one on the stairs, one at the door. Only females working the labour jobs. A crew of two cookers working the stoves, cooking the shit up nice, and five packers sitting at a table packing rocks into vials, vials into bags, bags that runners took to the corners, to the houses . . . All overseen by Julio the Blade. A stone-cold wizard with cutlery, in his mid-twenties, he'd done a three-spot in the Zoo for attempted murder back when I was a ten-and-under. Attempted murder? Shit, there was nothing "attempted" about it. If Julio the Blade wanted you out of the equation – simple math, you was out. That Puerto Rican mafocka could carve his initials on a nigga's chest faster'n you can say Swiss Army.

The females cooking and packing were naked, their clothes locked up so they couldn't rip us off – which no doubt they would given half a motherfuckin' chance. The heat in the place was on high. Bitches were sweatin'. They were allowed to smoke a pipe every two hours of their eight-hour shift, but that was it. Smoke a few pipes and take some shit home at a discount, but work time was just that. They worked. Bitches earned their head-candy.

"Whussup, Piss?" Julio dropped fingers with the big man. And then he saw me. "Frankie? Bienvenida, Cannibal! Gimme some love!"

He hugged me.

"Lookin' good, m'nigga!"

"*Doublemint Gum, Julio*," I said, quoting the ancient ad starring exact mirror-image twins. "Keepin' your ass busy here?"

"You know it, bro. Suckas out there smoke the rock so fast we barely got time to shit or go blind or eat a slice of pizza . . ."

Julio went over to the changing room and let seven new naked females into the room. They sat on a couch. All sizes, all shapes, all ages. All naked.

"Yo, Frankie. It's shift change time. You want to do the honours?"

"Nah," I said. "I'll watch."

"You know the drill," Julio said to the females.

The bitch packing on the far end of the table stood up. Her spot at the table was instantly taken by one of the couch bitches who didn't miss a beat and stuffed a rock into a plastic vial, then put that vial into a plastic bag with others. The table was shiny with plastic bags and rock cocaine. Bags full of vials. Money tree ripe with fruit. Bitches packing away like machines, brown fingers moving fast, titties bobbling, sweat rolling down their brown bodies like widow's tears. The room smelled of coke and sweat and pussy.

"C'mere, girlfriend," Julio said, snapping on a pair of surgical gloves. "Gotta watch these bitches like a hawk, Frankie. They got hidey-holes everywhere."

He checked her oral cavity. Clean.

He checked her frontal cavity. Clean.

He checked her rear-end cavity . . .

"Hey," he said, mad, looking deep and reaching. "What's this?"

He pretended to pluck a quarter out of her ass.

"Bitch be shittin' money!"

Piss and I laughed. Julio grinned.

"Okay," he said, slapping the empty ass. "Next."

We watched him work. He was fast, he was good. And the bitches knew the drill. Soon's one stood up, one sat her ass down.

"Julio," I said, when the shift was all changed, as we drank a beer away from the work area. "I got something for the Blade."

"Bueno," he said, smiling, patting his pocket. "Who is it."

"A nobody," I said. "A stockboy at a supermarket . . ."

Colombia is a fertile fucking country. Don't believe what the government tells you 'bout the war on drugs. Ain't no war on drugs. Drugs just a weapon in the war on niggaz. And Colombia be the nation's partner in the war on niggaz.

Like the coke, the heroin comin' out of Colombia was fine. Strong. Muscular. Fine product. Competitive product. Less travel and less middlemen than the Asian shit.

As Piss and I watched G-love and the boys cut and package that good Colombian heroin, I knew: Ronny Dewitt's days as the King of Dope were numbered. Zoo Crew on the way up. Rigor mortis for Nigger Mortis. Adios, Ronny.

The little white boy hassling the doorman at the B Street crackhouse when we showed took one look at Piss and shit, he nearly pissed his pants.

We'd been still cruising the town that first night, checking out the spots, letting the niggaz know that the Cannibal was in town and that all work and no play would be rewarded with hard cash and friendship.

A fucking limousine was pulled up out front the crackhouse. What kind of conspicuous dumb-ass white motherfuckers ride the hood in a white stretch limo?

"But I've been here before, sir." The white boy begged Piss. "We're cool . . ."

The doorman looked out the slot in the heavy steel door.

"That true?" asked Piss. "You know the gentleman?"

"Never seen him," said the doorman.

"I was here, I swear."

Motherfucker goin' to a crackhouse in a limo? An invitation to the heat, invitation to get taken down.

"Who's in the limo, Bubba?" I asked.

"Friends," said the skinny white boy. "Look, bro, we got cash to spend. We wanna cop five hundred dollars worth."

"Bring your friends in," I said. "And tell the limo you'll call for a pick-up when you all nice and crispy."

I was watching the white kids piping up and lemme tell you, those suburban punks was as doggy for the rock as any broom-pushin' janitor on payday. And there were a few of those there too. All of them, black and white, rich and poor, sprawled out on old mattresses sucking hits like Hoover vacuums. The white kids'd smoked their five hundred dollars, were moving up on the seven-hundred-dollar mark, all their ready cash, but I didn't give a platinum-plated shit about the money. I was watching the blonde. The blonde bitch with the blonde curls.

Now's a good moment for a quick rundown on my relationship with the drug. You see, me being born a crack baby, undersize and jonesing for the buzz from the jump, I steered clear of the shit. I sniffed a line now and then, but if I smoked it, it was always just a rock or two mixed with herb. I wouldn't let myself become a pipe jockey. No way, José.

The thing about rock is that it wipes out colour and class. Everyone equal behind the pipe. The democracy of compulsion. Money and need the common denominator. And now that the white kids were out of money, their need was through the roof.

I'd been watching them – watching the bitch to be exact. Watching them smoke – watching the bitch smoke. Watching them laugh – watching the bitch laugh. Watching them kiss – watching the bitch kiss. Yeah, watching her kiss . . . I was sitting there, my dick hard under my red silk under my fur coat, watching the blonde bitch with blonde curls kiss the pushy little front boy she called Morton . . . I watched her kiss him and I smiled . . .

"I want another hit, Morton," the blonde bitch whined, breaking off the clinch.

"We don't have any more money," said the boy.

"Give them your watch," said blondie.

We was sitting there, me and Piss, silent, watching.

The white boy came over and handed me a fresh Rolex. It was real. I could tell. Had the weight, the shine, the silence.

"How much?" he asked me, looking over at the girl, pissed.

"Nice copy like this?"

"Copy?" he almost screamed. "Dude, it's real."

"Fake shit like this you can buy from an African brother on the street for twenty. Maybe ten if he ain't had his foo-foo yet that day."

"Dude . . ." He had the beggar's whine in his voice.

I nodded at the brother holding the house stash.

"Give them four bottles, Terrence," I said.

"Four bottles!" Morton whined. "That's twenty dollars!"

"Take it or leave it. Leave it and you leave here."

It was a done deal, I knew. The blonde bitch was licking her lips. Blue eyes bright and sick with the rock fever.

"Do it!" she cried. "Tell your father you got ripped off!"

"Yeah," I said. "Tell Daddy Bigbucks the bad *niggaz* ripped you off."

Morton was about to be funny-style. I shook my head.

"Careful," I said to him, passing the watch to Piss.

Morton sighed and nodded his head, looked sadly at his watch on Piss's redwood wrist. Shit, the band wouldn't even close.

"What time is it, Piss?" I asked.

"Party time, bro."

"Party down, friends," I said.

The blonde was already piping it up. She was a freak for the shit, her long legs were loose from the buzz. She looked over and smiled at me. Yeah, this was gonna be fun.

The new bottles were finished now.

"One more," she said to me. "On the house."

"No freebies," I said. "What else you got?"

I looked her up and down. Licked my lips.

"Let's go," said the boy, getting up. And the other kids got up too. All except the blonde.

"Don't be such a party pooper, Morton," she said with a pout.

"Let's go, Mary." Morty was nervous. The kids were at the door.

Mary didn't want to go.

"We're tapped out, Mary."

"Give him a credit card." She giggled.

"Get serious," he said.

"I take credit cards," I said, winking at Mary.

"You have a machine?" Morton asked.

"No, bitch, I 'take' credit cards."

Piss laughed. Mary laughed. The other white kids giggled nervously.

"Just fuckin' with you." I nodded at Piss. "Give her a hit," I said. "For the road. And make it Hollywood style."

Piss smiled. He packed a stem with a rock.

"Come here, Mary," he said.

Mary stood, wobbly on those long legs. Morton grabbed her arm.

"Mary, let's go. I don't like this."

"Fuck you," she said to him, coming and squatting in front of us. Her skirt hiked high, panties visible. White thighs open, coat over her arm. I could see her pee-pee pressing wet against her panties. Could almost count the silky snatch hairs.

Piss hit the stem with a Bic. Sucked and sucked and sucked, coke crackling like a baby bonfire, Mary staring, blue eyes mesmerized, as Piss sucked that smoke deep. And then he reached a big hand and took that curly blonde head and brought it close. Blondie knew what to do. She closed her eyes, Hollywood style, and kissed Piss, Piss blowing smoke into her grill, filling her lungs as she sucked, him licking her lips, the endless smoking fade-out Hollywood kiss, and she tumbled back on her ass, a smile on her face, hair smoking, lips smoking sweet like a hot gun: pure crack ho bliss.

"*Gone With The Wind,*" I said.

Morton's face was a blushing mask of pink anger.

"We're going, Mary." He pulled her to her feet. Mary grinning goofy.

I nodded at the doorman to open sesame. Mary wobbly on her pins, her brain spinning.

"Thanks," she said to me and Piss.

"Anytime," I said. "You come back anytime and ask for Frankie."

"Thanks, Frankie," she said, looking at me curious-like.

I smiled, passed her a bottle of rock to clinch things. She tucked it in her bra like any good little crack ho.

"Beats the shit out of a mothball, Mary, don't it?"

As I lay there in bed that night in my new crib, watching Kali and the white girl Madrid lick each other, the city twinkling pretty as a jewelry showcase out the window – the jeweller with a gun to his head, the gems ready to be snatched – I thought about Mary. She'd known who I was. As the door closed, the recognition light bulb had popped on in her head. She'd known . . . Mary, little golden Mary . . . She'd be back, uh-huh, and when she came back, I had a surprise for that fine little rich bitch. Oh yeah, little golden Mary was in for a real lesson in democracy.

"Hello, Ayesha," I said.

"My God, Frankie?"

"It's me, Ayesha, all growed up."

She came out of the shitty little apartment, into my arms and hugged me. A baby started crying behind her. Looked like the same shitty little apartment I'd come up in. Shitty little ghetto apartments all look the same. Look the same and feel the same. Ayesha deserved better. Hell, I thought, it won't be long now.

"You still married, Eesh?" As if I didn't know.

"Still married, Frankie," she smiled and showed me her ring, still heavy and big and cheap, soon to be meaningless.

"Come on in," she said. "Rasheed be home soon."

I went in. She sat me down.

She took the baby in her arms, rocked it, shushed it up fast.

"How'd you find me, Frankie?"

"I asked around for the most beautiful girl in the world and all roads led here."

She smiled. "You still sweet."

"For you, Ayesha, always."

"You graduate?" she asked.

"With honours," I said. "Phi Beta Cappa."

Phi Beta *Cap-a-nigga*.

"I told Rasheed what you did for me . . ." Then her face fell. "Frankie, my grandma Hortense, she told me that the boy who tried to mess with me . . . I heard he . . ."

"Wasn't me, Ayesha. It was unrelated. I swear. I let him slide. I swear . . ."

"You swear?"

"I promised you I wouldn't hurt him."

"Well, I'm relieved." She looked at her watch. "Rasheed should a been home by now."

"I'll take you both out for a fine meal," I said.

"What about the baby?"

"Uncle Frankie pay for a babysitter." I pulled a wad of cash.

"We couldn't. It'll be our treat. Rasheed workin' steady and today's Friday. Payday."

Payday. The eagle shits on Friday. Niggaz gotta be careful when they step in eagle shit. That shit's slippery . . .

"Frankie," she asked, all concerned. "Where you getting money? You working already?" Her eyes took in my fur coat. "And that fur . . .? Can I take your coat?"

That's when the phone rang.

"May I?" I took the baby. Looked into the little motherfucker's eyes. He had her eyes. Poor little fucker. I knew what it was like to grow up without a father.

"He's called Kareem," she said, then picked up the phone, spoke into it. "Hello . . . Yes, that's me . . ."

Her eyes went big and scared and she looked over at me . . . And as I tickled Kareem, she screamed.

Poor Rasheed. Niggaz gotta be careful on payday . . . As I said before, if Julio the Blade wanted you out of the equation . . . Simple math – minus one. Ayesha, sweet Ayesha, was a single mother.

Talking about single mothers . . . Mama was out. It was a couple days later. I'd paid for Rasheed's funeral. Paid a month's rent for Ayesha. I'd held her hand when she buried her old man. Yup, single motherhood was tough as a motherfucker. She'd need all the help she could get . . .

"Where's Mama?" I asked the old dude.

"Boy," he said, looking at my fur with contempt. "I don't want you sniffin' round here."

"Where's Mama?" I asked again. Piss gave the old nigga the cold one-eyed stare.

"If I knew I wouldn't tell you. I can smell the evil on you hoodlums like blood in a slaughterhouse. You stay away from her, you cross-dressin' fool."

"Or what?"

"Or the Lord shall smite thee."

"Let the nigga try. One smite per customer."

"That's all it takes, smartmouth. One strike and you out."

Piss and I just laughed.

"Hello, Frankie," said the white plainclothes waiting for me outside my crib later that day. "Your doorman wouldn't let me up."

"Those his orders, chief. The only white dudes allowed up are Jesus and Santa Claus. And those blue-moon niggaz steer clear of this part of town."

"I could get a warrant."

"For what?" I asked. "And let's see some ID."

"For what?" he asked, pulling a badge. "For the fuckin' whole menu, asshole."

"Detective Charles," I said. "Name's familiar."

"You don't remember?"

"I usually remember bad shit, and man, you smell like somethin' runnin' out of a sick dog's ass. But I can't say I remember you."

The dude was making weird shapes with his hands. He nodded to the shadow on the wall. And the years peeled back like a rotten banana peel.

"That's a lion, Frankie. The lion that eats the nigger. Remember the shadows? The shadow puppets on the precinct wall?"

"Shit," I said, remembering. "You that nice motherfucker who took me in back in the day."

"That was me. But I'm not so nice anymore and neither are you from what I hear. And I hear everything."

"So, you wanna shoot the shit, motherfucker? Talk over old times like some barbershop homies? Catch up and shit?"

"Sorry, baby barracuda. I got a message for you."

"So deliver it, messenger boy."

"Ronny Dewitt says, 'Go back to the rockpile, Candy Balls. Or else.'"

"Else what, man?"

"Else?" The cop laughed. "Else he'll fuck you where you live."

"That it?" I asked. Piss had the car waiting.

"One more thing," he said. "Do me a favour and open your coat."

"Sure," I said, opening up. "For Nigger Mortis's pet cop, I give a prime-time fashion show . . . You like?"

"Now I seen it all," he said, spitting. "A gangstah in a red dress."

And then he laughed. I walked to the car, his laugh eating at me from inside my brain. Echoing.

"One laugh per customer," I said back at him.

And the motherfucker just laughed.

"That's two," I said under my breath. "Over the limit."

"Hello, Mary," I said to the blonde as she piped up on a mattress in the crackhouse. "I'm glad you made it back."

"Frankie," she said, giggling goofy. "The same little Frankie I used to play with."

"I know," I said, laughing with her, sitting. "It's a small damn funny damn world, ain't it?"

"No shit," she said. "How's your mother?"

"She fine," I said. "Forgive me if I don't ask the same after yours."

Mary laughed.

"She really did a number on you. I'm surprised you remember."

I remembered alright. Something hurts bad enough, it sticks with you like stink on shit.

"So Mary," I said. "Let's celebrate new times."

"New times," she said, stuffing a rock in the pipe.

"The party's on me," I said, showing her a rock the size of the Ritz in a plastic bag. Rock the size of . . . a giant mothball. "Let's take a ride."

"Cool," she said, getting up, taking my arm, smiling at the poor niggaz piping up. "This is so much cooler than hanging out with college kids."

"I'm takin' you to school, honey," I said as we headed arm in arm for the door. "Education is everywhere. Just gotta be open to it."

She was open to it. Wide open. And I was pounding that tight white blueblood "pee-pee" in the back of the

Mercedes like there was no tomorrow, no yesterday, like there was only now now now now now.

"Yes yes yes yes yes!!!!!" she screamed. "More!"

I slowed up, pulled out to the gate. Packed a rock in the pipe, put the pipe in her grill, hit it with a Bic. She sucked greedily. And when her lungs were full – WHOOOSH – I slammed home.

"Frankie-ee-ee-eeeeee!" she moaned, eyes rolling. "Man, I think I love you."

"That's good, Mary," I said, not a speck of back-at-ya love in my voice.

"Frankie," she said, lounging in her crack ho bliss.

"Yeah?"

"I'd do anything to feel this way always."

"Yeah?"

"Yeah."

"She yours," I said to the pack of winos living under the bridge. Maybe ten of them ragged sad motherfuckers.

"She sick?" asked the head nigga, a giant slobberpuss so dirty you couldn't tell he was black or white.

"Sick?" Piss threw Mary on the mattress. She was high as a motherfucker. High on dope, high on rock. Stinking of puke and sex. Moaning for another hit. "This is some fine high-class society pussy. She just love to party. Ain't nothin' sick about that. Right, Mary?"

"Gimme a hit," she moaned.

The big bum looked at me, looked at Piss.

"What are you waitin' for?" asked Piss. "That's your invitation into high society, nigga."

"Go ahead," I said. "She all yours."

The big motherfucker drooled and went to his knees, opening his pants.

Piss and I got back into the car. And as we drove away, the big motherfucker tore Mary's clothes off and got busy. And the other bums touched themselves. Waiting their turn.

"Democracy in action," I said.

Ayesha still in black. Mourning. We were walking along the river. Piss watching our backs from the car.

"Your mama loves Kareem," she said. "It's nice she's watchin' him for me."

"Mama's a sweetheart."

Ayesha sighed.

"They haven't caught the guy yet," she said. "Rasheed dead for a stupid two-hundred dollars."

"They might never catch him," I said. "And even if they do . . . I know you still hurtin', Ayesha. I know you still love him . . . but . . ."

"But what, Frankie?"

"I don't got no right to say this . . . But you gotta think about Kareem . . . And you gotta . . ."

"What, Frankie?"

"No," I said. "I shouldn't say it."

"Say it, Frankie."

"You gotta start thinkin' about you."

"Thanks for caring, Frankie Lawrence," she said, taking my hand and looking at me with those beautiful eyes. "You're a real gentleman."

"No way, nigga!" screamed the naked fifteen-year-old strapped in the chair in the crackhouse basement. "I ain't talkin'!"

Piss gave him a medium strong backhand cross the face. His nose exploded bloody and the little motherfucker screamed.

"You broke my nose!" he wailed.

"Give your ugly monkey face some character," I said.

Piss laughed. I didn't. The little motherfucker and his crew had come at us hard in a Cherokee, spraying our war zone Benz with semi-auto bullets.

We'd followed them, cut them off, taken two out with our 9's and then pulled this punk from the wreck. The driver was left crunched like a dead candy wrapper in the front seat.

"Now I ain't fuckin' around," I said to the little nigga. "Tell me where Nigger Mortis holed up."

"I talk I walk?"

"You talk you walk," I said. "My word is my bond."

"All right," he said . . . And then he broke off an address.

"That wasn't so hard," I said, cutting his ropes. "Now get y'ass up."

"I can go?" he asked, surprised, flexing his wrists, wiping his bloody face.

"Nigga," I said. "I said you can walk. Now walk."

He walked over for his clothes. I nodded to Piss. Piss kicked his clothes cross the room.

"Have a nice walk?" I asked. Piss laughed.

"Lyin'-ass nigga!" the kid spat out. "Lyin'-ass nigga in a red dress! Fuckin' faggot!"

I was over there in one big step, slammed that naked mafocka against the wall, his teeth breaking and tumbling onto the floor like snake-eyes dice. I rammed my Beretta right up where the sun don't shine.

"Faggot this!" I said, pulling the trigger, the caps barely muffled by his skinny ass.

"Motherfucker," he said soft, as his insides turned to creamed corn and poured out his smoking ass as he slid down the wall into a broken heap. "Shit . . ."

"For the last time," I said, wiping my Beretta in his hair.

"Hello, Mama," I said. I'd been waiting on whatever-that-motherfucker's-name-was to leave. Sitting in the ride and waiting. Had a crew staking out Ronny Dewitt cross town. Ronny hanging tight in his fortress. Getting reports about my boys taking out his boys, reports that some of his boys had jumped ship to my side. Old-fashioned street war.

Mama opened the door wider and let me in.

"Mama, you supposed to be over with Ayesha. Helpin' with the baby."

"I know, Frankie. I'll go soon. I'm not feelin' so good today."

"Mama," I said. "You don't look so good. What's-his-name treatin' you bad?"

"Your father's name is Larry, Frankie." She sighed.

"Whatever," I said. "Mama, I want you to move out of here."

She wandered over to the bathroom. I heard her making pee-pee.

"Frankie," she called. "You see the TV news? That little

white girl Mary whose folks I used to work for? They found her dead in the river. Drugged and raped and beaten to death."

"That so . . .? Mama, I'm gonna have to get a place for you and Ayesha away from all this. A nice place. A nice house outside the city. Place with a washer-dryer. You won't never have to go outside again you don't want to. You and Ayesha both be safe."

"Frankie, I can't move," she said, coming out. "I can't leave your father."

I smelled her breath as she came close and looked me in the eyes. Breath bad. Sour with wine, stanky with . . .

"Mama, you ain't smokin' rock . . .?"

"Frankie . . ."

"Mama, say it ain't so. You know that shit is poison for us."

"Just a little, baby. Just a little when the blues get me down."

"What's-his-name knows?"

"He knows, but he stickin' by me like I stuck by him. Your father's a good man."

"What'd that nigga ever do for you and me, Mama? 'Cept get his ass locked up and leave us holdin' a bag of hurt."

"You don't know what he did," she said. "Maybe if I told you . . ."

"I know all about it, Mama. I know he tried to take down Ronny Dewitt. I know he smoked Ronny's boy Lucius. I know he took five caps. I know I know I know. And it don't change a damn thing. He wasn't there for us."

"He was there for me, Frankie. You don't understand. Me and Ronny . . . See, him and me . . . I was confused . . . Your daddy and Ronny was partners back then, best friends, and I was Ronny's girl first and then I fell for your daddy hard . . . We got married . . . But Ronny he had me hooked on the pipe . . . Your daddy was tryin' to save me . . ."

"That's History Channel shit, Mama. Nigger Mortis goin' down."

"Frankie, promise me you won't mess with Ronny. He don't take no prisoners."

*   *   *

Detective Charles was actually whistling. I thought that shit was strictly movie-time macho. But the nigga was whistling and workin' his fronts with a toothpick as he left the restaurant. I'd bribed the parking lot jockey to let me in his car.

"Have a nice dinner?" I asked, putting my 9 against the motherfucker's head as he drove.

"Well, what have we got here?" he said looking in the mirror with a smile.

"A situation," I said. "Keep driving."

Later, Ayesha and I were eating a simple dinner. Kareem was sleeping a deep peaceful baby sleep. I finished my chicken and greens and wiped my plate clean with an extra slice of white bread.

"You always were generous with the starch, Eesh."

"You always were a funny man, Frankie."

Yeah, I thought, funny as a motherfucker. But old Detective Charles wasn't laughing. Or whistling . . . Or anything.

Ayesha smiled at me. She still wore black. I still wore red. I helped her wash the dishes. I was whistling as I washed the dishes.

"You want to go to a club, tonight, Eesh? Go somewhere nice?"

She shook her head.

"Frankie, thank your mother again for helping with the baby."

"It was her pleasure," I said. "She isn't workin' now and it makes her happy."

"She's not exactly happy, Frankie. Not with you. Not with what you're doing these days."

"What am I doin' these days?"

"Frankie, we ain't exactly stupid . . ."

"I'm clockin' dollars, Eesh. Bankin' the clink."

"You're playing with fire."

"I'm wearin' asbestos. This red dress keep me safe."

I smiled. Ayesha didn't.

"She told me about it."

"About what."

"About the dress. How you come up . . . Everything."

"Ayesha," I said. "Don't play psychologist on me. What's past is past and that's just the way it is."

The words came out of my grill, sure, but I didn't really believe them. The past is a resilient motherfucker. Pop right up like a jack-in-the-crack and hit a mafocka in the face with a shit and whipped cream pie. The History Channel feed into CNN and vice motherfuckin' versa . . . They both owned by the same corporation.

"Yeah," she said. "But new stuff comes along, changes everything."

"New? Like what."

"Like . . ." She came close. "Like this," she said, kissing me.

I kissed back, tasting love and hope instead of . . .

"I'm falling in love with you, Frankie."

I looked in her eyes.

"I'd do anything for you, Ayesha."

"Anything?"

"Anything."

"Then take off that damn red dress, Frankie Lawrence. Take it off and take me somewhere nice."

We went somewhere nice. We stayed home and went to heaven.

The cell phone wailing broke a peaceful sleep.

"Talk," I said.

"Frankie," said Piss. "Your Mama –"

"Black Jimmy and Little Uzi and Cisco watchin' Mama."

"Man, they got jacked by Ronny's boys. Cisco still alive, but barely. Called in on his cell. Your daddy shot up too. Ambulance took him and Cisco."

"Mama?"

"Snatched. But she alive."

"Okay," I said, taking a deep breath. "Where she now?"

"She inside Ronny's."

I left Rocco the Wop on guard outside Ayesha's door. His cell phone on speed dial to me.

"Rocco, anything smells the littlest bit off, you call me."

"You got it, Frankie."

I took the stairs, careful. Nothing. G waiting in the car.

"Ronny's place, G, and make it now."

Outside Ronny's. Quiet.

"Where's Piss?" I asked Smitty. My 9 in hand, ready to rock.

"Piss gone to pick you up," Smitty said.

"But I had my ride! What the fuck's goin' on? Piss knew G was waitin' on me . . ."

My cell phone rang.

"Talk," I said.

"It's fallin' apart on you, boy."

"Who this?"

"Motherfuckin' destiny callin', Red Dress."

"We can deal, Ronny."

"I'm callin' the shots, faggot. Your Mama sure do love to get busy. Freaky little thang. An oldie but goldie."

I heard the cold laughter.

"Leave her go, Ronny. I give you back your turf plus a hundred grand."

He laughed.

"You comin' up, Frankie?"

"Lemme talk to her," I said.

"Frankie?" Mama.

"Mama, you cool?"

"Frankie, Ayesha in trouble—"

Ronny took the phone from Mama.

"Looking forward to meetin' you, boy. But sorry about your bitch." The laughter was cold, man. Cold as the winter wind.

And then he clicked off.

We drove fast back to Ayesha's. Guns in hand. Took the stairs. In the hall, Rocco the Wop dead, knife in the heart, blade broke off inside. The door was open.

I heard a moan, like a wounded animal, a deep moan . . . Shit, it came from me.

Ayesha . . .

Ayesha . . .

Ayesha . . . Wearin' that eternal smile, throat laid open ear to ear, hanging by a thread of spine. Lovely honey lying there still and cold in a pool of blood, holding her baby, his poor little head crushed like an egg . . .

I laid my fur coat over them, closed my eyes.

"Damn, Frankie," said G-love. "What you cryin' about? You seen bodies before."

"You never been in love, G?"

"Love? Damn, bro, that's sucker action. Bad muhfuk-kahs don't fall for bitches. That some dangerous shit."

G was right. Love was sucker action, dangerous, bad for the health. Oughta put warning labels on that emotion . . . I'd loved Ayesha – shit, I love her still – but it had made me a sucker, made me soft. And Mama . . .? Hell, she was my original bitch. Tried to soften my ass up with the damn dress . . .

"Yo, G," I said. "I got the hundred-grand question . . . Where's Piss?"

Guns in hand. Ronny's building was quiet. Not a fucking sound. No Piss, no Smitty. No nobody. Ronny had cleared the motherfuckin' decks.

I carried the suitcase. Packed with a hundred grand . . .

We took the stairs. No nobody.

Top floor. One door open. Light pouring into the dark hall like spilt milk.

Me and G . . .

We approached the door. Me first . . . Threw the suitcase inside, then I sidestepped, grabbed G by the coat, shoved G through the door in front of me . . .

POP POP POP.

G hit hit hit, doin' a herky-jerky dance, blood spurting.

"Motherfuckah!" screamed G as I dived past him into the room gun firing. Julio, Piss, Popeye, Smitty – I saw them all in a flash. Tore off a full clip of caps before they could fire back. I rolled behind a couch . . . Snapped another clip in . . .

Looked out: Julio dead, shot in the head. Popeye crawling

in circles, shot in the chest, dying. Smitty runnin' out the door. G damn dead . . . Piss lying there, holding his gut.

"Double-crossin' set-up niggaz," I said, comin' from behind the couch. "Thanks for fuckin' up my faith in brotherhood, Piss."

"Fuck off, Frankie," he said, groaning, holding his gut.

"Why you do it, Piss? Why you take Ayesha and the baby out? They didn't do shit to you. Why you cross me?"

"Bottom line, Frankie, you fuckin' crazy. You out there in some twilight zone . . . Ronny all about business, you all about . . . I dunno, crazy red dress shit . . . You out of control. You don't respect the limits. Shit, the blonde bitch was bad enough, but you don't waste a cop, nigga . . . That shit get us all popped . . . You and that red dress, crazy . . ."

"Piss," I said, stroking his face with my gun. "What happened to loyalty?"

"You ate my mafockin' eye, bitch. I never forget that."

"You can forget about it now," I said, leaning down and screwing my piece into his one eye . . .

Piss laughed.

"Yeah, go out hard. Adios, motherfucker," I said, and shot the nigga. His body flopped once and his brains leaked onto the carpet slow out the hole in the back of his head. "See you in hell, Piss, but you won't see me."

I called out: "Where you at, Ronny?"

"In the bedroom, boy. If you're through fuckin' around, come on in."

"Mama, you okay?" I called.

"Get out of here, Frankie!" she called.

"I ain't leavin' without you. Ronny, I got a hundred grand you let her go."

"Let's discuss it like businessmen, Frankie. Come on in."

I picked up the suitcase. Cautious, low . . .

In the doorway to the bedroom.

"Gun down," ordered the baldhead nigga sittin on the bed with a gun at Mama's head. Mama naked, a string coming out of her snatch. Ronny flicking a Bic up near that string.

"This a stick of dynamite up there, Frankie. This'll stop her period . . . Period. Instant menopause."

Nigger Mortis laughing. Waves of coldness blowin' cross the room.

"You still an ugly muhfukkah," I said, remembering a long-ago night, a younger Ronny Dewitt smoking rock naked with Mama in bed . . .

"Frankie, get out!" Mama ordered. "He won't do nothin'!"

"Your mama always was a dynamite piece of pussy!"

"You a sick muhfukkah, Ronny. Take you money and gimme my mama."

"Put the money and the gun down and put your hands up."

"Untie her."

"You wanna save your mama, nigga, give up the roscoe."

"Frankie," said Mama. "Get out of here!"

Ronny slapped Mama with his 9.

"Shut up, bitch. This between me and the pup . . . I only wish Larry was here – make it complete . . . Shit, I could a had old Double L dusted any time I wanted those years he was inside . . . But I wanted the pleasure of doin' it myself."

"Ronny," Mama said. "You leave them both alone, I stay with you."

Nigger Mortis laughed.

"You? You think I want an old worthless bitch like you? An old dime-a-dozen crack ho bitch dry like Death Valley? I don't want you, bitch . . . They a billion bitches out there for me. Younger, better lookin', better in the sack, give better head."

"Enough!" said a voice from behind me . . .

Old Larry Lawrence, holding Piss's gun. His shoulder heavy with bloody bandages.

"Welcome, Preacher," laughed Ronny. "The family that hangs together, dies together."

"Get out of here!" screamed Mama, the tears rolling down her face.

"Hey, Larry," said Ronny. "Don't you think little Frankie looks like me?"

"Let her go, man," said my old man.

Ronny laughed, raised his pisol, aimed at Double L . . .

The old man aimed at Ronny.

"Mama," I said. "Which one of these niggaz my daddy?"
Ronny laughed.

And that's when the old man fired, bullets tearing Ronny's grill apart, teeth and lips and cheek and tongue ripped away. A moan coming from the basement of his hellish guts.

"One strike and you're out," said the old man, heading for Mama. "It's over, baby."

But Ronny Dewitt had one move left.

Nigger Mortis flicked that goddamn Bic and lit the fuse. Sizzle . . .

The old man bolted across the room, threw himself at Mama, reaching for the source of all our troubles . . .

VII

It's just one of those things. A fact of life. I'm naked. Naked and alone. I don't hold it against Mama for locking me up naked and leaving me alone. Ain't her fault I'm in a cage on death row, headed for the chair . . . That's just the way it is . . . Being locked up naked and alone is just one of those things . . .

And the winter wind keeps on blowing . . . I waived all my appeals. I laughed at the priest. I ate my Big Mac. I'm writing these words . . . There ain't no windows here in this coffin, but the winter wind keeps on blowing . . .

When the SWAT team busted into Ronny's crib and found me there, sitting on the floor, Mama blown into chunks, Larry Lawrence dead, Ronny dead without a face, me eating that thing I was eating, one of those hard sharpshootin' armoured robots actually puked behind his Darth Vader mask. Had to take the damn thing off he was puking so hard and heavy.

I laughed.

"What's the matter?" I asked. "Ain't you never saw a boy eatin' his mama's heart?"

I laughed and laughed and chewed it good, just like Mama always told me . . .

So here I am, naked and alone. Naked and alone. Naked and alone. Just like the old days, locked up naked and alone. And the winter wind keeps on blowing . . .

"You done good," the wind just say in my brain. "You exceeded all my expectations. You gave me value for my entertainment dollar. Frankie, baby, you one bad motherfucker . . ."

"Shut up, motherfuckin' devil," I say. "You push my ass, push my ass, push my ass, and now you got me where you want me, huh? Naked and alone . . ."

"I love you, Frankie," say the wind. "I love you. You my own very special little nigga."

"I don't love you," I say. "I love Ayesha. That's the way it is. Just one of those things. I don't love you."

"We'll see about that," say the wind, blowing cold. "You'll love me when you down in hell. You'll love me. You'll love me and beg me for some cold wind then . . . They're coming . . ."

I can hear them, the jailers. I can hear them, the other death-row niggaz rattling their cups against their bars. Frankie's gonna die today, they say. The Cannibal's going down . . . But shit, Frankie can't die . . . Man ain't never been alive can't die . . . You see, Frankie born dead. Born dead into a dead world . . . But shit, nigga, I had a helluva run for a dead man in a dead world . . .

I'm puttin' on the red dress. Red dress keep me safe. Mafockin' wind can't touch me. That devil wind can talk all the shit it wants, but the mafocka can't touch me . . .

Yeah, I be seein' you niggaz around the block. I be seein' you niggaz in the bank. I be seein' you down in hell . . . But remember this: When you start feelin' all safe and shit and you think the time is ripe and you can let your guard down and have a motherfuckin' laugh at my expense, that's when I reach out and teach you sorry-ass niggaz a lesson about respect . . . One laugh per customer, that's all you get . . .

Adios, motherfucker . . .

Caravan to Tarim

David Goodis

E leven miles out of Maglaf, the caravan ran into a mob of Bedouins. It started out as a pleasant negotiation with rifles.

Kelney cursed the Arabian sand and the Arabian sun and said, "Who gave them rifles?"

A bullet ran past Tiggs's cheek and he muttered, "Anyway, it's better than knives." Tiggs had three knife scars from the Bedouin blades. He had been working back and forth across the desert for nine years. He was used to this sort of thing.

The Bedouins were moving in now. They knew all about Kelney's caravan, the spices and perfume and rugs that were being taken to the market in Tarim.

Kelney cursed and started up, wielding his pistol. He tried to leap over the parapet formed by the spine of his camel. Tiggs pulled him down. And the next bullet came sailing across his crouching body and went on going and hit one of the Arabian guides in the forehead.

Kelney was not used to this. He was an American, big but not tall. Five seven and one ninety. He was thirty-six years old and for almost a quarter of a century he had been a drifter. His hair was whitish gold and his eyes were bottle green. His skin was oak. He wasn't a happy man; he was a bit too tough.

"Don't waste bullets," Tiggs said. He was an Englishman. His philosophy was that life was very short and a man had to do as he damned well pleased, provided he didn't cause grief to nice people. Tiggs was a year shy of forty and looked younger. He was tall and thin and dry. His eyes were colourless. He seemed very tired.

With Tiggs and Kelney there were seventeen honest Arabians. And in a semicircle behind the sand dune thirty yards away there were thirty-odd dishonest Arabians. There was nothing to do but crouch down behind the camels and listen to the bullets whining.

"Let's rush them," Kelney said.

"That wouldn't be wise," Tiggs murmured. "They've got the elevation. They've got too much sand in front of them. Wait. Let them use more bullets."

"They're killing us all."

"It's bad," Tiggs admitted. "But there's nothing we can do about it right now."

"That's one man's opinion," Kelney said. His dark green eyes became black.

In shabby Arabian he shouted an order. The guides whimpered. Kelney repeated the command and the Arabians still held back. He jumped out of cover, and his pistol shoved lead. The Arabians were following him. Even Tiggs joined up. They were running now, running and weaving, some of them falling as they went across the sand. The Bedouins stood up, shot downwards.

Kelney saw Tiggs go down. The Englishman rolled over a few times, and then his face was to the sun and his mouth was open. Blood dribbled from his lips. Kelney didn't see the need for further study. He concluded that Tiggs was dead and that was unfortunate but then this whole business was unfortunate.

The Bedouins were coming out from behind their dune. Kelney saw his men start to run. The Bedouins were laughing and shooting them down. A bullet tore flesh from Kelney's thigh.

In another minute, the Bedouins were walking out to get him. They were grinning.

They looked mean, and their women liked to see white men die slowly, with a lot of groans and screaming. Kelney put the pistol to his head and pulled the trigger.

He had forgotten that the chamber was empty. The Bedouins had him, and he was shouting curses, squirming, kicking with his good leg.

The leader came over and told him to be quiet.

In fuming Arabic, Kelney told the leader what he could do. But then his eyes became green again and he gave the Bedouin chief a half grin.

The Bedouin was not very tall and not very wide. But his eyes and nose and jaw line were bladelike and hard. His smile was a thread. He wore a lot of green and yellow silk, and shining belts of silvery leather. His men wore rags. Kelney, sizing it up, decided that the leader had a mixture of brains and vanity and could be talked to.

"There is precious stuff in the bags," Kelney said, pointing with his chin towards the corpses of the camels. His wrists were already behind his back and the Bedouins were drawing the hemp in tight knots.

"Why do you wish me to know that?" the Bedouin leader said.

Kelney shrugged. "It is good to know the joy of looking forward to a treasure."

"I know all about the treasure. I know all about you."

Kelney forced a laugh. He looked down to see blood fountaining from his thigh. The Bedouin reached down, arranged a somewhat capable bandage.

Then Kelney was placed on a camel and the Bedouin mob ribboned across the lake of sand.

The leader rode beside Kelney. He said, "I was in Tarim when you brought in the last shipment. I followed you. I know that you have more spices, perfume, rugs —"

"Not quite. But I know where to get more." Kelney said it wincing.

The Bedouin smiled at the sun. "We will speak of this later."

It was all very unpleasant, the sticky heat and the smell of too many unwashed camels and the general filth of a Bedouin camp. But Kelney wasn't thinking in terms of the present. He went so far as to eat and drink from the same big dish shared by a group of Bedouins.

The leader, who had introduced himself as Sheik Nadi, was saying, "You do not mind the food?"

"Why should I?"

"It is bad food. We are very poor. Do you know why?"

Kelney shrugged.

"We are the forgotten people," Nadi said. "We are kept out of the villages. This tribe was not always nomadic by nature. They took our grazing lands away and now we are slowly starving. That is why we come out on the desert with our rifles."

"How did you get the rifles?" Kelney's tone was conversational.

"Theft," the Bedouin said. "We have been forced to make our own laws. And we will benefit. When our treasure is sufficient, we will take trade away from the stingy merchants in village bazaars. We will be the scornful rather than the scorned!"

"And why not?" Kelney gazed directly into Nadi's eyes.

Nadi breathed deeply through his nose. He folded his arms and looked past Kelney's shoulder. "You know where to get these treasures," he said. "You pay a small price, then you take the stuff to Tarim and reap a high profit."

"You have it wrong," Kelney said. "I am not my own employer. I work for Mezar, the richest merchant in Tarim. He sends me to the coast of the Red Sea. There I trade with European vessels that slip up through the Indian Ocean. I can negotiate better than the Arabian tradesmen."

He was telling the truth. He was seeing hate sparkle in Nadi's eyes.

"Mezar," the Bedouin said. "I know him well. A jackal. It is he who controls the city of Tarim. And you work for him."

"No more," Kelney said.

Nadi went into his tent, brought out water pipes. For a while the two men sat smoking quietly. Kelney made the first bid. He said, "I will get you more treasure."

"Of course." Nadi smiled. "That is why you are alive now. That is why the knives of our women remain idle."

"I will go to Tarim," Kelney said. "Mezar will send me out with another caravan."

"Am I a fool?" Nadi said. "Do I speak with fools?"

"Another caravan," Kelney said.

"And heavily armed, yes?"

Kelney nodded. "Heavily armed – with blank cartridges."

"If you would cheat Mezar, you would cheat me."

"I have more to gain by cheating Mezar."

Nadi sucked at the water pipe. He looked at Kelney and then he looked at the sand. He said, "You think wisely. Work for me and your rewards will be plentiful. But revenge can come in equal quantity if you attempt betrayal."

"I wait for your word," Kelney said.

"My word is this – you will leave Tarim with the new caravan. You will be unmolested during your journey to the sea. This time you will bring back a treasure greater than any in the past. And once again you will meet me in the desert. There will be no fighting. You will tell your men to surrender. We will take their rifles and camels."

"And my men?"

"They will die in the desert. Under the sun. Thirsting."

Kelney put down the tube of his water pipe. "Must they die?"

"They are from the city," Nadi said. "They would happily see my tribe die the slow death. We will likewise be happy to see them crawling across the desert, their tongues black."

"What about me?" Kelney said. "How can I murder my own men?"

"Speak now!" Nadi was standing. "Your life is no longer your own. The knives of my women are waiting."

Deep inside, Kelney shivered. He said, "It is agreed."

He would start out the following morning. There were no complex details. A single Bedouin would accompany him.

Alone in his tent, Kelney laughed without sound. He had never expected it would be this easy. He had given his word to Nadi, but Nadi was a bandit and a killer and you're not obliged to keep promises to the Nadis.

Kelney was awakened at dawn by an old Bedouin, who informed him that his camel was ready. He was offered food and gulped it down hurriedly. Walking towards the camel, he turned to the man and said, "Sheik Nadi?"

"Gone," the old Bedouin said. "Out of the desert, waiting for another caravan. A great one, our chief."

"Yes," Kelney said. "And very clever."

"Cleverer than you think," the old man said.

After a moment the old man nodded. "You will keep your word. Because I will tell you that Nadi is a man of honour and he believes that honour means more than life itself. There have been those who have broken their word to Nadi, and they have died. I could tell you how they died but I will let you imagine it for yourself. They thought they had tricked Nadi; they thought once they were out of the desert they were free of him. But he followed them. And eventually he caught them. One by one. When Nadi decides to pursue a man, the man never gets away."

It hit Kelney with the force of a hammer. He had the ability to recognize profound truth when he heard it, and he was hearing it now.

The old man was saying, "Your fellow traveller will be the tongueless fool who waits now on his camel."

Kelney got a look at the man who would journey with him for two hundred miles across sand. It wasn't a pleasant look. The ragged Bedouin had a face that could turn a stomach. Some terrible disease had left scars, blotches and pulpy masses that distorted his features into a hideous mask. The diseased one opened his mouth to speak and his lips moved but he made gurgling sounds and nothing more.

Shuddering, Kelney said, "I must travel with that?"

The old man grinned. "It is the wish of Sheik Nadi."

Kelney was climbing onto his camel. His body jerked violently as the beast rose from a placid crouch, shook itself to get blood into its legs.

The old Bedouin looked up at Kelney. "Your camel is strong," he said. "May your will have the same strength."

Kelney nodded slowly. He really meant it as he said, "Thanks for the tip."

And the two camels, bearing silent riders, went eastward, towards Tarim.

Short and fat and sloppy, Mezar wallowed in his wealth. Once he had been a whining, begging seller of spices. In a miserable, hollowed-out space, he had made his living not on routine sales, but on certain practices that at times offered themselves when a customer was careless.

Slowly Mezar had pulled himself up, and now he had wealth. He was powerful and he had many persons working for him and it was good to think about all this, particularly the efficient white men he had working for him, this Kelney, this Tiggs, with their crisp, clear way of doing business. In short time, if things kept on the way they were going, his wealth would be doubled.

A servant came in, babbled loud and fast.

"Send him in!" Mezar said.

Kelney came in. His jacket and white linen breeches were rags. His pith helmet was cracked. He limped. But it was his face that made Mezar stare. His face was pale; the eyes had deepened in green until they were almost black.

The Arabian leaped up and almost choked on a mouthful of figs.

Kelney was in there first. He waved wearily at the fat merchant, he folded his arms and gazed at the floor and said, "Bedouins."

"But the shipment —"

"I had more luck than the others," Kelney said. His nerves were a sunbroiled mass dangling from an ever-thinning thread. He wanted to hit Mezar in the face.

"The shipment!" Mezar screeched. He was leaping around the silk-curtained room. "The shipment is gone! Why did you let the Bedouins —" He coughed on the figs. His eyes were glass. Then he saw the silent man standing in the doorway and he looked at the pulpy, scarred face and he said, "Who is that?"

"The man saved me," Kelney said, just as he had rehearsed it. "I do not know who he is. He has no tongue."

Mezar was slowing down. His eyes were retreating into the fat folds of his face. He walked past Kelney, kept walking towards the mute. As he did so, he clapped his hands, twice.

Then he stood in front of the mute, hitting his palms together lightly, smiling as he stood there waiting.

"He befriended me," Kelney said.

Two tall, half-naked Arabians entered the room. They were sweating, breathing hard. When you worked for Mezar you were always sweating, always groping for more energy.

Mezar pointed to the mute and said, "Take him."

Kelney saw the mute struggling in the grasp of the two big men. He pushed Mezar's elbow and said, "Leave him be. Reward him and let him go."

"He is a Bedouin," Mezar said.

Kelney was very tired. He was nearly broken in two. He said, "If any harm comes to the mute one, I will leave your employ. The Englishman is dead, and you will have no one to get the low prices. Hear me, Mezar."

"But he is a Bedouin!" Mezar insisted. "Can you know how I hate them? Can you understand what a plague they are?"

"This one is sick and harmless," Kelney said.

"I will make sure that he will always be harmless," Mezar replied, and now his smile had enjoyment in it. Gesturing towards the writhing, gurgling Bedouin, the fat merchant addressed the tall men and said, "Take him out and cut off his ears and the tip of his nose."

Then, as Mezar changed the smile to a laugh, Kelney cursed. He sensed himself going across the room, his hands shaping a couple of fists. He landed a hard one on an Arabian's chest and the tall man lurched. The other man moved towards Kelney and at that point the mute became an eel, went sliding away. His gurgling was now an awful sort of laughter, fading quickly as he made his escape down a narrow street.

Kelney had nothing to do and no place to go and he stood there and waited until the two tall men came back. They looked at Mezar. And Mezar nodded.

Mezar had seated himself and now he studied Kelney's face. He said, "You seem to like the Bedouins."

"There are good and bad in all tribes."

"I do not understand."

"It's very necessary to understand," Kelney said. "Every nation and every tribe has its good people and its bad. Does it take much intelligence to get that?"

Mezar rubbed a finger across a huge carbuncle amethyst that dangled from his neck. "All Bedouins are fiends," he said. "You know that, as I do. But you helped the mute one to escape. I want to know why."

Biting his lip, Kelney looked at Mezar and let out a sigh and said, "I told you why."

"I do not believe it," Mezar said. "I will tell you, Kelney, I expected that at some time you would try to trick me, but I did not suppose that you would be so foolish as to enlist the help of Bedouins. You are working with them now, is it not so?"

"Don't be a fool."

"The Englishman, too. And all the rest of the caravan. All working with the Bedouins. And you arranged it. Tell me with your own lips. Say it now!"

"All right," Kelney said. "Go to hell."

Then he squirmed and tried to get away, knowing that it was a crazy idea, knowing it would be a tough process from here on in. The violent part of it lasted about a minute. Afterwards they were able to half carry him out of the room, and he felt himself going down some corridor. And then he got the feeling of metal clamps fastened around his wrists, and he was vertical and his boots and socks were being pulled away; his naked feet just about tagged the floor.

"You will be alone for a while," Mezar said. "I will grant you complete darkness and silence. In an hour I will be back here with gifts of agony. It is my hope that you will tell the truth."

Footsteps were going away, a door was closing, and Kelney was calling himself the same names he had called Mezar. It occurred to him that perhaps he had deserved this sort of thing for a long, long time and now there was nothing to do but take it with philosophy.

Blank cartridges, he was thinking. That was a lovely arrangement and for that deal alone he deserved to get his head kicked in. Even though he hadn't been given the opportunity to go through with the transaction, the fact remained that he had agreed to it and he certainly would have gone through with it to soften his own mattress. And that made him a thousand varieties of louse and he was lower than any Bedouin.

He had to grin. It was so easy to feel this noble remorse, this inner cleansing, when the four surrounding walls were walls of odds. Give him a chance to get out of this and he would go back to the strategy, the fencing, the scummy bargaining that he always engaged in when he was bargaining with what he recognized as scum.

But was Nadi scum? What about those Bedouins? Were they really scum? He gave himself a picture of them, their rags, the food they ate, the sad faces of their children. On another canvas he was seeing fat Mezar with a mouthful of figs, and gems against fleshy fingers and all the silk. He thought about the good Arabians, honest and fairly decent men crawling across sand and dying of thirst because a noble soul named Kelney had placed blank cartridges in their rifles. He heard the door again, and then the footsteps.

Slanting light straightened itself out as Mezar placed a torch in a wall bracket. Mezar was alone and breathing hard.

This is going to be good, Kelney thought.

But he hadn't dreamed it would be this good, because Mezar was unfastening the clamps and saying, "I am humble."

Kelney rubbed his wrists. "Say it again."

The fat Arabian said it again.

"So what brings about the change of heart?"

"Tiggs is here."

"You can say that again, too."

"Tiggs has been brought in. He was picked up by another caravan coming this way from the coast. He was dying. They had a physician with them, a famous man from Charfa. An operation was performed in the desert, and a bullet was taken from Tiggs's body. He is recovering fast. And he has told me what happened with the Bedouins. I know now that you spoke the truth."

"Thanks," Kelney said, "for nothing."

"Let us forget this unpleasant affair," Mezar said. "In a short time Tiggs will be well again. You will take out another caravan —"

"I want more payment," Kelney said.

"Of course. You are a good tradesman, Kelney, and I am happy to reward my best workers."

"I don't work for you," Kelney said. I only deal with you. Remember that. And here's another thing. I don't want to wait around for Tiggs to get back on his feet. I'll take out the next caravan as soon as you make out your buying schedule."

"But Tiggs knows the route better –"

"I'm in a hurry."

"Yes, but Tiggs –"

"The buying is the important thing." Kelney was thinking of the blank cartridges, calling himself a skunk even as he called himself a nice guy for making this attempt to save Tiggs.

"You say that you do not work for me." Mezar's tone was level. "I tell you that you are wrong and that my word is the last. You will wait until Tiggs recovers and he will go with you on the next caravan."

All at once Kelney was very tired. He shrugged and said all right, he would wait for Tiggs.

It was an ordeal in itself, counting the days, pacing them in ratio with Tiggs's recovery. The day when Tiggs sat up. The day when he walked around. The day when he was able to eat and drink as a normal man. Kelney watched him come back to full life and realized that it would not be long before Tiggs was back there with death. The bargain with Nadi must be kept, otherwise Nadi would come creeping. And Nadi would find him.

There came a day when the caravan set out across the desert, aiming at the string of ports on the Red Sea coast. Kelney and Tiggs walked ahead of their camels. And following were thirty Arabians, whom Kelney had supplied well with water and food and rifles and cartridges. The cartridges were blank.

"I'd like to meet the Bedouins again," Tiggs said.

"A bullet can't settle an issue."

"In a way you're right," Tiggs said. "But I've had a lot of pain. I'd like to make at least one Bedouin go through what I've been through."

Kelney glanced to the side and saw that Tiggs's lean, dry face was working slightly. Tiggs's lips were drawn like expanded rubber and his eyes aimed ahead like rifle muzzles.

The caravan reached the coast in eleven days. It had been slow going. On the trip northward however, along the coast, Kelney made good progress. His negotiating was more clever than it had ever been. When the caravan was headed back towards Tarim, the packs were loaded with quality that would make Mezar smile.

They moved onto the desert, and the big sun was there to greet them. They watched it as it floated along with them. There was half a day of this, and hardly any talk, and then during a rest period Tiggs was lighting a cigarette and saying, "Well, we have our treasure. Now let the Bedouins try to take it away from us."

Kelney leaned his head towards the match in Tiggs's fingers. "Maybe we shouldn't talk about it too much."

For a while Tiggs was quiet. Then he said, "I've been wondering about something. That mute Bedouin who guided you back to Tarim. Rather odd that any of them would do something like that, don't you think?" And when there was no reply, Tiggs went on, "They're clever as well as mean, those buzzards. You've got to be careful."

"All right," Kelney said. "What's on your mind?"

They looked at each other, and Tiggs said, "What's on yours?"

"I'm not worrying about a thing," Kelney said.

They had moved another mile or so when Tiggs suddenly darted ahead. Something was on the sand, writhing out there in front of them.

It was a dying camel, left there by another caravan. They looked it over and Tiggs said it was no use, there was no saving the beast. And then Tiggs lifted his rifle, pointed it at the camel's head.

Kelney knocked down the rifle.

"Why not?" Tiggs said. He didn't move. There was no expression in his eyes. Kelney was rolling invisible dice, telling himself that Tiggs had examined the cartridges in his rifle. Anyway, there was a quick means of finding out for sure. "All right," he said, "if you think you're being merciful, go ahead and give it a bullet."

The Englishman said, "I can't do it, Kelney. I adore these animals. You take the job."

Kelney breathed hard, trying to keep his relief from showing. He told himself everything was fine now. But as he took the pistol from its holster he wondered about it. And as he pulled the trigger he asked himself if he was actually as clever as he thought he was.

Ninety miles out of Maglaf, Tiggs said, "They're about due."

"Who?"

"Bedouins."

"Bad ones?"

"They're all bad," Tiggs said.

Injecting it with a stiff dose of sarcasm, Kelney said, "How long does it take to learn all about Arabia?"

Tiggs laughed. "I've been here nine years and I'm just beginning to learn."

"Maybe you're slow to catch on," Kelney said. "Sometimes I think –"

A bullet cut in on that one. It came from a rise in the sand about seventy yards away. There was a string of bush fringing the rise, and above its meagre green there were bits of white that were Bedouin headdress.

Kelney acted electrically. His eyes made a chart of the surrounding sand. He saw that a deviation in the slope would afford a barrier against bullets. He yelled an order, his voice slicing hard. The Arabians backed up, swayed their camels behind the sand barrier. During all this there was quiet and Kelney knew what it meant. Nadi was waiting it out, waiting for a rifle response. Nadi wanted to see if the American was playing him clean.

Tiggs's voice barged in. "Well, you're in charge. What do we do?"

"Just wait," Kelney said. He was flat on his belly behind the barrier, and Tiggs, at his side, was inching up to peep over the barrier.

"Stay down," Kelney said. He raised his voice to give the command in Arabic. "Stay down – hold fire!" He knew it was loud enough for Nadi to hear.

Kelney waited for the Bedouin bullets and they didn't come and he pushed his tongue over dry lips. He didn't like the quiet. He didn't like himself. He had brought these men out to die.

"You don't look well," Tiggs said.

Kelney heard that clearly but it didn't mean anything to him. He sensed that he was breaking up inside. And all at once the break came and he realized that he could not let this thing go on. He had to do something drastic and he had to do it alone. He looked at Tiggs and he looked at the Arabians and he started to crawl backwards down behind the barrier.

"What's the object?" Tiggs said.

"I'm going roundabout," Kelney said. "I'm edging out to skirt that bush and get in behind them. I want to see what their plans are. Don't do anything, just stay here and hold fire. I don't want a single bullet wasted."

Then, without waiting for Tiggs's reply, he kept on moving back and he was following the barrier around its shape of an arc. He became older by a few years as he worked wide of the bush, then came in behind the bush, and all the time there was just that same thick quiet, and he knew that Nadi was wondering about the cartridges. Pressed flat against the sand, he crawled another twenty yards and then he was back there behind the Bedouins. He could see Sheik Nadi, the green and gold distinct against the colourless rags of Nadi's followers.

Kelney stood up and walked forward. A few Bedouins became conscious of his approach, raised their rifles, then lowered them as Nadi shouted something. Kelney stopped and waited as Nadi came towards him. When they faced each other they were both smiling and Nadi lowered his rifle and that was when Kelney made a subtle gesture with the pistol. Nadi lost the smile.

"A trick?" Nadi said.

"No trick. I have kept the agreement. My men are holding rifles that have blank cartridges. But in this pistol are real bullets. If you cry out I'll kill you. Now walk with me and try to be patient."

They walked back and away from the Bedouin position. Nadi was smiling. "Before you kill me let me tell you that my followers will someday find you, and your death will be a terrible thing."

"Aw, knock it off," Kelney growled in his own tongue. Then, going back to Arabic, he said, "I said that I had kept our agreement, and I was not lying. All I ask now is that you spare the lives of my men. I will see that you get the entire shipment."

"You are loyal to Mezar."

"I am loyal to myself. I hate Mezar even as you do, even as my men do. Your followers and my men are brothers."

Nadi lowered his head and rubbed his chin and it was done perfectly. The change of pace was also perfect, because Nadi was a streak as he smashed with both hands. The pistol went out of Kelney's grasp and Kelney went back with the Bedouin tearing at him. They went down together, grappling, and Kelney grinned as he thought of every other man who had tried to use this method of argument with him. And a few moments later he was upright again and he was frowning. And Nadi, who had gone sliding out of a bear hug to take the pistol, now had it pointed at Kelney's chest.

"It's too bad," Kelney said. "I was trying to be fair."

And he was telling himself that it didn't pay, there was no logic to it. If he had handled it from the evil side, if he had kept it dirty according to the original idea, he would have been in the cream.

He blinked and waited for the bullet.

And then he heard Nadi saying, "I cannot."

"You're not teasing me. I'm dead already and I know it." He was trembling, he was very frightened, very agitated, because he was a man who got real taste out of life and this was a sure and final thing that would happen to him.

"I cannot kill you," Nadi said.

"I'm listening."

Nadi's smile was vague. "When you went back to Tarim, I went with you. I was the mute."

Kelney stared.

"I did not trust you," Nadi said. "I wanted to be sure. I used a clay-and-rice paste to mask my face. But I was foolish enough to stay with you when you reported to Mezar. He would have given me death, slow and with agony. And you saved me. I cannot kill you. I want to, but I cannot. I will give you back your pistol and you will return to your men. Go on to Tarim. You will not be molested. But from now on you must take a different route. I do not want us to meet again."

Butt foremost, the pistol was handed back to Kelney. And Nadi turned and started back towards the rise where his men faced the Mezar caravan, and where all the rifles were silent and waiting.

Tiggs turned when he heard Kelney coming up. He smiled with sincerity and said, "It's a surprise. I never thought you'd come back."

"You mean that?"

"Of course," Tiggs said. "I thought they'd spot you and shoot you down."

"Oh," Kelney said. "I thought you meant something else." Then he bit his lip for a few seconds. "We'll move on. They won't bother us."

They shouted orders but the entire party was watching the Bedouins who were now moving away, a string of ragged figures on bony beasts, winding into the yellow distance.

Among the Arabians there were murmurs of puzzlement. Even the camels made questioning noises. The caravan formed line and moved on. Tiggs and Kelney walked ahead, saying nothing, and it went on like that for a long chain of hollow minutes.

Finally Tiggs laughed softly. "A good thing the Bedouins went home."

Kelney stopped and faced the Englishman and said, "Whatever you've got to say, say the whole thing now."

"I made a little change in our ammunition," Tiggs said. "I took out the blanks and put in the genuine."

Kelney had a feeling that he was two feet tall. "Which shows," he said, "how much you trusted me."

"Which shows how much I trust anyone before I come to know him," Tiggs said. "I always make a private inspection of the rifles before a caravan goes out. Every once in a while a guide makes a deal with the Bedouins. The blank cartridge business is an old trick. But this is the first time I ever watched a man change his mind."

"You knew I'd change my mind?"

"Let's say I was hoping for it so strongly I made myself believe it. It's this way, Kelney – you and I work well together and I've been planning that we should break away from Mezar and start our own little trade."

"Hold it," Kelney said. "After what's happened out here, you think I can be trusted? I'm not exactly a saint."

Tiggs's voice was as gentle as his smile. "Not exactly," he said, "but you've got possibilities."

The Lady Who Left her Coffin

Hugh B. Cave

I

Lincoln Street was deserted. The big clock in Park Street Church, uptown, had finished tolling midnight. In front of the Surety Building at Lincoln and West, Mr Loring Everett Newton leaned forward on the rear seat of his enormous car and nervously tapped his chauffeur between the shoulders, then clung to the upholstery as the car nosed towards the kerb.

The machine purred to a stop and with the assistance of the chauffeur Newton gingerly got out. "Better go home now, Andrews," he said. "And remember – if my son or daughter should ask where I am, you drove me to the club."

Loring Everett Newton was senior partner in the insurance firm of Newton, Hackler and Fern. Bony hands shaking and watery eyes wide in his white face, he let himself into the Surety Building and wearily climbed the stairs to the fourth floor, which was devoted in its entirety to the offices of the firm over which he presided.

He lit a light and left his topcoat and hat in the outer office. Thumbing a second light-switch in his own private sanctum, he closed the door and lowered his frail body into the chair behind the desk.

He was here to keep a midnight tryst with a woman who had died three months before, and he was quite unaware that his every movement was being observed by the keen grey eyes of Mr Martin Lane, investigator of the occult and supernatural.

For more than half an hour Martin Lane had been sitting

very quietly in a straight-backed chair behind an ungainly, old-fashioned filing cabinet. He was hardly noticeable sitting there, his slender, wiry frame blended so easily with the shadows.

Finding him there, Newton might have thought him merely one of the office clerks who had gone to sleep, perhaps, and forgotten to go home. Newton would probably have made the fatal mistake made so frequently by others – the mistake of classifying Martin Lane as "rather ordinary".

Only in appearance was Martin Lane ordinary, and only then because he desired to be. That studied colourlessness concealed a cobra-quick alertness, a mind keener than any microscope. That pale, thin face and those slumped shoulders hid hair-trigger muscles more responsive than those of a racing greyhound. Beneath the surface lightly slept a cyclone.

Men looked at Martin Lane, classified him as hardly worth remembering, and accordingly forgot him. That very lack of glitter was his major ace in the hole. It enabled him, time and again, to intrude where angels feared to tread; had helped him to face death without dying. It meant he could come and go without being labelled.

That, when one constantly poked one's nose into the supernatural, was an accomplishment not to be lightly regarded.

Martin Lane was alert now – and Newton did not discover him.

Bony hands still shaking, Newton produced four rubber-banded packages of bills and placed them on the desk. Then he carefully counted the bills in each package, mumbling the count as he did so.

It was a lot of money. Twenty thousand dollars in all, and in cash. Perspiration gleamed on Newton's high forehead as he paced nervously into the outer office and extinguished the light.

Returning, he darkened the inner office also, then seated himself at the desk again and waited.

Martin Lane, eyes narrowed and thin lips scowling, remained motionless behind the cabinet and knew that, unless something went wrong, the ghost of a dead woman would soon appear in the shadows.

Yesterday morning the attractive, twenty-two-year-old daughter of Loring Everett Newton had driven to Martin Lane's Chestnut Hill home and begged Lane's assistance. It was the first time she had come face to face with the famed investigator of psychic phenomena and she had seemed surprised to find him so utterly unglamorous in appearance.

He had been working in his photographic darkroom, and his hands were streaked with green dye, his slender stoop-shouldered body encased in an old rubber apron. Photography was only one of Martin Lane's many hobbies.

"I've come to you because I'm desperate," Ruth Newton said, "and because I've heard so much about you, Mr Lane. It's about my father. Possibly you've heard of him."

Most people had heard of her father, Lane told her with a smile. When a man controlled a mammoth insurance company and possessed several million dollars, his name became public property.

"For three months now," Ruth Newton said, "my father has been acting strangely. We thought at first it was due to mother's death. She was killed in that horrible accident, you know."

Lane knew. The wife of Loring Everett Newton had been found dead in the charred wreckage of her foreign-made car at the foot of Baker's Cliff on the lake road, six months ago.

"We thought he was brooding over her death," the girl said. "Then he took to going out at night, every night, alone. He talked about mother continually. When Paul and I demanded an explanation, he said that mother had come back to him. Then I began following him when he went out at night."

Lane, dye-streaked hands flat on his knees, peered at her and waited for the rest of it. The penetrating gaze of the girl's eyes did not trouble him, nor did her sudden hesitation. He guessed that she was thinking what many another person had thought – that he was somehow too mild, too ordinary, to be equal to his reputation.

She had expected, perhaps, a creature with glittering eyes and a bristling beard, seated cross-legged upon Oriental rugs and gazing into a crystal ball flanked by columns of incense-smoke. Ah, well . . .

"Night after night my father went to his office," Ruth Newton said at last, evidently steeling herself to go through with it. "He still goes there, Mr Lane. I can't stand it! He's not my father any longer; he's a total stranger to me and Paul. He is surely going insane!"

"I shall be more than glad to look into the matter," Lane said quietly.

That had happened yesterday.

Now, in darkness, Loring Everett Newton sat alone in his private sanctum, waiting for the arrival of his dead wife, while Lane watched from his place of hiding.

The office was a large one. In addition to Newton's huge desk and the filing cabinet, it contained another large cabinet that extended from floor to ceiling on the far side of the room. Newton, rigid in his chair and breathing heavily, expectantly faced that second cabinet.

There had been a great deal of talk, Martin Lane remembered, about the gruesome accident that had claimed Mrs Newton's life. The disaster had occurred late at night while the woman was returning from a camp near Spring Lake. The newspapers had subtly and suggestively wondered *why* she was returning from so isolated a place at so late an hour.

Through their scandal columns the papers had done a good deal of wondering about Loring Newton's wife over a period of years. She seemed to enjoy seeing her name in print, no matter how shady the circumstances. There were rumours, for instance, that she and Mr Arthur Fern, her husband's junior partner, had been very much more than casual friends.

Martin Lane watched and wondered. Then suddenly he had something more tangible to wonder about.

A creaking sound informed him that the door of the large cabinet had slowly swung open. Other sounds indicated that Loring Newton had stiffened convulsively in his chair and was leaning forwards one hand nervously pawing the edge of the desk.

Near the open door of the cabinet a thin, tenuous light undulated weirdly along the floor!

Martin Lane put his hands hard on his knees but otherwise sat still. The unearthly light wavered, grew larger, and began slowly to assume shape as it gained height. No flashlight was making it, that was certain; the weird glow possessed life and motion of its own. It wavered dimly in the room's darkness and became an amazingly soft, vaporous glow, swaying sluggishly as it assumed the form of a woman.

Then Lane saw the face.

It came into view as slowly and weirdly as a photographic face emerging in a darkroom developer-tray. The luminous vapour blurred away from it, sinuously coiling, and the face itself was indistinct, nebulous, with an unearthly beauty that drew Martin Lane's eyes forward in their sockets.

With a slow gliding motion the woman swayed forward, and then Loring Newton hoarsely whispered her name. "Marguerite!"

"You have brought the money, Loring?"

"I – yes – most of it." Newton's voice, issuing from lips that must surely be quivering, was a frightened whisper wandering in the room's murk. "You don't seem to realize how hard it is for me to raise more cash. I've given you so much!"

"You will give me much more, Loring, before your debt is paid in full."

Martin Lane could see only the woman; the man was invisible in darkness. He took note of her amazing beauty and recalled that newspaper portraits had invariably revealed Marguerite Newton to be lovely beyond comparison.

But there was something evil in the ethereal, ever-changing luminosity of that lovely face as the woman came closer. Softly she murmured, "Where is the money you have brought for me tonight?"

"You should not ask for more!" Newton groaned. "My God, I told you that the last time! My money is gone, all of it. I've had to borrow. I've had to steal from my company. Now must I steal from our own children?"

"Would you have them know the manner of my death, Loring?"

"No, no!"

"Would you have me go to them and say, 'It was not an accident, my children. When I left the camp that night, your own father was waiting for me and strangled the life from my earthly body while I screamed for mercy. Your own father murdered me and then set fire to the car and –'"

"No, no! My God, no! I'll pay you! I'll pay whatever you demand!"

Soft, mocking laughter answered him. "I have no love for my children, Loring. You knew that, even before you destroyed my earthly form and made me a wanderer in this dark world of death. I want this money because it *is* theirs. Because they love you, they too must pay for your sin."

Spectral hands reached forward to the dim black outline of the desk, and Martin Lane guessed they were avidly closing over the bills that lay there. Then, slowly, the woman retreated.

The vaporous contour of her face was blurred again by undulating shadows and began slowly to dissolve. Her unearthly form lost shape, became a wavering, uncertain glow in the darkness. A voice whispered softly, "I shall come again, Loring. Be here tomorrow night . . ."

The last wavering thread of light vanished. The door of the cabinet creaked shut.

Martin Lane remained where he was, unmoving. For a while the darkness was full of low, throaty sobs emanating from the man at the desk; then the legs of a chair scraped the floor and footsteps were audible. A light-switch clicked under Newton's groping fingers.

The man looked around him and shuddered, his face drenched with sweat, eyes wide with pure terror. He opened the cabinet door and peered into the murky interior. Finally, still sobbing, he snapped out the light and walked out of the office.

When the door of the front office had clicked shut, Martin Lane straightened and strode quickly past the desk. A flashlight glowed in his hand as he stepped into the cabinet.

He examined every inch of the walls, gazed intently at the ceiling, and on hands and knees explored the floor. It took

him a long time. When he walked out of the office, pulling
the door shut behind him, a suspicion of moisture gleamed
on his forehead and his lips were tight-pressed in a face
darkly scowling.

The fourth-floor corridor of the Surety Building was a
black tube of silence. Lane felt his way along it towards the
stairs – slowly, because he needed time to think.

He had stumbled upon a secret tonight which if reported
to the police would send a terrified man to the death-house.
Loring Newton's wife had not died accidentally; her own
husband had strangled her, then set fire to the car and sent
it hurtling over Baker's Cliff, where the flames had effectively destroyed evidence of his guilt.

Martin Lane, hired by Newton's terrified daughter to
investigate this case, held the life of Loring Everett Newton
in his own two hands.

Pondering his problem in ethics, Lane paced slowly past
the row of elevator shafts. He was looking ahead, not
behind, and the thing came without warning.

A hurtling shape crashed into him, slamming him off his
feet. He had no chance.

The grilled door of the nearest elevator shaft should have
stopped him, but the door was open. Lane frantically pawed
empty air as he staggered drunkenly through the aperture.
He tripped, sprawled headlong, and shot down horizontally
with nothing beneath him to stop his fall. The elevator was
at the bottom.

The blood in Lane's body ran cold as he squirmed
frantically to right himself. Cables tore skin from his face
and burned across his writhing legs. Above him a soft
feminine voice, hellishly familiar, laughed in vile triumph
at his plight.

A man more susceptible to terror would have screamed
until his plummeting body crashed in a mangled heap on
the roof of the elevator. Lane silently got his hands on the
cables and clung to them despite the agony that burned into
them.

Like slippery serpents they slid through his fingers until
he braked the speed of his descent. Then between the seond
and first floors he came to a full stop, wrapped his legs

around the cables, and hung there with blood streaming down his corded wrists.

Minutes passed before he was able to move again.

Gently, then, he lowered himself until his feet found the roof of the elevator. One hand groping, he searched for and found the grill-work of a door just above him and pulled it open. Miraculously still alive, he stepped up into the building's second-floor corridor.

With an automatic pistol gripped in his bloody right hand, he tiptoed silently up the stairs to the landing from which he had been pushed.

He searched the darkness first, then found a light-switch and explored every inch of the insurance company's labyrinth of offices. His assailant wouldn't be there, of course, but he had to look, to make sure. Undoubtedly by now the owner of that mocking voice had vanished.

Vanished where? Back into the nameless dark world of death from which she had apparently come prowling?

II

The Second Attempt

Miss Ruth Newton looked anxiously into Martin Lane's sombre face the next morning and said falteringly, "Must I answer your question?"

"I assure you I had good reasons for asking it," Lane murmured.

"Very well then, it is true that Paul and I had no love for our mother. She hated us, and I suppose we also hated her. She was a wicked woman who abused Father terribly. Now will you tell me what happened last night?"

"Your father has told you his version?"

She shook her head. "Andrews drove Father to the club last night and returned here without him at half-past one this morning. That is, he *says* he drove father to the club. But I know father wasn't there, because I called to find out. I don't know where to turn, Mr Lane. I thought I could trust Andrews when he came to us three months ago, but now –"

"Andrews returned here at half past one?" Lane asked,
scowling.

"Yes."

"Where is your father now, Miss Newton? At his office?"

"No. He said he had a number of errands to do and would
return here for lunch."

Lane nodded, wondering whether Loring Everett Newton were at this moment endeavouring desperately to raise
money to meet the demands made upon him. He looked
around him. Here in Newton's home he had talked for a
long while with the son and daughter of the man he was
trying to help. It was a pretentious home but an unhappy
one. Dread had taken possession.

"What happened last night is of little importance, Miss
Newton." Lane shrugged, rising. "Tonight may tell a
different story."

In the hall he again encountered the girl's brother, and
the young man glared at him without even a nod of greeting.
There was something strange here, Lane thought. The girl
was almost fanatically anxious to help her father. Paul, on
the contrary, seemed bitterly resentful of intrusion by
strangers. Less than half an hour ago he had angrily
requested Lane not to meddle further in the family's private
affairs.

Lane drove downtown to the Surety Building and got
there in ten minutes, took an elevator to the fourth floor and
asked for Mr Henry Hackler. "Please tell Mr Hackler," he
said to the girl, "that Dr Philip Washburne wishes to confer
with him in the interests of Mrs Newton."

"Dr Philip Washburne?"

"Yes."

It was a chance he had to take, a chance he had taken
dozens of times before with few disastrous results. At times
like this, his facility in self-effacement was invaluable. Men
who had met him less than twenty-four hours earlier – men
who thought themselves discerning – frequently accepted
him as a total stranger upon encountering him again.

He was ushered with some ceremony into the private
office of Newton's partner and realized presently that one
listened a lot and spoke little while in Hackler's presence.

Big, red-faced Henry Hackler enjoyed the sound of his own booming voice.

"Dr Philip Washburne? I haven't the honour of knowing you, sir, but if you are here in the interests of our senior partner I'll do all I can to help. Absolutely all I can, and gladly. Mr Newton has been ill for some time. We've noticed it, I assure you. He seems upset, worried, on the verge of a breakdown, I'd say. That mustn't happen, doctor. That simply must not happen. We need Newton and can't do without him."

"Mr Newton is a very taciturn man," Lane said patiently. "I find it difficult, Mr Hackler, to get inside him and discover just what is worrying him so. Perhaps you can help me."

Hackler made a business of puffing his cheeks and gusting breath from his generous mouth. "Well, doctor, he began losing his grip on things when Mrs Newton was killed in that ghastly accident. Yes, that started it, I'd say. Wait a minute, though. I'll get Mr Fern. Our junior partner knew Mrs Newton better than any of us."

"So I understand," Lane murmured.

"Eh?"

"I understand they were – ah – very good friends."

"Oh, that. Newspaper talk, doctor. Nothing to it, I assure you. They were friends, of course, but why not? I'll get Fern, let you talk to him."

Arthur Fern was younger and better looking than Hackler. Exceptionally handsome, in fact. He looked Lane over carefully, listened indifferently to Hackler's elaborate introduction, then sat and took a cigarette from a monogrammed silver case and said with an exhalation of tobacco smoke, "I prefer not to be drawn into a discussion of this sort, doctor."

With a murmured, "Thank you, gentlemen, thank you," Lane went out and drove to his own home on Chestnut Hill.

It was an unpretentious home amid trees and shrubbery on a short deadend street. Woods crowded close on two sides. Neighbours, of whom there were few, never pointed the house out to visitors and said, "There lives Martin Lane." Driving past, they might possibly notice the slen-

der, uninspiring figure of Martin Lane puttering about in
his garden, but they knew little or nothing about the man
himself and few had ever set foot over his threshold.

He closed the door behind him now and softly called,
"Jonathan!"

From the kitchen at the rear a diminutive English servant
came hurrying in response.

"Whisky and soda, please, Jonathan," Lane requested.
"In the living room."

He strolled into the modestly furnished living room and
slumped into his favourite thinking-place – a large club
chair near the fireplace. Jonathan appeared quietly with the
desired refreshment.

"I want you to call Dominic Corsi," Lane said, "and ask
him to pay me a visit this evening about eight."

"Yes, sir." Jonathan turned to walk to the telephone but
didn't get there. A double blast of gunfire smothered the
soft whisper of his slow footsteps and sent him spinning
backwards like a startled antelope. Martin Lane clapped a
hand to one shoulder and groaned, pitching sideways in the
big chair.

Outside, visible through an open window, a long-legged
figure raced at top speed across the lawn.

The face of the servant was a study in terror as he
frantically flung himself forwards and pawed at Lane's
crumpled body. "Are you injured, sir? Are you hurt?"
His voice was a high, thin wail.

"I'm all right, I think, Jonathan." The words came with
an effort from the wounded man's lips. "Get after him, will
you? Find out who he is!"

"But you're wounded, sir!"

"I'm all right, I tell you. Get moving!" Lane struggled to
sit up. "If he has a car, take mine and try to follow him!"

Jonathan departed, slamming the door behind him.
Martin Lane, groaning, groped erect and stared down at
the chair in which he had been sitting. Two shots had been
fired through the open window. One bullet had caught him
in the left shoulder; the other had tunnelled the chair's
upholstery, missing its human target by the breadth of a
hair.

"Out to get me," Lane muttered. "Second attempt, that was. Next time I might not be so lucky."

The wound was more painful than serious. Before a full-length mirror in the bedroom he stripped off his blood-stained shirt and undershirt and carefully doctored the gash, using instruments to remove the bullet.

When Jonathan returned an hour later, Martin Lane was again sitting complacently in the big living-room chair.

"The gentleman drove to a large house on the other side of the city, sir," Jonathan said excitedly. "I noted the address as one-thirteen Eastern Avenue."

Lane nodded. One-thirteen Eastern Avenue was the address of Mr Loring Everett Newton. "You got a good look at him, Jonathan?"

"Yes indeed, sir."

"Well?"

Omitting nothing, the competent Jonathan described the man he had trailed.

"Newton himself," Lane muttered. "I thought as much. Get Miss Ruth Newton on the phone, will you?"

The servant did so. Lane took the instrument, spoke for some time in a low, unruffled voice to the daughter of the man who had attempted to murder him, but did not mention the attempted slaying.

"Eleven o'clock tonight, then," he said finally. "You're sure you can make it? That will give us an hour – ample time, I'm sure – to finish our little programme before the other show begins."

He put the phone down, turned. "You were about to call Dominic Corsi, Jonathan," he said gently, "when we were interrupted."

At twenty minutes past ten that night Martin Lane let himself into the insurance company offices on the fourth floor of the Surety Building. With him was Mr Dominic Corsi, a tall, swarthy Italian to whom for the past half hour Lane had been carefully issuing instructions.

Lugging a suitcase, Dominic Corsi entered behind Lane and carefully closed the door which, with master-key and pick-lock, Lane had laboured to open.

At eleven o'clock to the minute, Loring Everett Newton

and his daughter climbed the stairs and entered Newton's private sanctum. They found Lane seated there at the desk.

Newton stopped short with a spine-jarring jerk and stared with eyes that swelled to amazing proportions. "Martin Lane!" he whispered hoarsely.

"And very much alive," Lane murmured.

Apparently suspecting he had walked into some carefully prepared trap, Newton looked wildly around him.

Lane said softly, "I seldom go to the police with my personal problems, Mr Newton. You've nothing to fear. Unless, of course, you repeat your clumsy attempt to kill me."

"To kill you?" Ruth Newton whispered, horrified.

"This afternoon, through an open window of my home. Just why did you attempt it, Newton?"

Newton's face, twitching, was the colour of chalk. He knew he was trapped and evidently feared the worst. "I–I was ordered to," he mumbled. "I had to obey."

"Last night?"

"No, no. A letter this morning from my – from –"

"From your dead wife?"

Newton wearily nodded.

Lane stood up. "Later, I'd very much like to see that letter," he said. "We haven't time now before your appointment here. I want you to sit at the desk, Newton, just as you did last night. Ruth, you may sit here." He pushed a chair against the filing cabinet behind which last night he himself had remained hidden. "And now – let's have the room in darkness."

Pacing forwards, he put a hand on the light-switch but turned before snapping it. Newton, rigid at the desk, was bewildered and apparently terrified. His daughter nervously watched Lane's every movement.

"No matter what happens," Lane said softly, "I want both of you to sit absolutely still." He glared at the girl's father. "If you've a gun on you, Newton, leave it in your pocket. I see rather well in the dark and have no intention of being shot, so don't try it. Just sit still."

The room was suddenly in darkness. Martin Lane paced to the far side of it, stood flat against the wall, and waited.

A soft creaking sound informed him that the door of the large cabinet was slowly swinging open. A thin, wavering glow materialized near the door and grew larger.

That weirdly undulating luminescence increased in size and assumed human form precisely as it had the night before during the ghostly resurrection of Newton's dead wife. It became the vague outline of a woman – a gloriously beautiful woman with translucent features, body outlines wavering as if composed of mist.

Loring Newton's quavering voice rode on wings of terror through the darkness. "Oh, my God, it's – it's –"

"Yes, it is Marguerite," the woman answered softly.

Martin Lane, smiling, said triumphantly, "Well done, Dominic. Very well done indeed. Now we'll have a light and show Mr Newton just how –"

The words died to a whisper as Lane's eyes widened. The woman had turned slowly to face him and was staring straight at him. Something in that sluggish movement was hostile, sinister. About to step forward, Lane held his ground and stood stiff as wood.

"Why have you brought this man here, Loring?" the woman asked harshly. "I told you never to bring a companion! I warned you what would happen!"

Martin Lane waited for no more. As if shot from a sling he hurtled forward, both arms outflung, head lowered like that of a charging ram. He heard Loring Newton wailing an answer to the woman's threat, heard a shrill scream of abject terror from Newton's daughter.

Then, too late, Lane saw the outline of a gun in one of those spectral, luminous hands!

He tried to hurl himself sideways but the momentum of his charge was too great. A streak of flame spewed amid reverberations of ear-splitting thunder from the gun's muzzle. Lane staggered, bent double with agony as the bullet gouged into him.

As he crashed to his knees, the gun-barrel descended with skull-splintering force to the back of his head. A spectral hand stabbed down towards him, fastened in his hair, and dragged him towards the cabinet.

Loring and Ruth Newton, both paralysed with terror,

made no move to come to his assistance and the woman from hell, facing them, was saying in a husky voice pregnant with hate, "Before many hours have passed you will pay for this, Loring Newton. You will learn what it means to disobey the commands of those who return from the farther world!"

Then Martin Lane lost consciousness.

III

Corpse Twin

He came to slowly with a pounding torment in his head and a burning pain in his thigh where the bullet had seared tender flesh. The darkness was black as soot because the tight, agonizing weight around his eyes was a blindfold. A gag filled his mouth. His wrists, crossed behind him, were caught in heavy shackles.

Below him a woman's voice was faintly audible.

Lane listened dully, realizing he must be in a room above Loring Newton's private office. Intuition told him he had been unconscious for a long time; no man could recover immediately from so vicious an assault. The voice of the spectral woman in the room below him spoke words that were grimly significant.

". . . at once, Loring, and be sure you are not followed when you come here. You will find Martin Lane in your office, handcuffed to the chair behind your own desk, and this time you must not blunder in performing the task assigned to you. Unless Lane dies within the hour, your son and daughter will be told the truth about my death. Do you quite understand what I mean?"

The woman was evidently using the telephone on Newton's own desk. Had time enough elapsed, then, for Newton to return to his own home? Probably it had. After Martin Lane's inexplicable disappearance from the office, Newton and his daughter had undoubtedly fled in terror. Now the man was being told to return here.

"If you disobey me or fail again in carrying out my orders," Lane heard the woman's voice softly threaten, "you know what the penalty will be. That is all, Loring. I shall be here waiting."

The phone clicked into its cradle and Lane heard soft scraping sounds as of someone slowly ascending a short flight of stairs. He feigned unconsciousness again. In a moment strong hands seized his legs and shoulders and raised him from the floor.

The woman's voice said softly, "You have been asleep a long while, Martin Lane. Death will be easier if you remain that way."

Lane felt himself being lowered carefuly through space into upstretched hands that were waiting to receive him. Again he was carried forward, this time but a short distance before he was dumped onto a chair. The chair, he guessed, was the one behind Loring Newton's massive desk.

Strong hands held him while others, strangely cold and damp, removed the bracelets from his wrists. His arms were jerked then through the slats of the chair and his wrists secured again with the same steel cuffs.

Then he was left alone, knowing that in a very short while, perhaps less than an hour, Loring Newton would come to murder him.

With grim determination he went to work.

The blindfold received his attention first. Judging from the feel of it, it consisted of a long strip of bandage wound tightly around his head. It could be moved, then, by clever and persistent manipulation of the facial muscles.

He laboured mightily for ten minutes. At the end of that time the bandage was high enough for him to see through a tiny slit beneath it. His head ached fiendishly from the torment of his efforts, and his ridged forehead was sleek with sweat.

The room was dark. He was safe then in continuing his attempts to free himself. But his hands, manacled behind the slats of the chair, were growing numb from lack of circulation.

Every muscle in Martin Lane's lean body suffered agony as he coiled his legs around one side of the chair and brought one foot within reach of his hands. The pain of it sickened him, and thé task required all of fifteen minutes when minutes were terribly precious.

Working slowly, with perspiration dripping like water from his convulsed face, he removed the lace from one shoe. Handcuffs – those of regulation pattern, at least – could sometimes be opened with a strong shoelace if one knew how. The primary requisite was to use both hands with equal dexterity, and Martin Lane was master of his own lean body.

Laboriously he looped the shoestring, forced it into the lock, and coiled it around the end of the screw. A dozen times then he exerted sudden pressure, yanking the string with all his strength while both arms maintained a cramped, nerve-numbing position that produced agony all but un-endurable.

When the bolt finally yielded, he had to steel himself against a return of unconsciousness. The ordeal was finished, though. He was free.

Then before he could capitalize on that hard-earned freedom a door lock clicked in the darkness. With horrible abruptness he was aware of the doom-march of advancing footsteps!

Lane sat rigid, wrists still resting in the open shackles behind him. With head tilted back he stared through the thin slit beneath the blindfold. The slow march of footsteps began again as the unseen intruder paced sluggishly towards him.

A light-switch clicked. The sudden glare stabbed Lane's eyes and momentarily blinded him. When the blindness passed, he saw what had happened. Loring Everett Newton had returned in obedience to the murder-command issued by the veiled woman from the grave!

Standing there against the opposite wall, Newton peered at his intended victim. Terror had brought him here. Terror was apparent in his bulging eyes, in the convulsive twitching of his whole big body. His right hand, holding a small automatic pistol, trembled violently at his side.

Martin Lane sat motionless, feigning unconsciousness.

Newton slowly advanced towards him, never once ceasing to stare. Halfway to the desk he stopped, and a low, liquid sob drained what little determination was left in his warped soul. He looked fearfully at the gun in his trembling fist, raised it, lowered it again, and moaned, "I can't do it. Oh, God, Marguerite, I can't do it! It would be cold-blooded *murder* . . ."

Martin Lane did not move a muscle.

It would be over in a moment, Lane was certain. The gun in Newton's fist would wobble into firing position and that trembling trigger-finger would tighten. The man would do it because he was too utterly terrified to disobey the hell-woman's command. He had already committed murder once – perhaps in good cause – and now his mind was twisted and torn by dealings with the dead. He was on the verge of insanity.

He would come closer to the desk and then take aim. And then Martin Lane would lunge sideways in the chair, leap erect and grapple with him before the gun could again blast out its murderous chant.

But Newton was retreating. Still staring with horribly wide eyes, still mumbling to himself, he paced slowly backwards towards the door. Lane watched every move and saw the man's left hand reach to the light-switch, saw the right hand, holding the gun, come slowly up for action.

Lacking courage to do the job in a lighted room, Newton was going to plunge the office into darkness and then squeeze the trigger!

With palsied fingers Newton pressed the switch.

Martin Lane went into action.

Shielded by darkness, Lane slid both arms through the slats of his chair, lunged forward, and began crawling. When the gun roared its death chant he was a full ten feet from the desk and slowly straightening to his feet.

The echoes of the blast crashed and jangled around him, choking the office with thunderous reverberations. No need now to creep soundlessly! No need for caution! Loring Newton was lurching forward, sobbing like a frightened child.

Lane leaped with catlike quickness, extended both arms, and slapped a two-foot length of bandage across Newton's

mouth. The bandage had been a blindfold. Now it provided
an effective gag and kept the man from screaming.

With one hand Lane held the twisted ends. With the
other he wrenched the gun from Newton's fist, then pushed
an upthrust knee into the man's back and jerked him to the
floor. The whole thing was done so swiftly the echoes of the
gun-blast were still alive in the room when Lane hurled
himself down upon his struggling victim.

A single well-placed blow stifled the terrified man's
attempt to put up a fight. Gun in hand, Lane dragged
him across the floor and thrust him behind the filing
cabinet. When Martin Lane straightened, the office was
once again a sinister abode of silence and darkness.

Swiftly, soundlessly, Lane strode to the cabinet on the
opposite side of the room.

He knew what was coming and set himself to wait for it.
Only one shot had been fired. To the veiled woman that
shot could mean only one thing – that Loring Everett
Newton had obeyed her instructions.

Footsteps were audible in the depths of the cabinet. In
there someone was cautiously descending a flight of stairs
or a ladder. Hidden hands pushed the door open. A crouching shadow-shape stepped into the room.

The gun in Martin Lane's fist crashed solidly down on
the intruder's stooped head, and without a sound the shape
crumpled to the floor at Lane's feet. In a half crouch Lane
pushed the door shut and scratched a match.

The face that gleamed yellow in the flickering light from
his cupped hand was the hard face of Andrews, Loring
Newton's chauffeur.

Martin Lane's lips curled in a thin smile of triumph. He
waited a moment, then quietly drew the cabinet door open
again. With Newton's automatic still gripped in his right
hand, he groped with his left and felt the shafts of a ladder.
Light spilled down through an open trap in the ceiling.

As he slowly ascended, Lane heard voices in the room
above.

He gripped the gun harder. A man and woman were
doing the talking, and he thought he knew who the man
was. Evidently the pair had not expected Andrews to

complete his mission for quite some time and were patiently awaiting the chauffeur's reappearance.

Lane took the last two rungs of the ladder at top speed and telescoped erect on the floor above. A man and a woman whirled to face him.

The woman, young and attractive, was a stranger. The man was Mr Henry Hackler of Newton, Hackler and Fern.

Lane stepped forward, thinking that in his wrinkled blue suit he probably looked like a helpless, middle-aged clerk holding a gun he did not know how to use. It was not to be so easy, though. While anticipating trouble, he was startled by the suddenness of its coming. Obviously he had under-estimated Mr Henry Hackler's potential.

Without a word of warning, Hackler leaped!

The man showed his true character in that leap, or at least demonstrated contempt for his slender, unsmiling adversary. Had his fear of Martin Lane been greater – had he known the dynamite that lay dormant beneath that apparently unimpressive exterior – he might have made for the door and chanced a bullet. With the room but dimly lighted, his chance of escape might even have been a good one.

Instead, he chose to reach for his attractive female companion. His big hands gripped her shoulders and swung her around. She made a good shield.

With a sneer on his lips then, Henry Hackler backed slowly to the door, dragging the girl with him. And when Martin Lane jerked forward to halt him, the big man abruptly changed grips.

His thick right arm coiled around the girl's throat. His left hand leaped to a pocket of his coat. Lane, halfway across the room, faced failure unless he chose the alternative of shooting through a squirming, terrified target.

"Stop right where you are!" Hackler snarled.

Lane obeyed, even when the gun came out of Hackler's pocket to menace him. Retreat was impossible, and the chances were about even that Hackler would squeeze the trigger. Even so, with a squirming woman in his grasp Hackler could easily miss.

Twice before, the insurance man had made arrangements

to have Lane put out of the way. Of that Lane was certain.
Now, though, he evidently felt that Martin Lane was not
worth shooting at. Sneering, he said with extreme self-
confidence, "You're quite the meddler, aren't you? Quite
the famous meddler! I ought to kill you, but you're not
worth the effort. I'll let Andrews do it for me." Then,
savagely: "Walk backwards to the opening in the floor!"

Lane took a slow step backwards, his gaze fixed on the
man's face. His own gun was still gripped in his fist. So far,
Hackler had overlooked that. Given time enough, the man
would surely thrust some part of his beefy body out from
behind his human shield. Then –

But Hackler's next words annihilated that hope. "Drop
the gun!" he snarled.

With no alternative, Lane let his weapon fall to the
floor.

"Now do as I told you! Walk backwards to the trap!"

Lane took two more backward steps. Then something
unforeseen interrupted Hackler's grim programme. Behind
him the door of a closet clattered open and, like an uncaged
wild man, Mr Dominic Corsi stormed from the closet's
depths!

IV

The Silence of the Grave

Corsi had been confined for some time in his dark little
prison and now was livid with anger. He emerged with his
arms flailing the air, his face crimson, his mouth spewing a
lurid blast of Sicilian vituperation.

He looked extremely formidable – much more so, of
course, than did Lane. Henry Hackler, startled, swung to
confront him. "Get back!" Hackler yelled.

Dominic Corsi was far too angry to think of obeying any
such command. Cursing, waving his arms, he advanced.
The gun did not scare him until he was almost on top of it
and Hackler had screamed again, "Get back!"

Unobserved, Martin Lane stepped forward. In the presence of such an outraged Vesuvius he seemed even less

obtrusive, more harmless, than before. A sudden panther-like leap closed the gap between him and Hackler.

Hackler's right hand, brandishing the gun, was suddenly caught in a grip of steel fingers.

Martin Lane whirled with his knees bent and, with an enormous heave of shoulders more muscular than they seemed, jerked the amazed Hackler off his feet.

Like a flung side of beef the big man's body hurtled through space. The wall stopped him with a bone-splintering crunch that made Lane wince. Hackler thudded to the floor and lay still.

The girl stood numb with terror as Lane scooped up Hackler's gun. Turning, Lane took her by one arm and curtly ordered her towards the trap door, while Dominic Corsi stood with mouth agape, torrential outburst of oaths silenced by amazement.

Then abruptly Lane stopped, and the smile of triumph that had begun to form on his lips was suddenly gone again. A man's head had lurched into view above the trap's opening, and the snarling face into which Lane stared was one he had forgotten. It belonged to Andrews, the chauffeur.

The gun in Andrews's big fist was aimed squarely at Lane's chest and, behind Lane, Corsi shrieked a warning.

One savage thrust of Martin Lane's arm sent the girl stumbling out of danger. He himself spun sideways as the weapon belched thunder.

Twice within the past few hours the gods of luck had deflected bullets from the vital parts of Lane's anatomy. This time the potential death that sprayed towards him came in a triple dose as the gun barked three times.

Reeling in a wild sidewise leap, Lane went unhit while his own gun roared its staccato challenge.

Andrews screamed. With a shoulder shattered by Lane's bullet he staggered on the ladder, clawed for an instant at the edge of the floor and then crashed down into the cabinet. Martin Lane descended after him.

The man was groaning on the cabinet floor when Lane reached him. Roughly Lane jerked him erect, dragged him to the chair behind Newton's desk, and propped him there.

When Lane reached the top of the ladder a moment later, Dominic Corsi was bending over the sprawled body of Henry Hackler.

"He is shot," the Italian said.

Lane stared. Two of the three bullets fired by Loring Newton's chauffeur and intended for Martin Lane had found a final resting place in Hackler's big body. Either would have been fatal.

"I should call the police?" Corsi asked.

"No." Lane frowned. "I think not."

Downstairs in Newton's private office Lane pushed the girl into a chair and shook Loring Everett Newton out of a terror-induced stupor. "Now listen," he said softly, "and get this straight, Newton. It may mean a lot to you."

Newton listened, staring.

"In the beginning," Lane declared, "Henry Hackler somehow found out the truth about your wife's death. Have you any idea how he did that?"

Newton was slow in answering. "I – can only guess," he said finally. "He may have been driving along the road that night, or walking along it, when –" He shuddered. "You see, he owned a cottage on the lake. It is just possible he may have witnessed the – the –" He bogged down again, staring hopelessly at Lane. "You see, my wife went there with Arthur Fern that night, to Fern's camp."

"I'm convinced," Lane said, scowling, "that Fern had nothing to do with what happened after your wife's death. Hackler played his game alone. He wanted your money and control of the company, and reasoned correctly that you'd be nervous and high-strung enough to be an easy victim for anything that seemed the least bit supernormal. He began by planting Andrews in your home as your chauffeur. Recall how he did that, do you?"

"He – he said Andrews was a deserving fellow out of work."

"Ha! I can't swear I'm right, but I believe Andrews is a former professional medium who worked under the name of Swami Sandrana." Lane turned to the girl. "Is that right?"

She nodded.

"Hackler hired Andrews to put on a show for you," Lane declared, "and the young lady here was brought into it by Andrews to impersonate your wife. Hackler probably intended to carry it just so far and then wind it up by sending you to jail, Newton, charged with the murder of your wife and perhaps of me as well. He'd have the company under his control then, and your ghost-story alibi wouldn't have convinced a jury of morons. You were an easy victim because you were scared half to death even before he began working on you. Are you beginning to understand?"

Loring Newton wagged his head up and down slowly but then gazed at the girl and mumbled, "I – don't know what you mean about this girl and my wife. Surely –"

"I'll show you. Or, rather, Corsi will. Corsi, you see, is a member of the Society of Magicians."

Dominic Corsi, nodding, went quickly to the room upstairs and returned with a cardboard box which he dumped on the floor.

"This," said Lane quietly, "is what might be called a property box. I brought equipment of my own tonight when I invaded that upstairs office, but found this stuff already there. With Corsi's help I intended to duplicate the psychic phenomena you've been witnessing night after night in this room. Something –" he gazed ruefully at the Italian "– went wrong with my plans."

"Something went very wrong indeed!" Corsi corroborated vehemently. "I waited up there for the lights to be turned out in this room. This man Andrews crept up behind me and slugged me, then he and Hackler threw me most ignominiously into a closet while this girl took my place for the performance! They tied me with ropes, but ropes are poor things with which to ensnare a magician, no? What I wish to know, Mr Lane, is why you did not inform me what to expect. Nothing did I know except my instructions. Nothing was I prepared for. Never was I –"

Lane put a stopper on the flow of words by saying softly, "I think we know the rest of it, Dominic." Then, turning to Newton, he said, "The equipment in this box is really rudimentary. It consists of a face-mask and rubber gloves sprayed with a dilution of Balmain's Luminous Paint, and a robe of finest French bridal veiling, thin as gauze, which has been dyed with the same preparation. After exposure to bright light, this stuff will glow with a soft, weird luminosity in the dark.

"Undoubtedly you investigated that cabinet in daylight, Newton, and found it empty. You explored the floor and walls but neglected to pay much attention to the ceiling, which was less accessible. Through the trap-door in the ceiling Andrews was able to lower a padded ladder by which the young lady could descend into your office.

"She came in darkness. She herself was invisible until after clever manipulation of the luminous gauze fabric she finally draped the veil over herself and appeared in human form.

"So you see, Newton, it was really quite simple. Professional mediums have used that stunt, or variations of it, for years."

Newton nodded slowly. He was sitting on a chair near the door, and the expression of utter despair on his face indicated the nature of the thoughts crawling in his dazed brain. He was a murderer. He faced the ultimate penalty. Martin Lane, staring at him, felt sorry for him but felt sorrier for the man's son and daughter, who would bear the brunt of it.

"Well," Lane said finally, "it's time to go, Newton. Time to —"

He didn't finish. Andrews, the chauffeur, silent for a long while behind the desk, chose that moment to lurch madly to his feet. He, too, would have a penalty to pay when his fate was weighed on the scales of justice. Evidently he feared it.

With one hand he scooped up the gun that Martin Lane had placed on the desk. It was not Lane's weapon; it had belonged to Henry Hackler. Lane's own gun, seized long ago from Newton and retrieved from the floor in the room upstairs where he had dropped it at Hackler's command, lay now in Martin Lane's pocket. It came out with alacrity.

But Loring Everett Newton was erect, blocking Andrews's escape.

The gun in Andrews's fist whipped high as the fleeing man hurled himself at the door. Newton had no chance.

The girl and Dominic Corsi stumbled out of the way, both screaming. Martin Lane's trigger finger, ready for action, curled a fraction of a second too late. Not intentionally too late, not deliberately, but at the same time not of necessity. It could perhaps have curled in time. It didn't.

In that split second Martin Lane's agile mind had flashed to the only merciful solution of the entire problem. Instinct held his hand.

The gun in Andrews's fist roared, sending a bullet into Loring Everett Newton's heart. Then, almost but not quite at the same instant, the gun in Martin Lane's hand spewed a bullet, and Andrews, leaping wildly for the door, twisted in mid-air, cried out in agony, and fell across the sprawled body of his victim.

Martin Lane strode forward, made a careful examination of the two lifeless bodies, then turned to the girl.

"I'm going to give you an even break," he said grimly, "even though I personally owe you something for pushing me into an elevator shaft. Undoubtedly you've heard a lot, but just as surely you know nothing. You could talk until doomsday and get no one to listen to you. However –" he gazed coldly into the girl's terrified eyes "– just remember that the charge of extortion is a serious one, and too much talk will bring it crashing down on your head. You're free to go now. I'll personally escort you to the nearest railroad station."

He turned to Corsi and held out his hand. "Thanks, Dominic, for what you've done." Then, gazing at the sprawled body of Loring Everett Newton, he said softly, enigmatically, "For what I've done, Newton has a very lovely daughter who will in the end, I'm sure, be much happier. She need never know now that her father was anything less than she believed him to be."

Death at the Main

Frank Gruber

O liver Quade had perused both the *Social Register* and *Bradstreet's Journal* on a number of occasions and he calculated mentally that there was easily a billion dollars worth of blue blood here tonight in this big renovated barn. Reggie Ragsdale, the host, was worth a hundred million if he was worth a cent; the average fortune of the two hundred-odd other men could be estimated conservatively at five million.

Long Island didn't see many cocking mains. Cocking wasn't a gentleman's sport like horse racing and fox hunting. In fact, many of Long Island's bluebloods had shaken their heads when Young Ragsdale took up cock-fighting. But they had eagerly accepted invitations to the Ragsdale estate to witness the great cocking main between Ragsdale's birds and the best of the Old South, the feathered warriors of George Treadwell.

Ragsdale had cleared out this large barn, had built tiers of seats in the form of a big bowl surrounding the cockpit. The place was ablaze with lights, and servants in uniforms scampered about with liquid refreshments for the guests.

Oliver Quade had crashed the gate and was enjoying himself immensely. He'd heard of the cocking main quite by accident; and, being a Southerner by birth and a cocking enthusiast, he'd "crashed". He'd brought along a bagful of books, too. After a long and varied career he never knew when the opportunity might present itself to dispose of a few volumes and he wanted to be prepared for any contingency.

He chuckled at the thought of it. Two hundred

millionaires, protected daily by business managers, secretaries and servants; few of them had ever been compelled – or privileged, depending upon your viewpoint – to listen to a really good book salesman. And Quade *was* a good book salesman, the best in the country. Oliver Quade, the Human Encyclopedia, who travelled the country from coast to coast, selling books and salting away twenty thousand dollars every year.

The fights had already been started when Quade bluffed the doorkeeper into letting him into the Ragsdale barn. For an hour he rubbed elbows with the Long Island aristocrats, talked with them and cheered with them while the feathered warriors in the pit fought and bled and died.

The score stood at eight-all now, with the seventeenth and last bout of the evening to come up, which would decide the superiority of Ragsdale's Jungle Shawls and the Whitehackles of George Treadwell. Ragsdale rose to make an announcement as the handlers carried out the birds after the sixteenth fight.

"There'll be a short intermission of ten minutes before the final bout, gentlemen."

Quade's eyes sparkled. This was his golden chance, the one he'd waited for all evening. Perhaps they'd throw him out, but Quade had been thrown out of places before. Chuckling, he climbed upon a bench. He held out his hands in a supplicating gesture.

"Gentlemen," he cried out suddenly in a booming voice that surprised people who heard it issue from such a lean body, "give me your attention for a minute. I'm going to entertain you – something entirely new and different."

A couple of attendants looked with surprised eyes at Quade. Reggie Ragsdale, on the other side of the pit, frowned. Quade knew that he'd have to talk fast – catch the interest of the audience before Ragsdale tried to stop him. He had confidence in his oratorical powers.

"Gentlemen," he continued in his rich, penetrating voice. "I'm Oliver Quade, the Human Encyclopedia. I have the greatest brain in the United States, probably the greatest in the world. I know the answers to all questions: what came first, the chicken or the egg; the population of Sydney, Australia; the dates of every battle from the beginning of history; the founders of your family fortunes. Try me out, gentlemen. Any question at all – any! History, science, mathematics, general interest. You, sir, ask me a question!"

Quade, knowing the hesitation of any audience to get started, pointed to a man close to him, whose mouth was agape.

The man flushed, stammered. "Why, uh – I don't know anything I want to ask – Yes, I do! At what price did NT & T close today?"

"Easy!" cried Quade. "You could read that in today's newspaper. National Telephone and Telegraph closed to-day at 187½. A year ago today it was 153. Ask me something harder. You, sir," he pointed. "A question; history, science, mathematics –"

"What is the distance to the moon?"

"From the centre of the earth to the centre of the moon the distance is approximately 238,857 miles. Next question!"

The game was catching on. Quade didn't have to point at anyone now. The audience had gathered its wits and the next question came promptly.

"What is ambergris?"

"Ambergris is greasy substance spewed up by sick whales and is used in the manufacture of perfumes. It comes in lumps and is extremely valuable, a chunk of approximately thirty pounds recently found in the North Atlantic bringing $5,200. Next!"

"How do you measure the thickness of leather?" That was evidently a wealthy shoe manufacturer, but his question didn't phase Quade in the least.

"By irons," he shot back. "An iron is one seventy-second of an inch. The ordinary shoe sole is eight irons thick, although some run as thick as twelve irons and those on dancing pumps as thin as four irons – And now –"

Quad stooped, snapped open his suitcase and extracted a thick volume from it. He held it aloft. "And now I'm going to give each and every gentlemen here tonight an opportunity to learn the answers *themselves* to any question that may arise, today, tomorrow or any time during the year. This book has the answers to ALL questions. *The Compendium of Human Knowledge*, the knowledge of the ages crammed into one volume, two thousand pages. Classified, condensed and abbreviated."

Quade paused for a brief breath and shot a glance at Reggie Ragsdale. The young millionaire, who had assumed a tolerant, amused expression a few moments ago when he saw that Quade's game was catching on with the guests, was frowning again. Entertaining the guests was all right, but selling something to them, that was different! Quade knew that he'd have to work even faster.

He launched again into his sales talk, exhorting in a vibrant, penetrating voice that was famous throughout the country. "The price of this magnificent volume is not twenty-five dollars as you might expect, not even fifteen or ten dollars, but a paltry two ninety-five. It sounds preposterous, I know, but it's really true. The knowledge of the ages for only two ninety-five! Yes, Mr Ragsdale, you want to ask a question before you purchase one of these marvellous books?"

"I don't want to buy your confounded book!" cried Ragsdale. "I want to know how you got in here."

Quade chuckled. "Why, your doorkeeper let me in. I told him I was a book salesman and thought this gathering would be ideal for selling books. Really, Mr Ragsdale, that's exactly what I told him and he let me in. Of course, if he didn't believe me, that's not my fault."

A roar of laughter swept the audience. None doubted that Quade had actually made his entrance in that manner. His audacity appealed to the thrill-jaded aristocrats. Even Ragsdale grinned.

"All right, you can stay. But put up your books now; they're coming in with the birds for the last fight. After it, you can sell your books. I'll even buy one myself."

Quade was disappointed. He'd made his pitch, built up his audience to the selling point and he didn't like to quit before collecting. But he couldn't very well cross Ragsdale – and sight of the handlers coming in with the birds was making the sportsmen turn to the pit. The best book in the world couldn't compete against a couple of fighting roosters.

Quade closed his sample case, walked down to Reggie Ragsdale's ringside seat and prepared to watch the last fight of the evening. Ragsdale grinned at him.

The handlers were down in the pit now. Ragsdale's handler, Tom Dodd, carried a huge, red Jungle Shawl and Treadwell's handler, Cleve Storm, a fierce-looking Whitehackle.

"Treadwell must have a lot of confidence in that Whitehackle," Quade remarked. "He's battle-scarred. Been in at least four professional fights."

Ragsdale looked at Quade in surprise. "Ah, you know that cocks are at their best in their first fight?"

"Of course," said Quade. "I was raised down in Alabama and fought a few cocks of my own. That Whitehackle must be one of those rare ones that's improved with every fight instead of deteriorated. Ah!"

The referee had finished giving the handlers their instructions and Storm and Dodd retired to opposite sides of the sand-covered pit.

The referee looked at first one handler, then another. He hesitated a moment, then cried, "Time!"

Both handlers released their birds. There was a fluttering of wings, a rushing of air from both directions and a sudden rumbling of voices from the audience. For the Jungle Shawl faltered in his charge, turned yellow. An unforgivable weakness in a fighting bird.

It cost the Shawl his life, for with a squawk and flutter of wings the Whitehackle hurtled through the air and pounced on his opponent. His vicious beak hooked into the hackle of the Shawl and for a second he straddled the bird, then the two-inch steel gaffe slashed down and the Jungle Shawl was dead!

"Hung!" cried Tom Dodd.

Both handlers rushed forward. Quade looked at Reggie Ragsdale. The young millionaire was rising to his feet, his lips twisted into a wry grin. Quade looked across the cockpit at George Treadwell and gasped.

Treadwell was still seated, but his arms and head hung

over the top of the pit and even as Quade looked, his hat fell from his head and dropped to the sandy floor. At the distance Quade could see that Treadwell's eyes were glassy.

"Treadwell!" Reggie Ragsdale exclaimed. He, too, had glanced across the pit.

Ragsdale brushed past Quade and hurried around the pit to Treadwell's side, Quade following. Other spectators saw Treadwell then and a bedlam of noise went up.

"Don't anyone leave!" thundered Ragsdale, his bored manner gone. "Treadwell is dead!"

"*He's been murdered!*"

The three words rang out above the rumble of noise. Quade looked down into the pit at the awe-stricken face of Cleve Storm, Treadwell's handler.

"Don't be a fool, man!" he cautioned. "You can't make an accusation like that! Mr Treadwell probably died of heart failure."

"He's been murdered, I tell you!" cried Storm. "There wasn't nothin' the matter with his heart."

Ragsdale straightened beside Quade. "Doctor Pardley!" he called.

A middle-aged man with a grey-flecked Vandyke came up. He made a quick examination of George Treadwell, without touching the body. Then he frowned at Ragsdale. "Hard to say, Reggie. Might have been apoplexy except that he's not the type."

Ragsdale blinked. "He was a dead game sportsman. I'll see that his widow receives my cheque at once."

"That ain't gonna bring him back to life!" cried Cleve Storm. "I – I warned him not to come up here."

"Why?" snapped Ragsdale testily.

Cleve Storm looked around the circle of hostile faces, for most of the men here were personal friends of Ragsdale. He gulped. "Because he didn't have a chance, not against your money. You always win."

Ragsdale winced. It was the deadliest insult any man could have hurled at him: to accuse him of not being a real sportsman. His lips tightened.

Quade came to Ragsdale's assistance. "I'd advise you to keep your opinions for the cops."

Ragsdale flashed him a wan smile of thanks. "That's right, we've got to call the police. And when the newspapers hear of this!"

Quade knew what he meant. Cock-fighting was an undercover sport. A murder on the Ragsdale estate – cock-fighting. The tabloids would have a scoop.

Ragsdale signalled to a steward. "Telephone for the Charlton police, Louis," he ordered. "Tell them someone died here – might possibly be a murder." He did not spare himself.

Quade looked at his leather case full of books and shook his head. Well, this shattered his hopes of making sales. The prospective customers wouldn't be in the mood now for buying books, even if Quade had the bad taste to try selling them with a corpse just a few feet away.

Wait – a thought struck Quade. The police! They'd be here in a few minutes. This might be a murder after all and everyone here knew everyone else – except Quade. He was a gate-crasher – and he was *not* a millionaire. Why – why, he might even have some very bad moments trying to explain his presence here.

The police came, four of them, led by Chief Kells. With them came the county medical examiner. There was deference in the chief's manner as he approached Ragsdale.

"Cock-fighting, sir? It's going to make quite a stir in town. It's – it's against the law!"

"I know," replied Ragsdale wearily. "Go ahead, do your duty."

The chief looked importantly at the medical examiner who was already going over the body of George Treadwell. "Very well, sir, you might begin by telling me just what happened."

Ragsdale sighed. "Our birds were fighting in the pit – the last bout. My bird lost. When I looked across the pit, there was Treadwell, head hanging over the railing, dead."

"Who was beside him?" asked the chief.

Ragsdale shook his head. "I don't know, several of my guests, I suppose. I know only that I was directly opposite him across the width of the pit. But no one – excepting myself – had any motive for wishing his death."

"And why yourself?" The chief pounced on Ragsdale's self-accusal.

"Because I had a bet with Treadwell and lost."

The chief looked worried, but just then the medical examiner came up. He, too, was frowning. "Not a mark on him," he said. "Yet I'd swear that it wasn't apoplexy or heart failure. Symptoms indicate he's been poisoned, but I can't find anything on him. I'll have to do a post-mortem."

Cleve Storm, who had released his Whitehackle in the pit and come up, sprang forward. "I knew he was poisoned. I knew it."

"How did you know it?" asked Chief Kells sharply. "And who are you anyway?"

"He was Treadwell's trainer," explained Ragsdale. "A loyal employee."

Kells shrugged his shoulders hopelessly. "It would have to be murder. All right, Mr Ragsdale. I've got to do some questioning. How much money did you have bet on the final outcome of these cock fights?"

"Ten thousand – no, wait. Thirty-five thousand altogether. Ten thousand with Treadwell and twenty-five thousand with a man down in the South."

"Who? Is he here?"

"No, and I really don't know the man except by reputation. The bet was made through correspondence. A cocking enthusiast who lives in Nashville; C. Pitts is the name."

The chief's eyes narrowed. "That sounds screwy. You mean this Pitts guy just up and sent you twenty-five thousand as a bet?"

"Not exactly. Pitts sent the money to the editor of the *Feathered Fighter*," explained Ragsdale. "I gave my own cheque to Mr Morgan when he arrived here."

"That's true," said a heavy-set man, stepping forward. "I have both cheques in my pocket right now."

Kells bit his lip. "You know this Pitts fellow?"

"Not personally," said the magazine man, "but by reputation. He bets on many of the cocking mains and I've held stakes for him before. The arrangements have always been made by mail."

Kells grunted. "How long you been raising roosters, Mr Ragsdale? I thought horses was your game."

"They are, but a few months ago Treadwell got me interested in game cocks. To tell you the truth, I've only raised a few birds and they're still too young to fight. All the cocks I fought here tonight were purchased specially for the occasion. It's quite ethical, I assure you."

Quade perked up his ears. This was ironical indeed. Ragsdale with millions at his command and intensely interested in winning in everything he did, had probably spent an enormous sum for his fighting birds – and yet they'd lost, against ordinary fighting birds raised by Treadwell himself. Quade began to take a more serious interest in the situation. There might be something here yet that would prove interesting, perhaps afford Quade an opportunity to use that marvellous brain of his.

"From whom did you buy your roosters?" Kells again.

"Terence Walcott, who lives in the state of Oregon. Tom Dodd brought the birds East and handled them for me, during the fights. Dodd!"

Tom Dodd came forward. He was a little bandy-legged man of about forty.

"You the chap who raises these roosters?" questioned the chief.

"Yes, I work for Mr Terence Walcott of Corvallis, Oregon. I been working around game cocks all my life."

"Where were you when Treadwell was kil – died?"

"In the pit, of course."

Kells looked at Ragsdale for confirmation. The latter nodded. "That's right. He was down in the pit. In the opposite corner from Treadwell. Treadwell's handler, Cleve Storm, was in the other corner, just under Treadwell's seat. Federle, the referee, was all around the pit."

"And everybody was watching them? That sorta lets those three out. Well, who was close by Treadwell at the moment?"

"I was," a lean, middle-aged man spoke up. "I was right beside him on his left. I was so excited over the fights down in the pit, however, that I didn't even know anything had happened to poor George Treadwell until Ragsdale came dashing around."

The chief looked at the man with suspicion-laden eyes. "What's your name?"

"Ralph Wilcoxson. Treadwell was my business partner. Treadwell & Wilcoxson, Lumber."

The chief looked even more hostile than before. "And who was on the other side of him?"

"I was," said Morgan, the editor of the *Feathered Fighter*.

The chief snorted in disgust. "Hell, everyone here is a friend of someone and respectable as a deacon. What chance have I got?"

Louis, the steward, who was standing behind his master, coughed. "Pardon, sir, everyone here isn't a friend. I – I let the gentlemen in at the door – and one of them didn't have a card."

Quade swore softly. Ragsdale, the sportsman, hadn't seen fit to betray him, but the servant, who'd been the butt of Quade's harmless joke a while ago, couldn't take it. This was his revenge.

"He means me, Chief," he said, beating the traitorous steward to the punch.

The chief's shoulders hunched, and his teeth bared. Here was someone who didn't belong. "Who are you?" he asked, in a voice that almost shook the rafters.

Quade grinned impudently. "Oliver Quade, the Human Encyclopedia, the man who knows the answers to all questions." The introduction rolled glibly off Quade's tongue. It was part of his showmanship.

The chief's mouth dropped open. "Human Encyclopedia! What the hell you talkin' about?"

"Just what I said. I'm the Human Encyclopedia who knows everything."

"Ask him who killed Treadwell," called out a wag in the crowd.

Quade winced. His wits had been wool-gathering, otherwise he'd never have left himself open for that. The chief pounced on it, too. "All right, Mr Encyclopedia – who and what killed Treadwell?"

Quade gulped. "Ah, now, Chief, you're not playing fair! Even Human Encyclopedias have a code of professional

ethics. We don't go into competition with other pro-
fessions. You wouldn't think it fair for cops to take in
laundry on the side or sell moth tabs from door to door?"

Chief Kells tried to look stern but made a failure of it.
"So you're not so smart after all."

"Well," said Quade, "it's against union rules, but I'll
help out a bit." He pointed at the body of Treadwell.
"Notice how the arms are hanging over the pit. I suggest
you look at the hands!"

The medical examiner sprang forward, reached down
and picked up Treadwell's limp arms. He exclaimed almost
immediately. "He's right. There's a tiny spot of blood right
in the palm of his right hand. And it's inflamed. Looks like
he's been struck with a hypodermic!"

The chief whirled and levelled a finger at Cleve Storm.
"You – you're the man!"

The cock handler's jaw dropped and his eyes threatened
to pop from his head. "Me!" he cried.

"Yes, you! You been doing all the hollering about murder
around here and you're the only one *could* have done it!"

"I could not!" screamed Storm, suddenly panic-stricken
that the tables had been turned on him. "I was down in the
pit when he was killed."

The chief nodded grimly. "That's why I'm accusing you.
Look," he pointed at the body of Treadwell. "He's hanging
over the pit right over the side where you was waiting while
the roosters were fighting. Dodd was over on Ragsdale's
side, so it couldn't have been him. And the referee was
moving all around, which lets him out."

The chief's reasoning was sound, but the expression on
Cleve Storm's face caused Quade to pucker up his brow.
Storm didn't act like a murderer – and if he really was, he'd
been damned dumb a while ago to insist on murder when
everyone else was willing to let it go as heart failure.

He looked down into the cockpit. The Whitehackle was
still down there and was now quietly scratching away in the
sand, hopefully trying to find a worm or bug. But where
was the Jungle Shawl's carcass?

Chief Kells spat out a stream of tobacco juice. "I'm
arresting you, Storm. If I find a hypodermic anywhere

around here you're as good as burned right now. Oscar!" He signalled to one of his policemen. "Go over that pit down there, inch by inch. Look for a needle or hypodermic. You, Myers and Coons, you go over this place with a fine-tooth comb!"

Kells turned to Reggie Ragsdale. "I don't believe there'll be any more now, Mr Ragsdale. Of course you know I got to bring charges about the cock fighting. That'll mean maybe a small fine or suspended sentence. You'll be notified when to appear in court."

Ragsdale nodded. "Of course, Chief, and thanks for the way you've handled things here. I'll speak to the board of councilmen about you."

The chief's eyes glowed. He rubbed his hands together and began shouting orders. Men bustled around. The body of Treadwell was carried out on a stretcher. Cleve Storm, still protesting his innocence, was led out. Guests began to leave.

Quade gathered up his bagful of books and topcoat. He walked over to Ragsdale. "Sorry about the trouble. Hope everything will work out all right."

"Thanks." The young sportsman smiled wanly.

Quade nodded and swung around. His topcoat caught on the top of the railing. He gave it a jerk and it came away with a slight ripping sound. Quade swore softly. The coat was only about a year old. He reached out to touch a nail on which the coat had caught.

He stopped his fingers an inch from the point and his eyes narrowed suddenly. It wasn't a nail on which the coat had caught, but a needle. It stuck up about a sixteenth of an inch from the top of the flat railing. This was the exact spot behind which Treadwell had sat.

At that moment one of the policemen down in the pit yelled. "I've found it!" He held aloft a shiny hypodermic needle. The medical examiner hurried down into the pit and took the needle from the policeman's hand. He sniffed at it. "Not sure," he said, "but it smells like *curare*, that stuff the South American Indians put on their blow-gun arrows. Kills instantly. Figured it was something like this that killed Treadwell," he said triumphantly.

Quade shook his head. *Curare* at a cock fight! Things were getting complicated. A scrap of information in the back of Quade's head bothered him. He had a habit of filing away odd bits of information in his encyclopedic brain and, when he had time, marshalling them together like the pieces of a crossword puzzle. A marvellous memory and this faculty of fitting together apparently irrelevant bits of information was largely responsible for his nickname – the Human Encyclopedia.

Quade deserved that name. Fifteen years ago he'd come into possession of a set of the *Encyclopedia Americana*, twenty-five large volumes. Quade read all the volumes from *A* to *Z* and then when he had finished, began at *A* again. He was now at *PU* on the fifth trip through the volumes. Fifteen years of reading the encyclopedias, plus extensive reading of other books, had given him a truly encyclopedic brain.

What was this odd bit of information that puzzled him? It had something to do with the mix-up here tonight – something he'd observed or heard. Storm? No, because Quade was quite sure Storm was innocent. Something about the birds?

He hesitated for a moment, then sauntered over to the rear door of the barn. He slipped out quietly.

The yard was pitch dark. In the front of the building he could hear voices and automobiles, but back here it was as still and dark as the inside of a pocket. There was no moon or stars. A long black shadow loomed up ahead. Quade made his way towards it.

As he approached the building he recognized it for a Cornell-type laying house. There was a door at one end of the building. Quade set down his bag and tried it. It was unlocked. He pushed it open. He stepped inside and struck a match. By the light of it he saw a light switch beside the door. He turned it and electric lights sprang on.

Quade saw that the building was evidently used as a conditioning room for poultry. Wire coops, sacks of feed, a bench on which stood cans of oil, remedies, tonics and other paraphernalia. Quade examined the objects and grinned. There was even a box of face rouge. Having raised birds himself he knew that breeders often used rouge to touch up the ear lobes of the birds. Baking soda was used to bring out the colour of the red Jungle Shawl birds. The oil was for slicking up the feathers.

A large gunny sack on the floor caught his eye. There was a small pool of dark liquid beside the sack. Quade stooped and picked up the sack. He dumped out the contents – four Jungle Shawl cocks – dead.

Four? Nine of Ragsdale's birds had met defeat. Quade hadn't seen all the bouts, but he'd been informed by other spectators that six of the losing Shawls had been killed, three merely wounded. Well, where were the other two carcasses? The bag was large enough to have held all of them. That didn't make sense. If Tom Dodd had brought the carcasses here why hadn't he brought them all? Or hadn't Dodd brought them here?

A sound behind him caused Quade to whirl. He was just in time to see the door push open and a couple of hairy arms reach in. The hands held a huge, red fighting cock. Even as Quade looked, the cock was dropped to the floor and the door slammed shut. Quade heard the hasp rattle outside and knew that the person who had thrown in the Jungle Shawl had locked the door on the outside.

Quade's eyes were focused on the fighting cock. The bird was ruffling up his hackles and uttering warning squawks. Quade gasped. He'd known game cocks down in the South to kill full-grown sheep with their naked spurs and those were ordinary games. These Jungle Shawls were only one generation removed from the wild ancestors of the Malay jungles.

This particular cock was well equipped for fighting. It had needle-pointed steel gaffs on his spurs which seemed to Quade longer than those the birds in the pits had used. They were at least three inches long.

One slash of those powerful legs and the needles would rip through clothing, skin and flesh. They would lay open a thigh to the bone.

Quade was given no time for thought. With a sudden vicious squawk the Jungle Shawl hurled himself at Quade, half running, half flying. Quade sprang backwards and collided with a sack of egg-mash. He stumbled on it and tripped to the floor. He rolled over on his side as quickly as he could and just missed the attack of the angry rooster. One wing brushed his face. He sprang to his feet and put a safe distance between himself and the bird.

The cock whirled and uttered a defiant screech. Then it charged again. Quade sidestepped and began stripping off his topcoat which he'd donned before leaving the big barn. He held the coat a foot or so before him and waited.

The bird charged. Quade flicked out the coat like a bull fighter teasing a bull and lashed out with his foot at the same time. The bird hit the coat and there was the ripping sound of cloth. At the same moment Quade's foot caught something solid and a sharp streak of pain shot through his leg.

The kick hurled the bird several feet backward and Quade looked down. The steel gaffs had slashed the topcoat clean through, pierced Quade's trouser leg and the skin underneath. Quade felt the warm blood course down his shin and cursed aloud.

He was fighting a losing fight, he knew. The bird seemed hurt by the kick but was preparing for another charge. Quade tossed his coat aside and sprang across the room for a heavy broom that stood against the wall.

Glass tinkled as Quade hefted the broom. His eyes shot to the little window beside the door. A red galvanized pail appeared in the opening and its liquid contents poured onto the floor with a tremendous splash. The fumes of gasoline hit Quade's nostrils and he gasped. The distraction fortunately had also attracted the attention of the fighting cock, for if it had charged just then it would have been too bad for Quade.

The hair on Quade's neck bristled. He had a feeling that he was in the most dangerous spot of his entire life. In front of him a fighting cock – and on the side –?

The rooster was cackling again. Quade took the fight to the bird now. He rushed across the room and met him in full charge. The smack of the broom as it hit the rooster could have been heard a hundred yards away. The cock screeched as it was lifted off its feet and hurled against the wall. Quade followed up his attack, smashed the bird again as it hit the floor.

Then – then the entire room shot up in one terrific blaze of fire. The attacker outside the shed had tossed a blazing piece of newspaper into the gasoline. One entire side of the room was a sheet of flame, from floor to ceiling. Quade rushed back from the crippled bird and stared, panic-stricken, at the fire.

The door was locked on the outside. The windows were small and had wire mesh nailed outside of the glass. He could never get through one of them – not in time at least. This building was made of dry spruce boards. It would be in ashes inside of ten minutes.

Quade was trapped.

Heat from the huge flames scorched Quade's face. Fire! Of what use now was his encyclopedia knowledge when he was trapped in a burning building? Was there anything in the *Encyclopedia Americana* that would tell him how to get out of such a predicament?

Fire – what would extinguish a fire? Water. There was none in here. Chemicals. There were none – Wait!

Chemicals – no – but baking soda! Why, there were three large cartons of it right here behind him on the bench. Baking soda, one of the finest dry fire extinguishers in the world. Quade had read about it in his encyclopedias and had tried it out – as he had many other things that particularly interested him. He'd built a fire of charcoal wood and paper, had let it blaze fiercely. Then with an ordinary carton of baking soda he'd put out the fire in an instant. That had been an experiment on a small scale, however, would it work on a large scale – when it was an absolute necessity?

Quade reached behind him and snatched up a five-pound carton of baking soda. He reached in, drew out a handful and hurled it into the midst of the big blaze. A flash of white leaped high and was followed by greyish smoke. Quade's eyes, looking sharply at the floor where the soda fell, saw that the fire burned less fiercely there.

He advanced on the fire then. It seared his face and hands, but he threw the baking soda full into the flames, handful after handful. Then, finally, with a desperate gesture, he emptied the box. He whirled his back on the fire and started back for the second box. He caught it up, ripped open the cover and turned it on the fire.

A wild surge of joy rose in him. Why, there was a wide swathe of blackened flooring now leading to the door. The fire still blazed around the edges but the heart was cut out of it. Quade attacked the fire with renewed effort. He hurled soda right and left. His eyes smarted, his lungs choked and his skin was scorched, but he persisted. The second box of soda went and now the fire was but a few flickering flames around the edges. It required only a few handfuls from the third box to put out the last little flame.

Quade surveyed the fire-blackened wreckage and let out a tremendous sigh of relief. A stench of burnt flesh penetrated his nostrils. A mass of smoking flesh and feathers told of the fate of the fighting cock that had attacked him.

Five minutes later Quade leaned against the doorbell of the big Ragsdale residence. A butler opened the door, gasped and tried to close the door again, but Quade shoved it open smartly and stepped into the hallway.

"Mr Ragsdale in?"

The butler rolled his eyes wildly. "Why – uh – I don't think so."

Quade heard voices and the tinkling of glasses ahead. He brushed past the butler. A wide door opened off the hallway into a luxuriously furnished room, containing about twenty men. Ragsdale, standing just inside the door caught sight of Quade and cried out in astonishment. "Why – it's Oliver Quade. Good Lord, man, what happened to you?"

Quade walked into the room. His eyes searched the crowd, picking out familiar faces – Morgan, Wilcoxson, the medical examiner, even Tom Dodd. Then his eyes came back to Ragsdale. "One of your hen houses caught on fire and I put it out," he explained.

"Good for you!" exclaimed Ragsdale. "We all left the barn right after the police found the hypodermic which pinned Treadwell's murder on Cleve Storm."

"Storm didn't kill Treadwell," Quade said buntly. "The murderer is right here in this room. He's the same man who poisoned your Jungle Shawls and made you lose the cocking main."

"He's a liar!" Tom Dodd, face black as a thundercloud, came forward. "Your birds weren't poisoned, Mr Ragsdale. I handled them myself and examined each one before I pitted them."

Quade looked insolently at the furious handler. "I didn't see all the bouts but I did see four Shawls in a row get killed – and each one of them was killed because he apparently turned yellow – and faltered. But they didn't really falter. They were poisoned –"

"That's a lie!" screamed Tom Dodd. "The Shawls lost because they were up against better birds."

Quade grinned wolfishly. "Say – whose side are *you* on?" he asked. "You brought those Shawls here and claimed they were the best in the world."

"That's right!" snapped Ragsdale. "I paid Walcott a fancy price for those birds and he guaranteed them to beat the best in the country."

"I think they would have," Quade assured him. "They were real fighters. One of them almost killed me – but let that pass for the moment. Mr Ragsdale, just to prove my point, pick up that phone there and call Mr Terence Walcott, of Corvallis, Oregon."

"Why should he call up the boss?" cried Dodd. "I'm the handler. I've raised fighting cocks all my life!"

"Have you?" Quade didn't seem impressed. "I've raised a few birds myself. By the way, have you gentlemen noticed that we Southerners use different cocking terms than Northerners? For example, up here you say 'stuck' when a bird is wounded. Down South we say 'hung'. Am I right, Mr Morgan?"

"That's right, Mr Quade," the editor replied. "There's quite a difference in the terminology of the South and North. I've published articles on the subject in my magazines."

"Well, did any of you notice that every time a Jungle Shawl was hung, Tom Dodd cried out, 'Hung'? Yet Mr Dodd says he comes from the *North*!"

The silence in the room was suddenly so profound that

Tom Dodd's hoarse breathing sounded like a rasping cough. Quade broke the silence. "By the way, Dodd, that's a peculiar ring you're wearing. Mind letting me take a look at it?"

Tom Dodd looked down at the ring on his left hand. His lips moved silently for a moment, then he looked at Quade. "No – I don't mind. Here –"

He started towards Quade, who, to the surprise of everyone in the room, suddenly lashed out with his right fist. He put everything into the blow, the pent-up emotion and anger he'd accumulated in the burning poultry house. The fist caught Dodd on the point of the jaw, smashed him back into a couple of the guests. They made no move to catch him and Dodd slid off them to the floor. He lay in a huddle, quiet.

"There's your murderer!" cried Quade, blowing on his fist.

That broke the spell. Men began shouting questions. Quade stooped down, slipped the ornate ring from Dodd's finger. He held it up for all to see. "See this little needle that shoots out on the inside of the ring?" Heads craned forward.

"That's why those birds of yours died without fighting, Mr Ragsdale," Quade explained. "Just as Dodd would let them go, he'd prick them with this needle. There's poison on it, which took effect almost instantly."

Ragsdale shook his head in bewilderment. "But Treadwell –"

"Was killed in a similar fashion, but not with the ring. Remember there was an intermission before the last fight – during which I tried to sell you men a few books," Quade grinned. "That's when Dodd stuck a little poisoned needle into the flat top of the railing where Treadwell sat. Perhaps he'd noticed Treadwell eyeing him with suspicion. Suspecting that he was poisoning the cocks. Dodd worked out the whole thing pretty cleverly. Took no chances. Witness the hypodermic which he tossed into the sand. That was for a blind.

"He'd figured out that when Treadwell's bird won the last and deciding bout that Treadwell would probably smack the railing in his excitement – maybe he'd watched him doing it after other bouts. Well, that's exactly what Treadwell did. The needle's still in the railing. I ripped my coat on it when I started to leave."

"But what made you suspect Dodd?" asked Ragsdale.

Quade grinned. "My encyclopedic brain, I guess. In the excitement of learning that Treadwell was murdered, Dodd was still cool enough to remove the carcass of the Shawl. That was the first thing that got me to thinking. Then the matter of terminology stuck in my mind. I didn't catch it at first. Dodd cried out 'hung' every time. Well, that's a Southern term and Dodd was supposed to have come from Oregon: claimed he'd lived there all his life."

"You mean to say that Dodd does not actually come from Oregon?" exclaimed Ragsdale. "Why – that would mean that he isn't really Dodd at all?"

"Right," said Quade. "And Treadwell must have known that. He'd probably met the right Dodd at some time or other. I suspect you'll learn after talking to Walcott on the phone that the real Dodd doesn't look like this one at all. Where he is, I don't know. This chap may have bought him off – murdered him perhaps. That isn't so important because he'll burn for the murder of Treadwell anyway. It's enough that we know this chap took the real Dodd's place somewhere between Oregon and here."

"Yes – but who is he?" asked Ragsdale.

Quade screwed up his lips. "I think you'll find that he sometimes uses the name of C. Pitts. In fact, I'm willing to lay odds that a handwriting expert will declare the signature on that cheque Morgan has, was made by this chap. Twenty-five thousand is a lot of money and Mr Pitts wanted to make sure he won."

"I'll be damned!" said Ragsdale. "You've certainly figured everything out. And – I believe you. I can understand now why they call you the Human Encyclopedia."

Quade's eyes lit up. "That reminds me – I didn't get finished out there in the barn. So if you have no objections, I'll continue with my little talk about the *Compendium of Human Knowledge*. 'All the knowledge of the ages condensed into one volume.'"

Red Goose

Norbert Davis

I t was a long, high-ceilinged hall, gloomy and silent. The air was musty. Tall, barred windows on one side of the hall let in a little of the bright sunlight where it formed waffle-like patterns on the thick green carpet. There was a polished brass rail, waist-high, running the length of the hall on the side opposite the barred windows.

Shaley came quietly along the hall. He was whistling softly to himself through his teeth and tapping with his forefinger on the brass rail in time with his steps.

Shaley was bonily tall. He had a thin, tanned face with bitterly heavy lines in it. He looked calm; but he looked like he was being calm on purpose – as though he was consciously holding himself in. He had an air of hardboiled confidence.

A door at the end of the hall opened, and a wrinkled little man in a grey suit that was too big for him came hurrying out. He carried a framed picture under one arm, and had dusty, rimless glasses on the end of his nose. He had a worried, absent-minded expression on his face, and mumbled in a monotone to himself.

Shaley stepped in front of him and said: "Hello."

"How do you do," said the little man busily. He didn't look up. He tried to side-step around Shaley.

Shaley kept in front of him. "My name is Shaley – Ben Shaley."

"Yes, yes," said the little man absently. "How do you do, Mr Shaley." He tried to squeeze past.

Shaley put out one long arm, barring his way.

"Shaley," he said patiently. "Ben Shaley. You sent for me."

The little man looked up, blinking through the dusty glasses.

"Oh!" he said. "Oh! Mr Shaley. Of course. You're the detective."

Shaley nodded. "Now you're getting it."

The little man made nervous, batting gestures with one hand, blinking. Apparently he was trying to remember why he had sent for a detective.

"Oh, yes!" he said, snapping his fingers triumphantly. "The picture! Yes, yes. My name is Gray, Mr Shaley. I'm the curator in charge. Won't you step into my office?"

"Thanks," said Shaley.

Gray trotted quickly back down the hall, back through the door. It was a small office with a big, flat desk next to another barred window. Gray dodged around the desk and sat down in the chair behind it, still holding the framed picture.

Shaley sat down in another chair, tipped it back against the wall, and extended his long legs comfortably.

Gray held up the picture and stared at it admiringly, head on one side. "Beautiful, isn't it?" he asked, turning the picture so Shaley could see it.

"Too fat," said Shaley.

Gray blinked. "Fat?" he said, bewilderedly.

"It's a picture of a dame, isn't it?" Shaley asked.

"It's a nude," Gray admitted.

Shaley nodded. "She's too fat. She bulges."

"Bulges?" Gray repeated in amazement. "Bulges?" He looked from the picture to Shaley. "Why, this is a Rubens."

Shaley tapped his fingers on the arm of his chair. "I suppose you had some reason for calling me?"

Gray came out of his daze. "Oh, yes. Yes, yes. It was about the picture."

"What picture? This one?"

"Oh, no. The one that was stolen."

Shaley took a deep breath. "Now we're getting somewhere. There was a picture stolen?"

"Of course," said Gray. "That's why I called you."

"I'm glad to know that. When was it stolen?"

"Three days ago. Mr Denton recommended you. Mr Denton is one of the trustees of the museum."

"Denton, the lawyer?"

Gray nodded. "Mr Denton is an attorney. He said something about setting a crook to catch a crook."

"I'll remember that," said Shaley.

"I hope I haven't offended you?" Gray said anxiously.

"You better hope so," Shaley told him. "I'm bad medicine when I get offended. There was a picture stolen from the museum, then, three days ago. What kind of picture?"

"The *Red Goose*, painted by Guiterrez about 1523. A beautiful thing. It was loaned to us by a private collector for an exhibition of sixteenth century work. It's a priceless example."

"What does it look like?" Shaley asked.

Gray peered at him closely. "You never saw the *Red Goose*?"

"No," said Shaley patiently. "I never saw the *Red Goose*."

Gray shook his head pityingly.

Shaley took out his handkerchief and wiped his forehead. "Listen," he said in a strained voice. "Would you mind giving me a description of that picture?"

"Certainly," said Gray quickly. "It's twelve inches by fifteen. It's a reproduction of a pink goose in a pond of green water lilies. A beautiful work."

"It sounds like it," Shaley said sourly. "How was it stolen?"

"It was cut out of the frame with a razor blade. I never heard of such an act of vicious vandalism! They cut a quarter of an inch off the painting all around it!"

"Terrible," Shaley agreed. "When was this done?"

"I told you. Three days ago."

Shaley took a deep breath and let it out very slowly. "I know you told me three days ago," he said in a deceptively mild voice. "But what time of the day was it stolen – at night?"

"Oh, no. In the afternoon."

"Where were your guards?"

"They were stopping the fight."

Shaley made a sudden strangling noise. He took off his hat and dropped it on the floor. He glared at Gray. Gray stared back at him in mild surprise. Shaley picked up his hat and straightened it out carefully.

"The fight," he said, his voice trembling a little. "There was a fight, then?"

"Why, yes," said Gray. "I forgot to mention it. Two men got into a fight in the back gallery, and it took four of the guards to eject them from the premises. And then we noticed that the picture was gone."

"That's fine," Shaley told him sarcastically. "Now would it be too much trouble for you to describe these men who fought?"

Gray said: "I noticed them particularly, because they seemed a trifle out of place in a museum. One was a big, tall man with long arms and short legs. He had four gold teeth, and he was bald, and his ear –" Gray stopped, hunting for the word.

"Cauliflower?" Shaley asked.

Gray nodded quickly. "Yes. Thick and crinkly. The man interested me as an example of arrested development in the evolutionary process."

Shaley blinked. He scratched his head, squinting.

"You mean he looked like an ape?" he asked.

Gray nodded again. "He had certain definite characteristics – the small eyes sunken under very heavy brows, the flattened nose, the abnormally protruding jaw – that have come to be associated with the development of the human race in its earlier stages."

"That's nice," Shaley said blankly. "What did the other one look like?"

"A nice-looking young man. A trifle rough-looking – but quiet and self-effacing. He had red hair and big pink freckles. The thumb on his left hand was missing."

"That's enough," Shaley said. "Have you notified the police of the theft?"

"Oh, no. Mr Denton advised us not to. He said the thieves might destroy the picture if they thought the police were after them." Gray shook his head sadly at the thought of such an outrage. "Mr Denton said to tell you to get it back for nothing if you could; but that the museum was willing to pay up to five thousand dollars. The picture must be returned undamaged. It's a matter of honour with the museum. It would be a terrible blow to our reputation if the property of a private collector should be lost while in our possession."

Shaley stood up. "I'll see what I can do."

"Mr Denton said he would take care of your fee."

Shaley said: "I'll take care of him. Calling me a crook."

Shaley drove his battered Chrysler roadster into Hollywood, entered a drug-store and went into one of the telephone booths in back.

He took a leather-covered notebook from his pocket, flipped through the pages, found the number he wanted. He put a nickel in the phone and dialled.

"Yeah?" It was a thin, flat voice.

"This is Ben Shaley, Mike."

"Oh, hello, Ben. Wait a minute." The voice pulled a little away from the telephone. "Turn that radio down. How the hell do you think I can hear?" The voice came closer again. "How are you, Ben? Long time no see."

"I'm okay, Mike. How you doing?"

"Damn good. I got the place all redecorated. I got a real bar now – a swell one – mahogany. Come on out, sometime, Ben."

"Thanks, Mike. Listen, is that guy that writes for *Ring and Turf* there – Pete Tervalli?"

"Yeah. He's upstairs playin' blackjack. You want him?"

"Uh-huh."

"I'll call him. Hold the phone."

Shaley waited, tapping out a complicated rhythm on the mouth-piece of the telephone and humming softly.

"Hello, Ben. This is Pete Tervalli."

Shaley said: "Pete, I want to ask you about a couple of guys. Number one is a big gook that looks like an ape. He's got gold front teeth, a flat snozzle, a thick ear, and he's bald. Know him?"

"Nope," said Pete. "He's a new one on me."

"All right. Here's the other one. He's red-headed and

sort of quiet, and he's got big pink freckles on his face. He's minus his left thumb."

"Sure," said Pete. "Sure. That's Fingers Reed. He fights in prelims at the Legion stadium sometimes. Been on at the Olympic a couple times, too. Had a semi-final down to Venice once – got knocked out."

"Where can I find him?"

"At Pop's gym down on main."

"Thanks a lot, Pete."

Shaley went up a flight of long, dark stairs littered with white blotches that were ground-out cigarette butts. He went along a short, dirty hall, through swinging double doors with frosted glass panels.

He was in a big high-ceilinged room that smelled strongly of tobacco, liniment, gin and sweat. A youth in a greyish sweatshirt was jumping rope in the middle of the floor. He skipped expertly and solemnly, first from one foot and then the other, counting aloud. In one corner a punching bag battered back and forth in a stuttering roar under the quick fists of a small, bowlegged Filipino. In another corner a fattish man made a rowing machine creak mournfully.

Shaley walked along the wall and entered an open door. It was a small office with a dusty desk in one corner. The walls were papered with the pictures of fighters in various belligerent poses.

Shaley said: "Hello, Pop," to the man sitting at the desk.

Pop was a small man with a shiny bald head. He wore a celluloid collar so high that it took him just under the ears and made him look like he was always stretching his neck. He had a dead brown-paper cigarette in one corner of his mouth.

"Hello, Ben," he said without enthusiasm.

"Where can I find Fingers Reed?"

"Fingers Reed?" Pop repeated absently. "Fingers Reed? I wouldn't know him. He a fighter?"

Shaley grinned. "Come on, Pop. Don't pull that stuff. I just want to give him twenty bucks. Which one is he?"

"Give me the twenty," Pop requested. "He owes it to me for gym fees. He's in the ring."

Shaley went out of the office, through another door and into a small room with seats in high, close tiers against three of its walls. There was a ring in the middle.

Fingers Reed, in a heavy sweatshirt and helmet, was sparring with a tall, spider-legged middleweight. The middleweight danced around very fancily, stepping high. Fingers Reed shuffled after him, his left poked out in front of him, his right held back shoulder high. He was much too slow for the middleweight. He crossed his right again and again — long, heavy blows that the middleweight slipped easily.

A little man in a chequered cap stood beside the ring. He had a watch in one hand and a string in the other. He pulled the string as Shaley watched. The gong boomed.

Fingers Reed and the middleweight patted each other on the back and started walking back and forth in the ring, breathing deeply and swinging their arms.

Shaley said: "Fingers!"

Fingers Reed stopped and looked down at him.

"I want to talk to you a minute," Shaley said.

Fingers Reed nodded. He slid through the ropes, jumped down on the floor. With the thumb of his right boxing glove, he hooked a rubber tooth protector out of his mouth. He spat on the floor and ran his tongue over his front teeth.

"What?"

Shaley said: "Who paid you to put on that fracas at the museum?"

Fingers Reed pulled up the front of his sweatshirt. He had an inner tube, cut open, wound tightly around his stomach. He loosened the inner tube a little. Then he rubbed his nose with the back of one glove, squinting sidewise at Shaley.

"I had an idea there was something sour about that."

Shaley said: "I don't want to get hard about it, but there was a picture lifted while you were having that little to-do, and I want to know about it."

"Sure," said Fingers. "Somebody tells me that they got some pictures of some old fight scenes over in his museum in Pasadena and, me not having nothing to do, I think I will go over and take a look at them. So I do, and they are pretty good pictures, too. After I am done looking at them I walk around to take a look at the rest of the stuff, and while I am looking up comes this big monkey and steps on my foot." He stopped and nodded at Shaley.

"So what?" said Shaley woodenly.

"Well, so I ask him what the hell he thinks he is doing, dancing with me? And then he hauls off and pops me, so I pop him back, and pretty soon a few guys in monkey suits come along and toss us both out on our ears." Fingers gestured with the boxing gloves. "So that's that."

Shaley said: "You wouldn't know this big monkey's name?"

Fingers shook his head. "Never saw him before or since."

Shaley took a twenty-dollar bill out of his vest pocket and folded it lengthwise and looked at Fingers calculatingly.

"That's too bad," he said regretfully. He poked the twenty back into his vest pocket. "Well, I'll be going, then. Thanks."

"Wait, now," said Fingers. "Wait a minute. Don't get in a rush."

Shaley took the bill out of his pocket and gave it to him.

Fingers said: "Here, Jig. Keep it for me." He tossed the folded bill to the timekeeper.

"Let's have the real dope," Shaley requested.

"Well, it's like this. The big monkey's name is Gorjon. He's the stooge for a gent by the name of Carter. The two of them come around the gym here a couple of times, and then they put this proposition up to me. Would I put on a phoney fight at the museum for ten bucks? I was flat, so I said sure, why not? So I did."

"Where can I get hold of these boys?"

Fingers shrugged. "By me."

Shaley said gently: "You wouldn't try to be smart with me, would you, Fingers? You wouldn't try to shake me down?"

Fingers held up one gloved hand, palm out. "So help me. I never see them but three times."

Shaley said: "It'd be worth a hundred to me if I could locate them."

Fingers blinked thoughtfully, rubbing his nose with the glove on his right hand. "Hm. The big boy is a fight fan. You might stake out the stadiums around here."

"You do it. You might get some of your pals to help. I could make it fifty for the guy that found them and a hundred to you."

Fingers nodded. "Okay."

When Shaley came into his office, Sadie, his secretary, was tapping away briskly on the typewriter with glossy, pink-nailed fingers.

"Hi-yah," said Shaley, tossing his hat on the hat-rack and heading for the inner office.

Sadie raised her sleek, dark head and watched him. She didn't say anything.

Shaley got to the door of the inner office, then turned around and came back to her desk.

"Well, what's your trouble?"

Sadie said: "A woman called you up. Who is she?"

"How do I know who she is? Who'd she say she was?"

Sadie sniffed. "She wouldn't tell me her name. Talked like a blonde though."

"How'd you know she was blonde?"

"Humph! I can tell, all right. Talking baby talk – all about a red goose. Who ever heard of a red goose?"

"Did you get her number?" Shaley demanded.

"Certainly I did. I always remember to ask people their number."

"Hell – Give me that number."

Sadie shoved a pad of paper along the desk. Shaley picked up her telephone and began to dial the number.

"And my mother was saying just last night," said Sadie righteously, "that she didn't think this office was the proper place for a young girl to work. All these questionable people coming in and out all day long and you swearing and yelling at me all the time and –"

"Shut up," said Shaley absently.

"Hello." It was a nice voice – small and clear and sweet – shyly innocent.

"This is Ben Shaley. Did you call my office?"

The nice voice said: "Oh, yes."

"About the *Red Goose*?"

"Yes, Mr Shaley. I called the museum, and they told me you were in charge. Are you looking for the picture?"

Shaley said suspiciously: "Who're you? A reporter?"

"Oh, no. I'm the one that has the picture."

Shaley nearly dropped the telephone. "What?"

"Well, Mr Shaley, I haven't exactly got it right here. But I can get it for you. Do you want it?"

"Where are you?" Shaley demanded. "When can I see you?"

"I'll be home tonight at seven-thirty. It's the Hingle Manor apartments on Harcourt just south of Sunset, in Hollywood. Apartment seven. The name is Marjorie Smith."

"I'll be there, Marjorie," Shaley said cheerfully, hanging up.

He put the telephone slowly back on Sadie's desk, frowning thoughtfully. He picked up her pencil and drew a pattern of squares on the desk-pad, still frowning.

"You know," he said absently, "someway or other I didn't like the sound of that. It sounded just a little screwy. I wonder if somebody is trying to lay me an egg?"

"Humph!" said Sadie. "Blondes!"

Hingle Manor was a long, neat, two-storey stucco building with turrets on the four corners and blue pennants on each of the turrets. Floodlights placed on the front lawn and slanted up made the building look larger and newer than it was.

Shaley found the card that said: "Marjorie Smith," and buzzed the bell under it. After a while the latch clicked. Shaley pushed open the door and was in a small, narrow hall, thickly carpeted.

He looked around, then went up a short flight of stairs. At the end of the hall an open door made a yellow square of light that was like a picture frame for the young woman standing there.

Shaley was reminded of an old-fashioned tintype he had once seen in a family album. The woman wore a neat blue dress, modest and plain. She had wide blue eyes and corn-coloured hair wound around her small head in thick braids. Given a sun-bonnet and a slate she would have been a perfect copy of a school girl of fifty years ago.

She smiled and curtsied a little and said shyly: "Won't you come in, please?"

Shaley went into a small, well-furnished living-room and stood there holding his hat in his hands and shifting from one foot to the other uneasily.

The woman came into the room, shutting the door. She sat down on a couch and folded her hands neatly in her lap.

"I'm Marjorie Smith," she said, smiling nicely.

"I'm Ben Shaley."

Marjorie Smith smiled up at him with admiring blue eyes. Shaley watched her uncomfortably. Something was wrong with all this. Marjorie Smith didn't fit in with the rest of the picture – with Fingers Reed and Carter and Gorjon.

"Who lives here with you?" he asked.

She shook her head, wide-eyed. "No one."

"Are we here alone?"

She nodded. "Oh, yes."

Shaley grunted. He scratched his head, scowling. He said:

"Listen, Marjorie, I'm just a nasty man with mean suspicions. The only kind of fairy stories I believe are the kind they tell about the boys who carry handkerchiefs in their cuffs. Just sit right here while I sniff around."

"Oh, surely," said Marjorie.

He nosed through the rest of the apartment – kitchen, bedroom, bathroom, closets. He shot the bolt on the back door. He came back into the front room, opened the front door, peered out into the hall. He sat down in a chair and stared at Marjorie Smith.

"Well, I'll be damned," he said blankly.

She put her hand up over her mouth. "Why, Mr Shaley!"

"Excuse me," said Shaley. "But this is over my head like a tent. Let's talk business."

"Oh, yes," said Marjorie Smith. "Oh, yes. Business." She leaned forward and watched him with big blue eyes.

"You've got the painting I want – the *Red Goose*?"

She nodded earnestly. "Yes."

"Where'd you get it?"

"A man gave it to me – a man by the name of John Jones."

"That was nice of him," Shaley said.

"He said you would pay me two thousand dollars for it."

"He's an optimist," Shaley said sourly.

"It seems like a lot of money, doesn't it?" Marjorie Smith asked earnestly. "But John Jones assured me that it was worth that much. Have you got the money, Mr Shaley?"

"Huh!" said Shaley. "Where's the picture?"

"John Jones said I was not to give it to you until you gave me the money."

"John's a smart fellow," said Shaley. "But I can't give you the money until I know if you have the picture."

"Oh, but I have got it."

"Yes, yes. But I want to see it. Where is it?"

She shook her head regretfully. "Not until you give me the money. Then I'll give it to you. Really I will, Mr Shaley."

Shaley took a deep breath and held himself in. "Listen, Marjorie, I don't want to get hard with you, but if I were you I'd hand over that picture right now."

"But, Mr Shaley, I explained –"

"Once more – will you give me that picture?"

"But, Mr Shaley –"

Shaley jumped for her. He grabbed her by the shoulders and hauled her off the couch and shook her.

"Now, you little dummy –" he snarled.

She made no resistance. Her body was soft and relaxed in his hands. She moved just enough to bring her right hand up under Shaley's nose.

She held a small bottle in her hand, uncorked.

Shaley got one whiff of the contents of that bottle. He choked suddenly. He let go of Marjorie Smith and jumped backwards, gasping.

"Acid!" he said, one hand over his nose.

"Yes," she said, smiling just as nicely as before. "Touch me again, and I'll throw it in your face."

Shaley swallowed hard. The picture wasn't out of focus any more. Marjorie Smith fitted right in.

"Wow!" said Shaley in an awed voice, backing away from her warily. He backed clear to the door, keeping his eyes on the bottle.

"Now listen, boob," said Marjorie Smith in her clear, childlike voice. "Let me tell you something –"

The door behind Shaley opened suddenly, bunting him forwards. He whirled around, one hand inside his coat, and looked squarely into the blunt, round muzzle of an automatic. His hand came out, empty.

"Take it easy, baby."

Gray had given a good description. This man Gorjon looked like an ape. He had enormously broad, sloping shoulders, hunched forwards. He stood there, swaying a little easily. The gold front teeth gleamed as he grinned at Shaley.

Another man was standing in the doorway behind Gorjon. This man didn't look at Shaley. He was looking at Marjorie Smith.

"Double-crossing little tramp," he said levelly.

He stepped around Gorjon and went towards her, walking springily on the balls of his feet. He was short and round and plumply dapper. He had thick red lips and a small black moustache. He wore a soft white felt hat. He was smiling a little.

Marjorie Smith had hidden the hand holding the acid bottle behind her. She watched the fat man. She waited until he put out a plump, white hand, reaching for her, and then she said something to herself in a tight whisper and hurled the acid at him with a quick sweep of her arm.

The fat man was astoundingly quick. He dropped into a crouch, ducking his head. The acid missed him, spattering on the wall in a bubbling brown stain.

The fat man bounced up again instantly and hit her with his fist. Marjorie Smith fell over a chair and lit on her hands and knees in the corner.

Gorjon hadn't moved either his eyes or the automatic from Shaley. He reached out one big hand and shut the door.

"Sit down, mister," he said to Shaley.

Shaley sat down slowly and tensely in the chair in back of him.

The fat man picked up Marjorie Smith effortlessly and planked her down on the couch. He was still smiling.

She didn't say anything. She watched the fat man expressionlessly. There was a red mark on her face where he had hit her.

The fat man turned to Gorjon. "Take his gun."

Gorjon reached inside Shaley's coat and pulled out the big automatic Shaley carried in a shoulder-holster. He hefted it, grinning.

"It's a .45. He goes loaded for bear. Maybe he's one of these here rough characters you read about in the papers."

The fat man said: "Who is he, Marj?"

Marjorie Smith said sullenly: "Ben Shaley. He's a private peeper – from the museum."

Shaley said: "And you are Carter."

The fat man smiled at him. "So you found Reed, did you? I knew that dead-head would blab all he knew. Yeah, Carter is one of my names. Take a good look at me. Me and Gorjon are gonna be your shadows until you get that money from the museum." He turned back to Marjorie Smith. "Where's the picture?"

"Try and find it."

Carter said: "I will," softly.

He picked her up by the front of her dress and slapped her in the face – quick, sharp slaps that rocked her head back and forth.

"Hey!" said Shaley.

Gorjon pushed his automatic into Shaley's neck. "I wouldn't poke my head out, boy."

Carter said: "Well?" and stopped slapping Marjorie Smith.

She spat at him. He hit her in the mouth with his fist and knocked her back on the couch.

"Rap that boob on the nut," he said calmly to Gorjon, "and take her shoes off. We'll have to get rough with her."

Marjorie Smith wiped her mouth with the back of her hand. Her lips left a little smear of blood on her hand.

"I'll tell you," she said thickly. "Tannerwell has it."

Carter watched her thoughtfully. "Tannerwell, huh? You wouldn't fool an old Civil War vet, would you, Marj?"

"Tannerwell has it."

Carter moved his plump shoulders. "So it was that artist sap, huh? I didn't think he had it in him. Where is he?"

"I don't know."

Carter said very gently: "Where is he, Marj?"

She shrugged impatiently. "I tell you I don't know. I've got his telephone number. I can get him to come here."

"That's just dandy," said Carter. "What's the number?"

"Rochester 2585."

Carter went over to the stand near the door and picked up the telephone. "I'll talk to him first, and then I'll let you. You tell him to come over here – and make it good. I'm going to be mad if you try something funny."

Marjorie Smith said: "He'll come."

Carter dialled the number. He waited, listening. Then he said:

"Hello, Tannerwell? This is Carter." He listened, grinning at Shaley. Then he said: "Yes. Your dear old pal, Carter. Now listen, smarty, while I tell you something. I'm over at Marj's apartment. You get that picture and come over here, or something sudden will happen to her. She's going to talk to you."

He held the mouthpiece of the telephone in front of Marjorie Smith.

She said brokenly: "Bill – Bill. Come quick. Bring the picture." Then she screamed suddenly, so loudly it made Shaley jump.

Carter pushed down the receiver hook with his thumb and put the telephone back on its stand. "Dandy, Marj. You should go on the radio."

"He'll be here in about fifteen minutes," Marjorie Smith said, still sullen.

Carter pulled up a chair and sat down. He tipped his hat back and began to whistle softly and patiently between his teeth, watching Marjorie Smith unblinkingly. Gorjon stood just behind Shaley's chair.

Shaley said: "How about sitting down? You make me nervous."

Gorjon chuckled. "Don't get too nervous, because if you start jiggling around this thing is liable to go off."

"Do you think you're going to put this over?" Shaley asked Carter.

Carter stopped whistling long enough to say: "I think so," and then began again. He stopped and looked at Shaley. "Just keep your nose out of this, baby. When I get that picture, then you and me will have a little talk. Until then you're just a kibitzer. Don't get the idea that anybody has dealt you a hand."

Marjorie Smith moved impatiently on the couch. "Can I have a cigarette?"

Carter said: "I don't smoke, dearie. You know that."

"There's some cigarettes in my right-hand coat pocket," Shaley said.

Gorjon fished the package out and tossed it on the couch. Marjorie Smith took one and used the lighter on the table at the end of the couch.

Carter got up and turned on the radio. He found a dance orchestra, nodded approvingly, sat down, and began to whistle in tune with it, tapping his foot.

They waited.

It took Tannerwell sixteen minutes. His footsteps came up the hall noisily, running. He rapped loudly on the door.

Carter got up quickly and got against the wall beside the door. He nodded at Marjorie Smith.

She said: "Come in, Bill."

Tannerwell came in with a rush. Carter pushed the door shut behind him.

Tannerwell didn't pay any attention to him. He went straight to Marjorie Smith and stood over her anxiously.

He didn't look like an artist. He looked more like a football player. He was tall, and he had wide, square shoulders. He was blond, and his features were evenly handsome, except for his nose, which had been broken and set crookedly.

"You screamed," he said to Marjorie Smith.

She sniffed a little, sadly. "D-did you bring the pic-picture, Bill?" She looked woebegone and bedraggled. She looked like a hurt child, crying there on the couch.

Tannerwell jerked a roll of parchment from inside his coat. "Sure. Here." He tossed it over his shoulder at Carter. He never took his eyes from Marjorie Smith.

Carter unrolled the parchment and examined it approvingly.

"Well," he said pleasantly. "Here we are at last."

"Marjorie," Tannerwell said. "Over the telephone. You screamed. Did they hurt you?" He put his hands out in front of him. He had big hands with long, thick fingers. He moved the fingers a little. "Did they hurt you, Marjorie?"

She sobbed. "Y-yes. Look." She pulled aside the neck of her dress and showed a round, ugly burn on the white skin of her shoulder. "Carter burned me with a cigarette to make me scream. He laughed when he did it."

Carter looked up from the picture. "Here!" he said, blankly amazed. "What —"

Tannerwell stared at the burn on Marjorie Smith's shoulder. Suddenly his face twisted crazily. He spun around and grabbed Carter by the neck with both big hands.

"Hey!" said Gorjon, starting around in front of Shaley.

Shaley braced his arms on the chair and kicked him savagely in the stomach with both feet. Gorjon doubled over, grunting.

Shaley jumped out of the chair. He got hold of the barrel of the automatic and twisted it out of Gorjon's hand.

Gorjon straightened up. He was grinning. He hit Shaley's wrist with the edge of one palm and knocked the automatic on the floor. He reached for Shaley.

Shaley swung on him with both fists, backing away. He hit Gorjon five times as hard as he could, squarely in the face. Gorjon shook his head, still grinning. He shuffled after Shaley, reaching.

Shaley hit him some more. It was like pounding on a wall. Gorjon didn't even try to block the blows. He let Shaley hit him. He even chuckled a little, his gold teeth gleaming. He was like a cat playing with a mouse. He had forgotten all about Carter and Tannerwell. He kept shuffling after Shaley, one hunched shoulder pushed forward, sidling a little.

Shaley bumped into a chair, and Gorjon got him. He got one big hand in the front of Shaley's coat. He pulled him forwards and hit him with the other hand.

Shaley's coat ripped, and he went backwards. He bounced off the table, fell over a chair. He got up quickly. He was breathing in gasping sobs. Over Gorjon's shoulder he caught a quick glimpse of the rest of the room and realized that all this was happening in seconds instead of hours.

Tannerwell was still shaking Carter by the neck. Carter's plump face was beginning to turn purple. He was trying to get a revolver from his pocket, but apparently the sight had caught in the cloth and, with Tannerwell shaking him, he couldn't get it free.

Marjorie Smith was still sitting on the couch. And she was laughing. She was laughing at Carter, pointing her finger mockingly at him.

Shaley slipped along the wall away from Gorjon's reaching hands. Gorjon got too close, and Shaley began to hit him again, putting everything he had in each blow. Gorjon grinned and shuffled after him.

Shaley tripped over a stool and fell. Gorjon dropped on him. He got Shaley by the neck, loosely, and began to pound his head on the floor slowly and methodically, chuckling gleefully to himself.

The room rocked in front of Shaley in a red haze. His fingers scrabbled on the floor, touched the barrel of Gorjon's automatic. He twisted and squirmed, scraping at the automatic with stiff fingers.

The red haze began to get black slowly. Gorjon's face was a long way above him – like a gleaming pin-point that nodded and bobbed and leered.

Shaley got his stiff fingers around the butt of the automatic, pushed the muzzle against Gorjon's side.

At its blasting report the room suddenly cleared in front of Shaley's eyes. Gorjon fell over sideways, very slowly, and hit the floor and lay there without moving.

Shaley got slowly to his feet, staggering a little. His nose was broken. He could feel the blood running down his face. He started towards Tannerwell and Carter.

Carter saw him coming and finally got his pistol free. He slapped Tannerwell on the side of the head with it. Tannerwell dropped him and bent over, holding his head.

Carter took a quick snap shot at Marjorie Smith that pocked the plaster just above her head. Then he whirled and ducked towards the door. He still held the roll of parchment in his left hand.

Shaley dived for him. He hit Carter's knees just as Carter was going through the door. They rolled out into the hall.

Carter was amazingly strong and quick. It was like trying to hold a squirming ball of soft rubber. He got one leg loose, kicked Shaley in the face. He hit Shaley's broken nose, and Shaley writhed on the floor, swearing thickly, losing his grip on Carter's legs.

Carter bounced to his feet instantly. He ran down the hall towards the stairs.

"Carter!"

It was Marjorie Smith. She was standing in the doorway, and she had the .45 automatic Gorjon had taken from Shaley in one small hand.

Carter whirled around like a dancer and jumped sidewise crouching. Marjorie Smith shot him.

The bullet caught Carter and slammed him back and down in a limp pile. His arms and legs moved aimlessly. After a second he got slowly to his feet and staggered down the hall.

Marjorie Smith shot him again, deliberately, in the back. Carter collapsed weakly and slid down the stairs, bumping soddenly on each step.

A woman was screaming somewhere close by.

Shaley got up off the floor. He walked down the hall, guiding himself with one hand on the wall and trying to keep his feet from walking out from under him. He got to Carter and leaned over to pick up the picture. He fell down and got up again slowly, holding the picture.

Marjorie Smith came running down the hall. She was pulling Tannerwell along behind her. She looked calm, sure of herself, as if she knew just where she was going. Tannerwell was shaking his head foggily, and he staggered a little as he ran.

They went by Shaley without even looking at him.

Feet were pounding up and down the hall overhead. A half dozen people were screaming for the police into telephones and out windows.

Shaley climbed the stairs, shuffled slowly towards the rear entrance.

A man opened a door, looked at him blankly, said: "Good God! He's all blood!" and slammed the door.

Shaley got out the back door into cool darkness. He fell over a hedge, got up, and ran heavily through a weed-choked lot, swearing to himself in a mumbling monotone. A siren began to moan in the distance.

Shaley had a piece of white court-plaster over his nose. It made his tanned face look darker and thinner. He had his hat tipped forward over his face because the back of his head was swollen.

He walked down a long, gloomy hall and found Gray at the end of it. Gray was on top of a high step-ladder carefully dusting a painting with a brush about an inch wide. He dusted in quick, dabbing strokes, stopping every minute to squint sidewise at the picture through his thick, dusty glasses.

Shaley said: "Hello!"

Gray said: "How do you do, Mr Shaley," without looking around.

Shaley leaned against the brass railing and watched him. "Well," he said. "It's a long story. Want to hear it?"

Gray dabbed busily at the picture. "Certainly, Mr Shaley."

"A guy by the name of Carter stole the picture. The fight was staged by a pal of his and another bird they had hired, to attract the guards' attention while Carter got the picture. Carter had spotted this scatter as an easy one to crack, but he didn't know anything about pictures. So he hired an artist to pick out the right one to steal. The artist selected the *Red Goose*."

Gray nodded. "A good choice, I must say. It's a very beautiful painting."

"Carter didn't care whether it was beautiful or not. He wanted something the museum would want back in a hurry – something that couldn't be replaced. So he took the *Red Goose*. But Carter had a girl by the name of Marjorie Smith. The artist fell for her. She got ideas. She stole the picture from Carter and lit out with it and the artist. She got in touch with me, intending to sell me the picture for the museum. But Carter found her, just about that time. Are you listening?"

"Yes, yes," said Gray absently. "Go on."

"The artist had the picture. Carter had Marjorie Smith. She pulled a fake screaming act over the telephone to get the artist to bring the picture to Carter. Then, when the artist got there, she double-crossed Carter again. She told the artist that Carter had actually tortured her to make her scream over the telephone. She had burned herself with a cigarette to make it look better. The artist is nuts about her, and he went screwy and tackled Carter. Carter and his pal got themselves killed in the excitement, and I got a broken nose, and Marjorie and her friend Tannerwell got away."

"Tannerwell," said Gray thoughtfully. "Tannerwell. Oh, yes! He's the man that brought back the picture."

There was a long silence.

At last Shaley said: "Brought back – the picture?" in a strained voice.

Gray looked down at him. "Oh, yes. I must have forgotten to notify you. A man by the name of Tannerwell came around yesterday afternoon some time after you left. He had the *Red Goose*, and I paid him three thousand dollars for it. We had promised not to ask any questions about how he happened to have it – we only wanted the picture back."

Shaley took the roll of parchment from his coat pocket with fumbling fingers. "What's this, then?"

Gray trotted down the step-ladder. He examined the picture, holding it up to the light and nodding in a pleased way to himself.

"Yes. Nice work. Of course it hasn't the depth, the colour blending of the original, but it's very nice work."

Shaley said thickly: "It's – it's a copy?"

"Oh, yes. Couldn't you see that? Mr Tannerwell told me, after it came into his hands he had made a copy of the picture to keep for himself."

Shaley said: "That little tramp. She had Tannerwell copy the painting, intending to shake me down with it. Then when Carter butted in, she just switched her plans a little."

Gray smiled at him. "I'm sorry you were deceived, Mr Shaley. You could say that the *Red Goose* was a sort of red herring, couldn't you?"

"I could say a lot worse than that," said Shaley.

The First Five in Line

Charles Willeford

"Them that dies'll be the lucky ones."
LONG JOHN SILVER

MEMO: (Confidential)
FROM: Doremus Jessup, Vice-President for Programming, NBN
TO: Russell Haxby, Director of Creative and Special Programmes
SUBJECT: "The First Five in Line . . ."
Dear Russ, this is merely an informal memo on the eve of your departure for Miami to wish you Godspeed, and to mention some other assorted shit that has been on my mind.

I'm not, for example, satisfied with the programme title, even though, at the present moment, it seems to fit, in an honest way, with the theme and projected format. The ellipsis following the title implies that others will eventually join the line, and that this experiment is only the beginning of a long line of various titillating programmes to attract more jaded viewers, but I'm still not certain whether the ellipsis is a valid addition or not. Do not waver in your thoughts for a better (exciting?) alternative title. We (the Board and I) are very receptive to a title change, and you should submit periodic alternatives right up until deadline.

The Board is quite excited about the entire concept. In ancient Rome it was possible for theatre-goers to see actual fornication on-stage (including rapes), actual crucifixions and ritual murders (usually with unwilling Xian actors), and it does not seem unlikely to me that in the not so distant future we shall see planned murders on our home screens as well as the unplanned, i.e., Ruby shooting Oswald, the colonel shooting the prisoner in Saigon, the female newscaster's on-the-air suicide in Sarasota, etc. And NBN may very well start the trend with our innovative "TFFIL . . ." The design is already apparent, with from 30 to 35 simulated murders per night on the tube, as if every network were preparing the viewers' minds for the real thing. The latest estimate indicates that the average viewer, by the time he reaches 65, will have seen 400,000 simulated murders and maimings on TV, discounting the murders and maimings he has also seen in movies. I saw the handwriting on the bloody wall as far back as "The Execution of Private Slovik". The huge audience for this show was predicated on the sure knowledge that Slovik would, indeed, be executed before the end of the programme. Such knowledge was foreshadowed by the revealing title, even for those viewers unfamiliar with Huie's book. That's one of the reasons I'm not too happy with "The First Five in Line . . ." as a title. In line for what? A viewer may very well ask; so keep thinking about an alternative.

But I also agree with you that real TV murders must be led up to gradually, if we are ever to see them at all. To jump right in with them without prolonged and careful audience preparation, even though the actors – victim and killer – were to sign releases, would still not absolve the network from the many legal problems that would surround such programmes, at least initially. When the time is right, we shall have them, of course, and it will always be in keeping for NBN to pioneer in the most dramatic and exciting programming we can provide for our loyal viewers. As a possible title, however, just off the top of my head, for such a show in the distant future, what about "Involuntary Departures"?

But back to "The First Five in Line . . ." The Board concluded that it must run for the full thirteen (13) weeks, not for just the six (6) weeks you and I had planned. This means, Russell, that you're going to have to come up with a good many innovative ideas to stretch out the series, and without the watering down of the entertainment values. Suspense, of course, is the key – but then I don't need to tell you how to do your job. Money is no problem; don't worry about the money. We will have the sponsors, all right; and it will also mean extra money for the five volunteers, even though they are not to know about any money in advance, which would screw up the statistical nature of the selection, as you know. At any rate, the go-go decision for a full 13 weeks puts us right up in there in the Emmy running for a new series, whereas a six-week mini-series would not. And I think we do have a No. One Emmy idea.

You will have to handle Harry Thead, the station manager of WOOZ, with kid gloves – a last-minute reminder of this requirement. The programme idea was his in the first place, which is why we have to originate from Miami instead of St Louis, even though the latter was a much better location demographically wise. But Harry Thead had no objections to you as the overall creative director, just so long as he could play an active behind-the-scenes part in the production. He wants the series credits, which he needs and you may tell him that he will be on the credits, network wide, as "Associate Producer for Miami". The credit is rather meaningless, but it will look good on the crawl and I think he'll be happy with the title. The main thing is to keep Harry Thead informed at all times of what you are doing, so that he'll have the right answers for the WOOZ owners. You could also use Harry as your coordinator with the Miami office of Baumgarten, Bates, and Williams, who will handle the national advertising. They are also very excited about the commercial possibilities.

Harry Thead did not have to come to us with his idea, even though WOOZ is an affiliate. He could have run the show as a local Miami show, which would have blown the idea for the network. So we have a lot to thank Harry Thead for. When he asks questions, answer them; he's behind us and the new programme 110%, and he respects your creative genius.

I wish you had been present when I sold the idea to the Board. I won't bore you with it, except to say that some of the reactionary reactions were predictable, ranging as they did from pretended shock to forced indignation; but we soon settled into the specifics, and your overall tentative plan (except for the addition of another seven weeks, which reveals their true enthusiasm) was accepted in toto, without any major modifications. Mr Braden, who was in favour of Miami over St Louis all along, pointed out that the high crime rate in Miami has prepared the local audience there for violence better than St Louis which is quite religious-oriented, as Mr Braden mentioned, whereas Miami has only a few organized religious groups, i.e., Hare Krishna, Unitarian, and a few other sects. The former isn't taken seriously in Dade and Broward counties, and the latter discredited itself with Miami businessmen several years ago when they, the Unitarians, protested putting up a cross on the courthouse lawn at Christmastime.

Another update factor, which comes as good news from a statistical standpoint: unemployment in Miami has increased 3.7% since Harry Thead's original demographic study, which, in turn, increases the predictable volunteers in Miami from 6.9 to 7.1. If I was apprehensive about anything, it was the 6.9 predictability, but the larger range to 7.1 ensures the required five volunteers. (The new 7.1 figure includes the overlap into Broward County, as well as Dade County.)

You, your staff, and the five volunteers, when you have them, will all stay at the Los Pinos Motel; the third floor on the wing facing the bay has been reserved, as well as the third floor conference room. The motel is less than three blocks away from the 89th Street Causeway location of WOOZ. Billy Elkhart, the unit manager, is already down there, of course, and he has everything under control, including rental cars. Phone him before you leave Kennedy, and he'll pick you up at the Miami airport.

One last item, and it's not unimportant. Harry Thead is a Free-Mason, with all 32 degrees. Before you leave the city, pick up a blue stone Mason ring (blue is the 4th degree, I think), and wear it while you're down there. Stop by Continuity and ask Jim Preston (I know he's a Mason) to teach you the secret handshake that they use. It will help you gain rapport with Harry Thead (call it insurance), even though he'll be cooperative anyway.

From time to time, send me tape cassettes about your

progress; and don't worry about the budget. Simply tell Billy Elkhart what you need, and let him worry about the budget. He has the habit of thrift, anyway, and if he goes over it'll be his ass, not yours. You have enough pressure creative-wise; I don't want you worrying about money.

"The First Five in Line . . ." is undoubtedly the greatest concept of a television series ever to hit the air in modern times, Russell, and we (the Board and I) have every confidence in you as the creative force behind it.

Good luck, and Godspeed!

Is/DJ

Violette Winters

Ms Violette Winters, 36, had short, slightly bowed legs, a ridiculously wide pelvis, and tiny, narrow hurting feet. She wore size 5AAA shoes, slit at the big toe with a razor blade to relieve the pressure on her bunions, usually nurse-white with rippled rubber soles, and cotton support hose. So far she did not have varicose veins, but she lived in dread of their purplish emergence, and she hoped that the white cotton support hose would hold them in abeyance for as long as possible; but she was fully aware that varicose veins were the eventual reward of the full-time professional waitress. Violette's broad, blubbery hips and thick thighs, even with her girdle stretched over them, were mushy to the touch, and she bruised easily without healing quickly. Her ankles and calves, however, were trim. In her low-heeled white nurse's shoes, she was five feet four, but appeared to be taller because of her narrow-waisted torso, petite breasts (with inverted nipples), long neck, and the huge mass of curly marmalade hair, which she wore with a rat, piled high on top of her head. When she worked, her hair was covered by a black, cobwebby net, which darkened her curls to an off-shade of dried blood. Her cerulean eyes were deep-set, well-guarded by knobby, bony brows and thick brown eyebrows. Any time a male got within seven feet of her person, her eyes narrowed to oriental dimensions. Her face had been pretty when she was a young girl, and she would have been handsome still if it were not for the harsh frown lines across her broad forehead and the deeply grooved diagonals that ran from the wings of her nose to the corners of her turned down mouth. Her retroussé nose was splattered with tiny pointillistic freckles.

Violette always moved swiftly at her tasks around the restaurants where she worked, rarely made a mistake in addition, and her large white fluttering hands could deftly carry up to six cups of coffee, on saucers, without spilling a drop. A highly skilled waitress, when the time came for her to quit a job, every manager she had ever worked for regretted her departure. By all rights, Violette should have made more money in tips than the other waitresses, if efficiency was a factor, but she was the kind of woman (and men knew this, as if by instinct) who would accept a miserly ten percent tip without making a fuss. Shrewder, middle-aged men, after taking a sharp look at her, left no tip at all. As a consequence, she made much less in tips than the other waitresses.

So far, at this midway point in her life, which frequently – at thirty-six – seems even more than a midway point to women than it does to men, Violette had had three husbands. By her standards, by anyone's standards, they had been losers to a man.

Her first husband, Tommy, was the same boy she went steady with all of the way through junior and senior high in Greenwood, Mississippi. They had moved into Tommy's parents', after getting married upon graduation from high school, but three months later Tommy left Greenwood with a carnival that was passing through town, and no one had ever heard from him again. Two years after Tommy's departure, Violette got a divorce, after giving Tommy notice in the classified section of the Greenwood paper for three weeks in a row.

At the time, in a less than liberal region, it had been embarrassing for a divorced woman to live in Greenwood, so Violette added the extra "te" to her name, and moved to Memphis. She obtained a job as a roller-skating car-hop at the Witch Stand.

After only three months on the job she was hit by a red MG that pulled into the lot at 55 miles per hour. Even then, she would have been able to dodge the MG okay, the manager told the police (Violette was a terrific skater), but she had tried to save a tray full of cheeseburgers, double fries, and two double choc-malts at the same time she tried to make good her escape from the vehicle.

During her stay in the hospital, Violette fell in love with an alcoholic named Bubba Winters, who was recovering from double pneumonia. Bubba had passed out in a cold rain, down by the levee, and had almost died from exposure before being discovered by an early morning fisherman. They were married two days after their release from the hospital, and Violette went back to work, this time as a waitress at the Blue Goose Café, and still wearing a cast on her left leg. She had to pay off both hospital bills, and support them both, as well, because Bubba's old boss at the Regroovy Tyre Centre, claimed that Bubba, with his weak chest and all, wasn't strong enough to change tyres all day.

To show her love for Bubba, Violette tried to drink with him at night when her work-day was over, but she didn't have the head for it. Bubba, who had learned to drink in the Marines, where he had served three years out of his four-year hitch in Olongapo, on Luzon, had a great capacity for gin. In addition to ugly hangovers, Violette awoke one morning to discover that she had a tattoo on her right forearm, a tattoo she had assented to woozily the night before to show her devotion to Bubba. In addition to a tiny red heart, pierced with a dark blue dagger, there was a stern motto in blue block letters below the heart: DEATH BEFORE DISHONOUR. The twin to Violette's tattoo, although it was slightly larger, both heart and lettering, was on Bubba's right forearm, and had been there since his first overnight pass to San Diego from Boot Camp, and somehow, the tattoo looked right on Bubba. But it looked a little funny on Violette's forearm, and because the Blue Goose patrons made remarks about it all the time, she was forced to wear long-sleeved blouses to work. She never drank again.

When Bubba's unemployment cheques ran out, and Violette was unable to keep him in gin, because of the exorbitant doctor and hospital bills, so did Bubba. When Violette finished paying off her debts, she moved to

Jacksonville, Florida. She didn't want to risk the possibility that Bubba might come back to Memphis.

Violette retained Bubba's surname, however, after divorcing her third husband, a civil service warehouseman (G-S3) in the Jacksonville Naval District, because she had never gotten around to divorcing Bubba Winters before she married him. The warehouseman, Gunter Haas, who didn't drink or smoke, was a compulsive gambler. Every two weeks, when he got paid, he lost his money in the regular warehouse crap game before coming home to Violette. Violette, who worked as a waitress at Smitty's Beef House in downtown Jax, rarely had two dimes to rub together all of the time she was illegally married to warehouseman Haas.

One night, on a pay night, after Haas had lost all of his pay, he brought three of his fellow warehousemen home with him at one a.m. to show them Violette's tattoo. Unbelievers, they had foolishly bet Haas five bucks apiece that his wife did not have a tattoo on her forearm. She showed them the tattoo, so Haas could collect his winnings, but the next day she left Haas and Jacksonville for Miami on the Greyhound bus. Except for his low IQ and penchant for gambling, Haas hadn't been a bad husband, as husbands go, but the insensitivity to her person in bringing three men into her bedroom, and her with just a nightie on, had been too much for her. Besides, as she wrote her married sister back in Greenwood, "We were married in name only. Legally, I'm still married to Mr Winters, even though I'll never love anyone as much as I loved Tommy."

Three sorry marriages to three sorry losers had made Violette wary of romance. She suspected, wisely, that she could fall in love again, and that she was susceptible to losers. So she solved her problem by staying away from men altogether, except in line of duty as a waitress. Gradually, week by week, Violette was finally building a little nest egg for herself, depositing ten dollars of her tips each week in the First Federal Savings Bank & Trust Company of Miami.

In Miami, Violette had found a job, almost immediately, in the El Quatro Lounge and Restaurant, on the Tamiami

Trail (Eighth Street). The El Quatro, because of its peculiar hours (it opened at four a.m., and closed at noon), attracted a unique clientele. The first arrivals, at four a.m., were mostly drunks who came from other bars, or party diehards who had decided to carry on the party elsewhere. By six a.m. another group arrived, mostly hard-working construction workers who liked steak and eggs for breakfast. There were also large breakfast wedding parties two or three mornings a week. By ten-thirty a.m., a good many secretaries arrived, in twos and threes, to eat early lunches. They would be needed to answer the telephones in their offices during the noon hour when their bosses went out for longer and much more leisurely martini lunches. As a consequence, Violette worked hard at the El Quatro, and never quite got accustomed to the hours.

Violette rented a room, with a private bath, from a Cuban family on Second Street. She said very little to the members of the Duarte family because they made it a practice – a dying stab at the preservation of their culture – to only speak Spanish at home. Violette did not sleep very well, that is, for any prolonged stretch at a time. The family was noisy, but that wouldn't have bothered her much; it was the peculiar working hours. Exhausted by the time she arrived home at one p.m., she napped fitfully, off and on, and watched television until it was time to go to work again. She ate two meals at El Quatro, and rarely fixed anything to eat on the hotplate she had in her room. She ate a good deal of candy between meals, mostly Brach's chocolate-covered peanut clusters and chocolate-covered almonds.

On her day off (Monday) she took the bus to Key Biscayne and rented a cabana at Crandon Park. She would wander around the zoo, sit in the shade of her cabana looking at the muddy sea, and browse idly through the magazines she brought along. Her favourite magazines were *Cosmopolitan* and *Ingenue*, with *Modern Romances* a close third. She also subscribed to *The Enquirer*, but she read that at home. On these lazy, off-days, Violette almost forgot sometimes that she was a waitress, but she always remembered to pick up her clean uniforms for the week on her way home.

Violette hated being a waitress, but she knew there wasn't anything she could do about it because of her astrological sign. She had read it in the *Miami News*, when she checked her daily horoscope on her birthday. "An Aries born on this date will be a good waitress."

And it was true. Violette was a good waitress: she was waiting: and she was an Aries.

Tape Cassette (undated)

Whihh, whihh, wheee! Hello test, hello test. Okay. Note to Engineer. Please make a dub of this cassette for my file, and mail the original to Mr Doremus Jessup, Veep for Programming, NBN, New York.

Hi, Dory, this is Russell Haxby, and I want you to know first off that the quarters at the Los Pinos are el fino, as they say down here in Miami. Harry Thead and I, you'll be glad to know, are getting along fabulously. In fact, we already have a bond in Quail Roost, and Harry isn't into Scotch like so many TV station-managers. So we drink Quail Roost, and, thanks to you, the fraternal idea of being Masons together has worked out rather well. Incidentally, Jim Preston, in Continuity, gave me a pretty damned hard time when I asked him to show me the secret handshake. I had to show him your memo ordering him to give it to me before he came across with it. Don't reprimand him, or anything like that, but I hope you'll bear it in mind when cost-of-living time rolls around. No man loyal to the network should put some sort of weird lodge on a level higher than the organization he works for.

Numero uno. The soundproof glass boxes are being built now at the station, according to the specs. We plan to use the narrow parking lot behind WOOZ, which faces Biscayne Bay. This area, ordinarily, is the staff and VIP parking area, but there is plenty of parking space out front, so Harry said to preempt it. A good part of the Miami skyline is in the b.g., so for the interview shows, we can do them outside, putting the skyline in the background when the MC talks alone, or goes from booth to booth. We will be able to hear the volunteers, but they won't be able to hear each other. The speaker in each box will pick up the MC's voice, and for control, my mike from the director's booth.

Two. At Harry's suggestion, we are going to lodge the five volunteers, when we have them, but not the staff, in a fairly large two-storey houseboat that's moored about fifty feet down the causeway from the studio property. The houseboat belongs to a friend of Harry's, and it will make everything much simpler. No transportation problems, and we can put the psychiatrist in there with them, and station a couple of security men at the gangplank for absolute control. The staff will remain at the Los Pinos. I told Billy Elkhart to work out some kind of fair rent deal with Harry's friend, even though we were offered the houseboat gratis. It's better to lock up a rental contract at a minimum fee, so he doesn't all of a sudden need his goddamned boat back in the middle of things.

Point three. As it turned out, it was a good idea to select the resident psychiatrist down here instead of bringing one down from New York. Not only was it cheaper – twenty applicants from the Miami area answered our ad in *The American Psychiatrist's Journal* – but these Miami doctors are more familiar with Florida mental profiles than New York doctors. Dr Bernstein, by the way, is enthusiastic as hell about the programme. He thinks he'll get a book out of it, poor bastard. A New York doctor would have understood the release he signed, or at least have had his lawyer read it. I didn't tell Bernstein any different; I'll lay that bomb on him after he turns in his pre-and-post programme studies. On the release he signed, he won't even be able to retain his notes.

Eliminating the other nineteen psychiatrists was simpler than Harry and I thought it would be. The first five we interviewed had nasal Midwestern accents, so we let them go immediately. Four others hadn't published anything in the last two years, one of our main requirements. As you know, I won't even go to a goddamned dentist if he doesn't write and publish in his field. And three were against the programme morally, or said they were, so I let them go. We narrowed down the others on the basis of videotape screen tests, and their publications. Bernstein's recent article in

The Existential Analyst's Journal was the most objective, and if you want to read it let me know and I'll send you a xerox. He can also fake a fairly good German accent that's still intelligible. He used to imitate and mock his old man, he said, and that's how he learned to do it. He's photogenic, wears a short white goatee, and his crinkly eyes will look kindly – with the right make-up. Also he has a head full of salt-and-pepper hair, and a little below-the-belt melon paunch. If it weren't for his bona fides, he could've been sent over by Central Casting. In fact, he looks so much like a psychiatrist, we're going to have him wear a suit instead of a white doctor's coat when we go on the air.

Problems. A few. And I don't mind suggestions. WOOZ has got six camera operators. Five are women, and one is a fag. Harry says the five women are all good, and he hired them a couple of years back to keep the women's lib people down here off his ass. The same with the fag, who's the secretary/treasurer of the North Miami Gay Lib Group. The women have degrees in Communications, two of them with MA's from Southern Illinois. So there's no way we can fire any of them for cause or incompetence. I talked to them, and none of them object to the programme idea. Why should they? They're pros, and they have union cards. But – and here's the problem – these women, being women, and a fag, being a fag, might faint during the operation scenes. They've never seen anything like the stuff we've got coming up, you know. What I wanted, and we discussed this in New York, was some ex-combat Signal Corps cameramen who were used to the sight of blood. These female operators sure as hell wouldn't stand for any stand-by cameramen, either. They want to do a network show, more for the prestige than for the extra money. Anyway, we've still got plenty of time, and if you have any ideas, let me know soonest.

Everything else is on schedule. We're working on the script for the TV spot announcements – to get the volunteers – this afternoon. Dr Bernstein is a help here, more help than the writer you sent me, Noble Barnes. He can't seem to forget that he's a novelist, and a black novelist at that. He's got to go. I've been around for a long time, Dory, and I've never seen a novelist yet who could do shit with a spot or a screenplay. Noble can't spell, and he leaves the "esses" and "ee dees" off his words as well. On a programme as important as this one, I've got to have another writer. "The First Five in Line" isn't "Amos and Andy" for God's sake.

– Sorry, Dory. I know we have to have at least one black on the staff, but if we're lucky enough to get a black volunteer, I'm shipping Noble Barnes's black ass back to Harlem. How, I'll always wonder, did this fucker ever get through CCNY?

Tomorrow we meet with the Miami account exec from Baumgarten, Bates, and Williams, who wants to discuss national accounts at this end. I'll send you a tape or a transcript of the minutes. The WOOZ engineer has rigged up the conference room at the Los Pinos, and we're going to tape everything. It's quite possible that Mr Williams himself might come to this meeting, according to the account exec. A good sign, don't you think?

Some possible alternative titles from my notes:

"The Five Who Fled"; "The Finalist Quintet"; "The End of the Line"; "Doctor, Lawyer, Indian Chief, Cowboy and Lady"; "Five Fists Full of Dollars".

I'm not crazy about any of these titles, but they're on the record, so you can kick them around.

Ciao, J.D. And that's a ten-four.

John Wheeler Coleman, Col., AUS (Retired)

A good many men in America, if they had to do it at all, would have rather done it John Wheeler Coleman's way than the more conventional method, but Coleman had always felt cheated by the failure of his father to get him into the US Military Academy at West Point, or, failing that, into the Virginia Military Institute where General Marshall had matriculated. In other words, despite Coleman's distinguished military career, he had never managed to become a Regular Army officer.

His failure to become RA had coloured his life brown. Coleman had obtained his commission as a second lieutenant at Fort Benning, at The Infantry School, by attending Officer's Candidate School, and he had served his country well for twenty-four years. He had retired as a lieutenant colonel, with a "gangplank" promotion to full colonel on the day before his retirement, from the AUS (Army of the United States) instead of the USA (United States Army).

The difference between the AUS and RA, in Coleman's case, would have made all the difference to his career. As a Reserve officer on active duty – instead of being a Regular Army officer on active duty – Coleman's active duty status was in jeopardy every single day of the full twenty-four years he served. Every Reserve officer on active duty knows this, but Coleman had never been able to adjust to the idea of sudden, peremptory dismissal. There wasn't a day that went by that the possibility of a letter, informing him that he would be "riffed", would land on his desk. The term "riff" is an acronym coined by Louis Johnson, during his tenure as Secretary of Defence, from "RIF," reduction in Force. Many thousands of officers were able to stay the full distance for twenty years, and retirement, but many more thousands were riffed; and when an officer was riffed there was no way that he could find out the reason, if, indeed, there was a reason other than a further reduction in force.

Coleman often thought bitterly (never voicing it, to be sure) about General Douglas MacArthur's fatuous remark, "There is no security, there is only opportunity."

Sure, a man who was RA could say that, and MacArthur had gone to West Point; but if MacArthur had been a Reserve officer, he would have whistled a different tune.

As a combat officer, serving in Korea and Vietnam, Coleman had been decorated with the Distinguished Service Cross; the Silver Star, with one Oak Leaf Cluster; the Bronze Star, with V Device; and two Army Commendation Medals. As a Reserve officer, Coleman had always tried harder than regular officers of the same rank, but the positive knowledge that he could be booted out of the service any day, without a reason, unlike RA officers, and without getting a dime in severance pay, either, had affected his decision-making ability. Coleman never hesitated about making a decision, of course (if he had, he never would have lasted the full twenty-four years), but his decisions were always determined by thinking first what kind of decision his immediate superior officer (the officer who made out his bi-annual Effectiveness Report) would have made in the same situation. He had been very successful at this kind of thinking, although the overall pattern of his career, as a consequence, made his record a somewhat eccentric mixture of inconsistencies. A brilliant record, to be true, but a strange one if examined closely, because it reflected the thinking of more than 100 different superior officers. Despite his Superior Effectiveness Reports, with only one Excellent Report to mar his record (the time, when he was a First Lieutenant, and a Supply Officer for Company "A", 19th Infantry, and someone had stolen ten mattress covers from the supply room), Coleman had served under a good many officers who had made dumb decisions. His decisions, under dumb officers, had been equally dumb – but that had been the game he had had to play if he wanted to stay on active duty.

With his daring combat record as a junior officer, Coleman, by all rights, should have been a full colonel with his own regiment at least five years before his retirement, but he had performed so brilliantly in Command and General Staff School, at Fort Leavenworth, he had been marked down for staff work. Without ever getting into command, of at least a battalion, he was doomed to staff work from then on, and no matter how brilliant a staff man happens to be, he is always considered a No. Two man, which means he is passed over for command more often than not.

The key year, for an officer with reserve status on active duty, is his eighteenth year of service. If the officer is allowed to serve for eighteen years, he cannot be riffed (except for a very serious cause) until he has served twenty years and is eligible for retirement. But even when Coleman passed safely through his eighteenth year, and then his twentieth, he was still unable to relax his vigilance. He tried even harder, in fact, feeling now that there was still a chance to make RA before his retirement and then stay for thirty years. If he could stay for thirty, or until he became sixty-five, those extra years would make the possibility of becoming a general officer a certainty. But he never made it. He languished as a regimental S-3, and was finally riffed after serving twenty-four years.

One morning, as he had been expecting for all of those years, a letter riffing him from the service appeared on his desk.

If a man is single, and Coleman had never married, a colonel's retirement is sufficient to live on, providing his needs are simple. He lived frugally in The-Bide-A-While Rec. Centre. Once a week he visited the officers' club at Homestead Air Force Base, on Bingo Night. The rest of the time, he watched TV, or took long nature walks in the nearby Everglades State Park. He drove a Willy's Jeepster, and sometimes drove to the Keys, just to have somewhere to go. After a few months of this boring retirement, he took a course in Real Estate, like so many other retired officers living in Florida, and passed the examination for Agent. During the long hot days after getting his licence, he sat in empty houses for eight hours a day, and sold at least one house a year. His commission was usually $1200 for each house he sold, and he added it to his savings. His savings, more than $100,000 in Gold Certificates, were kept in the Homestead Air Force Base Credit Union, at eight per cent. Sitting in empty houses gave him something to do, and he considered the commissions he made as hedges against future inflation.

Coleman had made few friends in the army, and he found it even harder to make friends on the outside. He was a lonely man, and he was ashamed of his military career, which many men would have been proud of – for one reason.

Despite his combat decorations for bravery under fire, Coleman felt as if he had never been tested. Coleman, who had never known any real joy, had never known any real pain, either. He had never been sick a day in his life. He was trim, athletic, and ate with small appetite. Nor had he ever been wounded in combat, or even hurt. He had never known the joy – or pain – of marriage and fatherhood. In short, by normal standards, many men would have considered him to be a lucky bastard all the way round. Although he kept his hair in a brush cut, with white side-walls, he had even retained his hair.

But when a man has never been tested, truly tested to the limits of his endurance, how does he know that he can meet the test? There is only one way, and that is to take the test.

Coleman thought about this a lot, especially during the long days when he watched the soap operas as he sat in empty houses, thinking about the emptiness of his life.

Tape Cassette

Hi Russell, this is D.J. I'll be sending this tape down with Ernie Powell, who'll also bring along some notes, including the comments from Doctor Glass of Bellevue. Ernie's been hired by the unit manager as a production assistant for TFFIL, but he's really a procurer. He has a rep in the trade, in case you haven't heard of him, of being able to get any prop, or anything else for that matter, within twenty minutes. He worked for seventeen years as a stage manager in summer stock, so you know how valuable he is. Ernie's worked with Billy Elkhart before, so I know Ernie'll be glad to have him on the staff.

First, those titles you reeled off were terrible. I'm putting a couple of Columbia grad students on the title. They'll be working free at NBN for two weeks, for two college credits, and they might as well learn something about TV the hard way. It will give them some incentive. I told them that if they came up with a useable title, great, but if they didn't, I wouldn't recommend them for the two college credits. It's obvious from your last tape that you don't have time to think creatively about an alternative title, and I want your mind to be free for all of the things you have to do.

We're paying Dr Glass a bundle, and you'll see by his notes that he's finally come up with some valuable stuff, except it's about two months too late. The gist is that the last three weeks in August and the first week in September would be the best time of the year to get volunteers. Our predictions show, as I said in my memo, a possibility ratio of 7.1, counting the new Miami unemployment figures, for volunteers. But in August, plus the first week in September, Glass claims that ninety percent of the Miami analysts, psychologists and psychiatrists, go on their vacations to North Carolina. This means that there are approximately five thousand or more neurotics stumbling around down there without a doctor to turn to for advice. At loose ends, these analysands would undoubtedly boost the probability factor for volunteers. Now, don't think I'm worried, but it's just too bad that Dr Glass's information was a month late, or as L.B.G. used to say, and "a dollar short".

We also need a black man as a volunteer, or failing that, a Cuban. But Glass said we would never get a black volunteer, never. They're too practical, he said; but at least they won't be able to holler discrimination when we're playing this game straight and we can prove it. So you'll be stuck with Noble Barnes as a writer. At any rate, Glass's figures will be helpful if we get another season out of the show — and next time we'll go to St Louis where there is a bigger percentage of blacks.

Re the women (and fag) camerapersons. No sweat, here. Hustle their ass over to the emergency ward at Jackson Memorial Hospital and make them watch a few emergency operations from the car wrecks. There will be amputations a-plenty, so make them watch a few. If any of them pass out you can replace them before rehearsals begin, and they can't squawk to the union. Anyway, hire at least one ex-Signal Corps cameraman as an advisor only, and have him stand by for emergencies during the actual programming. Too bad we decided to do this live, instead of on tape, but we do need the immediacy that a live show engenders.

Are you getting any, Russell? If not, ask Ernie, and he'll have a broad in your room within twenty minutes. It'll be good recreation for you, and you should do it anyway, even if you aren't interested, just to see Ernie work. Here he'll be, with this tape and the notes, right from the airport, and in a strange new city, and I'll bet you a case of Chivas to a case of Quail Roost that he can get a broad in your room within twenty minutes. And a free one, too. It's rather uncanny, when you come to think about it.

I called the Los Angeles office, and it's firm. Warren

Oates will be the MC. We might have to work around his movie schedule, but that'll be Billy Elkhart's problem, not yours. You *will* have Warren Oates as your MC. Warren used to work a live game show with Jimmy Dean back in the early fifties, and he did a lot of TV work before going into films. He'll be a great MC, and he has a positive image for this kind of thing. The only snag in his contract is that he gets to wear his dark sunglasses on the show. I had to concede this point, but you may be able to talk him out of it. By the way, when Warren comes out there from Hollywood next week, do not, do not under any circumstances, ask him what he's carrying in that burlap sack he lugs around with him. He's very sensitive about this point. Okay? Okay.

This is D.J., and a ten-four and God Speed.

Leo Zuck

Leo Zuck (nee Zuckerman), at 82, was a dapper dresser, even by Miami Beach standards, although sartorial standards on Miami Beach are not very high. Leo owned a white gabardine suit and a burnt orange linen suit, which, in various combinations, gave him four different changes. He possessed two white-on-white drip-dry-never-iron shirts, and twenty-five pink neckties. (He had had the neckties made to order out of the same bolt of cloth at a bargain price.) He also owned a red silk dinner jacket, with a ruffled pink shirt and maroon bow-tie to go with it, as well as blue-black tuxedo trousers and the cherry red patent leather pumps to round out the costumes. He did not, unhappily, have any underwear, and he had only two pair of black clock socks left in his wardrobe. The white suede shoes he wore with his suits-sports outfits, although they were clean enough, were very bald.

Leo Zuck, living in very reduced circumstances, was mostly front. Leo had lost his job as the MC at the Saturday night pier dance, and he did not know what he was going to do for the little luxuries that extra ten dollars a week had provided him with: a daily cigar, Sen-Sen (for his notoriously bad breath), and an occasional Almond Joy. But now he had to give up these small luxuries.

If Leo had learned or invented some new material each week, he could have, in all probability, kept the MC job indefinitely. Abe Ossernan, who ran the weekly dances (Admission 25 cents) and owned the pier concessions on South Beach (as South Miami Beach is called) was not a mean man; and Abe had hinted to Leo more than once that he should brighten up his faded material. But Leo paid no attention to Mr Ossernan; Leo loved his material, and he had it down ice cold. Leo had purchased his act in 1925 for $150, when $150 *was* $150, and he had sharpened and refined the material to perfection on the Keith-Orpheum Vaudeville circuit for fifteen years. An excellent mimic, with a rubbery, if deeply lined face, Leo did accurate and extremely funny imitations of Charles Ray, George Bancroft, Emil Jannings, and Harry Langdon. He was also able to sing "I'm a Yankee Doodle Dandy" raucously out of the side of his mouth in a near-perfect imitation of George M. Cohan. This act of Leo's had wowed the hicks in the sticks for years, but the material was so old now it baffled even his nostalgic audiences at the pier dance on Saturday nights.

Leo had a large scrapbook filled with yellowed clippings from every large city and from most of the small cities in the United States and Canada, attesting to how good his act was – or had been – and, in Leo's opinion, the act was still as good – if not better than ever. Except for minor alterations in timing, the only addition to Leo's act since 1925 (a socko finish!) was made in 1945. In this cruel year, Leo had had his remaining teeth removed, and was fitted with a full set of upper and lower white plastic choppers. Because of his thick, fairly long nose and pointed, rather long chin, Leo could perform a reasonably accurate imitation of Popeye the Sailor by removing both plates. Except for elderly persons with very keen memories, however, Popeye the Sailor was the only imitation most audiences recognized.

When vaudeville died out forever, as it had in 1940, Leo had been fortunate enough to get in the US Army Special Services during the war, joining various variety companies as they were put together in New York; and he had entertained troops in the South Pacific, England, and eventually, Italy. Between overseas tours he had made the rounds of stateside Special Service shows, as well. GI audiences are not critical, and they had applauded his old gags and imitations of long dead movie stars with cheerful tolerance. They liked especially his introduction:

MC: And now, straight from the Great White Way, the famous star from the Keith-Orpheum vaudeville circuit, Leo Zuck!
(Enter Leo Zuck.)
Zuck: Suck what?
Audience: (Laughter.) And so on. . . .

When the war and his teeth were finished, Leo obtained summer employment in the Catskills and Poconos at third-rate hotels on the Borscht circuit. Social directors did not care greatly for Leo's act, but he was a great success with the old ladies, mostly widows, who sojourned at these cheaper mountain hotels. Leo had never married, and single men were a premium in the mountains.

In his red satin dinner jacket under a pink spot, Leo was distinguished-looking on stage. He knew how to apply make-up for maximum effect, and his full head of blue-white hair reminded many old ladies of Leopold Stokowski. Leo sported a well-trimmed white toothbrush moustache, and it was almost as white (except in the centre where it had turned brownish from cigarette tar and nicotine) as his flashing false teeth.

Except for his own act, which was practically engraved on his brain, Leo's memory was not consistent, but no one in the Poconos minded when he put on his reading glasses and introduced the various acts, in his MC capacity, by reading the names and remarks off three-by-five inch cards with a flashlight.

In the mid-1960's, however, Leo had been unable to get any more work – even in the Poconos – and he had retired to South Beach to a residential hotel. He drew the minimum in Social Security benefits, of course, because, like many entertainers, he had preferred to be paid in cash for most of his theatrical life, but the minimum had been enough to pay for his room and meals for several years. He had also supplemented his meagre income, from time to time, by playing a few dates at parties and social functions. He had been interviewed twice on WKAT radio (for free), and once on a late night talk show on Channel Four. When the host on the Channel Four Talk Show introduced him, Leo said automatically, "Suck what?"

Because of three irate phone calls, Leo wasn't invited back to the TV station, but he was still a kind of celebrity to the retired old people who make up the general population of South Beach. With inflation, Leo's Social Security cheque was barely enough to cover the rent of his hotel room, and when the rent was raised again – which it soon would be – he would have to find a cheaper room, although there were no rooms cheaper in South Beach than the one he had. After paying the rent, there was no money left over to eat with, and he had to be satisfied with the one free noon meal he got each day at the Jewish Welfare Centre. The loss of his MC job at the pier, and the tax-free ten dollars that went with it, was a disaster for Leo and, for the first time since 1940, Leo Zuck, the old trouper, began to doubt seriously that vaudeville would ever come back.

We realise this is just a tantalising glimpse of what could have been, and the reader will wonder where the other men in line are, but sadly this is all there is of a novel which the legendary Charles Willeford began writing in 1975 and never completed.

There are so few short examples of Willeford's noir work available, with its distinctive absurdist incarnation of pulp, that its inclusion in this anthology was warranted, we feel. As to the rest of the story, we leave that to the reader's imagination . . .

Where There's a Will There's a Slay

Frederick C. Davis

I

The Package

Changing his course, Barney Chance squeezed himself into the doorway of Klamer's Dry Goods Store. The store was small, dark, and locked. The doorway was shelter, but not enough. He stood there impatiently, a briefcase in one sun-browned hand, an overnight bag in the other, water trickling off his hat-brim, the wet snow still reaching him.

He paused there only a moment. Barney Chance, as always, was in a hurry. He had certain important matters on his mind. From the overnight bag that had served his needs during a ten-day trip to Chicago, he removed his raincoat. He fought the coat until he had it buttoned on. Then his rangy stride carried him back along the sidewalk, his baggage again gripped tight, his head lowered against the stinging snow, a young man in no mood to let a little unexpected moisture hold him up.

The storm had struck without fair warning while he was heading towards the centre of town from the taxiless Pennswick station, where the 7:40 train had deposited him. Apparently its peak had been waiting for him to arrive. The full moon had greeted him by sneaking behind a black curtain of clouds – a high wind had commenced blowing down Main Street, lashing sleet and snow into huge drifts which piled against the store fronts. Barney looked like an animate snowman after walking the few blocks from the station.

The snowstorm, full-grown in seconds, had become one more minor item in a long list of tribulations that had been ganging up on Barney Chance for months past. But, like his business troubles, which had kept him in his home town of Pennswick much longer than he'd originally planned to stay, this snow had its good points.

It was pretty – fluffy white drifts in front of the lighted drugstore windows, red and violet icicles hanging from the familiar neon sign of the Pennswick Inn. It was ice crystals dancing on the sidewalk, cotton piling in the gutters. It was also like those instantaneous precipitations that had drenched him times without number in New Guinea, except that it was colder, this being southeastern Pennsylvania in early December.

The worst part of it had caught him only a block from his office. He was across State Street now, and it was letting up a little. So far as Barney Chance could see, only one other person had ventured out.

A man was standing at the mailbox just beyond the corner – standing none too steadily, hatless, his coat sagging open. The snow sprinkled on his curly black hair as he held onto the green box with one hand, balancing himself. His other hand held a long brown envelope poised, as if he were uncertain of getting it into the slot.

The man at the mailbox was Guy Farrish, who'd had the law practice of the firm of Lytham & Farrish all to himself since the death of his senior partner two months ago. Having known Guy as long as he'd known anyone, Barney wasn't too surprised at his evident condition. Guy had always been a conscientious drinker and lately he'd been working at it even harder than usual.

"Take it easy, pal," said Barney, who rarely took it easy himself.

Guy Farrish didn't answer, but stood swaying slightly, the envelope still in his hand. Barney grinned back at him, swinging past, still in a hurry. He didn't see Guy Farrish's eyes shift slowly and become fixed on him – fixed and brighter, in spite of the weariness and pain in them, nor did he see Guy sprawl in the snow, then painfully pull himself erect again.

The Lytham Building stood halfway between State and Court Streets, an old-fashioned brick structure three storeys high. Its entrance was unlocked and the foyer lights were burning, indicating that someone was staying late in one of the six offices inside.

Barney climbed the wooden stairs to the second floor, passed the door labelled *Lytham & Farrish: Attorneys-at-Law*, turned to another on the opposite side of the hallway that said *Filmore Electronic Corporation of Chicago: Eastern Representative*, and used his key.

Switching on the lights and dropping his bag, he tossed his coat into a chair with his hat. He had a white scar in the tan of his forehead which gave his left eyebrow a quizzical lift. The Jap whose bullet had put it there hadn't intended to make Barney look distinguished, but that was the effect.

He opened the briefcase at his desk. His big, awkward-looking hands moved decisively as he removed sheaves of memoranda, then a thick, folded mat of blueprints. They were the plans for a branch factory which the Filmore Corporation desired to construct for the postwar production of electronic equipment.

Mr Stewart Filmore, president of the firm, thought this an important project in his programme of expansion. Barney Chance agreed, particularly since it was he who had sold Mr Filmore on Pennswick as the location for the new plant, Pennswick being only two hours from New York City, forty minutes from Philadelphia and nearer still to Barney's heart. His home town should be delighted to welcome a new industry of such vast potentialities, Barney felt, but to judge from the results he'd obtained so far, you'd never think so.

The site had been bought without a hitch during the first two weeks of Barney's negotiations, but months had passed since then and still not a spadeful of earth had been broken. Ten days ago, Barney had journeyed back to the Chicago office to explain in detail just why this was. He'd left feeling frustrated, the reasons being obscure and involved, and only his powers of persuasion had postponed Mr Filmore's decision to abandon Pennswick in favour of a more receptive community.

Having gone this far with it, and not being one to give up, Barney had made it entirely his own responsibility now. Tonight he'd returned to Pennswick, determined to butt his way through to the finish of the job, and, if necessary, to throttle a few short-sighted local bureaucrats with skeins of their own red tape.

As he pored over the plans, footsteps came haltingly to his door. Guy Farrish sidled in. He dropped into the chair facing Barney's desk and his eyelids drooped heavily as he fumbled for something in his raincoat pocket.

"How's it working, Guy?" Barney said. "I mean your programme for forgetting Eve. Make lots of money, spend it fast and drink enough, and losing her might not hurt so much. Does it work?"

Out of his coat pocket Guy Farrish pulled a small package wrapped in brown paper and tied with red string. He leaned forward, extending it, his manner earnest.

"Give it to her, Barney," he said.

Curiously, Barney took it. It bore no postage stamp, but it was addressed. *Miss Eve Ranie*, 646 *East* 54*th Street, New York City*.

"A peace offering?" Barney asked. "But why pass it on to me? Why don't you mail it to her?"

"Give it to Eve," Guy said with an effort. "Don't mail it. She'll come. You give it to her then. But don't open it."

Barney looked up, a little incensed. Guy, drunk or not, should know him better than that. He wasn't the sort who'd poke into a package that had been entrusted to him, a forlorn gift from a man to the girl who was his fiancée no longer.

"Of course not, Guy," Barney said. He put the package aside and reverted to business. "Just before I left for Chicago you told me why I'm having such a hell of a time getting the necessary permits for this new plant."

Guy leaned back in his chair wearily. He didn't seem to be listening.

"Did I get it straight?" Barney went on. "I've made the

mistake of not greasing certain palms, is that it? You said I ought to see Chabbat." His face showed his deep distaste. "In other words, the permits can be had, but at a price. First I've got to butter somebody's popcorn."

Holding himself in his chair, Guy seemed about to doze off.

"The hell with that!" Barney said emphatically. "I'll get this plant built honestly or not at all."

Guy roused himself and spoke without apparently having heard Barney at all. "And don't tell anybody." He was referring anxiously again to the little package. His intent manner said this was more important to him than Barney's new plant. "Don't tell anybody about it. Not anybody."

"I won't. But about –"

"Your word on that?"

Barney wanted to sock him. "I said it, Guy, didn't I?" He rose impatiently. He'd always liked Guy, without approving of the man's dog-eat-dog outlook on life, but he had work to do. "I'd better take you home to bed before you pass out cold."

Guy sighed: "Get a doctor."

Astonished, Barney rounded the desk. Guy had eased back in his chair, chin down. Barney could smell the liquor on him – it was powerful.

He was bending over Guy when he heard the furtive noise at the door. Turning his head, he saw a shadow on the pane, a faint dark blur cast by the hallway lights. Someone was just outside the office, evidently listening. And at that moment Guy took hold of himself enough to speak again.

"Remember, don't open it. Don't tell anybody, not anybody! Just give it to her."

"Sure," Barney said. "Sure, Guy."

The shadow was gone now. Barney moved quietly to the door. When he eased it open, the corridor was empty, but there were sounds below. Someone was hurrying down the stairs.

Barney went to the window at the head of the hallway. A car was parked halfway between the Lytham Building and the corner of Court Street. It had been there a few minutes ago, when he'd come in, Barney remembered. It had been waiting. His bird's-eye view told him little about the man who was just then ducking into it. Light coat, black hat and shiny shoes. That was all.

The man was inside the car now and the door on its opposite side was opening. A girl slid out. She had a red beanie on her honey-blonde hair, her coat was beige and her shoes black, spike-heeled, with cute, big black bows. She turned back to the man at the wheel, said something, and then, as the car veered from the kerb, she ran along the sidewalk in the opposite direction, from which Barney and Guy had come.

Barney tried to watch both the car and the girl at once. The car swung again at Court Street, heading into the parking space that fronted the inn. Barney couldn't read its licence number before it passed from sight. Turning his head, he glimpsed the girl again just as she disappeared against the buildings near the State Street end of the block.

He retraced his steps and just inside his office he paused. Guy wasn't there. The little package still sat on the desk where Barney had put it, but Guy had left.

Barney picked up the box curiously, wondering why Guy wasn't taking care of it himself. Why had he said, "She'll come," meaning Eve Ranie, who hadn't once visited Pennswick since leaving for New York immediately after breaking off her engagement to Guy? There was something strange about this business of the package, Barney felt, and somehow he didn't like it.

He liked it still less, distinctly less, the moment he saw the dark spot on the floor.

The spot was directly beneath the chair Guy had occupied. It was wet to Barney's touch, and red. It had dripped off the hem of Guy's coat while he'd sat there.

Then Barney saw the other spots, smaller ones, a row of them, a dotted line leading out the door. He followed them diagonally across the hall, unconsciously carrying the little package with him into Guy's office.

Guy was seated at his desk, his arms crossed on the blotter before him, his head resting on them. The red stuff was still dripping slowly from the hem of his coat. And Guy wasn't alone here. Alma Remsen lay awkwardly against the wall in the far corner.

Barney hurried first to Alma. In his concern for her he was scarcely aware that he put the little package on the floor beside her. There were two large bruises on the left side of her face, both turning an ugly green-black. Her red hair was matted behind her left temple. The cut in her scalp there had parted its lips – it looked like a small snarling mouth. A steam radiator stood directly behind her. Evidently she'd struck her head against it when falling away from the brutal blows delivered to her face.

She was Guy's secretary, but she couldn't have been working with him tonight – she wasn't dressed for it. Her gown was long and full-skirted, of sea-green tulle, and her satin evening pumps matched it. She had a coronet of gardenias pinned on her red hair – crushed now. The blow behind her left ear might have killed her, but she wasn't dead. Barney found her pulse, a faint ragged beat.

He turned quickly to Guy, forgetting the package he'd left beside Alma. Guy hadn't moved. There was no doubt at all about his pulse. He had none. He'd left Barney's office to come back here to die at his own desk.

Barney peeled Guy's coat open and found a smear inside it, the blood still dripping from a puncture high in Guy's left side. Barney felt sick. He'd tried to talk business with a dying man. But then, he hadn't known, hadn't had a hint until Guy had asked for a doctor. Even Guy, perhaps sensing that his gunshot wound was fatal, had considered it less important than other things – for example, the little package he wanted Eve to have.

Barney didn't go back to the package at once. He found his hands trembling and swore at himself for it. He thought he'd grown used to seeing dead men. In the South Pacific he'd seen them die every day. Yet this was different. Guy was an old and good friend, but that wasn't it. Some of those Joes in New Guinea had been Barney's friends, too. This was out of place. This wasn't war. It was a peaceful little town which the war had scarcely touched. Now, suddenly, the terrors Barney had known seemed less far away. He found himself feeling that nowhere on earth was there security from attack and bloodshed and the relentlessness of death.

Because movement always helped his nerves in moments of stress, he circled the office once. He stopped at Guy's telephone, wanting urgently to call a doctor for Alma, then the police, but he drew back, remembering the matter of fingerprints. He crossed the hall, leaving the little package still lying beside the unconscious girl, forgotten again.

His own telephone was ringing. He was inside his door, still moving fast, before he realized his office lights were out. He glanced around once, uneasily, but lifted the receiver.

"Hello?"

No voice answered him. Instead, he heard music faintly, far away. It wasn't the jive of a juke-box, as it would have been if this call were coming from a pay-station in a bar. It was solemn, celestial, the strains of an organ. What was the selection? *O Promise Me.*

"Hello!" Barney said again.

The music was cut off, the connection severed, and no voice had spoken.

Barney stood still, slowly lowering the instrument. Someone was behind him. He'd heard a movement in the darkness and now hard pressure came to the small of his back.

Barney's reaction was not caution and fear, but swift counteraction. The feeling of a gun poked against his body was intolerable. Months ago, during those black, steamy nights in jungle clearings half a world away, when any sneaking sound or stir of motion might be a prowling Jap, he'd learned to strike first and look into it later. He turned quickly, but he'd lost some of his instinctive alertness during the eight months since his medical discharge. He turned not quite quickly enough.

The blow slashed across the base of his skull. Barney fell into a sort of helpless dream. He wasn't entirely out, but could feel himself being pulled at and rolled, and he couldn't do anything about it. After a vague interval, he heard someone running away. It was quiet now, and dark, but still not entirely calm, like a foxhole just after the last hostile plane has passed.

He found his chair, climbed into it and sat holding his head. After a few minutes he groped to the wall-switch. His desk was messed up, his papers scattered. Two of his pockets were hanging inside out. He went to the wash-bowl behind the screen in the rear corner and was splashing cold water into his numb face when he remembered.

The package! His attacker had come after the little package. There was nothing else here that anyone could possibly want.

Across the hall again, back in Guy's office, he saw slight changes in the scene. Guy's desk was also disturbed now. Barney felt the prowling presence that had come and quickly gone, and anger still smouldered in him. But the package was still there, still on the floor beside Alma. Barney gazed on it incredulously and took it up.

His shoulders were stubbornly set. Like all the comparatively less important difficulties he'd found in the way of the new Filmore plant, things were piling up on him without letting him know why. But he recognized there was no way of finding out at once, and this wasn't helping Alma, who needed help.

Back at his own desk, he first put the package in a drawer and locked it in. Then he twirled the dial on his telephone. He had called Dr Whitlock and was spinning the dial again, when a voice spoke from the doorway.

"You calling the police now?"

Barney hadn't heard the big man's approach. The big man stood in the doorway, his head ducked so his hat wouldn't brush the top of the jamb. He wore his clothes snugly. His face was square and his features blunt, yet peculiarly sensitive. Barney saw subtle, indefinable expressions coming and fading in his blue eyes and around his thin-lipped mouth.

The big man said it almost with a sigh: "Never mind calling. I'm the police."

Barney turned, still dizzy. "How did you know? Who told you to come here?"

Instead of explaining, the big man identified himself. "Captain Craddock." And as Barney rose: "You stay put. I'll be back."

"But – don't you want to hear about it?" Barney asked in confusion. "There's a dead man in the office across the hall, Guy Farrish. He was shot, murdered. Alma Remsen's there, knocked out."

Captain Craddock nodded, as if he already knew all that. Subtle glimmers of varying expressions continued to cross his face – hardness and grimness, intermingled with curious little flashes of tenderness. Barney told himself it was impossible to know just what kind of man this was, what his inner feelings were.

"I'm in charge," Captain Craddock said. "We'll have a talk about it. You stay right here."

Barney listened to his slow, measured steps across the hall. The door of Guy's office closed with a snap, a sharp sound of exclusion. Now Captain Craddock was moving about the dead man's office, his sounds seeming secretive. There was something about the man, Barney felt – brusqueness, even a capacity for ruthlessness, mixed with a queer, compassionate sort of understanding – something that brought Barney a cold twinge of apprehension.

II

Blonde in Distress

It was such an ordinary-looking little package. A four-inch cube, it was neither heavy nor light. Its contents rattled softly when Barney shook it, and it gave off a faint and pleasant odour, an Oriental sort of scent. Something exotically perfumed, he reflected, inside common brown paper and common red string – yet something uncommonly important.

Barney's head ached as he examined it, and he wondéred why he'd been slugged.

Before taking up the telephone, Barney listened down the hall. Low voices rumbled. Policemen had gone into Guy's office, Dr Whitlock next, then two white-coated ambulance men who had carried Alma Remsen out on a litter. Nobody had come to ask Barney any questions. That was another disquieting thing about Captain Craddock. Without making inquiries, he seemed to know.

Barney asked the long-distance operator to get Miss Eve Ranie, at 646 East 54th Street, Manhattan. He heard the connections progress as far as New York exchange, where they were stymied. The operator reported: "There's no phone listed under that name."

"Miss Ranie may be staying with friends or renting a room in somebody's apartment," Barney said. "Ask the superintendent."

Minutes later, the operator reported again. "Miss Ranie seems to be out, sir. Shall I leave a message for her to call you?"

"Yes, operator. It's an emergency."

He had time to get the package back into the desk drawer before Captain Craddock's deliberate footfalls reached his door. Craddock was tracing the line of blood drops. One of his hands was covered by a handkerchief and on the flat of it he carried a blue revolver.

"What did Farrish want with you, Mr Chance?"

"It must have happened before I reached the building," Barney said, disturbed by Captain Craddock's quiet directness. He told how he'd passed Guy at the mailbox in the street, and how Guy had followed him in. "He asked me to get a doctor, then went across to his office. He didn't explain anything. I thought –"

"But what else did he want with you?"

The package! Guy had said: "Don't open it. Don't tell anybody about it, not anybody!" Not even the police? Did Barney's promise to Guy include the withholding of evidence in a murder case? "Give it to Eve when she comes, but don't open it. Don't tell anybody, *not anybody*!"

And Barney had said: "I won't." He hadn't sworn it on a Bible – he'd simply said it. But that was enough, particularly if Guy had known instinctively he was close to death, as Barney believed.

"She'll come," Guy had told him, and he'd meant: "Because I'm going to die."

Captain Craddock took keen notice of Barney's hesitation. "You're holding out."

"I'm trying to get it straight. Somebody was sneaking around inside this building." Barney was glad he had this information to add. Craddock's steady gaze made him feel he was explaining it in too much detail, but it helped him to sidestep the subject of the package. Simultaneously, he conjectured about it – thought that Eve might tell the police about it herself, if she wished, after he'd delivered it to her – while talking about the attack in the dark. "He was gone when I pulled myself back together. I don't know who he was."

"Or what he was after?" Captain Craddock didn't even allow Barney an opportunity to evade the question. "Better sleep on it. It isn't smart to hold out. You can go now."

"What the hell!" Finding himself brushed off, and outmatched in the technique of evasion, Barney was full of sudden resentment. "I walked right into the thick of this business, and that's all you're going to ask me about?"

Eyeing him astutely and turning back to the door, Craddock paused, reminded of the revolver lying on his handkerchief-covered palm. "Farrish's. Found it under his desk. Shot with his own gun." This secretive man was unexpectedly volunteering information, no doubt for purposes of his own. And he added enigmatically, in an edged tone: "If you can't trust the police, Mr Chance, whom *can* you trust?"

Behind those last words, Barney sensed mockery.

Locking his office door behind him, Barney saw Marsha Barrow coming up the stairs. The daughter of the late Jonathan Lytham, formerly Guy Farrish's senior partner, Marsha was married to Lieutenant Commander Wallace Barrow, who was seeing service in Barney's old battle area. Her hair and eyes were vividly dark. Always blithely carefree, she sang out, "Why, hello, Barney!" and gave him her quick smile as she turned to the door behind which Guy sat dead.

Barney stopped her before she reached it. "What are you doing here, Marsha?"

"Why, Guy phoned me, Barney, dear." She used terms of affection indiscriminately. They meant nothing more than generous friendliness. "Darling, you look so terribly burned up about something!"

Barney was, but he didn't take time to explain. "When did Guy call you? What did he say?"

"It was less than an hour ago, and he said he had something for me, but he couldn't bring it, so he wanted me to come right down. He was very mysterious about it, Barney, dear – wouldn't tell me what it was, but said I should hurry, and he sounded so out of breath. I couldn't rush right out, of course. First I had to find a girl who'd come in and sit with the children –"

Marsha's voice faded, sparks of alarm in her dark eyes as she gazed over Barney's shoulder. Captain Craddock had opened the door. His bulk, physical power and puzzling face were enough, Barney felt, to startle any woman at first glance.

Craddock startled Marsha further by taking her arm without a word and drawing her into the office. There was something overwhelming and uncompromising about his manner. It said she'd made the mistake of talking to the wrong man, and he'd have no more of that. Then the door was closed again and the office beyond was silent except for a throaty moan from Marsha.

To Barney, the legend on the pebbled pane seemed to warn, *Keep Out – This Means YOU*. Craddock wanted it that way, and Craddock was no man to buck inadvisedly, in Barney's estimation. He went down the stairs with a frown, the little package now tucked inside his overnight bag.

The snow had almost stopped. Breathing the clean-washed air, Barney paused halfway to the State Street corner. It was here he'd seen the car parked, an unknown man getting in after eavesdropping at Barney's door, an unknown girl getting out.

Barney picked a black object from the slush near the kerb. It was a bow of suede, apparently lost from one of the girl's shoes – evidence of a sort, Barney surmised. He had no intention of going back to Craddock with it. Not to Craddock now. It could wait until the captain got around to him again. Barney pushed the suede bow into his raincoat pocket and strode on.

He had an apartment on Sycamore Street, only three blocks from his office. As a boy, he'd lived in this neighbourhood. He liked the reminiscent fragrance of its old gardens in the spring mornings, its midsummer tranquillity, its moon-shade these brisk winter nights. Tonight, however, it seemed unfamiliar and dark, too much like those tropical nights that had concealed stealthy dangers. Barney told himself he'd grown soft – he'd had enough for one night, and he'd rather not believe he was hearing footfalls behind him, quick footfalls trailing him.

He wasn't sure just when the footsteps had started, but they were coming closer. Glancing back, he sensed rather than saw a figure nearing him, dodging along against the wet hedges.

Barney was keenly conscious of the little package shut inside his overnight bag. His immediate intention was to get it safely out of anyone else's reach. He turned sharply to the left, ran up the stoop of the house where he lived, got his key out and slipped it into the lock.

He'd drawn the bolt open when he heard a girl's gasping cry of fright. The footfalls became more distinct and quickened into a rapid tick-tick of high heels. Barney saw the girl halt on the sidewalk just beyond the stoop. She looked around quickly as if in desperate search for shelter, then broke towards him. Suddenly at Barney's side on the stoop, she pressed herself against him, her eyes white flashes.

"Don't let him get me!"

"You're all right," Barney said.

Necessarily, he lowered his bag, feeling he might need both hands free. He went down the steps and gazed back along the street. The sycamores stirred in the night wind and snow sprinkled off them. He took slow steps along the sidewalk. Presently he paused, shrugging. If someone had been trailing the girl there was no sign of him now.

Barney turned back. The girl was no longer on the stoop. He opened the door of his ground-floor apartment, swung his bag in, snapped the switch and, as he'd expected, rediscovered her. She was huddled against the wall just inside, looking less frightened now.

Her hair was honey-coloured, like that of the girl who had got out of the car in front of the Lytham Building, but in other ways she was different. She wasn't, for example, wearing a red beanie – she was bare-headed. Her jacket wasn't tan, but red plaid. Her high-heeled shoes were black suede, but they had no bows.

She gave him a strained smile of thanks, but Barney didn't smile back. He couldn't shake the feeling that he'd seen this girl before, earlier tonight, under circumstances that weren't the sort to smile about.

"Who was he?" Barney asked. "What did he want?"

"I don't *know*!" The girl's eyes widened, very blue eyes trying to be very innocent. "If you hadn't been here, I – I don't know what would have happened!"

"Do you live on this street?"

She shook her head, estimating him. "I've got a room above Colby's Market."

That was four blocks from here. She added no explanation as to what she was doing alone in this neighbourhood. Not that it was dangerous territory, but even though someone else had evidently been following her, she may have been following Barney, and that possibility still troubled him. He turned uneasily to the telephone and as he spun the dial, she quickly came to his side.

"You calling the cops? Oh, please don't do that!"

He eyed her. "Why not? If someone was after you –"

"Please." She put her hand over the contact bar and held it down tightly. "It wouldn't do any good." He couldn't know exactly what she meant by that, but her voice carried a strange note of sincere concern. "Please don't."

The telephone itself settled the argument by ringing at that moment. Lifting it, Barney heard the operator say: "Mr Chance? New York City calling."

It was Eve Ranie. Barney looked up at the girl, wanting her out of here. "Do you mind?" She bit her lower lip as he indicated the bedroom. After she'd gone in, he noticed she'd left the door ajar. The little witch! He turned from the telephone long enough to pull it shut. What the hell, he wondered, was that girl up to? The package again?

"Barney?" Eve sounded shaken. "Barney, how did it happen?"

"You know already?" Barney had a feeling of events

rushing ahead, always a little beyond his reach. "Who told you? How?"

"A Captain Craddock. He found my phone number in Guy's address book. He wouldn't tell me very much."

"But why should Craddock choose to call you?"

Eve was softly crying. "I'm coming, Barney, of course."

"Listen," Barney said urgently. "Guy gave me something for you – a little package. It seems to be damned important, not only to Guy and you, but to others as well." The ache in the back of his head wouldn't let him forget that. "Any idea what's in it?"

"No. Open it, Barney. Tell me now what it is."

"Guy asked me not to open it," Barney explained. "I don't know why. But I told him I wouldn't and I've funny ideas about keeping my word. Nobody else is even to know about it, Guy said. When will you be here, Eve?"

"The first through train in the morning."

"I'll meet you and give it to you then." Despite their broken engagement, Barney knew she'd gone on loving Guy, just as he'd gone on loving her. Barney had never clearly understood what had separated them. "Chin up, Eve."

Had the bedroom door moved just as Barney disconnected? He wasn't sure of that, but he was certain he wanted to get rid of the blonde girl. He found her sitting on his bed, her trim feet tucked under her, looking too innocent again. He couldn't waste time deciding what her game was.

"This way, please."

With a curious sort of obedience she followed him from the bedroom. He said, "Wait here," took up his overnight bag and went back with it, closing the connecting door. After a quick glance around he decided that the bookcase was as good a hiding-place as any. He concealed Guy's little package behind several technical works on electronics, then returned to the living room. The girl was waiting for him, puzzled, a pleading look in her eyes.

He took her arm and firmly escorted her out. The snow had stopped. Her steps were quicker than his as they went along the icy street. She gazed up at him questioningly, but let him direct her.

"My name's Barney Chance," he informed her, wondering if she didn't already know. "What's yours?"

"Dorelle Dale."

He almost laughed. Dorelle Dale! It couldn't be anybody's real name.

"I'm a hostess at the Merry-Go-Round," she added, seeming to feel herself that the name needed something to back it up.

She wasn't the hard-skinned, catch-as-catch-can sort, Barney thought, but on the other hand a certain type of sucker would go for her. The Merry-Go-Round catered to war-plant workers with money to spend, and to well-heeled servicemen on furlough. It was a roadhouse located a mile outside of town, a glorified clip-joint operated by one Victor Gartin, as the Big Tent had been.

The recent, early-morning fire that had destroyed the Big Tent had also destroyed the lives of four army men. Charges of manslaughter and failure to maintain adequate fire protection had been brought against Gartin, but only this week the district attorney had dropped the case. It was a noisome affair, smelling to high heaven of hush-hush influences and bribery, overlaid with rumours that Gartin was merely the front man for someone bigger who couldn't be touched. This might or might not be a power-behind-the-throne politician named Chabbat. By working for such crooks, Barney reflected, Dorelle Dale wasn't recommending herself to the esteem of decent people.

"Where are you taking me?"

They were in the centre of town now, near the inn, and walking fast. "Home," Barney said.

She stopped short. "But I can't go home! I'd be alone there. I'd be scared!"

He eyed her again. "What've you got to be afraid of now?"

She didn't answer, but stamped her foot a little, and seemed about to burst into furious tears. Barney took her arm again, regardless, and again she hurried along beside him, curiously but without resistance. He guided her across the porch of the pre-Revolutionary inn, past a row of empty rocking chairs and into the lobby. It was also deserted.

George Sawyer, the proprietor, wasn't behind the desk. Impatiently, Barney banged the bell on it, facing the girl with a frown.

"Who was with you," he asked her flatly, "in the car that was parked near the Lytham Building at eight o'clock tonight?"

"Where?" Again her eyes were very large, very blue. "I wasn't with anybody. I wasn't there."

She was pretty. She was lovely – a very lovely little liar, probably, Barney judged.

"Got money enough for a room? You'll be safe here, won't you – as safe as anywhere?"

She squinted at him through her eyelashes, her lips pursed. "I'll be perfectly all right!" Barney couldn't remember anyone having hated him so intensely on such short acquaintance. "You don't need to bother about me. I'll get along fine without any help from you, you big lug!"

"I think so, too," Barney said, smiling wryly. "Good night," and he left her.

III

"If You Can't Trust the Police . . ."

Captain Craddock was leaving the Lytham Building. Light-footed for one of his bulk, he walked rapidly along Court Street. Barney felt it was his turn to do a little trailing. It would be justified – he was certain Craddock's purposes were not entirely official. "If you can't trust the police," the captain had said sourly, "whom *can* you trust?" Barney couldn't trust the captain.

Craddock led him to the Pennswick Hospital. A low brick building sitting behind a broad lawn, most of its lights were out. As soon as Craddock had gone in, Barney crossed the waiting room and looked down the corridor. The captain had disappeared into one of the private rooms. No nurses were moving about. Barney went quietly down the hall, neither liking nor disliking the idea of eavesdropping. He simply couldn't trust Craddock.

There were subdued voices behind one of the swinging doors. Tall enough to look over it, Barney took one quick glance. Dr Whitlock was still with Alma. She lay on the bed, gauze bandages bound around her red hair. An efficient, resourceful, tireless young woman, her stamina had brought her back quickly. Her eyes were clouded only a little as she gazed at Captain Craddock.

"Suzie's wedding," she was whispering. "Poor Suzie. I was going to be my little sister's maid of honour – and I never got there."

"Don't worry about that," Craddock said brusquely. "Suzie went ahead and married Neal Lytham anyway. They're on their way here now. Did you stop into Farrish's office on your way to the church?"

"Mr Farrish phoned me," Alma Remsen whispered. "Said it was important – take only a few minutes. I thought he must have a wedding present for Suzie and Neal." After a moment she resumed. "When I went in the office, Mr Farrish was sitting at his desk with a queer look on his face. He didn't say anything. It scared me. Then all of a sudden the closet door opened – and a man rushed out."

"Who was that man?"

Alma's respiration quickened. She was reliving a moment of high emotional stress. Without answering Craddock, she carried it through. "He rushed at me like a wild man and hit me terribly hard."

"Describe him," Craddock insisted relentlessly.

She was silent another moment. "He had a handkerchief tied over his face – coat and hat – so I couldn't see much. He moved like an animal, gliding, but very fast. He was heavy, powerful, big. The bigness of him as he came at me – it was awful."

Barney straightened, the scar on his forehead giving his left eyebrow a twist of alarmed astonishment. Did Alma realize she was describing, vaguely yet accurately, too, the very man who was questioning her – Captain Craddock?

Someone else was coming into the hospital. Barney retreated along the corridor to the accident ward entrance. Outside, but looking in through a diamond-shaped pane, he saw a party of three hurrying towards Alma's room. A slender, petulant-faced girl – Alma's sister Suzie, Barney surmised – came between two men.

The man on her right was Neal Lytham, Marsha's brother and Suzie's husband as of tonight. The other was fat, short and pink-jowled – the Benson Chabbat whose name carried such overtones of obscure power in the county, and who was, in addition, Barney remembered now, the uncle of Suzie and Alma Remsen. Both men wore tails. A third man in a tuxedo, whom Barney didn't recognize, stepped into the corridor behind them.

It was adding up somehow, Barney felt as he turned away, but in indefinable terms. Guy Farrish had been fatally shot, and Alma Remsen had been viciously knocked out, at almost the same time that Alma's younger sister was marrying Neal Lytham with Ben Chabbat's blessings. A strange juxtaposition of events, particularly since the wedding had gone on regardless, evidently with a substitute maid of honour. It must have significance, and Barney felt sure this business wasn't yet finished. He was still mulling over it when he reached his apartment.

Leaving the door wide open, he halted to stare. His living room looked like something left behind by a high wind. The cushions of his couch were tossed about, the drawers of his desk were turned upside down on the floor, the rugs peeled up. In a chair in the midst of this shambles, her ankles bound to a rung, her wrists fixed together behind her and a gag in her mouth sat the girl who had called herself Dorelle Dale.

Dorelle Dale wriggled in her bonds, silently beseeching Barney to get her loose. She wasn't hurt, he saw. Going past her, he found his bedroom also upset, a window open. A dozen volumes had been swept out of the bookcase. And the amazing thing, the thing that stunned Barney, was that Guy's little package was still there.

He blinked over it. It was intact. The person, who had ransacked the apartment hadn't bothered to open it, had shown no interest in it whatever!

In the living room, Dorelle Dale was squealing. Barney went back, wagged his head at her, then untied her. The strips of cloth he unwound had been a pair of his fanciest pyjamas. She glared at him spitefully, as if it were all his fault.

"Why did you come back here, Dorelle? How'd you get yourself into this fix?"

"There wasn't any vacancy at the inn," she told him, evidently considering this his fault also, "and somebody'd broken into my own room. I didn't exactly want to stay there and get murdered in my bed. I had to go somewhere, didn't I?"

Barney laughed outright. As an explanation it was ridiculous. Surely she had friends who would have taken her in for the night.

"If you think I came back because I like you, you're crazy," she said evenly, rubbing her ankles, her eyes flashing at him even more hotly because he'd laughed. "Your front door was locked, but one of the back windows was open, so I climbed in. First thing I knew, somebody grabbed me and did that to me. Holy cats, I was scared!"

Appraising her, Barney felt inclined to believe this much. "There's a question that's getting asked a lot tonight," he said. "Who was that man?"

"My gosh, how should I know?" she flung at him. "It was dark. He used a flashlight and he was careful not to show me his face. After he got me all done up, he just went around, wrecking the place."

"A big man?" Barney asked quietly.

"No, thin. I could see that much. He was thin, like –"

"Like someone you remember?"

"Like *anybody* who's thin, for gosh sakes! What're you staring at me for? What do you think I am anyway?"

"I wish I knew," Barney said wryly, touching the scar on his forehead. It felt tight. "What about the police now? Don't you want them in on this either?"

"What could they do about it now? You haven't lost anything anyway. You've still got the package."

Barney narrowed his eyes at her. "What package?"

She bounced up to face him indignantly. "Guy Farrish gave it to you tonight. I heard you saying so over the telephone. You're being a perfect fool about it."

Barney closed one fist.

"You're a man of honour, aren't you?" Dorelle said bitterly. "You promised Guy Farrish and you're going to keep your word even if it kills you." Now she challenged him. "What difference would it make to a dead man? Instead of being so disgustingly noble about it, you should have told people that Guy Farrish gave you just a little package and nothing else. Then you wouldn't have girls getting tied up by burglars in your living room!"

It dazed Barney. She seemed to know so much and she was so vehement about it! Her knowing made him feel his trustworthiness was undermined, that somehow he'd failed Guy. This girl seemed to him to be a treacherous little snooper. He strongly desired to sock her on her wagging jaw, but he didn't.

"It's strictly none of your damned business," he said. "You can clear out of here now. And this time stay out!"

She plumped herself down on his couch, gazing at him defiantly, almost tearfully. "I'm not going!"

"Oh, God!" Barney said. She was getting to be more than he wanted to take. "Will you *please* get the hell out of here?"

"I won't." More quietly, appealing to him, she added: "I can't. I'm afraid to go. I'm in a jam."

"What kind of a jam?"

"You wouldn't understand." She was scornful again. "Nobody'll come back here. It ought to be safe. I know *you* wouldn't touch me with a ten-foot pole, anyway. I'm not leaving and that's that."

She kicked her shoes off and tucked her stocking feet under her in a manner of finality. Barney made a gesture of despair. He couldn't throw her out bodily. However, there was a simpler way of getting her out of his hair. He opened the outer door and left.

The Dutch Colonial house on Elder Street was the home of Marsha Barrow. But it wasn't Marsha who answered Barney's ring at the door. Her brother Neal looked out – first expectantly, Barney thought, then with an odd, tight sort of disappointment.

"Come in, Barney."

Still wearing his white tie and tails, Neal had evidently come directly from the hospital. Rather handsome, he was lithe, sandy-haired and usually easy-mannered. The peculiar thing about Neal Lytham was that his mind seemed forever busy with speculations which he rarely divulged to anyone else.

His bride sat in Marsha's living room, sobbing childishly. Pretty in a frail way, Suzie had been thoroughly pampered by her older sister, Alma, who had brought her up. Marsha, darkly beautiful and light-hearted as always, was trying to cheer her.

"Alma's going to be perfectly all right, Suzie, darling. The doctor said she can go home tomorrow."

"But what about *me*?" Suzie wailed. "My wonderful wedding all spoiled, and now my honeymoon plans all upset! It isn't fair!" She went on sobbing, pitying herself.

Marsha turned from Suzie, her glance at Barney commenting that Neal had picked himself a choice little brat for a wife, hadn't he? Neal himself seemed only slightly concerned for her. He moved about nervously, his mind elsewhere. He seemed to be listening for something.

Certainly Neal could have done better than this, so far as the girl herself went, Barney reflected. Why *had* Neal married this self-centred little nonentity? Because she was Ben Chabbat's niece, of course. He had deliberately married into Chabbat's power. Suzie, however, instead of sobbing her heart out over trifles, should consider herself fortunate. Upon the recent death of their father, Jonathan Lytham, Neal and Marsha had inherited his estate equally. An accruement of generations, it amounted to more than a million dollars for each of them.

Barney asked of Marsha: "What did you find at Guy's office?"

"Nothing, Barney, dear."

"He called you down there in a hurry, especially to give you something important, and there was nothing?"

"Not a thing that we could find, darling. I can't imagine what it might have been." Marsha gave her agitated brother a puzzled smile. "Queer sort of nuptials you're having, Neal, dearest. Why on earth don't you take Suzie somewhere?"

Neal sat. "We're staying here."

It precipitated a cross-fire of discussion. Suzie wailed, Marsha protested. Neal answered obdurately. In the midst of it Barney attempted to say good night, but nobody heard. He left with the impression that Neal, in spite of his bride and his sister, would spend his wedding night right here in Marsha's room, for reasons he wouldn't explain.

Barney entered his apartment again to find Dorelle curled up on his couch, apparently asleep. Crossing the room, he unintentionally kicked one of her shoes. He picked it up and noticed frayed threads. In an instant he was smouldering. Her coat, he discovered, was reversible – red plaid now, but beige when turned inside-out. From one of its pockets, he pulled a red beanie. Out of the other came a black suede bow exactly like the one he'd found in the street.

He turned on her angrily. She was sitting up now, warily watching him.

"You little liar! You deliberately changed your appearance, even to pulling the bow off your other shoe so nobody'd notice you'd already lost one."

"I can explain," Dorelle said contritely.

"I'll bet you can," Barney remarked, sounding sour. "You'll do a beautiful job of explaining."

"I didn't want to get mixed up in it, that's all," she went on quickly. "Not with Vic."

"Vic Gartin?"

She nodded, shivering a little. "Vic drove us – Alma and me. Suzie and Neal and Ben Chabbat were already at the church, but Alma had to stop at Guy Farrish's office on the way. Vic didn't go in with her. He waited in the car with me and a minute later we heard the shot."

"The shot fired at Guy," Barney said.

"We didn't know what had happened," Dorelle continued earnestly. "Guy Farrish went out of the building and down to the corner, then came back. We kept waiting for Alma, but she didn't show up, so Vic went in to look for her."

So it was Victor Gartin who had prowled in the building, Barney mused.

"Then Vic came out and told me there'd been a shooting,

all right – probably Guy Farrish – and Alma looked dead, too. He wanted to get away from there fast. I wouldn't go with him, wouldn't leave Alma like that, so I got out of the car and Vic went on".

"You weren't too concerned for Alma," Barney reminded her. "You didn't go into the building."

She studied him a moment, inimically, saying nothing. Remembering the organ music he'd heard over the telephone, Barney could fill in the rest of it. Vic Gartin had driven no farther than the inn. From there he'd phoned Ben Chabbat at the church. No doubt Chabbat had given Gartin certain instructions, for next he had returned to the building to search for something. That was why he had invaded Barney's office, and why Chabbat had called Barney's phone, expecting Gartin to answer and wanting urgently to learn whether the search had been successful.

If Barney was right about this, it was Gartin who had clipped him – a personal score still to be settled.

"A neat job you've done," Barney said, giving Dorelle a sceptical smile. "It's a wholesale alibi for Guy's murder – an alibi for Gartin, Neal, Suzie and yourself, as well."

She peered at him through her lashes. "That's why I'm scared. I don't know who or what's behind all this. It must be something big and terrible. I'm afraid something else will happen now."

She sank back on the couch, looking really frightened. "Having you around makes me feel safer somehow, you high-principled mule. We don't like each other a nickel's worth, and that helps. So I'm staying here tonight."

Looking out his bedroom door next morning, Barney didn't feel too surprised. Dorelle Dale had gone, but he'd rather expected that, and he was glad of it. In a way he was glad. She was nice to look at, but too damned disturbing.

He'd overslept. A glance at a Reading timetable hurried him. He had time to shave, shower and dress, but not breakfast, before Eve Ranie arrived.

The little package in his pocket, he drove into the Pennswick station yard half a minute late. The train had already pulled in. Still in his car, he saw Eve Ranie alighting from a coach – willowy, ash-blonde, photogenic Eve. She'd gone back to modelling after breaking her engagement to Guy. Everywhere she went she was recognized by those who'd seen her smiling from magazine covers and drug store windows, and this morning was no exception.

A man stepped towards her and turned his lapel. A detective, Barney thought, sent by Captain Craddock, of course. A station wagon in front of Barney held him up as he backed into a parking stall, and Eve didn't hear him call her. The man – narrow-faced and sly-looking, Barney saw – escorted her to a waiting sedan. It swung into the street, accelerated and disappeared.

Barney stared after it with rising alarm. It hadn't turned towards police headquarters, but had veered off in the opposite direction.

He blared his horn urgently and somehow squeezed through. Once in the street, he sighted the black sedan travelling almost a block ahead. Its licence plate was bright, new. He could make out the number – PD7-604. That much was right; all local police cars carried PD plates. But this one was taking Eve in the wrong direction and travelling too fast.

Suddenly Barney braked. Directly in front of him, a railroad-crossing watchman was wagging a red paddle, a bell was clanging a warning, the barrier was swinging down to close the street. Barney fumed because the other car was past and he glared at the freight train rumbling through endlessly.

Impatiently he U-turned. There was no quick way around the freight, but police headquarters sat on this side of it.

The police department occupied a building which in earlier days had been a fashionable home. Captain Craddock's office overlooked Main Street from the second floor. The captain wasn't there.

Pacing, Barney noticed a yellow sheet of paper on Craddock's desk. It was a carbon copy letter addressed to Benson Chabbat and consisting of one terse sentence: *As of this date our relationship as attorney and client is permanently terminated.* The late Jonathan Lytham must have written that letter, Barney knew, and Craddock must have removed it from Lytham & Farrish's files last night. Lytham, although conservative, had possessed an ability to touch pitch without becoming defiled by it, but apparently he'd been unwilling to handle Chabbat's brand beyond a certain limit.

The date of the letter, August 17 of this year, stirred Barney's memory. It was also the date of the Big Tent fire, and Jonathan Lytham's death from chronic myocarditis had occurred only two days thereafter.

Barney heard Craddock's deliberate footfalls and stepped back. Entering, Craddock immediately slipped the letter into a drawer. Again his face was shadowed by a series of fleeting expressions springing from secret causes.

"Where have you had Eve Ranie taken?" Barney asked bluntly. And as Craddock answered with lifted eyebrows, he insisted: "You sent a man to the station for her. He hasn't brought her here."

Those strange expressions flitting across Craddock's face suggested astonishment, sympathy, ruthlessness. "On the phone last night Miss Ranie told me she'd go to Mrs Barrow's home," the captain said. "I'd intended to talk to her there." He looked over Barney's shoulder. "What is it, Kelsey?"

A man paused in the doorway. Seeing Barney, he mumbled, "Later," and began to move off.

"Kelsey!"

Craddock's hard tone forced the plain-clothesman to confess his embarrassment before a non-official witness. "Lost my badge. Don't know what became of it. Gone, that's all."

Barney stepped closer to the desk. "That tears it. It was someone posing as a detective, using this man's badge. Now he's got Eve."

Craddock's eyes turned stony as he signalled Kelsey away.

"But he had an official car." Barney pressed his hands on the desk. "I got the licence number. PD7-604."

Craddock turned to a file cabinet. He looked at a typewritten list. "Sure you got that number right, Mr Chance?"

"I'm positive. A low-priced, black, two-door sedan, number PD7-604."

Craddock's face put a chill into Barney, it was so cold, his eyes so icy. "There's no such licence number. It doesn't exist."

Watching him consulting the telephone directory, Barney felt an almost wild impulse to get out of here, to tackle this emergency on his own. Craddock called Marsha Barrow's home, asked curt questions, then put the phone down with a thump.

"Miss Ranie isn't there." He looked as massive as a monolith and as feelingless, yet his voice sounded compassionate. "I'll handle this. Don't make the mistake of underestimating the danger to Miss Ranie. Kidnapping is a capital offence. There'll be no worse penalty if she's killed. Outside interference might cause her death. *I'll* take care of this." Then he said it again, with the same mocking twist of his mouth: "If you can't trust the police, Mr Chance, whom *can* you trust?"

He trudged from the office, leaving Barney full of fighting resentment, brushed off again.

IV

Suicides Are a Nuisance

Barney had left his car parked beside a sign reading, *Police Parking Only*. He sat in it, the scar itching above his left eyebrow, feeling he'd at least wasted precious time in seeing Craddock, suspecting that the captain meant to accomplish nothing. Minutes later, the right-hand door of his car opened. Dorelle Dale sat herself beside him, smiling too brightly.

"Hello," she said, as if they were the best of pals.

She wore comfortable-looking moccasins and a red topper over a simple green dress, all of which made her look like a guileless schoolkid. The effect was calculated – Barney knew very well she was nothing of the sort.

"What do you want?"

"I thought you might drive me down to the Merry-Go-Round. Vic didn't like the way I ran out on him last night, so I'd better try to square myself." She added: "That is, if you've nothing better to do."

"I have." He studied her. "Why are you dogging me? What makes you tick? Whose team are you on?"

She lifted her chin. "I'm minding my own business, believe it or not. Why don't you mind yours and let the rest alone? Why do you insist upon making it tougher?"

"Make what tougher? Make it tougher for whom? What *is* your business, Dorelle? Go on, let's have it."

"All I want from you," she said, flicking him with a glance, "is a ride down to the Merry-Go-Round. But my gosh, I can walk."

He caught her arm as she began to slide out. She didn't resist – she slid right back in again. For some reason of her own she wanted to stay with him, but without giving him any information about herself. In one way she was like Craddock. He couldn't decide what she was, whether friend or foe. Hers was a game two could play, however. While she watched him, he could watch her and sound her out.

Not starting the car, he sat in thought, and presently he said: "I need to find a sign painter."

"A what?"

The question subjected her to a subtle sort of test. Before going on, Barney checked over his reasoning and felt it was sound. Eve Ranie had been spirited away in a car carrying a new licence plate with a non-existent number on it. The plate had to be a fake contrived for the purpose of covering Eve's kidnapper. It was by no means a crude job. The bright paint and exact lettering indicated professional skill.

"A sign painter," Barney repeated, alert for Dorelle's reaction. "Somebody in town."

"New night clubs need painters and decorators," she said thoughtfully. "Vic Gartin always uses the same firm. They sell second-hand bar equipment, too. It's the Ajax Hotel Supply Company, on lower Ashland Street. Ben Chabbat owns it – through a dummy, of course."

Barney stared at her. She looked pleased with herself, but slightly scared, too. Without another word, he swung his car from the kerb. On Ashland Street he parked again. The Ajax Hotel Supply Company occupied an old store now used as a warehouse. It's dusty show-windows were crammed full of bar stools, gilded chairs and pin-ball games.

They watched it without speaking, and ten minutes later a light truck rolled out of the alleyway flanking the building. Barney started after it. Dorelle was curious and jittery, but she asked no questions. The truck turned south at Main Street and continued along the highway until, a mile outside of town, it pulled around to the rear of the Merry-Go-Round.

Barney stopped in the broad parking lot beside the roadhouse. The truck driver began unloading panels of heavy cardboard painted in circus colours.

"This is where I get off," Dorelle said lightly. "Thanks for the ride."

She hurried to the Merry-Go-Round's front entrance. It was a sprawling frame building, old, flimsy of construction, which should have been condemned and razed long ago. Barney noted its few narrow doors, thought of what would happen in case of a panic and knew no crowd should ever be permitted inside it. Just as the Big Tent had been, it was not only sucker-bait but a fire-trap awaiting a spark, a new tragedy in the making, but flagrantly operating regardless.

The truck was emptied now and pulling away. About to start after it, Barney saw Dorelle hurrying back. She climbed in beside him, looking anxious. She kept her fist closed whitely over a little wad of currency, while Barney followed the truck back towards Pennswick.

"I've been fired." She spoke too lightly. "In fact, I'm being run out of town. Vic gave me this money for a railroad ticket. He was very sweet – so sweet he made me shudder. I'd better make myself scarce or else."

"Or else what?" She didn't answer and Barney looked hard at her. "When are you leaving?"

"I'm not." Her voice sounded peculiarly resolute but it shook a little. "I'm sticking around – only I wish I could get over being scared, more scared all the time."

She meant that. She was really, deeply fearful. But, as before, she wasn't saying why.

Barney stopped again on lower Ashland Street. The truck had returned to the Ajax storehouse. Empty time passed while Barney thought coldly and blankly of Eve, his hunch having come to nothing at all.

Night had fallen upon a day that had seemed years long. Dorelle had left Barney before noon, with another of her evasive excuses, and he'd doggedly gone on watching the Ajax warehouse. It was so much time lost. Now, aching with nerve-strain, he was again in Craddock's office. For once the captain's expression was explicit, a darkly hostile frown.

"This is the fifth time you've been in here today, Mr Chance. There's still no news of Miss Ranie. When I find her I'll let you know. I'm still trying."

"Are you?" Barney said tersely. "Pennswick's a small town. There aren't many places where she might be hidden."

"Tell me, Mr Chance." Craddock's voice was ugly. "Tell me how to do my job."

Other voices spoke behind Barney. Two men were leaving an office directly across the hall. One, his uniform decorated with a gold shield, was moon-faced, bald-headed, unctuous in manner. The other was thin, sly-looking, and at sight of him Barney stiffened.

"That's the man!"

Craddock drawled in a forbidding tone: "What man, Mr Chance?"

The pair in the hallway, having heard, gazed at Barney curiously. He stepped towards them, Craddock following.

"That's the man who met Eve Ranie at the station this morning!"

"Him?" Craddock said heavily. "Vic Gartin?" He gestured in irritation towards Gartin's uniformed companion. "Mr Chance, this is Chief of Police Blount." And to Chief Blount he added: "I'm afraid Mr Chance has gone off half-cocked here."

"I'm not mistaken." Barney said it emphatically, but inwardly he was shaken. All day he'd scanned the faces of passersby, hoping to spot Eve's snatcher – and now he'd found him in police headquarters, of all places. Victor Gartin! Neither Gartin nor Chief Blount seemed in the least disturbed by Barney's accusation. "I tell you, this is the man who grabbed Miss Ranie!" but Gartin looked smugly unmoved and Chief Blount blinked stupidly.

"Surprising, very surprising, I must say," the chief rumbled. "Let's see now. Miss Ranie arrived on the 9:50, didn't she, Captain? Now, at 9:50, Mr Gartin, you were – ah –"

"At my home, gentlemen."

This was a new voice, edged and commanding. A third man had stepped from the chief's office. Benson Chabbat, as always, was expensively-groomed. His deep-set eyes were clouded for a moment, but then he produced his pink-cheeked smile. "At nine o'clock this morning, gentlemen, Mr Gartin came to my home to talk business, and he was there until eleven. This is Mr Chance, isn't it? What were you saying, Mr Chance?"

"Mr Chance was jumping at conclusions, Mr Chabbat," Captain Craddock put in quietly. "If Mr Gartin was with you at 9:50 this morning, he was with you, not somewhere else."

Chief Blount was wagging his shiny ball-like head. "You should try to be more careful, young man. This sort of mistake could be serious. Fortunate, very fortunate indeed, that Mr Chabbat was able to nip it in the bud. I think you owe Mr Gartin an apology."

Barney boiled. He still felt certain he was right, but even more certain that his position was hopeless. He suspected this incident had been prearranged, boldly and badly staged. He was staggered to find a chief of police glibly accepting an obviously falsified alibi. The police here were not an agency of the law, he told himself, but the instruments of criminals – they were not a bulwark of security, but the tools of predatory menaces.

Barney stood speechless as he watched Chief Blount deferentially escorting Gartin and Chabbat to the stairs, the three of them laughing together over the absurdity of Barney's accusation. But Captain Craddock did not laugh. His face hinted a callous sort of regret, and inner fierceness.

"Get wise," he said, his voice a subdued growl. "Keep quiet and get wise."

Barney turned on his heel. He was overwhelmed with a

sense of subtly hostile forces, of obscure and inimical powers, shutting him off from Eve. He felt terror in the realization that there was no protection from evil here, no support to be found against it, no hope in fighting it.

Chabbat and Gartin had driven off. Barney sat in his car, weighed down by his sense of helplessness and his dark anxiety for Eve. He saw Captain Craddock leaving headquarters. More than ever, Craddock had become the focus of Barney's suspicions. His mocking hardness, his deep secretiveness had become a challenge that Barney felt impelled to meet.

Craddock trudged purposefully as Barney followed him. He turned into Oak Street, a section of modest homes, and his pace slowed. In the darkness, he seemed to glide – and Barney remembered coldly Alma Remsen's description of the masked assailant in Guy's office.

Then Barney realized that Craddock was no longer moving along the shadowed sidewalk, no longer in sight.

Barney paused at the spot where Craddock had vanished. Nearby, a picket gate stood open and a path led to a bungalow that sat forward in a deep lawn. There was still no sign of Craddock, but light shone from a broad front window and Ben Chabbat and Vic Gartin were inside.

While Barney watched them, they talked unpleasantly, with sharp gestures. Gartin broke off the argument to lift his head, and listen, then step through a doorway towards the rear of the house. Chabbat sat alone, frowning, rolling a cigar in his lips. After a moment, not waiting for Gartin to return, Barney went to the front door.

Chabbat answered his knock. Chabbat was poised, calmly but enormously self-confident, not easily surprised. "Mr Chance again," he said without rancour. "This is my niece's home, so I suppose you've come to call on her?" He allowed Barney to step in. "Alma's upstairs. I'm afraid she's not seeing anyone."

"I don't know exactly why I'm here," Barney answered, looking around at tasteful furnishings, at logs burning in the fireplace. "But it's not to apologize."

Chabbat chuckled. "That really isn't necessary. We all make mistakes." He gestured Barney to a chair, but Barney shook his head. "We haven't met, Mr Chance, but I've heard of you. Building some kind of plant here, aren't you?"

"Trying to," Barney said briefly. "Firetraps like the Big Tent and the Merry-Go-Round get their permits without a hitch, but I can't get them for a modern, fireproof factory."

"Well-l," Chabbat said, examining his cigar, "there are certain borough ordinances, Mr Chance. Some of them are out of date and pretty hard to get around. I'm not a holder of public office, you understand, so I wouldn't know exactly what's causing your trouble. But perhaps you haven't gone about it the right way."

"That's right," Barney agreed ironically. "I haven't shelled it out your way, and I don't intend to – but I'll get that plant built."

The first gunshot came without warning, a flat, slapping noise behind the house. Chabbat started, and Barney heard a sound of alarm from upstairs. The second report followed quickly, then, after an interval, the third.

The echoes hadn't yet bounced away before Alma Remsen appeared on the stairs. She was barefoot, wearing a black lace nightgown. Bandages still bound the wound behind her left ear. She stared at Chabbat, deathly pale.

"Where's Vic?"

Barney was first out the back door, with Chabbat close behind him and Alma fearfully trailing them both. The yard was deep and dark. Hurrying past the white garage, Barney heard the rippling of a brook. He came to it, a shallow, spring-fed stream, winding across the rear of the property. They found Vic Gartin sprawled on the bank, both legs immersed.

"Vic!" Alma screeched his name, fell to her knees beside him, tugged at him. "Vic, Vic!"

A single bullet had pierced Gartin's right temple and the hole was blackly rimmed by a powder-burn. Both his hands clawed at the pain, smearing blood across his cheeks. Then they dropped, limp. Beside him in the wet gravel lay a revolver.

Barney stepped back while Chabbat attempted to pull the hysterical Alma off the dead man. He turned his head, listening. Foliage rustled faintly. Someone was stealing along the brook. Barney moved towards the street. He ran to the picket gate, paused there and saw a man appear on the sidewalk three houses below. It was a big man who glided away rapidly – Captain Craddock.

Barney went after him again. Nearing the lights of Main Street, Craddock slowed to his trudging stride. Swinging only one arm, he pressed the other against his body, as if holding something concealed under his coat. Barney's sense of stunned incredulity mounted as he watched the captain turning to the entrance of headquarters.

Craddock was at his desk, sealing the flap of an official file envelope, when Barney stepped in. The telephone was ringing. Ignoring Barney, Craddock answered the call at once. He spoke in monosyllables, his face sad, his eyes flinty. Lowering the instrument, he gazed steadily at Barney.

"That was Mr Chabbat," he said regretfully. "He tells me Vic Gartin is dead."

"I was there at the house," Barney said tersely.

"From what Mr Chabbat says, it looks like suicide."

"There were three shots. I heard three." Barney leaned over the desk. "But there's only one hole in Gartin's head."

"Two bad tries, then," Craddock said tonelessly. "It often happens. A man nicks his throat once or twice before he works up enough nerve to make a good cut. In the same way, Mr Gartin must have flinched the first two times."

Then Craddock did a strange thing. From his hip he brought forwards a pocket holster containing his police gun. Swinging out its cylinder, he ejected the cartridges. There were six, all intact. Next he produced a short cleaning brush and a square of cotton cloth. He pushed the cloth through the bore and it came out white. Quite deliberately, he'd made Barney a witness to the fact that his gun had not been fired.

"Suicide!" Barney scoffed, unconvinced, feeling that this move of Craddock's was evidence, instead, of shrewd and ruthless trickery. "Why should Vic Gartin kill himself?"

"Who knows?" Craddock returned his holstered gun to his hip. "Suicides don't talk much about their reasons afterwards."

His telephone rang again. This time he said only, "Craddock," listened for several seconds, then hung up. Barney had faintly heard the voice on the wire – a young woman's. Craddock's eyes hardened again at him.

"As a business man, Mr Chance, you know the value of advice. You've got in my way. Don't do it again. Keep out of my way, Mr Chance." He seemed to smile mockingly. "Now if you'll excuse me, I'm busy. A suicide is a nuisance, but not as much of a nuisance as a murder."

Leaving Barney standing there, he went out carrying the file envelope. Barney stared after him through the doorway, too dazed for a moment to move. In his mind he called Captain Craddock a killer, a killer behind the law.

V

Will You be My Valentine?

This time Craddock turned at Court Street and went past the inn. If he were responding to Chabbat's call, he was going a block out of his way. He paused beside a parked car, handed the file envelope into it, spoke and listened briefly, then trudged on.

Observing this, Barney also stopped to gaze into that car. Dorelle Dale sat behind the steering wheel. Her eyes lifted to his, startled. Then she hastily slipped something under the seat. Craddock's envelope, of course. Barney felt sickened. All too plainly, the murderous police officer and this girl were conniving together.

Now she gazed past him, her lashes lowered. "Get in," she whispered. "Get in!"

Barney looked over his shoulder at a man who was leaving the taproom of the inn. He recognized the truck driver for Ajax. With an exasperated "Oh, holy cats!" Dorelle opened the car door and tugged at his arm. "Will you get in?"

He did, frowning at her, immediately reaching beneath the seat. The envelope contained something flat and inflexible. Barney ripped it open and drew out an automobile licence plate. It felt slightly damp to his fingers. The number PD7-604, bright and new, had been painted over an old number which was embossed in the metal and still discernible on the reverse side. The old number, Barney realized, might be a valuable lead. And the plate somehow lay behind Craddock's shooting of Vic Gartin.

Dorelle hadn't attempted to interfere. Her interest was concentrated on the man who had just left the inn.

"I saw him in the A. & P. just before it closed. He was buying canned goods and milk – and candles." She repeated significantly: "Candles."

"I'm going to get this straight," Barney said. "What's Craddock to you? Why are you –"

"There he goes," Dorelle interrupted, pressing one neat foot against the starter pedal.

The Ajax truck rolled unhurriedly along Court Street, then turned, not towards the warehouse. Dorelle kept her distance without losing sight of it.

"Let's get this straight, I said," Barney persisted. "You're working with professional crooks, including the worst kind of crooked cop. You –"

"Oh, shut up!" Dorelle said with stinging vehemence. "You make me tired!"

Just what was there about him that made her "tired", Barney wondered? The fact that he was actively concerned for a kidnapped young woman, a friend? The fact that he was fulfilling, as best he could, the mission entrusted to him by a dead man? That he was determined to buck a corrupt police department because it was a dangerous evil which he couldn't decently shrug off?

Barney wished he knew exactly what the hell Dorelle Dale was. She possessed a quality of forthrightness that contradicted the rest of her suspicious makeup. She was lovely, spirited, she had a head on her, and she was full of deceit. At the Merry-Go-Round she'd functioned as sucker-bait for pay. To Barney she might be pure poison. He didn't want her to be poisonous to him – and as for that, there was something reassuringly earnest and wholesome about her. He would like to figure her out, especially because he felt she really didn't dislike him as much as she pretended, even though he was getting in her way – and Craddock's.

She was trailing the Ajax truck skilfully. It was outside the main residential section and still rolling.

"Have you still got that little package?" she asked abruptly. "Of course you haven't opened it!"

She'd put him on the defensive, made him the one who must explain himself. It angered him.

"Never mind that. I want to know what the devil I'm messed up in. Murder, kidnapping, God knows what else! I didn't ask for any part of it. All I wanted was to build a factory."

"You'll never get it built as long as Chabbat's running this show – not without paying plenty for the privilege. He won't come to you! You'll have to go to him. And don't think he wants your money for himself. He doesn't. He makes his in bigger ways. He wants his boys in office to get their cut."

Barney knew that now, but he was startled to hear Dorelle putting it into words, wisely and earnestly.

"Chabbat's no novelty in politics," she went on. "There are thousands like him all over the country – the men who deliver the votes. But he's smarter than most, he keeps his office-holders happy. For example, your plant would be a big thing for this town, but Chabbat wants it to be a big thing for his boys first. You can't see it that way, so you'll keep right on running into one impossible legal tangle after another, as long as Chabbat goes on ruling this roost."

Gazing at her, Barney asked quietly: "What's your real name?"

She didn't answer. The Ajax truck was slowing now, turning into a driveway. It stopped behind a house of pointed stone that stood completely dark against the grove behind it. Barney opened his eyes at the house while Dorelle drove past. Guy Farrish had bought it, intending it to be his and Eve's home, and it had remained empty ever since.

Dorelle swerved to the shoulder of the road and switched off the headlamps. After a few moments, the truck reappeared, turning in the opposite direction, towards town. Dorelle backed her car quickly, then swung it into the driveway and stopped short behind the house. Barney beside her, she ran to the rear door.

On the steps sat a carton containing groceries, left there by the Ajax driver. The door was locked. Barney thumped his shoulder against it. On the third thrust the old lock snapped. He stepped in and struck a paper match, Dorelle holding her breath at his side. They listened and heard not a sound.

Dust lay thick on the floor, marked by footprints leading to the cellarway. Barney and Dorelle followed them down. The darkness below was almost liquid. Under the rear of the house, and behind a heavy door of oak, there was a windowless, damp, stone-walled room that felt like a cell in a dungeon.

Eve Ranie huddled against a hand-hewn post, her wrists corded together behind it, her eyes flickering whitely in the unsteady shine of Barney's match.

Shivering Eve shrank down in the seat between Barney and Dorelle. He kept his arm tight around her. She whispered, "I'm all right now, I'm all right," but she couldn't stop shivering.

She hadn't been hurt physically, but she was nervously exhausted and the chill and the terror of that dark underground room clung to her. Dorelle, all solicitude, drove rapidly. Eve sighed with relief when the car stopped in front of Marsha Barrow's home.

"Marsha's there," Barney said. "She'll fix you up. A hot tub and a stiff drink will help."

"Thanks – thanks for finding me," Eve said, pressing one of her cold hands over Barney's.

"Don't thank me, Eve. Dorelle did it."

"I did not!" Dorelle retorted. "You figured out the licence. The rest wasn't anything."

She was eager to avoid taking the credit, Barney suspected. What did that fact tell him about her? Had she led him to Eve with inside knowledge, because the purpose behind the kidnapping had then been accomplished or had failed? He intended to get those questions answered in a hurry, but his immediate concern was for Eve.

"Can you tell me about it now?" he asked gently.

Eve shivered again. "He wanted something – something he thought I had. He tried to find it in my hatbox and it wasn't there. Then he tried to make me tell him what I'd done with it, but I had no idea what he meant."

"Didn't he tell you what it was he wanted to get his hands on?"

She shook her head. "But he wanted it desperately. He made me feel he'd stop at nothing to get it."

"Eve, it couldn't have been this." Barney removed the little package from his coat pocket. "At first I thought this was the reason behind everything that's happened, but now I know it isn't. Still, it's important. It was so important to Guy that he had to make sure you'd get it. That's why it's been so damned important to me, too."

Eve gazed at the little package and took it into her hands almost tenderly. Barney and Dorelle watched her as she loosened the red string. The removal of the brown paper disclosed an ordinary small gift-box. Eve's fingers trembled as she raised the lid. Then her head sank and she closed her eyes on sudden tears.

Dorelle squirmed to peek into the box and Barney stared, a frown darkening his face. First he saw a small cake of soap. That accounted for the scent. The lettering stamped on the cake was blurred, as if it had been used once or twice. Beside it lay one red lollipop. And underneath both was a cheap little heart-shaped greeting card that asked, *Will You Be My Valentine?*

Barney felt a crazy impulse to laugh, but the laugh wouldn't come. Sharp bitterness choked it off. He felt Guy had tricked him trivially in the name of friendship, he felt betrayed by a ridiculous whim. This was the solemn trust Guy had placed in him! This was the mission Guy had asked him faithfully to complete, upon his word of honour – to deliver a cake of soap, a lollipop and a valentine!

Getting out of the car, Barney shut the door with an angry slam. Dorelle hurried ahead to the house. The entrance had scarcely opened before Marsha had her arms around Eve. There followed a flurry of anxious "darlings" and "dears" while Marsha rushed Eve upstairs. Barney found no opening to introduce Dorelle, but apparently it wasn't necessary. Together, Marsha and Dorelle got Eve out of her damp dress, ignoring Barney in the process. In another moment she was wrapped in a warm robe and Marsha was bringing her a drink. She put it aside to gaze again at Guy's little box, her chin quivering.

"Does it mean anything?" Barney asked, still fuming.

"A great deal, Barney," Eve said quietly. "A very great deal." She smiled wanly over the lollipop and valentine. "Guy and I didn't know each other when we started going to the same school. He was such a bashful little boy, he couldn't even say hello to me. He'd just smile and shy away, until one day he handed me a soiled envelope, then ran for dear life. Inside was an old valentine and a bright red lollipop – and it was weeks past Valentine's Day. It was his way of telling me he liked me."

There were tears in Eve's eyes. "And much later he proposed to me in just the same way, by giving me a lollipop and a little card asking me to be his valentine for life." Then she really burst into tears. "I know it's silly, it's terribly silly, but I adored it."

Barney waited until she'd taken hold of herself. He understood now why Guy had wanted no one else to see the contents of the box. It was one of those intimate, closely-guarded bonds, personal and tender, cherished between a man and a woman in love, like a song first heard together, which someone else might injure with ridicule. To Barney it seemed no longer frivolous.

"And this time he was asking you to come back to him?"

"Yes," Eve spoke softly. "The rest is something I've never told anyone before. I don't like telling it before Marsha."

"It probably won't be news to me, Eve, dear," Marsha said. "To begin with, nobody needs to tell me my darling brother is a stinker, but I've never let it bother me much."

Eve's eyes widened. She clasped Marsha's hand and turned to Barney. "You know the kind of a man Guy had become – out for all he could get and not too particular about how he got it. But did you know that Guy's senior partner, Jonathan Lytham – Marsha's and Neal's father – had cut loose from Ben Chabbat? And why? And that immediately after Mr Lytham's death, Guy took Chabbat back as a client?"

"My father was a grumpy old darling," Marsha put in. "A stubborn, close-mouthed old bear, but honest as they come. He hated his chiselling clients, Ben Chabbat most of all, and finally the old dear reached the point where he couldn't stomach Chabbat another day. That was the day of the Big Tent fire."

Barney listened intently as Eve went on. "I learned all this from Guy. Vic Gartin operated the Big Tent, acting as the owner's front man. Chabbat wanted the charges against Gartin quashed, of course, and expected Mr Lytham to fix it. Mr Lytham wouldn't. Then Chabbat tried to put pressure on him by revealing that the real owner of the Big Tent was his own son, Neal."

Barney's eyebrows went up. Marsha merely looked at him levelly, not at all surprised.

"That was one straw too many for Father," she said simply. "He was perfectly furious – ordered Chabbat out and swore he'd never forgive Neal. He died only two days later – the emotional shock did it, I know – still detesting Neal for it." Marsha added: "I loathe him, too, for using his inheritance for more of the same nasty sort of business. The Merry-Go-Round is only a new beginning. Terribly skunky, that darling brother of mine."

"Neal's money plus Chabbat's influence, you see, Barney," Eve said, "with Guy pulling the legal wires for them. When Guy took Chabbat back as a client, I considered it unforgivable, a betrayal of his old partner, but Guy just shrugged. Chabbat meant big fees. His first job was to get Vic Gartin off the manslaughter rap, which he later did. It was too much for me to take. I saw Guy heading into more and bigger dirty work, and I couldn't decently go along with him."

Eve's eyes misted over as she gazed into the little box. "I was horribly disappointed in Guy. The showdown came in the apartment I had here. We were in a hopeless clash over it. I told Guy I wouldn't marry him, and then I stepped into the bathroom, of all places, to cry it out where he wouldn't see me. He came in anyway and begged me not to break off our engagement. Then I handed him this cake of soap, this same cake. It sounds melodramatic, but we were both worked up. I told Guy I still loved him, but I wouldn't take him back until he could come to me with clean hands, and that was final. He turned away without another word and left the apartment, taking the cake of soap with him. It was fresh then, unused."

Barney bounced up. "But now it's been used. He used it and knew you'd see instantly what it meant. He'd cleaned his hands – for some reason he'd broken with Chabbat." Barney sat again, overwhelmed by the significance suddenly acquired by this apparently trivial token. "And that's why he was killed, Eve. Somehow, that's why Guy was murdered."

Eve broke then, sobbing unashamedly. Marsha promptly dispensed with Barney and Dorelle. They went down to the living room. There he faced her.

"I've got a hold on this thing now," Barney said. "I'm going to get the right answers, and all of them – from you next."

His tone, like a dash of cold water, caused her to draw a little gasp. "But telling you won't do any good. It may do a lot of harm. This thing's not finished yet, and somebody's not stopping at murder. But you've just got to know regardless, don't you?"

"I've got to know," Barney said. "Especially about you, Dorelle."

"That isn't my name," she answered, shaking her head very seriously. "It was my mother's, sort of – her stage name when she was in musical comedy. One of the servicemen killed in the Big Tent fire was Private First Class Johnny Vernon. He was my kid brother. My name's Jean."

"Jean Vernon." Barney liked the sound of it. "That's much better. I hope the rest is as good."

Her eyes clouded over. "I had to come here to identify Johnny's body, and I stayed. Nobody in Pennswick knew me. I simply changed my name and got a job at the Merry-Go-Round because I wanted to learn who was really responsible. Now I've found out – the combination of Chabbat and Neal Lytham chiefly, but what can I do about it?"

Barney said quietly: "That's not all of it. You're holding something out."

"Last night I got acquainted with you deliberately, if that's what you mean," she went on. "Nobody was following me. I just had to see what you added up to. Later, when I went back to your apartment, I was still trying to find out as much as I could from you. I did learn something was going terribly wrong for Chabbat and his inner circle. It was Vic Gartin who ransacked your place. He fired me from the Merry-Go-Round and warned me to make myself scarce because his finding me at your apartment had told him I was playing a game on my own."

"You're still holding out," Barney insisted. "All this wasn't your own idea. Somebody's behind you."

She pressed her lips together, and at that moment a knock sounded. The door opened at once. Captain Craddock took a gliding step inwards, his face enigmatically hinting a sense of regret which was somehow ominous.

A glance passed between him and the girl. It seemed to Barney to convey a mutual warning. Then Craddock closed the door and came closer. From inside his coat he produced a long brown envelope.

"Do you know what this is, Mr Chance?" he asked.

Barney's gaze fixed on it. In one corner it bore the printed return address of Lytham and Farrish. Marsha Barrow's name and address had been scrawled across it, but the ink had been almost entirely washed off while still fresh. There was no postmark. It had been slit open.

"Guy Farrish was mailing a letter like that when I first saw him last night," Barney said cautiously. "How did you get hold of it?"

"He didn't mail it," Craddock said, sounding brusque. "He thought he did, but he missed the slot of the mailbox. It dropped to the wet sidewalk, but he didn't know that and he left it there."

"How did you get it?" Barney repeated. "What's in it?"

"This young lady saw it fall," the captain continued, while Barney suspected his purpose in revealing this.

"That's why she left Vic Gartin's car first chance she found. She went to pick it up. I've had it since last night and now I'm going to use it."

"Use it for what?"

"Mr Chance," Craddock said wearily but tensely, "we're in a spot, the three of us. We've found out too much at a time when it was never more unhealthy to find out too much. If you and Miss Vernon should turn up dead —"

"Suicides?" Barney put in wryly.

"As murder victims," Craddock went on softly, "the case will stay in the unsolved file — you can bank on that. As for me, one word from Chief Blount can break me. Then I'll just be another casualty, powerless. In other words, we'd better be smart and careful. Now please get Mrs Barrow down here."

The note of urgency in Craddock's voice carried through Barney's confusion. He called up to Marsha. Craddock approached her at the base of the stairs.

"Eve's going to sleep now, I think," she told Barney. "Captain Craddock? What is it?"

"Mrs Barrow, Guy Farrish was the executor of your father's estate. Did he know the details of the will prior to Mr Lytham's death?"

"I'm sure he didn't," Marsha answered. "He didn't even know he was to be the executor until a few hours before Father's death. I remember Guy coming out of Father's bedroom after hearing about it, and asking me if I knew about the will. I said, no, he'd never talked about it."

"Did your brother Neal know?"

"Really, Father never mentioned his will to either of us. I'm sure he didn't tell Neal anything at the last minute. He wouldn't see Neal. Guy and I were with Father when he died, but Neal was downstairs, excluded, so —" Marsha broke off to ask: "Why are you asking me this?"

"You'll soon know, Mrs Barrow. Thank you."

Captain Craddock glanced at Jean Vernon, his darkened eyes commanding her. Both moved towards the door.

"Hold it," Barney said, going after them. "Captain, you look to me like a man who's trying his damnedest to hit the jackpot and dreading it. You don't want me, but I'm in it too deep to get out now. Well? Don't hang back on my account."

VI

Where There's a Will There's a Slay

Barney paused beside Craddock's car. The captain was at the wheel, Jean Vernon beside him. She was frightened and trying not to show it. Craddock returned Barney's gaze, tight-nerved.

"You killed Vic Gartin," Barney said.

"Gartin was a suicide."

"You killed him and tricked it up."

Craddock seemed to sigh. "Have it your way. But don't noise it around. Get in, if you're coming."

Despite his cold confusion, Barney felt determined to keep his hold on this thing. He slid onto the seat beside Jean and felt her trembling. Captain Craddock drove ponderously.

"You saw Gartin snatch Miss Ranie," he said, "but you heard Chabbat alibi Gartin. There was no way around that. No legal way."

Barney listened.

"Miss Ranie was taken away in a black sedan. Gartin's own car was a sky-blue convertible. I wondered if he'd borrowed Alma Remsen's black sedan without her knowledge while she was laid up. He was practically living at her place. That was the hunch I played."

Craddock turned at a corner, still driving slowly.

"I found the fake licence plate in the brook, where Gartin had thrown it. The new number was painted over an old one registered in Gartin's own name. He'd heard me prowling around and caught me fishing the plate out of the brook. He had a gun, so I had to jump him. His first shot missed me and the second went into the sky while we wrestled. Then I twisted the gun up to his temple."

Craddock stopped the car.

"It was much better that way, Mr Chance. A cop doesn't

openly kill one of Chabbat's boys and get away with it, even in performance of his duty. Suicide settles Gartin's score and leaves me where I am, on the Force, still able to work at my job as I see it. I doubt that Chabbat's satisfied, though. That's why I'm calling the play tonight."

Barney thought back. When fighting the Japs he hadn't worried at all about doing it nor had the enemy. When a man is defending his life he doesn't fret over the niceties of the Marquis of Queensberry rules. Barney could clearly see the parallel in Craddock's position.

"There are only two ways a cop can crack a case honestly when his chief is a big-shot crook's dummy, Mr Chance," the captain added quietly. "One way is crack it so wide open that the whole thing falls apart, which is the hard way, the almost impossible way. The other is to chip away at it under cover. That's more dangerous, because they can hit back under cover also. Until now it's been my method. But it's no good any longer. The covers are coming off."

He trudged to the door of Alma Remsen's home. Barney tried to doubt him no longer. It wasn't easy. Craddock was a shrewd, ruthless man – courageous, admirably and self-lessly devoted to his own code, but ruthless nevertheless – a hard man to take on faith.

Barney caught Jean Vernon's arm and stopped her on the walk. "You've helped Craddock all along, beginning with the job he got you to take at the Merry-Go-Round. You sounded me out for him, you're holding evidence and testimony for against the day when he might use it. But now you're showing yourself with him here. Why?"

"He told you, Barney. We've got to face them openly now," Jean said, keeping a grip on herself. "This is what we've worked for. This is it."

The door had opened and Neal Lytham was looking out. Barney and Jean followed Craddock into the living room. Chabbat was seated before the warm fireplace with a cigar. He smoked as imperturbably as always, but Neal was inwardly agitated. Astonished, Barney noted a change in Craddock's manner. The captain became almost apologetic.

"Sorry to disturb Miss Remsen," Craddock murmured. "Just routine, for the record."

Neal led them up the stairs, his weakly handsome face pale with apprehension. Alma Remsen was sitting up in bed. Bandages no longer bound her red hair – instead, a patch of gauze covered the wound behind her left ear.

Her sister, Suzie, was there, munching chocolates. Neal signalled Suzie out, and she complied pettishly. He watched from the foot of the bed while Craddock deferentially drew a chair.

"Just routine, Alma," the captain said again, "and it won't take long. You were Jonathan Lytham's secretary until he died, then you became Guy Farrish's. Tell me all you know about Mr Lytham's last will."

"You mean the one he wrote just a couple of days before he died?" Alma said, her greenish eyes becoming thoughtful. "But that one doesn't even exist any more. Mr Lytham changed his mind again and destroyed it."

"How do you know he did?"

"Mr Farrish told me Mr Lytham tore up the new one, and that made the old one good again."

"Go on, Alma," Captain Craddock encouraged her quietly. "Tell me how it all happened."

Readily, Alma went back to the beginning. "It was the last day Mr Lytham was ever at the office. He was very upset because he'd had a terrible blow-up with Mr Chabbat that morning. He wasn't feeling at all well, poor man, but before he left he dictated a new will."

"One cutting off his son and leaving everything to his daughter?"

"Yes," Alma said, gazing at Jonathan Lytham's son. "In it he gave everything to Marsha and cut Neal off with only a dollar."

Neal gestured disarmingly. "It doesn't matter now. Alma told you my father had a change of heart and tore up that new will before he died."

Craddock nodded. "Just for the record, Neal. Go on from there, please, Alma."

"It was late in the afternoon," Alma continued, "and the bank was closed. Mr Lytham couldn't put the new will in his safety deposit box, or take the old one out, so instead he put the new one in the office safe. Then he went home to bed and he never got up again. Two days later he was dead. That was the day when Mr Farrish told me –"

She pushed herself higher against the pillows, as if in an effort to get every detail straight. "First Marsha phoned the office, saying Mr Lytham couldn't live much longer and he wanted Mr Farrish to bring a certain envelope from the safe and come to the house. It was that new will. When Mr Farrish came back, he told me Mr Lytham had changed his mind about it and had torn it up. Then, after Mr Lytham was dead, Mr Farrish got the other one out of the safety deposit box – the old one leaving everything to Neal and Marsha equally. That's all I can tell you. It's all right, isn't it?"

Barney saw Craddock shake his head. "No, Alma, it's not all right. Farrish lied to you about the new will. Actually, Mr Lytham hadn't forgiven his son. That's proved by the fact that he died without allowing Neal to see him again."

Alma's lips parted as she gazed at Craddock.

"What Mr Lytham actually told Farrish was that a new will existed and he wanted it to stand. He didn't destroy it. On the contrary, he gave it to Farrish, his executor, to be acted upon. But Farrish didn't probate it. Instead, he betrayed the old friend and partner who'd trusted him to honour his dying wishes. Farrish concealed the new will, which gave everything to Marsha, and instead probated the old one, which divided the estate equally between Marsha and Neal. No doubt of it, Alma. You see –" again producing the long brown envelope from his coat, Craddock held it without opening it "– I have the new will right here."

Barney swallowed, stunned by this revelation of trickery on Guy's part, and stared at Neal. Neal's face had turned waxy – he could say nothing.

"It was easy to do," Craddock went on. "In Pennsylvania, no witnesses to a will are required. Mr Lytham was close-mouthed. He'd told no one about the new will, not even Marsha. Farrish made sure of that, which meant you were the only living person who knew about it, Alma, other than himself. So he simply told you Mr Lytham had torn up the new will, and you naturally believed him."

"But –"

"Easy and simple," Craddock added, gazing now at Neal, his face stony. "It dropped more than a million dollars into your lap, Neal, money not rightfully yours. Farrish wanted a good cut of it and started getting it. He showed you the new will and warned you he could 'find' it and probate it at any time. That would jerk the million right out of your lap again, except for one lone dollar. But as long as he kept the new will under wraps, both of you would collect – you directly, he through you. And that's the way it went."

Craddock rose heavily, the unopened envelope still in his hand. "That's all, Alma, thank you," and he turned to the stairs.

Barney followed Craddock, revolted and heartsick. Was this the extent of the captain's purposes – to show that Guy Farrish, now dead, had turned crooked? Barney resented it, despite his conviction that Craddock was right, but when he went into the living room after Craddock he began to see its broader, deeper aspects. Actually, he realized now, the captain was striking at a cabal, at a conspiracy of powers – Neal's dishonestly acquired wealth, unequalled in Penns- wick except by Marsha's, plus Chabbat's entrenched in- fluence.

Chabbat still sat comfortably before the burning logs in the fireplace, rolling his cigar in his lips. He must know what Craddock had done, Barney thought coldly, but he was still superbly unperturbed. Neal Lytham, in contrast, was profoundly shaken. Coming in after Jean Vernon, he stared fearfully at Craddock. He didn't attempt to explain or defend himself – he couldn't speak at all.

"Wait a minute," Barney said. "Guy tried to mail the new will to Marsha. That means he was washing his hands of the whole dirty business." His figure of speech recalled to Barney's mind that strange but significant token which Guy had wanted Eve to see – the used cake of soap. "Guy was putting the whole thing straight again, and he was killed because somebody wanted to stop him."

Craddock must know this, he reminded himself, but Craddock said nothing. For reasons of his own the captain was letting Barney take the lead. Barney sensed the danger in that. Chabbat's silent scrutiny of him was more than ominous. Neal's inner agitation was growing, threatening to break. In Jean's widened eyes there was anxiety for Barney. But he couldn't stop now.

"Why?" he said. "Why did Guy want to put it straight? He'd reached his limit, just as Jonathan Lytham had. Why? He'd got Vic Gartin off the manslaughter charges, in connection with the Big Tent fire. Do you mean that was too much for him to stomach once he'd done it?" Suddenly Barney felt he had the real answer. "The wedding. Neal's marriage to Suzie. Ben Chabbat's niece. Chabbat's power married to Neal's wealth. The founding of an evil dynasty."

Craddock dourly permitted Barney to continue.

"And more. Guy must have seen himself becoming its victim. He had to keep the new will, because without it he'd have no hold on Neal, but his hold wasn't secure. He could be sloughed off, frozen out, eliminated entirely, and he knew Chabbat and Neal would sooner or later do exactly that in order to consolidate and safeguard themselves. And Guy saw it coming." Barney's eyes opened wider. "He may even have seen that Neal was set up as a murder victim, because if Neal should die all his money would go to Suzie, a brainless little doll to be manipulated as Chabbat pleased."

The skin around Neal's eyes became dead white as he stared at the man seated before the log fire. Barney felt sure that until now Neal hadn't realized his marriage might be turned into an instrument of treachery. Chabbat smiled faintly and smoked. And still Captain Craddock permitted Barney to hold the dangerous reins.

"Guy decided to strike first, to wreck Chabbat's plans even while they were forming. He could do that very simply, by revealing the existence of the new will. Perhaps he hoped Marsha would never take legal action against him, but he must have known it would mean his finish at Chabbat's hands – and he tried to do it anyway."

Guy had tried and had been killed. Barney gazed from Chabbat to Neal, feeling suddenly at a loss. He remembered a statement of Jean's which he'd doubted at the time but must believe now, a statement providing an alibi for Gartin, who had been with her when Guy was shot, for Neal and Chabbat – both of whom had been at the church, for –

A crash of glass came sharply. They turned – Barney, Jean, Craddock, Neal, and even Chabbat hoisted himself halfway from his chair, startled out of his complacency – to stare across the room. A figure stood outside the window, visible only from the waist up, looking both threatening and ridiculous. A shapeless felt hat pulled low on its head, a topcoat hung loosely across its thin shoulders and a hand-kerchief curtained its face, so that only a pair of eyes was visible in the shadow of the hat-brim.

But the gun pointing from its gloved hand was not ridiculous.

They were still until Chabbat sank slowly back into his chair. Jean moved closer to Barney's side, her hand reaching for his. He saw tense alarm in Neal and knew it was real. Captain Craddock, also seated, turned quietly in his chair to face the figure outside the window.

The gun watched them through the hole broken in the glass. The handkerchief-mask puffed a little as the mouth behind it spoke in a disguised whisper.

"Get his gun."

The eyes were peering at Barney and the voice meant Craddock. The captain moved a hand towards his hip but a warning exclamation from the window stopped him. Again the shadowed eyes commanded Barney. He complied. Reaching under Craddock's coat, he removed the pocket-holster.

"Take the shells out."

This was a preliminary, Barney knew. Something more was coming, but first the captain's revolver must be made harmless. He told himself it must be the only weapon in the room, but he was forced to go on obeying. He swung out the cylinder and ejected the shells. They rolled on the rug, glittering.

"Fireplace," the whisper ordered.

Barney looked at Craddock in despair. The captain shrugged slightly, his face picturing resignation mingled with a queer sort of tenacity. The other gun outside the window was shining a threat at Barney and turning on Jean.

Barney tossed Craddock's revolver. It fell behind the burning logs, into a bed of red embers. In a few moments it would grow too hot to touch.

"Now that envelope."

Craddock still holding it, didn't stir.

"Throw it in the fire."

Jean's move startled Barney. Reaching to the envelope, she snatched it from Craddock's fingers. Quickly she drew out and unfolded a single sheet of paper. Her chin lifted in defiance of the figure outside the window. She put it into Barney's hands.

"Read it, Barney!"

The voice commanded again, hoarsely: "Throw that in the fire!"

"No, Barney, read it!"

Barney stared at the typewritten lines, fearful for Jean. The will was short, the terse pronouncement of an embittered man. "I, Jonathan Lytham, being of sound mind . . ." Exactly as Craddock had said, it disinherited Neal. Jonathan Lytham's signature looked decisive, final.

"In the fire!" The voice carried a note of impatience, desperate impatience at the point of breaking. "Now!"

Jean's next move startled Barney even more. She seized the will again. Turning, she crumpled it into a wad and threw it onto the logs. Before Barney could grasp what she had done, the paper was flaming up. He started towards it in dismay, but Jean tugged him back. Chabbat, smiling faintly again, grasped up the poker and stirred its ashes. Now it was hopelessly lost.

Barney stared at Jean, numbly cold, yet smouldering with a sense of betrayal. She didn't glance at him, but gazed at the masked figure behind the window.

A new gleam had come into the shadowed eyes. The figure remained there, not moving, the gun steady. It was still purposeful. The realization struck Barney that the destruction of the will wasn't enough. Still more was coming. It could be only one thing – the destruction of witnesses in addition. To Barney that meant Jean, Craddock, too, himself, and perhaps Neal as well. The mere thought was incredible to Barney, but it was the purpose in a murderer's mind, in the mind behind the gun at the window.

"There was a red smear on that will." Barney heard himself speaking. "Guy's blood. He was shot before he put it in that envelope."

Barney wondered crazily why the gun in the window didn't shoot. It was as if his words were keeping the bullets back. He hurried on, feeling Jean's hand in his again.

"Guy was shot even before he phoned Marsha. That's why he sounded so short of breath to her. He had something for her, but he couldn't take it to her because he had a bullet in his body. She'd have to come down for it, he said. But then he felt his strength failing. Feeling he couldn't wait any longer, he sealed the will inside an envelope, wrote Marsha's address, stuck on stamps and actually went down to the mailbox. He thought that would get it safely to her after he was dead."

A strange fascination seemed to have closed over the figure outside the window.

"Vic Gartin didn't know that. He overheard Guy talking to me in my office. Guy said, 'Give it to her,' meaning the little package he intended for Eve, but Gartin thought he'd given me the will and that meant I should give it to Marsha. That's why Gartin ransacked my office first, then my apartment – trying to get the will, so it could be destroyed, so Neal could stay dishonestly rich."

Barney now spoke to Neal.

"But then you learned that Guy had gone about mailing the will. That's why you stayed at Marsha's house on your wedding night, Neal. You expected the postman to bring the will there. You meant to get hold of it before Marsha saw it. But it didn't come. Then you decided Guy must have mailed it to Eve instead, so Eve could plead with Marsha on Guy's behalf. So Gartin kidnapped her, but she didn't have the will either. You were at your wits' end, suspecting one another, preparing to back-stab one another for its sake, until just now, when you learned Craddock had it."

Barney was conscious of a slight movement, not at the window, but behind him. Chabbat was easing forward in his chair. Barney didn't shift his gaze from the slitted eyes in the shadow.

"The story you told doesn't hang together, Alma," he said. "You might have done better if you hadn't been suffering from shock. Actually there wasn't any masked man hiding in Guy's office when you went in. The description was one you faked on the spur of the moment. If there had been such a man, he wouldn't have left without the will, not with Guy already shot and you knocked unconscious. Guy attempted to mail it *after* you'd gone in. He decided on that because he couldn't know how much longer he'd last, and he wanted most of all to keep it out of your hands."

The handkerchief mask was swaying, moved by a succession of quick breaths.

"After Jonathan Lytham's death you began suspecting that Guy had concealed the new will, Alma. For one thing, Guy was becoming too prosperous on too few cases. Soon you challenged him on it. A few words from you to the bar association and the income tax people would play hell with him, so he was forced to cut you in. You became one of the dynasty based on Neal's crooked money – Neal himself, Chabbat, Guy and even Suzie, who was soon to marry Neal. Small wonder Guy wasn't long reaching the limit of his dishonesty."

The voice said sharply, recognizable as a young woman's now: "That's enough!"

"When Guy called you into his office just before the wedding, it was to give Neal and Suzie a gift, sure enough. The gift was dynamite, enough of it to blow up everything. He gave you fair warning that he meant to turn the new will over to Marsha at once. You had to stop that, Alma. You got Guy's own gun out of his desk and over it you demanded the will."

The eyes of Alma Remsen shone as hard as the metal of the weapon she held.

"He refused. The only way you could stop him now was to shoot him. With your bullet in his body, he hit you, knocked you down and took the gun away from you. Then he went on, first calling Marsha. Next, wanting to hurry, he put the will in the envelope. You saw him doing it when you got up off the floor. You tried to get at the gun again, but he knocked you down a second time, hard enough to keep you down. You see, Alma, you're the only one who could have known of Guy's intention to mail the will to Marsha, the only one who could have tipped off the others about that. Now we know all of it."

Now it was coming.

"You, too, Neal," Barney said. "When she starts shooting she won't leave you out. Suzie will inherit then. She thinks she's fairly sure of getting away with the whole thing with Chabbat's help. She may be wrong on that point. Not even Chabbat can hush up so many murders –"

A gasp broke from Jean's lips. Alma's gun had swung at Neal. Craddock moved heavily, but in a quick glide, just as its hammer lifted. The report wasn't loud, but the bullet carried a power that spun Craddock half around. He fell against Neal, holding his left shoulder with his right hand, while Neal braced against the wall, unhurt. Dazed, Barney knew Craddock had done it deliberately, had protected Neal Lytham with his own body.

The second gunshot broke behind Barney. Chabbat was out of his chair. In one hand he held his cigar, balancing a long ash on it, and in the other he held an automatic. Chabbat, the only man in the room who might consider himself safe from Alma's fire, was turning his own gun on her. Because, as Barney had said, this madness of hers would be more than even he could hush up. Because the death of Alma Remsen, a proved murderess, done in what he would claim to be self-protection, would help him to preserve his power.

He had fired one shot and missed. The masked girl stood rigid outside the window, too stunned by Chabbat's act to grasp its treacherous meaning. Craddock was heaving himself across the room again when Chabbat fired the second time. Alma screamed and fell away. Craddock took a grip on Chabbat's automatic. He twisted it free and slashed Chabbat once across the face. Chabbat fell.

Barney found Jean suddenly in his arms. With an impulse of fear and gladness she'd thrown her arms around his neck – gladness because he was unhurt. He felt her body shaking and with equal suddenness she flung herself away.

Barney hurried out the door after her, with Captain Craddock trudging behind him. Neal was at the window now, still speechless, looking down at Alma Remsen.

With his one usable hand Craddock opened her coat. Beneath it she was wearing a nightgown. The stain was on her left side, just below the ribs. She was as unconscious as when Barney had first found her in Guy's office.

"Bad," Craddock said, rising with a sigh, "but it doesn't have to be fatal. She knows Chabbat shot her and why, and she won't forget it. She's the hating kind. She'll get back at him and talk."

"And you, Neal," Craddock added to the stricken man at the window. "You'll talk, too, because you know what her plans for you were. Between the two of you, there'll be no more Chabbat."

For the first time Barney saw a smile on the captain's face, a smile of bitter gratification. "I don't see how we could have asked for anything better, Barney." He looked like a man who had won without ever having really hoped to win.

Jean was in Barney's arms again, her head pressed to his shoulder, sobbing a little.

"You burned the will," Barney heard himself mumbling. He wasn't sure of his voice but he was certain he was holding her tightly. "You burned it!"

"But it doesn't matter, Barney!" She lifted her head, her eyes widened. "Really it doesn't. You and I can swear to the authenticity of that will. Captain Craddock, too. The writing's gone, but Jonathan Lytham's last wish will remain in force. The court will uphold it."

"How do you know that? You're talking like a – a –"

"A law student? I am one, Barney. There just hasn't been time for us to get really acquainted with each other, has there?" She put her head back on his shoulder, shivering.

Barney was dizzy. The small task that Guy had entrusted to him had become a mission fulfilled. And Jean. She surprised him endlessly. He wanted her to go on surprising him endlessly, although he knew he'd never get used to it.

"There'll be time now, darling," she said, and he freed one hand long enough to grip the strong, comradely hand of Captain Craddock.

Ride A White Horse

Lawrence Block

A ndy Hart stared unbelievingly at the door of Whitey's Tavern. The door was closed and padlocked, and the bar was unlighted. He checked his watch and noted that it was almost 7:30. Whitey should have opened hours ago.

Andy turned and strode to the candy store on the corner. He was a small man, but his rapid walk made up for his short legs. He walked as he did everything else – precisely, with no waste motion.

"Hey," he asked the man behind the counter, "how come Whitey didn't open up yet?"

"He's closed down for the next two weeks. Got caught serving minors." Andy thanked him and left.

The news was disturbing. It didn't annoy him tremendously, but it did break up a long-established routine. Ever since he had started working as a book-keeper at Murrow's Department Store, eleven years ago, he had been in the habit of eating a solitary meal at the Five Star Diner and drinking a few beers at Whitey's. He had just finished dinner, and now he found himself with no place to go.

Standing on the street corner, staring at the front of the empty bar, he had a vague sensation that he was missing something. Here he was, thirty-seven years old, and there was nowhere in the city for him to go. He had no family, and his only friends were his drinking companions at Whitey's. He could go back to his room, but there he would have only the four walls for company. He momentarily envied the married men who worked in his department. It might be nice to have a wife and kids to come home to.

The thought passed as quickly as it had come. After all,

there was no reason to be broken-hearted over a closed bar. There was undoubtedly another bar in the neighbourhood where the beer was as good and the people as friendly. He glanced around and noticed a bar directly across the street.

There was a large neon sign over the doorway, with the outline of a horse and the words "White Horse Café". The door was a bright red, and music from a juke box wafted through it.

Andy hesitated. There was a bar, all right. He had passed it many times in the past, but had never thought to enter it. It seemed a little flashy to him, a little bit too high-tone. But tonight, he decided, he'd see how it was on the inside. A change of pace wouldn't hurt him at all.

He crossed the street and entered. A half-dozen men were seated at the bar, and several couples occupied booths on the side. The juke box was playing a song which he had heard before, but he couldn't remember the title. He walked to the rear, hung his coat on a peg, and took the end seat.

He ordered a beer and sat nursing it. He studied his reflection in the mirror. His looks were average – neatly-combed brown hair, brown eyes, and a prominent chin. His smile was pleasant, but he didn't smile too often. He was, all in all, a pretty average guy.

The time passed slowly. Andy finished his beer and ordered another, and then another. Some of the people left the bar and others entered, but he saw no one he recognized. He was beginning to regret coming to the White Horse. The beer was fine and the music was nice enough, but he had no more company than the four walls of his room provided.

Then, while he was drinking his fourth beer, the door opened and she entered. He saw her at once. He had glanced to the door every time it opened in the hope of seeing an acquaintance, and each time he had turned back to his glass. This time, however, he couldn't turn his eyes away from her.

She was tall, very pretty, with long blonde hair that fell to her shoulders. She took off her coat and hung it up and Andy could see that she was more than just pretty. Her skirt clung to her hips and hugged her thighs, and her breasts threatened to break through the tight film of her sweater. Andy couldn't stop looking at her. He knew that he was staring, but he couldn't help himself. She was the most beautiful woman he had ever seen.

He was surprised when she walked over and sat down on the stool beside him. Actually, it was natural enough. There were only two other empty stools at the bar. But to Andy it seemed like the rarest of coincidences.

He was glad that she was sitting next to him but at the same time he was embarrassed. He felt a desire for her which was stronger than anything he had experienced in years. He had neither needed nor wanted a woman in a long while, but now he felt an instantaneous physical craving for her.

The girl ordered a sidecar and sipped at it, and Andy forced himself to drink his beer. He wanted desperately to start a conversation with her but couldn't think of a way to begin. He waited, listening to the music, until she finished her drink.

"Miss," he said nervously, "could I buy you another?"

She turned and looked at him for a long moment, and he felt himself flush. "Yes," she said at last. "Thank you."

He ordered a sidecar for her and another beer for himself, and they began talking. He was amazed to discover that he was able to talk freely and easily to her, and that she in turn seemed interested in everything that he had to say. He had wanted to talk to anybody in the world, and talking to her was almost the answer to a prayer.

He told her everything about himself – his name, his job, and the sort of life he led. She didn't have much to say about herself. Her name was Sara Malone and she was twenty-four, but that was all she volunteered.

From that point on the time flew by, and Andy was thankful that Whitey's had been closed. He wanted the evening to pass more slowly. He was happy, and he dreaded returning to his empty bed in his tiny room.

Finally she glanced at her watch, then smiled up at him. "I have to go," she said. "It's getting late."

"One more drink," he suggested.

"No," she said. "We've had enough. Let's go."

He helped her on with her coat and walked outside with her. He stood there on the sidewalk, awkwardly. "Sara," he said, "when can I see you again?"

She smiled, and it was a warm, easy smile. "You could come home with me. If you'd like to."

They walked quickly, with the blackness of the night around them like a blanket. And when they reached her apartment they kissed and they held each other. He took her, and lying there in her arms, with her firm breasts warm against his chest, he felt complete and whole again.

When he woke up the next morning she was already awake, and he smelled food cooking. He washed and dressed, then went into the kitchen for breakfast. It was a fine breakfast, and so very much better than toast and coffee at the Five Star Diner. He had to keep looking across the table at her to make sure that he was really awake and that she was really there. He couldn't believe what had happened, but the memory of last night was too vivid to leave room for doubt.

They didn't talk much during breakfast. He couldn't talk, afraid that he might do something to spoil it all. When he finished his second cup of coffee, he stood up regretfully.

"I have to go now," he said. "I have to be at work by nine."

"When will you be home? I'll have dinner ready."

"Right after work," he said. "About 5:15 or so. Don't you have to work?" He remembered that she hadn't mentioned it last night.

"No. I have enough money for a while, so I don't work." She smiled. "Would you do me a favour?"

"Of course."

"I checked a package at the Public Library yesterday and forgot to pick it up on the way out. You work across the street from the library, don't you?"

He nodded.

"Here," she said. She took a ticket from her purse and handed it to him. "Will you get it for me?"

"Sure." He put the ticket in his pocket and slipped on his overcoat. He walked slowly to the door, and when he turned she was in his arms suddenly, kissing him. "I love you," he said. He walked lightly down the street, and she closed the door softly behind him.

His work went easily and quickly that day. He was anxious for five o'clock to roll around, but the memory of last night and the promise of the coming one made the time pass. At noon he picked up her parcel at the library, a small box wrapped in brown wrapping paper. He brought it home to her that night, and she put it on the top shelf in the closet.

Sara cooked him a good dinner, and he helped her with the dishes. They sat in the living-room, listening to records, until it was time for bed. Then they made love, and he knew that he could never live without her again, that he could never sleep without her beside him.

Days passed and the nights. Andy had never been so happy and contented in his life. He settled into a routine once again, but it was a groove rather than a rut. His life before had lacked only a woman like Sara to make it complete, and now nothing was missing.

From time to time he thought of asking her to marry him. But, for some reason, he was afraid to. Everything was so perfect that he was hesitant to chance changing the arrangement. He let things remain as they were.

He knew very little about her, really. She seemed reluctant to talk about her past life. She didn't say how she was able to afford the luxurious apartment they lived in, or what she did during the days while he was at the office. He didn't press her. Nothing mattered, just so long as she was there for him when he arrived home.

She had him pick up packages frequently – about twice a week or so. They were always the same type – small boxes wrapped in brown wrapping paper. Sometimes they were in a locker at the bus depot, sometimes at the library, sometimes in a safety deposit box at the bank. He wondered idly what the boxes contained, but she wouldn't tell him, and he suspected it was some sort of medicine which she didn't want to mention. The question nagged at him, though. It bothered persistently. He didn't care about her earlier life, for that was beyond her now. But he wanted to know everything about her as she was now, wanted to share all of her life.

Inevitably, one evening he brought home a package and she was not home. He sat waiting for her, the package in his lap. He stared at the package, turning it over and over in his hands, as though he were trying to burn a hole in the wrapping paper with his eyes. Five, ten minutes passed, and he couldn't stand it any longer. He untied the string, removed the wrapping paper, and opened the box.

The box was filled with a white powder. He looked at it, smelled it, and tasted a flake of it. It was nothing that he could recognize. He was wondering what the devil it could be when he heard a key in the lock, and he began guiltily to rewrap the package. Sara entered the room while he was still fussing with the string.

"Andy!" she cried. "What are you doing?"

"The package came undone," he said lamely. "I was rewrapping it for you."

She looked at him accusingly. "Did you see what was inside?"

"Yes," he said. "What was it, Sara?"

She took the box from him. "Never mind," she said. "Just some powder."

But this time he would not be put off. He had to know. "What is it? I'll find out anyway."

She let out a sigh. I guess you had to find out. I . . ."

He waited.

"It's . . . horse, Andy."

"What!"

"Horse. Heroin."

"I know what 'horse' is," he said. "But what are you doing with it? You're not an addict, are you?" He couldn't believe what she had told him, but he knew from the expression on her face that she was telling the truth. Still, it was hard to believe, and he did not want to believe it.

"No," she said. "I'm not an addict. I'm what they call a pusher, Andy. I sell the heroin to addicts."

For a moment he could not speak. Finally he managed to say, "Why?"

She hesitated. "Money," she said. "I make lots of money.

And it costs money for an apartment like this, and for good clothes and steak for dinner."

"You'll stop. I'm making enough money for us both, and you'll stop before you get caught. We'll get a smaller place somewhere and . . ."

"No," she cut in. "I won't get caught, Andy. And I want to keep on like this. I like steak, Andy. I like this place."

He stared at her. His mouth dropped open and he shook his head from side to side. "No! Sara, I won't let you!"

"I'm going to."

"I . . . I can't pick up any more packages for you."

She smiled. "Yes, you can. And you will, because you need me." She threw back her shoulders so that her breasts strained against the front of her dress. "We need each other, don't we?"

He stood up, and the package fell to the floor. He reached for her and lifted her in his arms, carrying her to the bedroom. And they came together fitfully and fiercely, as though the force of their bodies could erase everything else.

Later, when he was lying still beside her, she said, "In a way, it's better that you know. I'll need help with the business, and you can quit your job and help me. I guess it's better this way."

At that moment Andy began to distrust her. His love slowly dissolved eventually to be replaced by an ever-increasing hatred.

The following morning he quit his job. It had never been an especially exciting job, but he had liked it. He liked the office and the people he worked with. He hadn't wanted to quit.

But he could never give up Sara. He couldn't live without her, couldn't sleep again in an empty bed. She had become a habit, a part of his routine, and he had to have her no matter what.

The days that followed were hell for him. Sara taught him the business step-by-step, from pick-ups and deliveries to actual sales. He learned how to contact an addict and take his money from him. He watched feverish men cook the heroin on a spoon and shoot it into a vein. And he watched Sara refuse a shot to an addict without money, and watched the man beg and plead while his hands twitched and his knees shook.

He thought he would lose his mind. He argued with Sara, telling her what a rotten thing she was doing, but he couldn't sway her. He saw her for what she was – cold, mercenary, and ruthless. And in her arms at night, he couldn't believe that she was the same woman.

Bit by bit, piece by piece, he learned the business. It became a routine after a while, but it was a routine which he hated. He settled into it, but he had trouble sleeping nights. Time after time he tried to leave her, but it was impossible.

One night he was sitting in the living room, trying to read a magazine. She came over and sat beside him taking the magazine from his hands. She handed him a brown cigarette, loosely-packed. "Here," she said, smiling. "Smoke this."

"What! This is marijuana, isn't it?"

"That's right. Smoke it."

"Are you crazy?"

She smiled slowly and ran her hand up and down his thigh. "Don't be silly. I've been smoking pot for a long time now, and it doesn't hurt you. It makes you feel real fine. Try it?"

He drew away from her, his eyes searching hers. "I don't want to become an addict, Sara. I've seen the poor fish suffer, and I don't want it."

She laughed. "It's not habit-forming. I've been smoking since I was seventeen, and I just have a joint whenever I want one. You want to stay clear of horse, but this won't hurt you."

He drew a deep breath. "No," he said, firmly. "I don't want it."

Her hand worked on his thigh, and with her other hand she toyed with the buttons on her blouse. "You want me, though," she said, huskily. "Don't you, Andy?"

She put the cigarette between his lips and lit it, and made him smoke it quickly, drawing the pungent, acrid smoke deep into his lungs. At first he was dizzy; then his stomach churned and he was sick. But she only made him smoke another, and this time the smoke took hold of him and held him, and the room grew large and small and large again, and he made love to her with a thousand voices shrieking warning inside his brain.

And so marijuana, too, became a part of Andy's routine. He smoked as an alcoholic drank, losing his worries in the smoke. It was more a habit with him than it was with Sara. He grew to depend upon it, mentally if not physically.

And he learned things, too. He learned to smoke the joint down to a "roach", or butt, in order to get the maximum charge from it. He learned to hold as much smoke as he could in his lungs for as long as possible, in order to intensify the effect. He learned to smoke two or three joints in a row.

At the same time, he learned his business from start to finish. He bargained with contacts and squeezed the last cent from customers, burying his conscience completely. He gained an understanding of the operations of the narcotics racket, from the Big Man to the smalltime pusher. Everything he did became part of him, and part of his routine.

He sat alone in the apartment one day, just after selling a cap of heroin to an addict. He opened a glassine envelope and idly poked the powder with the point of a pencil.

Horse, he thought. White Horse, the same as the bar where they had met. Valuable stuff. People killed for it, went through hell for it.

He sat looking at it for a long time, and then he folded a slip of paper and poured some of the powder on it. He raised the paper to his nose, closed his eyes, and sniffed deeply. He drew the flakes through his nostrils and into his lungs, and the heroin hit home.

It was a new sensation, a much bigger charge than marijuana had given him. He liked it. He threw away the slip of paper, put the heroin away, and leaned back to relax. Everything was pink and fuzzy, soft and smooth and cool.

He started sniffing heroin daily, and soon he noticed that he was physically aware of it when it was time for a fix. He began increasing the dosage, as his body began to demand more of the drug. And he didn't tell Sara anything about it.

His hate for her had grown, but it too became habitual.

He learned to live with it. However, when they had a disagreement over the business, he realized that she was standing in the way.

Andy wanted to expand operations. He saw that, with a little effort and a little muscle, he and Sara could move up a notch and have a crowd of pushers under them. He explained it to her, step by step. It couldn't miss.

"No," she said, flatly. "We're doing fine right where we are. We make good money and nobody will want us out of the way."

"We could make more money," he said. "Lots more. The cops wouldn't be able to touch us."

"It's a risk."

He shrugged. "Everything's a risk. Walking across the street is a risk, but you can't stay on your own block forever. It's a chance we've got to take."

She refused, and once again she used her body as a bargaining point. At last he gave in, as always, but the hate was beginning to boil in him.

A few days later an addict came whining for a shot. Andy saw the way he trembled and twitched, but the spectacle didn't bother him any longer. He had seen it time and time again, until it was just a part of the day's work.

"Sorry, junkie," he said. "Come back when you raise the dough."

The man begged, and Andy started to push him out the door when a thought came to him. He opened the door and let the man in.

"C'mere," he said. "You got a spike?"

The addict nodded dumbly and pulled a hypodermic needle from his pocket. Andy took it from him and inspected it, turning it over and over in his hand. "Okay," he said at length. "A shot for your spike."

The man sighed with relief, then demanded, "How am I gonna take the shot without a spike?"

"Take it first; then get out."

Andy followed the addict into the bathroom and watched him heat the powder on a spoon. Then he filled the syringe and shot it into the vein in his arm. It hit immediately, and he relaxed.

"Thanks," he said. He handed the syringe to Andy. "Thanks."

"Get out." The addict left, and Andy closed the door after him.

He washed the syringe in hot water, then put some heroin on a spoon. He deftly filled the syringe and gave himself a shot in the fleshy part of his arm.

It was far more satisfying than sniffing the powder. It was stronger and faster. He felt good.

As the heroin became more and more a part of his life, he switched to the mainline, shooting it directly into the vein. It was necessary to him now, and he itched to build up his trade until he controlled narcotics in the town. He knew he could handle it. Already, he had virtually replaced Sara. She was the messenger now, while he handled the important end. But she still called the shots, for she still held the trump card. And no matter how he argued, she would simply rub herself up against him and kiss him, and the argument would be finished. So he could do nothing but wait.

And, at last, he was one day ready.

He took a long, sharp knife from the kitchen drawer and walked slowly to the bedroom, where she lay reading. She looked up from the magazine and smiled at him, stretching languorously.

"Hi," she said. "What's up?"

He returned the smile, keeping the knife behind his back. "I have news for you," he said. "We're expanding, like I suggested. No more small-time stuff, Sara."

She sighed. "Not again, Andy. I told you before . . ."

"This time *I'm* telling *you*."

"Oh," she said, amused. "Do you think you can get along without me?"

"I know I can."

"Really?" She threw back the bedcovers and smiled up at him. "You need me, Andy."

He forced himself to look at her. He ran his eyes over the firm breasts, the soft curves of her hips. He looked at her carefully, waiting for the familiar stir within him. It didn't come.

"I don't need you," he said, slowly. "Look."

He held out his right hand, the hand that held the knife. He unbuttoned the sleeve and rolled it up slowly, showing her the marks of the needle. "See? I'm a junkie, Sara. I only care about one thing, baby, and it isn't you. You don't show me a thing."

But her eyes were not on the marks on his arm. They were on the knife in his hand, and they were wide with fear.

"I don't need you at all," he went on. "I don't need liquor, I don't need sex, I don't need you. You're just dead wood, Sara."

She rose from the bed and moved towards him. "Andy," she cooed. "Andy, honey." Her whole body seemed to reach out for him, hungrily.

He shook his head. "Sorry," he said. "It just won't work any more. I don't care about it. Just the horse is all that matters."

She looked into his eyes, and they were flat and uncaring. "Wait," she said. "We'll play it your way, Andy. We'll expand, like you said. Anything you say."

"You don't understand. I don't *need* you."

"Please!" she moaned. "Please!"

"Sorry. It's time for my shot." And he lowered the knife.

He moved towards her and she tried to back away, but he kept coming, the knife pointed at her. "No!" she shrieked. And she started to say something else, but before she could get the words out the knife was in her heart.

Best Man

Thomas Walsh

C arver, plain-clothesman on homicide, left the elevator at the fourth floor, and stepped out to a wide marble corridor flanked by glass-panelled doors on either side. "To your right," the operator said. Carver nodded and turned.

It was a very long corridor, running the length of the Gresham Building. There was a stairway at the side farthest from him, and as he turned around a short man in a camel's hair coat was going down this. He wasn't hurrying; Carver, reading the labels on the office doors, didn't pay him much attention.

The fourth door he came to was marked Tammany and Sutorius, Attorneys At Law. He was reaching for the knob when a bald fat man with mildly puzzled eyes stepped out into the corridor from an office on the opposite side.

The fat man looked curious. "You hear anything?" he asked. When Carver shook his head he stopped a little uncertainly, peered up and down, grunted: "Well," and drew back into his room. Carver stared after him a moment, pinching his nose thoughtfully.

The door of Tammany and Sutorius was locked. Carver rattled it once to make sure, then rapped his knuckles heavily against the frosted glass panel.

He waited perhaps sixty seconds before rapping again. Inside a man's voice was speaking shrilly, rapidly. At Carver's second knock it choked off, a phone hook was banged down; footsteps inside hobbled across a hard wood floor, and the voice of Abel J. Sutorius, high and a little hysterical, came thinly to him:

"Who – who is it? You'll have to smash the door." He

stopped; Carver heard his loud gasping, saw the feeble shadow of his hands beating at the glass. Then his whimper: "My God! My God!"

Carver got his broad knuckles under the knob, lifted it, and crashed his shoulder against the door's wooden edge. Metal splintered and snapped, and the door swung in unevenly. He saw Sutorius kneeling on the floor of the small office, above another man whose body was prone, whose light brown coat was stained with blood.

Sutorius turned to him, his face very white. He babbled: "The man! The one that just left – Did you see him, Carver?"

Coming fast across the rug, Carver didn't answer him. The prone man's eyes were closed, but he was still breathing, with a rapid, liquid sound; he had a long thin face, narrow lips, a small black moustache. There was blood on his checked tie and on the white breast of his shirt.

Sutorius wrung his hands together, gasped as Carver reached for the phone: "I called the police – the ambulance. My God, Carver, do something! Perhaps he's still downstairs. He was wearing a camel's hair coat, a dark hat. I couldn't see his face – he had a handkerchief over it – but he was short and pretty broad. He came in while I was talking to De Villier; he didn't say anything. Just shot and ran out –!" He wiped his face.

"You gave him two minutes' start," Carver said gravely. He looked up sidewise at the crippled attorney. "This building has three exists and a subway station in the cellar. He could have used any of them in sixty seconds."

Sutorius breathed heavily, looking down at the wounded man. He shuddered again. "It was horrible, Carver. That fellow came in just after Frenchy got here. He closed the door to the hall and fired twice without speaking at all, before I could get out of my chair. Then he went out and locked it after him. It didn't seem to take a moment. I phoned for help first, of course. Then I heard you knocking –"

The fat, bald man stood in the doorway, with other faces crowded over him. He was staring at De Villier, and there wasn't much colour in his pudgy cheeks. He said to someone behind him: "I got the office just across the hall. Yeah, I heard the shots but I thought maybe they were backfires. I asked that man —" Carver pushed him out tiredly with one hand on his fat stomach and closed the door. His light eyes were cold, expressionless, and not sorry. He said: "Don't throw a convulsion, Sutorius. Frenchy got it the way he gave it — in the back. It was way past due.".

The lawyer got up, groaning as his weight went on to his withered leg. "It's horrible," he repeated faintly. "It means my practice will be ruined. Shot down in my office —"

Carver said: "Think of that the next time before you play with crook trade!"

In the street under him a siren screamed, and as it died an ambulance bell jangled tinnily on the avenue. A minute later the room was filled with people; two stretcher bearers, an interne in white, two blue coated patrolmen and a detective in plain-clothes who looked surprised and said: "Hello, Joe," when he saw Carver there.

Carver nodded to him, pushed out through the crowd at the door and went downstairs to the lobby. He bought some cigarettes at the stand there, then went up again slowly, using the stairs, after the stretcher was brought down. The plain-clothesman was questioning Sutorius in the office.

The lawyer's voice was calmer now, but his narrow mouth was still white and nervous. He made aimless little gestures as he spoke, wiped his cheeks twice with a linen handkerchief.

When he had finished Carver said: "I saw this bird in the camel's hair coat go downstairs, Barnes. Only I didn't know what was wrong until I got in the room here. If Sutorius had hollered through the door when I knocked first I could have got him."

Sutorius wiped his lips again. "But, Carver, in a position like that you don't do logical things. My first thought, of course, was to phone the police. I was doing that when you came."

Carver grunted and got up. He took the elevator down with Barnes and got in the police car with him. After two blocks he said: "I don't like coincidences. I don't like Sutorius. The whole thing smells, Barnes. Sutorius called me an hour ago and said he wanted to see me about something very important. When I get up here I'm just in time to see this bird leave. Sutorius doesn't holler to me what's wrong; he just lets out a few squeals and runs back. When I find out what it is, camel's hair has two minutes' start. Too late to catch him."

Barnes shrugged. "Open and shut to me, Joe."

"Too much," Carver growled. "That's the point. Me, I have to back up that shyster's story. It looks like a plant, and I don't like plants. Not even when they smell nice. This one doesn't."

He stared plaintively out at Park Avenue traffic, worrying at his lips.

Al Tammany, his partner Sutorius, Carver and a broad-shouldered young man, whom Carver didn't know, were in the hospital reception room waiting for news of the wounded man.

Al Tammany stopped being genial when the door behind him opened. His head turned quickly on its beefy neck, and his heavy jowls, his small merry eyes, took on concern in the instant that he waited. Watching him, Carver thought that his eyes were like a pig's – a happy, plump pig that was trying unsuccessfully to look sad.

He asked: "What's the news, doctor?"

The doctor was a lean-jawed, very clean man in surgical white. He closed the door behind him and made twin black arches with his brows across a narrow, grave face. "Unfortunate," he said, spreading his hands. "De Villier died on the operating table. I don't see how he lasted an hour with his right lung blown apart."

Abel J. Sutorius let out a long breath without much sound to it. Tammany said: "Poor Frenchy," and shook his head dolefully. The young man in the corner whom Carver didn't know looked briefly at the doctor with steady and cold black eyes. His hair was dark, brushed back like a cap of smooth enamel, and he was dressed quietly and very well in grey tweeds. His face, too, was dark and oval, handsome, but the eyes and the strong chin took away weakness from it. Carver eyed him narrowly. Pretty enough, this lad, but not just that. Hard, too. Who the hell was he?

The doctor said: "Sorry, gentlemen," and went out. A strong reek of antiseptic swept in around them from the whitewashed hospital corridor as he left. Carver wrinkled his nose against it, got up, and smoothed out his overcoat with the palm of one hand.

Sutorius sighed, hobbled forward to the desk, took his hat. The dark young man rose after him and crossed to the door, closed it quietly, without turning.

Carver stared after him. "Who's the Valentino, Abel?"

"Jack Miller?" The cripple looked surprised. "I thought you knew him. Everybody does. He was Frenchy's collection man in the racket before repeal."

Carver prodded a front tooth thoughtfully. "What's he in now?"

"A fine thing to ask me," Sutorius cackled. "How would I know? He's quite a dancer; Frenchy told me once he intended to quit the game and work at that. I think he was at Harry Caddis's place for a while, doing tangoes."

"Let's go," Tammany growled. His little eyes seemed uneasy, moving away from Carver's. "I got that brief to prepare yet, Al."

Carver frowned at them faintly and followed them out. His coolness seemed to annoy Tammany; his red face swung back once across his shoulder, but he did not say anything.

They went along the hall and through the glass doors at the end that led to the street. It was very cold outside; a late afternoon snow fell softly, and sounds from the avenue beyond came through it muted and dull. Sutorius limped down the steps first and got into the only taxi in line. Tammany crouched and entered after him, and as the door swung shut Carver grabbed the knob and drew it out again.

"You don't mind dropping me uptown?" he said.

Tammany grunted, settling back. Little Sutorius pulled in his wizened cheeks, smiled. "Honoured," he said. He turned abruptly to his partner. "We can drop you at the office first, Al."

Carver lit a cigarette without offering them around.

Smoke from it spiralled up slowly in the dim interior, and clung in small thick swirls to the icy windows. When they were stopped by a traffic light on Broadway, Tammany roused himself and looked at Carver.

"Now, don't get me wrong on this," he growled. "Whatever you police had against Frenchy he was a good client of ours and I liked him. I hate like hell to see some yellow rat plug him and get off scot free. You have any line on his killer?"

"Sure," Carver said. "We got a perfect description from Abel J. He had a camel's hair coat and a dark hat. We figure to pick him up any minute on that. Maybe he'll turn out to have two eyes and a nose too."

Tammany said ha, ha, very loudly, disgustedly. "That's funny as hell, Carver." He didn't speak again until the cab swung up on the Grand Central ramp, crossed it, turned into a side street and stopped. Then he barked: "See you later, Abel," and slammed the door after him.

The cab started again. Sutorius leaned forward and lit a slim brown panatella. He murmured, blowing out smoke: "I might like you if you weren't so clever, Carver. But really you annoy people – people who might be able to help you." His large, greenish eyes slid to Carver, with a bright glitter of something undefined far down in their depths. The something seemed to amuse him hugely. "And that, of course, makes them decide not to. You're left out in the cold when you might be warming yourself at a nice log fire. I may say –"

Carver shrugged. "I get along."

Sutorius nodded gravely. "You do," he said. He looked through the window and puffed on his panatella; he didn't speak again. When the cab turned off Park and rolled the short block to Lexington, Carver stepped on his cigarette and got out.

With the door half closed behind him he stopped it with his hand, put his head back in. "That something important, Sutorius, you wanted to see me about this morning. It still on your mind?"

Sutorius stroked his narrow chin with yellow fingers, smiled above them. "You get along," he said.

Carver shrugged again and closed the door. He had taken three steps across the pavement when it opened and Sutorius peered out. He said: "Merely in the interests of justice, Carver. Jack Miller, the man you saw at the hospital, has a bungalow on Gibson's Island, in the Sound. I went up there with Frenchy three days ago, after I freed him on those income tax charges." He smirked, preened himself. "Which was really a nice piece of work, if I may say so."

"Not bad," Carver said. "How many jurymen have you fixed?"

"Tut, tut." Sutorius waved his hand easily. He leaned forward and clasped skinny fingers around one wrist, smiled up at Carver with dry, very bright eyes. "I proved to the satisfaction of a court of law that my client had made no money in the past five years."

Carver said: "Abel J. Sutorius, of the Legal Aid Society. Big hearted Abe. What'd he pay you with? Empty bottles?"

"That," Sutorius pronounced, smiling, "is beside the point. You asked me what Miller was doing. I wondered myself, when I found him on that island in midwinter. There's nobody else there from October until May. He had a charming girl with him – I caught a glimpse of her in the bedroom. She looked uncommonly like Mary Flood Harrington." The lean smile darted up once more at Carver; then Sutorius bowed, waved, closed the door. The cab rolled away. Carver stared after it until snow got on his brows and began to melt down over his cheeks.

He got a paper on the way to a restaurant, read it as he was finishing his coffee. De Villier's picture was on the front page under headlines that screamed blackly across its breadth, but Carver didn't pay much attention to that. There was a photo on an inner page, with a thinner black caption under it – a photo of a very beautiful young girl with large eyes, apparently a blonde. The leader under it was: *Harrington Girl Feared Kidnapped; Father Still Silent.* Then, in smaller letters: *Parent Refuses to interview Police; Believed Fearing for Girl's Safety.*

Carver read this through to the end, then stared for some moments, thoughtfully, at the ceiling. Later he paid his bill, walked over to a garage on Third Avenue, and took out his roadster.

His headlights picked out the sign fifty yards ahead. He slowed as he came to it, swinging the nose of his car slightly in. It said: *A. Johnson – Boats for Hire – 75c an Hr.*

At the far end of the long, low building set back from the road a rectangular line of window shone yellow. Carver turned his roadster in on the faint markings of the gravel and parked it before the stoop. It was bitterly cold, though without wind; snow still fell, heavy and soft, and under the flakes he could smell the salt strong freshness of the Sound.

In a room just off the porch a big yellow haired Swede sat at the centre table, reading a paper. He asked: "Yah?" in a heavy, surprised tone when he saw Carver, took the pipe slowly out of his mouth and lowered his shoes from the table edge.

Carver knocked the snow off his coat before speaking. Then he said: "You know where Gibson's Island is?" A. Johnson nodded, watching him with great, candid blue eyes. Carver took a five-dollar bill from his wallet and tossed it to him. "They told me at the Point that the ferry doesn't run there after October. One of the men said you could take me over. The five's yours if you do."

A. Johnson got up, his face puzzled. He said earnestly, and his voice was almost a roar: "But t'ere iss nobody t'ere now, in vinter. You know t'at? T'e island iss what t'ey call a summer resort. In vinter t'ere iss –"

"Nobody there," Carver said. "I got good ears, Axel."

A. Johnson smiled. "It iss Adolph," he said. "'T'ere iss no axles in a boathouse, yah?" He rumbled laughter. "But I tak' you if you wantta go."

Carver grinned sourly, crossed with him to a door in the rear. There was a long damp shed off this, that smelled heavily of wet wood, with tiers of rowboats lined on either side, and the varnished sides of canoes glinting in the light. From somewhere below came the faint slap-slap of water.

At the end the shed lay open to the Sound, and they walked from it to a narrow descending gangplank that ran to a floating dock. Carver stepped into a long hooded black motorboat at the side, while A. Johnson busied himself with ropes.

Presently the motor purred and they slid away from the dock; behind them on the black bosom of the water a wake of foam whiter than the snow stretched out from the stern in a fantastic V. Soon the lights on shore vanished under the soft, endless flakes; they sliced ahead faster, and spray stung Carver's cheek. He shivered closer into his coat, dug his hands deep into his pockets.

The Swede spun the wheel, and they veered. Carver could see nothing but the whiteness of snow, the blackness of water. The breeze here came fresher, icier, and they rolled slightly in long, gentle swells. After ten minutes something dark and shapeless loomed up on their right, and the Swede slowed, circled in with a soft grunt. In a moment the white bones of a pier jutted out before them, and, barely moving, they slid up to it.

After the boat was fast Carver got out and stamped his feet on the planks. He could see a vague shoulder of land beyond, with the faded green and yellow of summer bungalows bulking up on it like a stage scene backdropped to the snow.

"Yah," A. Johnson said, nodding his head. "Like I told you, mister. Vinter, t'en t'e people all go."

Carver grunted. "How big is it around?"

A. Johnson thought, stroking his chin. He said at last: "It might be two miles. T'ere is a road round from t'e pier. It goes past all t'e bungalows."

"I might be an hour," Carver answered. "Take it easy."

The Swede's face grew pleading, anxious. His heavy voice chased Carver down the planks. "That Sue faller, mister – Ed Vine – he talks on t'e radio tonight. Ay want to hear him. You coom back by t'en, eh?" He stared up from the boat like a huge child.

Carver growled: "Wait, squarehead," and went down the pier.

At its end he struck off to the left along the faint depression of a path. Bungalows were lined closely here along the water's edge, but he could see no lights, hear no sounds. He came to a blank space which in summer might have been the beach; the ground before him was even, white, unmarked, and on the farther side tree branches were laced blackly against the low solidity of the sky.

He plunged across this, shoes crunching through the hard surface of the snow. Past the trees on the far side he came out to another clump of houses, with the black sheet of the Sound below them, on the left. He had passed the first of these when he heard gun shots a distance ahead: three, perhaps four, the reports hammering over each other so fast that they were almost simultaneous.

Carver began to run. His shoe soles struck against the polished white sheen of ice and he lunged forwards through the air, burying his shoulder in dry, cold particles of snow. Some of it sifted through his pocket flap to fingers numbed on the steel butt of his automatic. He cursed and got up, went forward more cautiously.

A second clump of bungalows swam up around him. But their windows were dark, and he could hear nothing. He passed the dirty, unlit window of a store and stopped suddenly on the ridge of a plank path. Sound came from somewhere, faint, fast, harmonized.

There was a small grey building on his left, isolated from the others. Its windows were dark as the rest. Carver crossed to it carefully and saw the reason. Steel shutters were locked over the panes, a dark shade pulled down across the glass panel of the front door. But the rhythm was plainer now: a saxophone's soft complaint, the muted syncopation of cornets. He put his hand on the knob and pushed, found it smoothly turning, silent, and unlocked.

The room inside was warm, brightly lit, but there was nobody in it. From the console cabinet of a radio in the far corner dance music swirled out drowsily. There were many floor lamps around, and a gas flame glowed in the brick fireplace. It was very well furnished. Cigarette smoke was thin in the air.

Carver closed the door softly and remained a moment careful and rigid against it. The room ran from side to side of the bungalow; there were two doors at the back, ten feet apart. Both of these were closed.

He took the automatic out of his pocket and walked across

a deep rug on the balls of his feet, choosing first the door on the left. It opened to darkness and a stale smell of fried steak; before him the metal hood of an electric range glittered whitely. He closed it, crossed to the other, listened with his ear against the wood, heard nothing and jerked it out with a twist of his hand.

On a big bed in the centre of the room a pyjamaed girl was sprawled face-down. She didn't seem to hear the sound of the door; she was making a funny noise deep in her throat, and there was blood on the cloth twined roughly around her right arm. Carver walked lightfooted to the side of the bed and looked at her with uncertain eyes. He was bending down when a voice behind him said: "Don't move, Carver."

Carver let his body drop across the girl, seeing in the bureau mirror the man who stood in the doorway. In the narrow space at the footboard Carver turned, waving his automatic through the bars.

"Check!" he said.

The man was Jack Miller, whom Carver had seen in the hospital reception room. Miller made a tired movement with his shoulders as he came fully into the room. There was a roll of cotton draped over his left arm and a white basin in his right hand. His eyes were cold and luminous against the olive face.

He said: "You shouldn't have done that, Carver. Been stupid if I'd had a gun."

"Sure," Carver said. "Only I could see you in the bureau mirror. I don't scare yet at basins."

Miller lowered his head slightly and looked at the mirror, at Carver. He shrugged again.

"Sit down," Carver said. From the bed the girl stared at him wide eyed. He kept watching Miller and backed around to her, bent one leg and squatted down. "How's the wound? Bad?"

She said it wasn't. Her voice, underneath a surface steadiness, struggled for balance. It ran up in little ripples of shrill sound that bordered on hysteria. "But you mustn't think that – that he shot me." Her gaze flicked to Miller, away. "It came from outside, through the window. We –"

Even before the report it seemed to Carver that something like the blow of an iron bar smashed against his shoulder, numbing it, knocking him to the floor. The girl screamed, and Miller flung himself to the light switch on the wall. Then Carver whirled, sprawling his body out flat as darkness snapped over the room, while from the window in back orange spurts of flame stabbed viciously through a deafening ricochet of sound that bounced against his eardrums like the beat of hollow metal hammers.

Carver fired rapidly, wildly, as his body rolled over and over out of direct range. Crouched by the bureau and protected by it, a narrow streak of grey showed him the unshuttered half of the window. It was empty now; silent. He did not fire again.

After a minute Miller said: "I guess he's gone. That's what happened just before you came. The shutter hinges must have been sliced through so he could pull it loose."

There wasn't much strength in Carver's arm. He believed a shoulder bone had been touched. The numbness was wearing off and his whole arm was beginning to ache. When he spoke it was an effort to keep his voice steady. "Don't put on the light. Any way out here, from the back?"

"Through the kitchen," Miller answered. The door behind him, pushed in, revealed the fainter darkness of the passage.

Carver said: "The girl better get out of this room," and waited until he heard the creaking of the bed springs. In the blackness he crawled after the dim coloured splotch of her pyjamas through the small lobby that connected, through another door, with the kitchen and bath.

Sheltered in this, he got up and felt his shoulder with the fingers of his left hand. It was still throbbing, but he could detect no blood. As he moved something wobbled under it – the thick leather holster he carried at his armpit. He prodded a forefinger through the hole in the side where the bullet had been deflected, grunted. The damned thing felt like it had smashed his shoulder. He asked Miller: "Where's the door?"

Huddled behind the stove, the girl watched them as they

went out. He kept Miller before him as they rounded the house, and still ahead as they followed footprints on the snow a hundred yards in the woods. The prints were wide apart and deep, as if the man was running. Carver stopped, heard nothing, and turned back.

The girl was waiting in the kitchen for them when they got back to the house. They went in together and Carver said: "You can put on the lights. What's the story, Miller?"

"I told you," the other man said. His black eyes were grim, worried; he was watching the girl. "Five minutes before you came someone fired through the living-room window. They shot Mary – the girl – in the arm. I ran outside but I couldn't see anyone. I was too excited to notice if the shutters in the bedroom were safe. Then I went in again and started to fix her arm, and when I came out of the bathroom you were there."

Carver said: "Where does Sutorius fit in?"

Miller's face got careful, vacant. "I didn't think he did."

Carver turned to the girl. "You're Mary Flood Harrington?"

She didn't answer him. She looked at Miller, terror in her face and something else that Carver couldn't fathom. After a while she said: "Yes," with difficulty. Carver closed the outer door and followed them through to the living-room. There he looked at her wound and tightened the rough bandages that Miller had put on.

"That'll do till we get you to a doctor. Now get dressed, in the bathroom. We'll wait here."

She was gone five minutes. Jack Miller sat in a chair and put his elbows on his knees, his face between his hands. Once he looked up at Carver and started to speak. He was haggard now and not so handsome with the black gloss of his hair rumpled and the narrow mouth set deeply. He was very nervous; he kept rubbing the side of his cheek with one hand, pulling his lips in and out with the other.

"Give me a break on this, copper. I –"

"It's late," Carver said. "I'm cold. Speak your piece at the house."

Miller's mouth widened and turned down. He said very emphatically: "To hell with you." He lit a cigarette.

Music still droned from the radio in the far corner and Carver hummed the words until the girl came out again. As Miller took a coat from the closet Carver fixed cold eyes on it.

"Camel's hair," he said, pointing the gun. "That makes it bad. Frenchy De Villier's killer was dressed in one. You wouldn't have a revolver in one of the pockets?"

Miller shrugged, held up his arms to be searched. After a moment Carver stepped away from him and grunted: "All right. We're getting out of here. You first, Miller."

He followed them through the front door and turned off the light switch as he passed. Out on the path he put the automatic in his pocket, and kept his hand on the butt. Three paces behind Miller, he hummed a little going along; none of them spoke.

But when they came to the white ridge of the pier Carver cursed. The Swede was gone; the boat was gone. He looked out at the narrow stretch of Sound visible and let his lips droop ferociously. "Where in the hell –"

It was nine-thirty by his watch. When he saw that he whistled a long note, nodding his head. Ed Wynn, of course; he came on at nine-thirty and stayed until ten. And the lousy squarehead wanted to –

"Let's get back," he said irritably, without explaining. "My ferry won't come back until after ten. It's too cold to wait here."

They returned along the path, following their own tracks. Snow got inside Carver's shoes and began to melt coldly on his socks. He thought a good deal about Adolph Johnson, not nice thoughts.

As they turned off the path up from Miller's bungalow the girl stopped suddenly. Following her gaze, Carver saw a yellow streak of light staring out from the sagged shutter of the bedroom.

Miller turned, faced Carver. "The pop-pop boy," he said. "He probably saw us go."

Carver nodded, his lips thin. They crossed the porch, the girl behind them, and Carver tried the front door, opened it softly. He saw Abel J. Sutorius standing in the centre of the room, his bad leg favoured slightly, his long fingers caressing the sharp small angle of his chin. He was smiling, and at Carver's approach he didn't lose the smile.

"Ah," he said, eyes darting to Miller. "Delightful, really, to see you here. I wasn't sure whether my hint –"

Carver didn't return the smile. He pulled the lawyer around to him and ran his fingers over the man's slight form, down to the steel brace that held up his withered right leg.

Sutorius raised his brows. He murmured: "Forgive me if I don't quite understand. You seem –"

Carver moved his eyes up at him. "I don't get it," he said, "and I don't like things I don't get, weasel. You gave me a tip this afternoon that the Harrington girl was here. Well, she was. Only I can't figure why you spilled it. It didn't mean money in your pocket."

The lawyer's thin smile, the mild gesture of his hand, were bland, self deprecating. "Perhaps it is too simple for your – shall we say unduly suspicious? – mind. I am, after all, a man of warm emotions, Carver; I am quite capable of doing the little in my power to assist a grieving parent. This morning I phoned you, intending to tell what I knew, but unfortunately before you came De Villier –" He looked sad, spreading his hands.

Carver said nothing. He swung the automatic slightly on his index finger, pinching his nose, watching Sutorius with narrowed, puzzled eyes.

Sutorius began again: "And I can assure you –"

Carver growled: "Don't bother. I wouldn't believe you anyway. Someone slammed off at me with a .45 a half hour ago. He came damn' near blowing me apart. I think you are kind of lucky you aren't carrying a gun."

"Violence!" Sutorius protested, in a very loud voice. He moved closer to the window as he spoke, looking horrified. "My poor young friend, your delusions run away with you if you seriously imagine that I would have anything to do with that." He stopped, gave an exclamation of pitying wonder, then added: "There is a limit, I remind you, to what a respectable professional man will endure at your hands."

His voice was rising higher, though his eyes were

without anger; for an instant Carver was puzzled by that.

He went on: "There is a question, also, of your method of handling this case. When you keep this poor young girl away from her parent instead of restoring her to him as soon as humanly possible –" His shrug was nasty, a shade too elaborate, too careless; under cover of it his eyes darted to the clock.

Carver read it then. He cut in, sharp toned: "Get back from the window. Keep quiet. Sit in that chair facing the door and don't move until I tell you you can."

Sutorius's face got dark. He began: "I don't intend to –" Something in Carver's stare stopped his words; he wet his lips with his tongue, sat down.

Carver kept watching him. He told Miller: "You and the girl get back here, by me. Where anyone that comes in won't see you."

They stood by the wall, to the left of the door. The pleasant sheen was gone from the cripple's face. It was naked and savage, the lips twisting silently. He started once to rise, then changed his mind, sat back. His hands were gripped very hard on the arms of the chair.

Three minutes went by – quietly, save for the quick, high breathing of the girl. At her side Carver began to worry at his lips. Sutorius expected someone, of course – someone he wanted to warn. Thus the loud voice, the stand near the window, where he had a better chance of being heard outside, the glance at the clock. If that someone had already heard . . .

Even as he thought it a sliding, crisp sound came from outside, materialized into the brisk patter of steps on the porch. The door came back fast and hit Carver's shoulder; a big man shot past its end.

"Abel," he said, panting. "I got lost in those damned woods. I was afraid to follow them too close and I missed the path. But the boat was gone when I got to the pier. So they must have –"

The cripple's frozen face stopped him. He stuttered: "What – what –" and turned his head. Carver saw the beefy red face of Al Tammany glaring at him.

He waved his automatic gently. "Don't let me stop you," he said.

Tammany swore, whirled about at Miller and the girl. He looked back to Sutorius and heavy bluster came into his voice and his eyes.

"What the hell's the matter with you? Point your gun at that thug and not at me. By God, Carver, you've acted the wise boy long enough. I'll have your badge off you by morning. I'll –"

Some of the redness went out of his cheeks when Carver stepped up to him, and he went a pace backwards, against the wall, wriggled there as if only that stopped him from retreating further. Carver prodded the automatic into his belly and smiled; it wasn't a nice smile. When he took a .45 out of Tammany's coat pocket the smile died on his lips and left them narrow and white.

Tammany put his hands before him and pushed at the air. He said: "Don't – don't look that way, man. I –"

Carver lifted the gun and smelled it, watching him from under his brows. His lower jaw came out a little and he brought his own automatic up to Tammany's chin, breaking the flesh. The fat man wiped dazedly at the blood.

Carver said in a soft voice without moving his lips much: "You fired through the window at me a half hour ago. I want to know why, Tammany. Now."

Tammany didn't seem to feel the pain. His eyes, veering to Miller, were bewildered. "I thought it was –"

Sutorius snarled, came halfway out of his chair. Carver put one hand against his chest and flung him back.

"There's a part of it missing," he said. "You told me today that the girl was here, Sutorius. You knew it for three days but didn't spill until De Villier was dead. Then you tell me. Why? So I'd come up and get her and Miller, take them away. Then you decide maybe Miller knows too much about this missing piece; you figure it will be better to have him shut up too. He might spoil your act. So Tammany tries twice to get him but he has lousy eyes. The first time he wings the girl, the second time he mistakes me for Miller. You couldn't do the shooting yourself; with your game leg you couldn't get away fast enough."

Sutorius's eyes glittered like green glass. He snarled: "You're insane. This girl was kidnapped – there's her abductor. He was holding her here for ransom. And instead of taking them in you stand here questioning my partner and myself. I –"

"I'll take them in," Carver said. "I'll do it right now if you tell me what you came here for. That's the part that's missing. What the hell are you here for?"

Sutorius smiled viciously. He said: "Maybe the country air. This island isn't private. As a matter of fact, I came to see if it really was the Harrington girl, I thought perhaps you hadn't taken me seriously and I wanted to do what I could to help if it really was she."

Carver didn't seem to hear him. His brows were wrinkled in a thoughtful, cold frown.

"You wanted the place left empty, Sutorius; that's it," he said, "and the first gag you thought up was for me to take Miller and the girl away. I guess you were afraid to tackle him alone. Then you decided to kill him, but Tammany spoiled that. He even messed things up when you sent him after us to make sure we left the island. When he saw us go off he was supposed to come back here and tell you. Then you'd hunt for the thing that's here – the thing you wanted so much you'd kill for it."

Tammany's glance, in panic, moved from Sutorius to Carver, to his partner again.

"Wait a minute. You're not getting it straight. Abel and I naturally wanted to free the girl, but we were afraid to speak while Frenchy was alive. I thought he was in on the snatch with Miller. Then –"

"Shut up," Carver said. He used the gun again on Tammany's chin, lightly but effectively. "So now I want to know what that thing was, Sutorius. You're going to tell me."

"You don't need me," the cripple sneered. "You're smart. You're Joe Carver."

Miller came out from the wall, frowning.

"The whole thing's a joke, Carver. There's nothing here. I used it because –" He glanced at the girl; very pale, she was watching him, her hands clasped together. He repeated: "There's nothing here. We had no visitors until tonight. De Villier came three days ago, but he only stayed an hour. He left me –" He stopped suddenly.

Sutorius looked up at him with nothing human in his eyes.

Carver asked: "What'd he leave?"

"Two bags." Miller's voice was slow, queer. He was turning slowly, facing Sutorius, his dark face like stone. "I didn't look in them; I don't know what's inside. They're in the closet. I'll get them now."

"Uh-huh," Carver said. "Miss Harrington gets them. You stay here."

Miller stopped, shrugged. The girl went across to the bedroom and vanished inside. When she came out she had a small travelling bag in each hand. Sutorius's breathing was heavy.

"All right," Carver said. "I guess we'll start. You first, Sutorius. Tammany carries the bags."

The cripple ran a hand over his withered leg, winced. "I presume I may adjust my brace," he said nastily. Under Carver's eyes he bent and gripped his pants leg.

Tammany's lips wobbled with a queer sound; there was perspiration on his forehead but he didn't seem to mind it. He kept watching Carver and there was terror in his face. Carver was amused. He said: "Take a good look at the bogey man, Al. When they open the bags at Headquarters I'll have you and Abel J. –"

The girl saw it first. She screamed. Whirling, Carver had no more warning than the split second glitter of steel as Sutorius's hand swept out from the brace.

Then he felt a shock, a hot flash streak across his left side like the burn of a steel rod at white heat. A moment later he opened his eyes. He was lying on the floor, but he hadn't remembered falling. His left side was powerless, and gunpowder smelled acrid in the room. Tammany, with his frightened face, was bending for the automatic Carver had taken from him and Carver's own gun, and Sutorius was by the wall, speaking to the others in a queer whine that didn't make words for Carver.

The room blurred in, ran together in Carver's mind like a dissolve shot in a film. It was very hard for him to think. He came unsteadily to his feet under Sutorius's gun, but his mind was queerly hazy.

He knew that when they left the house they turned left, away from the pier where the Swede would be waiting; he tried to tell Miller that but his voice only made mumbling noises. Later he fell – it seemed a long, long way – and his face touched snow; then he was walking again, and Miller's arm was holding him up.

It had stopped snowing, and the air was thin, cold, biting. Between grey clouds there were stars, small and bright. Presently his head grew clearer, though he felt very weak, and the pain from his side seemed unendurable. They were walking through woods that thinned gradually to an open space of beach, and on the left the Sound lay huge, black and silent.

They crossed the beach, and Miller helped Carver up to a thin row of boards that led out across the water. The girl went first, they followed, and behind them came the sounds of Tammany's heavy tread, the uneven clip clop of the cripple, Sutorius. Then they stood huddled by one side, the girl and he, with Sutorius and Miller before them, and Tammany jumping down, crouched, from the dock's edge.

By the tip of the pier a big launch was moored, with a glassed cabin running forward. But Tammany had not gone to this; he had dropped down further back, and there came to Carver heavy sounds like the beating of a mallet on wood. Later Tammany crawled back to the planks, his eyes veering swiftly to Carver and the girl.

"Hell, Abel!" he said. "You can't do it. Not to the girl."

Sutorius cursed him, waved the gun. He said: "Be very careful, Miller. You're getting a chance. When I tell you, cut the rope."

Miller nodded. Sutorius watched him narrowly, holding the automatic. "The girl first," he said. Miller lowered her to the boat, and then he and Tammany helped Carver forwards, lifted him in after her.

They were in a small rowboat, layered by dirty snow. But as Carver looked down the snow turned colourless, and specks of it floated around. The launch motor purred and they slid out from the dock, a rope from their bow stretched taut to the rail of the big craft.

The girl was holding Carver's arm, peering into his face. She breathed: "What are you going to do? They're not —"

Carver didn't answer her. He tried to drag himself forwards to the rope that connected with the launch. As he crawled water swept coldly about his ankles, filled the bottom of their boat almost to the seats. The nose of it wobbled unsteadily from side to side.

When he got to the rope there was no strength in his left arm, not enough in his right.

He tried twice to pull them up to the launch hand over hand, but his fingers slipped and his head jerked down against the gunwale. He lay there, panting. Behind them the dark spread of water grew wider, the shore line sank lower and lower into the grey sky. For a moment Sutorius smiled down at him from the launch, then turned and hobbled away.

Carver pulled again at the rope. It was like iron. Their boat was very deep in the water now; the tip of a wave slapped in over the wobbling side. Jack Miller came to the rail and bent from it, something that glittered extended in his hand. Carver's mouth twitched a little; he watched him, panting.

But Miller didn't use the knife. His body heaved once and their craft slid up to the launch. Then he bent and his arms went over Carver to the girl; her weight bore Carver down as she crept forwards, and under the pressure water swirled up coldly to his armpits. He was struggling weakly, trying to grip the rail, when Miller caught him by the collar, drew him up and over, into the launch as easily as a child.

On a raised space before the cabin Tammany stood at the wheel, his back to them. Beside him Sutorius talked, pointing one hand forward. Tammany nodded and Sutorius stepped down to the deck, started to turn. He called: "All right, Miller. We're out far enough. Now you —"

He stopped very quietly, in the middle of a stride, staring at the girl; he didn't seem to see Carver behind Miller. In the faint light his narrow white face became wax. He said to

Miller: "You fool," without much viciousness, without any force. "There's more than enough for you – for me, for Tammany. You can't hope to save her for ransom again. She knows too much. She dies with Carver."

Miller's body bent slightly, faced Sutorius, balanced and light on spread feet. He said softly – a kind of dreadful softness: "I told you back there it was a joke. It is, Sutorius. I didn't kidnap her. She's my wife."

Sutorius made a long sound with his lips. His face remained motionless and pale in the half light, the green surfaces of his eyes steady and depthless, but after the pause his arm rippled in to his body smooth and effortless and fast. Yet Miller's movement was faster; he stepped in and his lean shoulders pivoted once, hard.

Carver heard the blow. Sutorius groaned, not loud. He fired once but he fired at the deck, as if he couldn't bring the gun up. Then Miller struck again; the tall slight body staggered back, balanced across the rail. It wobbled a little there, and after an instant, very gently, almost silently, slid out to the black water. Miller didn't try to catch him.

Tammany, at the wheel, made frightened sounds, words to which no one paid attention. Miller had picked up Sutorius's gun and covered the fat man.

Miller took over the wheel, throttled down to little more than drifting and told the others to get under shelter and fix up Carver.

In the cabin, after Carver's side had been bound up, Tammany talked freely enough. He was crying, his fat face distorted, like a baby's; he kept pulling at Carver's arm with pleading fingers.

"Sutorius got me into it," he said. "I didn't know he was going to kill De Villier until I got out in the hall and heard the shots; then I was in so deep that I couldn't back out. Later he said you'd seen me on the stairs, and that he'd tell you who it was if I didn't do what he said."

Carver nodded, tired. "I was a plant. I figured that. But how did he time things so nice?"

"He was a clever devil," Tammany shuddered. "He phoned you at the precinct just before De Villier came;

then he told me to watch from the window, that you'd come straight across Fiftieth Street. When I saw you coming I nodded to him, and he told me to go over to the court house for some papers. I still didn't know what he meant to do – De Villier had just got there and they were talking about the tax case.

"Then, when I got halfway down the hall I heard the shots – I knew then what they meant, why he asked me to lock the door as I left. I didn't dare go back, but I should have. I just walked downstairs and out of the building on the Forty-ninth Street side. When he told me that you'd seen me leaving, and that you'd probably recognize my coat if he told you who it was, I was afraid to say anything; I had to do everything he wanted. God knows I didn't want to shoot Miller or the girl or you; but that devil –" He shuddered again.

Carver grunted. "He pulled it smart. With the door locked and the key gone, no one would figure he'd shot De Villier – it didn't occur to me that he might have had someone lock it for him. That was the angle of the story that didn't fit. He kept the gun in his brace, of course, like he did here; nobody would look there and he had a perfect story."

There was a bottle of Scotch on the table and Carver took a long drink. Then his glance moved down to the two travelling bags at his feet, packed with neat stacks of currency row on row. "How'd he know De Villier had all this money?"

"We defended Frenchy on those income tax charges," Tammany answered. "He'd been our client for years, and Sutorius had been warning him not to keep books or bank his earnings. He said the government would get after the boys on tax charges sooner or later. That was the reason he gave why Frenchy should keep all his earnings in cash, on him; maybe he had this plan in his mind all the time.

"After the case fell through – since nobody could prove where Frenchy's assets were – he told De Villier that the Federal men were watching him, and that he'd better put the cash some place where they wouldn't search. He went with Frenchy while he took the bags to Miller's place. Then things started."

The girl nodded. "They came up to us three days ago. I didn't want anyone to see me, so I kept in the bedroom, but he must have had a glimpse of me some way. But Jack closed the door quick and I suppose with all the paper talk he thought that I'd been kidnapped."

"Who didn't?" Carver growled. "Your father know you're married?"

"Yes." Her chin came up; her eyes flamed. "I met Jack three months ago when he was dancing at Harry Caddis's club. I think I fell in love with him the first moment. Last week we got married. I knew father would raise an awful row so I didn't tell him until it was done. Then father told me I'd disgraced the family, things like that. I told him that he needn't worry, that nobody would ever know we were married. It was foolish, of course, but he made me terribly angry. So I didn't tell any of my friends, and Jack kept it quiet, too. We came up here where we could be alone, where there'd be no one to bother us."

Carver grinned up at her. "You should be spanked," he said. "Happy?"

"Terribly," she smiled. "Jack never had a chance – I'm going to see that he gets one now. Oh, he isn't bad, Mr Carver; it was only that money was so easy to make in bootlegging, and so hard to get other ways. But he had broken with Frenchy even before I met him; he didn't want to take the bags from him that day he came up to the bungalow until Frenchy almost begged him. He said he was in terrible trouble."

Carver sighed. "You gave me enough of that when your father wouldn't say where you'd gone or deny what some smart reporter doped out that you'd been kidnapped and that he was negotiating privately with the ransom gang. We were all suckers enough to believe it, even Sutorius."

He took another drink of the Scotch and went on: "It was lucky for us that he did. He thought things out smart all through but he slipped on that and he was afraid to put Miller in the boat with us because he had only one gun, and he figured if the two of us rushed him and Tammany one of us might get to him. He didn't, of course, have to be afraid of Miller squealing, since he figured Jack would have to keep quiet to save his own hide. The plan was to cut the rope when we were out far enough, and let us sink. If our bodies were ever found it would look like we'd swamped escaping from the kidnappers. That would let him out clear."

Mary Miller got up, smiling at him. "Jack wanted to tell you about us back there, but I think he decided to wait – and then things happened. When they put us in the boat I was a little afraid, but I knew Jack would help us the first chance he got. Then when the water got so high –" She shivered slightly.

"It got higher for Sutorius," Carver said. He pulled a minute, reflectively, on his long nose. "Things work out funny. A big dumb Swede he never heard of wanted to listen to Ed Wynn. That was the only thing he didn't figure."

Mary Miller smiled. She held out her finger and Carver saw the wedding ring.

"That too," he said, grinning back at her.

Dog Life

Mark Timlin

There wasn't anything they could do for Billy Dukes when they found him. There hadn't been anything anyone could do for him for quite a while. Two boys found him. Brothers. One twelve, the other ten. The pair had been trawling for anything they could find on the filthy beach left by the receding tide round the Isle of Dogs in east London. Once upon a time the boys would have been called mudlarks. Urchins. And they would've had the backsides hanging out of their trousers. But these two were dressed in the height of fashion for the time, the second year of the new millennium. They didn't often find much when they wet their new trainers in the Thameside mud. Mostly old truck tyres, supermarket trolleys and the occasional used condom, knotted at the top, the gases inside blowing up the rubber like balloons. Billy Dukes had blown up too, his arms and legs sticking straight out from his torso like the Michelin man in those old advertisements. His body had been damaged by the water, bruised black and blue, and green with rot. But it hadn't been just the river that had taken its toll. Someone else had done that before he'd been thrown in the water. Someone had taken a baseball bat to his knees and elbows and head. And then someone had cut his eyes out with a knife leaving two empty sockets staring up at the grey, London sky.

The boys looked at the body for a long time, but they didn't touch it. Not that it would have worried them to do so. They were too young to realize that one day, maybe sooner, maybe later, they too would stare with sightless eyes at some stretch of sky as they joined Billy wherever he had gone.

The eldest boy used his newly acquired mobile to call the police. He felt very grown-up dialling three nines and telling the faceless voice on the other end what he and his brother had found.

The young police constable first on the scene knew all about mortality though, and he disgorged the egg, bacon, sausage, tomato, fried bread and two cups of strong tea he'd eaten in the station canteen a few hours before behind one of the massive wooden breakwaters that stuck out into the river at that point, in the shadow of the Millennium Dome just across the river. As he held onto the rotten wood it peeled off under his fingers just like the flesh of the dead man lying a few yards away, still under the watchful eyes of the two boys, would if touched.

The two detectives who arrived a few minutes later were made of sterner stuff, but they still took on something of the colour of Billy's face after they had shooed the boys and the constable off and stood looking down at the dead body that looked up at them, but could see nothing.

The two plain-clothes coppers called for Scenes of Crime Officers, although they knew that it was unlikely that anything on the beach would throw up any information about the crime as the body would have been subject to the tidal flow of the Thames. SOCO duly arrived as the river started to come in again and the body was swiftly transferred to a coroner's wagon to be taken to the police mortuary in Lambeth as the detectives spoke to the brothers who had now been joined by their mother, also called on the eldest boy's mobile from the flats where the family lived just a short walk away.

Before the body was taken away, SOCO discovered a sodden wallet in the deceased's back pocket which itself contained nothing but a single ten-pound note, a phone card and the remains of a UB40 that the social security department would eventually identify as belonging to Billy Dukes, a fact confirmed when the pathologist expertly removed the skin from his fingertips and checked the prints thus found with the police central computer files on convicted felons.

The funeral was a low-key affair attended only by Billy's

wife, their two sons, his mother and a lone detective. Billy was planted in Greenwich cemetery close by the river where he had been thrown by person or persons unknown, and if Billy's family could have afforded a headstone, it would have looked out over the river to the exact spot he had been found.

No one was ever arrested for the murder of Billy Dukes, and as the days after his discovery turned to weeks and months, the case was consigned to the unsolved file, and eventually almost forgotten by the overworked Metropolitan police.

The Dukes had lived in a tower block on the south side of the river, a single concrete slab that stood tall and gave the finger to the surrounding low-rise buildings in the area. When the man who came looking for Billy's wife found the block he expected the front door to be smashed in, the foyer daubed with graffiti and stinking of urine, and the lifts to be out of order. But, in fact, the local council had taken pity on the residents and restored the flats, so that the door was firmly locked against intruders, a concierge sat at a desk inside in front of a bank of CCTV monitors, the foyer was freshly painted and smelled only faintly of disinfectant and the four lifts ran smoothly. The concierge admitted the man, confirmed that the Dukes lived on the twenty-first floor and allowed him entry to the bank of elevators that transported him up into the sky. The man walked around the corridor with its magnificent view of London, found flat twenty-one-oh-six and rang the bell.

The woman who answered the door was overweight, with greasy, stringy hair and the look of defeat that her visitor had seen in many countries in the world.

"Yes," she said, with the air of one who expected the Jehovah's Witnesses or someone to cut off the electricity.

"Mrs Dukes," said the man politely.

"Who wants her?"

"My name's Vincent. Vincent Graves. I was a friend of your husband's."

"Billy. He didn't have any friends. Only the bookies. And that's because he left most of his dole behind the counter.

And a few publicans. They got the rest behind the jump."

"I haven't seen him for years," said the man. "I only just heard what had happened. I wonder if I might talk to you." He had a gentle voice, and kind eyes, and Veronica Dukes, Ronnie to her friends, found herself, almost against her will, opening the door wider and allowing him inside.

"Come through to the kitchen," she said. "I'm just making a cuppa. Want one?"

The man smiled and nodded and he followed her down the hall.

If he had half expected the place to be a tip, he was surprised again. Pleasantly so. The flat was warm and spotlessly clean. The carpet through to the kitchen a deep red and thick under the soles of his boots. And the kitchen itself sparkled under the fluorescent lights, the tops wiped and everything in its place. A young boy sat at the table reading a comic and he looked up when his mother and her visitor entered.

"Go and watch TV, Jim, there's a good boy," Ronnie Dukes said, and without a murmur the boy concurred and a minute after he left they could hear the sound of Homer Simpson's voice from another room. "Half term," Ronnie explained. "That's Jimmy, my youngest. Little Billy's doing the shopping. They're good boys, thank God. Not like their father."

Vincent Graves stood awkwardly for a moment before sitting unbidden on the seat the boy had vacated as Ronnie Dukes found the makings of tea. When two mugs were prepared she set one in front of him and sat opposite with her own and looked at him. He wasn't tall, just average size and dressed all in black. His monkey boots were cracked and down at heel and toe, but highly polished. His black Levis were worn white at the knees, and under a scuffed leather jacket he wore a black sweatshirt. But, despite the shabbiness of his clothes, he looked neat and contained, as if waiting for inspection. Between his feet lay the black leather bag he had been carrying on his arrival. Ronnie looked closer at his face. He was, she guessed, about the same age as her husband, his tanned skin, lined and worn, his hair the colour of cigarette ash, thin and cropped close to his skull.

He looked tired, but there was something in his eyes that she liked.

"I'm sorry about Billy," he said, taking a pair of glasses from inside his jacket. They were rimless, and one ear piece had been attached with a piece of fuse wire. He saw her notice and pulled a face. "One day I'll have them fixed," he said.

"Why are you here?" she asked.

"Like I told you. I was sorry to hear about Billy."

"I'm glad someone is. He didn't owe you money, did he?"

He shook his head at the question. "No. We were old friends."

"He never mentioned you."

"Did he not?" The man didn't seem surprised.

"No."

"We went to school together."

"You can't have seen much of him then. From what I've heard he was hardly ever there."

"Nor was I."

She laughed mirthlessly and found a packet of cigarettes on one of the kitchen tops, offered the man one which he refused and lit one for herself.

"What exactly happened?" the man asked after a moment.

"God knows," she said. "Billy must've done something out of order. Nothing new there. They cut out his eyes."

She started to cry then and the man put his hand over hers. "I'm sorry," he said. "I didn't mean . . ."

"No. I'm the one that's sorry," she said and wiped her eyes on her sleeve. "It's just that no one's done anything."

"The police."

She laughed again without humour. "What do they care?"

He made no reply.

"He was a grass," she went on. "An informer. That's what they do to grasses round here. To warn anyone else off. They broke his knees and elbows and cut out his eyes, then tossed him into the river like so much rubbish. He wasn't much, my Billy, but I loved him. And now there's no one." She looked past him with red-rimmed eyes and saw only a future alone.

"I'm sorry," Vincent said again. "If I'd've known I'd've come sooner, but I've been . . . away."

"Prison?" Ronnie asked.

The man shook his head. "No. But it's been close a couple of times."

"Billy did time."

"I know."

"How?"

"Sorry."

"How do you know about him? Being in prison. Being dead."

"I keep in touch as much as I can. Of course, as time goes on it's harder. People move. People die."

"You can say that again."

"He saved my life once," said Vincent.

"Did you pay him?"

"No." He looked surprised at the question.

"Because he didn't do much for free, my Billy."

"He did that. It was a long time ago," Vincent explained. "When we were kids. Out there." He gestured towards the kitchen window with its view of the river sparkling in the autumn sunshine. "When it was still a working river. He dared me to swim out to a boat and see what I could find. I did it. I was a puny kid then and I got into trouble. The wash from another boat. I nearly drowned. He jumped in and saved me."

"Blimey," said Ronnie. "He never mentioned that either. Mind you, Billy's life was all secrets."

Vincent nodded as if his too had its share, which it had.

"So you have no idea who did it?" he asked at length.

She shook her head.

"I'll find them," he said.

"Who, you? What can you do?"

"What I said."

"Fat chance."

Outside, a helicopter flew low over east London.

"Do you really think you can?" she asked when it had passed by.

"Yes."

She shook her head. "If the cops can't . . ."

"I'm not the cops."

"You can say that again. I don't fancy your chances."

"You don't know me."

"No, I don't."

"Then trust me."

She smiled ruefully as if trust was a currency in short supply in her life. "OK," she said. "You're better than nothing, I suppose."

He made no reply to that.

"How will I know?" she asked.

"What?"

"That you've found them. Him. Whatever."

"You'll know."

"How?"

"You just will."

The look in his eyes convinced her and she nodded.

"But now I'd better go. I don't have much time," he said.

"Something important on?" she asked.

He smiled. "Not really. But I have to be somewhere. Anyway, thanks for your time."

"That's all I've got these days."

"You have your sons."

"For how long? They'll be gone too soon. That's what kids do."

"That's what everyone does."

She nodded in agreement and he got up to go.

"Thanks for coming," she said as she opened the front door to let him out.

"I owed him at least that. Goodbye, Mrs Dukes. I hope things go well for you."

She shook her head and she was still shaking it as he waited for the lift and entered it.

She never saw him again.

Vincent Graves spent the next three days visiting pubs in Rotherhithe, Greenwich and the Isle of Dogs. He walked for miles, sipping halves of lager, water and juice as he watched and listened, occasionally ingratiating himself into conversations and questioning bar staff. The day he'd visited Ronnie Dukes he found a room in a boarding house in Poplar run by a fat Asian gentleman. The toilet was unusable and the bathroom was filthy and Vincent smiled at the thought of how many time he had been ordered to clean latrines with a toothbrush until they sparkled, and wondered how the Asian would take to being forced to do the same, but did nothing about it. It was a place to flop, that was all. Cheap, and handy for his search. But when he went out in the morning he always took his bag, because the lock in his room door appeared to have been forced as many times as it had been opened with a key.

On the evening of the third day, the sun had set early behind banks of low, purple clouds, and the rain had started as the rush hour began. Vincent had walked to a pub that stood above the northern entrance to the Blackwall Tunnel and looked at the traffic speeding in both directions before entering. The line of cars coming from the north were stuck solid and looked like a diamond necklace with their headlamps full on, and the vehicles heading back in that direction like a string of rubies, and the man smiled to himself before entering the pub.

It was quiet at that hour and he only stayed long enough for one glass of mineral water. When he left and walked onto the island, the rain had stopped, the puddles on the pavement were as black as ink and reflected the sodium street lights.

There was a new hotel on one corner and another pub at the end of that street and he decided to investigate. But before he could reach the warmth of the bar, his walk was interrupted as a man stepped out of a concealed entrance and blocked his path. Vincent felt a surge of adrenalin through his body. He knew that eventually this was bound to happen. Sooner or later someone would mark his progress and do something about it.

"Oi, you," said the figure in front of him. "What's your game?"

"Game?" Vincent replied without rancour. "No game."

"You interested in Billy Dukes, the dirty grass," the figure said, and Vincent sensed more movement behind him and turned so that his back was against the wall that surrounded the hotel. Two other figures had appeared from the hotel car park. One was carrying a baseball bat. The man noted that it was made of wood. Somewhere he remembered reading a story where two assassins discussed the merits of wooden bats versus metal. He couldn't remember where, or who had written the story.

"That's right," said Vincent, dropping the bag he was carrying and taking off his glasses and slipping them into the inside pocket of his jacket.

"Well, you'd better forget about him and go home."

"Did you kill him?" asked Vincent.

"Killed his bloody self. With his gob."

"Shut up," said the one with the bat. "Let's get this done." And with that he swung the bat hard at Vincent's head. Hard enough to take it off his shoulders if the blow had connected. But it didn't. Almost faster than the eye could follow, Vincent lifted his left hand and caught the fat end of the bat on his palm with the sound of an axe hitting a tree, stopping the weapon dead, about three inches from his skull. Then, as easily as most men would have taken a lollipop stick from a small child, he twisted the bat out of his assailant's hand, transferred the handle to his right, and smashed him on the outside of his left knee with exactly the same sound, plus the unmistakable noise of at least one bone snapping. The erstwhile attacker screamed then, a sound so high that only the dogs that lived on the eponymous island that they made their home could hear. Then Vincent broke the bat across his knee as easily as another man would have broken the same lollipop stick.

If the trio of attackers had the wit to realize how difficult a task this would be, the bat being almost three inches in diameter at its thickest point, that would have been the time to realise that discretion was the better part of valour and go home to cocoa and a warm bed. But neither wit nor time was on their side and they decided to continue.

The original speaker produced a knife from inside his Puffa jacket and stabbed at Vincent's stomach. He moved smoothly aside, allowing the point of the knife to slide past his belt, took hold of the attacker's arm at the elbow joint and pressed hard. Another scream and the clatter of the knife hitting the pavement as Vincent twisted the joint and the crack of the break echoed off the bricks. Vincent tossed the man into the gutter and turned his attention to assassin number three, who he lifted up by his throat and asked without pausing for breath, "Who sent you?"

The third man's feet lifted off the ground and he kicked frantically as he searched for purchase on something solid. "Jimmy Silver," he gasped.

"Who is he?" asked Vincent.

"He owns it round here."

"Owns what?"

"Let me down, please."

Vincent could see the man's face reddening almost to black under the pressure of his fingers and he dropped him back on his feet where he doubled up searching for air. "Owns what?" Vincent asked again, kicking the man with the broken knee in the ribs as he tried to crab away to somewhere safe where his reputation as a hard man was still intact.

"Everything," said the third man, holding his hands to his throat. "Fags, booze, dope. Everything."

"Where do I find him?"

"You don't. He finds you."

Vincent backhanded him casually around the face. "He must have a place," he said. "Don't mess around or I'll really hurt you."

The third man considered what pain he'd already felt, and what being "really hurt" would entail.

"The Golden Hind pub on the island," he said. "It's his place. He's there all the time. Lives upstairs in the week."

Vincent considered the three men littered about around him. Broken Knee was now lying holding his ribs, at least one that Vincent had felt crack as he kicked him. Broken elbow lay in the gutter unconscious, his snorting breath disturbing a pool of rainwater. The third one was leaning against the hotel wall, his head bowed. "I suppose the first thing you'll do will be to call Jimmy Silver," said Vincent.

"No. No, mate. I'm off."

"Liar," said Vincent.

"Don't hurt me no more, mate," said the third man. "I just did this as a favour."

Vincent smiled. "No good deed goes unpunished," he said. He knew he had two choices. Kill all three or walk away. But this was London, and a triple murder wouldn't go unnoticed, and he had no time or means to hide the bodies. "Tell Silver I'm coming," he said and, picking up his bag, he walked away.

Back at the boarding house Vincent looked up the address of The Golden Hind in the tattered directory next to the pay phone in the narrow corridor that acted as a foyer, under the watchful eye of the proprietor as if he was about to steal it. Next he checked his A-Z and found the street, a narrow thoroughfare close to the DLR railway between Mudchute and Island Gardens. It was not a pub he had visited previously.

That same evening he went on a recce. It was a worn out house with peeling paint and a wonky sign that creaked in the breeze. But it was busy. Mostly locals, he surmised, being far from the glittering towers of Canary Wharf, and advertised all-day breakfasts, live music and karaoke. From where he was watching there was a constant toing and froing of punters, but there was also a suspiciously large presence of big men in leather jackets with heavy boots and shaven heads. Obviously the word was out that the three stooges had been taken apart and Jimmy Silver was taking no chances.

Vincent stood in the shadows for more than an hour, then, after slipping on a pair of thin leather gloves, went into a nearby council estate, looking for a warmer and safer reconnaissance point.

He found it in the shape of an old Ford Thames van which he broke into and started easily. The petrol gauge showed just under half full, and with the lights off he pulled out of the estate's car park, then switched on the sidelights and drove back to the pub. Once there he parked a hundred yards or so down from the front door in the darkest space he could find, killed the engine and lights and climbed into the back. The van was obviously used by some sort of handyman and was littered with tools and old, paint-covered sheets that Vincent made into a nest which he lay upon with a clear view of the pub through the back windows. He didn't know how long it would be before the owner noticed the vehicle missing, but as he had seen little police presence on the island on his travels, and considering the dilapidated state of the Ford, he surmised it would not be on the local coppers' high priority whatever happened, and he hoped he would only need it for a few hours.

Chucking-out time seemed to be a movable feast at the Hind. Drinkers drifted out in ones and twos from eleven-thirty onwards, and the lights in the bar were not dimmed until after midnight. Vincent lay patiently in the van and waited.

Lights also went on and off in the rooms above the bar but, finally, around twelve-thirty, the downstairs lights went down to a dim glow and through the glass on the front doors he saw someone snap the bolts at the top.

He gave it another twenty minutes before he stretched his stiffening muscles, crawled back into the front of the van and exited from the driver's door. First of all he headed away from the building, then took a circuitous route around the back that was protected by high walls trimmed with barbed wire. Then he strolled around to the front and sensed a human presence, before he saw one of the large men standing by the corner smoking a cigarette, facing away from him. Vincent sucked in a breath and, silently, on the toes of his rubber-soled monkey boots drifted closer to the smoker.

The man never saw or heard a thing until Vincent propelled him by the back of his neck into the brick wall of the Hind, where his cigarette burst in a cloud of sparks and his nose broke with an audible snap. A rabbit punch finished the assault and Vincent dragged the unconscious body into a gap between the pub and the next-door building and left the man snoring quietly, a bubble of blood popping out of one nostril with each exhalation.

Where there's one there's usually two, he thought, and walked round the corner, almost bumping into a twin of the first man. "Sorry," said Vincent, doing a body-swerve around the surprised heavy before smashing him in the kidneys with the extended three fingers of his right hand and breaking his jaw with the palm of the other. The man slumped to the ground and Vincent pulled him out of sight between two parked cars.

He went straight back to the van, found a sharp screwdriver amongst the tools in the back, started the engine, then, leaving it running, went to the back of the vehicle, screwdriver in hand, found the fuel tank and ruptured it with one straight stroke of the blade. He ran back to the driver's seat, smacked the Ford into gear and did a screeching U-turn, drove up onto the pavement and stopped by the front doors. He pulled open the back doors which he'd unlocked from the inside, collected the pile of sheets and ran across the road to where the trail of spilt petrol lay like a rainbow on the damp tarmac. He lit a match and dropped it onto the liquid, watched as flame ran across the street and headed to the back of the pub again as the petrol tank exploded like a bomb. There was one more explosion as the engine caught, and he pulled himself up the pub wall, tossed the sheets over the barbed wire and rolled over to drop into the pub's back area amongst a pile of crates and empty beer barrels.

As lights came on at the top of the house, Vincent kicked the back door in and ran upstairs. He had no idea of the layout inside the building but trusted his instincts to find who he was looking for. As he ran, thick smoke filled the stairwell and he covered his mouth and nose with his sleeve.

A door opened in front of him and a man ran out and hammered on the next door. "Are you all right, Jimmy? I've called the fire bri –" Vincent didn't let him finish. On his travels he had noticed that there was a fire station less than a mile away, and he didn't have much time. Vincent hammered the man to the carpet and opened the door. Inside was a bedroom. In the bed were two figures, one female, one male. The female sat up pulling the bedclothes over her ample breasts. Next to her, clearly visible in the light leaking through the curtains, was a moustachioed man just coming awake.

Outside, Vincent could already hear the sound of sirens.

"Who the hell . . . ?" said the woman above the noise, but Vincent was at her side of the bed in an instant and silenced her with a punch to the jaw.

The man sat up too, his face indignant.

"Jimmy?" said Vincent.

The man said, "Who wants to know?"

"I'm a friend of Billy Dukes," said Vincent. "You're Jimmy Silver."

But Silver wasn't paying attention. He was staring at the door, and suddenly Vincent felt a strong arm around his throat, and another clamped his arms to his side. His breathing was constricted and the light from the window darkened. With all his strength Vincent stamped back with one boot heel. Once, twice, three times on the instep of his captor, who loosened his grip enough to allow Vincent to strike back with his elbow. The breath whooshed out of the man and Vincent felt for his groin. He found the man's balls tight in denim, and he twisted hard. Hard enough so that he could feel the rupture grow in his hand as the man screamed and loosed his hold. Vincent spun round and flat-footed him hard in the stomach, and he dropped to the carpet. When Vincent turned back, Silver was groping for something in the drawer of the bedside cabinet. Vincent vaulted the bed and slammed the drawer shut on Silver's wrist.

"Bastard," said Silver.

"Goodbye," said Vincent and broke Silver's neck with one hand as at least one fire engine skidded to a halt outside. Vincent pulled Silver out of bed and with both thumbs dug into his eye sockets and popped out both eyeballs. He broke the strings and gathered the two damp orbs into one gloved palm before leaving.

Outside the bedroom the smoke was thicker, more fire engines had arrived, and helmeted figures appeared at the foot of the stairs.

Vincent ran down, his arm covering his face again. "Upstairs," he yelled at one of the firemen. "There's people trapped," and ran past as the firemen clattered up past him. As the last one went by, Vincent shouted, "Hey."

The fireman turned and Vincent said, "These belong to

the boss here," and he dropped the eyes from his gloved hand into the fireman's own.

"What?" said the confused man, looking down through the breathing mask he was wearing. "What's this?" But Vincent was already through the back door and saw that the gate to the street had been opened, and he pushed through into the fresh air. He jogged down the road and lost himself in the council estate.

Vincent cut across the island and went back to the boarding house to collect the bag he had left with the owner. Then he left the area never to return. When the story of the fire at The Golden Hind broke, the various assaults meted out to customers and staff, and the death of its owner, Jimmy Silver, by person or persons unknown, much was made of the grisly nature of the way Silver's eyes were given to the fire officer. Up on the twenty-first floor of the tower block in Rotherhithe, Ronnie Dukes read the story in her morning paper and knew what Vincent had promised her had come true.

The next time she visited her late husband's grave she found a wilted, blood-red rose dropping its petals on the dirt. It was held fast by a stone. Under the stone was a single sheet of paper torn from a notebook. On it was written one word – *Goodbye*.

Don't Look Behind You

Fredric Brown

J ust sit back and relax, now. Try to enjoy this; it's going to be the last story you ever read, or nearly the last. After you finish it you can sit there, and stall a while, you can find excuses to hang around your house, or your room, or your office, wherever you're reading this; but sooner or later you're going to have to get up and go out. That's where I'm waiting for you: outside. Or maybe closer than that. Maybe in this room.

You think that's a joke, of course. You think this is just a story in a book, and that I don't really mean you. Keep right on thinking so. But be fair; admit that I'm giving you fair warning.

Harley bet me I couldn't do it. He bet me a diamond he's told me about, a diamond as big as his head. So you see why I've got to kill you. And why I've got to tell you how and why and all about it first. That's part of the bet. It's just the kind of idea Harley would have.

I'll tell you about Harley first. He's tall and handsome, and suave and cosmopolitan. He looks something like Ronald Colman, only he's taller. He dresses like a million dollars, but it wouldn't matter if he didn't; I mean that he'd look distinguished in overalls. There's a sort of magic about Harley, a mocking magic in the way he looks at you; it makes you think of palaces and far off countries and bright music.

It was in Springfield, Ohio, that he met Justin Dean. Justin was a funny-looking little runt who was just a printer. He worked for the Atlas Printing & Engraving Company. He was a very ordinary little guy, just about as different as possible from Harley; you couldn't pick two men more different. He was only thirty-five, but he was mostly bald already, and he had to wear thick glasses because he'd worn out his eyes doing fine printing and engraving. He was a good printer and engraver; I'll say that for him.

I never asked Harley how he happened to come to Springfield, but the day he got there, after he'd checked in at the Castle Hotel, he stopped in at Atlas to have some calling cards made. It happened that Justin Dean was alone in the shop at the time, and he took Harley's order for the cards; Harley wanted engraved ones, the best. Harley always wants the best of everything.

Harley probably didn't even notice Justin; there was no reason why he should have. But Justin noticed Harley, all right, and in him he saw everything that he himself would like to be, and never would be, because most of the things Harley has, you have to be born with.

And Justin made the plates for the cards himself and printed them himself, and he did a wonderful job – something he thought would be worthy of a man like Harley Prentice. That was the name engraved on the card, just that and nothing else, as all really important people have their cards engraved.

He did fine-line work on it, freehand cursive style, and used all the skill he had. It wasn't wasted, because the next day when Harley called to get the cards he held one and stared at it for a while, and then he looked at Justin, seeing him for the first time. He asked, "Who did this?"

And little Justin told him proudly who had done it, and Harley smiled at him and told him it was the work of an artist, and he asked Justin to have dinner with him that evening after work, in the Blue Room of the Castle Hotel.

That's how Harley and Justin got together, but Harley was careful. He waited until he'd known Justin a while before he asked him whether or not he could make plates for five and ten dollar bills. Harley had the contacts; he could market the bills in quantity with men who specialized in passing them, and – most important – he knew where he could get paper with the silk threads in it, paper that wasn't quite the genuine thing, but was close enough to pass inspection by anyone but an expert.

So Justin quit his job at Atlas and he and Harley went to New York, and they set up a little printing shop as a blind, on Amsterdam Avenue south of Sherman Square, and they worked at the bills. Justin worked hard, harder than he had ever worked in his life, because besides working on the plates for the bills, he helped meet expenses by handling what legitimate printing work came into the shop.

He worked day and night for almost a year, making plate after plate, and each one was a little better than the last, and finally he had plates that Harley said were good enough. That night they had dinner at the Waldorf-Astoria to celebrate and after dinner they went the rounds of the best night clubs, and it cost Harley a small fortune, but that didn't matter because they were going to get rich.

They drank champagne, and it was the first time Justin ever drank champagne and he got disgustingly drunk and must have made quite a fool of himself. Harley told him about it afterwards, but Harley wasn't mad at him. He took him back to his room at the hotel and put him to bed, and Justin was pretty sick for a couple of days. But that didn't matter, either, because they were going to get rich.

Then Justin started printing bills from the plates, and they got rich. After that, Justin didn't have to work so hard, either, because he turned down most jobs that came into the print shop, told them he was behind schedule and couldn't handle any more. He took just a little work, to keep up a front. And behind the front, he made five and ten dollar bills, and he and Harley got rich.

He got to know other people whom Harley knew. He met Bull Mallon, who handled the distribution end. Bull Mallon was built like a bull, that was why they called him that. He had a face that never smiled or changed expression at all except when he was holding burning matches to the soles of Justin's bare feet. But that wasn't then; that was later, when he wanted Justin to tell him where the plates were.

And he got to know Captain John Willys of the Police Department, who was a friend of Harley's, to whom Harley gave quite a bit of money they made, but that didn't matter either, because there was plenty left and they all got rich. He met a friend of Harley's who was a big star of the stage, and one who owned a big New York newspaper. He got to know other people equally important, but in less respectable ways.

Harley, Justin knew, had a hand in lots of other enterprises besides the little mint on Amsterdam Avenue. Some of these ventures took him out of town, usually over weekends. And the weekend that Harley was murdered Justin never found out what really happened, except that Harley went away and didn't come back. Oh, he knew that he was murdered, all right, because the police found his body – with three bullet holes in his chest – in the most expensive suite of the best hotel in Albany. Even for a place to be found dead in, Harley Prentice had chosen the best.

All Justin ever knew about it was that a long-distance call came to him at the hotel where he was staying, the night that Harley was murdered – it must have been a matter of minutes, in fact, before the time the newspapers said Harley was killed.

It was Harley's voice on the phone, and his voice was debonair and unexcited as ever. But he said, "Justin? Get to the shop and get rid of the plates, the paper, everything. Right away. I'll explain when I see you." He waited only until Justin said, "Sure, Harley," and then he said, "Attaboy," and hung up.

Justin hurried around to the printing shop and got the plates and the paper and a few thousand dollars' worth of counterfeit bills that were on hand. He made the paper and bills into one bundle and the copper plates into another, smaller one, and he left the shop with no evidence that it had ever been a mint in miniature.

He was very careful and very clever in disposing of both bundles. He got rid of the big one first by checking in at a big hotel, not one he or Harley ever stayed at, under a false name, just to have a chance to put the big bundle in the incinerator there. It was paper and it would burn. And he made sure there was a fire in the incinerator before he dropped it down the chute.

The plates were different. They wouldn't burn, he knew

so he took a trip to Staten Island and back on the ferry and, somewhere out in the middle of the bay, he dropped the bundle over the side into the water.

Then, having done what Harley had told him to do, and having done it well and thoroughly, he went back to the hotel – his own hotel, not the one where he had dumped the paper and the bills – and went to sleep.

In the morning he read in the newspapers that Harley had been killed, and he was stunned. It didn't seem possible. He couldn't believe it; it was a joke someone was playing on him. Harley would come back to him, he knew. And he was right; Harley did, but that was later, in the swamp.

But anyway, Justin had to know, so he took the very next train for Albany. He must have been on the train when the police went to his hotel, and at the hotel they must have learned he'd asked the desk about trains for Albany, because they were waiting for him when he got off the train there.

They took him to a station and they kept him there a long long time, days and days, asking him questions. They found out, after a while, that he couldn't have killed Harley because he'd been in New York City at the time Harley was killed in Albany but they knew also that he and Harley had been operating the little mint, and they thought that might be a lead to who killed Harley, and they were interested in the counterfeiting, too, maybe even more than in the murder. They asked Justin Dean questions, over and over and over, and he couldn't answer them, so he didn't. They kept him awake for days at a time, asking him questions over and over. Most of all they wanted to know where the plates were. He wished he could tell them that the plates were safe where nobody could ever get them again, but he couldn't tell them that without admitting that he and Harley had been counterfeiting, so he couldn't tell them.

They located the Amsterdam shop, but they didn't find any evidence there, and they really had no evidence to hold Justin on at all, but he didn't know that, and it never occurred to him to get a lawyer.

He kept wanting to see Harley, and they wouldn't let

him; then, when they learned he really didn't believe Harley could be dead, they made him look at a dead man they said was Harley, and he guessed it was, although Harley looked different dead. He didn't look magnificent, dead. And Justin believed, then, but still didn't believe. And after that he just went silent and wouldn't say a word, even when they kept him awake for days and days with a bright light in his eyes, and kept slapping him to keep him awake. They didn't use clubs or rubber hoses, but they slapped him a million times and wouldn't let him sleep. And after a while he lost track of things and couldn't have answered their questions even if he'd wanted to.

For a while after that, he was in a bed in a white room, and all he remembers about that are nightmares he had, and calling for Harley and an awful confusion as to whether Harley was dead or not, and then things came back to him gradually and he knew he didn't want to stay in the white room; he wanted to get out so he could hunt for Harley. And if Harley was dead, he wanted to kill whoever had killed Harley, because Harley would have done the same for him.

So he began pretending, and acting, very cleverly, the way the doctors and nurses seemed to want him to act, and after a while they gave him his clothes and let him go.

He was becoming cleverer now. He thought, What would Harley tell me to do? And he knew they'd try to follow him because they'd think he might lead them to the plates, which they didn't know were at the bottom of the bay, and he gave them the slip before he left Albany, and he went first to Boston, and from there by boat to New York, instead of going direct.

He went first to the print shop, and went in the back way after watching the alley for a long time to be sure the place wasn't guarded. It was a mess; they must have searched it very thoroughly for the plates.

Harley wasn't there, of course. Justin left and from a phone booth in a drugstore he telephoned their hotel and asked for Harley and was told Harley no longer lived there; and to be clever and not let them guess who he was, he asked for Justin Dean, and they said Justin Dean didn't live there any more either.

Then he moved to a different drugstore and from there he decided to call up some friends of Harley's, and he phoned Bull Mallon first and because Bull was a friend, he told him who he was and asked if he knew where Harley was.

Bull Mallon didn't pay any attention to that; he sounded excited, a little, and he asked, "Did the cops get the plates, Dean?" and Justin said they didn't, that he wouldn't tell them, and he asked again about Harley.

Bull asked, "Are you nuts, or kidding?" And Justin just asked him again, and Bull's voice changed and he said, "Where are you?" and Justin told him. Bull said, "Harley's here. He's staying under cover, but it's all right if you know, Dean. You wait right there at the drugstore, and we'll come and get you."

They came and got Justin, Bull Mallon and two other men in a car, and they told him Harley was hiding out way deep in New Jersey and that they were going to drive there now. So he went along and sat in the back seat between two men he didn't know, while Bull Mallon drove.

It was late afternoon then, when they picked him up, and Bull drove all evening and most of the night and he drove fast, so he must have gone farther than New Jersey, at least into Virginia or maybe farther, into the Carolinas.

The sky was getting faintly grey with first dawn when they stopped at a rustic cabin that looked like it had been used as a hunting lodge. It was miles from anywhere, there wasn't even a road leading to it, just a trail that was level enough for the car to be able to make it.

They took Justin into the cabin and tied him to a chair, and they told him Harley wasn't there, but Harley had told them that Justin would tell them where the plates were, and he couldn't leave until he did tell.

Justin didn't believe them; he knew then that they'd tricked him about Harley, but it didn't matter, as far as the plates were concerned. It didn't matter if he told them what he'd done with the plates, because they couldn't get them again, and they wouldn't tell the police. So he told them, quite willingly.

But they didn't believe him. They said he'd hidden the plates and was lying. They tortured him to make him tell. They beat him, and they cut him with knives, and they held burning matches and lighted cigars to the soles of his feet, and they pushed needles under his fingernails. Then they'd rest and ask him questions and if he could talk, he'd tell them the truth, and after a while they'd start to torture him again.

It went on for days and weeks – Justin doesn't know how long, but it was a long time. Once they went away for several days and left him tied up with nothing to eat or drink. They came back and started in all over again. And all the time he hoped Harley would come to help him, but Harley didn't come, not then.

After a while what was happening in the cabin ended, or anyway he didn't know any more about it. They must have thought he was dead; maybe they were right, or anyway not far from wrong.

The next thing he knows was the swamp. He was lying in shallow water at the edge of deeper water. His face was out of the water; it woke him when he turned a little and his face went under. They must have thought him dead and thrown him into the water, but he had floated into the shallow part before he had drowned, and a last flicker of consciousness had turned him over on his back with his face out.

I don't remember much about Justin in the swamp; it was a long time, but I just remember flashes of it. I couldn't move at first; I just lay there in the shallow water with my face out. It got dark and it got cold, I remember, and finally my arms would move a little and I got farther out of the water, lying in the mud with only my feet in the water. I slept or was unconscious again and when I woke up it was getting grey dawn, and that was when Harley came. I think I'd been calling him, and he must have heard.

He stood there, dressed as immaculately and perfectly as ever, right in the swamp, and he was laughing at me for being so weak and lying there like a log, half in the dirty water and half in the mud, and I got up and nothing hurt any more.

We shook hands and he said, "Come on, Justin, let's get

you out of here," and I was so glad he'd come that I cried a little. He laughed at me for that and said I should lean on him and he'd help me walk, but I wouldn't do that, because I was coated with mud and filth of the swamp and he was so clean and perfect in a white linen suit, like an ad in a magazine. And all the way out of that swamp, all the days and nights we spent there, he never even got mud on his trouser cuffs, nor his hair mussed.

I told him just to lead the way, and he did, walking just ahead of me, sometimes turning around, laughing and talking to me and cheering me up. Sometimes I'd fall but I wouldn't let him come back and help me. But he'd wait patiently until I could get up. Sometimes I'd crawl instead when I couldn't stand up any more. Sometimes I'd have to swim streams that he'd leap lightly across.

And it was day and night and day and night, and sometimes I'd sleep, and things would crawl across me. And some of them I caught and ate, or maybe I dreamed that. I remember other things, in that swamp, like an organ that played a lot of the time, and sometimes angels in the air and devils in the water, but those were delirium, I guess.

Harley would say, "A little farther, Justin; we'll make it. And we'll get back at them, at all of them."

And we made it. We came to dry fields, cultivated fields with waist-high corn, but there weren't ears on the corn for me to eat. And then there was a stream, a clear stream that wasn't stinking water like the swamp, and Harley told me to wash myself and my clothes and I did, although I wanted to hurry on to where I could get food.

I still looked pretty bad; my clothes were clean of mud and filth but they were mere rags and wet, because I couldn't wait for them to dry, and I had a ragged beard and I was barefoot.

But we went on and came to a little farm building, just a two-room shack, and there was a smell of fresh bread just out of an oven, and I ran the last few yards to knock on the door. A woman, an ugly woman, opened the door and when she saw me she slammed it again before I could say a word.

Strength came to me from somewhere, maybe from Harley, although I can't remember him being there just then. There was a pile of kindling logs beside the door. I picked one of them up as though it were no heavier than a broomstick, and I broke down the door and killed the woman. She screamed a lot, but I killed her. Then I ate the hot fresh bread.

I watched from the window as I ate, and saw a man running across the field towards the house. I found a knife, and I killed him as he came in at the door. It was much better, killing with the knife; I liked it that way.

I ate more bread, and kept watching from all the windows, but no one else came. Then my stomach hurt from the hot bread I'd eaten and I had to lie down, doubled up, and when the hurting quit, I slept.

Harley woke me up, and it was dark. He said, "Let's get going; you should be far away from here before it's daylight."

I knew he was right, but I didn't hurry away. I was becoming, as you see, very clever now. I knew there were things to do first. I found matches and a lamp, and lighted the lamp. Then I hunted through the shack for everything I could use. I found clothes of the man, and they fitted me not too badly except that I had to turn up the cuffs of the trousers and the shirt. His shoes were big, but that was good because my feet were so swollen.

I found a razor and shaved; it took a long time because my hand wasn't steady, but I was very careful and didn't cut myself much.

I had to hunt hardest for their money, but I found it finally. It was sixty dollars.

And I took the knife, after I had sharpened it. It isn't fancy; just a bone-handled carving knife, but it's good steel. I'll show it to you, pretty soon now. It's had a lot of use.

Then we left and it was Harley who told me to stay away from the roads, and find railroad tracks. That was easy because we heard a train whistle far off in the night and knew which direction the tracks lay. From then on, with Harley helping, it's been easy.

You won't need the details from here. I mean, about the brakeman, and about the tramp we found asleep in the empty reefer, and about the near thing I had with the police in Richmond. I learned from that; I learned I mustn't talk to Harley when anybody else was around to hear. He hides himself from them; he's got a trick and they don't know he's there, and they think I'm funny in the head if I talk to him. But in Richmond I bought better clothes and got a haircut and a man I killed in an alley had forty dollars on him, so I had money again. I've done a lot of travelling since then. If you stop to think you'll know where I am right now.

I'm looking for Bull Mallon and the two men who helped him. Their names are Harry and Carl. I'm going to kill them when I find them. Harley keeps telling me that those fellows are big time and that I'm not ready for them yet. But I can be looking while I'm getting ready so I keep moving around. Sometimes I stay in one place long enough to hold a job as a printer for a while. I've learned a lot of things. I can hold a job and people don't think I'm too strange; they don't get scared when I look at them like they sometimes did a few months ago. And I've learned not to talk to Harley except in our own room and then only very quietly so people in the next room won't think I'm talking to myself.

And I've kept in practice with the knife. I've killed lots of people with it, mostly on the streets at night. Sometimes because they look like they might have money on them, but mostly just for practice and because I've come to like doing it. I'm really good with the knife by now. You'll hardly feel it.

But Harley tells me that kind of killing is easy and that it's something else to kill a person who's on guard, as Bull and Harry and Carl will be.

And that's the conversation that led to the bet I mentioned. I told Harley that I'd bet him that, right now, I could warn a man I was going to use the knife on him and even tell him why and approximately when, and that I could still kill him. And he bet me that I couldn't and he's going to lose that bet.

He's going to lose it because I'm warning you right now and you're not going to believe me. I'm betting that you're going to believe that this is just another story in a book. That you won't believe that this is the *only* copy of this book that contains this story and that this story is true. Even when I tell you how it was done, I don't think you'll really believe me.

You see I'm putting it over on Harley, winning the bet, by putting it over on you. He never thought, and you won't realize how easy it is for a good printer, who's been a counterfeiter too, to counterfeit one story in a book. Nothing like as hard as counterfeiting a five dollar bill.

I had to pick a book of short stories and I picked this one because I happened to notice that the last story in the book was titled *Don't Look Behind You* and that was going to be a good title for this. You'll see what I mean in a few minutes.

I'm lucky that the printing shop I'm working for now does book work and has a typeface that matches the rest of this book. I had a little trouble matching the paper exactly, but I finally did and I've got it ready while I'm writing this. I'm writing this directly on a linotype, late at night in the shop where I'm working days. I even have the boss's permission, told him I was going to set up and print a story that a friend of mine had written, as a surprise for him, and that I'd melt the type metal back as soon as I'd printed one good copy.

When I finish writing this I'll make up the type in pages to match the rest of the book and I'll print it on the matching paper I have ready. I'll cut the new pages to fit and bind them in; you won't be able to tell the difference, even if a faint suspicion may cause you to look at it. Don't forget I made five and ten dollar bills you couldn't have told from the original, and this is kindergarten stuff compared to that job. And I've done enough bookbinding that I'll be able to take the last story out of the book and bind this one in instead of it and you won't be able to tell the difference, no matter how closely you look. I'm going to do a perfect job of it if it takes me all night.

And tomorrow I'll go to some bookstore, or maybe a newsstand or even a drugstore that sells books and has other copies of this book, ordinary copies, and I'll plant this one there. I'll find myself a good place to watch from, and I'll be watching when you buy it.

The rest I can't tell you because it depends a lot on

circumstances, whether you went right home with the book or what you did. I won't know till I follow you and keep watch till you read it – and I see that you're reading the last story in the book.

If you're home while you're reading this, maybe I'm in the house with you right now. Maybe I'm in this very room, hidden, waiting for you to finish the story. Maybe I'm watching through a window. Or maybe I'm sitting near you on the streetcar or train, if you're reading it there. Maybe I'm on the fire escape outside your hotel room. But wherever you're reading it, I'm near you, watching and waiting for you to finish. You can count on that.

You're pretty near the end now. You'll be finished in seconds and you'll close the book, still not believing. Or, if you haven't read the stories in order, maybe you'll turn back to start another story. If you do, you'll never finish it.

But don't look around; you'll be happier if you don't know, if you don't see the knife coming. When I kill people from behind they don't seem to mind so much.

Go on, just a few seconds or minutes, thinking this is just another story. Don't look behind you. Don't believe this – *until you feel the knife.*

College-Cut Kill

John D. MacDonald

I

Brethren, Here's to Death

It was half past twelve on one of those early September days in Manhattan when the streets are Dutch ovens and a girl who can look crisp is a treasure indeed. I was completing the last draft of the current three-part blast, with Dolly sitting at my elbow noting the changes I wanted.

Miss Riven came in simultaneously with her crisp rap at the door, and said, "Mr Engelborg wishes to see you immediately, Mr Arlin."

She did a Prussian drill-sergeant's about-face and went back through the door, shutting it with a crisp clack that only Miss Riven can seem to get out of a door.

"Her!" Dolly said. "Her!" She made it sound like a dirty name.

"She thinks I work here," I said. During the six weeks that I had been provided with office space and Dolly, she and I had become good friends. "Look, lovely. I can't see anything more we need. Type it up with three carbons and get one over to the legal eagles for checking."

I hesitated, decided against my coat, and went down through the offices full of common people to the shrine where Engelborg, the almighty, flings his weight around.

Miss Riven gave me a cool look, glanced at her watch and said, "You may go right in, Mr Arlin."

I pushed the door open. Engelborg, who looks like a giant

blond panda, said, "This is Arlin. Joe, meet Mr Flynn."

Flynn merely nodded but he stared at me intently. He was a big, sagging man in his late fifties with an executive air about him. There was a bloodhound sadness about his eyes.

"Arlin," said Mr Engelborg, "is just finishing up a hot series on real estate swindles."

"It's all done," I said. "Ought to be out of the typewriter tomorrow. That is, if the lawyers have no kick."

"Good," Engelborg grunted. "I want you to understand, Mr Flynn, that Arlin isn't a part of this organization. He works on a freelance basis and this particular job was so hot we wanted him right here so we could coordinate more closely. What are your plans, Joe?"

I didn't like the sound of that. I said, "I am going to wait until I get page proofs on the first instalment and then I am going to go to Maine."

"I understand," Flynn said, "that you're out of college two years. The University of Wisconsin. You were a Gamma U there?"

"That's right." I couldn't smell which way this was going. Flynn looked at me as though he resented me in a tired way.

"He looks young enough, doesn't he?" Engelborg said. Flynn nodded.

That has been a sore point with me. When I was twenty I looked fifteen. Now, at twenty-eight, I look twenty. Professionally that has its limitations. Emotionally it's all right. I play on their maternal instincts.

"So I look young," I said. "Gee, thanks."

"Take it easy, Joe," Engelborg said. "Real easy. Don't get upset. How'd you like to go to college?"

"Thanks, I've been."

Flynn spoke heavily. "Let me talk, Arlin. My son is dead. He died last June at the age of nineteen. Everyone says he hung himself. I went down there. He was at West Coast University in Florida. I cannot believe he hung himself. He was a Gamma U. Other boys in that house died last year. In different ways. Automobiles. One drowned. Too many died. I cannot get help from the police. A private investigation firm would be too heavy-handed.

"Mr Engelborg has been my good friend for many years. Last night I talked to him about this. He mentioned you. We discussed it. I want to pay you to go down and register for this fall term which starts very soon. I have certain influence and so does Engelborg. It can be arranged. We have a friend at the University of Wisconsin. The first three years of your credits will be transferred so you can enter as a senior. I know the secretary of the national chapter of Gamma U. There will be no trouble from that end."

I sat down. I kept my voice as calm and logical as I could. "Mr Flynn, I appreciate your problem. There are many inexplicable suicides among young people."

"Teddy did not kill himself. I know that. I must have it proven. I have two other boys, younger boys. I don't want this thing hanging over them."

"Which would be better? Suicide or murder? If it isn't one it's the other."

"Suicide is a sign of basic weakness. Teddy was not weak. I want you to go down there and live in that house and find out what happened." He was as positive and undeniable as an avalanche.

I appealed to Mr Engelborg. "Look, that isn't my line. I find things out to write them up."

Engelborg said, "You've done some very slick investigatory work, Joe. Those dock gangs, the Bermuda dope setup."

"I'm my own man," I said. "I do what I please."

"That's right, Joe," Engelborg said.

"I don't want to go to college. I want to go to Maine. Brother, it's hot down there now. I'm tired. I want to go fishing."

"You'll wonder," Flynn said, "all the rest of your life. You'll wonder what kind of a thing you might have uncovered. What kind of a twisted, diseased thing it is that causes the deaths of fine young boys."

"I won't do it," I said.

"You will be paid all expenses, plus a thousand a month plus a bonus of five thousand when it is all over, no matter what your conclusion is."

"I hate Florida," I said.

*   *   *

The blue gulf sparkled on my right as I drove south. The sun glinted off the chrome of the convertible, needling through the dark glasses. My luggage was stacked in the back end and I had not had to change to college cut clothes because the veterans pretty much took that aspect out of higher education. I had been one myself, the navy taking out a four-year chunk so that I got out when I had turned twenty-six.

The town of Sandson where the university was located turned out to be half on the mainland and half on a long island connected to the mainland by a half-mile public causeway. The university was inland from the mainland half of the town, perched on a hill a hundred feet high – which made it a mountain in that locality.

The timing was good and I arrived on the last day of registration. I dumped cash and traveller's cheques into the Sandson National Bank and drove east along the wide main drag. The university turn-off was to the right just beyond the city limits. A curving road led up to the haphazard collection of Moorish, Neo-Gothic, Spanish and Twentieth Century Lavatory construction. The bright young girls walked and cycled by in their thin dresses, brown legs flashing, eyes measuring me and the car for possible future reference.

I told myself this was a wild goose chase, a big mistake, a bunch of wasted time. I told myself again. Then I stopped telling myself. It was too much fun dropping back into the college frame of mind. But this time I was doing it the way I wished I had been able to do it at Wisconsin. At Wisconsin I had been knocking myself out, wondering how tough it would be to make a living later. Here I was getting paid for the deal.

Temporary cardboard signs were tacked up, pointing the way to Administration and Registration. I parked beside the indicated building, took the transcript of my three years out of the glove compartment and went in. There were tables with people working at them, filling out the desired schedules of classes. I took one of the catalogues and one of the blanks and went to work. I laid out six courses.

Literature IV (Creative Writing), Psychology VIII (Abnormal), Philosophy III (Ethics), Political Science VI (Ecology of nations), Modern History II (1914–1950).

Lastly, I dipped for an elective into the Business School, Accounting I (Basic Methods), because I have never been able to see quite eye to eye with the Collector of Internal Revenue.

Then I joined the line leading to the window titled A to K. The young lady was very crisp. I gave the name we had agreed on – Rodney J. Arlin. It's my name. The one my stuff has been published under is R. Joseph Arlin, and we thought the name might be just a shade too familiar to the reading public of one certain large magazine.

She checked her card file. "Arlin, Rodney J. We have you listed as a transfer. You have your transcript?" I handed it over. She checked it carefully.

"We can give you full credit for the hours shown here, and admit you as a senior. As a senior you are not restricted to living on the campus. Do you have a place to live yet?"

"Not yet."

"Advise us immediately when you have an address. Your schedule is approved. Tuition will be three eighty-five for each semester. Yes, a cheque is acceptable. Take one of the getting acquainted bulletins as you leave. They're on that far table. Class hours and rooms are posted on all bulletin boards. Compulsory meeting tomorrow morning at nine. As a senior you will attend the meeting in the Science Building auditorium. Next, please."

I found the cafeteria, had a quick lunch and went off in search of the brethren. I found them in a rambling Miami-type house of cinderblock, with a big overhang to kill the heat of the sun, sprinklers turning lazily on the green lawn. There was a parking area to the left of the house with a dozen cars lined up in it, eight of them convertibles of recent vintage. I parked and went around to the front. The door was open. The interior looked dim and invitingly cool.

I punched the bell and stepped inside. Two of the brethren came into the hallway and stared at me curiously, warily. One, with heavy bone-structure, I immediately type-cast as a working guard or tackle. The other was the smooth-dan type that inhabits all major fraternities. Careful, casual, a shade haughty and a bit too handsome.

I picked him to slip the grip to. "Brother Arlin," I

announced. "Beta chapter at Wisconsin. Just transferred here as a senior."

He looked slightly pained. "Nice to see you, Arlin. I'm Bradley Carroll and this is Brother Siminik."

He was giving me the inch-by-inch survey – and I knew right then that it was a political house. By that I mean one with cliques, possibly two strong ones. Bradley was trying to decide whether I'd be any addition to his clique, or whether I might be permitted to join the other as dead weight. We were like a couple of dogs that circle each other, stiff-legged.

I sighed inwardly. The next move was too obvious. "I put my wagon in the parking area. Hope it's all right there." I took out a pack and offered him a cigarette. Siminik refused it. I lighted Bradley Carroll's with a gold lighter, wide-ribbed, a thing I would never buy for myself, but something that a girl named Ann thought I ought to have.

"You drove down?" he asked politely. "*Where from?*" is what he was trying to say.

"From New York. Three days on the road."

"Oh, you live in New York?"

"No, I just took a place there for the summer. Everybody says it's a hell of a place to spend a summer. Not me."

He was still wary, but warmer. "Say, we're being pretty inhospitable, Arlin. Come on back to my room."

It was an exceedingly pleasant room. The bottle on the coffee table was the very best bourbon. Siminik wasn't drinking. Carroll mixed me a stiff one. He kept his good-looking slightly bovine eyes on me during our casual talk. I let him know without saying as much that I had no financial worries, that I was neither an athlete nor a bookworm, that I intended to sandwich a very good series of very good times in between the necessary study.

We went through the slightly oriental ceremonies until it was time to come to the point. "Would you recommend living in the house?" I asked.

He hadn't expected the question that way. "It's . . . very pleasant. The food is good." He suddenly realized that he was on the defensive, an unthinkable position. "But of course," he said quickly, "I can't say whether there'd be room for you. I mean a private room, of course."

"The house is too small?"

"Not that. Seniors are entitled to private rooms if they wish to live in the house. Juniors go two to a room and sophomores bunk in the dorm. There are only eight private rooms and all those are spoken for this semester."

Siminik said, "Brad, the room that Flynn was going to –"

Brad Carroll said hastily, "Quent is taking that one, Al. I thought you knew."

"Somebody drop out?" I asked very casually.

"No," Siminik said, "he –"

"– won't be here this year," Carroll said. I let it go. No point in pushing.

"You'll have to see Arthur Marris anyway," Brad Carroll said. "He's house president and he handles the quarters problem. You might care to bunk with one of the juniors. That's been done before and I think there's one vacancy."

I yawned. "I don't know as I want to stay in the house anyway. I want to look around first. Maybe I can get some sort of a layout on the beach."

"On the beach," said Al Siminik, "it costs like there's a river of oil under the land."

Brad looked at him as though he had made a rude noise in public. He gave me an apologetic glance that said, *"What else can you expect from knuckled-headed athletes?"*

As I was leaving, promising to be back for dinner, I met two more of the brethren, one a shy, blond likeable sophomore named Ben Charity, with a Georgia accent, the other a lean, hot-eyed, dark-haired, less-likeable junior named Bill Armand. I got over to the beach part of Sandson at about three-thirty. I found a small rental office inhabited by a vast, saggy female with an acid tongue.

"How much can you go for?" she said without hesitation. "If you want it through the winter it'll come high. From now until Christmas I can find you something for peanuts."

We went in my car to three places. I went back and took the second one, mostly because of its isolation. Bedroom, bath and kitchen made one side of an L and the living room made the other side. The L enclosed a small stone patio overlooking the gulf. It was sparkling new, completely furnished, and though the gulf front lot was small, a high thick hedge on either side kept the neighbours out. The car port was at the rear and it was ample protection against salt mist off the gulf. Two-eighty a month until the end of December. Four hundred after that.

I paid my two months in advance, unpacked, raided a package store for all the necessary, bought a typing table and still had time for a dip in the warm gulf before dressing to run back over to dine amid the brethren.

The house was noisy when I went in. In the lounge somebody had racked a bunch of very poor bop on the machine. There was laughing and shouting going on back in the bedroom wing. Suitcases were stacked in the hall. Through the doorway to the dining room I could see the waiters setting the big table in the middle, the smaller tables around the walls.

A little redheaded sophomore with the face of an angel collared me. "Are you Brother Arlin? Come on with me. Brother Carroll said to wait for you and take you back to his room."

I told him I could find it and went back by myself. Brother Carroll was being the merry host. He smiled at me with what I guessed was his nearest approach to friendliness and steered me over to a tall boy. I found myself liking him immediately. He had gauntness and deep-set eyes and a firm-lipped wide sensitive mouth. He was older than the others.

"I'm Arthur Marris," he said. "I'm glad to know you, Arlin. You do have a first name."

I swallowed hard and said it. "Rodney. Rod, usually."

Siminik was there, drinking ginger ale, and another senior named Step Krindall, a bulging, pink, prematurely bald boy.

"Martini all right?" Brad asked. I nodded and took the cool cocktail glass he handed me.

"I think we'll be able to make you comfortable if you'd like to move into the house, Rod," Arthur Marris said.

"I can see you're pretty crowded and I'm an outsider," I said. "I've taken a place on the beach. Turn left at The Dunes. Right at the end of the road. I see no reason why it can't be the Gamma U annex."

Arthur Marris looked a little hurt. He glanced at his watch. "One more round and then we'd better go in," he said.

The names and faces were slightly blurred at dinner. I knew I'd get a chance to straighten out in my mind. Brad Carroll, with Siminik as a stooge, ran the opposition to Arthur Marris. The controlling group in the fraternity during the past years had been composed of veterans. Marris was one of the last of them in school. Bald-headed Step Krindall and Marris were the only two left in the house.

Brad Carroll was the leader of the group trying to get the reins of authority back into the hands of the younger non-veteran group. His biggest following was among the sophomores. Better than half the seniors and almost half the juniors seemed allied with Marris. With enough voting strength, Brad Carroll could effectively grab the power from Marris this year, even though Marris would retain the title as president of the house.

I found that there were thirty-three members. Ten seniors, nine juniors and fourteen sophomores. They hoped to take in fifteen freshmen who would not be permitted to live in a house until their sophomore year. Of the active members living in the house, eight were seniors, seven were juniors and ten were sophomores. My presence brought the number of seniors up to eleven.

After dinner, much to Brad's poorly concealed concern, Arthur Marris took me off to his room. Daylight was fading. He lit his pipe, the match flare flickering on his strong features.

"How do you like the chapter?" he asked.

"Fine. Fine! Of course, I'm not acquainted yet, but everything seems —"

"You're not a kid, Rod. You don't handle yourself like a kid. You spoke of the navy at dinner. How old are you?"

"Twenty-six," I said, chopping off a couple of years.

"I'm twenty-five. I can talk to you as man to man. That sounds corny, doesn't it? I want to ask you if you've noticed the tension. I can feel it. It's all underneath, you know. I brought you in here to talk to you about it. Part of my job is to protect the reputation of the chapter. You'll make friends outside the house. They'll gossip. I prefer that you hear the bad things from me, not from outsiders."

I shrugged. "So the boys get a little rough sometimes. Is that serious?"

"This is something else. This is a jinxed house, Rod. I want to tell you a little about last year. I was a junior. The house president was a senior named Harv Lorr. In October, just as the rushing season was about to begin, two sophomores on their way back from Tampa rolled a car. Both of them were killed."

I whistled softly. "A tough break."

"That's what we all thought. Just before Christmas vacation one of my best friends went on a beach party. His body was washed up two days later."

"Accidents in a row like that aren't too unusual."

His voice was grim. "In March a boy, a senior, named Tod Sherman, was alone in his room. The guess is that he was cleaning his gun, an army .45. It was against the rules to have it in the house. His door wasn't locked. It went off and killed him."

"Maybe they come in threes."

"In June, during the last week of school, one of the most popular kids in the house hung himself. A boy named Teddy Flynn. He was a senior, a very bright boy. He was graduating a week before his twentieth birthday. He hung himself in this room. I took it for this term because no one else wanted it. He used heavy copper wire and fastened it to a pipe that runs across the ceiling of that clothes closet."

It bothered me to think that it had happened in this room. It made the whole situation less of an academic problem. It made me realize that I had taken a smartalec attitude from the beginning. Now that was gone. There was a tangible feeling of evil. I could taste it in the back of my throat.

"Let me get this straight, Arthur. Why are you telling me this?"

"One, two or three deaths might be written off as accident and coincidence. I think five can, too, in this case. But outsiders don't see it that way. They think it's fishy."

"Do the police?"

"Oh, no. I didn't mean that responsible people consider it

fishy. The kids in the other houses do. By next year, it will all
be forgotten. The transient population will take care of that.
But this year is going to be rough. It'll affect our pledge total.
There'll be a lot of whispering. For those inside the group
it'll mean a stronger unifying force, I suppose. I thought
you, as a senior transfer, should know all this."

"Why did the Flynn boy kill himself?"

"We'll never really know, I guess. His gal was really
broken up. She was a junior last year."

"Did she come back?"

"I saw her at registration. Her name is Mathilda Owen.
Tilly. You'll probably run into her sooner or later. This is a
big school, but she'll travel in our group, I imagine."

"The five boys that died, Arthur. Outside of their being
members of the fraternity, is there anything else to tie the
five of them together?"

"No. Nothing."

"Teddy Flynn hung. Tod Sherman shot, two sophomores killed in a car and one unnamed guy drowned."

"That's it. The boy who drowned was Rex Winniger.
The sophomores were Harry Welly and Ban Forrith. It was
. . . a pretty bad year here."

"I can imagine."

He leaned over and put on the desk lamp. Evil was thrust
back into the far shadows. He smiled without humour and
said, "There had better not be any accidents this term."

I made myself laugh. "Hell, all the accidents for the next
ten years are used up now. We're over the quota."

II

Axes to Grind

The creative writing deal met once a week for a two-hour
session, Friday from ten to twelve. It was taught by a dry
but pompous little man who, the year before, had hit one of
the book clubs with a novel that had little to recommend it
but the incredible size of the heroine from the waist up and
the frenzy with which she met all emotional experiences.

Tilly Owen was in the class. I located her at the first

session, a tallish dark-haired girl, almost plain. Her face showed nothing and I was disappointed in her. She took notes meekly, her dark head bent over the notebook. But when she walked out, I did a quick revision. The tall body had an independent life of its own. Her face showed a clear and unspectacular intelligence, an aloofness – but the body was devious and complicated and intensely feminine, continually betraying the level eyes. She went off with a few other girls before I could make an intercept.

During the week leading to the next session when I saw her again, I enlarged my circle of friends inside the fraternity. Brad Carroll thawed a great deal, particularly after I had a few of them out to the beach house for cocktails. I began to learn more about the insides of the brethren.

Step Krindall, with the baby blue eyes and the pink head, was as uncomplicated and amiable as a dancing bear. Arthur Marris had too deep a streak of seriousness in him, verging on self-importance. His touch was thus a shade too heavy. The better house president knows when to use a light touch. Every house has its types. Bill Armand, the dark, vital junior, was the house sceptic, the cynic, the scoffer. Ben Charity, the shy blond Georgia boy, was the gullible one, the butt of most practical jokes. The angel-faced red-headed sophomore named Jay Bruce was the house clown. There was the usual sullen, heavy-drinking kid on his way off the rails – one Ralph Schumann, a senior.

The rest of them seemed to merge into one composite type, a bunch of well-washed young men in a stage in their development when clothes, women, snap courses and hard-boiled books had a bit too much importance. They talked easily and well, made perhaps a shade too confident by their acceptance into one of the most socially acceptable groups on the campus. And, in many ways, they were exceedingly silly, as the young of any species is likely to be.

Their silliness pointed up the vast gulf that my two years out of college had opened up. I could see that in their group mind I was becoming rated as one hell of a fellow, a quick guy with a buck, a citizen who could handle his liquor, keep his mouth shut.

I found that I had not lost the study habit. Necessary

research during the two intervening years had kept me from losing the knack. The courses were amazingly stimulating. I had expected boredom, but found intellectual excitement.

On Friday came the second writing class. As per instructions, the entire class had done a short-short apiece and dropped it off on the previous Wednesday at the instructor's office.

He gave us a long beady stare and we became silent. "I should like to read one effort handed in," he said. He began to read. I flushed as I recognized my own master-work. I had banged one out with an attempt to give him the amateur stuff he expected.

He finished it and put it carefully aside. "I shall not tell you who wrote that. I read it because you should all find it interesting. I do not care to be laughed at. That story had complete professional competence. No doubt of that. And it is a devilishly clever parody of the other stories that were turned in. It is a tongue-in-cheek attempt to cover the entire scope of the errors that beginners make.

"Yet the perpetrator of this – this fraud, could not conceal his ability, his very deft turn of phrase and control of emotion. I am mystified as to why he or she should be taking my course. I suggest to this unnamed person that he or she give me credit, next time, for a bit more intelligence."

I shot a wary look to either side. No one was watching me. I forced myself to relax. Another dumb stunt like that and I would destroy my purpose, if I hadn't done so already.

At noon I elbowed my way through the mob and went down the steps behind Tilly Owen. I fell into step beside her and said, "My name is Rod Arlin, Miss Owen." I gave her the very best smile. "I offer lunch, an afternoon on the beach, early dinner in Tampa, and a few wagers on the canines at Derby Lane."

She quickened her pace. "Please, no."

"I come well-recommended. Arthur Marris will vouch for me."

"I have a date."

I caught her arm above the elbow and turned her around. Anger flashed clear in her grey eyes.

"And a Mr Flynn in New York considers me to be a bright kid, if that means anything."

The anger faded abruptly and her eyes narrowed. "If this is some sort of a –"

"Come on. My car's parked over in the lot behind Administration." I gestured.

She sat demurely beside me in the car. I parked in front of her sorority house. She dropped off her books, changed to a pale green nylon dress beautifully fitted at the waist and across the lyre-shaped flare of her hips, and came back out to the car with swim suit and beach case in an astonishing twenty minutes. She even smiled at me as I held the door for her.

At lunch she said, "Now don't you think you ought to tell me why . . ."

"Not yet. Let's just get acquainted for now."

She smiled again, and I wondered how I had managed to think of her as plain. I got her talking about herself. She was twenty-two, orphaned when she was eighteen. A trust fund administered by an uncle was paying for the education. During the summer she had gone north to work at a resort hotel. She adored steaks, detested sea food, kept a diary, lived on a budget, hated the movies, adored walking, wore size eight quad A shoes and thought the fraternity and sorority system to be feudal and foul.

She gave me a surprised look. "I don't talk like this to strangers! Really, I'm usually very quiet. You have quite a knack, Rod. You're a listener. I never would have thought so to look at you."

"What do I look like?"

She cocked her head to the side and put one finger on the cleft in her chin. "Hmmm! Pretty self-satisfied. Someone who'd talk about himself rather than listen. And you're older than I thought. I never noticed until just now those little wrinkles at the corners of your eyes. Quite cold eyes, really. Surprisingly cold."

"Warm heart."

"Silly, that goes with hands not eyes."

We drove out to the beach. She was neither awed by nor indifferent to my layout. "You should be very comfortable here," she said.

The sun bounced off the white sand with a hard glare. I spread the blanket, fiddled with the portable radio until I found an afternoon jazz concert. The gulf was glassy. It looked as if it had been quieted with a thick coat of blue oil. Porpoise played lazily against the horizon and two cruisers trolled down the shore line. Down by the public beach the water was dotted with heads.

She came across the little terrace and down across the sand wearing a yellow print two-piece suit. Her body was half-way between the colour of honey and toast, fair, smooth and unblemished. I rolled onto my elbows and stared at her. It put a little confusion into her walk, a very pleasing shyness – with the mind saying don't and the body saying look. That kind of a girl. That very precious kind of a girl.

"Well!" I said. She made a face at me.

She sat on the blanket, poured oil into the palm of her hand and coated herself. We lay back, the radio between us, our eyes shut, letting the frank Florida sun blast and stun and smother us with a glare that burned through closed lids with the redness of a steel mill at night.

"Now," she said sleepily. "Now tell me."

I reached over and closed the lid of the radio. "Have you made any guesses?"

"Just one. That was your story he read today, wasn't it?"

It startled me. "A very good guess indeed. Mind telling me how you made it?"

"Too simple, really. Somebody in the class had to be there on . . . false pretences. I'm a senior here, you know. So I happened to know everybody else in the class except you."

I told her why I had come.

She didn't answer. When I glanced over I saw that she was sitting up, her forehead against her knees. She was weeping.

I patted her shoulder. It was a very ineffectual gesture. The oil she had used was sticky.

She talked without looking at me. "I didn't want to come back here. I wanted to go to some other school. Every day I see places where . . . we were together."

"Do you feel the way Mr Flynn does?"

"That Ted didn't kill himself? Of course. We were going to be married. Almost everybody knew that. And now they look at me and I can see in their eyes that they are full of nasty pity. The girls won't talk to me about dates or marriage. I thought I'd die this summer. I worked every day until I was too exhausted to think about anything, just go to sleep."

"If he didn't kill himself, somebody else did."

"That's the horrible part." She turned and looked at me. Her eyes were red. "That's the awful part, having to accept that. And that's why I came back. I thought I would try to find out. The first thing is to find out why anyone should kill Ted, why anyone should want him dead."

I took her in on my reasoning thus far. "If you assume that he was killed, you have two choices. The other deaths in the house were either accidents or they were caused too. If they were accidents, somebody was after Ted as an individual. If they were not accidents, then you have two further choices. Were they linked, or were they separate crimes? If they were linked, there is no use looking in Ted's history for an enemy. If they were linked, he and the others were killed as symbols, not as individuals. Do you follow me?"

"Of course. I've been thinking the same way. But you've organized it better."

"That may be the reason I'm here. The use of orderly thought processes acquired through feature work now applied to murder. Do you think you would slip in public if you called me Joe?"

"No. I'm Tilly, of course. But let's get on with it. Five died. Sherman, Winniger, Welly, Forrith and Ted. Suppose they were killed as a symbol. It had to come from someone inside the house, or an outsider. Each guess leads to a different set of symbols, Joe."

"You are doing very nicely. Keep going."

"If they were all killed by a fraternity brother, it had to be because of jealousy, spite, house politics . . . all that doesn't satisfy me, Joe. Those reasons seem too trivial somehow. And if it came from outside the house, you have to agree that it was a male who was willing to take the chance of being seen inside the house. There the risk is greater, but the motives become stronger. The fraternity system is based on a false set of values. Kids can be seriously and permanently hurt by the sort of cruelty that's permitted. A mind can become twisted. Real hate can be built up.

"When I was a freshman, one sorority gave my roommate a big rush. She wanted to join and so she turned down the teas and dances at the other houses. When the big day came she was all bright-eyed and eager. The stinkers never put a pledge pin on her. She offended somebody in the house and in the final voting she was blackballed. But she had no way to fight back."

"What happened to her, Tilly?"

"She left school before the year was over. She wrote once. The letter was very gay, very forced. But even though it hurt me to see what happened to her, I was too much of a moral coward to turn down my own bid that night she cried herself to sleep."

"Then," I said, "if this is a case of a twisted mind trying to 'get even' with Gamma U, we have to find out who took an emotional beating from the brethren in the pledge department, eh?"

"Doesn't it look that way to you? And you can find that out, you know. There are six thousand kids in the university. Two thousand belong to clubs and fraternities and sororities. Four thousand are what we so cutely call barbarians. Barbs. Outcasts. Spooks, creeps, dim ones. There, but for the grace of the Lord –"

"It can be narrowed down a little, Tilly," I said. "The first two were killed last year just before the rushing season started. That means that if the assumption we're making is correct, the jolt came the year before and the party brooded about it for almost an entire year before taking action. That would fit. He would be a junior.

"Assume, with the even split between male and female, there are seven hundred and fifty juniors. Five hundred of them are barbs. Out of that five hundred, probably fifty were on the Gamma U rush list two years ago. Out of that fifty, I would guess that fifteen to twenty were pledged. The rush list should be in the files. If we both work on it, we ought to be able to narrow it down pretty quickly."

She looked at me and her eyes filled again. "Joe, I . . . some day I want to tell you how much it means that you've come here to . . ."

"Last one in is a dirty name," I said.

She moved like I thought I was going to. As I reached the edge, she went flat out into a racing dive, cutting the water cleanly. She came up, shook her wet hair back out of her eyes and laughed at me.

We swam out, side by side. A hundred yards out we floated on the imperceptible swell. "Ted and I used to swim a lot," she said in a small voice. And then she was gone from me, her strong legs churning the water in a burst of speed. I swam slowly after her. When I caught up with her, she was all right again.

"It's clear today," she said, going under in a surface dive. I went down too, and with my eyes squinted against the water I could see the dance of the sunlight on the sandy bottom. I turned and saw her angling towards me, her hair streaming out in the water, half smiling, unutterably lovely. I caught her arm and, as we drifted up towards the surface, I kissed her.

We emerged into the air and stared at each other gravely. "I think we'd better forget that, Joe," she said.

"That might be easier said than done, Tilly."

"Don't say things you don't mean, Joe. Ever."

Only three to go. I parked in the shade and was glad of it when I found he hadn't come back yet. It was a tourist court and trailer park. The layout had been pasted together with spit and optimism. Neither ingredient had worked very well. Dirty pastel walls, a litter of papers and orange peels, a glare of sun off the few aluminium trailers, some harsh red flowers struggling up a broken trellis. I watched his doorway. The sign on it said *Manager*. A half hour later a blonde unlocked the door and went in.

I walked over and knocked. She came to the door, barefoot. In another year the disintegration would have removed the last traces of what must have once been a very lush and astonishing beauty. That is a sad thing to happen to a woman under thirty.

"Maybe you can't read where it says no vacancy," she said.

"I want to see Bob Toberly," I said.

"If it's business, you can talk to me. I'm his wife."

"It's personal."

She studied me for a few moments. "Okay, wait a sec. Then you can come in and wait. He's late now." Her voice had the thin fine edge that only a consistently evil disposition can create.

She disappeared. Soon she called, "Okay, come on in."

Her dress was thrown on the unmade bed. She had changed to a blue linen two-piece play suit that was two sizes too small for her.

"I gotta climb into something comferrable the minute I get in the house," she said defiantly. "This climate'll kill you. It's hell on a woman." She motioned to a chair. I sat down. She glared at me. "Sure I can't handle whatever it is you wanna see Bob about?"

"I'm positive."

She padded over to the sink, took a half bottle of gin out of the cabinet and sloshed a good two inches into a water tumbler. "Wanna touch?"

"Not right now, thanks."

She put an ice cube in it, swirled it a few times and then tilted it high. Her throat worked three times and it was gone. The room was full of a faint sour smell of sweat.

The room darkened as Bob Toberly cut off the sunlight. He came in, banging the screen door. He was half the size of a house, with hands like cinderblocks. He looked suspiciously at me and then at the bottle on the sink.

"Dammit, Clara, I told you to lay off that bottle."

"Shaddup!" she snapped. "I drink what I please, when I please, with no instructions from you."

He grabbed her arm and twisted it up behind her. He pushed her to the door, shoved her outside. "Wait out there until I tell you to come in."

He turned to me, ignoring her as she screamed at him. "Now what do you want?"

"I'm making a survey of local students who were turned down by the local chapter of Gamma U. It's for a magazine article condemning fraternities. I got my hands on the rush list for two years ago. Your name was on it."

He rocked back and forth, his lips pursed, staring down at me. Suddenly he grinned. "What do you want to know?"

"What was your reaction when you weren't pledged? How'd you take it?"

"I wanted to go bust those smart guys in the chops."

"Did you know why they turned you down?"

"Sure. They were rushing me because they figured me for eventual All-American here. But the timing was bad. In early practice I got a bad shoulder separation. It happened during rush week. They got the spy system operating and found out I was out for the year, probably out for good. From then on I was just another guy with muscles."

"Has it made any change in your life?"

He frowned. "I got stubborn. I decided I wanted to stay in school. But they dropped me off the athletic scholarship list. I married Clara. Her daddy had just died and left her this place. It brings in enough to swing the school bills." He turned and stared at the door. Clara stood outside looking in through the screen. "I didn't know at the time she was no good."

Clara screamed more curses at him. He went over casually and spat through the screen at her. A charming little family scene. I got out as quickly and quietly as I could. As I drove out onto the road I could still hear her.

III

No Suicides Today

The next to the last was a washout, the same as Toberly. The last was a kid named Harley Reyont. I found him at his room in the dormitory and I took him down the street to a beer joint. I knew he had seen me around the campus so I had to use a different approach with him.

I said, "I'm a transfer and I've been thinking of whether or not to hook up with the local chapter of my fraternity. But I don't like some of the things I've seen around there. I thought the smart thing to do would be to find somebody they gave the dirty end of the stick to."

I saw his hand shake as he reached for his stein. He was a pale, thin, pleasant-looking boy. "What makes you think I got the dirty end of any stick, Arlin?"

"I saw the rush list. They didn't pledge you and neither did any other group."

"They did me a favour, that bunch."

"Just how do you mean that?"

His mouth curled bitterly. "I was just as wide-eyed and eager as any of the rest of them. Hell, I thought I'd die when I wasn't tapped on pledge night. I thought something was wrong with me, that maybe I was a second-class citizen. I've smartened up since that night, believe me. My clothes weren't right during rush week and my conversation wasn't smooth enough to suit those snobs. They could see I wasn't going to be an athlete. So I got passed over in the rush."

"Was that good?"

"Take a good look at them, Arlin. A good look. Then come back and tell me what you think of their set of values. It's a damn superficial life, fraternity life. If they'd take me in I'd be like the rest of them now. Cut out of the same pattern."

"But you resented them at the time. Maybe you still do."

He frowned down at his stein. "No, I don't think I still resent them. I feel a little bit sorry for them."

"Didn't you want to get even?"

He looked up quickly. "I see what you mean. I suppose so. I sublimated it. I hated them and I had to show them. I turned in straight As for the freshman and sophomore years. I'll do it again this year. But not because I still resent them – because in the process of acquiring the high grades, I learned that I'm actually pretty bright. I enjoy the work." Again the bitter smile.

"You could say the brothers helped me find myself." He sighed. "Hell, Arlin, I guess I still resent it. I'll resent it all my life. Sour grapes, I suppose. Only I went for a walk along fraternity row during one of the big weekends. I could see them through the windows, dancing with their tall cool women, all wearing that same satisfied smirk. I wanted to bust the windows with rocks. I wanted to be inside there, one of them.

"I wanted to be Brother Reyont, the Big Man on the Campus. I walked back to the dorm and read Kant. He always puts me to sleep in short order. It took twenty pages that night. But I don't blame Gamma U. Any other house would have done the same thing. I was a pretty dim little freshman, that I can assure you."

"Thanks for being so frank with me."

"You're buying the beer, aren't you? . . ."

When I drove in I saw that my lights were on, and I knew that Tilly had used the key I had given her. I parked quietly and stopped and looked through the window. She was in the big chair wearing that green dress I liked. Her legs were tucked up under her and she was reading a news magazine. The lamplight brought out the very fine line of her cheek and throat.

She looked good to me. Having her waiting there for me made me play too many mental games. It wasn't healthy. On a crap table the wise man plays the field. Anybody who bets all night on the same number loses his shirt.

I went in and she came up eagerly out of the chair.

"Aha!" I said. "So you are here about the mortgage! Heh, heh, heh."

"Please, sire! The night is cold. You will not throw me and my piteous child out into yon snow."

"Mind your tongue, girl, or I shall feed you both to the wolves."

We laughed together. Silly people. She stopped suddenly and said, "Oh, Joe, it seems so long since I could laugh like this."

"Easy, easy," I said warningly. "Go weepy on me and I'll turn you over to the dean of women. They'll hang you for – dawn! I'm sorry, Till. Foot in the mouth disease."

"That's okay. How did you do?"

"Reyont is off the list. And he's the last one, that is if you covered your boy. Did you?"

"That's why I came, Joe. I saw him. He . . . he's very odd. He frightens me a little. His name is Luther Keyes."

"Do you think he's capable of – what happened?"

"I don't know. I just don't know. You'd better talk to him tomorrow. He's in my nine o'clock class, room fourteen

in the Arts Building. I'll arrange to walk out with him.
We'll come out the west door.

"Done. What did you tell him? What sort of a story did
you give him?"

"I played the gossip. I asked him if he thought one of the
Gamma U men had been killing his fraternity brothers.
You know, dumb innocent questions. Baby stare. I won't
tell you how he reacted. You be the judge of that." She
looked at her watch. "Gosh, it's late."

"And a bright moon and a warm breeze. It just so
happens that I picked up a suit the other day that ought
to fit you."

She stared hard at me. "No, nonsense, Joe?"

"Promise."

I waited for her in the living room. She went out first. I
turned off the lights. There was a trace of phosphorescence
in the waves as they broke against the shore.

We went out too far. The fear came without warning. She
was surging along, ten feet ahead of me. All knowledge of
the shore line was gone. We were in the middle of an ocean.

"Tilly!" I called. "Till!" She didn't stop. I put on a burst
of speed that I knew would wind me completely if I had to
continue it for long. As I made a long stroke, my fingertips
brushed her foot. I reached and caught her by the ankle.

"No, Joe," she gasped. "Let me go! Oh, please let me go!
Don't stop me!"

She fought to get free but I wouldn't let her go. "What
good would it do? You're trying to run away from something."

Suddenly she was passive. "All right, Joe. I'm all right
now."

"Come on, we'll get you in." That was easy to say. In the
struggle we had become turned around. I could get no clue
as to the direction of the swells. I could see no lights on
shore. I knew then that we were out so far that the lights
were too close to the horizon for us to see them from our
angle of vision.

"Which way, Joe?" she asked, her voice tautening with
panic.

Oh, fine, I thought. *This was your idea and now you don't care for it much.*

Then, like a letter from home, I saw the pink on the sky, the reflected lights of Sandson.

"That way," I said. "Come on. Take it easy."

After a long time I was able to correct our course by the lights of a familiar hotel. It seemed that we would never, never make it – and then my knee thumped sand. She stood up, swayed and fell forwards. I tried to get her up. She was out cold. I got her over my shoulder and weaved up to the house. I dumped her, dripping wet, on the couch. I turned on the hooded desk light, got big towels.

Her lips were blue. Her eyes opened and her teeth were chattering so badly she couldn't speak. It was a warm night. I poured a shot and held her head up while she drank it. She gagged but she kept it down. I got blankets, covered her. She cried for a long time, softly, as a tired child will cry. I sat beside her and rubbed her forehead with my fingertips until she went to sleep.

After she was asleep, I sat for a long, long time in the dark and I knew, without her telling me, just how it had happened. She had grieved for Ted. But not enough. She had been strongly attracted to me, as I was to her. With a person of her intense capacity for loyalty, it seemed an unthinkable deceit. It made a strong conflict within her. What she had done had seemed to her at the time to be the only solution.

I knew that when she awakened, her reaction would tell me whether or not I had guessed right about her feelings.

I sat there until the eastern sky was grey shot through with a pink threat of tomorrow's sun. She stirred in her sleep, opened her eyes and looked at me with no alarm or surprise. She held her arms up and I kissed her. It was as natural and expected and unsurprising and sweet as anything I ever knew.

"I had a nightmare," she whispered.

"A long, long bad dream, darling. It's all over now. For good."

"Don't ever say anything to me that you don't mean, Joe. Ever."

"Promise."

"And Joe . . ."

"Yes, darling."

"Please. Go away from me for a little while. Way over there. I feel like a hussy. I don't want to be one." She grinned. "Not quite yet."

"We ought to get you back."

"Isn't today Saturday?"

"Don't ask me like that. I always look at my watch when anybody asks me too quickly what day it is. Yes, it's Saturday."

"No classes, Joe. I can cook. How do you like your eggs?"

"After a swim at dawn, of course."

"Then go on out and swim, dear. You're dressed for it. I'll call you when it's ready. How's the larder?"

"Full of ambrosia."

"Come here, Joe. Now go swimming. Quickly, Joe. Quickly."

I swam. She cooked. She called me. I ate. We kissed. We made silly talk. Words are no good. Ever.

That Ted had himself a girl, he did. I was glad he was dead. To be glad for a thing like that gave me a superstitious feeling of eternal damnation. Bad luck. It gave me a shiver. She saw it. We held hands. No more shivers. No more bad luck, I hoped.

During that week, after I rubbed Keyes off our list, we plotted. I could speak more freely because now I could talk about Ted without it rocking her as badly as it had in the beginning.

I said, "We tried one way. I have a hunch that guy you mistrust is just another zany. Now we go at it from the other direction. We forget motive and try opportunity. We back-track on the beach party, the return trip from Tampa, the gun-cleaning episode. Ted's apparent suicide. Now from the motive viewpoint you brought out that the case is stronger for an outsider.

"From the opportunity point of view, the case is stronger against one of the brethren. Two of the incidents happened inside the house. At the beach party most of the members were present. The car accident is the hard one to figure out. I suggest that we drop it for the time being. Maybe it was a legitimate accident. Maybe it just served to give the murderer his idea. Were you on the beach party? Yes, I know you were, because I know Ted was there. And it was all couples."

"You want me to tell you about it."

We were in deck chairs side by side on the little terrace, our heads in shade, our legs stretched in the sun. She took a cigarette. I held the lighter to her.

She leaned back. "The beach party was just before Christmas vacation started. It was a fraternity affair, but there were a few outsiders, guests. Rex Winniger, the boy who drowned, was with a casual date, a snakey little blonde that I disliked on sight. Rex had broken off with Bets, a girl in my house. It seemed too bad. He was very popular and a good athlete, but not much of a swimmer. He came from Kansas, I think."

"Where was the party?"

"On a long sand spit called Bonita Island. We used a big launch belonging to Harry Fellow's father. Harry graduated last year. We moored it on the mainland side of the island and we had to wade ashore. We got there in mid-afternoon. Everybody swam and toasted in the sun. The drinking started a little later. Nearly everybody drank too much. The party got a little wild.

"The party broke up a little after midnight because some of the boys had passed out and their dates were yammering to be taken home. Somebody thought of counting noses. Rex and the little blonde were missing. Some of the group thought it would be a big gag to leave them marooned there. Then they went looking with flashlights. They found the little blonde asleep on the sand. They got her awake and she said she hadn't seen Rex in she couldn't remember when. You could feel people getting a little worried and a little soberer then.

"The boys made a line across Bonita holding hands – it's only about seventy feet wide. They went right from one end to the other. Quite a few of the other boys could have swum to the mainland as a joke. But Rex really couldn't swim that well. Then we all hoped that maybe he'd tried it and made it all right. But on the way back people were laughing in that funny nervous way that worried people do. Ted whispered to me that he didn't like the look of it at all. We girls were taken home.

"In the morning Ted met me and he looked haggard. He said that Rex hadn't showed up. They reported it early that same morning. Hundreds of people looked for the body. The papers made a big story of it and the blonde got her picture on the front page, looking tearful. Well, you know the rest. The beach party was on a Thursday night. They found his body on the beach on the mainland on Saturday afternoon, about three miles below Bonita Island."

"Did you notice if he got drunk at the party?"

"Everybody was drinking. Some of them got pretty sloppy. But I don't remember that Rex was sloppy. We talked about that later. We compared notes. After dark everybody was in the water at one time or another, because the surf was coming in beautifully."

"Was there any incident, any trouble that caught your eye?"

She thought for a few moments. "No . . . I guess not. Nothing really unusual. When people drink they say things they normally wouldn't say. There were quarrels and poor jokes and some spiteful talk. Harv Lorr was president of the house. He saw that things weren't going too well. He tried to keep all the boys in line. Arthur Marris helped him, even though Arthur was only a junior then. Ted could have helped but he didn't want to leave me alone for as long as it would take."

"All in all, a bust party, eh?"

"Not a nice party, Joe. Full of undercurrents."

IV

Sweating Bullets

At that moment a car drove in. I heard it stop. Till gave me a quick look. I got up out of the chair. Bill Armand, the faintly vulpine junior, and Brad Carroll came around the side of the house, carrying suits and towels. One of Armand's dark eyebrows went high in surprise as he saw Tilly.

"Why, hello, Tilly!" Brad Carroll said in his careful voice. "Hi, Rod. I didn't know you two were acquainted. Rod, we decided this was the day to take you up on your standing invite."

"Hello, Brad," Tilly said. "And Bill. I met Rod in our writing class. The guy is persuasive."

"We've noticed that," Bill said. "Tilly, you're looking wonderful."

"Thank you," she said gravely.

There was a moment of awkwardness. I said, "The bar is the kitchen shelf, mates. Select your venom and some for us. Till's is rum and Coke, and I'm on bourbon and water if you feel industrious. You can change in the bedroom."

They went inside. Tilly reached over and touched my arm. "Joe, darling. This is going to give them a very choice bit of gossip."

"Do you really care?"

"Uh uh."

"That's my girl."

They came back out bearing drinks. Bill clowned it, his towel over his arm like a waiter's napkin. He bowed low as he handed Tilly her drink, murmuring, "Madame." In trunks he was deeply tanned, whip-lean, with long smooth muscles. Brad was whiter, softer, thickening a bit in the waist, with a small roll of fat over the top of his yellow trunks.

Bill sat on the edge of the terrace turned towards us, with one eyebrow still high enough to give him a knowing look. Brad said, "We didn't do this right. We should have come armed with charming blondes and a couple of jugs to salve our conscience. We thought you hadn't had time yet to live dangerously, Rod."

"I keep telling you that we're underestimating the guy," Bill said.

"Where's Al Siminik, Brad?" I asked. It seemed odd to see Brad without his shadow.

"By the time we see him again, we'll have forgotten what he looks like. He's earning his keep, throwing his muscles around," Bill answered.

I eyed Bill. "What's your sport, Armand?"

He laughed. "Molly."

Tilly bristled. "That isn't a nice thing to say, Bill!"

"Protecting your sisters?" he jeered.

I was amazed at how cold Tilly's grey eyes could get. "The only thing I have against Molly is that she's stupid enough to find you attractive, Bill Armand."

He held up his hands in mock defence and ducked his head. "Hey! Take it easy."

Talk became more casual. After a while Bill drove to the main road and phoned Molly. He came back and said that Brad's girl, Laura, was coming out and bringing Molly with her. Shortly after that, Bill and Tilly went in for a swim. Brad moved over into the chair where Tilly had been.

His smile was very engaging. "Rod, you strike me as being a pretty canny guy."

"Oh, thank you, sir."

"No gag, Rod. I mean it. You're smart enough to see how things stand at the chapter. Arthur is one of the best friends I've got." He was working the knife out of the sheath very slowly and I knew why he'd decided to come out. Carroll, the tireless politician.

"But . . ." I said.

He gave me a quick look. "Oh, you see it too?"

"Better tell me what you see, Brad."

"I'll be frank. I wouldn't want this to go any further. I see a sweet guy who completely lacks the executive touch. He's too heavy-handed. Now take Harv Lorr. There was a great president. We used to have a penny-ante poker game going on weekends in his room. Will Arthur go for that? Not for a minute. It says in the book no gambling in the house. The boys resent that rule-book attitude, Rod. But a lot of the fellows figure it this way. They say that Arthur was elected and he'll graduate in June, so why not play along with him."

"And what do you say?"

"I say that this is a whole year out of our lives. Why let Arthur make it a poor fraternity year? Every member has a vote. Right now, because of some people's sense of duty, Arthur swings the majority. But if the rest of us who don't quite agree with some of his measures could consolidate our vote, we could do just about anything we pleased."

"In other words, let Arthur have the title and let you have the real push."

"I didn't say that!" he said in a hurt tone.

"Doesn't it amount to the same thing?" I asked disarmingly.

He pretended to think it over. Well, it would be one way to put it, Rod."

"Let's get it out in the open. You want me to vote with you."

"Only if you sincerely believe that it's the thing to do."

"Let's take the gloves off, Brad," I said. "I'm a transfer. I'm a senior. I'm not living in the house. As I see it, there's no reason for me to get messed up in local chapter politics. With either you or Arthur running things, the food is going to be good, the lounge is going to be comfortable, the dances are going to be fun. I don't care about anything else."

"That," he said firmly, "is what I consider an irresponsible and selfish attitude."

"Consider it anything you want to."

"Then I may take it that you'll vote with Arthur?"

I saw I had hurt his feelings. Or at least he had decided that should be his attitude. "You may take it this way. I'm not for you or again you. When I attend chapter meetings I'll refrain from voting. Then you won't have to worry about a counterbalancing vote."

His smile was full of satisfaction. "I'm glad to hear you say that. Frankly, a lot of the younger boys would be willing to follow your lead in preference to mine, even. You've made quite an impression, Arlin. Quite an impression."

"Do you want some advice?"

"What do you mean?"

"Take it or leave it. You're creating tempests in teapots, Carroll. You're misdirecting a very strong itch for power. Find some new direction for it."

He dropped all expression. "Am I to judge from that that you consider the fraternity to be unimportant?"

"Take it any way you please."

"You damn veterans are all alike. Everything is a big joke. Arthur is the only one I ever saw who takes things seriously. Just because you fought a war, you've got this superior attitude. Frankly, Arlin, it makes me sick to my stomach."

"Vote for Carroll!" I said. "Vote for a square deal!"

"Go to hell!"

"Now you're being stupid. Offend me too much and I'll get interested enough to bust a few spokes out of your big wheel."

He chewed that around in his mind for a while. I was rewarded with his most charming smile, an outstretched hand. "Sorry, Rod. I get too worked up."

"Forget it," I said, yawning.

He stood up. "I'm glad to see Tilly dating, Rod. Poor girl. She needs a few good times."

"I'll tell her you said so."

He flushed. "You're damn difficult to talk to sometimes."

At that point a car stopped behind the house. We heard a girl's voice over the sound of the surf. They came around the side of the house. Bill and Tilly came out of the water to meet them. Molly had a trim little figure, chestnut hair, a set of large trusting eyes and a vulnerable mouth. Her eyes glowed as she watched Bill Armand walk towards her. Laura was as dark as Tilly, but taller, a shade leaner, with a face so patrician that it looked inbred. Her speech was a finishing-school drawl.

Molly was a giggler. Bill treated Molly with affectionate amusement. Brad treated Laura as a girl who had earned the right to share in his reflected glow as a large wheel around the university. Both girls tried without success to conceal an intense curiosity about Tilly and me and our current status.

Tilly turned feline on me, and in the process she was as cute as a bug. I saw her wondering how to handle the problem. Finally she gave me a meaningless stare and said, "Rod and I are so glad you could come out here. What are you drinking? Rod, fix them up, like a dear, will you?"

Laura gave Molly a meaningful look.

It was a complete essay, that look.

We swam, we loafed in the sun – three couples on a late Saturday afternoon. To any onlooker we were young and carefree and casual. Uncomplicated, I lay with Till sprinkling sand on the back of my arm and thought about us.

One vulnerable little girl heading for heartbreak, one icy maiden as ambitious as her grasping boyfriend, one young cynic complicated by a streak of ruthlessness, one lovely girl who had been persuaded the night before that this was not the time to die – and one pretender, a young man who had thought it possible to come to this place and solve a pretty problem without becoming emotionally involved, and who was slowly finding it impossible.

The police station at Sandson and the fire department shared the same building. It looked vaguely like a Moorish castle.

The man they steered me to was a Lieutenant Cord. He was an unlikely six foot six with a stoop that brought him to six three. He had a corded throat, heavy wrists and a slack liver-spotted face.

"What can I do for you, Mr Arlin?"

"I'm at the university, Lieutenant. I've been doing some work in psychology. One of the case histories assigned to me is the case of Tod Sherman, who was killed during March this year."

I made it pretty breezy. He leaned back in his chair and for the first time I noticed a very alert intelligence hiding behind his sleepy grey-green eyes.

"Let me get you straight. I remember Sherman. How does it hook up with psychology when a lad had a bad accident like that?"

I took a deep breath. I had to make it better than I thought. "You know, of course, about accident-prone people and how they contribute the lion's share of motor vehicle accidents and accidents in the home. The study of such people is a legitimate part of modern psychology. I have reason to believe that Sherman was an accident-prone. Actually it is the death wish operating on the subconscious level, or else the result of a childish desire for attention."

"What do you want from me?"

"If it wouldn't be too much trouble, a summary of what happened. I've talked to the other members of the fraternity who were there at the time. Their reports are confusing."

He looked at the wall clock. "I guess it won't take too much time. We got the call on a Sunday afternoon. They don't operate the dining room at that house on Sundays and nearly everybody was out. A boy named Flynn, the one who hung himself three months later, was the one who heard the shot and traced it to Sherman's room. Flynn was in the lounge at the time, and it took him, he said, maybe ten minutes to find out who and what it was.

"One other lad, a sophomore named Armand, was in the house at the time. He was asleep and the shot didn't awaken him. Flynn was smart. He phoned the campus infirmary and then us. He didn't touch the body. He checked the time. We got there as the ambulance did. The doctor pronounced him dead. We were both there a little less than twenty minutes after the shot according to Flynn's watch. Sherman had been sitting at his desk by the window. There was an oily rag and a bottle of gun oil on top of the desk. The gun was a .45 Army Colt.

"The slug had caught him under the chin and gone up through the roof of his mouth, exploding out of the top of his head to lodge in the ceiling. He had fallen to his left between the chair and the window. The gun was under his desk. The ejected cartridge case was on the window sill. A full clip was on the desk blotter beside the oil bottle. It was the standard mistake. Ejecting the case and forgetting the one in the chamber.

"As I see it, he was holding it pointing up towards him, and he pulled the slide down so he could look through the barrel. His hand was oily and the slide got away from him. When it snapped up, it fired the shell in the chamber."

"Were you completely satisfied with the verdict of accidental death, Lieutenant?"

He smiled humourlessly. "Now what kind of a fool question is that, Arlin? If it wasn't an accident it would screw up this psychology report, wouldn't it?"

I tried again. "Did you investigate to see if anyone said he was depressed?"

"Sure. Lots of guys are cagey enough to do a hell of a good job by faking an accident when they want to knock themselves off. But in that case there is an insurance angle, usually, and the guy himself is older. No, this Sherman was apparently a pretty popular guy in the house. He wasn't depressed. He'd busted up with his girl, but he had a new one pretty well lined up. He had enough dough, a good job after graduation, and his health."

"You've been very kind, Lieutenant." I stood up.

"Any time," he said.

I went to the door. As I turned the knob he said, "Just a minute." I looked back at him. He smiled. "Do me a favour, Arlin. Come around some time and tell me what the hell it was you really wanted."

"I don't think I know what you mean."

"See you around, Arlin."

I went out and sat in the car. There was a coldness at the nape of my neck. Up until the talk with Cord, I had been willing to go along with the theory of a chain of accidents. I had tried to be thorough for the sake of the pay I was getting. Mr Flynn had just been a man pathetically anxious to prove his son was not a suicide. Tilly had been a girl who had not been able to understand how Ted Flynn's mind may have been unstable, along with his undeniable brilliance.

But now everything had a new flavour. It was something that Cord had said, and yet, going over his words again and again, I could not pick it out.

I knew, sitting there in the sun, as well as I knew my own name that the odds were in favour of someone else's finger pulling that trigger. I was sweating and yet I felt cold.

For the first time I realized that my operations were a bit transparent. If someone had killed Sherman – and I didn't know why I was so sure they had – then that someone might still be in the house. If so, he was watching me. It would be natural for him to watch me. I was a stranger. I was an unknown factor.

I sensed a quiet and devious intelligence at work. A mind that could plan carefully and then move boldly.

I drove away. My hands were too tight on the wheel and my foot was shaky on the gas pedal.

V

Accidentally – On Purpose

I cut the History class. Tilly cut her class at the same hour and we drove down Route 19 through Clearwater to Largo and then turned left to Indian Rocks Beach. I found a place where we could park in the shade and watch the placid gulf. On the way I told her of the talk with Cord.

She took my hand, looked into my eyes and said, "For the first time it's real to you, isn't it, Joe?"

"That's one way to put it."

"It's been real to me all along. You know how when people go with each other, they talk about everything under the sun. Once Ted and Step were arguing about suicide. It was after Sherman had died. Step couldn't see that it was wrong – but Ted told us that the only time he could see the remotest justification was when a person was painfully and incurably ill – that the world is too wide and wonderful a place to leave before the time you have is up. He wasn't just talking, Joe."

"I think I would have liked him, Till."

"You would have. I know it. When they told me he'd hung himself, I found out later that I'd screamed that he didn't do it, that someone had done it to him. I'm still just as certain of that as I was during the first moments. He was incapable of it. They were holding the last meeting of the year, the election of officers for the next year it was. They waited and waited and then they went looking for him.

"Brad cried like a baby. They cut him down and then he was shipped north for the funeral. I couldn't go to that. I couldn't even go to the memorial service for him in the chapel at school. I was too sick. They had me in the infirmary. When I got out I went north and took that job."

"Up until now," I said, "I've been playing an intellectual game. Mental musical chairs. Now it isn't a game any more."

"For me it never has been." She bit her lip. "Joe, you'd better not let anything happen to you. You'd just better not."

I kissed her then, there in the cool shade with the warm

wind touching our faces, and she came alive in my arms in a way I've never before experienced. Holding her was holding flame and purpose and a clean, wanting strength. It shook me, and shook her too. We sat apart from each other.

We said very little on the drive back. I left her off at the sorority house. I went to a bar and had a few. I arrived at Gamma U in time for dinner. I talked and I listened politely and the table conversation went over the surface of my mind while below the surface a tallish, faintly awkward girl walked, and her eyes were more than promise . . .

I woke with a start at dawn. The bedroom had an outside door. I had left it open and latched the screen. A tall figure was silhouetted there.

"Rod," he said. "Rod, let me in."

I went to the door. "Oh, Arthur! Man, it's a little after six. I didn't know you boys were going to drop in at this time of day."

I unlatched the door. He brushed by me, walked to the bed and sat down, staring at his big hands. His faintly Lincoln-esque appearance was more pronounced. The eyes had sunk deeper into his head. His cheeks were more hollow. I suddenly knew that this was no time for patter and laughter.

"I can't depend on anybody else," he said. "You've got to help me."

I sat beside him and reached over and took my cigarettes from the bedside table. I lit both cigarettes with my lighter. "What is it?"

"The most awful mess yet, Rod. The worst. Everybody's running around like headless chickens. I came out here to talk to somebody with sense. This time it has rattled me."

"Get to it, Arthur. What happened?"

"The police phoned the house at three this morning. It happened at the Onyx Court." I barely concealed my start of surprise. That was the court and trailer outfit owned by the Toberlys.

"They said that they had a body tentatively identified as Bradford Carroll. I dressed and went over along with Bill Armand. The place was swarming with police. Brad's throat had been cut. I told them that it was Brad all right. I still feel sick. There was blood all over . . ."

"Take it easy, Arthur."

"They were still questioning Bob Toberly. He's a student too. We rushed him a couple of years ago and passed him over. He runs the place along with his wife. It's a sort of crummy place. Toberly said that Brad and his wife, a tall dark girl that he recognized as a student, had registered in at about ten for the night. He said they'd done it many times before. He said that they were secretly married.

"Well, Bill, standing beside me, said 'Laura!' They turned on Bill and made him admit that he thought it sounded like Laura Trainor. They got the name of the sorority house and two cops went to pick her up. They're holding her now. I've done all I could. I wired Brad's parents, and the sorority sisters phoned Laura's father. I heard he's on his way down. Rod, it would be bad enough without all that trouble last year, but this is absolutely the worst. I don't know what's going to happen."

I left him sitting there and made him a stiff drink. Laura was one of Tilly's sorority sisters, along with Molly. So Tilly would know already. I made a second stiff one for myself. He took his glass numbly and drank it as though it were water.

"The razor was right there," he said. "I saw it. A straight razor. He used them. I guess it was an affectation. I guess he had a kit with him so he could get cleaned up and go directly from the Onyx Court to class."

"Do you think Laura did it?"

He shuddered. "How do I know what to think? I don't think she's capable of a thing like that. But they could have quarrelled."

"What will happen?"

"It was too late for the morning papers but the afternoon papers will give it a big play. They'll bring up all that stuff from last year. There were reporters there. Toberly's wife put on her best dress. To her it was like a party. They're giving Toberly a bad time. Brad voted against Toberly, of course, two years ago. Most of us did. They'll twist and turn until they made a motive out of it."

"How can I help?"

He gave me a tired smile. "You've helped by listening. I have to go back now. I have to get everybody together and tell them to keep their damn mouths shut. Then I have to pack Brad's things. A policeman is going to help me. He'll be looking for evidence. He's in the house now, sitting on a chair outside Brad's room. He was there when I left anyway."

"What about Brad's people?"

"They'll be down, I suppose. I ought to make a reservation for them at the hotel. Look, would you do that for me?"

"Sure thing."

He stood up and put the glass on the bedside table. "Thanks, Rod. That drink helped a lot."

"Let me dress. I'll go in with you."

"No, I'll go along. I'll be at the house. See you there."

Some of the brothers were having an early breakfast when I went in. The single waiter acted jittery. Lieutenant Cord was sitting in the lounge. He came over to me and said, "Is this another one of those accident-prone guys?"

I kept my voice low. "Do you think he cut his throat?"

Cord shrugged his big sloping shoulders. "He could have. The razor's in the right place. At least it was. But usually people that take a hack at their own throat, they're timid about it. This was a good try. He damn near slashed his head off – that is, if he did it. Now I got what the boys call an unhealthy interest in you. Want to talk right here?"

"It doesn't matter to me."

"You come in and give me a queer line of chatter and the next thing I know one of your friends is dead. I like to get all the loose ends pasted in or clipped off. Let's you stop trying to kid me."

"How do you mean?"

"I checked your schedule after you left and had a few words over the phone with your professor. I didn't mention your name. He told me somebody was kidding me and that the department wouldn't send a student out like that. So talk, Arlin."

"Suppose I tell you that my reason was good but that it's my business?"

"First let's see how you check out last night. You had dinner here and left. Where did you go?"

"Right back to my place on the beach. I studied until about eleven, wrote a few letters and went to bed at about quarter to one."

"No proof?"

"Not a shred."

"Now this Toberly tells me that somebody was around asking him questions about how Gamma U turned him down. The guy said it was for a magazine article on fraternities. He didn't give a name. Toberly gave me a description. It fits you pretty good, Arlin. Want to come on down to see if Toberly can make identification?"

"I give up. It was me."

"Now don't you think you better tell uncle?"

Two sophomores walked through into the dining room and stared at us curiously. "Someday I'll get smarter," I said. "Come on out and sit in my car for a little while."

The sun was climbing higher. Cord's face was drawn with fatigue. I told him my situation. He listened with a sour expression.

"What answer have you come to, Arlin?"

"I can't give reasons. It's just a very strong feeling. I say that four of them were murdered. Carroll is the fourth. I don't know about the automobile accident. We'll skip that one."

"And you think," he said bitterly, "that three murders took place right under our noses. You think we're that stupid!"

"It's not that you're stupid, Lieutenant. It's that the guy behind it is one clever operator. Take the beach party. No trick to get Winniger out into the surf and drown him. No special trick to take advantage of the empty house on a Sunday, start a conversation with Sherman, and trick him. And if a guy were disarming enough, he could talk the Flynn boy up onto a chair in the closet on some pretext.

"And now Brad. This last one is bolder than the others. This last one was permitted to even look a little like murder. Was it hard to find out where Brad and Laura had a habit of going? Would it be difficult to wait until Laura left to go back to her sorority house? There was a moon last night. What time did it happen?" I asked Lieutenant Cord.

"Around two, I guess. The way it was discovered so fast,

this Toberly couldn't sleep. He went for a walk around the place. He saw the light on and it bothered him. He took a quick look and phoned. We were there at quarter to three. Doesn't that spoil the moon angle?"

"Not completely. Sneak in there and find the razor and let him have it. Then snap on the light on the way out to make it look more like suicide."

Cord studied me. "You talk a good game, Arlin. You almost get me believing it. Except for one thing. Why would anybody do all that? What the hell reason would he have?"

"Are you going to expose me, Lieutenant?"

He shrugged. "There's no point in that. Keep playing your little game if you want to, as long as you're getting paid for it. But stay out of my way. Don't foul up any of my work."

He got out of the car. He regarded me soberly. "And don't leave town. I'm taking a chance on believing you, but that doesn't mean I'm not going to do some checking to make sure."

I had no heart for the classes. I ate and went over to pick up Tilly. She came running out to the car. She climbed in beside me and her fingernails bit into my wrist. "Oh, Joe, I can't take it any more! All this horror! I keep seeing him the way he was out at your place. Smiling and happy."

"How did Laura take it?"

"They had to stop questioning her. She's in the Sandson General Hospital. Shock and hysteria. They're fools to bother her," she said hotly. "Laura goes all green if somebody steps on a bug."

"Have you eaten?"

"No, I couldn't. And I couldn't stand going to classes today, Joe. Start the car. Take me away from here. Drive fast, Joe."

We didn't get back until late afternoon. We bought a paper and read it together.

MYSTERY DEATH OF COLLEGE STUDENT.

That's the way they covered it, speaking neither of suicide nor murder, but hinting at murder.

Bradford Carroll, accompanied by a coed to whom he was secretly married, registered in at a local tourist court at ten o'clock last night. He was discovered shortly before three this morning by the proprietor of the court – who was attracted by the light which was left on. His throat had been cut with a straight razor which was found near his right hand.

Police took the coed into custody. She had returned to her sorority house some time before the body was discovered. Police report that before his wife collapsed, she testified that Carroll had been alive when she left, at approximately ten minutes of two.

Carroll, a senior at West Coast University, was a member of Gamma U, that same hardluck fraternity which lost through suicide and accidental death, five members during the previous school year.

From there on the article went into his history and the school groups of which he was a member.

"It's a ghastly thing," Tilly said.

"The police," I said, "promise an early solution of Carroll's mysterious death."

A friend of Tilly's came over to the car. Tilly introduced us. The girl said, "How do you like a new ruling, kids?"

"Haven't seen it yet."

"No? It's on all the bulletin boards. Curfew for all students living on the campus in either houses or dorms. All special senior privileges rescinded. Now we stand a bed check just like the lower classes. All absences from living quarters after eleven are to be reported to the office of the dean until further notice. How do you like that?"

"I don't," Tilly said. "But what else can they do? Anxious parents will be giving the school a very bad time. They've got to have some sort of an answer."

I dropped Tilly with a promise to pick her up later, and went to the house. Step Krindall looked as glum as his round pink face permitted.

"Special meeting tonight," he said.

Bill Armand was standing in the lounge, staring out the

windows towards the palms that bordered the drive. He gave me a crooked smile.

"Come to college for a liberal education," he said. "Where have you been all day?"

"Comforting the shaken."

"Tilly? When you need a stand-in, let me know."

I was surprised at the sudden feeling of jealousy. "Sure, Bill," I said easily. "What's the voting around here? Murder or suicide?"

"The dopes, which I might say covers about ninety percent of our membership, favour suicide. They overlook the very real argument that Brad was too selfish to kill himself. He wouldn't think of depriving the world of his presence for the next forty years."

"I thought he was your friend!"

"Is friendship blind, like love?"

"Armand, the adolescent cynic. Who stepped on you, Bill? And how hard?"

His lips tightened and his face turned chalk white. He turned on his heel and walked away.

I ate with placid Step Krindall, Arthur, Al Siminik and a quiet senior named Laybourne at a table for four. It was a very subdued meal. Once I went to a slaughter-house. I saw the look in the eyes of the steer after that first brutal smack between the eyes. Siminik wore that look. Arthur ate doggedly, as though from a sense of duty.

After coffee, Arthur looked up at the dining-room clock. He rapped on his glass with a knife. "We'll go up to the meeting room in five minutes. You, Step – you other latecomers – hurry it up."

We filed up to the meeting room. It was a meeting without ritual, the lights on full. Arthur took the chair. "We'll dispense with the minutes of the previous meeting and with the treasurer's report. This is a special meeting called for a special purpose. What happened last night was a severe shock to all of us. Brad was . . . our brother and our friend."

Siminik startled the group by sobbing once aloud. He knuckled his eyes like a small boy.

Arthur went on. "I have talked with the police, just

before dinner. It begins to appear that the verdict of the coroner's jury will be death by his own hand."

"Nuts!" Bill Armand said loudly.

Arthur rapped for order. "That's enough, Armand. If you can't control yourself, I'll order you out of the meeting. Lieutenant Cord has made it clear to me that he anticipates that some of you will find a verdict of suicide hard to believe and will make some foolish, amateurish attempt to uncover evidence turning it into a crime. Murder. I have called this meeting to tell you that the police intend to deal with any such quixotic impulse very harshly. I will deal with it very harshly from this end. What happened is police business and will be handled by the police. I hope I've made myself clear.

"Now for my second point. The students will ask us Gamma U's innumerable questions. Was Brad depressed? Did we know about his marriage? It will be the duty of each and every one of you as a Gamma U to politely but firmly evade all such questions. It is our duty as Brad's friends to keep our mouths shut. By that I do not mean to go about with mysterious and knowing looks. Brad is dead. Nothing can alter that. The policy of this house will be to say that Brad had been troubled lately and that we did not know the cause. Any comment?"

"Yeah, what was he troubled about?" Armand asked.

"I consider that question impertinent, Armand. Any other comments?" He stared around the room. "All right, then. This meeting is adjourned. Wait. One more point. This is for you boys that live in the house. The bed check and curfew will be adhered to rigidly."

Chairs were shoved back. Arthur walked out first. I went down the stairs and out the door. Tilly was sitting in my car.

"I walked over," she said. "I didn't want to be stood up."

"How did you know I was going to?"

I turned on the lights and motor. She moved over close to me. "We're going to your place and talk, Joe. I can think more clearly now."

VI

Shooting at Windmills

She went in ahead of me and put the lights on, as I put the top of the car up against the dew. The gulf was rough, the waves thundering hard against the beach. We dragged chairs out onto the terrace. I held her tightly against me for a moment. "Hey," she said, "I want to keep on thinking clearly for a while. Leggo!"

"Chilly woman."

"Hush!" She sat down and after three tries we got our cigarettes going. "This," she said, "is probably silly. You'll have to let me know. Remember when we talked about what the dead boys had in common except the fraternity?"

"I remember."

"Brad's death makes the pattern more clear, Joe. Can you guess what they had in common?"

I thought for a time. "No, give."

"Rex Winniger, Tod Sherman, Ted and Brad were all very positive people. Strong personalities. They had influence in the fraternity. Every house has a certain quota of nonentities. But there was nothing wishy-washy about any one of that four. They had power in the house and on the campus. Is that going to help?"

I felt the excitement. "That *is* going to help. You are a lovely and intelligent gal. I was so close to it I didn't even see it. Wait a minute now. Let me think. It doesn't make motive any stronger from a sane person's point of view, but it does make it clearer. Jealousy. Lust for power. If the pattern is anything other than accidental, it means we have to look among the membership for our boy. And we said a long time ago that insiders would have the edge by far on opportunity."

I guess we got it both at the same time. She reached over and held my hand. Her hand was like ice. "It couldn't be, Joe. It just couldn't be."

"Come on inside. I want to read you something."

We went in and shut the terrace doors against the wind. I found my lecture notes from the abnormal psychology class. They were fragmentary, but I could piece them together.

"Listen, Tilly. One of the types of insanity least vulnerable to any known treatment is the true psychopath. It's as though the person were born with some essential part missing. Conscience. The psychopath has no understanding of right and wrong. To him, the only thing is not to get caught. Has reasonable-sounding motives for all his actions.

"This type of person, if displeased with service, will set fire to a hotel and think nothing of the consequences as long as he is not apprehended. Entirely blind to the other person's point of view. Many murderers caught and convicted and sentenced are true psychopaths. Motive for crime often absurdly minor. True psychopath shows high incidence of endowment of brains and charm of manner. Is often outstanding. Often basically arrogant.

"Delights in outwitting others. Capable of carrying on long-range planning. Constantly acts in the presence of others. Often a liar as well, with amazingly intricate and well-conceived fabric of untruth. Society has no good answer as yet to the true psychopath."

I put the notebook away. She frowned at me. "But Joe! He's such a sweet guy! Gentle, understanding. He was so nice to me after Ted . . . died."

"High endowment of charm of manner. Constantly acts in the presence of others. Delights in outwitting others."

"But with all he's got on the ball, he'd be almost as big without . . . going to such crazy heights."

"Motive for crime often absurdly minor."

"But to kill . . . just for the sake of fraternity house politics. Joe, it's crazy!"

"A true psychopath is an insane person. He hides among us normal jokers because he looks and acts and talks just like one of us . . . up to a point."

"Will the police listen to you?" she finally asked.

"They'd laugh in my face. What proof have I got? We've got to show that each murder helped him, even though it helped him in a minor way."

She crossed the room. "Hold me tight, darling. I'm scared. I don't want to think about him. I wish it were

Bill, or Step, or little Jay Bruce, or even Al Siminik. Anybody except Arthur Marris."

"We've got to get hold of Harv Lorr, the fellow who was president last year. He can help us straighten out the timing on those other deaths. He's probably in North Dakota or some equally handy place."

"He's a Tampa boy. He's working in the family cigar business. With luck, Joe, we can be talking to him in an hour or so."

Harv Lorr came across from the door to our booth. "There he is," Tilly said. I looked up and saw a tall man approaching. He was prematurely grey and there were deep lines bracketing his mouth. He wore a light sports coat and an open-collared shirt.

"It's nice to see you again, Tilly," he said. His smile was a white ash in his sun-darkened face.

I had slid out of the booth. "Meet Joe Arlin, Harv," she said. We shook hands and murmured the usual things. We all sat down.

Harv ordered beer. He sat beside Tilly. He turned so he could look at her. "You sounded a little ragged over the phone. What's up?"

"It's about Brad," she said.

Harv frowned. "I read it this evening. Terrible thing. How do I fit?"

Tilly looked appealingly at me. I took over. "Mr Lorr, I want to ask you some pretty pointless-sounding questions. If you stop me to ask me why I'm asking them, it will just take that much longer. Believe me, there's a definite pattern in the questions. First. The two sophomores who were killed in that automobile accident. Were they of any particular importance in fraternity politics? Were they active?"

Harv looked puzzled. "They were two votes. At the election of officers the previous June they'd voted for me as house president for the next year, rather than Ted Flynn."

"We'll move on to the next question. We weren't particularly interested in those two sophomores anyway. The next guy we care about is Rex Winniger. Was he active?"

"He was the outstanding man in the junior class. If he'd lived, I don't think there was any doubt of his becoming house president during his last year. It was a blow to all of us."

"He died in December. Then in March of this year it was Tod Sherman. He was a classmate of yours, as Flynn was. Was he active in house politics?"

"Everybody is to a certain extent, Arlin. When I won out over Ted, Ted gave up having any pronounced opinions. There is usually a couple of strong groups in the house. Tod Sherman was my opposition. We fought each other tooth and nail, but it was good-natured. At the time he died, we were pretty well lined up for the June elections. I wanted Arthur Marris for president and it was understood that Tod Sherman was pushing Brad Carroll.

"In a house that size the cronies of the pres get the gravy. You know that Tilly said over the phone you were in the fraternity up at Wisconsin. You know then how a president on the way out through the graduation route tries to get one of his boys in for the following year."

"And so after Sherman died, Ted Flynn took over the opposition."

"If you knew all that, why ask me?"

"I didn't. I just guessed."

"I don't see how you could guess a thing like that. Ted was quite a boy. He went to work on the membership. It began to look as though Brad was going to give Arthur a very close race or squeak in himself in Arthur's place. But, of course, it was all shot to hell when Ted killed himself. In fact, we had to vote by mail during July, after school was out. I handled it.

"Arthur made it by a good ten votes. If Ted had lived to give his little talk in favour of Brad, it might have been a different story. Probably would have been, as Arthur sometimes makes a pretty poor impression in spite of his ability."

I leaned towards him. "And what would you say if I told you that Brad had organized a pretty effective resistance to Arthur and was hamstringing him very neatly by having acquired a majority of the voting strength?"

Harv gave me a quizzical look. "Now wait a minute, Arlin, let's not go off –"

"Can't you see the picture? First, Winniger, then Sherman, then Ted, and now Brad. Which did each death help? Which man? Arthur. Every time."

He gave me a long scornful look. "Now hold it up, Arlin. That's kid stuff and you know it. Sure, the boys play politics. It's a game. It's good training. But nobody – nobody *ever* took it that seriously! Man, are you trying to tell me that old Arthur goes around killing people so he can get to be house president and then so he can keep his authority?" He turned to Tilly. "You ought to know better than that!"

Tilly counted it for him on her fingers. "Winniger, Sherman, Flynn, Carroll. All in the way, Harv. All dead, Harv. You know the law of averages. If you don't care for our answer, give us your answer."

I could see it shake him a little. But he kept trying. "People, you don't kill guys for that sort of thing. Look! It's a college fraternity."

Then Tilly carefully explained to him about psychopaths. I was surprised at how much she remembered. She told it well. When she was through, Harv Lorr knew what a psychopath was.

"It seems so incredible!" he complained. But I saw from his eyes that we had him.

"If it was credible," I said, "somebody would have found out a long time ago. If there'd been a million bucks at stake or something like that – some motive that everybody would be willing to accept, the whole thing would have looked fishy and friend Arthur would have been stopped in his tracks. But this way, for a goal that seems unimportant to the common man, he can hack away almost without interference."

"What do you want me to do?" he asked humbly. He had given up. He believed us.

"Just sit tight," I said. "Be ready to give over the facts when they're called for."

"What do you two plan to do?" he asked.

I looked at Tilly. I kept my eyes on hers. "We've got to

give the guy a new reason," I said, "and then jump him when he jumps."

Her lips formed a soundless, "No!"

"There's no other way," I said. And there wasn't. I wanted her to talk me out of it. I was ready to be talked out of it. I wanted no part of it. But she saw the logic of it, the same as I did.

"Keep your guard up," Harv said.

"I'll make him be careful," Tilly said.

I looked at my watch. "If we can make fifty miles in fifty minutes, you stand a chance of not being expelled, Miss Owen."

We left. I got her back in time. I went out to my place on the beach and wished I was in Montreal. I wished I was in Maine looking at the girls in their swimsuits. I wore myself out swimming in the dark, parallel and close to the shore. I had a shot. I tried to go to sleep. I had another shot. I went to sleep. I dreamed of Arthur Marris. He had his thumbs in my jugular . . .

I waited for the coroner's jury. I told myself it was the smart thing to do. They might force the issue. Then they returned a suicide verdict and sad-eyed people shipped Brad to his home state in a box. Laura went abroad . . .

Call it a ten-day wonder. A small town might have yacked about it until the second generation. A college has a more transient sort of vitality. Life goes on. Classes change. New assignments. Next Saturday's date. Call it the low attention factor of the young. A week turns any college crisis into ancient history.

Tilly and I talked. We talked ourselves limp. The conversations were all alike.

"We've got to get him to make the first move, Tilly."

"But to do that, Joe, you've got to be a threat to his setup. You've got to take Brad's place."

"You don't think I can engineer a strong opposition move?"

"I know you can. That's the trouble."

"What's the trouble?"

"You fool! I don't want you being a target."

"The other boys didn't have their guard up. Not one of them knew until the very last moment. It must have been a horrid surprise. He won't be able to surprise me."

"How can you be sure?"

"By never being off guard."

"People have to sleep, don't they?"

"Now you're handing me quite a sales talk, Till."

We talked. At the drive-ins, between races at the dog tracks, on my small private beach, riding in the car, walking from class.

I didn't tell her, but I was already starting the programme. I took over Brad's sales talk. I buttonholed the brethren and breathed sharp little words into their ears.

I racked up a big zero.

It was funny. When I had no axe to grind, I was Rod Arlin, a nice guy, a transfer, a credit to the house. As soon as I started to electioneer I became that Arlin guy, and what the hell does he know about this chapter, and why doesn't he go back to Wisconsin . . .

Arthur tapped me on the shoulder after dinner. "Talk for a while, Rod?"

"Why, sure."

We went to his room. He closed the door. I glanced towards the closet. I sat down and the little men were using banjo pics on my nerves. But I worked up a casual smile. "What's on your mind, Arthur?"

I didn't like him any more. That warm face was a mask. The deep-set eyes looked out, play-acting, pretending, despising the ignorance of ordinary mortals.

He stood by his desk and tamped the tobacco into his pipe with his thumb. He sucked the match flame down into the packed tobacco with a small sound that went *paaa, paaa, paaa*. He shook the match out.

"It pleased me that you transferred here, Rod. I liked you when I first met you. I considered you to be a well-adjusted person with a pretty fair perspective."

"Thanks."

"Lately you've been disappointing me."

"Indeed!" I made it chilly.

"This job I have is fairly thankless. I try to do my best. I could understand Brad Carroll when he tried to block me in my job. Brad was a professional malcontent. Not mean – just eager. You know what I mean?" He was bold. He half sat on the edge of his desk.

"I know what you mean."

"When you try to operate in the same way, I fail to understand you, Rod. What have you got to gain? You're only spending one year in this school. I want this chapter to run smoothly. The least thing we can have is unity among the members."

"And you're the great white father who's going to give it to us."

"Sarcasm always depresses me a little, Arlin."

"Maybe you depress me a little. Maybe I think that if you can't run the house right, a voting coalition should take the lead away from you."

"Look, Arlin. You have your own place on the beach. You have a very pleasant girl to run around with. You have a full schedule of classes. If you still have too much energy left over, why don't you try taking on a competitive sport?"

"Is it against the house rules to buck the pres?"

He sighed. "I didn't want to say this. But you force me. You may have noticed that there is a certain coolness towards you among the membership."

I nodded. I had noticed it.

"The membership feels that you are stirring up needless conflict among the more susceptible boys. We had a small closed meeting of the seniors the other day. It was resolved that I speak to you and tell you to cease and desist. If you had any chance of being successful, I wouldn't speak to you this way. But you have no chance. You just do not have enough influence as a transfer."

"If I don't?"

"Then I can swing enough votes to deny the privilege of the house to you."

"That takes a three-fourths majority."

"I have more than that."

I knew that he did. It was no bluff. I made my tone very

casual. "Well, you've taken care of me a lot easier than some of the others."

He took his pipe out of his mouth. "I don't think I quite understand that, Rod."

"Then we'll drop it right there." I stood up.

He put his hand out. "No hard feelings?"

I ignored his hand. "Isn't that a little trite?"

He was good. He actually looked as though he wanted to weep. "That isn't the Gamma U spirit, Arlin."

"You take your job pretty seriously, Marris."

"I do the best I know how."

"What man could do more!" I said breathlessly. I turned and walked out.

VII

Setting Up the Kill

Tilly had stayed up until three, she said, finishing a story for our mutual Friday class. She wanted me to read it. She had brought her carbon with her, in her purse.

"Right here?"

"No. The atmosphere has to be better than this, Joe. Wine, soft music."

"At my place I can provide the wine and the soft music. Would you okay the background?"

"Look, I'm blushing about the story. I thought it was something I'd never try to put on paper. Maybe I don't want you to read it."

It was Friday afternoon. We went out to my place. I put on dark glasses and took the carbon out on the beach.

Tilly said, "One thing I'm not going to do is sit and watch you read it, Joe." She walked down the beach away from me. I watched her walk away from me. No other girl had such a perfect line of back, concavity of slim waist, with the straightest of lines dropping from the armpits down to the in-curve of waist, then flaring, descending in a slanted curve to the pinched-in place of the knee, then sleekly curving again down the calf to the delicacy of ankle bone and the princess-narrow foot.

She turned and looked back and read my mind. "Hey, read the story," she said.

I read it. She'd showed me other work and I'd been ruthless about too many adjectives, about stiltedness. This one was simple. A boy and a girl. The awkward poetry of a first love. The boy dies. Something in the girl dies. Forever, she thinks. She wants it to be forever. She never wants to feel again. But as she comes slowly back to life, she fights against it. In vain.

And one day she has flowered again into another love and she cannot fight any more – and then she knows that the bruised heart is the one that can feel the most pain and also the most joy. There was a sting at the corners of my eyes as I finished it.

"Come here," I called. My voice was hoarse.

She came running. I held her by her sun-warm shoulders and kissed her. We both wept and it was a silly and precious thing.

"I do the writing in this family," I said. "I thought I did. Now I don't know. Now I don't think so."

"In this family? That is a phrase I leap upon, darling. That is a bone I take in my teeth and run with."

"Trapped," I said.

"I release you. I open the trap."

"Hell, no! I insist on being trapped. I want to be trapped. I am a guy who believed in a multiplicity of women. I still do. You're all of them. You'll keep well. You'll last. How will you look at sixty?"

"At you."

"I'll be six years older. I'll sit in the corner and crack my knuckles."

"With me on your lap it'll be tough."

"We'll manage."

"Is it good enough to hand in, my story?"

"Too good. We won't hand it in. We'll whip up something else for the class. This one we keep. Maybe someday we'll sell it." Something stirred at the back of my mind. She saw then the change in my expression.

"What is it, Joe? What are you thinking about?"

"Let me get organized." I got up and paced around. She watched me. I came back and sat beside her. "Look. I can't power Arthur into trying anything. It won't work. I can't become dangerous. But there's another way."

"How?"

I tapped her story with one finger. "This way."

"How do you mean?"

"I write it up. Other names, other places, but the same method of death in each case. I'll twist it a little. I'll make it a small business concern. The similarity will be like a slap in the face."

"You'll have to write an ending to it. How does it end, Joe?"

"I won't end it. I'll take it right up to a certain spot."

"Then what are you going to do with it?"

"Easy, my love. I'm going to leave it in Arthur's room and wait and see what happens. I am going to have it look like an accident. I am going to do it in such a way that he's going to have to give some thought to eliminating one Joe Arlin."

"No, Joe. Please no!"

"I've got to finish it off. One way or another."

She looked at me for a long time. "I suppose you do," she said quietly.

"Be a good girl. Play in the sand. Build castles. I want to bang this out while it's hot."

Dust clouded the page in the typewriter and I put the desk lamp on. Tilly sat across the room reading a magazine. I could feel her eyes on the back of my head from time to time.

I had brought my bad guy up to the Sherman death.

". . . stood for a moment and took the risk of looking to see that nothing had been forgotten. The gun had slid under the desk. The body was utterly still. He saw the full clip on the desk beside the bottle of gun oil and . . ."

"Hey!" I said.

"What, darling?"

"I've got a slow lead in my head. So has Lieutenant Cord. So had the murderer."

She came up behind me and put her hand lightly on my shoulder. "How do you mean?" I pointed at the sentence I had partially finished. "I don't see anything."

"Angel," I said, "Lieutenant Cord spoke of a full clip. I do not think he meant seven or six. I think he meant eight. A clip will not hold nine. There was one shell in the chamber. So how did it get there? To load a .45 with nine you put in a full clip, jack one into the chamber, remove clip, add one more to the clip and slap it back into the grip. A guy loading with nine is not likely to forget he has done so. Let us go calling . . ."

Lieutenant Cord was about to leave. He frowned at me, looked appreciatively at Tilly. I put the question to him.

"Yes, the clip was full, but what does that prove? Maybe that one had been in the chamber for months. It even makes the case stronger my way. The guy takes out the clip, counts eight through the holes and forgets the nine load."

"Or somebody else palms another shell out of the box he had and puts it in the chamber."

"What kind of tea do you drink, Arlin?"

"Be frank with me, Lieutenant. Doesn't this make the whole thing just a little more dubious to you?"

"No," he said flatly.

"You," I said, "look at life through a peashooter. You can focus on one incident at a time. Don't you ever try to relate each incident to a whole series?"

"Not this time."

"Miss Owen and I know who did it, Lieutenant."

"She drinks tea too, eh?"

"You don't want to know?"

"Not interested. Go play games. Go play cop. Maybe it's part of your education."

We left. "For a time there he seemed brighter than that," I said.

We got into the car. "Joe," she said. "Joe, why don't you go back to New York? Why don't you tell Mr Flynn that in your opinion Arthur Marris did it? Why don't you let him take over? He could build a fire under the lieutenant. Why don't you go to New York and take me with you?"

"Shameless!"

"Determined. You're not getting out of my sight again, Joe."

"I propose and what do I get? A blood-hound yet."

"Take us home, Joe."

"Home! Haven't you ever heard the old adage about street cars?"

"Yes, but you have a season ticket. Home, Joe."

What can you do? . . .

I finished the unfinished yarn, folded one copy carelessly and shoved it into my pocket. I finished it Saturday. Tilly, who'd driven down early, was singing in the small kitchen, banging the dishes around.

"I go to leave the epic," I said.

"Hurry back. And, Joe, bring two of the biggest steaks you can find. The biggest. I've never been so hungry."

I felt like a commuter going to work. Kissed in the living room. Kissed at the door. Waved to. Told to be careful, dear.

Although the brethren with Saturday morning classes were at them, the others were in bed, most of them, with a few others looking squinty-eyed at black coffee in the dining room. I had some coffee with Step Krindall. This morning his baby-blue eyes were bleary.

He moaned at forty-second intervals, wiping his pink head. He said, "that wristwatch of yours, Rod. Could you wrap it in your handkerchief and put it in your pocket? The tick is killing me."

"A large evening?"

"I don't know. I haven't counted my money yet. I missed the curfew and the bed check and the last bus out here."

"Seen Arthur around this morning?"

"He was coming out of the communal shower as I went in. A ghastly memory. He smiled at me. He slammed the door."

I finished my coffee.

"You slurp a little, don't you?" he said weakly.

I gave him a hearty slap on the back and went back to the row of senior rooms. I tapped on Arthur's door.

"Come in!" He looked up from the desk. He was studying. He frowned and then forced a smile.

"I came in to tell you I was a little off the beam the other day, Arthur. I'm sorry. Must be the heat."

"You don't know how glad I am to hear that, Rod. Frankly, you had me puzzled. I was going to suggest a check-up at the infirmary. Sometimes the boys get working too hard. A lot of times you can catch them before they crack."

I looked at him blandly. "Too bad you didn't catch Ted Flynn in time."

He nodded. "I've felt bad about that ever since. Of course, it was Harv Lorr's responsibility then. But all upperclassmen should look out for all the other brothers, don't you think?"

"I certainly think so." I pushed myself up out of the chair, said good-bye and left quickly before he could call my attention to the folded second-sheets I'd left tucked visibly between the cushion and the arm. I had written it up without my name so that anyone would naturally read it to find out whose it was. And I was depending on the narrative hook I'd inserted in the first sentence to keep the reader on the line until it broke off on page nine.

I went and bought two steaks as thick as my fist, frozen shrimp, cocktail sauce, an orchid with funny grey petals edged with green, a bandanna with a pattern of dice all adding up to seven or eleven, gin and vermouth, both imported, and a vast silly shoulder bag of woven green straw. I wanted to buy her the main street, two miles of waterfront beach and the Hope diamond, plus a brace of grey convertibles that would match her level eyes. But I had to save something to buy later.

When I got back, she was gone. I stowed the perishables in the freezing compartment and jittered around, cracking my knuckles, humming, pacing and mumbling until she came back at quarter to one.

"Just where do you think you've been?" I demanded.

"Hey, be domineering some more. I love it."

"Where did you go?"

"I took a bus to school and found Molly and talked her out of this." She took it out of her purse and handed it to me. It was ridiculously small. On the palm of her hand, it looked as vicious and unprincipled as a coral snake.

"Her father gave it to her," Tilly said.

I took it and broke it and looked at the six full chambers. I put out one load and snapped the cylinder shut and made certain the hammer was on the empty chamber.

"I thought we ought to have one," she said in a small voice.

"You're cute," I said. "You're lovable. Come here." I opened the bottom bureau drawer and took out the .357 Magnum. If the one she brought was a coral snake, this is a hooded cobra. "Now we've got an arsenal."

"How was I to know, Joe?"

"Look at me! Am I a bare-handed type hero? Am I a comic-book buccaneer? Uh uh, honey. At moments of danger you will find Arlin huddled behind the artillery. You should have seen me in the war. Safety-first Arlin, they called me. The only man in the navy who could crawl all the way into a battle helmet."

Suddenly she was in my arms and shivering. I laid the weapons on the corner of the bureau and paid attention. "I'm scared, scared, scared," she said.

"Hold on for twelve hours," I said. "To yourself – not to me. Junior will move fast. He has to. The chips are on the table. The mask has slipped. The hour is on the wing and the bird in the bush has become a rolling stone."

"You're not making sense."

"What do you expect? Get out from under my chin. Stand over there. Okay. This is the order of battle. Arthur will show. He has to. He will show in one of two ways, but first night must fall. He will either come in here playing house president looking for an opening, or he will sneak.

"We will have the daylight hours in which to be gay. Then, come night, we must be boy scouts. We must guard against the sneak play. The surf makes considerable racket. A sneak will come from the beach.

"Thus, the answer is to be invisible from the beach and to be brightly lighted. The south corner of the living room answers that purpose very neatly. We will move the couch there and sit pleasantly side by side with weapons available and wait. In that way we shall be facing the door at which he will knock, should be decide to come openly. Should he knock – you, in great silence, will dart into the living room closet.

"Either way, we shall have two witnesses, you and me. Should he come openly, you must rely on my reflexes and my glib tongue, darling."

"I love your reflexes."

"On the ice you will find two mastodon steaks, shrimp that need no cleaning and one wild flower. The wild flower is for you.

"If the steaks turn out poorly, due to the cooking thereof, I shall take away the flower."

Oh, we were glib and gay throughout that long afternoon. We swam, drank, ate, told jokes, sang, held hands. Nothing did very much good. Our laughter was too brittle and high, and our jokes were leaden.

There were ghosts lurking behind our eyes.

Violence belongs in damp city alleys and shabby tenements and sordid little bars. It doesn't fit into an environment of white sand and the blue-green gulf water, and the absurd and frantic running of the sand pipers, and the coquinas digging into the wash of wet sand. Murder doesn't go with the tilt of white gull-wings against the incredibly blue sky, or the honeyed shoulders of the girl you love.

From time to time during that afternoon I would almost forget, and then it would come back – the evil that hid behind the sun and under the sand, and under the water and around the corner of the house.

VIII

Booby-Trap

The sun sank golden towards the gulf and then turned a bank of clouds to a bloody fire that was five thousand miles long. Dusk was an odd stormy yellow, and then a pink-blue and then a deep dusty blue. A cool wind came from the northwest, and we shivered and went in and changed. We were as subdued as children who have been promised punishment.

It was possible that he might listen. As night gathered its dark strength and the sea turned alien, we sat in the brightness in the corner and read silently together from the same book, but even that was not powerful enough to keep us from starting with each small night noise. The wind grew steadily. The Magnum was a hard lump by my leg. She had clowned possession of the .32, stuffing it under the bright woven belt she wore, but it did not look particularly humorous.

When the knock came, firm and steady, we looked at each other for a moment frozen forever in memory. Her face was sunbronzed, but the healthy colour ran out of it so that around her mouth there was a tiny greenish tint. I squeezed her hand hard and pointed to the closet. I waited until the door was closed so that a thin dark line showed.

"Come on in!" I called. I let my hand rest casually beside me so that in one quick movement I could slap my hand onto the grip inches away.

Arthur Marris came in. The wind caught the door and almost tore it out of his hand. He shut it. The wind had rumpled his hair so that strands fell across his forehead. It gave him a more secretive look.

He smiled. "The night's getting wild."

I made myself put the book aside very casually. "Sit down, Arthur. I wrenched my ankle in the surf. If you want a drink, you'll have to go out into the kitchen and make it yourself. I want to stay off the foot."

I admired his tailor-made concern. "Oh! Too bad. Can I fix you one too?"

"Sure thing. Bourbon and water. Plain water."

I sat tensely while he worked in the kitchen. He brought me a drink and I was relieved to see that he had a drink in each hand. I took my drink with my left hand and as I did so I braced myself and moved my fingers closer to the weapon. He turned away and went back to the chair nine feet away. He sat down as though he were very weary.

I lifted the drink to my lips and pretended to sip at it. I set it on the floor by my feet, but I did not take my eyes off him as I set it down. It made me think that this must be the way a trainer acts when he enters the cage for the first time with a new animal. Every motion planned, every muscle ready to respond, so much adrenalin in the blood that the pulse thuds and it is hard to keep breathing slow and steady.

"I'm troubled, Rod," he said.

"Yes?" Casual and polite.

"This is something I don't know how to handle."

"Then it must be pretty important."

He took the folder copy out of his pocket. "Did you leave this in my room by accident?"

"So that's what happened to it. No, don't bother bringing it over. Toss it on the desk. I can see from here that it's mine."

"I read it, Rod."

"Like it?"

"What do you intend to do with it?"

In the game of chess there is move and countermove, gambit and response. The most successful attacks are those, as in war, where power is brought to bear on one point to mask a more devastating attack in another quarter. But before actual attack, the opponents must study each other's responses to feints and counterfeints.

"It's an assignment for my Friday class. Due next week."

"I suppose you realize, Rod, that you've patterned your story, so far as it's gone, on the series of misfortunes we've had in the house. You've twisted it a bit, but not enough. The method of death and the chronology are the same."

"I still can't see how you're troubled."

He frowned. "Is that hard? I had two other people in the house read it this afternoon to see if their slant was the same as mine. You can't hand that in the way it is. Your instructor would really have to be a fool not to tie it up with what has happened, particularly because Brad Carroll's death is still fresh in everyone's mind."

"What if he does?"

"You've made an amazingly strong case, Arlin, whether you know it or not. Until I read, your . . . story, I thought it was absurd to think of what has happened as anything except a series of tragic accidents and coincidences. No one can read your story, Rod, without getting, as I have, a strong suspicion that there is some human agency behind this whole affair. Absurd as the motives may seem, I have been wondering if . . ." He frowned down at the floor.

"What have you been wondering?"

"I took a long walk this afternoon. I tried to think clearly and without any prejudice. I want to ask you to hold up sending in that assignment for a time. Is the original copy here?"

"In that desk."

"Are there any other carbons?"

"No. You've seen the only one."

"I'd like to have you come back to the house with me, Rod. Right now. We might be able to clear this up."

I smiled and shook my head. "Not with this ankle."

He stood up and came two steps towards me. "I'll help you, Rod. You see I want you to come back there with me, because even though your reasoning might be right in that story, the conclusion is . . ."

Marris stopped short and stared at the levelled weapon. He licked his lips. "What's that for?"

"What do you think it's for? How do you like the end of the road."

He smiled crookedly. "Look, Arlin. You can't possibly believe that I . . ."

The room was gone as abruptly as though the house had exploded. Too late, I remembered the fuse box on the outside of the house, in typical Florida fashion. We were alone in the sighing darkness, in a night that was utterly black. The outside door banged open and the sea mist blew in, curling through the room, tasting of salt.

I moved to one side, towards the closet, as fast and as quietly as I could go. I took three steps when somebody ran into me hard. A heavy shoulder caught my chest and I slammed back against the closet door, banging it shut. The impact tore the gun out of my hand and I heard it skitter across onto the bare floor beyond the rug. I touched an arm, slid my hand down to the wrist and punched hard where the head should be.

I hit the empty air and the wrist twisted out of my grip.

Something hard hit me above the ear and I stumbled, dazed and off balance. I fell and had sense enough to keep rolling until I ran up against a piece of furniture. I had gotten twisted in the darkness. I felt of it and found it was the desk. Tilly screamed at that moment and the scream was far away because of the closed closet door.

Crawling on my hands and knees, I patted the floor ahead of me, looking for the gun. Somebody rolled into me and there was a thick coughing sound. I slid away. There was a thumping noise. The shots came, fast and brittle against the sound of the sea. There was an angry tug at my wrist and then a liquid warmth across my hand.

The terrace doors we had locked splintered open and the white glare of flashlights caught me full in the face as I sat back on my heels.

Two figures tramped towards me and around me. I turned and saw that they had gone towards a moving mass in the centre of the room. One of the figures who had come in towered over the other. I got to my feet and reached the closet door and opened the closet. At that moment the electricity came back on.

Tilly stared up at me and said, "I thought you were . . . I thought you were . . ." She leaned against the wall of the closet, closed her eyes and sank slowly towards the floor.

I turned and saw Lieutenant Cord pulling a man off Arthur Marris. Arthur lay on his back. His face was dark and the breath was whistling in his throat. His eyes were closed.

"Back up against that wall," Cord said quietly to the other man who had risen to his feet.

Step Krindall blinked his baby-blue eyes. Droplets of sweat stood on his pink bald head. He stared incredulously at Arthur. He said, "I thought I had my hands on Arlin! My heaven, I thought it was Arlin! I was strangling Arthur." He worked the fingers of his fat pink hands convulsively.

"You were trying to kill Arlin like you killed Carroll?" Cord asked, very casually.

"Sure," Krindall said. "And the other ones. My heaven, I have to take care of Arthur. He's not smart you know.

He'd let them push him around, Arthur would. I've been watching out for Arthur now for a long time." He looked appealingly at Lieutenant Cord.

"He knew what you've been doing?"

"Oh, no! He wouldn't like it even though it helped him a lot. I never told him. He won't die, will he?"

Arthur stirred. He opened his eyes. He gagged and rubbed his throat as he sat up.

Krindall took a step forward, ignoring Cord. "Arthur, you're not sore at me, are you? I knew you wouldn't be sore. I was helping you. And then when you showed me that story today, I just thought Arlin would make trouble for both of us and it would be better is he was dead."

He reached down as though to touch Arthur's shoulder. Arthur pulled himself away, violently, hunching along the floor.

Step looked at Arthur for one incredulous moment and then began to blubber, his eyes streaming, his hands making helpless appealing flapping motions.

"Who was shooting?" Cord demanded.

That reminded me forcibly of Tilly. I turned back to her.

She was sitting on the closet floor staring at me. She wore a curious expression. "I felt myself fainting. I sort of expected to wake up on the couch. Only – I didn't."

Cord saw the punctured door, thin plywood splinters protruding. "You were shooting from inside the closet?" he asked incredulously.

"I was locked in," Tilly said with dignity as I helped her to her feet. "I thought Mr Arlin was being killed. I wanted to create a diversion."

"Great diversion," Cord said dryly, staring at my hand. The blood was dripping from the tips of my index and middle fingers. Tilly looked down. This time I was ready. I caught her and put her on the couch.

Arthur stood up shakily. He said, "Rod, that's what I wanted to talk to you about. You built such a strong case you got me thinking about Krindall. Little things that I had half forgotten. I still couldn't believe it."

Krindall stood, weeping silently. But there was a gleam in his tear-damp blue eyes. I said,

"Look at him! Great emotion. Great acting. He's standing there trying to figure an angle. All this doesn't actually mean anything to him. This great devotion to Arthur is just a sham."

The tears stopped as abruptly as though they had been turned off with a pipe wrench. He looked like an evil, besotted child. "I could have got you, Arlin," he said. "I could have got you good. I rode Rex under the water and towed him out to where it was deep. I got Tod into an argument about guns and slipped a round into the chamber. The argument was whether you could see any glint of light down the barrel.

"I fixed the noose for Ted and got him on the chair to tell me if it was water pipes in the top of the closet. He didn't see the noose until I slipped it over his head and yanked the chair away. Then I had to keep pulling his hands off the pipe for a little while. I knew about Brad and his wife. When she left, I went in. It didn't take long. All of them were stupid. All of them. I've been smarter than any of you."

"Yeah, you're real bright," Cord said speculatively. "Real bright. We got some mind-doctors who can check on you."

"Doctors! You think I'm crazy!"

He made a dive to one side. Even as he moved, I saw the but of the Magnum peeping out around the edge of the chair leg. I needn't have worried. Cord took one step and swung a fist that was like a bag of rocks on the end of a rope. The fist contacted Step Krindall in mid-flight. It made a sound like somebody flopping an over-ripe cantaloupe. Cord sucked his big knuckles and stared down at Krindall.

"Real bright," he murmured. He looked over at me. "You worried me, Arlin. I thought it wouldn't do any harm keeping an eye on this place."

Tilly revived and Krindall came to enough to be walked out. As I held my punctured epidermis under the cold water faucet, I apologized to a glum Marris.

We were alone again and the night wind still blew, but it was not alien. The sea sighed, but it was a domesticated beast.

Then we had a solemn nightcap together. Tilly said that she thought I ought to drive her back to the campus and I said why of course. We put the top up and I took her back as though we were returning from a very average date.

Ten days later I hit rain as I crossed into Georgia. I took the coast road and the rain stayed with me. The wipers clicked back and forth and the blacktop was the colour of oiled sin.

I thought of facing one Mr Flynn and telling him what had happened, what I had found out. He would have some of the details from the papers. There were others he should know, and others I would spare him. It wouldn't be pretty, but it was something that had to be done. Krindall would be institutionalized.

Tilly stirred and yawned and stretched like a sleepy cat and smiled at me. Depression went away as though the sun had come out.

"Hungry?" I asked.

"Mmm. Famished. Let's find a place to eat and then go find a nice court to stay in. We'll stay there until a sunny day comes along, huh?"

"What'll thinkle peep, honey? It's eleven o'clock in the morning."

"Who cares what they think, huh? Show 'em the licence."

"Hunting, driving or marriage?"

"Hunting, of course. No, I'll tell 'em we had to get married."

"Then they'll ask why."

"Then I'll say because you got me expelled from junior high."

"You don't look old enough to have been in junior high."

She curled against me. "Just old enough to know better, hey?"

It was raining like crazy in Georgia and the sun was shining bright.

The Lost Coast

Marcia Muller

California's Lost Coast is at the same time one of the most desolate and beautiful of shorelines. Northerly winds whip the sand into dust-devil frenzy; eerie, stationary fogs hang in the trees and distort the driftwood until it resembles the bones of prehistoric mammals; bruised clouds hover above the peaks of the distant King Range, then blow down to sea level and dump icy torrents. But on a fair day the sea and sky show infinite shadings of blue, and the wildflowers are a riot of colour. If you wait quietly, you can spot deer, peregrine falcons, foxes, otters, even black bears and mountain lions.

A contradictory and oddly compelling place, this seventy-three-mile stretch of coast southwest of Eureka, where – as with most worthwhile things or people – you must take the bad with the good.

Unfortunately, on my first visit there I was taking mostly the bad. Strong winds pushed my MG all over the steep, narrow road, making hairpin turns even more perilous. Early October rain cut my visibility to a few yards. After I crossed the swollen Bear River, the road continued to twist and wind, and I began to understand why the natives had dubbed it The Wildcat.

Somewhere ahead, my client had told me, was the hamlet of Petrolia – site of the first oil well drilled in California, he'd irrelevantly added. The man was a conservative politician, a former lumber-company attorney, and given what I knew of his voting record on the environment, I was certain we disagreed on the desirability of that event, as well as any number of similar issues. But the urgency of the current situation dictated that I keep my opinions to myself, so I'd simply written down the directions he gave me – omitting his travelogue-like asides – and gotten under way.

I drove through Petrolia – a handful of new buildings, since the village had been all but levelled in the disastrous earthquake of 1992 – and turned towards the sea on an unpaved road. After two miles I began looking for the orange post that marked the dirt track to the client's cabin.

The whole time I was wishing I was back in San Francisco. This wasn't my kind of case; I didn't like the client, Steve Shoemaker; and even though the fee was good, this was the week I'd scheduled to take off a few personal business days from All Souls Legal Cooperative, where I'm chief investigator. But Jack Stuart, our criminal specialist, had asked me to take on the job as a favour to him. Steve Shoemaker was Jack's old friend from college in Southern California, and he'd asked for a referral to a private detective. Jack owed Steve a favour; I owed Jack several, so there was no way I could gracefully refuse.

But I couldn't shake the feeling that something was wrong with this case. And I couldn't help wishing that I'd come to the Lost Coast in summertime, with a backpack and in the company of my lover – instead of on a rainy fall afternoon, with a .38 Special and soon to be in the company of Shoemaker's disagreeable wife, Andrea.

The rain was sheeting down by the time I spotted the orange post. It had turned the hard-packed earth to mud, and my MG's tyres sank deep in the ruts, its undercarriage scraping dangerously. I could barely make out the stand of live oaks and sycamores where the track ended; no way to tell if another vehicle had travelled over it recently.

When I reached the end of the track I saw one of those boxy four-wheel-drive wagons – Bronco? Cherokee? – drawn in under the drooping branches of an oak. Andrea Shoemaker's? I'd neglected to get a description from her husband of what she drove. I got out of the MG, turning the hood of my heavy sweater up against the downpour; the wind promptly blew it off. So much for what the catalogue had described as "extra protection on those cold nights". I yanked the hood up again and held it there, went around and took my .38 from the trunk and shoved it into the outside flap of my purse. Then I went over and tried the door of the four-wheel drive. Unlocked. I opened it, slipped into the driver's seat.

Nothing identifying its owner was on the seats or in the side pockets, but in the glove compartment I found a registration in the name of Andrea Shoemaker. I rummaged around, came up with nothing else of interest. Then I got out and walked through the trees, looking for the cabin.

Shoemaker had told me to follow a deer track through the grove. No sign of it in this downpour; no deer, either. Nothing but wind-lashed trees, the oaks pelting me with acorns. I moved slowly through them, swivelling my head from side to side, until I made out a bulky shape tucked beneath the farthest of the sycamores.

As I got closer, I saw the cabin was of plain weathered wood, rudely constructed, with the chimney of a woodstove extending from its composition shingle roof. Small – two or three rooms – and no light showing in its windows. And the door was open, banging against the inside wall . . .

I quickened my pace, taking the gun from my purse. Alongside the door I stopped to listen. Silence. I had a flashlight in my bag; I took it out. Moved to where I could see inside, then turned the flash on and shone it through the door.

All that was visible was rough board walls, an oilcloth-covered table and chairs, an ancient woodstove. I stepped inside, swinging the light around. Unlit oil lamp on the table; flower-cushioned wooden furniture of the sort you always find in vacation cabins; rag rugs; shelves holding an assortment of tattered paperbacks, seashells, and driftwood. I shifted the light again, more slowly.

A chair on the far side of the table was tipped over, and a woman's purse lay on the edge of the woodstove, its contents spilling out. When I got over there I saw a .32 Iver Johnson revolver lying on the floor.

Andrea Shoemaker owned a .32. She'd told me so the day before.

Two doors opened off the room. Quietly I went to one and tried it. A closet, shelves stocked with staples and canned goods and bottled water. I looked around the room again, listening. No sound but the wail of wind and the pelt of rain on the roof. I stepped to the other door.

A bedroom, almost filled wall-to-wall by a king-sized bed covered with a goosedown comforter and piled with colourful pillows. Old bureau pushed in one corner, another unlit oil lamp on the single nightstand. Small travel bag on the bed.

The bag hadn't been opened. I examined its contents. Jeans, a couple of sweaters, underthings, toilet articles. Package of condoms. Uh-huh. She'd come here, as I'd found out, to meet a man. The affairs usually began with a casual pick-up; they were never of long duration; and they all seemed to culminate in a romantic weekend in the isolated cabin.

Dangerous game, particularly in these days when AIDS and the prevalence of disturbed individuals of both sexes threatened. But Andrea Shoemaker had kept her latest date with an even larger threat hanging over her: for the past six weeks, a man with a serious grudge against her husband had been stalking her. For all I knew, he and the date were one and the same.

And where was Andrea now?

This case had started on Wednesday, two days ago, when I'd driven up to Eureka, a lumbering and fishing town on Humboldt Bay. After I passed the Humboldt County line I began to see huge logging trucks toiling through the mountain passes, shredded curls of redwood bark trailing in their wakes. Twenty-five miles south of the city itself was the company-owned town of Scotia, mill stacks belching white smoke and filling the air with the scent of freshly cut wood. Yards full of logs waiting to be fed to the mills lined the highway. When I reached Eureka itself, the downtown struck me as curiously quiet; many of the stores were out of business, and the sidewalks were mostly deserted. The recession had hit the lumber industry hard, and the earthquake hadn't helped the area's strapped economy.

I'd arranged to meet Steve Shoemaker at his law offices in Old Town, near the waterfront. It was a picturesque area full of renovated warehouses and interesting shops and restaurants, tricked up for tourists with the inevitable horse-and-carriage rides and t-shirt shops, but still pleasant. Shoemaker's offices were off a cobblestoned courtyard containing a couple of antique shops and a decorator's showroom.

When I gave my card to the secretary, she said Assemblyman Shoemaker was in conference and asked me to wait. The man, I knew, had lost his seat in the state legislature this past election, so the term of address seemed inappropriate. The appointments of the waiting room struck me as a bit much: brass and mahogany and marble and velvet, plenty of it, the furnishings all antiques that tended to the garish. I sat on a red velvet sofa and looked for something to read. *Architectural Digest, National Review, Foreign Affairs* – that was it, take it or leave it. I left it. My idea of waiting-room reading material is *People*; I love it, but I'm too embarrassed to subscribe.

The minutes ticked by: ten, fifteen, twenty. I contemplated the issue of *Architectural Digest*, then opted instead for staring at a fake Rembrandt on the far wall. Twenty-five, thirty. I was getting irritated now. Shoemaker had asked me to be here by three; I'd arrived on the dot. If this was, as he'd claimed, a matter of such urgency and delicacy that he couldn't go into it on the phone, why was he in conference at the appointed time?

Thirty-five minutes. Thirty-seven. The door to the inner sanctum opened and a woman strode out. A tall woman, with long chestnut hair, wearing a raincoat and black leather boots. Her eyes rested on me in passing – a cool grey, hard with anger. Then she went out, slamming the door behind her.

The secretary – a trim blonde in a tailored suit – started as the door slammed. She glanced at me and tried to cover with a smile, but its edges were strained, and her fingertips pressed hard against the desk. The phone at her elbow buzzed; she snatched up the receiver. Spoke into it, then said to me, "Ms McCone, Assemblyman Shoemaker will see you now." As she ushered me inside, she again gave me her frayed-edge smile.

Tense situation in this office, I thought. Brought on by what? The matter Steve Shoemaker wanted me to investigate? The client who had just made her angry exit? Or something else entirely . . . ?

Shoemaker's office was even more pretentious than the waiting room: more brass, mahogany, velvet, and marble; more fake Old Masters in heavy gilt frames; more antiques; more of everything. Shoemaker's demeanour was not as nervous as his secretary's, but when he rose to greet me, I noticed a jerkiness in his movements, as if he was holding himself under tight control. I clasped his outstretched hand and smiled, hoping the familiar social rituals would set him more at ease.

Momentarily they did. He thanked me for coming, apologized for making me wait, and inquired after Jack Stuart. After I was seated in one of the clients' chairs, he offered me a drink; I asked for mineral water. As he went to a wet bar tucked behind a tapestry screen, I took the opportunity to study him.

Shoemaker was handsome: dark hair, with the grey so artfully interwoven that it must have been professionally dyed. Chiselled features; nice, well-muscled body, shown off to perfection by an expensive blue suit. When he handed me my drink, his smile revealed white, even teeth that I, having spent the greater part of the previous month in the company of my dentist, recognized as capped. Yes, a very good-looking man, politician handsome. Jack's old friend or not, his appearance and manner called up my gut-level distrust.

My client went around his desk and reclaimed his chair. He held a drink of his own – something dark amber – and he took a deep swallow before speaking. The alcohol replenished his vitality some; he drank again, set the glass on a pewter coaster, and said, "Ms McCone, I'm glad you could come up here on such short notice."

"You mentioned on the phone that the case is extremely urgent – and delicate."

He ran his hand over his hair – lightly, so as not to disturb its styling. "Extremely urgent and delicate," he repeated, seeming to savour the phrase.

"Why don't you tell me about it?"

His eyes strayed to the half-full glass on the coaster. Then they moved to the door through which I'd entered. Returned to me. "You saw the woman who just left?"

I nodded.

"My wife, Andrea."

I waited.

"She's very angry with me for hiring you."

"She did act angry. Why?"

Now he reached for the glass and belted down its contents. Leaned back and rattled the ice cubes as he spoke. "It's a long story. Painful to me. I'm not sure where to begin. I just . . . don't know what to make of the things that are happening."

"That's what you've hired me to do. Begin anywhere. We'll fill in the gaps later." I pulled a small tape recorder from my bag and set it on the edge of his desk. "Do you mind?"

Shoemaker eyed it warily, but shook his head. After a moment's hesitation, he said, "Someone is stalking my wife."

"Following her? Threatening her?"

"Not following, not that I know of. He writes notes, threatening to kill her. He leaves . . . things at the house. At her place of business. Dead things. Birds, rats, one time a cat. Andrea loves cats. She . . ." He shook his head, went to the bar for a refill.

"What else? Phone calls?"

"No. One time, a floral arrangement – suitable for a funeral."

"Does he sign the notes?"

"John. Just John."

"Does Mrs. Shoemaker know anyone named John who has a grudge against her?"

"She says no. And I . . ." He sat down, fresh drink in hand. "I have reason to believe that this John has a grudge against me, is using this harassment of Andrea to get at me personally."

"Why do you think that?"

"The wording of the notes."

"May I see them?"

He looked around, as if he were afraid someone might be listening. "Later. I keep them elsewhere."

Something, then, I thought, that he didn't want his office staff to see. Something shameful, perhaps even criminal.

"Okay," I said, "how long has this been going on?"

"About six weeks."

"Have you contacted the police?"

"Informally. A man I know on the force, Sergeant Bob Wolfe. But after he started looking into it, I had to ask him to drop it."

"Why?"

"I'm in a sensitive political position."

"Excuse me if I'm mistaken, Mr Shoemaker, but it's my understanding that you're no longer serving in the state legislature."

"That's correct, but I'm about to announce my candidacy in a special election for a senate seat that's recently been vacated."

"I see. So after you asked your contact on the police force to back off, you decided to use a private investigator, and Jack recommended me. Why not use someone local?"

"As I said, my position is sensitive. I don't want word of this getting out in the community. That's why Andrea is so angry with me. She claims I value my political career more than her life."

I waited, wondering how he'd attempt to explain that away.

He didn't even try, merely went on, "In our . . . conversation just prior to this, she threatened to leave me. This coming weekend she plans to go to a cabin on the Lost Coast that she inherited from her father to, as she put it, sort things through. Alone. Do you know that part of the coast?"

"I've read some travel pieces on it."

"Then you're aware how remote it is. The cabin's very isolated. I don't want Andrea going there while this John person is on the loose."

"Does she go there often?"

"Fairly often. I don't; it's too rustic for me – no running

water, phone, or electricity. But Andrea likes it. Why do you ask?''

"I'm wondering if John – whoever he is – knows about the cabin. Has she been there since the harassment began?"

"No. Initially she agreed that it wouldn't be a good idea. But now . . ." He shrugged.

"I'll need to speak with Mrs Shoemaker. Maybe I can reason with her, persuade her not to go until we've identified John. Or maybe she'll allow me to go along as her bodyguard."

"You can speak with her if you like, but she's beyond reasoning with. And there's no way you can stop her or force her to allow you to accompany her. My wife is a strong-willed woman; that interior decorating firm across the courtyard is hers, she built it from the ground up. When Andrea decides to do something, she does it. And asks permission from no one."

"Still, I'd like to try reasoning. This trip to the cabin – that's the urgency you mentioned on the phone. Two days to find the man behind the harassment before she goes out there and perhaps makes a target of herself."

"Yes."

"Then I'd better get started. That funeral arrangement – what florist did it come from?"

Shoemaker shook his head. "It arrived at least five weeks ago, before either of us noticed a pattern to the harassment. Andrea just shrugged it off, threw the wrappings and card away."

"Let's go look at the notes, then. They're my only lead."

Vengeance will be mine. The sudden blow. The quick attack. Vengeance is the price of silence.

Mute testimony paves the way to an early grave. The rest is silence.

A freshly turned grave is silent testimony to an old wrong and its avenger.

There was more in the same vein – slightly Biblical-flavoured and stilted. But chilling to me, even though the safety-deposit booth at Shoemaker's bank was overly warm. If that was my reaction, what had these notes done to Andrea Shoemaker? No wonder she was thinking of leaving a husband who cared more for the electorate's opinion than his wife's life and safety.

The notes had been typed without error on an electric machine that had left no such obvious clues as chipped or skewed keys. The paper and envelopes were plain and cheap, purchasable at any discount store. They had been handled, I was sure, by nothing more than gloved hands. No signature – just the typed name "John".

But the writer had wanted the Shoemakers – one of them, anyway – to know who he was. Thus the theme that ran through them all: silence and revenge.

I said, "I take it your contact at the EPD had their lab go over these?"

"Yes. There was nothing. That's why he wanted to probe further – something I couldn't permit him to do."

"Because of this revenge-and-silence business. Tell me about it."

Shoemaker looked around furtively. My God, did he think bank employees had nothing better to do with their time than to eavesdrop on our conversation?

"We'll go have a drink," he said. "I know a place that's private."

We went to a restaurant a few blocks away, where Shoemaker had another bourbon and I toyed with a glass of iced tea. After some prodding, he told me his story; it didn't enhance him in my eyes.

Seventeen years ago Shoemaker had been interviewing for a staff attorney's position at a large lumber company. While on a tour of the mills, he witnessed an accident in which a worker named Sam Carding was severely mangled while trying to clear a jam in a bark-stripping machine. Shoemaker, who had worked in the mills summers to pay for his education, knew the accident was due to company negligence, but accepted a handsome job offer in exchange for not testifying for the plaintiff in the ensuing lawsuit. The court ruled against Carding, confined to a wheelchair and in constant pain; a year later, while the case was still under appeal, Carding shot his wife and himself. The couple's three children were given token settlements in exchange for dropping the suit and then were adopted by relatives in a different part of the country.

"It's not a pretty story, Mr Shoemaker," I said, "and I can see why the wording of the notes might make you suspect there's a connection between it and this harassment. But who do you think John is?"

"Carding's oldest boy. Carding and his family knew I'd witnessed the accident; one of his co-workers saw me watching from the catwalk and told him. Later, when I turned up as a senior counsel . . ." He shrugged.

"But why, after all this time –?"

"Why not? People nurse grudges. John Carding was sixteen at the time of the lawsuit; there were some ugly scenes with him, both at my home and my office at the mill. By now he'd be in his thirties. Maybe it's his way of acting out some sort of midlife crisis."

"Well, I'll call my office and have my assistant run a check on all three Carding kids. And I want to speak with Mrs Shoemaker – preferably in your presence."

He glanced at his watch. "It can't be tonight. She's got a meeting of her professional organization, and I'm dining with my campaign manager."

A potentially psychotic man was threatening Andrea's life, yet they both carried on as usual. Well, who was I to question it? Maybe it was their way of coping.

"Tomorrow, then," I said. "Your home. At the noon hour."

Shoemaker nodded. Then he gave me the address, as well as the names of John Carding's siblings.

I left him on the sidewalk in front of the restaurant: a handsome man whose shoulders now slumped inside his expensive suitcoat, shivering in the brisk wind off Humboldt Bay. As we shook hands, I saw that shame made his gaze unsteady, the set of his mouth less than firm.

I knew that kind of shame. Over the course of my career, I'd committed some dreadful acts that years later woke me in the deep of the night to sudden panic. I'd also *not* committed certain acts – failures that woke me to regret and emptiness. My sins of omission were infinitely worse than those of commission, because I knew that if I'd acted, I could have made a difference. Could even have saved a life.

I wasn't able to reach Rae Kelleher, my assistant at All Souls, that evening, and by the time she got back to me the next morning – Thursday – I was definitely annoyed. Still, I tried to keep a lid on my irritation. Rae is young, attractive, and in love; I couldn't expect her to spend her evenings waiting to be of service to her workaholic boss.

I got her started on a computer check on all three Cardings, then took myself to the Eureka PD and spoke with Shoemaker's contact, Sergeant Bob Wolfe. Wolfe – a dark-haired, sharp-featured man whose appearance was a good match for his surname – told me he'd had the notes processed by the lab, which had turned up no useful evidence.

"Then I started to probe, you know? When you got a harassment case like this, you look into the victims' private lives."

"And that was when Shoemaker told you to back off."

"Uh-huh."

"When was this?"

"About five weeks ago."

"I wonder why he waited so long to hire me. Did he, by any chance, ask you for a referral to a local investigator?"

Wolfe frowned. "Not this time."

"Then you'd referred him to someone before?"

"Yeah, guy who used to be on the force – Dave Morrison. Last April."

"Did Shoemaker tell you why he needed an investigator?"

"No, and I didn't ask. These politicians, they're always trying to get something on their rivals. I didn't want any part of it."

"Do you have Morrison's address and phone number handy?"

Wolfe reached into his desk drawer, shuffled things, and

flipped a business card across the blotter. "Dave gave me a stack of these when he set up shop," he said. "Always glad to help an old pal."

Morrison was out of town, the message on his answering machine said, but would be back tomorrow afternoon. I left a message of my own, asking him to call me at my motel. Then I headed for the Shoemakers' home, hoping I could talk some common sense into Andrea.

But Andrea wasn't having any common sense.

She strode around the parlour of their big Victorian – built by one of the city's lumber barons, her husband told me when I complimented them on it – arguing and waving her arms and making scathing statements punctuated by a good amount of profanity. And knocking back martinis, even though it was only a little past noon.

Yes, she was going to the cabin. No, neither her husband nor I was welcome there. No, she wouldn't postpone the trip; she was sick and tired of being cooped up like some kind of zoo animal because her husband had made a mistake years before she'd met him. All right, she realized this John person was dangerous. But she'd taken self-defence classes and owned a .32 revolver. Of course she knew how to use it. Practised frequently, too. Women had to be prepared these days, and she was.

But, she added darkly, glaring at her husband, she'd just as soon not have to shoot John. She'd rather send him straight back to Steve and let them settle this score. May the best man win – and she was placing bets on John.

As far as I was concerned, Steve and Andrea Shoemaker deserved each other.

I tried to explain to her that self-defence classes don't fully prepare you for a paralysing, heart-pounding encounter with an actual violent stranger. I tried to warn her that the ability to shoot well on a firing range doesn't fully prepare you for pumping a bullet into a human being who is advancing swiftly on you.

I wanted to tell her she was being an idiot.

Before I could, she slammed down her glass and stormed out of the house.

Her husband replenished his own drink and said, "Now do you see what I'm up against?"

I didn't respond to that. Instead I said, "I spoke with Sergeant Wolfe earlier."

"And?"

"He told me he referred you to a local private investigator, Dave Morrison, last April."

"So?"

"Why didn't you hire Morrison for this job?"

"As I told you yesterday, my –"

"Sensitive position, yes."

Shoemaker scowled.

Before he could comment, I asked, "What was the job last April?"

"Nothing to do with this matter."

"Something to do with politics?"

"In a way."

"Mr Shoemaker, hasn't it occurred to you that a political enemy may be using the Carding case as a smokescreen? That a rival's trying to throw you off balance before this special election?"

"It did, and . . . well, it isn't my opponent's style. My God, we're civilized people. But those notes . . . they're the work of a lunatic."

I wasn't so sure he was right – both about the notes being the work of a lunatic and politicians being civilized people – but I merely said, "Okay, you keep working on Mrs Shoemaker. At least persuade her to let me go to the Lost Coast with her. I'll be in touch." Then I headed for the public library.

After a few hours of ruining my eyes at the microfilm machine, I knew little more than before. Newspaper accounts of the Carding accident, lawsuit, and murder-suicide didn't differ substantially from what my client had told me. Their coverage of the Shoemakers' activities was only marginally interesting.

Normally I don't do a great deal of background investigation on clients but, as Sergeant Wolfe had said, in a case like this where one or both of them was a target, a thorough look at careers and lifestyles was mandatory. The papers described Steve as a straightforward, effective assemblyman who took a hard, conservative stance on such issues as welfare and the environment. He was strongly pro-business, particularly the lumber industry. He and his "charming and talented wife" didn't share many interests: Steve hunted and golfed; Andrea was a "generous supporter of the arts" and a "lavish party-giver". An odd couple, I thought, and odd people to be friends of Jack Stuart, a liberal who'd chosen to dedicate his career to representing the underdog.

Back at the motel, I put in a call to Jack. Why, I asked him, had he remained close to a man who was so clearly his opposite?

Jack laughed. "You're trying to say politely that you think he's a pompous, conservative ass."

"Well . . ."

"Okay, I admit it: he is. But back in college, he was a mentor to me. I doubt I would have gone into the law if it hadn't been for Steve. And we shared some good times, too: one summer we took a motorcycle trip around the country, like something out of *Easy Rider* without the tragedy. I guess we stay in touch because of a shared past."

I was trying to imagine Steve Shoemaker on a motorcycle; the picture wouldn't materialize. "Was he always so conservative?" I asked.

"No, not until he moved back to Eureka and went to work for that lumber company. Then . . . I don't know. Everything changed. It was as if something had happened that took all the fight out of him."

What had happened, I thought, was trading another man's life for a prestigious job.

Jack and I chatted for a moment longer, and then I asked him to transfer me to Rae. She hadn't turned up anything on the Cardings yet, but was working on it. In the meantime, she added, she'd taken care of what correspondence had come in, dealt with seven phone calls, entered next week's must-do's in the call-up file she'd created for me, and found a remedy for the blight that was affecting my rubber plant.

With a pang, I realized that the office ran just as well – better, perhaps – when I wasn't there. It would keep functioning smoothly without me for weeks, months, maybe years.

Hell, it would probably keep functioning smoothly even if I were dead.

In the morning I opened the Yellow Pages to Florists and began calling each that was listed. While Shoemaker had been vague on the date his wife received the funeral arrangement, surely a customer who wanted one sent to a private home, rather than a mortuary, would stand out in the order-taker's mind. The listing was long, covering a relatively wide area; it wasn't until I reached the R's and my watch showed nearly eleven o'clock that I got lucky.

"I don't remember any order like that in the past six weeks," the clerk at Rainbow Florists said, "but we had one yesterday, was delivered this morning."

I gripped the receiver harder. "Will you pull the order, please?"

"I'm not sure I should –"

"Please. You could help to save a woman's life."

Quick intake of breath, then his voice filled with excitement; he'd become part of a real-life drama. "One minute. I'll check." When he came back on the line, he said, "Thirty-dollar standard condolence arrangement, delivered this morning to Mr Steven Shoemaker –"

"*Mister?* Not Mrs or Ms?"

"Mister, definitely. I took the order myself." He read off the Shoemakers' address.

"Who placed it?"

"A kid. Came in with cash and written instructions."

Standard ploy – hire a kid off the street so nobody can identify you.

"Thanks very much."

"Aren't you going to tell me –"

I hung up and dialled Shoemaker's office. His secretary told me he was working at home today. I dialled the home number. Busy. I hung up, and the phone rang immediately. Rae, with information on the Cardings.

She'd traced Sam Carding's daughter and younger son. The daughter lived near Cleveland, Ohio, and Rae had spoken with her on the phone. John, his sister had told her, was a drifter and an addict; she hadn't seen or spoken to him in more than ten years. When Rae reached the younger brother at his office in LA, he told her the same, adding that he assumed John had died years ago.

I thanked Rae and told her to keep on it. Then I called Shoemaker's home number again. Still busy; time to go over there.

Shoemaker's Lincoln was parked in the drive of the Victorian, a dusty Honda motorcycle beside it. As I rang the doorbell I again tried to picture a younger, free-spirited Steve bumming around the country on a bike with Jack, but the image simply wouldn't come clear. It took Shoemaker a while to answer the door, and when he saw me, his mouth pulled down in displeasure.

"Come in, and be quick about it," he told me. "I'm on an important conference call."

I was quick about it. He rushed down the hallway to what must be a study, and I went into the parlour where we'd talked the day before. Unlike his offices, it was exquisitely decorated, calling up images of the days of the lumber barons. Andrea's work, probably. Had she also done his offices? Perhaps their gaudy decor was her way of getting back at a husband who put his political life ahead of their marriage?

It was at least half an hour before Shoemaker finished with his call. He appeared in the archway leading to the hall, somewhat dishevelled, running his fingers through his hair. "Come with me," he said. "I have something to show you."

He led me to a large kitchen at the back of the house. A floral arrangement sat on the granite-topped centre island: white lilies with a single red rose. Shoemaker handed me the card: "My sympathy on your wife's passing." It was signed "John".

"Where's Mrs Shoemaker?" I asked.

"Apparently she went out to the coast last night. I

haven't seen her since she walked out on us at the noon hour."

"And you've been home the whole time?"

He nodded. "Mainly on the phone."

"Why didn't you call me when she didn't come home?"

"I didn't realize she hadn't until mid-morning. We have separate bedrooms, and Andrea comes and goes as she pleases. Then this arrangement arrived, and my conference call came through . . ." He shrugged, spreading his hands helplessly.

"All right," I said, "I'm going out there whether she likes it or not. And I think you'd better clear up whatever you're doing here and follow. Maybe your showing up there will convince her you care about her safety, make her listen to reason."

As I spoke, Shoemaker had taken a fifth of Tanqueray gin and a jar of Del Prado Spanish olives from a Lucky sack that sat on the counter. He opened a cupboard, reached for a glass.

"No," I said. "This is no time to have a drink."

He hesitated, then replaced the glass, and began giving me directions to the cabin. His voice was flat, and his curious travelogue-like digressions made me feel as if I were listening to a tape of a *National Geographic* special. Reality, I thought, had finally sunk in, and it had turned him into an automaton.

I had one stop to make before heading out to the coast, but it was right on my way. Morrison Investigations had its office in what looked to be a former motel on Highway 101, near the outskirts of the city. It was a neighbourhood of fast-food restaurants and bars, thrift shops and marginal businesses. Besides the detective agency, the motel's cinder-block units housed an insurance brokerage, a secretarial service, two accountants, and a palm reader. Dave Morrison, who was just arriving as I pulled into the parking area, was a bit of a surprise: in his mid-forties, wearing one small gold earring and a short ponytail. I wondered what Steve Shoemaker had made of him.

Morrison showed me into a two-room suite crowded with

computer equipment and file cabinets and furniture that looked as if he might have hauled it down the street from the nearby Thrift Emporium. When he noticed me studying him, he grinned easily. "I know, I don't look like a former cop. I worked undercover Narcotics my last few years on the force. Afterwards I realized I was comfortable with the uniform." His gesture took in his lumberjack's shirt, work-worn jeans and boots.

I smiled in return, and he cleared some files off a chair so I could sit.

"So you're working for Steve Shoemaker," he said.

"I understand you did, too."

He nodded. "Last April and again around the beginning of August."

"Did he approach you about another job after that?"

He shook his head.

"And the jobs you did for him were –"

"You know better than to ask that."

"I was going to ask, were they completed to his satisfaction?"

"Yes."

"Do you have any idea why Shoemaker would go to the trouble of bringing me up from San Francisco when he had an investigator here whose work satisfied him?"

Headshake.

"Shoemaker told me the first job you did for him had to do with politics."

The corner of his mouth twitched. "In a matter of speaking." He paused, shrewd eyes assessing me. "How come you're investigating your own client?"

"It's that kind of case. And something feels wrong. Did you get that sense about either of the jobs you took on for him?"

"No." Then he hesitated, frowning. "Well, maybe. Why don't you just come out and ask what you want to? If I can, I'll answer."

"Okay – did either of the jobs have to do with a man named John Carding?"

That surprised him. After a moment he asked a question of his own.

"He's still trying to trace Carding?"

"Yes."

Morrison got up and moved towards the window, stopped and drummed his fingers on top of a file cabinet. "Well, I can save you further trouble. John Carding is untraceable. I tried every way I know – and that's every way there is. My guess is that he's dead, years dead."

"And when was it you tried to trace him?"

"Most of August."

Weeks before Andrea Shoemaker had begun to receive the notes from "John". Unless the harassment had started earlier? No, I'd seen all the notes, examined their post-marks. Unless she'd thrown away the first ones, as she had the card that came with the funeral arrangement?

"Shoemaker tell you why he wanted to find Carding?" I asked.

"Uh-uh."

"And your investigation last April had nothing to do with Carding?"

At first I thought Morrison hadn't heard the question. He was looking out the window; then he turned, expression thoughtful, and opened one of the drawers of the filing cabinet beside him. "Let me refresh my memory," he said, taking out a couple of folders. I watched as he flipped through them, frowning.

Finally he said, "I'm not gonna ask about your case. If something feels wrong, it could be because of what I turned up last spring – and that I don't want on my conscience." He closed one file, slipped it back in the cabinet, then glanced at his watch. "Damn! I just remembered I've got to make a call." He crossed to the desk, set the open file on it. "I better do it from the other room. You stay here, find something to read."

I waited until he'd left, then went over and picked up the file. Read it with growing interest and began putting things together. Andrea had been discreet about her extramarital activities, but not so discreet that a competent investigator like Morrison couldn't uncover them.

When Morrison returned, I was ready to leave for the Lost Coast.

"Hope you weren't bored," he said.

"No, I'm easily amused. And, Mr Morrison, I owe you a dinner."

"You know where to find me. I'll look forward to seeing you again."

And now that I'd reached the cabin, Andrea had disappeared. The victim of violence, all signs indicated. But the victim of whom? John Carding – a man no one had seen or heard from for over ten years? Another man named John, one of her cast-off lovers? Or . . . ?

What mattered now was to find her.

I retraced my steps, turning up the hood of my sweater again as I went outside. Circled the cabin, peering through the lashing rain. I could make out a couple of other small structures back there: outhouse and shed. The outhouse was empty. I crossed to the shed. Its door was propped open with a log, as if she'd been getting fuel for the stove.

Inside, next to a neatly stacked cord of wood, I found her.

She lay face-down on the hard-packed dirt floor, blue-jeaned legs splayed, plaid-jacketed arms flung above her head, chestnut hair cascading over her back. The little room was silent, the total silence that surrounds the dead. Even my own breath was stilled; when it came again, it sounded obscenely loud.

I knelt beside her, forced myself to perform all the checks I've made more times than I could have imagined. No breath, no pulse, no warmth to the skin. And the rigidity . . .

On the average – although there's a wide variance – rigor mortis sets in to the upper body five to six hours after death; the whole body is usually affected within eighteen hours. I backed up and felt the lower portion of her body. Rigid; rigor was complete. I straightened, went to stand in the doorway. She'd probably been dead since midnight. And the cause? I couldn't see any wounds, couldn't further examine her without disturbing the scene. What I should be doing was getting in touch with the sheriff's department.

Back to the cabin. Emotions tore at me: anger, regret, and – yes – guilt that I hadn't prevented this. But I also sensed that I *couldn't* have prevented it. I, or someone like me, had been an integral component from the first.

In the front room I found some kitchen matches and lit the oil lamp. Then I went around the table and looked down at where her revolver lay on the floor. More evidence; don't touch it. The purse and its spilled contents rested near the edge of the stove. I inventoried the items visually: the usual makeup, brush, comb, spray perfume; wallet, keys, roll of postage stamps; daily planner that had flopped open to show pockets for business cards and receipts. And a loose piece of paper . . .

Lucky Food Centre, it said at the top. Perhaps she'd stopped to pick up supplies before leaving Eureka; the date and time on this receipt might indicate how long she'd remained in town before storming out on her husband and me. After I picked it up. At the bottom I found yesterday's date and the time of purchase: 9:14 p.m.

"KY SERV DELI . . . CRABS . . . WINE . . . DEL PRAD OLIVE . . . LG RED DEL . . . ROUGE ET NOIR . . . BAKERY . . . TANQ GIN –"

A sound outside. Footsteps slogging through the mud. I stuffed the receipt into my pocket.

Steve Shoemaker came through the open door in a hurry, rain hat pulled low on his forehead, droplets sluicing down his chiselled nose. He stopped when he saw me, looked around. "Where's Andrea?"

I said, "I don't know."

"What do you mean you don't know? Her Bronco's outside. That's her purse on the stove."

"And her weekend bag's on the bed, but she's nowhere to be found."

Shoemaker arranged his face into lines of concern. "There's been a struggle here."

"Appears that way."

"Come on, we'll go look for her. She may be in the outhouse or the shed. She may be hurt –"

"It won't be necessary to look." I had my gun out of my purse now, and I levelled it at him. "I know you killed your wife, Shoemaker."

"What!"

"Her body's where you left it last night. What time did you kill her? How?"

His faked concern shaded into panic. "I didn't –"

"You did."

No reply. His eyes moved from side to side – calculating, looking for a way out.

I added, "You drove her here in the Bronco, with your motorcycle inside. Arranged things to simulate a struggle, put her in the shed, then drove back to town on the bike. You shouldn't have left the bike outside the house where I could see it. It wasn't muddy out here last night, but it sure was dusty."

"Where are these baseless accusations coming from? John Carding –"

"Is untraceable, probably dead, as you know from the check Dave Morrison ran."

"He told you – What about the notes, the flowers, the dead things –"

"Sent by you."

"Why would I do that?"

"To set the scene for getting rid of a chronically unfaithful wife who had potential to become a political embarrassment."

He wasn't cracking, though. "Granted, Andrea had her problems. But why would I rake up the Carding matter?"

"Because it would sound convincing for you to admit what you did all those years ago. God knows it convinced me. And I doubt the police would ever have made the details public. Why destroy a grieving widower and prominent citizen? Particularly when they'd never find Carding or bring him to trial. You've got one problem, though: me. You never should have brought me in to back up your scenario."

He licked his lips, glaring at me. Then he drew himself up, leaned forward aggressively – a posture the attorneys at All Souls jokingly refer to as their "litigator's mode".

"You have no proof of this," he said firmly, jabbing his index finger at me. "No proof whatsoever."

"Deli items, crabs, wine, apples," I recited. "Del Prado Spanish olives, Tanqueray gin."

"What the hell are you talking about?"

"I have Andrea's receipt for the items she bought at Lucky yesterday, before she stopped home to pick up her weekend bag. None of those things is here in the cabin."

"So?"

"I know that at least two of them – the olives and the gin – are at your house in Eureka. I'm willing to bet they all are."

"What if they are? She did some shopping for me yesterday morning –"

"The receipt is dated yesterday *evening*, nine-fourteen p.m. I'll quote you, Shoemaker: 'Apparently she went out to the coast last night. I haven't seen her since she walked out on us at the noon hour.' But you claim you didn't leave home after noon."

That did it; that opened the cracks. He stood for a moment, then half collapsed into one of the chairs and put his head in his hands.

The next summer, after I testified at the trial in which Steve Shoemaker was convicted of the first-degree murder of his wife, I returned to the Lost Coast – with a backpack, without the .38, and in the company of my lover. We walked sand beaches under skies that showed infinite shadings of blue; we made love in fields of wildflowers; we waited quietly for the deer, falcons, and foxes.

I'd already taken the bad from this place; now I could take the good.

The Pit

Joe R. Lansdale

For Ed Gorman

Six months earlier they had captured him. Tonight Harry went into the pit. He and Big George, right after the bull terriers got through tearing the guts out of one another. When that was over, he and George would go down and do their business. The loser would stay there and be fed to the dogs, each of which had been starved for the occasion.

When the dogs finished eating, the loser's head would go up on a pole. Already a dozen poles circled the pit. On each rested a head, or skull, depending on how long it had been exposed to the elements, ambitious pole-climbing ants and hungry birds. And of course how much flesh the terriers ripped off before it was erected.

Twelve poles. Twelve heads.

Tonight a new pole and a new head went up.

Harry looked about at the congregation. All sixty or so of them. They were a sight. Like mad creatures out of Lewis Carroll. Only they didn't have long rabbit ears or tall silly hats. They were just backwoods rednecks, not too unlike himself. With one major difference. They were as loony as waltzing mice. Or maybe they weren't crazy and he was. Sometimes he felt as if he had stepped into an alternative universe where the old laws of nature and what was right and wrong did not apply. Just like Alice plunging down the rabbit hole into Wonderland.

The crowd about the pit had been mumbling and talking, but now they grew silent. Out into the glow of the neon lamps stepped a man dressed in a black suit and hat. A massive rattlesnake was coiled about his right arm. It was wriggling from shoulder to wrist. About his left wrist a smaller snake was wrapped, a copperhead. The man held a Bible in his right hand. He was called Preacher.

Draping the monstrous rattlesnake around his neck, Preacher let it hang there. It dangled that way as if drugged. Its tongue would flash out from time to time. It gave Harry the willies. He hated snakes. They always seemed to be smiling. Nothing was that fucking funny, not all the time.

Preacher opened the Bible and read:

"Behold, I give unto you the power to tread on serpents and scorpions, and over all the power of the enemy: and nothing will by any means hurt you."

Preacher paused and looked at the sky. "So, God," he said, "we want to thank you for a pretty good potato crop, though you've done better, and we want to thank you for the terriers, even though we had to raise and feed them ourselves, and we want to thank you for sending these outsiders our way, thank you for Harry Joe Stinton and Big George, the *nigger*."

Preacher paused and looked about the congregation. He lifted the hand with the copperhead in it high above his head. Slowly he lowered it and pointed the snake-filled fist at George. "Three times this here *nigger* had gone into the pit, and three times he has come out victorious. Couple times against whites, once against another nigger. Some of us think he's cheating.

"Tonight, we bring you another white feller, one of your chosen people, though you might not know it on account of the way you been letting the *nigger* win here, and we're hoping for a good fight with the nigger being killed at the end. We hope this here business pleases you. We worship you and the snakes in the way we ought to. Amen."

Big George looked over at Harry. "Be ready, sucker. I'm gonna take you apart like a gingerbread man."

Harry didn't say anything. He couldn't understand it. George was a prisoner just as he was. A man degraded and made to lift huge rocks and pull carts and jog mile on miles every day. And just so they could get in shape for this – to go down into that pit and try and beat each other to death for the amusement of these crazies.

And it had to be worse for George. Being black, he was seldom called anything other than *"nigger"* by these psychos. Furthermore, no secret had been made of the fact that they wanted George to lose, and for him to win. The idea of a black pit champion was eating their little *honky* hearts out.

Yet, Big George had developed a sort of perverse pride in being the longest-lived pit fighter yet.

"It's something I can do right," George had once said. "On the outside I wasn't nothing but a *nigger*, an uneducated *nigger* working in rose fields, mowing big lawns for rich white folks. Here I'm still the *nigger*, but I'm THE NIGGER, the bad ass *nigger*, and no matter what these peckerwoods call me, they know it, and they know I'm the best at what I do. I'm the king here. And they may hate me for it, keep me in a cell and make me run and lift stuff, but for that time in the pit, they know I'm the one that can do what they can't do, and they're afraid of me. I like it."

Glancing at George, Harry saw that the big man was not nervous. Or at least not showing it. He looked as if he were ready to go on vacation. Nothing to it. He was about to go down into that pit and try and beat a man to death with his fists and it was nothing. All in a day's work. A job well done for an odd sort of respect that beat what he had had on the outside.

The outside. It was strange how much he and Big George used that term. *The outside.* As if they were enclosed in some small bubble-like cosmos that perched on the edge of the world they had known; a cosmos invisible to *the outsiders*, a spectral place with new mathematics and nebulous laws of mind and physics.

Maybe he was in hell. Perhaps he had been wiped out on the highway and had gone to the dark place. Just maybe his memory of how he had arrived here was a false dream inspired by demonic powers. The whole thing about him taking a wrong turn through Big Thicket country and having his truck break down just outside of Morganstown was an illusion, and stepping onto the Main Street of Morganstown, population 66, was his crossing the River

Styx and landing smack dab in the middle of a hell designed for good old boys.

God, had it been six months ago?

He had been on his way to visit his mother in Woodville, and he had taken a short cut through the Thicket. Or so he thought. But he soon realized that he had looked at the map wrong. The short cut listed on the paper was not the one he had taken. He had mistaken that road for the one he wanted. This one had not been marked. And then he reached Morganstown and his truck had broken down. He had been forced into six months' hard labour alongside George, the champion pit-fighter, and now the moment for which he had been groomed arrived.

They were bringing the terriers out now. One, the champion, was named Old Codger. He was getting on in years. He had won many a pit fight. Tonight, win or lose, this would be his last battle. The other dog, Muncher, was young and inexperienced, but he was strong and eager for blood.

A ramp was lowered into the pit. Preacher and two men, the owners of the dogs, went down into the pit with Codger and Muncher. When they reached the bottom a dozen bright spot lights were thrown on them. They seemed to wade through the light.

The bleachers arranged about the pit began to fill. People mumbled and passed popcorn. Bets were placed and a little, fat man wearing a bowler hat copied them down in a note pad as fast as they were shouted. The ramp was removed.

In the pit, the men took hold of their dogs by the scruff of the neck and removed their collars. They turned the dogs so they were facing the walls of the pit and could not see one another. The terriers were about six feet apart, butts facing.

Preacher said, "A living dog is better than a dead lion."

Harry wasn't quite sure what that had to do with anything.

"Ready yourselves," Preacher said. "Gentlemen, face your dogs."

The owners slapped their dogs across the muzzle and whirled them to face one another. They immediately began to leap and strain at their masters' grips.

"Gentlemen, release your dogs."

The dogs did not bark. For some reason, that was what Harry noted the most. They did not even growl. They were quick little engines of silence.

Their first lunge was a miss and they snapped air. But the second time they hit head on with the impact of .45 slugs. Codger was knocked on his back and Muncher dived for his throat. But the experienced dog popped up its head and grabbed Muncher by the nose. Codger's teeth met through Muncher's flesh.

Bets were called from the bleachers.

The little man in the bowler was writing furiously.

Muncher, the challenger, was dragging Codger, the champion, around the pit, trying to make the old dog let go of his nose. Finally, by shaking his head violently and relinquishing a hunk of his muzzle, he succeeded.

Codger rolled to his feet and jumped Muncher. Muncher turned his head just out of the path of Codger's jaws. The older dog's teeth snapped together like a spring-loaded bear trap, saliva popped out of his mouth in a fine spray.

Muncher grabbed Codger by the right ear. The grip was strong and Codger was shook like a used condom about to be tied and tossed. Muncher bit the champ's ear completely off.

Harry felt sick. He thought he was going to throw up. He saw that Big George was looking at him. "You think this is bad, motherfucker," George said, "this ain't nothing but a cake walk. Wait till I get you in that pit."

"You sure run hot and cold, don't you?" Harry said.

"Nothing personal," George said sharply and turned back to look at the fight in the pit.

Nothing personal, Harry thought. God, what could be more personal? Just yesterday, as they trained, jogged along together, a pick-up loaded with gun-bearing crazies driving alongside of them, he had felt close to George. They had shared many personal things these six months, and he knew that George liked him. But when it came to the pit, George was a different man. The concept of friendship became alien to him. When Harry had tried to talk to him about it yesterday, he had said much the same thing. "Ain't nothing personal, Harry, my man, but when we get in that pit don't look to me for nothing besides pain, 'cause I got plenty of that to give you, a lifetime of it, and I'll just keep it coming."

Down in the pit Codger screamed. It could be described no other way. Muncher had him on his back and was biting him on the belly. Codger was trying to double forward and get hold of Muncher's head, but his tired jaws kept slipping off of the sweaty neck fur. Blood was starting to pump out of Codger's belly.

"Bite him, boy," someone yelled from the bleachers, "tear his ass up, son."

Harry noted that every man, woman and child was leaning forwards in their seat, straining for a view. Their faces full of lust, like lovers approaching vicious climax. For a few moments they were in that pit and they were the dogs. Vicarious thrills without the pain.

Codger's legs began to flap.

"Kill him! Kill him!" the crowd began to chant.

Codger had quit moving. Muncher was burrowing his muzzle deeper into the old dog's guts. Preacher called for a pick-up. Muncher's owner pried the dog's jaw loose of Codger's guts. Muncher's muzzle looked as if it had been dipped in red ink.

"This sonofabitch is still alive," Muncher's owner said of Codger.

Codger's owner walked over to the dog and said, "You little fucker!" He pulled a Saturday Night Special from his coat pocket and shot Codger twice in the head. Codger didn't even kick. He just evacuated his bowels right there.

Muncher came over and sniffed Codger's corpse, then, lifting his leg, he took a leak on the dead dog's head. The stream of piss was bright red.

The ramp was lowered. The dead dog was dragged out and tossed behind the bleachers. Muncher walked up the ramp beside his owner. The little dog strutted like he had just been crowned King of Creation. Codger's owner walked out last. He was not a happy man. Preacher stayed in the pit. A big man known as Sheriff Jimmy went down the ramp to join him. Sheriff Jimmy had a big pistol on his hip and a toy badge on his chest. The badge looked like the sort of thing that had come in a plastic bag with a capgun and whistle. But it was his sign of office and his word was iron.

A man next to Harry prodded him with the barrel of a shotgun. Walking close behind George, Harry went down the ramp and into the pit. The man with the shotgun went back up. In the bleachers the betting had started again, the little, fat man with the bowler was busy.

Preacher's rattlesnake was still lying serenely about his neck, and the little copperhead had been placed in Preacher's coat pocket. It poked its head out from time to time and looked around.

Harry glanced up. The heads and skulls on the poles – in spite of the fact they were all eyeless, and due to the strong light nothing but bulbous shapes on shafts – seemed to look down, taking as much amusement in the situation as the crowd on the bleachers.

Preacher had his Bible out again. He was reading a verse. ". . . when thou walkest through the fire, thou shalt not be burned; neither shall the flame kindle upon thee . . ."

Harry had no idea what that or the snakes had to do with anything. Certainly he could not see the relationship with the pit. These people's minds seemed to click and grind to a different set of internal gears than those on *the outside*.

The reality of the situation settled on Harry like a heavy, woollen coat. He was about to kill or be killed, right here in this dog-smelling pit, and there was nothing he could do that would change that.

He thought perhaps his life should flash before his eyes or something, but it did not. Maybe he should try to think of something wonderful, a last fine thought of what used to be. First he summoned up the image of his wife. That did nothing for him. Though his wife had once been pretty and bright, he could not remember her that way. The image that came to mind was quite different. A dumpy, lazy woman with constant back pains and her hair pulled up into an eternal topknot of greasy, brown hair. There was never a smile on her face or a word of encouragement for him. He always felt that she expected him to entertain her and that he was not doing a very good job of it. There was not even a moment of sexual ecstasy that he could recall. After their daughter had been born she had given up screwing as a wasted exercise. Why waste energy on sex when she could spend it complaining?

He flipped his mental card file to his daughter. What he saw was an ugly, potato-nosed girl of twelve. She had no personality. Her mother was Miss Congeniality compared to her. Potato Nose spent all of her time pining over thin, blond heartthrobs on television. It wasn't bad enough that they glared at Harry via the tube, they were also pinned to her walls and hiding in magazines she had cast throughout the house.

These were the last thoughts of a man about to face death?

There was just nothing there.

His job had sucked. His wife hadn't.

He clutched at straws. There had been Melva, a fine looking little cheerleader from high school. She had the brain of a dried black-eyed pea, but God-All-Mighty, did she know how to hide a weenie. And there had always been that strange smell about her, like bananas. It was especially strong about her thatch, which was thick enough for a bald eagle to nest in.

But thinking about her didn't provide much pleasure either. She had gotten hit by a drunk in a Mack truck while parked alongside a dark road with that Pulver boy.

Damn that Pulver. At least he had died in ecstasy. Had never known what hit him. When that Mack went up his ass he probably thought for a split second he was having the greatest orgasm of his life.

Damn that Melva. What had she seen in Pulver anyway?

He was skinny and stupid and had a face like a peanut pattie.

God, he was beat at every turn. Frustrated at every corner. No good thoughts or beautiful visions before the moment of truth. Only blackness, a life of dull, planned movements as consistent and boring as a bran-conscious geriatric's bowel movement. For a moment he thought he might cry.

Sheriff Jimmy took out his revolver. Unlike the badge it was not a toy. "Find your corner, boys."

George turned and strode to one side of the pit, took off his shirt and leaned against the wall. His body shone like wet licorice in the spot lights.

After a moment, Harry made his legs work. He walked to a place opposite George and took off his shirt. He could feel the months of hard work rippling through his flesh. His mind was suddenly blank. There wasn't even a god he believed in. No one to pray to. Nothing to do but the inevitable.

Sheriff Jimmy walked to the middle of the pit. He yelled out for the crowd to shut up.

Silence reigned.

"In this corner," he said, waving the revolver at Harry, "we have Harry Joe Stinton, a family man and pretty good feller for an outsider. He's six two and weighs two hundred and thirty-eight pounds, give or take a pound since my bathroom scales ain't exactly on the money."

A cheer went up.

"Over here," Sheriff Jimmy said, waving the revolver at George, "standing six four tall and weighing two hundred and forty-two pounds, we got the *nigger*, present champion of this here sport."

No one cheered. Someone made a loud sound with his mouth that sounded like a fart, the greasy kind that goes on and on and on.

George appeared unfazed. He looked like a statue. He knew who he was and what he was. The Champion Of The Pit.

"First off," Sheriff Jimmy said, "you boys come forward and show your hands."

Harry and George walked to the centre of the pit, held out their hands, fingers spread wide apart, so that the crowd could see they were empty.

"Turn and walk to your corners and don't turn around," Sheriff Jimmy said.

George and Harry did as they were told. Sheriff Jimmy followed Harry and put an arm around his shoulders. "I got four hogs riding on you," he said. "And I'll tell you what, you beat the *nigger* and I'll do you a favour. Elvira, who works over at the cafe has already agreed. You win and you can have her. How's that sound?"

Harry was too numb with the insanity of it all to answer. Sheriff Jimmy was offering him a piece of ass if he won, as if this would be greater incentive than coming out of the pit alive. With this bunch there was just no way to anticipate what might come next. Nothing was static.

"She can do more tricks with a six-inch dick than a monkey can with a hundred foot of grapevine, boy. When the going gets rough in there, you remember that. Okay?"

Harry didn't answer. He just looked at the pit wall.

"You ain't gonna get nowhere in life being sullen like that," Sheriff Jimmy said. "Now, you go get him and plough a rut in his black ass."

Sheriff Jimmy grabbed Harry by the shoulders and whirled him around, slapped him hard across the face in the same way the dogs had been slapped. George had been done the same way by the preacher. Now George and Harry were facing one another. Harry thought George looked like an ebony gargoyle fresh escaped from hell. His bald, bullet-like head gleamed in the harsh lights and his body looked as rough and ragged as stone.

Harry and George raised their hands in classic boxer stance and began to circle one another.

From above someone yelled, "Don't hit the *nigger* in the head, it'll break your hand. Go for the lips, they got soft lips."

The smell of sweat, dog blood and Old Codger's shit was thick in the air. The lust of the crowd seemed to have an aroma as well. Harry even thought he could smell Preacher's snakes. Once, when a boy, he had been fishing down by the creek bed and had smelled an odour like that, and a water moccasin had wriggled out beneath his legs and splashed in the water. It was as if everything he feared in the world had been put in this pit. The idea of being put deep in the ground. Irrational people for whom logic did not exist. Rotting skulls on poles about the pit. Living skulls attached to hunched-forward bodies that yelled for blood. Snakes. The stench of death – blood and shit. And every white man's fear, racist or not – a big, black man with a lifetime of hatred in his eyes.

The circle tightened. They could almost touch one another now.

Suddenly George's lip began to tremble. His eyes poked out of his head, seemed to be looking at something just behind and to the right of Harry.

"Sss . . . snake!" George screamed.

God, thought Harry, one of Preacher's snakes has escaped. Harry jerked his head for a look.

And George stepped in and knocked him on his ass and kicked him full in the chest. Harry began scuttling along the ground on his hands and knees, George following along kicking him in the ribs. Harry thought he felt something snap inside, a cracked rib maybe. He finally scuttled to his feet and bicycled around the pit. Goddamn, he thought, I fell for the oldest trick in the book. Here I am fighting for my life and I fell for it.

"Way to go, stupid fuck!" A voice screamed from the bleachers. "Hey *nigger*, why don't you try, 'hey, your shoe's untied,' he'll go for it."

"Get off the goddamned bicycle," someone else yelled. "Fight."

"You better run," George said. "I catch you I'm gonna punch you so hard in the mouth, gonna knock your fucking teeth out your asshole . . ."

Harry felt dizzy. His head was like a yo-yo doing the Around the World trick. Blood ran down his forehead, dribbled off the tip of his nose and gathered on his upper lip. George was closing the gap again.

I'm going to die right here in this pit, thought Harry. I'm going to die just because my truck broke down outside of town and no one knows where I am. That's why I'm going to die. It's as simple as that.

Popcorn rained down on Harry and a tossed cup of ice hit him in the back. "Wanted to see a fucking foot race," a voice called, "I'd have gone to the fucking track."

"Ten on the *nigger*," another voice said.

"Five bucks the *nigger* kills him in five minutes."

When Harry back-pedalled past Preacher, the snake man leaned forwards and snapped, "You asshole, I got a saw-buck riding on you."

Preacher was holding the big rattler again. He had the snake gripped just below the head, and he was so upset over how the fight had gone so far, he was unconsciously squeezing the snake in a vice-like grip. The rattler was squirming and twisting and flapping about, but Preacher didn't seem to notice. The snake's forked tongue was outside its mouth and it was really working, slapping about like a thin strip of rubber come loose on a whirling tyre. The copperhead in Preacher's pocket was still looking out, as if along with Preacher he might have a bet on the outcome of the fight as well. As Harry danced away the rattler opened its mouth so wide its jaws came unhinged. It looked as if it were trying to yell for help.

Harry and George came together again in the centre of the pit. Fists like black ball bearings slammed the sides of Harry's head. The pit was like a whirlpool, the walls threatening to close in and suck Harry down into oblivion.

Kneeing with all his might, Harry caught George solidly in the groin. George grunted, stumbled back, half-bent over.

The crowd went wild.

Harry brought cupped hands down on George's neck, knocked him to his knees. Harry used the opportunity to knock out one of the big man's teeth with the toe of his shoe.

He was about to kick him again when George reached up and clutched the crotch of Harry's khakis, taking a crushing grip on Harry's testicles.

"Got you by the balls," George growled.

Harry bellowed and began to hammer wildly on top of George's head with both fists. He realized with horror that George was pulling him forward. *By God, George was going to bite him on the balls*.

Jerking up his knee he caught George in the nose and broke his grip. He bounded free, skipped and whooped about the pit like an Indian dancing for rain.

He skipped and whooped by Preacher. Preacher's rattler had quit twisting. It hung loosely from Preacher's tight fist.

Its eyes were bulging out of its head like the humped backs of grub worms. Its mouth was closed and its forked tongue hung limply from the edge of it.

The copperhead was still watching the show from the safety of Preacher's pocket, its tongue zipping out from time to time to taste the air. The little snake didn't seem to have a care in the world.

George was on his feet again, and Harry could tell that already he was feeling better. Feeling good enough to make Harry feel real bad.

Preacher abruptly realized that his rattler had gone limp. "No, God, no!" he cried. He stretched the huge rattler between his hands. "Baby, baby," he bawled, "breathe for me. Sapphire, breathe for me." Preacher shook the snake viciously, trying to jar some life into it, but the snake did not move.

The pain in Harry's groin had subsided and he could think again. George was moving in on him, and there just didn't seem any reason to run. George would catch him, and when he did, it would just be worse because he would be even more tired from all that running. It had to be done. The mating dance was over, now all that was left was the intercourse of violence.

A black fist turned the flesh and cartilage of Harry's nose into smouldering putty. Harry ducked his head and caught another blow to the chin. The stars he had not been able to see above him because of the lights, he could now see below him, spinning constellations on the floor of the pit.

It came to him again, the fact that he was going to die right here without one good, last thought. But then maybe there was one. He envisioned his wife, dumpy and sullen and denying him sex. George became her and she became George and Harry did what he had wanted to do for so long, he hit her in the mouth. Not once, but twice and a third time. He battered her nose and he pounded her ribs. And by God, but she could hit back. He felt something crack in the centre of his chest and his left cheekbone collapsed into his face. But Harry did not stop battering her. He looped and punched and pounded her dumpy face until it was George's black face and George's black face turned back to her face and he thought of her now on the bed, naked, on her back, battered, and he was naked mounting her, and the blows of his fists were the sexual thrusts of his cock and he was pounding her until –

George screamed. He had fallen to his knees. His right eye was hanging out on the tendons. One of Harry's straight rights had struck George's cheekbone with such power it had shattered it and pressured the eye out of its socket.

Blood ran down Harry's knuckles. Some of it was George's. Much of it was his own. His knuckle bones showed through the rent flesh of his hands, but they did not hurt. They were past hurting.

George wobbled to his feet. The two men stood facing one another, neither moving. The crowd was silent. The only sound in the pit was the harsh breathing of the two fighters, and Preacher who had stretched Sapphire out on the ground on her back and was trying to blow air into her mouth. Occasionally he'd lift his head and say in tearful supplication, "Breathe for me, Sapphire, breathe for me."

Each time Preacher blew a blast into the snake, its white underbelly would swell and then settle down, like a leaky balloon that just wouldn't hold air.

George and Harry came together. Softly. They had their arms on each other's shoulders and they leaned against one another, breathed each other's breath.

Above, the silence of the crowd was broken when a heckler yelled, "Start some music, the fuckers want to dance."

"It's nothing personal," George said.

"Not at all," Harry said.

They managed to separate, reluctantly, like two lovers who had just copulated to the greatest orgasm of their lives.

George bent slightly and put up his hands. The eye dangling on his cheek looked like some tentacled creature trying to crawl up and into the socket. Harry knew that he would have to work on that eye.

Preacher screamed. Harry afforded him a sideways glance. Sapphire was awake. And now she was dangling from Preacher's face. She had bitten through his top lip and was hung there by her fangs. Preacher was saying something about the power to tread on serpents and stumbling about the pit. Finally his back struck the pit wall and he slid down to his butt and just sat there, legs sticking out in front of him, Sapphire dangling off his lip like some sort of malignant growth. Gradually, building momentum, the snake began to thrash.

Harry and George met again in the centre of the pit. A second wind had washed in on them and they were ready. Harry hurt wonderfully. He was no longer afraid. Both men were smiling, showing the teeth they had left. They began to hit each other.

Harry worked on the eye. Twice he felt it beneath his fists, a grape-like thing that cushioned his knuckles and made them wet. Harry's entire body felt on fire – twin fires, ecstasy and pain.

George and Harry leaned together, held each other, waltzed about.

"You done good," George said, "make it quick."

The black man's legs went out from under him and he fell to his knees, head bent. Harry took the man's head in his hands and kneed him in the face with all his might. George went limp. Harry grasped George's chin and the back of his head and gave a violent twist. The neck bone snapped and George fell back, dead.

The copperhead, which had been poking its head out of Preacher's pocket, took this moment to slither away into a crack in the pit's wall.

Out of nowhere came weakness. Harry fell to his knees. He touched George's ruined face with his fingers.

Suddenly hands had him. The ramp was lowered. The crowd cheered. Preacher – Sapphire dislodged from his lip – came forward to help Sheriff Jimmy with him. They lifted him up.

Harry looked at Preacher. His lip was greenish. His head looked like a sun-swollen watermelon, yet, he seemed well enough. Sapphire was wrapped around his neck again. They were still buddies. The snake looked tired. Harry no longer felt afraid of it. He reached out and touched its head. It did not try to bite him. He felt its feathery tongue brush his bloody hand.

They carried him up the ramp and the crowd took him, lifted him high above their heads. He could see the moon and the stars now. For some odd reason they did not look familiar. Even the nature of the sky seemed different.

He turned and looked down. The terriers were being herded into the pit. They ran down the ramp like rats. Below, he could hear them begin to feed, to fight for choice morsels. But there were so many dogs, and they were so hungry, this only went on for a few minutes. After a while they came back up the ramp followed by Sheriff Jimmy closing a big lock-bladed knife and by Preacher who held George's head in his outstretched hands. George's eyes were gone. Little of the face remained. Only that slick, bald pate had been left undamaged by the terriers.

A pole came out of the crowd and the head was pushed onto its sharpened end and the pole was dropped into a deep hole in the ground. The pole, like a long neck, rocked its trophy for a moment, then went still. Dirt was kicked into the hole and George joined the others, all those beautiful, wonderful heads and skulls.

They began to carry Harry away. Tomorrow he would have Elvira, who could do more tricks with a six-inch dick than a monkey could with a hundred foot of grapevine, then he would heal and a new outsider would come through and they would train together and then they would mate in blood and sweat in the depths of the pit.

The crowd was moving towards the forest trail, towards town. The smell of pines was sweet in the air. And as they carried him away, Harry turned his head so he could look back and see the pit, its maw closing in shadow as the lights were cut, and just before the last one went out Harry saw the heads on the poles, and dead centre of his vision, was the shiny bald pate of his good friend George.

Clean Sweep

Roger Torrey

Dal Prentice stood with feet apart, heavy eyebrows meeting in a line above hard eyes. He stared at the blonde young woman, said: "And he just walked in and started shooting, eh? Where was you?" in a sceptical voice. His eyes didn't blink, held round and scowling.

The woman looked back defiantly, met the hard glare, turned her eyes towards the side of the room and away. She pointed, said: "I was in the kitchen. There. I let him in and he said, 'I want to see Margie,' and I called her. I knew he was her old man. I went in the kitchen and then the shooting started."

"And then?"

"Well, I waited a minute and heard him run out and then I went in."

"What didja wait for?"

"My gawd! Did *I* want to get shot?"

Prentice considered. He said: "Well, I s'pose not," in an easier tone, turned, called through the door of the bedroom at his right: "How 'bout it, Doc?" said: "All right, all right," to the irritable voice that called back a request for time, and swung to the blonde again. He asked: "Who was with her when he come?"

"Nobody."

He spoke to the lean man at his elbow. "Y'see, Al. He just comes in and starts shooting. What a honey!"

The lean man looked bored, offered: "Maybe he was sore," in a voice that showed a total lack of interest, and Prentice snorted: "Sore!" and slewed back to the woman.

"You said nobody?"

The blonde stuck out her lower lip.

"I said nobody."

"No?"

"No."

Prentice smoothed his voice and smiled. His eyes didn't soften. He said: "Now, now, be nice. Tell a man. Who was with her? This heel wouldn't have killed her if she'd been alone, would he?"

"He *did*."

"Now, now. You know what the score is. Let's tell secrets."

"You tell me one and I'll tell you one."

The blonde took in her lower lip, tried a smile, and the grin left Prentice's face and he snapped: "Okay! This Marge is a witness against Pat Kailor on the murder rap he's facing. *The* witness. If that's a secret, you're told. Who was with her?"

"Nobody."

"That's your story?"

"It's the truth."

Prentice gritted: "Like hell!" between his teeth, took a step ahead with his hand raised, and the lean man at his side caught his arm, held it, said: "Easy, Dal! Don't be a chump."

"She's lying."

"What of it?"

The blonde girl said: "You're Allen, aren't you?" and he dropped Prentice's arm, told her: "Yes."

"I'm not lying."

Allen slid between the scowling Prentice and the girl, said softly: "No . . . just stalling. Let me put it in a different way. Who was with her earlier if there wasn't anybody here when he came?"

The blonde said: "I . . . uh . . ." looked past Allen and caught Prentice's eye and finished: "There was three," in a hurried voice.

"Who?"

"Two of 'em I don't know. They been here before but they wasn't looking for anyone in particular. The other one wanted Margie."

"Who was he?"

"Hal Cross. That bird of a deputy District Attorney. If it wasn't that he'd have closed me up I wouldn't have let him in the house."

Allen flashed Prentice a look, said: "Oh, oh," with the accent on the first one. He asked the blonde: "You sure?"

"I should be. He stuck me on a liquor rap that cost me a hundred dollar fine. They only found part of a pint."

"What did he want?"

The woman shrugged. "Margie. Margie come in the room when I was talking to him or he'd never have seen her. I was just going to tell him she was out, but she come in and I flashed her not to crack wise and he says to her, 'I want to see you,' and she takes him in her bedroom."

"Why didn't you want him to see her?"

The muscles on the girl's jaw tightened. She flashed out: "A hundred dollars. Didn't you hear? He told me if I copped a plea he'd see it was suspended."

Allen laughed suddenly, said: "Tough break!" and to the man in the white coat who came out of the bedroom: "Howzit, Doc?"

The police surgeon had glasses jammed up on his forehead. He was wiping his hands on a towel but one sleeve had a bloody cuff. He shook his head, growled: "Dead. About two minutes after I got here. She was unconscious."

Prentice grunted: "How 'bout one of the slugs?" and the surgeon reached into the pocket of the white coat, pulled out a piece of lead and tossed it to him. The bloody cuff made a smear by the pocket and he swabbed at this with the towel, complained; "I put this on fresh, not an hour ago. Damn these shootings," added in a tired voice: "I suppose you'll want to know. Thirty-eight. Three times. Stomach and twice in the right lung. Almost centre, the last one. Looks like he turned that one loose just as she was falling. It slants. She never spoke a word. That cover it?"

Prentice looked at the bullet, tossed it from one hand to the other while he thought. He turned to the woman, asked: "You sure she and this heel that killed her was married?"

"Uh-huh! There was an argument once, and she showed me her certificate."

"What was *his* name on that certificate?"

She hesitated, just for an instant, then said: "Denzer – George Denzer."

The surgeon stopped pawing at his coat with the towel. He looked up from this at the two detectives and the woman, jerked out irritably: "Well! Is there any reason I've got to stay here? How about it?"

"Okay, Doc! We'll lock the room until the print and cameramen get here. Thanks a lot."

The doctor grunted: "For nothing! Be seeing you," and went out. The white coat made a grey blotch in the darkness as he climbed into the ambulance.

Prentice argued: "You don't get it, Cap! Here's this gal bumped. The story'll be her old man come back to town and finds her in a spot. He'll be supposed to've gone screwy and given her the works in a fit of rage. See. He'll either beat the rap or get at the most five years. See. He's got a swell defence. Outraged husband finds wife hustling. The only thing is, it ain't so."

Captain of Detectives Hallahan said: "Why ain't it, Dal?" in a weary voice.

"Well, for one thing, Hal Cross come to see her earlier in the evening. I could tell that the landlady was hushing something and I figured there was a man in the room with her when her husband came in. There wasn't. It turned out that Cross had been down and seen her and left."

"What of it?"

Prentice laughed. "Plenty! Three months ago I told you there was going to be trouble over the contract to run the new paving out on Seventh. That it'd be juicy enough to bring out all the sharpshooters. You said I was·screwy but here's the second killing over this same contract. Screwy, hell!"

"You *are* screwy. You add two and two and get nine. Or nineteen."

"Then nine or nineteen is the right answer. Cap, I know."

"You mean you guess."

"Listen. Hal Cross is the deputy in charge of prosecuting Kailor, who's charged with killing Grossman, who *was* chairman of the board of supervisors. There's one tie-up with the paving contract. Now this Margie gal would've proved Kailor guilty of that shooting. She was an eye-witness to it. Cross seeing her makes a further tie-up."

"You're screwy but go on." Hallahan leaned back in his chair and closed his eyes but the fingers of his right hand continued their nervous drumming on the battered desk.

"I hate to say it but Hal's mixed in some way. He went down to buy her off and she wouldn't go for the shot. He, or somebody, had it all arranged with this husband of hers to gun her out if she didn't."

"Cross is the prosecutor, not the defence attorney. It don't make sense. You got paving contracts on the brain and can't see anything else to it."

"Have I? It'd make sense if Hal was working for Izzy Schwartz as well as the DA. It all works in. Izzy Schwartz was after that big paving job. Grossman doesn't let him in and Grossman gets bumped. If Izzy don't clear Kailor on this Grossman rap, Kailor'll spill his guts. What was Cross down there for if he ain't mixed in the mess?"

Hallahan held his hand palm out. His eyes were half closed but his voice held heat. "You're dingy about the whole affair, Dal. Hal Cross is a good boy. You're trying to figure out angles when there ain't any angles. Even if you were right about Grossman getting killed over this paving steal, you're wrong about Hal being wrong. Kailor *might've* been working for Schwartz but Cross isn't. That's the trouble with you. You get a notion and let it ride you. Cross isn't mixed."

Prentice made his jaw lumpy, slammed the table. "Hal Cross *is*. Al and I've known that for two months or more." He slammed the desk for emphasis. "And . . . I'll . . . prove . . . it. I'm going out and pick up this rat that killed his wife and I'll prove it by him. A heel like that'll *talk*."

Hallahan brushed white hair back from his forehead, opened light blue eyes. He shrugged: "Go ahead if it makes you feel any better. I was going to put Peterson and McCready on it but you can have it. God himself couldn't blast an idea out of that pig head of yours."

"Allen thinks the same way I do."

"He does?" Hallahan looked questioningly up at Allen

and the lean man nodded, took a match from his mouth, said mildly: "Dal's right, Cap! He's *bound* to be." He looked at the frayed end of the match, threw it on the floor. "Once in a while. Let's go, Dal."

Prentice followed him to the door, turned and glowered at Hallahan. He said: "And I'll tell you what'll happen. If we *don't* find him, he'll come in by himself as soon as everything's fixed. Hal Cross'll have it set for him to prosecute. And the guy'll have the best lawyer Izzy Schwartz's money can buy and he'll beat the case. And mind you, I like Hal Cross. I *used* to think he was honest." He stared hard at Hallahan, jerked out: "You see! The rat!" without saying for whom the name was meant, and went out.

Hallahan didn't seem to have any doubt about whom was meant. He said: "Izzy Schwartz!" under his breath, as if he didn't like the words.

After putting out a general alarm for George Denzer, husband and killer of the woman, Prentice and Allen methodically contacted all of the stools they knew. This was without result for the first day but late in the afternoon of the next, Prentice answered the phone, talked, and banged the receiver down with a satisfied expression. He told Allen, seated across from him: "Toad Simpson. He says Denzer's holed up in a house on Alvarado. 1423 West Alvarado. Can't miss it, he says. As soon as it gets dark we'll take him."

Allen looked bored and agreed, asked: "Do we take a squad?" and Prentice said with rising excitement: "No! It'd cramp us. I'll sweat this frame out of him or break both hands. This Denzer thinks he's got power back of him and I'll show him a different kind."

"We might take McCready. He won't talk."

"Well, all right. He can cover the back and we'll crash it. You tell him."

Allen nodded, yawned, and sauntered out to the general room, leaving Prentice staring at one big-knuckled hand and muttering about wife-killers.

With McCready at the back door, Prentice and Allen went quietly, side by side, up on the porch, tried the door as softly, found it open and stepped inside, guns out and covering the blackness they met. The flashlight in Allen's hand clicked on with the light as far from his side as he could hold the torch, and as it ranged he said: "Too late!" in a hushed voice, holstered his gun and turned the house lights on from the switch the flash picked out. Prentice made no answer until he had soft-footed through the other three rooms and back and looked again at the body on the floor.

He finally said: "I knew he was stiff the minute I saw him. I can tell a stiff as far as I can see one." He motioned at the knife in the hollow of the dead man's throat, pointed out: "And whoever done it twisted the knife."

Allen still wore a bored look but his face was a shade whiter. "He ain't been dead long. There's still a little bleeding yet." He raised his voice, shouted: "Hi! Mac! Come in!"

The three men stood looking soberly at the body and finally Prentice knelt and taking his handkerchief from his pocket wrapped it around the haft of the knife. Allen said warningly: "Why not leave . . ."

With both the front and back doors open the shrill of the police whistle carried no hint of direction, and while McCready raced to the back door, both Prentice and Allen dashed out the front. The whistle shrilled again and Prentice cursed, cried out: "In the back!" and they circled the house with Allen tripping over a low hedge concealed in the shadow.

They came to the back, Prentice ten feet in the lead, saw McCready leaning against a garbage container, shoot into the blackness at the end of the lot . . . and saw a tongue of flame lance back from the black and McCready sit down suddenly and lean against the can. Prentice dashed past him, the marksman at the end of the lot fired again, and Prentice slid to his belly and shot back.

Allen shouted: "Roll to the side, you fool! The kitchen light's showing you!" He dived past the prone Prentice into shade, then ten feet ahead. He shot once, heard a door slam, shouted: "They're in the house that faces the back street. I'll head 'em off from the front of it. We got 'em boxed."

He got to his feet and running low, went past the side of the house and around to its front. Prentice slid back to

McCready, stooped over him, and the hidden gun blasted again and the can by his side clanged. He took McCready by the feet and drew him back into shelter, heard Allen bawl out: "I'm set. How's Mac?"

Prentice drew a whistle from his pocket and blew three times, called back: "In the body some place. Ambulance case and quick. He's bleeding from the nose and mouth." He heard Allen blow his own whistle three times . . . then three times more . . . heard an answering rattle of a night-stick some distance away . . . then another whistle at the same distance.

Lights were flashing on in the house next door and when Prentice saw the back door show a thread of light he called: "You there in the house! Come here quick! It's police!" The door opened wide; the marksman cornered in the rear house fired again and there was a frightened squawk and the door closed and the light went out. Prentice bawled impatiently: "You in there. Leave that light out and come here. You won't get hurt."

A side window opened and a voice quavered: "I . . . I'm af-f-fraid."

"Hurry and phone the police station to send riot cars and an ambulance to this address. Hurry, man! There's an officer dying here. Tell 'em Prentice said so."

"Riot cars and an ambulance?"

"Yes! Hurry, man! Riot cars and an ambulance. Hurry!"

The window went blank and in a moment he heard an excited voice say: "Operator! Operator! The police station. Quick!" He lifted McCready's head higher, McCready coughed bloody foam and he lowered him hastily.

Allen shouted: "How's Mac?"

Prentice felt McCready's wrist and found a strong pulse and shouted back: "He'll make it, I think, if they get him to a hospital quick."

The voice at the window asked: "He dead yet? The police are coming. With an ambulance."

"Good! Thanks! Stick out in front and tell 'em where I am and not to rush in here."

"I'll not leave my house."

"Go to the front window and holler then."

Another whistle shrilled and Prentice heard flat feet pounding down the sidewalk. He shouted: "In here. Come close to the house," and in a moment a uniformed man was alongside him. He said: "Take care of this man. No matter what, you stay here. Got it?" He slid close to the back door of the rear house, keeping in the shadow, shouted: "Al! They're on their way."

"Good. I found the guy that started this. The copper."

"Yeah!"

"He was laying alongside the house when I found him. He saw something moving and told whatever it was to come out. Nothing came so he blew his whistle and went in after whatever it was. He got crowned."

Prentice could hear a dissenting voice. "He says it wasn't a whatever. It was two guys."

"They must just have killed the guy and were making their sneak when he come along. Make him watch the other side."

"I have."

Prentice heard the moan of an ambulance siren, followed by a deeper, lustier roar that he identified as the riot squad cars and he heard and segregated the latter sound as belonging to three of these. He said: "Eighteen men and the works!" with an evil grin, hurried past McCready and the watching patrolman to the street and called: "Doc! Here he is. You need a stretcher."

He watched McCready get loaded on the stretcher, saw one limp hand trail along the ground as he was carried to the ambulance, hurried to the first of the riot cars drawn up along the walk and commandeered a shotgun and took command.

He ordered: "You six cover the front and where you can watch the sides. Snap it up. Lieutenant Allen is there and he'll tell you. You three get on this side and you other three on that one. They've got Lieutenant McCready already, so watch your step. You four, come with me. I'm going in, and you cover me."

He started with head down, walking fast towards the back door of the house that held the imprisoned men. One of the four men with him came along his side, said: "Here's a grenade, Lieutenant! For God's sake, don't go in with nothing but a shotgun."

The interruption shook Prentice out of the black rage the sight of the wounded McCready had bred in him and he stopped while yet in the shadow, bawled out: "Hey! You in there! Come out or we're coming in. Quick!"

There was a moment's silence, then a voice shouted back: "We got some people in here that ain't mixed in this. Can they come out?"

"Send 'em."

Prentice called a low-voiced warning and the four men with him scattered out, watching the house. The back door opened and a man and woman came out, the woman half-carrying, half-dragging the man. She stopped when just outside the door, and Prentice called. "Come on. Get clear."

The woman laughed hysterically, said: "They come in and pointed guns at us and my husband fainted." She wavered a moment, dropped the unconscious man and started to slump down, and Prentice stepped from the shadow of the bush and started towards her.

A gun crashed from the back window and he jumped back, slid to his belly, said: "She'll just have to faint," in a resigned voice. The gun blasted again and two of the men with him shot back at the pale tongue of flame. He said from the ground: "Hold 'em. I can't rush the back door with them two laying in front of it. I'll go in from the front with the pineapple."

He eased on his belly out of the range of fire from the back window and to the front, called softly: "Al! Oh, Al!" heard an answer and said: "Cover me. I'm on my way."

He got to his feet, pulled the pin on the grenade, took two steps towards the house and lobbed the bomb to the front porch with just force enough to carry it to the door, dropped, counted five before the crash and was on his feet again running as the shock came to him. He saw the front door hanging crazily on broken hinges, smashed into it shoulder first, with his pistol in his hand, and was in the hall and shooting at the dim shape outlined against the hall window when he heard Allen's feet pound the floor behind him. The shape fired back once, went down with the combined blast of his and Allen's guns, and he turned, cursed, said: "You would shoot in my ear. He was cold turkey for me. You wrecked that ear, sure as hell."

He heard Allen laugh and crept cautiously down the hall, heard a burst of pistol shots and the deep roar of a shotgun, stood up and said: "Broke out the back! It's curtains!" They heard a shout from outside that confirmed this guess, saw the man in the hall was a stranger and quite dead, went out the back door and found the guard placed there grouped around a body that had just cleared the window.

The woman by the steps sat up as they came out, said in a shaky voice: "They said they had shot a policeman and that they were afraid to give up." Allen patted her shoulder, said: "They were smart." He followed Prentice to the body and as they reached it one of the men snapped a light on, showing the dead face. Prentice asked: "Any of you know who . . . My good God! It's Williams, of the DA.'s office."

The silence held for a long minute – was broken by one of the uniformed men blurting out: "Jeeze!"

Dal Prentice nodded at Hallahan triumphantly and said: "Does that check?" in a tone that showed his satisfaction. He added: "I may be screwy about paving contracts but it's proving up." He turned to the new chairman of supervisors, who sat across the desk, said: "Didn't Mr Cross tell you where he heard this fairy story? Who's supposed to've told him all this, Mr Heilig?"

Heilig was florid-faced and heavy-chinned. One eyelid had a tic and this twitched as he said: "Mr Cross didn't reveal his source of information. I asked him but he refused to tell. Frankly, Lieutenant Prentice, I'll admit I believe him."

Allen, from the side, offered: "So do I."

Hallahan's voice was incredulous. "Do you mean, Mr Heilig, that because you hear a cock-and-bull story about why a man was murdered . . . a story without the slightest bit of proof or verification to back it up . . . you believe it? Do you realize that you are practically accusing Izzy Schwartz of having Grossman killed because he wasn't going to favour Schwartz on this paving business?"

Heilig shrugged and spread his hands. He said evenly:

"I'm telling you what Hal Cross told me. I'm frank in saying I believe him and I want protection." The tic became more pronounced. "Cross claims that I am in danger unless I *do* throw my influence in his way and I'll not do it." His face tightened. "Am I to understand you will do nothing about this?"

Hallahan said hurriedly: "I'll be very glad to detail a man or two men to go with you."

Prentice jeered: "So they'll make him an easier target, huh? This backs up what I think, don't it?"

"What you think!" Hallahan said, sarcastically.

"My reason for coming to your office, Captain," Heilig said, "wasn't alone this. I'm honestly nervous over this warning but there's another angle you seem to overlook. Sid Grossman was a damn' good man and a damn' good friend of mine. He was killed for *some* reason, and this is a good explanation. May I say that I don't understand your attitude towards this same explanation? It seems to me you should be interested in any possible lead."

Hallahan's face showed red. He snapped: "We got the man in jail that killed him. Lead, hell! We got the killer."

Allen's voice was very mild as he pointed out: "But he won't be convicted. There are no witnesses, *now*, that he *is* the killer."

Hallahan stood up, crossed to the wall and stared at a reward poster. His clenched hands were behind his back and showed the knuckles white. He didn't turn as Heilig said: "Lieutenant Prentice tells me that he believes Schwartz to be responsible for that. That he thinks Kailor was hired by Schwartz."

Hallahan turned and glared at him. He blurted out: "Lieutenant Prentice also thinks that Cross is mixed up in that. I've known that boy for ten years, helped him get his deputy job for that matter, and he's mixed, according to Lieutenant Prentice. All I hear this last few days is Cross, Kailor and Schwartz, and now more of it."

Heilig shrugged and Hallahan swung around to Prentice. "Dal! You're so damn' sure about this, *you* see that Mr Heilig is protected." He added with heavy sarcasm: "Why don't you go up and see Schwartz and tell him to tend to his paving business and quit the murder racket. Tell Cross, too, while you're at it."

"That's an idea at that."

"Mr Heilig, we'll see that you have two men with you that'll do everything but get in the bathtub with you. That is," he bowed to Prentice, "Lieutenant Prentice will see that you have. How's that? As far as Kailor being convicted for killing Grossman, I'm not the DA. I'm only in charge of the department that puts 'em in jail for the DA to convict. That isn't up to me."

Allen said to Heilig in the same mild voice: "That wasn't meant as a rib."

"I take it that Cross didn't threaten you," Hallahan said to Heilig . . . "that he warned you. Is that right?"

"That's the way I took it. He as much as told me that Schwartz was the man that hired Kailor to kill Grossman for that reason, and that I was in danger for the same reason."

"All right, Dal! This don't fit your pipe dream about Cross being in it."

"Why don't it fit? Maybe Cross is losing his guts. Maybe he figures that Mr Heilig will take it as a warning and throw the deal to Schwartz."

"Maybe!" Hallahan snorted contemptuously. "Maybe this, maybe that. I guess this and I guess that. But you don't know." He turned to Heilig. "Maybe you'll go for Schwartz then if you're so damn worried about this."

Heilig said: "I didn't ask to be appointed to the board in Grossman's place but . . ." His voice grew firm as he finished the sentence. "As long as I am, I'll do as I think best, regardless of threats." He walked to the door. "Then you'll see I'm protected, whether you believe there's a need or not. Is that right?"

"Right."

Heilig went out and Hallahan snapped out: "I'll be dingy if this keeps up."

"You and me both. C'mon, Al."

"Where you going?"

Prentice grinned: "Up and see Schwartz. That was an idea."

*   *   *

Prentice led the way down the hall and past the door that said: "Magna City Construction Company – Izadore Schwartz, President" . . . around a jog in the hall and to a door that said "Private". The door opened on an intersection with one branch corridor leading to the back and service elevators. There was no one in that corridor and it was apparently rarely used. He raised his hand to knock and the door opened under it and Schwartz, with his back partially turned to the opening door said: "Then, Gino, you go ahead and . . ." He turned from the man inside the room, said: "Why, why, hello, Lieutenant!"

Prentice shouldered past him, said: "I didn't know you had company," in an ironic tone. Allen followed him into the room, staring hard at the man called Gino, and Gino backed to the desk, sat on its edge.

Schwartz still held the door. He said: "Of course I'm always glad to see you, Lieutenant, but . . ." He coughed. "I have a secretary in the outer office to announce visitors. I might have been busy instead of all through with my talk." He made an almost imperceptible motion with his head towards the still open door, and Gino came to his feet, said: "I'll be seeing you then, Mr Schwartz."

"Come up any time. Lieutenant Prentice is an old friend of mine . . . such an old friend he doesn't bother to be announced." He slightly stressed the name.

Gino's sloe eye swivelled to Prentice. He said: "Prentice?" slowly, hesitated, again said: "Prentice?" with the same question in his voice and Prentice said: "Yeah!" He reached out, said: "I'll close the door," and Gino said: "But I'm just going!" Schwartz was still holding the door and Prentice took it and as Schwartz released his hand, closed it, asked: "Where? Not by any chance to see Heilig, were you?"

Gino said: "I don't understand!" in an angry voice, and Allen spoke from the side. "You got a permit for that gun you're packing there under your arm?" His eyes had not left Gino since he had entered the room but his face was blank.

"Yeah! I got one."

"Let's see it."

Gino produced a wallet and the permit from the wallet,

and Allen looked it over and handed it back. He said to Prentice: "It's from that heel of a police chief down at Colton. It's good any place in the county though."

Gino grinned. Prentice opened the door and Gino started towards it, but as he went out his eyes slewed back at Prentice, with a malevolent gleam.

Schwartz went back of his desk, asked: "What was it you boys wanted?" His tone was mild but his eyes were very cautious.

Prentice leaned over the desk, spoke bluntly. "To tip you to lay off Heilig."

"I don't get you."

"Why stall! Listen, Schwartz! We know why Grossman was killed. *Know*! Get that. Don't let it happen to Heilig."

"Don't be silly, Lieutenant: I'm running a reputable business and I won't stand for that kind of talk."

"No-o-o? You're running a contracting business that depends on what you can swing from the city hall." He leaned farther over the desk, his eyes dark and smoky looking, his lips curled over his teeth in a snarl. "Listen, Schwartz! You may be a big shot but you ain't big enough to murder in order to swing these same contracts. You can burn as easy as the next man. Don't forget that. Lay – off – Heilig!"

"Is that what you came up to tell me?"

"Just that!"

Schwartz laughed, mocked: "Just that! Listen, you heel! You make trouble for me and I'll have your job in twenty-four hours. Now get to hell out of my office."

Allen took hold of Prentice's arm, shook it. He said: "All right, Dal, that's enough. He's told. It's up to him." He started Prentice towards the door and Schwartz asked: "What makes you think I've got anything to do with Heilig?" but Allen laughed and ignored the question. He said: "Come on, Dal!" and opened the door, but turned there and said to Schwartz: "You'd be safer at that."

"What do you mean by that crack?"

"If you got our jobs in twenty-four hours. Be seeing you." He laughed again, as followed by Prentice, he went out.

The door slammed, cutting off Prentice's muttered: "In jail!"

The two men started down the dim back corridor that led to the service elevators. Allen wore rubbers heels, and only Prentice's footsteps made sound. They rounded a turn in the hall, passed a tiny closet reserved for the storage of janitor supplies and as they passed it Allen, who was behind, shouldered into Prentice, knocking him to one side. At the same time he caught Gino's arm, deflected the blade that was directed between Prentice's shoulders. Prentice turned, saw what was happening, and swung his gun from under his arm and against Gino's jaw with the same motion, and Gino slid to the floor between them. The knife clattered against the wall.

Allen panted out: "I saw a shadow. That's all. He was in the closet." He reached for the knife, added: "Hell! What a shiv!"

Prentice reached down and hauled Gino to his feet. He said: "I've seen this mug some place, or his picture. D'ya suppose Schwartz hired him for this?"

"Let's ask him."

They turned and started back the hall to Schwartz's office and when they reached it, grinned at each other, knocked, and when Schwartz opened the door filed through, carrying the unconscious Gino with them. Prentice said: "Look what we found in the hall, Schwartz," and threw Gino half across the room to where he fell on the desk and from there to the floor. In falling he took a dictaphone and two letter baskets down with him.

Schwartz stood by the door staring at Gino and Allen asked: "What d'ya know about him?"

"Nothing much. What's happened?"

"Not one damn' thing yet. He made a mistake and started to stick Dal with about a yard of shiv and we took it away from him. Didn't you expect it?"

"My God, no!" Schwartz's tone carried conviction.

"Who is he anyway?"

"Gino Petrone. He came up to see me about a job."

"Didja give him one?"

"No."

Prentice said slowly: "He'll have one for about five years now. Working for the state. That'll be a load off his mind."

"Surely you boys don't think that . . ."

"Hell, no, Schwartz! We don't think. We wouldn't be policemen if we did." Allen picked up Gino, who was showing signs of renewed interest in life, and hauled him to his feet. He said: "C'mon, boy friend. Let's go down and see what you think of our ailjay." He boosted him to the door, waved his hand at Schwartz and said: "Be seeing you, like I said we would." His voice was cheerful.

Schwartz said: "That's right, you *did* say that." He looked worried, cursed when he put the shattered dictaphone back on the desk.

Dal Prentice said: "But we have to see him tonight. We'll wait."

The maid had a tiny white apron over a black uniform and a white cap, that matched the apron, perched on one side of her head. She rattled the chain that held the door from further opening, explained again: "Mr Cross didn't leave any word," and Prentice, as patiently, said again: "Then we'll wait for him." She looked undecided and he showed her his badge and identification card, told her: "It's business from Mr Cross's office that's supposed to be a secret. Get it?"

"But Mr Cross didn't say . . ."

"He didn't know we were coming tonight or he'd have waited."

"It's my night off and I was going to a show."

"We won't stop you. We have to see Mr Cross tonight. It's important."

"Well, I guess it's all right."

"Sure it is, sister."

She opened the door, said: "I guess you could wait in the library," and Allen said: "That'd be fine." As they went in he poked a finger at the white cap, and she giggled and blushed.

Prentice asked: "Any idea where Mr Cross went?"

"He didn't say." She hesitated a second, offered: "But

you might get him at Mr Schwartz's house. I answered the phone just before Mr Cross went out, and Mr Schwartz was on the line. Shall I call and see?"

Allen said: "Oh, don't bother!" in a hasty voice. He was glancing at the flat desk and the pile of letters on it and the girl saw his glance and misunderstood. She blushed again. "It looks terrible but Mr Cross won't have me tidy it. He says that important papers might be misplaced or lost."

Prentice was looking at a decanter and tray of glasses on a stand made by a very small but very modern safe. He grinned at the flustered maid, said: "D'ya think a drink would be misplaced?" and Allen said: "Shut up, you chiseller."

The girl laughed, went to the door, asked: "Do you really think Mr Cross wouldn't be mad if I *did* go? I've had the date for a week."

Allen said: "I'm sure it will be all right. We'll take care of things." He was still looking at the papers.

The girl coughed and blushed again, asked: "Do you know a policeman named Kerrigan?"

"Don't believe so."

"I go with him steady."

"Lucky man!"

She went out and as she did, Prentice grunted: "Yeah! If he's deaf!" and lifted the decanter. Allen said nothing in return, sorted papers on the desk.

When they heard the front door slam a half hour later Allen had a bulge in his inner coat pocket and Prentice had a perceptible flush on his face. The level in the decanter was four inches lower than on their arrival and both men held glasses. Cross stopped in the doorway, blurted out: "What . . . how . . ."

"The maid let us in, Hal. She had a date."

"Sorry I was out, Prentice. Been waiting long?" He flashed a look at the desk, said sharply: "The maid should have taken you in the other room."

Allen chose to misunderstand and looked at the decanter. He said: "We figured you'd have bought a drink if you'd been here so we went ahead. Sorry if we overstepped." His grin did not show sorrow.

Cross reddened, said: "I didn't mean it that way, Lieutenant. You are very welcome. Lieutenant Prentice and I are old friends." He sat down back of the desk, worried eyes searching the litter, asked: "What is the trouble, or is it just a friendly call? I hate like the devil to talk business after I leave the office, Dal; you know that."

Prentice stared over the rim of his glass at him. "We could have seen you at the office as well as not. Or can see you, rather. It's up to you."

"I don't understand."

"What's the tie-up between you and Schwartz?"

Cross half rose from his chair, dropped back. His face turned white and his eyes bulged. He repeated: "Tie-up!" in little more than a gasp, pulled at his collar with his left hand while his right stirred the scattered papers on the desk.

Allen said: "They're here!" and tapped his breast pocket. "We thought you'd rather talk it over with us here than down to the office. You being a good friend of Hallahan and Dal both."

Cross choked and dropped his right hand below the desk top, while his left still pulled at his collar. Prentice took his eyes from his tortured face and stared back at the whiskey glass. He said: "It might make things clearer, Hal, if we tell you what we know. Would it?" in a mild voice.

Cross made a strangled noise and nodded.

"You're to get a cut from Schwartz if his paving deal goes through. So you go in on the Grossman deal. We put the finger on Kailor for that, and you go down and try to buy the witness that we dug up that saw the shooting. When she wouldn't pop you had her killed."

Cross made a motion with his left hand, still kept his right below the desk. He cried out: "Dal! No! You're wrong on that." His eyes were bulging and his voice was unrecognizable.

"Am I? You were in the Grossman deal."

"Yes, but not that way. I thought he was to be bribed. I was to talk to him on Thursday, and he was killed Wednesday night. That's the truth. I didn't know a thing about it."

"You were in it, just the same. Why were you fretting about Kailor taking the rap if you wasn't mixed in it?"

Cross hung his head, stared down at what his right hand held. He blurted: "I . . . I . . . couldn't help . . . I was . . ."

Prentice was leaning forward in his chair, whiskey glass poised in his hand, and Allen was listening with a half grin. Cross looked up, moving only his eyes, stammered: "I . . . I couldn't help it." He straightened his shoulders and tried to lift his head but the effort seemed too great and he motioned with his left hand towards the safe and said: "It's all in there. Signed and all. I was afraid . . ."

Prentice's eyes had followed the motion and when his glance came back to Cross he saw him bring his right hand up from under the desk. As he jammed the gun it held against his temple, Prentice threw the whiskey, glass and all, full into Cross's face and in the same motion was leaning across the desk and had Cross's wrist bent down and the gun pointing at the floor. He was in a position where he could not get leverage enough to free the gun from Cross and he cried out: "Al! Get it."

Allen had not moved from his chair. He said: "What for? I took the shells out of it when I went through the desk. I knew damn' well he'd try to do the Dutch when he got caught up with." He laughed, and at the sound Cross wilted and put his head down in his arms on the desk. Prentice sat on the edge of the desk, balancing the gun, and Allen asked: "Blackmailed into it, weren't you?"

The head nodded.

"Why didn't you tell us? That'd been better than getting mixed in a murder."

Cross looked up in horror, tear stains streaking his cheeks. "I wasn't in that. I went down there to warn her. I got thinking about Grossman being killed and thought she was in danger."

"She was in danger all right."

"I told her she'd better leave town and not tell anyone where she was going. I was afraid of Schwartz, but I didn't want any more people killed."

"Why were you afraid?"

Cross made a motion towards the safe, said dully: "It's all in there. I was in a jam for money and I took some from him. It was when those inspectors on the new Armoury job he contracted were under fire. I didn't make a case against them, and he could have ruined me at any time after that. I've just been getting in deeper all the time." He dropped his head, stared at his hands. "The only thing left is . . ." He shrugged and looked at the empty gun on the desk.

Prentice was staring at Cross, a question in his eyes. He jerked his head at Allen, said: "Al! See what you think of this," led the way to a corner of the room and talked, nodding his head at Cross from time to time. They came back to the desk and Prentice asked: "If we show you a way out of this, will you play ball with us?"

Cross spoke in the same dull voice. "There's no way out. Schwartz will have me killed when he knows I've talked. And the whole dirty business will come out."

"There is a way. A chance at least."

"I'll do anything you want." Cross's face did not lighten.

"It's compounding a felony."

Cross smiled with no mirth, shrugged.

"It'll take Schwartz and everyone else that knows a thing about your deals with him out of the way. It's dangerous, though. Plenty!"

Cross looked at the empty gun on the desk, shrugged again.

Cross opened the door to Schwartz, said: "How are you, Izzy?" and to the dim shape behind him: "And you, Kailor?" He told Schwartz: "Gino's here and I've let the maid go and my wife's out of town. I thought this would be a better place to meet than at your office."

Schwartz shrugged out of a topcoat, grunted: "It'd make no difference. What can't be proved, won't hang anybody," and Kailor, behind him, laughed and added: "Stiffs can't get up and testify."

Cross led the way to the library and as he stood at the door to let Kailor past him before closing it, Schwartz strolled to the desk and stood looking at the papers still littering its surface. He said without looking up: "That was good work getting Gino out," and nodded at the little Italian seated across from him. "If you hadn't pointed out to the judge that he was a stranger in town and had no motive for attacking those two coppers, I doubt if the judge would have gone for only five grand for bail."

Kailor walked behind Gino and sat down, still behind him and facing Schwartz, who was standing back of the desk. He grunted: "That jail is nobody's bargain, either. Before the writ and bond caught up with me, these same two coppers worked me over plenty, but didn't learn anything." He spat on the heavy rug, and staring at the back of Gino's head, said, "If I was a damn' wop I'd have spilled my guts."

Gino swung around, snapped: "What's that!" and Schwartz said: "Now, now boys!" He spoke to Cross. "Kailor got in a jam once and an Italian boy spoke his piece. I've told him that Gino ain't that way . . . that Gino's right."

Kailor grunted scornfully and Gino turned his eyes away from him and back to Schwartz, who was reading a letter he had picked up from the desk. Gino said: "Cross has been telling me that this Prentice came to see him when I was in jail." His voice had a slight accent but was soft and low.

Schwartz looked up from the letter, sat down at the desk, said: "He told me, too. What of it? They didn't learn anything."

"Cross did." Gino's eyes were black and glowing, and Schwartz looked puzzled. "Cross learned plenty."

"What do you mean by that?" Schwartz swung towards Cross but Gino rapped out: "I'm still talking!" and Schwartz turned back to him. "Cross said this copper told him he had a tip about my brother and Williams going to do the Denzer job. And that he was there waiting and that the only reason he didn't catch 'em in the house was because the job took no time. Did Cross tell you that?"

"Why, no," Schwartz said slowly. "I figured they were tipped to Denzer's hideout but that was all. He turned to Cross, asked: "Did they tell you that, Hal?" in a puzzled voice.

Cross said: "Yes, they did."

"Why didn't you tell me this?"

Cross shrugged: "I thought you knew it," turned his head away from Schwartz.

"Thought *I* knew it!" Schwartz shook his head and put the letter down on the desk. "What *is* all this?"

Gino slipped his right hand up his left sleeve, said in his soft, low voice: "Why shouldn't he think you knew it? The copper said your office called him and told him." His right hand slid out from the sleeve and an inch of steel followed it. "You told me and Mario it was a cinch. Told us that Denzer expected us to come there and pay off for you. I couldn't go, so Williams went with Mario instead. They run into a stake-out."

Schwartz burst out: "You're crazy!" His eyes were on the knife blade showing in the Italian's sleeve.

"Like a fox, I'm crazy! You had the girl killed because she knew too much. And Denzer. Why not my brother and me? If we were killed by the cops, *we* couldn't talk."

Cross, at the right, was leaning against the library door and was twenty feet from the group at the desk. Kailor was some five feet behind and directly in back of Gino, who faced Schwartz across the desk. Wide French windows, closed and draped, were at the left of the room. Schwartz looked over Gino's head, narrowed his eyes at Kailor, who nodded slightly in return.

Gino bent a little in his chair, whispered, "Well . . . ain't it so?"

His hand moved out of his sleeve a little more, and Kailor took a blackjack from his pocket and balanced it in his hand. He stood up and Gino heard the movement and turned his head. Schwartz squirmed in his seat, dragged a gun from his hip pocket, and Gino caught the motion and turned back. He said: "You would!" and flashed the knife all the way clear from his sleeve, and with this, Schwartz shot from below the desk.

Kailor had the sap halfway up to strike, but with the shot fell forwards on Gino. Gino twisted free, flinging him to the floor, and as Schwartz fired again, leaned across the desk. Schwartz cried out and made an attempt to lift his gun above the desk, but Gino was halfway across it with his right hand out, and the gun barrel hit the edge of the desk and clattered to the floor.

Gino lunged with the knife once more, turned his head towards the windows as they crashed open. Prentice, already half through the windows, flinched as Allen fired past his ear. Gino fell across the desk with his right hand still holding the knife in Schwartz's throat. Schwartz, with his hands around Gino's and the knife, wavered and slowly fell towards him and across him.

Prentice stepped gingerly towards the desk, gun in hand, watching Kailor, who had not moved since Gino had thrown him to the floor. He turned him over, said: "Deader than hell!" and to Cross, leaning whitefaced against the door: "Looks like a clean sweep. How did he get it . . . from what we heard it was between Gino and Schwartz."

"He fell when Schwartz shot the first time. Schwartz missed Gino and got him."

Allen was straightening the tangle on the desk. He said: "Gino ain't dead. Not yet. He won't last until the surgeon gets here, though." He bent over the Italian, asked: "Can you talk? Listen, you! Can you talk?" and straightened with a shrug when he got no answer except in muttered Italian.

Cross said: "Oh, my God!" in a sick voice. He retched and Prentice went to him and patted him on the back and told him: "You're okay now. You'll be a hero from now on. 'Deputy District Attorney traps band of yeggs.'" He turned to Allen, who was trying to telephone. "And you, you lug, that's twice you've blown my ear damn near off me. Is it a game?"

Captain Hallahan looked up when the two men came into the Homicide office, his red face shining, his white hair in an angry ruff. He bellowed: "That wop that tried to knife you is out on bail and so is Kailor and I've tried to get you since four o'clock to stop it. Cross stood there and let their lawyer plead 'em out on bail. Bail on a murder rap. That's what we've come to!" He snorted violently. "Don't stand there with silly grins on your faces. Where was you? In some speak drunk?" I'm going to the DA and build a fire under him that'll burn Cross out of his lousy job inside of twenty-four hours. You was right on him at least; he's a heel."

Prentice said: "Easy, Cap! You got high blood pressure!" in a calm voice and this calm infuriated Hallahan the more.

He exploded: "You may think it's a joke to have a hood like that out running around knifing people in the back, but by God I don't. Where was you? Hey! Don't you know you're supposed to phone in if you can't come in? Huh!" He added in a milder tone: "Lord! I been worried sick about you."

Prentice sat on the edge of the desk and swung his leg back and forth. He said: "We couldn't help it. We was busy and couldn't phone."

"Busy! You should've been out and picking them two up again. You could hold 'em on an open charge."

"Sure we could but why fret about them? They're dead."

Hallahan ruffled his hair, opened his mouth.

"They're dead and so is Schwartz."

Allen said: "They all killed each other. It was more fun!" and Prentice grinned: "Couldn't you buy a boy a drink?"

Hallahan reached blindly for the drawer in his desk. He said: "Is this a rib?" and jerked his hand away from the drawer, roared: "By God if you think you can come in here and . . ."

"It's no rib, Cap!" Prentice's voice was soothing. "They're all dead an we're damn near it from needing a drink. Come on and pop. We even took care of Hal for you."

Allen looked pointedly at the drawer.

"All right, all right. You chisellers!" Hallahan jerked the drawer open and Prentice sighed happily as he poured his glass over full. He waved it at Hallahan, a little of the whiskey splashed, and Hallahan cursed and moved a report blank out of danger. He said: "All right, I know you're two smarties. Tell it! What you been trying to do?"

Allen corrected: "Not trying. Doing. It worked."

Hallahan grimaced and spat towards a battered cuspidor. He snapped: "If it worked, it worked late. First the chairman of the Board of Supervisors killed. Then there's a girl shot, then a man knifed, then two more killed resisting arrest. One of them a detective assigned to working for the DA. Then three more killed, all at the same time, you say. Something worked." He snorted.

Allen said soberly: "Grossman was killed by Kailor. That wasn't our fault. Then the girl that could have proved this was killed by her old man. We couldn't help that either."

"I s'pose not. Dal had the notion that Cross was mixed in that." He snorted again.

Prentice tipped his head and drank and put the glass on the desk. He argued: "He was. The story I told you was all true . . . about the frame being this guy killed his wife because he caught her hustling. And Cross was supposed to see that the guy beat the case when it came up. The only thing was that Cross didn't know this and that the plan was changed. Cross wasn't in the change, either."

"Go on." Hallahan rapped nervous fingers on the desk.

"Schwartz hired two hoods to wipe out Denzer because he figured that'd be safer than having him stand trial. Gino and Mario Petrone. Gino struck a snag, got held in Centreville three days on a speeding charge, and Mario had to have somebody else go with him on the job. Schwartz got Williams, who was working for him just the same as Cross was to go. That's all there was to it. We got there right after they done their stuff and cornered 'em. Williams knew he couldn't beat it if he was caught but figured he might break free if he fought it out. He didn't but I'll always say he tried."

Allen took up the story while Prentice filled glasses. "Cross wasn't in this because Schwartz figured he'd lost his nerve. He was right because Cross went down and warned the gal but he was too late. We went up and tried to scare Schwartz into laying off Heilig and run into this Gino. The crazy hood knew it was us that killed his brother and tried to knife Dal. I don't think Schwartz had a thing to do with that."

Hallahan said: "Maybe not. You could've stuck Gino on that."

"Sure we could. And have him get not more than five years. We got hold of Cross and scared hell out of him. He was ready to crack and I think he had the notion that Kailor had spilled his guts to us when we give Kailor the works. We worked a frame with him, let him get Gino and Kailor out, and got him to set Gino against Schwartz. Gino was nuts about his brother getting the business and believed everything he was told. That's all there was to it. When the beef started, Schwartz tried to kill Gino and popped Kailor by mistake. That saved us the bother."

"And Gino killed Schwartz?"

"He surely did." Allen looked reflective. "And the funny thing is, it was with a knife and he stuck him in the same place his brother stuck Denzer." He tapped the hollow in his throat. "He even turned the knife the same way. I shot Gino through the chest but Schwartz had already hit him in the belly and he'd have died from that."

"What about Cross?"

"He's okay! He got blackmailed into working for Schwartz in the first place and he's such a weak sister he couldn't get guts enough to break loose. We're covering him on the whole thing. That's Dal's idea."

Hallahan argued: "But if he was in it?"

Prentice complained: "Oh, what the hell! It was just drag in a lot of dirt and he's smarted up now. What would we make by it?" He leaned forwards. "Look, Cap! If he hadn't worked with us we couldn't have proved a thing on either Schwartz or Kailor and Gino'd only got maybe five years. He helps us and they kill each other off. Ain't that better?"

Hallahan looked doubtful and Prentice persisted: "He got roped in on the whole damn' thing. Give the guy a break. He's been a friend of yours. And besides, the way politics are in this rotten town it's a damn good thing to know there's one deputy prosecutor that's honest."

Hallahan grinned slightly, said: "Even if he went crooked to get that way. Maybe you're right. I always liked Hal."

Prentice laughed suddenly, set his glass down. "I feel sorry for the poor guy. He's got the messiest rug I ever saw in my life." He grinned at Allen, added: "The hell he'll catch when his old lady gets home."

Eye of the Beholder

Ed Gorman

I

All this started one spring when I couldn't find any women. The weather was so beautiful it just made me crazier. I'd lie on my bed in my little apartment, feeling the moonbreezes and would ache, absolutely effing ache, to be with a woman I cared about. I was in one of those periods when I needed to fall ridiculously in love. It wasn't just that sex would be better – everything would be better. Fifty times a day I'd spot women who seemed likely candidates – they'd be in supermarkets or video stores or walking along the river or getting into their cars. The first thing I did was inspect them quickly for wedding rings. A good number of them were unburdened. But still, meeting them was impossible. If you just walked up to them and introduced yourself, you'd probably look like a rapist. And if you told them how lonely you were, you might not look like a rapist but you'd sure seem pathetic. I tried all the usual places, the bars and the dance clubs and some of the splashier parties, but I didn't see it in their eyes. They were looking for quick sex or companionship while they tended broken hearts, or simply a warm body at their dinner tables when too many lonely Saturday nights became intolerable. But they weren't looking for the same thing I was, some kind of spiritual redemption. Not that I didn't settle some nights for quick sex and companionship, but next morning, I felt just as lonely and disconsolate. I couldn't settle very often. I wanted my ideal woman, this notion I've had in my mind since I was seven or eight years old, this ethereal madonna I had longed for down the decades.

So of course the night I met Linda I wasn't even looking for anybody. I just walked into this little coffee shop over by the public library and there she was, sitting alone at the counter drinking coffee.

I wasn't sure she could rescue me, and I doubt she was sure I could rescue her, but at least the potential was there, so two nights later we started going to bed. Even though we were sort of awkward with each other, we kept trying till we got it right, and then we became pretty good lovers. The only thing that got me down was she was still pretty hung up on this football coach who'd dumped her recently. She kept telling me how it had only been for sex, and how he was an animal six, seven hours a night, which did not exactly fill me with self-confidence. I wasn't jealous of the guy but I didn't necessarily want to attend his testimonial dinner every night, either.

The only other thing that bothered me was her two teenaged daughters. They were usually around the house while Linda and I were making love. Linda always laughed when I got uptight. "Hey, what do you think they do in their bedrooms when they bring their boyfriends over here?"

Linda was one of those modern parents. I'm not. My two kids, daughter and son, were raised pretty much the way I was: what your parents don't know won't hurt them. One boozy New Year's Eve I actually heard this teenage girl talking to her mother about how her tenth-grade boyfriend wasn't any good at oral sex. Linda wasn't that far gone but she was a lot more liberal with her daughters than I would've been. Even when my wife and I split up, we agreed that our kids would be raised properly, at least as we defined "properly".

I kept wanting Linda to go to my place to make love, but one night she laughed and said, "But your place is such a pit, Dwyer. I'm afraid I'd have cockroaches walking up my thigh."

Linda was three years divorced from a very prosperous insurance executive. She'd gotten the big house and the big car and the big monthly cheque. She only had to work part-time at a travel agency to make her monthly nut.

So we made love at her place, and even though we both figured out pretty quickly that we weren't going to rescue each other, the thing we had was better than nothing. So we kept it up, even though I had the sense that she was vaguely ashamed of herself for liking me. Her previous boyfriends had run to MDs and shrinks and business executives. Security guard was a long way down the ladder.

Then one night I went over and she was late getting home from work. And that was the night it happened, with her sixteen-year-old daughter Susan, I mean.

Started out with an argument in the kitchen between Susan and Molly.

I was sitting in the living room watching a boxing rerun on ESPN. Linda had just called and said she was running late.

First I hear screaming. Then I hear cursing. Then I hear a cup or a glass being smashed against the wall. Then screaming again.

I run out there and find sixteen-year-old Susan slapping fifteen-year-old Molly across the face.

You have to understand, they were both extremely good-looking girls. But Molly was even more than extremely good-looking. She was probably the single most beautiful person I had ever seen, a madonna with just a hint of the erotic in her dark and brooding eyes. Her sister Susan had always been jealous of her, and now there was special trouble because Susan's boyfriend had developed this almost creepy fixation on Molly.

I got between them.

"Get the hell out of this kitchen," Susan said. "You don't even belong here."

"You shouldn't talk to him like that," Molly said.

"Why? Because our sweet mommy is fucking him?"

Molly shook her head, looked embarrassed, and left the kitchen. In moments, I heard her on the stairs, going up to the second floor.

Susan pushed past me and opened the refrigerator door.

She took out a can of Bud, popped the tab and gunned some down.

"I'm sure you'll tell my mother I was drinking this." Before I could say anything, she said, "By the way, she's sleeping with this new guy Brad at the travel agency. That's why she's late. She's going to tell you all about it. But she doesn't want to hurt your feelings." She smiled at me. "On the other hand, I don't mind hurting your feelings at all."

"So your boyfriend dumped you, huh?" Hell, I was just as petty as she was.

For the first time, I felt sorry for her. The anger and arrogance were suddenly gone from her face. She just looked sad and lost and painfully young. She even lost some of her sexiness in that moment, tiny sad pink barrette turning her into a little girl again. She was all vulnerability now.

She went over to the breakfast nook and sat down in the booth.

"You want a beer, Dwyer?"

"You gonna tell your mom I took one?"

She laughed. "I actually like you."

"Yeah, I could tell."

"I'm sorry I told you about Mom's new boyfriend."

Women know all the secrets in the world. All the important ones, anyway. Men just know all that bullshit that doesn't matter in the long run.

"It was bound to happen," I said.

"You're not gonna be heartbroken?"

"For maybe a week. Or two. Probably more my pride than anything."

"He's sort of an asshole. I mean, I met him a couple of times. Real stuck on himself. But he's real cute."

"I'm happy for him. Maybe I'll take you up on that beer."

I felt betrayed, stunned, pissed, sad and slightly embarrassed. I was more of an interloper than ever in this house. Very soon now, I'd be back to roaming my apartment and talking to imaginary women again.

I got a beer and sat down.

"You ever been in love?" she said.

"Sure."

"Really in love?"

"Uh-huh."

"It's terrible, isn't it?"

"Sometimes."

"This is the third one."

"Third one?"

"Yeah, the third boyfriend I've had who's fallen in love with Molly. The first one was in sixth grade. His name was Rick. I loved him so much, I'd get the Neiman-Marcus catalogue down and look at wedding gowns. Then one day I found a note he'd written her. It took me a year to get over it." She shrugged. "Or maybe I've never gotten over it."

"So it happened again."

"Yeah. Paul – you met him – he broke up with me six weeks ago and he's been calling her ever since. She doesn't encourage him – I mean, it's not her fault – but he follows her around all the time. Takes pictures of her, too. He's the photographer for the high-school paper. Real good with a telephoto lens." She stared out the window. "He was like part of the family. Mom liked him even. And she doesn't like many boys." She looked over at the sheepdog, Clarence, who was treated like the third child. Now he sprawled on the kitchen floor, watching her. "Clarence wouldn't bark at him or try to eat him or anything."

Reference to Clarence made her smile.

"If it isn't Molly's fault, why'd you hit her?"

She shrugged. "Because I hate her. At least a part of me does. If she wasn't so beautiful –" She looked at me. "She's even got one of her teachers in love with her."

"Really?"

"Yeah. One day I was afraid my boyfriend was writing her letters, and so I snuck into her room and started looking around and there was this letter from Mr Meacham, her English teacher. He said he loved her and was willing to leave his wife and daughter for her."

"Molly ever encourage him?"

She shook her head. "Molly is the most virginal person I know. Sometimes I think she's retarded. I really do. She's still a little girl in a lot of ways. She gets these crushes on her teachers. This year it's Mr Meacham. He's teaching her the Romantic poets and Molly keeps telling me how much she thinks he looks like Matt Dillon, who's her favourite movie star. To her, it's all very innocent. But not to Mr Meacham." She hesitated. "I even think she's started seeing him at nights. Last week I was out at Warner Mall and saw them sitting together in the Orange Julius."

"Does your mother know about this?"

"I haven't told her. She's got problems of her own with Molly. Well, with Brad."

"The guy at the travel agency?"

"Uh-huh. He's been over here a few times and it's pretty obvious he's fallen in love with Molly."

"You said he was young. How young?"

"Twenty-one."

"Well, that's better than Mr Meacham lately."

"He may be the one stalking her."

"Someone's stalking her?"

"Yeah. Grabbed her the other night in the breezeway. But she got away. And been sending her threatening notes." She sighed. "I want to be pissed off at her but I can't. She doesn't understand the effect she has on men. She really doesn't." Then: "I feel like shit. God, I can't believe I slapped her. I'd better go talk to her."

"Good idea. Tell your mom something came up and I had to go."

"Sorry I broke the news to you that way. I mean, about Brad."

"It's all right."

"Like Mom says, I can be a bitch on wheels when I want to be."

We stood up and she gave me a hard little hug and then I went away. For good.

II

So it was back to the streets for me the rest of the summer. I kept thinking about Molly and how beautiful she was and how otherwise sensible men, young and old alike, seemed to take leave of their senses when they were around her. While

I wasn't looking for virginal fifteen-year-olds, I was looking for the same kind of explosive love affair those men were, one that blinds you to all else, the narcotic that no amount of drugs could ever equal. In a few years, I'd be fifty. There weren't many such love affairs left for me. I'd had three or four of them in my lifetime, and I wanted one more before the darkness. So I went back to the bars, I became infatuated ten times a day in grocery stores and discount houses and even gas stations when I'd see the backside of a fetching lady bent slightly to put gas in her tank. But mostly my reality was my solitary bed and moonshadow, white curtains whipping ghostly in the rain-smelling wind, my lips silent with a thousand vows of undying love. A drinking buddy tried to make me believe that this was simply an advanced case of horniness but I said if it was, it was *spiritual* horniness and when I said "spiritual" he gave me a queer look, as if I'd told him that I'd started sending a lot of money to TV preachers or something.

The summer ground on. One of the investigators at Allied Security had to have a heart by-pass so they shifted me from security (which I like) to working divorce cases (which I hated). While I've committed my share of adultery, I can't say that it's ever pleasant to think about. Betrayal is not exactly a tribute to the human spirit. The men seemed to take a strange kind of pride in what they were doing. They didn't seem particularly concerned about being secretive, anyway. But the cheating women were all a little furtive and frantic and even sad, as if they were doing this against their will. Maybe they were paying back cheating husbands. Four weeks of this stuff before the investigator came back to Allied. My advertising daughter came to town just as August was starting to punish us. My son drove in from med-school in the east. Their mother had married again, third time a charm or so she said, a man with some means, apparently, whom they liked much better than husband number two, a bank vice-president with great country club aspirations.

"You've got to find yourself a woman," my daughter said right before she kissed me goodbye at the airport.

One night in late September, beautiful Indian Summer, I

came home and found Linda sitting in my living room.

"Your landlady let me in," she said. Then: "This is really a depressing place, Dwyer. You think we could go somewhere else?"

She didn't like any of the bars I recommended. Too downscale, presumably. We ended up in a place where businessmen yelled and whooped it up a lot about the Hawkeyes. The way they shouted and strutted around, you'd think they owned copper mines down in Brazil, where they could make people work for twenty-five cents an hour.

"Did you hear what happened to Molly? It was in the news about three weeks ago."

"I guess not."

"Somebody cut her up."

"Cut her up?"

"Slashed her cheeks. Do you remember a New York model that happened to a few years ago?"

"Yeah. She wasn't ever able to work again."

Linda's eyes glistened with tears. "The plastic surgeon said there's only so much he can do for Molly. She looks terrible."

"What're the police saying?"

She shook her head, sleek and sexy in a white linen suit, her dark hair recently cut short. "No leads."

"Molly didn't see her assailant?"

"It was dark. She'd parked her car in the garage and was just walking into the house – through the breezeway, you know – and he was waiting there. I guess this happened before – somebody in the breezeway I mean – but neither Molly nor Susan told me about it. Why should they tell me anything? I'm just their mother."

"She's sure it was a 'he'?"

"That's the assumption everybody's making. That it was a guy, I mean."

"She doesn't have any sense of who it might have been?"

Linda sighed. "Maybe."

"Maybe?"

She nodded. "I think she knows who it was but won't say."

"Why would she protect somebody?"

"I'm not sure." Pause. "I've been having terrible thoughts lately."

"Oh?"

"I've been thinking that Susan may have done this."

"Your daughter?"

"Yes." Pause. "She's very, very jealous of Molly. Molly – well, a few of Susan's boyfriends have fallen in love with Molly over the last year or so. About a month ago, Susan made up with this boy, Paul, the one who'd fallen in love with Molly. But then she came home one night and found Paul drunk in the living room putting the moves on Molly."

"You really think it's possible that Susan could do something like this?"

"She's been upstaged by Molly all her life. Even as a baby, Molly sort of unhinged people. I mean, she's the most beautiful girl I've ever seen. And I think I'm being objective about that."

"Anybody else who might have done it?"

"The police are talking to one of Molly's teachers, this Mr Meacham. That's another thing my girls didn't tell me until after this happened. It seems this Mr Meacham offered to leave his wife and daughter for Molly. He's forty-three years old. My God."

"Anybody else you can think of?"

After another drink was set down in front of her, she said, "I have to tell you something. It's so ridiculous, it pisses me off to even repeat it."

I just waited for her to say it.

"Last night, my dear sweet daughter Susan accused me of slashing Molly's face."

Calmly as I could, I said, "Why would she say something like that?"

"I'm kind of embarrassed telling you the rest."

"Maybe it'll make you feel better."

"I trashed Molly's room."

"When?"

"Late August, I guess."

"Why?"

"Brad."

"The guy from the travel agency?"

"Uh-huh. He'd started phoning her – Molly, I mean – when I wasn't there. Then one night he came right out and asked me. I mean, I suspected something was wrong. He hadn't touched me in two weeks. Then this one night he said, 'Would it really piss you off if I asked Molly out?' I didn't want to let him know how pissed I was, so I just said that I didn't think that was such a great idea. But I said it in this real calm voice. I told him that technically she wouldn't reach the age of consent until October, and he said he'd wait. Then after he left – I sat in the den and got really drunk and then I went upstairs and started screaming at Molly. Then I started trashing her room."

She started crying. "My own daughter, and I treated her that way."

I changed the subject quickly. "You mentioned Susan's ex-boyfriend."

"Paul."

"Tell me about him."

"Right. He calls Molly four times a day. He says he doesn't care about her face being cut up. He loves her. His parents have called me, they're so worried about him. He went from As to Ds last semester. They want him to see a shrink. When Molly won't come to the phone, he gets furious."

"And you think Molly might know who did it?"

"I think so. Would you talk to her?"

"It'd probably be easier if you went through the agency. Ask them to assign me to you. I don't really have much time for any freelance on the side."

"Fine. I'll call them tomorrow. I really appreciate this, Jack." Then: "Oh, God."

"What?"

"It's almost ten. I'm supposed to meet somebody at ten-fifteen way across town." She shrugged. "Met somebody new at the agency. He's a little older than Brad."

"Sixteen?"

She smiled. "Wise ass." Then: "I really am sorry. You know, about Brad and everything."

"I survived."

"I'd always be willing to see you again."

"I never take handouts except at Christmas time."

What the hell, it never hurts to sound dignified once in a while.

III

The next day, I told her about the breezeway incident. She led me up to the den on the second floor. "She sits in the dark. The blinds are drawn and everything, I mean. You'll get used to the shadows. She doesn't want anybody to see her. But I convinced her you only wanted to help her." Then she went away.

I knocked and a small voice said to come in and I went in and there she sat in a leather recliner by a TV set that was playing a soap opera. Just as I started to sit down in the chair facing her, a commercial came on, the bright colours flashing across the screen illuminating her face.

He'd done a damned good job. If it was a he. Long deep vertical gashes on both checks. The stitches were still on, and that just made her look worse. But even with the stitches gone, her beauty would be forever and profoundly marred.

"Remember me?"

She looked at me with solemn eyes and nodded.

"You think we could turn the TV down a bit?"

She picked up the remote and brought the volume down to a low number.

"Your mom wants me to make sure that you told the police everything, Molly. You understand that?"

Again she nodded. I had the unnerving sense that she'd also been struck mute.

"She told me what Susan said. About hearing somebody run away right after it happened. Is that true?"

Again, she nodded.

"I checked out your breezeway last night, Molly. That's where it happened, right?"

She said: "I wish I didn't have to go through this, Jack."

"I wish you didn't have to either, sweetheart."

"I mean your questions."

"Oh."

"My mom talked to the principal this morning. I'm going to finish my classes at home this year. So I don't have to see – anybody. You know, at school."

"You're going to sit in this room, huh?"

"Pretty much."

"With the blinds drawn."

"I like it when it's dark. When nobody can see me this way."

"Can I tell you about the breezeway, Molly?"

"The breezeway?"

"Uh-huh. I came out here last night and checked it out when everybody was asleep. You've got an alarm system that kicks on the yard lights whenever anybody approaches the house."

"I guess so."

"That means that when the person who did this to you ran off, you had a very good chance to see his face."

"Oh."

I waited for her to say more, and when she didn't, I watched her for a moment – she wore an aqua blouse and jeans and white socks – and then I said, "I think you know who did this to you. And I think that you're trying to protect him."

"You keep saying 'him,' Jack. Maybe it was a woman."

"Is that what you're telling me? That it was a woman?"

"No, but –"

"It'll come out eventually, Molly. One way or the other, the police are going to figure out who did this to you."

"I just want it to be over with. I've accepted it and I just want it to be over with."

"It was either Paul or Mr Meacham, wasn't it?"

"I don't want to talk any more, Jack."

"Your mother loves you, Molly."

"I know."

"And she's very worried about you."

"I know that, too."

"She doesn't like the idea that whoever did this is still out there running around free."

"It's over with, Jack. It happened. And I don't have any

choice but to accept it. People accept things all the time. There was a girl in my class two years ago who lost her legs in a tractor accident. She was staying on her uncle's farm. She'll never be able to walk again. People accept things all the time."

"He should have to pay for doing this, Molly. I don't know what's going through your head, but nothing justifies somebody doing this to you. Nothing."

I stood up.

"Susan is worried about you, too."

She nodded. "I'd like to watch this show now, if you don't mind." But smiled for the first time. Her scars were hideous in the flickering lights of the TV picture tube. "I appreciate you caring about me, Jack. You're a nice guy. You really are."

When I got downstairs, I found Susan and Clarence waiting for me. The big sheepdog lay next to the desk where Susan was working on her homework.

As always, the overtrained dog barked as I approached. I was going to get him some Thorazine for Christmas.

"Mom said to say goodbye. She had to run back to work." Then: "How'd it go with Molly?"

I told her about coming out here last night and testing the yard lights. "She had to've gotten a good look at the person who did this."

"You're sure?"

"Positive. Tell me one more time. You were sitting in here watching TV –"

"– and I heard her scream and then I ran out to the breezeway and I saw somebody at the edge of the yard running away. He went up over the white fence out there."

"You said 'he'. Male?"

"I think so."

"And Molly was –"

"Molly was in a heap on the breezeway floor. When I flipped on the light, all I could see was the blood. She was in pretty bad shape. Then Clarence came running out and he was barking like crazy." Then: "I think she knows. Who did it, I mean."

"So do I."

"But why would she protect him?"

"That's what I need to figure out. I'm going over to see our friend Paul."

"I'm trying to keep an open mind. The way he dumped me for Molly, I mean, I really hate him. But that doesn't mean he'd do something like this."

"No, I guess it doesn't," I said. I leaned over and gave her a kiss on the forehead. "Anybody ever tell you what a nice young woman you are?"

"Yeah," she said. "Paul used to tell me that all the time. Before he fell in love with Molly."

IV

Paul lived in a large Colonial house on a wide suburban street filled with little kids doing stunts on skateboards.

As soon as his mother learned who I was, her polite smile vanished. "You don't have any right to ask him any questions."

I was still outside the front door. "The family has asked me to talk to him."

"He didn't do it," she said. "I'll admit that he's been pretty – involved with Molly lately. But he'd never hurt her. Ever. And that's just what we told the police."

She was a tall, slender woman in black slacks and a red button-down shirt. There was a kind of casual elegance to her movements, as if she might have long ago studied dance.

Behind her, a voice said: "It's all right, Mom. I'll talk to him."

Paul was taller than his mother but slender in the same graceful way. There was a snub-nosed boyishness to the face that the dark eyes belied. There was age and anger in the eyes, as if he'd lived through a bitter experience lately and was not the better for it.

"You sure?" she said to Paul.

"Finish fixing dinner, Mom. I'll talk to him."

He wore a Notre Dame football Jersey and ragged Levi cut-offs. His feet were bare. There was an arrogance about him, a certain dismissiveness in the gaze.

His mother gave me a last enigmatic look and then vanished from the doorway.

"I don't have much time," he said.

"I just have two questions."

"The police had a lot more than two."

"Can you account for your time the night Molly was cut up?"

"If I have to."

"Meaning what?"

"Meaning I mostly drove around to the usual places."

"And 'the usual places' would be where exactly?"

"The mall and the parking lot next to the Hardee's out on First Avenue and then out to the mall again."

"And you can prove that?"

"Sure," he said. But for the first time his lie became obvious. His gaze evaded mine.

I said: "I saw her."

He didn't ask me who "her" was.

"When?"

"A few hours ago."

"Was she —"

"I didn't get a real good look at her. The room was pretty dark."

He surprised me, then, as human beings constantly do. His eyes got wet with tears. "The poor kid."

"She's a nice girl."

"She's a lot more than nice."

"Susan's nice, too."

"Yeah, she is. And I treated her like shit and I'm sorry about it." He cleared tears from his voice. "I couldn't help – what I feel for Molly. It just kind of happened."

"Molly's mother thinks you're obsessed with her. In the clinical sense, I mean."

"I love her. If that's being obsessed." He sounded a lot older and a lot wearier than he had just a few minutes ago.

"Her mother also thinks you were the one who cut her."

He smiled bitterly. "That's funny. I've been thinking it was her mother who did it."

"Are you serious?"

He nodded. "Hell, yes, I'm serious. Her mother's got a

real problem with Molly. She's very jealous of her. Molly told me how bitter she was when this Brad started coming after her. She pushed Molly down the stairs, bruised her up pretty bad."

"She show you the bruises?"

"Yeah."

"She wasn't exaggerating?"

"Not at all."

Somewhere inside, a telephone rang, was picked up on the second ring. His mother called: "Telephone, Paul."

"Maybe I'd better get that."

"You can prove where you were when Molly was being cut?"

He surprised me again. "No, I can't, Mr Dwyer. I can't. I was alone."

"How about the mall?"

He shrugged. "I just made it up."

"Then you were doing what?"

"Just driving around."

Mother: "Honey, somebody's waiting on the phone."

"Just driving around?"

"Thinking about her. Molly. I really have to go, Mr Dwyer."

"Honey!" his mother called again.

V

This was the kind of neighbourhood where college professors always lived in the movies of my youth, a couple blocks of brick Tudors set high up on well-landscaped hills. The cars in the driveways ran to Volvos and Saabs, and the music, when you heard it through the occasional open window, ran to Brahms and Mahler. At night, the professors would sit in front of the fireplace, a blanket across their legs, reading Eliot or Frost. Even if life here wasn't really like this, it was nice to think that even a small part of our world could still be so enviably civilized.

A knock and the door opened almost at once. A heavy woman in a green sweater and a pair of too-snug jeans stood there watching me with obvious displeasure. She wore too much make-up on her fleshy, bitter face. Women who lived in these houses were supposed to look dignified, not like aging dance club babes. "Yes?" she said. Her mouth was small and bitter. She'd sucked on a lot of lemons, at least figurative ones, in her time.

"I'd like to see Bob Meacham."

She did something odd, then. She smiled with a kind of nasty pleasure. "Oh, God, you're another cop, aren't you?"

"Sort of."

I showed her my licence.

"Well, come in, Mr Dwyer. Would you like some coffee?"

"No, thanks."

I couldn't figure out why she was so happy to see me suddenly. Why would the presence of a private detective bring her such pleasure?

She flung an arm to a leather wingback chair that sat, comfortably, near a fireplace. An identical chair sat just across the way.

"I'll be right back."

She didn't go far. The floor creaked a few times and then she said, "So it's all over, is it, you bastard? Well, guess who's here to see you? Another cop. Your little girlfriend must think you were the one who cut her up."

When he appeared, moments later, he kept looking over his shoulder at his wife, as if he was waiting for her to put a knife in his back.

He came over and said, "I'm Bob Meacham."

"Jack Dwyer. Nice to meet you."

We shook hands.

"What can I do for you, Mr Dwyer?"

"I wanted to ask you some questions about Molly."

"Oh. I see."

His wife, who stood to the side of him, smirked at me. "When we first got married, Mr Dwyer, I used to worry that my husband was secretly gay. I guess I should be happy he just has this nice heterosexual thing for underage girls."

Meacham obliged her by blushing.

Seeing that she'd scored a direct hit, she said, "I'll go

back to my woman's work now, and leave you two to
discussing the wages of sin."

"I know what you must think of her," Meacham said
softly after his wife left. "But it's my fault. I mean, I've
made her like this. I've – I've had a lot of affairs over the
years. We should've gotten divorced a long time ago but –
somehow it's just never happened."

He didn't fit the professorial mould, either. He was a
little too beefy and a little too rough in the face. He'd
probably played football at some point in his life. Or boxed.
His nose and jaw had the look of heavy contact with
violence. He wore a chambray shirt and jeans. His balding
head didn't make him look any more professorial, either. It
just added to the impression of middle-aged toughness. He
didn't belong in a Tudor house with a Volvo in the drive
and T.S. Eliot lying open on his knee.

"You said you've had some affairs."

"Yes."

"Were they with young girls?"

"Youngish."

"Meaning?"

"Always of consenting age, if that's what you're getting
at."

"Molly isn't of age."

"Molly's the first. A fluke. Being that young, I mean."

"You realize that hustling her has opened you up to
several legal charges if the cops want to press them."

"You may not believe this, Mr Dwyer, but I wasn't
hustling her. We haven't slept together. I don't plan to
sleep with her till we're married. I know people laugh at me;
I mean, I know I'm not much better than a dirty joke these
days, but I don't give a damn about anything or anybody
other than Molly."

He looked at me.

"You're smiling, Mr Dwyer."

"Are you seeing a shrink?"

"No."

"You should be."

"I'm in love with her."

"She's fifteen."

"She's also the most spiritually beautiful creature I've ever known. That's why I say I'm not hustling her, Mr Dwyer. That's why I say we won't make love till we're married."

"Or at least till he gets out of prison," Mrs Meacham said, walking back into the room.

For the first time, I saw the sorrow Meacham had hinted at. Saw it in the slump of her shoulder, saw it behind the pain and anger in her gaze. She looked old and sad and slightly adrift.

"He's going to lose his teaching job – the school is already seeing to that – and then the district attorney will charge him with contributing. He brought her over here one day while I was gone and they drank wine together. Isn't that sweet?"

She hovered at the back of his chair. The smirk was back.

"He said he's going to leave me everything, when he runs away with her. Probably Tahiti, is what I'm thinking. He's always been obsessed with Gauguin. He even got sweet Molly interested in him."

She started wandering around the living room. We watched her with great glum interest.

"He's going to leave me everything, Mr Dwyer. The mortgage. The car that has nearly 175,000 miles on it. The bank account that never gets above $2,000. And the cancer. I've had three cancer surgeries in the past four years, Mr. Dwyer. And I'll know in a few weeks if I need another one." This time there was no smirk, just grief in the eyes and mouth. "And you know the worst thing of all, Mr Dwyer? I still love him. God, I'm just as sick as he is but I can't help it."

After a moment, Meacham said, "Why don't you go upstairs and lie down? You sound tired."

She looked at me. "I'm sorry for all this, Mr Dwyer."

I didn't know what to say.

"That's why we don't have friends any more. Nobody wants to come over here and hear all this terrible bullshit we put each other through." Then: "Goodbye, Mr Dwyer."

After she left, he said, "I suppose you're getting a bad impression of me."

I almost laughed. He was pursuing a fifteen-year-old, cheating on a wife with cancer, and thinking of running away and leaving that same wife with all the bills. Gee, why would that give me a bad impression of him?

"My opinion of you doesn't matter."

He stared at me a long time. "I'm a romantic, Mr Dwyer. I believe in the ideals of art and beauty. That's why I was so drawn to Molly. She's beautiful in an idealistic way – perfectly untouched – a virgin of body and mind. That's why I want to take her away – to save her so that she doesn't become corrupted."

I thought of Brad dumping Linda for Molly; and Paul dumping Susan for Molly, and taking her picture all the time, and following her around obsessively; and I thought of how I'd been all summer, meeting perfectly fine women whom I rejected because they didn't fit my ideal. A dangerous thing, beauty. It brings out the best and worst in men. The trouble is, sometimes the best and the worst are there at the same time – Meacham here loving her in the pure way of a college boy dumbstruck by the beauty of art; and yet at the same time willing to hurt a wife who was sick and needed him. The best and the worst. Beauty has a way of making us even more selfish than money does.

"She said no."

"Who said no?"

"Molly."

"She told you that, Mr Dwyer?"

"In so many words."

"So you think that because she was taking some time to think it over –"

I sighed. "Meacham, listen to me. She wasn't thinking it over. There was no way she was ever going to run off with you. Ever. But maybe deep down you really understood that. And maybe deep down that's why you cut her face."

"My God, you really think I could do that?"

"I think it's possible. You're so obsessive about her that –"

"'Obsessive.' That's a word my wife would use. A clinical word. There's nothing clinical in my feelings for Molly, believe me. They're pure passion. And I emphasize *pure* and *passion*. There's no way I could cut her up. She's the woman I've waited for all my life."

I wondered if I happened to be blushing at this point in the conversation. I thought again of all the women I'd stayed away from because they weren't my ideal. Good women. There's nothing like hearing your own sappy words put into the sappy mouth of someone else. Then you realize how inane your beliefs really are.

"Were you here the night it happened?"

"No, Mr Dwyer, I wasn't. I was walking, actually."

"The entire night?"

"Most of it. You're wanting an alibi?"

"That would help."

"I don't have one – other than the fact that I'm a creator, Mr Dwyer, not a destroyer. I have created something with Molly that is too beautiful for anybody to destroy. Even I couldn't destroy it if I wanted to."

I had to agree with his wife. I don't know why she stuck it out all these years, either.

"I'll be going now, Mr Meacham."

A chill smile. "You don't like me much, do you, Mr Dwyer?"

"Not much," I said.

"You're like her," he said, and nodded upwards to where his wife lay in her solitary bed. "Very middle-class and judgmental without even understanding what you're judging."

"Maybe you're right," I said. "But I doubt it."

I left.

VI

Clarence started barking at me the minute I pulled into the drive. He was in the breezeway, where he spent a lot of time on these unseasonably warm autumn evenings. Linda came out and calmed him down and then let me in.

"I guess we should be grateful he barks so much, as a watch dog and all, but sometimes he drives me crazy."

Then, apparently out of guilt for saying such a thing, she bent down and patted his head fondly, and said in baby talk, "You drive Mommy crazy, don't you, Clarence?"

Susan was in the kitchen setting out placemats on the breakfast nook table.

"We're doing Domino's tonight," Susan said. "Are you going to join us, Jack?"

I still couldn't imagine either of them doing it, cutting her up that way, daughter to one, sister to the other.

"Pepperoni and green pepper," Linda said.

"You convinced me."

Susan got beers for her mother and me and a Diet Pepsi for herself. Just as we were sitting down in the nook, Clarence exploded into barks again. The Domino's man had pulled into the drive.

"Maybe Clarence needs some tranquillizers," Susan said.

"I put a twenty on the counter there, hon," Linda said to her.

While Susan was out paying the pizza man, and calming Clarence, Linda said, "Did you talk to them?"

"Yes."

"Any impressions?"

"They're both good possibilities," I said. "Especially Meacham. I've been learning some things about him. He's a real creep. His wife has cancer and he's still running around on her. He thinks he's the last of the Romantic poets."

"Good for him. He's the one I'd bet on. For doing that to Molly, I mean."

Susan came back with the pizza and we ate.

Halfway through the feast, Linda said, "Tell him about Mark."

"Oh, Mom."

"Go on. Tell him."

Susan shot me a you-know-how-moms-are smile and said, "Mark Feldman asked me to the Homecoming dance."

"Great," I said.

"Honey, Dwyer doesn't know who Mark Feldman is. Tell him."

"He's a football player."

"Jeeze, honey, you're not helping Dwyer at all. Mark

Feldman just happens to be the best quarterback who ever played in this state. He's also a very nice looking boy. Much better-looking than that creep Paul. And he's really got the hots for my cute little daughter here."

"God, Mom. The 'hots'. That sounds like something you'd get from a toilet seat."

We all laughed.

"Congratulations," I said.

"And she was worried that nobody'd want to ask her out any more, Dwyer. Pretty crazy, huh?"

A knock on the breezeway door.

Susan went out to the breezeway to see who was there. She came back in carrying two pans.

"Bobbi brought your cake pans back, Mom. She said the upside down cake was great and to thank you for the recipe, too."

"Thank Gold Medal flour," Linda said. "The recipe was on the back."

I guess it was the silence from the breezeway I noticed. Clarence tended to bark at strangers when they came up to the door and when they were leaving. But he hadn't barked at all with Bobbi.

"Why didn't Clarence bark just now?" I said.

"Oh, you mean with Bobbi?" Linda said.

"Right."

"He knows her real well. He doesn't bark with our best friends."

Then I remembered something that Susan had said to me back when I'd first met her.

I said, "He doesn't bark when Paul comes up, either, does he?"

"No," Susan said.

"The other night, when Molly was cut, you said you heard screams from the breezeway. But did you hear barking?"

Susan thought a moment. "No, I guess I didn't."

"Would Clarence have barked if Meacham had come up?"

"Absolutely," Linda said.

I tried not to make a big thing of it but they could see

what I was thinking. I finished my three slices of pizza and my beer and then said I needed to go and do some work.

VII

He wasn't too hard to find. I spent some time in the parking lot with some burglary tools I use on occasion, and then I went inside the mall looking for him.

He was hanging out with some other boys in front of a music store.

When he saw me, he started looking nervous. He whispered something to one of his friends.

Three good-sized boys stepped in front of him, like a shield, as I started approaching.

They were going to block me as he ran away.

"Molly wants to see you," I said over the shoulders of the boys.

He had just started to turn, ready to make his run, when he heard me and angled his face back towards mine.

"What?"

"She wants to see you. She sent me to get you."

"Bullshit," he said.

I shrugged. "All right. I'll tell her you didn't want to come."

The boy in the middle, who went two-twenty easy, decided to have a little fun with the old man. He stepped right up to me and said, "You want to rumble, Pops?"

The other kids laughed. Nothing kids love more than bad dialogue from fifties movies.

"Like I said, Paul, I'll tell her you didn't want to see her." I looked down at the tough one and said, "If that's all right with you, Sonny."

I hadn't kicked the shit out of anybody for a long time, but the tough one was giving me ideas.

"Fuck that 'Sonny' bullshit," the tough one said.

But Paul had a hand on his shoulder and was turning him back.

"She really wants to see me?"

"Yeah," I lied. "She does."

Paul looked at the tough one. "I better go, then, Michael."

"With this creep?" Michael said.

"Yeah."

Michael glowered at me. The others did, too, but Michael had done some graduate work in glowering, so he was the most impressive.

"Nice friends," I said, as we turned back towards one of the exits. I said it loud enough to get Michael all worked up again. "Especially the dumb one with the big mouth."

We sat in an Orange Julius.

"I thought we were going to Molly's."

"We are."

"When?"

"Soon as you explain this."

From my pocket, I took a stained paper sack. "Know what this is, Paul?"

"You sonofabitch."

"There's a hunting knife in there. A bloody one. I'll bet the blood is Molly's."

"You sonafabitch."

"You said that already."

"That's illegal."

"What is?"

"Getting into my trunk that way."

"Wanna go call the cops?"

"You sonofabitch."

"How about calling me a bastard for a while? Breaks the monotony."

"It isn't what you think."

"No? You ride around with a bloody knife in your trunk and you don't have an alibi for the other night and it isn't what I think? You're telling me you didn't cut her?"

He started crying then, sitting right there in Orange Julius. He put his face in his hands and wept. People watched us. Son and father, they probably figured, with the father being a prime asshole for making his son cry this way. I took out my clean handkerchief and handed it over to him. I felt sorry for him. I shouldn't have but I did.

Loving somebody can make you crazy. All the fine sane people in the mental health industry tell you that you shouldn't give into it so hard, but you can't help it. There was a poet named Charles Bukowski who said that the most dangerous time to know any man is when he's been spurned in love. And from my years as a cop dealing with domestic abuse cases, Bukowski was absolutely right. So I sat there hating him for what he'd done to poor poor Molly, and feeling sorry for him, too. He'd ended her life, now I was going to make sure that his life was ended, too. He'd be tried as an adult and serve a long, long sentence. The way all men who visit their rages on helpless women should be sentenced.

He started snuffling then and picked up my handkerchief and blew his nose and said, "You still don't understand, Dwyer."

"Understand what?"

"What really happened."

"Then tell me."

So he told me and I said, "Bullshit. I should beat your face in for even saying that."

"Let's go see Molly."

"Are you serious?"

"Absolutely."

I walked across to the pay phones, keeping my eye on him all the time. It was preposterous, what he'd said.

When Linda came on, I told her I was bringing Paul over and taking him up to the den to see Molly. I said I couldn't answer any of her questions. She did not sound happy about that.

Soft silvered shadows played in the darkness of the den. Molly wore a pair of jeans and a white blouse and sat primly in the chair next to the dead TV. There was no question of turning on the lights. Molly had pretty much decided to live her life in darkness.

Paul and I sat on the edge of the narrow leather couch.

"He told me something crazy, Molly," I said. "I just wanted to give you the chance to tell me he's lying."

"I had to tell him, Molly," Paul said. "I'm sorry."

I told her what he'd said and she said, "Paul loves me."

"I guess I don't know what that means, Molly," I said gently. I was starting to get goosebumps because it appeared that Paul had told me the truth, after all.

"He loves me. That's why he did it."

"Why he cut you up that way?"

"Yes."

"You wanted him to cut you?"

"I asked him to. He didn't want to. But I kept after him till he did it. I just couldn't take the way people acted around me. My face. It's why I was having all this trouble with my mother and my sister and my friends. I didn't ask for my face, Mr Dwyer. I'd be much happier if I was plain, because then I wouldn't have to have all these people after me – like I was some sort of prize or something." Then to Paul: "I finally made you understand, didn't I, Paul?"

"Yes," Paul said.

"And he said he'd love me just as much if I didn't have my looks. And he does, don't you, Paul, even though I'll never be beautiful again?"

Even in moonshadow, his young face looked set and grim. He nodded.

Then she started sobbing and Paul went over to her and knelt next to her and took her in his arms and held her with a tenderness that moved and shook me. This wasn't puppy love or lust. This was real and simple and profound, the way his young arms held her young body.

At that moment he was father and brother and friend and priest, and only coincidentally, lover. I let myself out of the den and went downstairs.

VIII

"I'm having one, too," Susan said, when her mother asked her to bring us beers.

She brought three and we sat in the breakfast nook and I told them what had happened.

Linda cried and Susan held her.

"You think we should go up there, Jack?" Susan said as her mother wept in her arms.

"I'd give them a few more minutes."

"Do you think she's sane?" Susan said.

I shrugged. "I think she probably needs to see a shrink."

Linda sat up suddenly. She was angry. "That little prick took advantage of her. That's why he cut her face that way. He figured if he made her ugly, nobody else would want her. He was just being selfish, that's why he did it."

She made a fist and muttered a curse beneath her breath.

"You think that's true, Jack?" Susan said.

"Maybe."

"Maybe he did it because he really loves her," Susan said.

"Maybe," I said.

"I'm not going to sit here and listen to this bullshit," Linda said. "I'm going up there."

And with that, she forced Susan out of the booth.

"Mother, maybe you'd better stay down here for a little while," Susan called.

"She's my goddamned *daughter*," Linda said, sounding hysterical. "My goddamned *daughter*."

She stormed off to the front of the house and the stairway.

Susan shook her head. "Maybe he really did do it because he loved her. Isn't that possible, Jack?"

She wanted to believe in love and romance, just the same way I wanted to believe in being redeemed by the right woman. There was a good chance we were foolish people. Maybe very foolish.

Then Linda was screaming and Molly was sobbing and a terrible rage and despair filled the house, like the scent of rain on a sudden chill black wind.

Susan said, "Could I hold your hand for a minute, Jack? For just a minute."

I did my best to smile but I don't think it was very good. Not very good at all.

"For just a minute," I said. "But not much longer."